Forever and the Night
For All Eternity

LINDA LAEL MILLER

Forever and the Night

For All Eternity

Rhapsody
Garden City, New York

This edition was especially created in 2003 for Rhapsody by arrangement with The Berkley Publishing Group.

Published by Rhapsody, 401 Franklin Avenue, Garden City, New York 11530.

ISBN: 0-7394-3816-6

Printed in the United States of America

Contents

Forever and the Night

I wrote this book for myself;
it was a gift from me, to me.
For that reason, and many others,
I dedicate it to the best of who
I am and to all that I hope to become.

Special acknowledgments are in order for Alex Kamaroff, who saw the vision more clearly than I did and helped me to bring it into focus; to Irene Goodman, who was a light in the darkness when things seemed hopeless; to Debbie Macomber, whose confidence in me seemed unwavering; and to Pamela Lael, who fearlessly marked errors of logic and spelling and raved in all the right places. Last but not least, I wish to thank my editor, Judith Stern, for her tireless efforts to make the book shine.

" 'Tis now the very witching time of night,
When churchyards yawn and hell itself breathes out
Contagion to the world: now could I drink hot blood,
And do such bitter business as the day
Would quake to look upon."

—*Hamlet,* Act III, Scene ii

Chapter

1

That year, on the afternoon of Halloween, great glistening snowflakes began tumbling from a glowering sky, catching the maples and oaks by surprise in their gold and crimson housecoats, trimming fences and lampposts, roofs and windowsills, in shimmering, exquisite lace.

Aidan Tremayne awakened at sunset, as he'd done every day for more than two centuries, and felt a strange quickening in his spirit as he left the secret place in the woods. He allowed himself a wistful smile as he surveyed the snowy landscape, for he sensed the excitement of the town's children; it was like silent laughter, riding the wind.

All Hallow's Eve, he thought. How fitting.

He shook off the bittersweet sadness that had possessed him from the moment he'd opened his eyes and walked on toward the great stone house hidden in the stillness of its surroundings. There were birch trees among the others, gray-white sketches against the pristine snow, and a young deer watched him warily from the far side of a small mill pond.

Aidan paused, his eyes adjusting to the dusk, all his senses fluttering to life within him, and still the little doe returned his gaze, as though caught in the glow of headlights on some dark and forgotten road. He had only to summon the creature, and she would come to him.

He was hungry, having gone three days without feeding, but he had no taste for the blood of innocents, be they animal

9

or human. Besides, the life force of lesser creatures provided substandard nourishment. *Go*, he told the deer, in the silent language he had become so proficient at over the years. *This is no place for you, no time to be abroad in the night.*

The deer listened with that intentness so typical of wild creatures, white ears perked as fat flakes of snow continued to fall, as if to hide all traces of evil beneath a mantle of perfect white. Then the creature turned and scampered into the woods.

Aidan allowed himself another smile—it was Halloween, after all, and he supposed the occasion ought to have some celebratory meaning to a vampire—and walked on toward the house. Beyond, at the end of a long gravel driveway, lay Route 7, the first hint of civilization. The small Connecticut town of Bright River nestled four and a half miles to the north.

It was the kind of place where church bells rang on Sunday mornings. Local political issues were hotly debated, and freight trains came through late at night, the mournful cry of the engineer's whistle filling the valley. The children at the elementary school made decorations colored in crayon, pumpkins or Pilgrims or Santa Clauses, depending on the season, and taped them to the windows of their classrooms.

Aidan still smiled as he mounted the slippery steps at the back of the house and entered the mudroom. He stomped the snow from his booted feet just as a mortal man might have done, but he did not reach for the light switch as he entered the kitchen. His vision was keenest in the dark, and his ears were so sharp that neither cacophony nor silence could veil the essence of reality from him.

Usually.

He paused just over the threshold, focusing his awareness, and knew in the space of a moment that he was indeed alone in the gracious, shadowy house. This realization was both a relief—for he had powerful and very treacherous enemies—and a painful reminder that he was condemned to an eternity of seclusion. That was the worst part of being the monster he was, the wild, howling loneliness, the rootless wandering over the face of the earth, like a modern-day Cain.

Except for the brief, horrified comprehension of his victims, flaring in the moment before their final heartbeat, Aidan knew no human contact, for he consorted only with other vampires. He took little comfort from the company of his fellows—except for Maeve, his twin, whom he loved without reservation—for they were abominations, like himself. As a rule, vampires were amoral beings, untroubled by conscience or a need for the fellowship of others.

Aidan sighed as he passed silently through the house, shoving splayed fingers into dark, unruly hair. The yearning to live and love as an ordinary man had never left him, even though older and wiser vampires had promised it would. Some remnant of humanity lingered to give unrelenting torment.

He had not known peace of mind or spirit since the night *she*—Lisette—had changed him forever. Indeed, he supposed his unrest had begun even before that, when their gullible and superstitious mortal mother had taken him and Maeve to a gypsy camp, as very small children, to have their fortunes told.

The old woman—even after more than two hundred years, Aidan still remembered the horror of looking into her wrinkled and shrewd face—had taken his hand and Maeve's into her own. She'd held them close together, palms upward, peering deep, as if she could see through the tender flesh and muscle to some great mystery beneath. Then, just as suddenly, she'd drawn back, as though seared.

"Cursed," she'd whispered. "Cursed for all of eternity, and beyond."

The crone had turned ageless eyes—how strange they'd seemed, in that wizened visage—on Aidan, though her words had been addressed to his now-tearful mother. "A woman will come to him—do not seek her out, for she is not yet born—and she will be his salvation or his damnation, according to the choices they make."

The ancient one had given each of the twins a golden

pendant on a chain, supposedly to ward off evil, but it had been plain, even to a child, that she had little faith in talismans.

The chiming of the doorbell wrenched Aidan forward from that vanished time, and he found himself in mid-pace.

He became a shadow among shadows, there in the yawning parlor. Cold sickness clasped at his insides, even though they had long since turned to stone. *Someone had ventured within his range, and he had not sensed the person's approach.*

The bell sounded again. Aidan dragged one sleeve across his forehead. His skin was dry, but the sweat he'd imagined had seemed as real as that of a mortal man.

"Maybe nobody lives here," a woman's voice said.

Aidan had regained his composure somewhat, and he moved to the front window with no more effort than a thought. He might have come as easily from his hiding place to the house, except that he liked to pretend he had human limitations sometimes, and remember how it felt to have breath and a heartbeat.

He made no effort to hide himself behind the lace curtain, for the woman and child standing on the porch would not see him—not consciously, that is. Their deeper minds would register his presence and probably produce a few spooky dreams in an effort to assimilate him.

The child, a boy no older than six or seven, was wearing a flowing black cape and wax fangs, and he gripped a plastic pumpkin in one hand. His companion, clad in blue jeans, a sweater, and a worn-out cloth coat, was gamine-like, with short brown hair and large, dark eyes. Their conversation went on, ordinary and sweet as music, and Aidan took the words inside himself, to be played over and over again later, like a phonograph record.

Perhaps the other side of him, the beast, willed solidity and substance to his body and made him open the door.

"Trick or treat," the small vampire said, holding up the grinning pumpkin. In his other hand he held a flashlight.

The woman and child glowed like angels in the wintry

darkness, beautiful in their bright innocence, but Aidan was aware of the heat and warmth pulsing through them, too. The need for blood made him sway slightly and lean against the doorjamb.

That was when the woman touched him, and parts of her past flashed through his mind like a movie. He saw that she liked to wear woolen socks to bed, that she was hiding from someone she both cared for and feared, that despite her close relationship with the child, she was as lonely as Aidan himself.

All in all, she was delightfully mortal, a tangle of good and not-so-good traits, someone who had known the full range of sadness and joy in her relatively brief existence.

Aidan felt a wicked wrench, in the darkest reaches of his accursed soul, a sensation he had not known before, in life or in death. It was both pain and pleasure, that feeling, and the possible significance of it dizzied him.

Why had he recalled the words of the gypsy, spoken so long ago, words tucked away in a child's mind and forgotten five minutes after they were offered, now, on this night?

A woman will come to him . . . she will be his salvation or his damnation . . .

No, he decided firmly. Even given all he knew of the world, and of creation, it was too fanciful a theory to accept. This was not the one who would save or damn him; such a creature probably did not even exist.

Still, the gypsy's prediction had been otherwise correct. He and Maeve had both been cursed, as surely as the rebellious angels had been, those banished from heaven so many eons before, following the legendary battle between Lucifer and the archangel, Michael.

"Are you all right?" the woman asked, pulling him sharply back from his musings. "You look a little pale."

Aidan might have laughed, so ludicrously accurate was her remark, but he didn't dare risk losing control. He was ravenous, and the woman and child standing before him could have no way of knowing what sort of monster they were facing all alone, there in those whispering woods.

Their blood would be the sweetest of nectars, made vital by its very purity, and to take it from them would be a bliss so profound as to sustain him for many, many nights. . . .

The soft concern in the visitor's manner was nearly Aidan's undoing, for he could not even recall the last time a woman had spoken to him with tenderness. He drew in a deep breath, even though he had no need for air, and let it out slowly, holding the inward demons in check with his last straining shreds of strength. "Yes," he said, somewhat tersely. "I've been—ill."

"If you don't have any candy, it's okay," the child put in with quick charity. "Aunt Neely won't let me eat anything I get from strangers anyhow."

Aidan was almost deafened by a rushing sound stemming from some wounded and heretofore abandoned place in his spirit. *Neely.* He made note of the woman's name—it was a detail that had seemed unimportant, in the face of the devastating affect she'd had upon him—and it played in his soul like music. His control was weakening with every passing moment; he had to flee the pair before he broke his own all-but-inviable rule and ravaged them both.

Still, he was so shaken, so captivated by this unexpected mortal woman, that movement was temporarily beyond his power.

"I have something better than candy," he heard himself say, after a desperate inner struggle. He made himself move, took a coin from the ancient cherry-wood box on the hallway table and dropped it into the plastic pumpkin the little boy held out to him. "Happy Halloween."

Neely's brown eyes linked with Aidan's, and she smiled.

He watched the pulse throb at the base of her right ear, imagined the vitality he could draw from her, the sheer, glorious *life*. The mere thought of it made him want to weep.

He did not risk speaking again.

"Thank you," she said, turning to start down the porch steps.

The small vampire lingered on the doormat. "My name's Danny. We're practically your neighbors," he said. "We live

14

at the Lakeview Trailer Court and Motel, on Route Seven. My dad is the caretaker there, and Aunt Neely cleans rooms and waits tables in the truck stop."

The blush that rose in the woman's cheeks only made Aidan's deadly hunger more intense. Just when he would have lunged at her, he thrust the door closed and willed himself away quickly—far away, to another time and another place, where he could stalk without compunction.

Aidan chose one of his favorite hunting grounds, a miserable section of nineteenth-century London known as Whitechapel. There, in the dark, narrow, stinking streets, he might select his prey not from the prostitutes, or the pickpockets and burglars, but from procurers, white slavers, and men who made their living in the opium trade. Occasionally he indulged a taste for a mean drunk, a wife-beater, or a rapist; circumstances determined whether his victims saw his face and read their fate there or simply perished between one breath and the next. He did not actually kill the majority of his victims, however, and he had never made vampires of his prey, even though he knew the trick of it only too well. It was all a matter of degree.

He kept a room over a back-alley tavern, and that was where he materialized on that particular night. Quickly he exchanged his plain clothes for an elegant evening suit and a beaver top hat. To this ensemble he added a black silk cape lined with red, as a private joke.

A cloying, yellow-white fog enveloped the city, swirling about the lampposts and softening the sounds of cartwheels jostling over cobblestones, of revelry in the taverns and whoring in the alleys. Somewhere a woman screamed, a high-pitched, keening sound, but Aidan paid no attention, and neither did any of the other shadowy creatures who haunted the night.

He'd walked only a short way when he came upon a fancy carriage stopped at the curb. A small man, clad in a bundle of rags and filthy beyond all bearing, was pressing a half-starved child toward the vehicle's open door.

Inside, Aidan glimpsed a younger man, outfitted in clothes even more finely tailored than his own, counting out coins into a white, uncalloused palm.

"I won't do it, do you 'ear me!" the little one cried, with unusual spirit for such a time and place. Although Aidan sensed that the small entity was female, there was nothing about her scrawny frame to indicate the fact. She couldn't have been older than eight or ten. "I won't let some *bastard* from Knightsbridge bugger me for a shilling!"

Aidan closed his eyes for a moment, filled with disgust; vividly recalling the human sensation of bile bubbling into the back of his throat in a scalding rush. After all the time that had passed since his making, it still came as a shock to him to realize that vampires and werewolves and warlocks weren't the only fiends abroad in the world.

"Get'n the carriage and tend to your business!" shouted the rag-man, cuffing the child hard between her thin shoulders. "I'll not stand 'ere and argue with the likes of you all night, Shallie Biffle!"

Aidan stepped forward, deliberately opening himself to their awareness. Closing one hand over the back of the rag-man's neck, instantly paralyzing the wretched little rodent, he spoke politely to the urchin still standing on the sidewalk.

"This man"—he nodded toward his bug-eyed, apoplectic captive—"is he your father?"

" 'ell, no," spat Shallie. " 'e's just a dirty flesh-peddler, that's all. I ain't got no father or mother—if I did, would I be 'ere?"

Aidan produced a five-pound note, using that special vampire sleight of hand too rapid for the human eye to catch. "There is a woman in the West End who'll look after you," he said. "Go to her now."

He put the street name and number into the child's mind without speaking again, and she scrambled off into the shifting murk, clutching the note she'd snatched from his fingers a second after its appearance.

The horses pulling the carriage grew restless, but the

dandy and his driver sat obediently, bemused, as helpless in their own way as the rag-man.

Aidan lifted the scrap of filth by the scruff of his neck and allowed him to see his fierce vampire teeth. It would have been the purest pleasure to tear open that particular jugular vein, to drain the blood and toss away the husk like a handful of nutshells, but he had settled on even viler prey—the wealthy pervert who had ventured into White-chapel to buy the virtue of a child.

He flung the procurer aside, heard the flesh-muffled sound of a skeleton splintering against the soot-stained wall of a brick building. *Fancy that,* Aidan thought to himself with a regretful smile.

He climbed easily into the leather-upholstered interior of the carriage, and there he settled himself across from his intended victim. With a thought, he broke the wicked en-chantment that had held both the driver and his master in stricken silence.

"Tell the man to take you home," Aidan said compan-ionably enough, examining his gloves to make sure he hadn't smudged them while handling the rag-man's dirty person.

The carriage was dark, but Aidan's vision was noonday perfect, and he saw the young nobleman swallow convul-sively before he reached up with a shaking hand and knocked three times on the vehicle's roof. The lad loosened his ascot as he stared at Aidan in confounded fear, his pulse plainly visible between the folds of silk.

Yes, Aidan thought with quiet lust, eyeing the man's throat. Soon, very soon, the terrible hunger would be satis-fied, at least for the time being.

"Wh-Who are you?" the nobleman finally managed to stammer out.

Aidan smiled cordially and took off his hat, setting it carefully on the leather seat beside him. "No one, really. You might say that you're having a remarkably authentic night-mare—Bucky."

The young man paled at Aidan's easy use of his nickname, which, of course, he hadn't given. Bucky swallowed again, gulped really, and a fine sheen of perspiration broke out on his upper lip. "If it's about the child—well, I was only looking for a little harmless diversion, that's all—"

"You are a man of peculiar tastes," Aidan said without expression. "Does your family know how you amuse yourself of an evening?"

Bucky squirmed in the seat. On some level, Aidan supposed, the specimen's mind was developed enough to discern that the curtain was about to come down on the last act. "If this is about blackmail—"

Aidan interrupted with a *tsk-tsk* sound. "For shame. Not all of us are willing to stoop to such depths as you do, my friend. Blackmail is far beneath me."

A flush flowed into Bucky's pasty face, sharpening Aidan's desire to feed to something very like frenzy. He would wait, however, allowing the prospect to grow sweeter, in much the same way he had let fine wine breathe before indulging in it, back in those glorious days when the only blood he'd needed was that which coursed through his own veins.

"What do you want then, if not money?" Bucky sputtered.

Aidan smiled, revealing his fangs, and watched in quiet, merciless resolution as a silent scream moved up and down Bucky's neck but failed to escape his constricted throat. He looked frantically, helplessly, toward the carriage door.

"There is no escape," Aidan told him pleasantly.

Bucky's eyes were huge. "No more—no more children— I swear it—"

Aidan shrugged eloquently. "I quite believe you," he conceded. "You will never again have the chance, you see."

The carriage rattled on through the foggy London night, and the trip must have seemed endless to Bucky. Indeed, for him it was surely an eternity. Finally, when Aidan knew time was growing short, that dawn would come soon, he decided he'd savored the salty, vital wine long enough.

Slowly he put his hands on Bucky's velvet-clad shoulders, drew him close, even snarled a little, as a media vampire might, to give the moment a touch more drama. Then he sank his teeth into the tender flesh of Bucky's neck, and the blood flowed, liquid energy, not over Aidan's tongue but through his fangs.

As much as he hated everything he was, feeding brought the usual ecstacy. Aidan drank until his ferocious thirst had been quelled, then snapped Bucky's neck between his fingers and flung him to the floor of the carriage.

Aidan rarely fed in Bucky's circles, and he frowned as he imagined the furor the finding of a dandy's blood-drained hulk would arouse in the newspapers. He felt some regret, too, for the confusion that would reign among the diligent, well-meaning souls at Scotland Yard when they tried to make sense of the incident.

They would, of course, blame the Ripper.

Aidan stopped the carriage by freezing the driver's already addled mind, bent to straighten Bucky's stained ascot, then climbed out onto a virtually empty sidewalk.

His sister Maeve's grand house loomed before him, beyond an imposing wrought-iron fence, its chimneys and gables rimmed with the first gray-pink tatters of dawn.

The vampire met the carriage driver's blank stare, dismissed him with no memory of visiting Whitechapel or even encountering a stranger. The vehicle lumbered away through the slow, silent waltz of the fog.

Aidan let himself into the house via a special entrance next to the wine cellar and took refuge in a dark, tomblike room where inhabitants had once hidden from Oliver Cromwell's men. He bolted the door, then removed his hat and the cloak and settled in a half-crouch against a cold stone wall.

He yawned as the fathomless sleep began to overtake him. He'd been careless, coming here, but after his dawdling with poor, misguided Bucky, there hadn't been time to return to his lair in twentieth-century Connecticut. Besides, satiation always dulled his wits for a while.

He would just have to hope—it was futile for a vampire

to offer a prayer—that none of his enemies had been watching when he came to this only-too-obvious place to rest.

Aidan yawned again and closed his eyes. He didn't fear most vampires, for all but a few had to hide from the sun just as he did, but there were other arch-demons, other abominations of creation, who preyed upon his kind, terrible, beautiful things that flourished in the daylight.

Usually Aidan did not dream. All consciousness faded to dense blackness when he slumbered, leaving him vulnerable while his being assimilated the food that made him immortal.

Tonight, however, Aidan saw the woman, Neely, on the stage of his mind, and the little boy with wax vampire teeth, and even in his stupor he was wildly troubled. In two centuries no mortal female had captured his imagination. This one, this Neely, was different.

It wasn't just her looks—she was pretty enough, though by no means beautiful—but something far deeper, an ancient and cataclysmic affection of the soul, a bittersweet paradox. It was as if he'd been captured by a cunning and much-feared foe and at the same time found a vital part of himself that he hadn't known was lost.

Again, the long-dead gypsy witch's ominous words echoed, fragmented and sharp as splintered glass, in his mind. *Cursed—damnation or salvation . . .*

When he awakened, many hours later, he knew immediately that he was not alone in the dark chamber.

A match was struck; the light flared, searing Aidan's eyes. Before him stood Valerian, majestic in his vampirism, a giant, beautiful fiend with chestnut-brown hair, patrician features, and a dark violet gaze that could paralyze any lesser creature in a twinkling.

"You are a fool, Aidan!" Valerian spat, and the motion of his lips made the candlelight flicker. Like Aidan, Valerian had no breath. "What possessed you to come *here*?" He waved one elegant arm in barely bridled fury. "Have you forgotten that she searches for you? That she needs neither darkness nor sleep?"

Aidan yawned and raised himself to his feet, using the wall behind him for support. " 'She,' " he quoted mockingly. "Tell me, Valerian, are you so terrified of Lisette that you will not even say her name?"

The older vampire's eyes narrowed to slits; Aidan could feel his fury singing in the room like the discordant music of a thousand warped violins. "I have no reason to fear Lisette," he said after a moment woven of eternity. "It is you, Aidan, who have incurred her everlasting hatred!"

Aidan scratched the back of his neck, another habit held over from mortal days. The only itch that ever troubled him now came from far beneath his skin, driving him to take blood or die in the cruelest agony of thirst. He arched one eyebrow as he regarded his long-time acquaintance.

"No doubt, if Lisette is near, it's because she followed you," he said reasonably.

Again Valerian's lethal anger stirred. "I am nearly as powerful as she is—I can shroud my presence from her when I wish. You, on the other hand, might as well have laid down to sleep in the full light of the sun as to take refuge here! How long will you walk about with your thoughts naked to whatever demon might be listening? Do you *want* to perish, Aidan? Is that it?"

Against his will, Aidan thought of the woman, Neely, who lived and breathed back in the cold, fresh air of twentieth-century Connecticut. He felt the most torturous and inexplicable grief, coupled with a joy the likes of which no fiend could expect to entertain. "Perhaps I do," he confessed raggedly. Then he lifted his eyes to Valerian's magnificent, terrible face and asked, "Do you never yearn for peace? Don't you ever grow so weary of what you are that you'd risk the wrath of heaven and the fires of hell to escape it?"

"Fool," Valerian spat again, plainly exasperated. "Why do I bother myself with such an idiot? For us, the pure light of heaven would be as great a torment as the blazes of Hades! We would escape nothing by fleeing this life!"

"This is not life," Aidan replied with unexpected fury.

21

"This is a living death. Hell itself could not possibly be worse!"

Valerian gentled, for he was an unpredictable creature, and laid his gracious hands on Aidan's shoulders. "Poor Aidan," he mocked. "When will you accept what you are and stop playing at being a man?"

Aidan turned away and snatched his cloak and top hat from the top of the wine crate where he'd left them that morning before giving himself up to a tempestuous sleep. Valerian's words had struck a chord of terror in his spirit.

Did the other vampire know about Neely and the little boy? Was that what he'd meant by "playing at being a man"? If Valerian had taken notice of their existence while Aidan's mind was unguarded in slumber, he might see it as his duty to destroy them.

In the next moment Aidan's worst fears were confirmed. "You are an even greater fool than I thought," Valerian said with rueful affection. "Imagine it, your being besotted with a fragile mortal!" He paused, sighed. "You do me injury," he murmured, before going on to say, in his usual imperious way, "Come with me, Aidan. I will show you worlds and dimensions you have never dreamed of. I will teach you to cherish what you are, to *relish* it!"

Aidan retreated a step, covered his ears with his hands, as though that could keep out the brutal truth of Valerian's words. "Never!" he gasped out. "And if you go near the woman or the child, I swear by all the unholy vows, whatever the cost may be, *I will destroy you!*"

Valerian looked stung, which was another of his many affectations, of course. Aidan knew the other vampire was not capable of anything so prosaic as getting his feelings hurt, and he certainly didn't fear a being of lesser powers.

The creature sighed theatrically. "Perhaps Maeve can reason with you," he said. "I am weary of the effort."

"Leave me," Aidan replied.

Miraculously Valerian conceded the point and disappeared.

Aidan tilted his head back as if to see through the thick

ceiling. His senses told him that Maeve was not in residence but off hunting in some other place and century.

A small, aching coil of loneliness twisted inside Aidan's breast. Whatever their differences, he cherished his sister. Her companionship would have been comforting, a warm hearth in the dark bewilderment that tormented him now.

He closed his eyes and thought of Connecticut, and when he looked again, he was there, standing in the darkness of a bedroom he never used.

Aidan tossed the top hat and cloak onto a wing chair upholstered in rich leather and wrenched at the high collar that suddenly seemed to constrict his throat. Somehow, in those few treacherous minutes when Neely had stood on his doorstep, escorting a little beggar in a vampire suit, Aidan had made a truly terrible error. He had brought the woman into his mind, just to admire her effervescence for a few moments, and she had taken up stubborn residence there.

What in blazes was this fascination he'd acquired?

He looked toward the bed, remembering what it was like to lie with a daughter of Eve, to give and take physical pleasure, and was possessed of a yearning so fierce that it horrified him. He had merely *glimpsed* this troublesome woman, and yet he found himself wanting her, not as sustenance, but bucking beneath him in wild spasms of passion, clutching his bare shoulders in frantic fingers, crying out in the sweet fever of ecstasy . . .

He had to see her again, if only to convince himself that he had built her up into something more than she was, to end this reckless obsession that could so easily end in obliteration for them both.

When he had regained his composure somewhat, Aidan exchanged his gentleman's garb for well-worn jeans and a wheat-colored Irish cable-knit sweater. He brushed his dark, longish hair—a style suited to the current century and decade—and formed a clear picture of Neely in his mind.

In the space of a second he was standing in the parking lot of the truck stop on Route 7, a soft Connecticut snow falling around him, and she was just coming out through the front door, scrambling into her cheap coat as she walked.

She stopped when she sensed his presence, met his gaze, and sealed his doom forever simply by smiling.

"Hello," she said. Her gamine eyes were bright with some hidden mischief, and the snowflakes made a mantilla for her short hair.

Long-forgotten and deeply mourned emotions wrung Aidan as he stood there, powerless before her innocent enchantment. "Hello," he replied, while sweet despair settled over him like snow blanketing a new and raw grave.

Somewhere deep inside him a spark kindled into flame.

It was true, then, what the gypsy sorceress had said so long before. Here, before him, stood the reason for his creation, the personification of his fate.

Chapter

2

It almost seemed that he'd been waiting for her.

Neely Wallace felt both an intense attraction and a rush of adrenaline as she stood in the parking lot of the Lakeview Café, gazing into that enigmatic pair of eyes. A spontaneous "hello" had tumbled over her lips before she'd given full consideration to the fact that this man was a virtual stranger.

Remembering that there were people in the world who wanted to silence Neely, or even kill her, she was surprised at her own reaction. Briefly, futilely, she wished she had never worked for Senator Dallas Hargrove, never found the evidence of his criminal acts, thus making herself a target.

He smiled, the snow drifting and floating softly between them, cosseting the land in a magical silence. Something about his gaze captivated her, made her want to stand there looking at him forever.

It was as though he had looked inside her, with those remarkable eyes of his, and awakened some vital part of her being, heretofore unknown and undreamed of.

Neely cleared her throat nervously but kept her smile in place. She should have taken the time to call her brother, Ben, when her shift was over, as he was always telling her to do, so he could come and walk her back to the trailer court. If she hadn't seen the man the night before, when she and Danny had gone out trick-or-treating, she might have thought he was a mugger or a rapist, or that her former boss had finally sent someone to make sure she never talked about his close association with drug dealers. "The café's closed," she said. "We'll open up again at five."

He came no nearer, this man woven of shadows, and yet his presence was all around Neely, in and through her, like the very essences of time and space. "Don't be afraid," he said. "I'm not here to hurt you."

Neely figured a serial killer might say the same thing, but the idea didn't click with her instincts. She realized she *wasn't* truly afraid, but her stomach was fluttery, and she felt capable of pole-vaulting over the big neon sign out by the highway. "I don't think I caught your name," she said, finally breaking the odd paralysis that had held her until that moment.

"Aidan Tremayne," he said, keeping his distance. "And yours?"

"Neely Wallace," she answered, at last finding the impetus to start across the lot, the soles of her boots making tracks in the perfect snow. Idly she wondered if she would end up as a segment on one of those crime shows that were so popular on TV. She could just hear the opening blurb. *Ms. Cornelia Wallace, motel maid and waitress, erstwhile personal assistant to Senator Dallas Hargrove, disappeared mysteriously one snowy night from the parking lot of the Lakeview Truck Stop, just outside Bright River, Connecticut....*

A high, dense hedge separated the parking area from the motel and trailer court beyond, and Neely paused under an arch of snow-laced shrubbery to look back.

Aidan Tremayne, clearly visible before in the glimmer of the big floodlights standing at all four corners of the parking lot, was gone. No trace of him lingered, and the new layer of snow was untouched except for Neely's own footprints.

She stood perfectly still for a moment, listening, but she heard nothing. She drew a deep breath and walked on at a brisk pace, making her way past the two-story motel and into the trailer court. Reaching the door of her tiny mobile home, which was parked next to Ben's larger one, she looked back over her shoulder again, almost expecting to see Tremayne standing behind her.

"Weird," Neely said to herself as she turned the key in the lock.

The trailer wobbled, as usual, when Neely stepped inside. She flipped on the light switch and peeled off her coat in an almost simultaneous motion. Then, as an afterthought, she turned the lock on her door and put the chain-bolt in place.

Her utilitarian telephone, a plain black model with an old-fashioned dial, startled her with an immediate jangle. She grabbed up the receiver, oddly exasperated.

"Damn it, Neely," her brother said, "I told you to call me when you were through closing up the café so I could come over and walk you home. Don't you read the newspapers? It isn't safe for a woman to be out alone so late at night."

Neely calmed down by reminding herself that Ben truly cared about her; except for Danny and her best friend, Wendy Browning, he was probably the only person in the world who did. She put away her coat, sat down on her hide-a-bed sofa with a sigh, and quickly kicked off her snow boots.

"I'm sorry, Ben," she responded, rubbing one sore foot. She frowned, spotting a run in her pantyhose. Even hairspray or nail polish wouldn't stop this one. "Yes, it's late, and that's exactly why I didn't call. I knew Danny would be in bed, and I didn't want you to have to leave him alone." She paused, drew a deep breath, and plunged. "Ben, what do you know about Aidan Tremayne, that guy who lives in the mansion down the road?"

Ben sounded tired. "Just that. His name is Aidan Tremayne, and he lives in the mansion down the road. Why?"

Neely was unaccountably disappointed; she'd wanted some tidbit of information to mull over while she was brushing her teeth and getting ready for bed. "I was just wondering, that's all. Danny and I went there on Halloween night. He struck me as sort of—different."

"I guess you could say he's a recluse," Ben said, barely

disguising his indifference. "Listen, sweetheart, I'm beat. I'll see you in the morning."

Emotion swelled in Neely's throat. She and Ben had more in common than their late parents. He'd lost his wife, Shannon, to cancer a few years before, along with his job in a Pittsburgh steel mill, and he'd been struggling to rebuild his life and Danny's ever since. Neely had been forced to give up an entire way of life—her work, her apartment, her friends—because she knew too much about certain very powerful people.

"Good night," she said.

Neely's trailer consisted of one room, essentially, with the fold-out bed at one end and a kitchenette at the other. The bathroom was quite literally the size of the hall closet in her old apartment.

Resolving to dwell on what she had—her life, her health, Danny and Ben—instead of what she'd lost, Neely took off her pink uniform and hung it carefully from a curtain rod. After showering, she put on an old flannel nightshirt and dried her hair. Then she heated a serving of vegetable soup on a doll-size stove and sat in the middle of her lumpy fold-out bed, eating and watching a late-night talk show on the small TV that had once occupied a corner of the kitchen counter of her spacious apartment in Washington.

Neely didn't laugh at the host's monologue that night, though she usually enjoyed it. She kept thinking of Aidan Tremayne, wondering who he was and why he'd stirred her the way he had. He was one of the most attractive men she'd ever met, and inwardly she was still reeling from the impact of encountering him unexpectedly as she'd left the café.

Not to mention the way he'd vanished in the time it took to blink.

She walked to the edge of the bed on her knees, balancing her empty soup bowl with all the skill of a good waitress, then got up and crossed to the sink. After rinsing out her dish, she returned to the bathroom and brushed her teeth. The thing to do was sleep; she would think about Mr. Tremayne another time, when fatigue did not make her overly fanciful.

Aidan was especially ravenous that night, but he did not feed. The hunger lent a crystalline sharpness to his thought processes, and as he sat alone in his sumptuous study, with no light but that of the fire on the hearth, he allowed himself to remember a time, a glorious time, when he'd been a man instead of a monster.

He closed his eyes and tilted his head back against the high leather chair in which he sat, recalling. Like most mortals, Aidan had not realized what it really meant to have a strong, steady heartbeat, supple lungs that craved air, skin that sweated, and muscles that took orders from a living brain. He had thought with his manhood in those simple days, not his mind.

Now he was a husk, an aberration of nature. Thanks to his own impetuous nature and unceasing pursuit of a good time, thanks to Lisette, he was a fiend, able to exist only by the ingestion of human blood. He longed for the peace of death but feared the possibilities of an afterlife too much to perish willingly.

Aidan could travel freely in time and its dimensions, but the Power that pulsed at the heart of the universe was veiled to him. He knew only that it existed, and that its agents were among his most dangerous enemies.

He could not bear to consider the fate that might await him should he succumb to the mystery of true death; he'd had enough religious training in his early years at school to sustain a pure and unremitting terror. Nor did Aidan choose to think of Neely Wallace, for to do that in his present mood would be to transport himself instantly into her presence.

He engaged in a sad smile, letting decades unfold in his mind, and then centuries. He'd been twenty-two when the unthinkable had happened. The year had been 1782, the place an upstairs room in a seedy English tavern, not far from Oxford. . . .

*   *   *

Lisette's waist-length auburn hair was spread across Aidan's torso like a silken veil, and her ice-blue eyes were limpid as she gazed at him. "Lovely boy," she crooned, stroking his chest, his belly, and then his member. "I can't bear to give you up."

Aidan groaned. They'd been together all night and, as always, as the dawn approached, she grew sentimental and greedy. He was amazed to feel himself turn hard, for he'd thought she'd drained him of all ability to respond.

Lisette was older than Aidan by a score of years, and her experience in intimate matters was vast, but other than those things, he knew little about her. One night a few weeks before, when Aidan had been out walking alone, a splendid carriage drawn by six matched horses had stopped beside him in the road. Lisette, a pale and gloriously beautiful creature, had summoned him inside with a smile and a crook of her finger. They'd been meeting regularly ever since.

Now she laughed at his reluctance to surrender even as his young body betrayed him.

She set the pace as the aggressor and the seducer. She took him, extracted yet another exquisite response from him, and left him half-conscious in the tangled bedclothes immediately afterward.

Aidan watched his lover through a haze as she paced the crude plank-board floor, once again clad in her gauzy, flowing gown, her hair trailing down her back in a profusion of coppery curls. He was glad it was nearly sunrise, that she would leave him then as always, because he knew that one more turn in her arms would kill him.

"See that you don't go dallying with a wench while I'm away," she flared. "I won't have it!"

He hauled himself up onto his elbows, but that was all he could manage. "You don't own me, Lisette," he said. "Don't be telling me what you'll have and what you won't."

She whirled on him then, and he saw something terrible in her face, even though there was no light but that of a thin winter moon fading into an approaching dawn. "Do not speak to me in that disrespectful way again!" she raged.

Aidan was a bold sort—indeed, his father's solicitor swore the trait would be his undoing—but even he did not dare challenge Lisette further. She was no ordinary woman, he'd guessed that long since, and she was capable of far more than ordinary mischief. He guessed that had been her appeal, along with her insatiable appetites and the envy her attentions generated among his peers.

Lisette cast a sullen glance toward the window, then glared at Aidan again, her eyes seeming to glitter in the gloom. They looked hard, like jewels, and they flashed with an icy fire. She made a strangled sound, a mingling of desire and grief, and then she was upon him again.

He tried to throw her off, for the sudden ferocity of her attack had unnerved him, but to his annoyance he discovered that she was far stronger than he was.

"Soon," she kept murmuring, over and over, like a mother comforting a fitful child, "soon, darling, all the earth will belong to us—"

Aidan felt her teeth puncture his neck, and his heart raced with fresh horror. He fought to free himself, but Lisette was like a marble statue, crushing him, breaking his bones. At that point he began to recede into unconsciousness; he was going to die, never see Maeve again, never laugh or paint or drink wine and ale with his friends.

He renewed his efforts, struggling to return to full awareness, even though there was pain and fear, mortal fear so intense that his very soul throbbed with it.

"Now, now," Lisette whispered, lifting her head to look into his eyes. "Your friends will think you're dead, poor fools, but you will only be sleeping. I will return for you, my darling, before they bury you."

Aidan was appalled and wildly confused. He felt strange; his body was weak to the point of death, and he could barely keep his eyes open, yet his soul seemed to soar on the wings of some dark euphoria. "Oh, God," he whispered, "what's happening to me?"

Lisette rose from the bed, but it made no difference that

she'd finally freed him, for Aidan could not move so much as a muscle.

"You'll see, my darling," she said, "but don't trouble yourself by calling out to God. He turns a deaf ear to our sort."

Aidan fought desperately to raise himself, but he still had no strength. He could only watch in terrified disbelief as Lisette's form disintegrated into a swirling, sparkling mist. She was gone, and even though Aidan was conscious, he knew full well that she had murdered him.

He could not speak, could not move. His heart had stopped beating, he wasn't breathing, and as the room filled with sunlight, his sight faded. His flesh burned as surely as if he'd been laid out on a funeral pyre, and yet Aidan knew the pain wasn't physical. He was dead, as Lisette had said, yet only too aware of all that happened around him.

A wench, probably come to fill the water jug and tidy the bed, found him later that morning. Her shrieks stabbed his mind; he tried to move, to speak, to show her he was conscious, but it was all for naught. Aidan was a living soul trapped inside a corpse.

He was aware of the others, when they came, for it was as though the conscious part of him had risen to a corner of the ceiling to look down on the lot of them. There were two men, the tavern owner and his burly, stupid son, but a priest soon arrived as well.

The boy took the door from its hinges, and they laid Aidan's helpless body out on that wooden panel. He could do nothing to resist them.

"Poor soul," said the priest, grasping the large crucifix he wore around his neck on a plain cord and making the sign of the cross over Aidan's mortal remains. "What do you suppose happened to him?"

"He died a happy man," the idiot-boy replied, leering. It didn't seem to bother him that he was addressing a man of God. "That's if the lady I saw him with and the sounds I heard comin' from this here room meant anything!"

Aidan returned to his wasted body from his vantage

point near the ceiling, struggled to move something, anything—an ear, an eyelash, one of the tiny muscles at the corners of his mouth. Nothing. Blackness covered him, swallowed him up, mind and soul, and he was no one, nowhere.

When Aidan wakened, he still could not move. He knew, with that peculiar extra sense he'd acquired soon after Lisette's attack, that he was in the back of the undertaker's shop, laid out on a slab, with coins on his eyes. At first light he'd be closed up in a coffin and probably sent home to Ireland in the back of a wagon, no longer a troublesome responsibility to his prosperous English father. His mother, a dark-haired tavern maid, a woman of light laughter and even lighter skirts, would mourn him for a while, but Maeve would suffer the sorest grief. Maeve, his twin sister, his childhood companion, the counterpart of his personality.

Hope stirred in Aidan's being when he felt a cool hand come to rest on his forehead; his hope died when he heard his murderess's voice. "There now, I told you I'd come back for you," she said, placing a frigid kiss where her fingers had been. "Sweet darling, have you been afraid? Perhaps you'll remember, after this, what it means to defy me."

Aidan knew a pure anguish of emotion, but he could say nothing. He cried out inwardly when she bent over him again, when he felt her teeth puncture the skin of his throat like pointed quills thrust through dry parchment. In the next instant, liquid ecstacy seemed to flow into every part of him; he could see clearly again and hear with crystal clarity, even though he still had no breath or heartbeat. An unearthly and wholly incredible power was spawning inside him, growing, grumbling, surging upward like lava thrusting at the inside of a mountain.

His muscles were flexible again; he sat bolt upright on the slab and thrust Lisette aside with a motion of his arm.

"What have you done?" he rasped, for the joy that seemed to crush him from the inside was the sort denied to mere men. It was dark and rich and evil, and he yearned to throw it off even as he embraced it. "In the name of God,

Lisette, *what manner of creature are you and what have you done to me?*"

Lisette thrust her arms up, as if he'd attempted to strike her again. "Do not speak of the Holy One again—it is forbidden!"

"Tell me!" Aidan bellowed.

There was a clamor beyond the door of the morgue, the sounds of rushing feet and muffled voices.

Lisette came to Aidan's side. Her mind filled the room, swirled around his like an invisible storm, swallowed it whole. When his awareness returned, when he knew that he was a separate entity, they were hiding together in a damp place with cold stone walls.

He was lying down once again, this time on an altar of sorts. In the flickering light of a half dozen candles, he saw Lisette, looming at his feet like some horrible angel of darkness.

"Please," he said, his voice a raw whisper. "Tell me what I am."

She smiled and came to stand beside him, smoothing his hair back from his forehead. He wasn't bound, as far as he could tell, and yet she must have been restraining him somehow, for he was utterly powerless once more.

"Don't be so anxious, my darling," Lisette scolded. "You are a most wonderful creature now, with powers others only dream of. You are a vampire."

"No," he protested. "*No!* It's impossible—such things do not happen!"

"Shhh," said Lisette, laying an index finger to her lovely, lethal mouth. "Soon you will adjust to the change, my darling. Once you've felt the true scope of your talents, you'll thank me for what I've done."

"Thank you?" Aidan trembled, so great was his effort to rise and confront her, and so fruitless. "If what you say is true—and I cannot credit that it is—then I shall curse you. But I will never, *never* thank you!"

Lisette's beautiful face became a mask of controlled rage. "Ingrate! You don't know what you're saying. If I thought you did, I would toss you out into the sunlight to burn in the sort of agony only a vampire can know! Count yourself fortunate, Aidan Tremayne, that I am mercifully inclined toward you!" She stopped, seemed to gather herself in from all directions, then favored Aidan with a smile made brutal by its sweet sacrilege. "Sleep now, darling. Rest. When darkness comes again, I will show you places and things you've never imagined. . . ."

In the nights to come, Lisette had kept her promise.

She had taught Aidan to hunt, and despise it though he did, he had learned his lessons well. She had shown him how to move as easily between eras and continents as a mortal travels from room to room. From Lisette, Aidan learned to find a safe lair and to veil his presence from the awareness of human beings.

From Lisette, Aidan learned pure, enduring, singular hatred, and all of it was directed at her.

He pitied his victims and often starved himself to the point of collapse to avoid taking blood. Then, one foggy winter night not so long after Lisette had changed him from a man into a beast, while sitting alone in a country tavern, pretending to drink ale, he'd been approached by another vampire . . . Valerian.

"Reminiscing about me? How touching."

Aidan started in his chair by the fire in his Connecticut house and muttered a curse. His unannounced and quite unquestionably arrogant caller leaned against the mantel, indolently regal in creased trousers and tails. He was even wearing the signature gold medallion, which meant he was in a mischievous mood.

Like Aidan, Valerian held the stereotypical media vampire in unwavering contempt.

"This is the second time in as many nights that I've taken you unawares," Valerian scolded, tugging at his immaculate white gloves. "You've become careless, my friend. Tell me, have you fed so well that your senses are dulled?"

Aidan raised himself from the chair and faced his visitor

35

squarely. Valerian was ancient, by vampire standards, having been changed sometime in the fourteenth century. He was a magnificent monster, given to sweeping displays of power, but only the stupid showed fear in his presence.

When Valerian sensed cowardice, he turned dangerously playful, like a cat with a mouse between its paws.

"I am allowed some introspection," Aidan said, pouring a snifter of brandy and raising it to Valerian in an impudent toast even though he could not drink. "I was remembering how I came to join the ranks of demons, if you must know."

Valerian chuckled, took the glass from Aidan's hand, and flung the contents into the fire. A furious roar preceded his reply. " 'The ranks of demons,' is it? Do you hate us so much as that, Aidan?"

"Yes," Aidan spat. "Yes! I despise you, I despise Lisette, and most of all, I despise myself."

Valerian yawned. "You have become something of a bore, my friend, always whining about what you are. When are you going to accept the fact that you will be exactly this until the crack of doom and get on with it?"

Aidan turned his back on his companion to stand facing one of the bookshelves, running one hand lightly over the spines of the leather-bound volumes he cherished. "There is a way to end the curse," he said with despairing certainty. "There has to be."

"Oh, indeed, there is," Valerian said cheerfully. "You have only to tell some crusading human where your lair is and let him drive a stake through your heart while you sleep. Or you could find a silver bullet somewhere and shoot yourself." He shuddered, and his tone took on a note of condescension as he finished. "Neither fate is at all pleasant, I'm afraid. Both are truly terrible deaths, and what lies beyond is even worse, for us if not for mortals."

Aidan did not turn from his inspection of the journals he had written himself, by hand, over the course of two centuries. His musings had kept him from losing his mind and, he hoped, given some perspective on history. He had written a full account of his vampirism as well.

"I don't need your lectures, Valerian. If you have no other business with me, then kindly leave."

Valerian sighed philosophically, a sure sign that he was about to pontificate. He surprised Aidan this time, however, by speaking simply. "Lisette stirs again, my friend. Have a care."

Aidan turned slowly to study his companion. When he'd grown beyond the needs of a fledgling vampire, and spurned her affections, Lisette had first raged, then sulked, then gone into seclusion in some hidden den. She had emerged on occasion and busied herself with her usual dalliances, but she had not troubled Aidan in years. In fact, he seldom worried about her, although Valerian and Maeve constantly chided him for his carelessness.

"She has long since forgotten me," he said. "I am but one of many conquests, after all."

"You delude yourself," Valerian replied tersely. "Lisette has indeed taken many lovers, and made many vampires. But you were the only one who dared to resist her advances. It's a miracle you haven't perished long before this, and I honestly can't say why I keep trying to save you when you seem determined to die."

Aidan clutched Valerian's silk lapels in both hands. He was not afraid for himself, but he did fear for Maeve, and the human woman, Neely. "Have you seen Lisette?" he demanded. "Damn you, stop your prattling and tell me!"

Valerian shrugged free of Aidan's grasp and seemed to settle his garments closer to his skin, the way a raven might do with its feathers. "I have not been so unfortunate as to encounter Lisette," he said with ominous dignity, "but certain of the others have. She is weak and feeds only sporadically, according to my sources. Nevertheless, she has roused herself, and sooner or later, as mortals so colorfully put it, there will be hell to pay."

Aidan shoved splayed fingers through his hair, his mind racing. "Where? Where was she seen?"

"Spain, I think," Valerian answered. He'd shifted his attention to a mechanical music box on Aidan's desk; Valerian loved gadgets. He turned the key, and the tinkling notes of a long-forgotten tune echoed in the room. "If you say you're going there to look for her," he said distractedly, "I swear I'll wash my hands of you."

"You've made that vow often enough," Aidan said tersely. "What a pity you never keep it."

Valerian chuckled, but the snap with which he closed the music box lid was a more accurate measure of his mood. "What an insolent whelp you are. Who but Lisette would change such a difficult human into an immortal, thereby subjecting us all to an eternity of pathos?"

"Who, indeed?" Aidan replied. He sighed, and his shoulders slumped slightly. He was faint with the need for sustenance, but the dawn was too close now. There was no time for a proper hunt. "I'm sorry," he said, even though he wasn't, not entirely, and they both knew it. "If you see Lisette, will you let me know?"

The older vampire regarded him coldly for a long time, then said, "You may encounter the creature before I do, Aidan." He frowned, adjusted his gloves, and set his top hat at a dashing angle. "And now, adieu. Dawn is nearing. Sleep soundly, my friend, and in safety."

With that, Valerian vanished. He often indulged in dramatic exits.

Aidan banked the fire on the hearth, put the screen in place, and left the house, moving through the silent, snowy woods as noisily as a man, instead of with a vampire's stealth. Maybe Valerian was right; maybe he was courting destruction, in the unconscious hope that there was no heaven or hell beyond death, but only oblivion.

In oblivion would lie peace.

Aidan's hunger tore at him as he moved closer and closer to the long-forgotten mine shaft that was his lair. He glanced toward the sky, reasoned that he had about fifteen minutes before the sun would top the horizon. There was time to go to Neely, time for one look to sustain him in the deathlike sleep that awaited him.

He shook his head. No. He dared not approach her now, when he needed to feed.

He wended his way toward his hiding place, lowered himself inside, crouched against one dank wall, and folded his arms atop his knees. Then he yawned, lowered his head, and slept.

The mansion had looked spooky to Neely on Halloween night, but now that she stood before it in the dazzling sunshine of that November afternoon, it seemed very ordinary and innocuous, except for its size.

She wasn't sure why she'd come; Mr. Tremayne certainly hadn't invited her to drop by. All Neely really knew was that she was drawn to that house and even more so to its owner. It was as if she'd always known Aidan Tremayne, as if they'd been close once, very close, and then cruelly separated. Encountering him had been a reunion of sorts, a restoration of something stolen long before.

Wedging her hands into the pockets of her coat, Neely proceeded up the walk and climbed the steps onto the gracious old porch. Then, after drawing a deep breath, she rang the bell.

There was no answer, so she tried a second time. Again, no one came.

Neely walked around the large house once, thinking she might encounter the owner in the yard, but she didn't catch so much as a glimpse of him.

Finally, feeling both relieved and disappointed, Neely turned and walked back along the driveway toward the highway. She had already cleaned the motel rooms that had been rented the night before, and she wasn't due back at the café until the supper shift. Danny would be in school until three o'clock, and Ben was busy repairing a water pipe under one of the trailers.

Neely was a free woman, and she was at loose ends.

She decided to borrow Ben's battered old Toyota and head into Bright River. Her emotions were churning; she tried to put Tremayne out of her mind and failed.

She would stop by the local library, she decided. There she would surely find back copies of the Bright River *Clarion*; she intended to scan the microfilm records for interesting references to Aidan Tremayne or his family. After all, she rationalized as she bumped along Route 7 in her brother's car, she needed to keep up her professional skills—especially in research. God knew, she couldn't work as a waitress and maid all her life; her feet would never withstand the strain.

Besides, the project gave her a legitimate reason to think about Aidan on a more practical level, and it would distract her from the riot of emotions and needs that had been bedeviling her ever since their first encounter.

Neely adjusted the car's temperamental heater and shivered in spite of the blast of hot air that buffeted her. Aidan was going to change her life, and she was going to change his; she knew it as well as if an angel had whispered the fact in her ear. There was a magical mystery afoot here, and she yearned to learn its secrets.

The trick would be to stay alive long enough to investigate.

She sighed and silently reminded herself that she knew too much about her ex-boss's source of campaign funds, among other things. Five years working in the nation's capital had cured Neely of starry-eyed illusion—even though Hargrove was an easygoing sort who would not relish the prospect of ordering her death or anyone else's, he loved the power of his office, and the status it gave him. The senator would never sacrifice money, position, and his marriage, much less his personal freedom, for Neely's sake.

She must be more careful now and stop pretending to herself that all was right with the world.

Chapter

3

When Aidan awakened, he was dangerously weak, a state that rendered him vulnerable to all manner of enemies. He had no choice but to hunt.

He rose slowly and stretched, this last being an unnecessary habit lingering from his days as a mortal. Aidan's muscles had long since atrophied to a stonelike condition beneath his skin. Even that was changed, he thought, extending his arms and gazing at his hands. The once-living flesh was now as cold and smooth and hard as marble.

Aidan did not stay long in his lair, for the hunger had grown merciless in its intensity, biting into his middle, sapping his strength, threatening his very reason. He climbed deftly up the smooth dirt wall to the surface of the ground. There, the moon shed a silvery light over a new layer of snow.

He thought first of Neely, and ached to be mortal and thoroughly ordinary so that he could be close to her, learn how her mind and heart worked, walk in sunlight with her. Most of all, he wanted to make love to her, feeling his own flesh warm and supple against hers, but that seemed the most impossible of all his dreams.

It was dangerous to think in such a fashion, he reminded himself. He would never be human again, and he would die at the hands of his enemies before he would turn Neely into what he was.

Aidan knew his vampire powers well, despise them

41

though he did, and he feared that the fervor of his emotions would draw Neely to him. If he were to encounter her now, when he was so desperate to feed, when his vile hunger for blood would be coupled with the elemental physical and emotional passion he felt for her, he could not be sure of restraining himself.

As it happened, thrusting Neely from his mind was not enough, for she clung tenaciously to the innermost cords and fibers of his heart.

Maeve hid herself in the chilly mists of the evening and waited. Through the foggy windows of the Lakeview Café, she could see Neely Wallace, the woman Valerian was so concerned about.

Valerian was Maeve's mentor, after a fashion, and he had made her an immortal when Aidan refused. Thus, she trusted Valerian, as much as one vampire ever trusts another, and since he saw the Wallace woman as a threat to Aidan, so had she. Maeve had come to this backward country, this century she heartily disliked, prepared to confront and destroy an enemy. Instead she found herself drifting with the breeze in a parking lot, like so much smoke, and questioning Valerian's judgment.

Miss Wallace was an attractive young woman, between twenty-five and thirty, Maeve guessed, with short, shiny brown hair and large gamine eyes. She smiled a lot, and the café customers seemed to like her, but she was clearly an ordinary mortal with no special powers of any sort.

How could such a creature be a menace to any vampire, even a reluctant one like Aidan?

Maeve was irritated and not a little bored. She'd fed early so that the evening would be her own, and now she was missing at least one very important social event—specifically Columbine Spencer's supper-dance in Charleston, South Carolina.

"Bother," said Maeve. In a fit of pique she willed herself to Aidan's house, solidifying herself very dramatically in the center of his parlor.

He was there, remarkably, sitting behind the antique library table he used as a desk, bent over one of those interminable volumes of his. Even though there was electricity in this crass century, and his house was wired for it, he worked by the light of a smelly oil lamp.

He raised his eyes at Maeve's appearance, grinned, and stood, as befits a gentleman vampire.

"Kiss, kiss," said Maeve, making an appropriate motion with her lips. She placed her hands on her trim waist—she was wearing an elaborate white dress decorated with hundreds of tiny iridescent beads, because of the Spencer party—and tossed her head impatiently. Her dark hair was done up in tiny ringlets and curls, her flawless white skin prettily flushed because she'd taken nourishment soon after awakening. "Honestly, darling, you're becoming the worst sort of curmudgeon." She held out a slender gloved hand. "Come. I'm on my way to a ball, and I know the Spencers would be delighted to have you among their guests."

Instead of lowering himself into his chair, Aidan perched on the edge of his desk, his arms folded. "I suppose all the very best fiends will be in attendance," he teased, arching one dark eyebrow.

Maeve was not amused. "The majority will be mortals, of course," she said, raising her chin. "Stage actors, an opera singer, some artists of various sorts, I suppose—"

"Along with a vampire or two, a handful of witches and warlocks—"

Color flared in Maeve's alabaster cheeks. "When did you become such a snob?" she demanded. She didn't wait for an answer. "Valerian told me you were developing a dangerous predilection for the society of humans. Even after a firsthand look at the supposed object of your fascination, I still thought he was mistaken. Now I'm not so certain."

All friendliness had vanished from Aidan's manner. His eyes narrowed as he regarded his twin in the smoky light of the oil lamp. "What do you mean, 'after a firsthand look at the supposed object of my fascination'?"

Maeve gathered all her formidable forces, as she sometimes did when she wanted to intimidate a particularly brazen human. "I went to see Neely Wallace," she said.

Aidan didn't move, and yet every fiber of his being seemed to exude challenge. *"What?"*

Maeve began to pace, folding and unfolding her silk and ivory fan as she moved. "So it's true, then. You're actually smitten with a human being." She stopped and gazed at her brother with tears glittering in her stricken blue eyes. "Oh, Aidan, how could you do something so foolish?"

She saw conflict in her brother's remarkable face, as well as pain. *"Smitten* is hardly the word for what I'm feeling," he confessed. "Maeve, I've encountered the woman exactly twice, and it's as if she owns my soul. I keep recalling what the gypsy woman said that day Mother took us to have our fortunes told. Do you remember?"

Maeve flinched inwardly, wanting to recoil from the memory and all it might mean, even after so many years, but unable to do so. "Yes," she said grimly, "I remember it perfectly well. We visited a flea-infested camp, and Mama, bless her simple heart, paid an old, ignorant crone to predict our futures."

Aidan gazed at her in quiet reflection for a long moment, and Maeve saw something uncomfortably like compassion move in his eyes.

She was indignant. "All right," she conceded, even though her brother had not actually challenged her, "the witch was right about some things—our being cursed, if you want to think of it as that—but there is no reason to believe—"

"That Neely is the woman the sorceress mentioned?" Aidan finished gently. "The one who would mean either my salvation or my destruction?" He paused, evidently gathering his thoughts, and frowned pensively when he spoke again. "Oh, to the contrary, my dear, there is every reason to believe it. I know almost nothing about Neely, and as you've so often pointed out, she is a mortal. And for all of that, when I saw her, it was as though my very soul leapt out of me and ran to her, desperate to lose itself in her."

44

Aidan looked so haunted, so beleaguered, that Maeve wanted to weep. She began in that moment to fear the Wallace woman, and to hate her, for if Aidan's theory was fact and not fancy, then the situation was grave, indeed.

"What are you going to do?" Maeve whispered, struggling to restrain all the wild, violent emotions that suddenly possessed her.

"Do?" Aidan countered softly. "My dear sister, there is nothing to 'do.' It is something that must unfold."

"No," Maeve protested, shaken, remembering that long-ago day in the gypsy camp as if it were a part of last week instead of a remnant from a distant century. "The crone said it depended on your choices, yours and hers, whether you would be saved or destroyed!"

Aidan came to her then and laid his hands gently to either side of her face. "But I can only control my own choices," he pointed out with infinite tenderness. "What Neely decides is quite beyond me—" He must have seen the rebellion brewing in Maeve's eyes, for he smiled sadly and clarifed, "Beyond both of us."

Maeve was full of fury and fear. "You want to perish!" she accused. "Damn you, Aidan, I followed you into eternity, and now you would leave me to take refuge in death!"

He released her, stepped away, turned his back to stand at one of the tall windows, gazing out upon the snowy night. "To be parted from you would be exceedingly painful," he admitted, almost grudgingly. "Still, we are brother and sister, Maeve, not lovers. Perhaps we simply were not meant to travel the same path."

Maeve steadied herself, called on all her vampire powers to sustain her, as the agonizing truth of Aidan's words settled over her spirit. "You've decided, then, that you will pursue this madness?"

"Yes," he replied wearily, without turning to face his sister. For the first time in all the winding length of Maeve's memory, he seemed unaware of her feelings. "Yes," he repeated. "For good or ill, I will see it through and find my fate at the end."

At last Aidan abandoned that wretched window to look at Maeve again, though he kept his distance. She knew the span was not merely physical, but emotional, too, and she was further wounded by this realization.

"You are not to interfere, no matter how consuming the temptation may be," he warned quietly but with the utmost strength of purpose. "I mean what I say, Maeve—if you value my wishes, if you care for me at all, you will avoid Neely Wallace at all costs."

Maeve was stricken, for she could not doubt that Aidan was grimly sincere. If she meddled in this threatening affair, he might never forgive her, and the thought of his scorn was beyond endurance.

Still, she was angry as well, and suspicious. "Can you possibly believe there is a need for you to defend her against me?"

Aidan did not relent. "I don't know," he answered bluntly, "but aside from wanting to let this thing run its course, be it curse or blessing, I am concerned for Neely's safety. As you well understand, your presence could draw the attention of the others to Neely. Suppose, for instance, that Lisette should learn of her?"

Maeve had heard the rumors that Lisette, the most vicious and unfortunately the most powerful of all vampires, had come forth from her tomb, but she had disregarded them as alarmist drivel. "Don't be an idiot," she replied. "Even if Lisette is stirring abroad now and again, she surely has no interest in the likes of your pitiful mortal."

"She is *not* pitiful in any way, shape, or form," Aidan retorted tersely. "Neely is a magical creature, like most humans, and part of her splendor lies in the fact that she is quite unaware of her own majesty."

Maeve examined her ivory-colored fingernails, which were perfectly shaped and buffed to a soft glow. She was still in turmoil, and her outward calm was all pretense. "You're right to be afraid of Lisette," she said with a lightness she did not feel. She was injured, and in her pain she needed to be cruel. "If your enemies suspect you are fond of the woman, they may use her to make you suffer." She paused a moment for effect, then went boldly on, aware that the attempt was futile even as she made it. "There is one way to solve the problem forever, Aidan. 'If thy right eye offends thee . . .' "

His rage was sudden and palpable; it filled the room with coldness. And it confirmed Maeve's worst suspicions.

"No." He whispered the word, but it had all the strength of an earthquake. "Neely is not to be touched, do you understand me? Her only sin is that she brought a child to my door one night, on an innocent errand—"

Maeve lifted one hand and laid an index finger to Aidan's lips to silence him. "You needn't raise your voice, darling," she said, again with a levity that was wholly feigned. "I will respect your wishes, you know that. Know also, however, that I love you and that I will do whatever I must to keep you safe."

They studied each other in silence for a long interval, equally determined, equally powerful.

"Please," Maeve cajoled finally. "Come to the ball with me. What better way to draw the attention of the others away from Neely Wallace?"

Aidan hesitated, then gave a grim nod.

He went upstairs to change into suitable clothing and quickly rejoined Maeve in the study. He was breathtakingly handsome in a top hat and tails, and for added affect he wore his silk cape.

Five minutes later, distracted and silent, he was entering the Spencers' antebellum ballroom with Maeve on his arm.

Once her shift was over, Neely lingered at one of the Formica-topped tables in the café, sipping herbal tea and poring over the information she'd collected earlier at the library. She became, by an act of will, the detached professional, putting her personal feelings about Aidan temporarily on hold.

She'd found a number of articles regarding the Tremayne family on microfilm and made photocopies of each one. According to the newspaper pieces, there had been an Aidan Tremayne living in the colonial mansion for well over a century. Each generation was as reclusive as the last, apparently marrying and raising their families elsewhere. There were no wedding or engagement announcements, no records of local births, no obituaries. The articles yielded only the most general information—in the summer of 1816, part of the house had been destroyed by fire. During the War Between the States, Union troops had moved into the downstairs rooms. In 1903 a young woman had disappeared after leaving a calling card at the Tremayne residence, and there had been a brief flurry of scandal, an earnest but fruitless police investigation. One of the earlier ancestors had been a painter of some renown, and several of his pieces had brought a fortune at auction in 1956.

Only when one of the chairs on the opposite side of the table scraped back did Neely bring herself out of her revelry. Lifting her eyes, she saw her brother sitting across from her.

Ben resembled nothing so much as a renegade biker, with his long hair, battered jeans, and black T-shirt, but in truth he was a solid citizen. He worked hard managing the motel, café, and trailer court, and he was a conscientious father to Danny.

"Digging up more dirt on Senator Hargrove?" he asked. The café was closed now, and the night cook and the other waitress had gone home for the night. They could talk freely.

Of course, Ben knew all about the discoveries she'd made while working in the senator's office as his assistant. She'd told him everything, from the very beginning, when she'd only suspected that her employer was consorting with criminals in general and drug dealers in particular, and he'd known about the documented proof she'd collected, too.

Neely shook her head in answer to his question; there was probably a lot more "dirt" to be dug up where Dallas Hargrove was concerned, but she was through playing detective. She'd given the FBI numerous papers and even photographs outlining the senator's exploits, and now she could do nothing but wait. And hope the Feds would bring Hargrove down for good before he decided to avenge himself.

"Not this time," she said, somewhat wearily. "I'm curious about the Tremayne family, but I haven't been able to come up with much. I'll try the courthouse tomorrow."

Ben looked puzzled and not a little uncomfortable. "Why, Neely? What interest could you possibly have in that place or those people? Hell, I've always thought it was a little spooky, the way that guy keeps to himself."

Neely propped one elbow on the table and cupped her chin in her hand. "I can't explain it," she answered, because honesty had always come easily with Ben. "It's almost like a compulsion. I've met Mr. Tremayne twice, and both times I felt some kind of paradigm shift—something I never even guessed it was possible to feel. Unless I watch myself, I think I could actually love him."

Ben shook his head and grinned, then got up to go to the pie keeper on the counter. He took out two slices of lemon meringue and returned to the table. Usually he wouldn't have stuck around, but Danny was spending the night in town with a friend from school, and there was no need to hurry home.

"Would that be so awful?" he asked. "If you fell in love, I mean?"

She picked up a fork and cut off a bite-size piece of pie. "When are you going to get married again, Ben?" she countered, purposely stalling. "Shannon's been gone for five years now. Isn't it time you had a romance?"

Ben chuckled, but there was sadness in the sound. "It isn't quite that easy," he said. "Nobody's likely to mistake me for Kevin Costner, for one thing, and for another, well, my job isn't exactly impressive. I have a young son who still looks for his mother to come home, a beat-up old truck that needs an overhaul, a small savings account, and medical bills roughly equal to the national debt. What woman in her right mind would tie up with me?"

Neely reached across the table and touched her brother's tattooed forearm affectionately. "None, if you're going to take that attitude," she scolded with a smile. "What about the fact that you're loyal—you stuck by Shannon through one of the worst ordeals a human being can experience, and you were there for her the whole time, even though you must have been reeling with pain yourself. You've raised Danny ever since, with love and gentleness, and you're resilient, Ben. A lot of other people would have given up, being widowed and laid off in the same year, but you kept going. You're a special guy, and there must be plenty of good women out there looking for somebody like you. All you've got to do is stop hiding behind that gruff exterior of yours."

A slight blush told Neely that her compliments had struck their mark. Ben concentrated on his pie for a time, chewing and swallowing several bites before he met his sister's eye and tried again. "How about you, Neely? Is it serious, what's happening between you and this Tremayne character?"

She looked away. "It could be," she admitted softly, after staring out at the snowy night for a long time. "At least on my side. For all I know, Aidan has never given me a second thought." It was time to steer the subject in another direction, however briefly. "The people Hargrove is involved with may wait years to strike, Ben, but sooner or later they'll see that I meet with an accident. It's bad enough that I'm hanging around here, in such an obvious place, endangering you and Danny. I can't drag some unsuspecting man into the situation, too."

Ben finished his pie and ate what was left of Neely's, since she'd pushed her plate away. "We're a pair, you and I," he said. "Still, the senator and his bunch are bound to go to prison, once the full extent of their sins comes to light. Then none of them will be a danger to you anymore."

Neely gave her brother a wry look, carried their plates into the café's small kitchen, and returned to gather up her photocopies before answering. "We've had this conversation before," she pointed out. "We keep going over the same ground, again and again, as if we believe on some level that the situation will change if we just *discuss* things enough."

With a sheepish shrug Ben stood, taking his lined denim jacket from the brass coat tree next to the door and putting it on. "Who knows?" He waited while Neely donned her pea coat and fetched her purse from behind the counter. "It seems to me that it's taking the FBI a long time to pull the investigation together and make a move. Maybe you ought to give the material you gathered to the producer of one of those tabloid TV shows. I'll bet *that* would bring some action."

Neely passed through the open café doorway ahead of her brother, raising her collar against the cold wind while she waited for him to turn out the lights and lock the door. There were several big rigs in the parking lot, their drivers either staying at the motel or sacked out in sleepers in the backs of their truck cabs.

"I may approach a journalist or a reporter," she said, "if the FBI doesn't do something soon." Neely had another set of copies of the incriminating documents stashed away in a safe place, but she'd never told Ben or anyone else where they were. It was something too dangerous to know.

A hard crust had formed on the snowy ground, and the sky was clear, full of icy stars. Misty clouds passing over the moon made it look blurry and slightly out of focus. Neely's clunky waitress shoes made a satisfying crunching sound as she and Ben walked toward home.

Ben escorted her to her trailer and waited while she worked the lock, opened the door, and turned on the lights.

"Tomorrow's your day off," her brother reminded her, hands in the pockets of his jacket. "Do something constructive with it, why don't you, instead of rooting around in the courthouse files or straining your eyes at one of those microfilm machines."

Neely smiled. "Good night, Ben," she said.

He chuckled, shook his head, and walked away toward his own nearby trailer.

After locking up and performing her usual nighttime ablutions, Neely folded out her sofa bed and collapsed. She'd meant to go over the newspaper articles she'd copied at the library once more, just in case she'd missed something. Instead she barely managed to switch out the lamp on the wall above the couch before she tumbled into an unusually deep slumber.

Almost immediately she began to dream.

Aidan Tremayne appeared at the foot of her bed, even more handsome than before in the kind of beautifully tailored dancing clothes leading men sometimes wore in movies made in the thirties and forties. He even had on a top hat, set at a rakish angle, and his dark cape rustled in the draft.

As the dreaming Neely raised herself on one elbow to stare at him, he winked.

Neely laughed. "See if I ever have a chili dog with onions for dinner again," she said.

Aidan smiled and tipped his hat, tumbling it down his arm and catching it in one gloved hand.

Neely clapped, and he bowed deeply. She hoped the dream wasn't over, that the lemon meringue pie would pick up where the chili dog had left off.

"Is this dream a talkie?" she asked. "Or are we going to use subtitles?"

He held out one hand, and she felt herself rising effortlessly from the bed, floating toward him. "It's wired for sound," he answered. He caught her in his arms, and she felt tremendous energy in him, as well as danger, and, within herself, a tumultuous need. "I'm afraid I'm quite bewitched."

Neely reminded herself that she was asleep and decided to enjoy the night fancy as much as possible before real life intruded. She allowed herself to revel in being held close against him, to savor the melting warmth in her most feminine parts and the bittersweet ache that had taken root in her heart.

"You're dressed for dancing," she observed.

The walls of the trailer seemed to disintegrate; there was

only Neely herself, and Aidan Tremayne, holding her, with all the universe silent and still around them. Stars fell in glittering arches and formed a twinkling pool beneath their feet.

Aidan's dark blue eyes sparkled more brightly than anything in the firmaments of heaven possibly could have. "Yes," he agreed. "You, on the other hand, are quite scantily clad."

Neely sighed. One nice thing about the imagination—a person could dance on the night wind in an oversize T-shirt without getting cold and give in to a scandalous attraction knowing that, come morning, it would no longer be real.

"This is wonderful," she said. "A girl can go her whole life without ever having a dream like this."

Aidan said nothing; instead, he drew her closer and bent his mouth to kiss her, and set her very soul to spinning within her like a skater on ice.

The kiss mended some parts of her that she had not guessed were broken, but shattered others, and Neely wept because she knew she loved Aidan Tremayne, that she would always love him, that this love was hopeless outside of her dream.

They waltzed along the treetops, up a staircase of stars, all around the moon. There was beautiful music, of course, for this was a celestial production number. The tune was unique, rife with a bittersweet poignancy, and it was still running through Neely's mind when she awoke with a thumping start, sitting up in the middle of her bed.

She was gasping for breath, feeling as though she'd been dropped from a great height. Her cheeks were wet with tears.

Neely hugged herself and rocked back and forth on her knees, possessed by a sudden and terrible sense of loss. The miraculous fantasy was evaporating, so she scrambled in the darkness for a pencil and a piece of paper in order to record it. She started to write, but the last of the memory faded, like a final heartbeat.

She switched on the light, trembling with this new grief,

and read what she'd written on the back of her telephone bill. All that was left of her magnificent vision was a single, hastily scrawled word.

Aidan.

Chapter

4

Aidan slept profoundly all the following day, beyond the reach of dreams and nightmares that trouble mortals. He awakened only a few minutes after sunset and was still assembling his wits when Maeve appeared, resplendent in a flowing white toga.

She looked around the dark mine shaft, noting its lacery of cobwebs with mild but still obvious disdain. "Your capacity for self-punishment never ceases to amaze me," she remarked.

Methodically Aidan dusted the sleeves of his evening coat. He arched one eyebrow as he regarded his sister. Maeve was dressed for some kind of Roman celebration, but not the authentic article; like most vampires, she was forbidden to venture back prior beyond the instant of her death as a human being. He made a *tsk-tsk* sound and shook his head.

"On your way to one of those debauched Victorian parties?" he inquired, taking off his coat to shake out the dust, then putting it on again.

"It isn't 'debauched,' " Maeve snapped, her blue eyes fiery. "The Havermails are perfectly nice—"

"People?" Aidan teased.

Maeve looked away for a moment. "Vampires," she said distractedly. "They're vampires, of course." Her temper flared anew. "Stop trying to change the subject. You left the ball early last night, Aidan. Where were you?"

Aidan had a yearning for fresh air, even though he could

not actually breathe the wonderful stuff. He pictured himself standing on the snowy ground overhead, and as quickly as that, he was there. Only a moment later Maeve was beside him.

The woods were quiet, except for the far-off hooting of an owl and the vague murmur of tires passing through slush on Route 7. Clouds hid the moon, and a sort of pale darkness had spread itself over the land.

"Where were you, Aidan?" Maeve persisted.

He started toward the house. He would change clothes and feed early that night, he decided, and then play his favorite, futile game by pretending to be a man again. "Assuming that's any of your business, which it isn't," he retorted without stopping, "why in hell do you care?"

Maeve stepped in front of him and glared up into his eyes. "You endanger all of us when you consort with humans, Aidan, you know that! If you truly want to throw away your own existence, I guess I'll just have to endure it, but you have *no right* to bring risk on the rest of us!"

Aidan winced, for her words stung. "All right," he said, feeling exasperated and weary, so unbelievably weary. He was like a guilty husband, hastening to explain a gap in his schedule, and he resented the comparison bitterly. "I left the ball, I came back here, and I settled in my lair to hibernate, like any good beast."

Maeve subsided a little and allowed Aidan to pass, rushing to keep up just as she had when they were children. "Valerian said you were dancing with—with that Neely creature."

"It was only a mental exercise, a shared fantasy," Aidan responded. He hated explaining even that much, but it was true that others might be threatened by his fascination with Neely. Too much association with mortals, for purposes other than feeding, of course, served to dilute a vampire's powers and dull his perceptions. Other fiends, such as Lisette, were frenzied by weakness, like sharks in bloody waters. "You don't think I'd dare to actually dance with her, do you, to hold her in my arms? A human woman?"

They reached the rear of the towering stone house and entered through the mudroom. In the kitchen, which contained almost nothing in the way of food, Maeve stopped her brother again, this time by reaching out and catching hold of his sleeve.

"Couldn't you simply put her out of your mind? Surely it isn't too late!"

Aidan gazed into his sister's face for a long time before answering hoarsely, "It was too late at the beginning of time," he responded. "Leave it alone, Maeve. There is no changing this."

"Put her out of your mind," Maeve pleaded, sounding frantic. "If you must play at romance, choose an immortal!" Tears glimmered in her eyes, and Aidan was touched; he was surprised that she'd retained the ability to weep.

He gripped Maeve's upper arms and squeezed gently. "I don't know what this is," he told her. "I don't pretend to understand what's happening to me. But I know this much—it can't be avoided. You, Valerian, the others—you must all stay away from me until it's resolved, one way or the other."

"No," Maeve said. "I cannot abandon you, Aidan—"

"You must!"

"I won't."

He hissed a swear word.

After a long interval of struggle, plainly visible in her expressive eyes, Maeve lifted one hand to touch his face. "Very well. I will do my best to keep my distance for as long as I can," she promised in a despairing whisper. "But hear this, Aidan, and remember it well: I will be guarding and nurturing my powers from this moment on. He—or she—who does you injury will feel the full force of my vengeance, and I will not trouble myself with mercy."

Aidan felt a mental chill. While his twin fed only on those humans whose souls were already damned, as he did, she did not share his aversion to the life of a vampire. To Maeve, the compulsion to consume human blood was a small price to pay for immortality, the capacity to travel through time and space at will, the heightening of the senses, and the fathomless physical energy.

"Stay away from Neely," he warned.

Maeve drew herself up, seeming to blaze with white fire. "If she brings about your destruction, she will die."

Before Aidan could respond, his sister vanished. He was alone in his shell of a kitchen, with its empty cupboards. He leaned against a counter, arms folded, full of despondency and yearning for ordinary pleasures, like the sound and scent of bacon sizzling in a skillet and the embrace of a woman, still warm from sleep.

What cruel irony it was, he reflected, that mortals never seemed to understand what a glorious gift it was, just to be human. If only they knew how they'd been blessed. . . .

Washington, D.C.

Senator Dallas Hargrove left his Georgetown house by a side door, wearing battered jeans, a T-shirt rescued from a bag of rags in the laundry room, sneakers, and a jacket so old that the leather had cracked in places. He pulled the collar up around his face and whistled tunelessly as he walked.

He was good at avoiding the press and other pests, and that night his luck held. He walked until he was some distance from the gracious room where his lovely, fragile wife slept, then hailed a cab.

The driver didn't recognize him—Washington was crawling with government types, after all—and drove him to a park at the edge of the city without question.

"Wait here," Dallas said. The snow was coming down harder, and not only was the wind picking up speed, but it also had a bite to it.

The man in the cab shifted uncomfortably. "I don't know, man," he said. "This ain't the *best* neighborhood in D.C."

Dallas handed over the fare, then flashed a fifty-dollar bill and a vote-getting smile. "Five minutes?"

The cabbie sighed, snapped up the fifty. "Five minutes,"

he agreed. "But that's all, and I mean it, man." He rested one arm in the open window of the battered, smoke-belching old cab and tapped the face of his watch with an index finger. "Once that sweep second hand has made five swings past the numbers, I'm out of here."

Dallas nodded, turned, and sprinted away into the park. There were a few derelicts sleeping on and under benches, but the wandering bands of thugs who usually frequented the place had apparently stayed in out of the cold. He walked quickly to the statue of a minor Civil War general mounted on a horse and stood in its long shadow.

His contact spoke up right away, though as usual Dallas didn't see more than a vague form. It gave him the creeps; the guy was like a ghost, moving without noise, materializing where he chose.

"It's time the Wallace woman was disposed of."

Dallas felt a twinge of guilt, even though logic told him Neely deserved whatever she got. She'd violated his trust, after all, sneaking around, going through his files and papers the way she had. Still, she was a pretty, vibrant thing and killing her would be like crushing an exquisite rose just opening to the sunlight. "Look," he said reasonably, "my friend at the FBI forestalled any problems we might have had. And Ms. Wallace hasn't made a move since or even tried to hide. She's living in Connecticut, for God's sake, helping her brother run a truck stop and motel. I say we leave her alone."

"She set out to bring us all down, Senator—you included. Who's to say she won't try again?"

Dallas ground his teeth, caught himself, and forcibly relaxed. He didn't want to see Neely die, despite the way she'd betrayed him, but he couldn't stand against these people. If he was foolish enough to try, he would be killed or crippled for his trouble, and then what would happen to Elaine? Who would take care of her if not him?

Once his beautiful wife had been vital and active, a successful journalist. Now she was confined to a wheelchair, suffering from a progressive muscular disease. Elaine's prognosis was grim, and he could not abandon her.

"You know where to find her," Hargrove said, rubbing his eyes with a thumb and forefinger. He had to think about his family, his backers, his constituents. What was one woman compared with so many others?

Almost five minutes had passed by that time, and Dallas was painfully conscious of the taxi driver's promise to leave when that small amount of time had elapsed. He handed over a packet of documents, and the man in the shadows reciprocated with a thick envelope.

It was all for Elaine, the senator told himself as he turned and hurried toward the curb. The cab was already moving when he landed inside.

Aidan washed, groomed his hair, and put on jeans and an Irish cable-knit sweater. He would hunt early, get the abominable task out of the way, and spend the evening next to the fire, working on his journal.

He guarded his thoughts carefully, for to think of Neely too intensely would be to summon her to his side. That would be embarrassing for him because he would have to come up with an explanation, and for Neely because she would suddenly find herself in his home with no memory of traveling there.

It was, he found, a little like that old schoolyard routine "Don't think of blue elephants." Fortunately the hunger was keen enough that night to provide sufficient distraction.

Aidan took a computer printout from a file cabinet against the wall, laid it on his desk, and ran his finger down the list of names. These men subscribed to the very basest of pornographic magazines, the kind even the most flagrant liberal would happily consign to the bonfire.

He selected a victim in the next county, closed his eyes, and vanished.

Only minutes later he was back.

*   *   *

Neely certainly didn't make a habit of walking alone along Route 7 at eleven-thirty at night, but she was too restless to stay inside her trailer. God knew, the place wasn't spacious, and that evening it seemed even smaller than usual. She'd felt like a grasshopper trapped in a pint jar.

As she walked, keeping to the far edge of the shoulder in an effort to avoid the headlights of passing cars, fat flakes of iridescent snow tumbled from the sky. She often found such weather peaceful, even festive, but just then it seemed eerie.

How ridiculous, Neely decided, to be so upset over a dream she could hardly remember. Aidan Tremayne had been part of it, she knew that much, and a wisp of weirdly beautiful music echoed in her mind.

As if all that wasn't enough, she had a sense that someone was stalking her, closing in slowly, watching and waiting.

She shivered and walked faster, stopping only when she reached the head of the Tremayne driveway.

"You're crazy," she told herself as a mud-splattered Blazer passed on the other side of Route 7, then slowed.

Neely's heart seemed to slide over an expanse of sheer ice, leaving her breathless. She bolted into the woods, stumbling in the deep snow. From the highway she heard the slam of a car door.

"Hey, lady, come back!" a man's voice called.

Neely ran on, tripped over a fallen birch limb, scraped her shin, scrambled to her feet again, and flung herself headlong toward Aidan's house. She could see the light on his front porch through the trees.

Behind her, the man from the Blazer crashed along in pursuit.

Neely looked back, half blind with unreasoning terror, and collided hard with something. At first she thought it was a tree, but then a pair of strong hands steadied her, and she looked up into the classically handsome face of Aidan Tremayne. She was too breathless to speak.

"You're all right now," he said in a low voice. For the

first time she noticed a hint of a brogue in the way he framed his words. "No one's going to hurt you." He glared into the woods with a chilling intentness for a long moment, then shifted his gaze back to Neely again.

He smiled, and some of the starch went out of her knees.

Vaguely she heard running footsteps, the crash of a car door closing, the squeal of tires on wet pavement.

"What you need is a cup of tea," Aidan said, as though it were perfectly normal for the two of them to be standing out there in the woods at that hour. He wasn't even wearing a coat, just jeans and a fisherman's sweater. "Come along now."

Neely allowed him to escort her through the woods; he politely cupped her elbow in one hand.

"Do you always go out walking at such odd times?" he asked. There was no irritation in the question, only a companionable kind of curiosity.

"No," Neely answered, somewhat weakly. "No, I don't. It's just that I've been feeling very restless lately—"

"Any idea who the rascal in the woods might have been?"

Neely shook her head, embarrassed. She was making one hell of an impression. "I ran into the trees when he stopped and turned around, and he followed. He was probably harmless, but—"

"But you don't think so?" he asked. They had gained the edge of Aidan's sloping lawn.

Again she shook her head. "I have some formidable enemies," she said.

"So do I," he replied. They mounted the steps to the porch, and he held the door open for her, waiting politely while she passed over the threshold.

He led her into a parlor, where oil lamps burned cozily and a fire blazed on the hearth. "Here," he said, depositing her in a large leather chair. "Have a seat and catch your breath. I'll get that tea. Or would you rather have brandy?"

"Brandy," Neely said without hesitation.

Aidan smiled, went to a sideboard, and poured amber

liquid into an etched glass snifter. He brought Neely the drink but stood well away from her chair while she sipped.

"I know I've already disrupted your evening," she began when her limbs had stopped quivering and her heart had slowed to its normal pace, "but I wonder if you'd mind driving me home. I'm afraid to walk, under the circumstances."

He was near the fireplace, arms folded, his back braced against the mantelpiece. The first two times Neely had encountered him, she'd been struck by the unusual fairness of his complexion, but that night his face looked quite normal, almost ruddy. "I'll bring the car around in a few minutes," he said in that refined voice of his.

Neely stared at him over the rim of her glass, wanting to blurt out that she'd dreamed about him, that she wondered why. But she only nodded.

"These 'powerful enemies' of yours," he said, watching her in a way that made her feel like some unparalleled work of art. "Can you tell me who they are?"

She sighed and sank back in the chair, slouching, running one index finger around the rim of the snifter. "It might not be wise to do that," she mused after a long time. "It's dangerous to know too much."

One moment he was halfway across the room, the next, Aidan was crouching beside her chair.

"It's often more dangerous not knowing enough, don't you think?"

Neely felt a purely elemental pull toward him and turned her head slightly in order to protect herself. She sighed. "I used to work for a United States senator," she said. "He was involved in some very crooked deals, and I gathered enough proof to put him, and the creeps he was dealing with, out of business. Or so I thought." Out of the corner of her eye she saw that he was looking at the base of her throat, and she felt a sudden and inexplicable desire to surrender to the dark magic she saw in his eyes. "Now it appears that they've decided to make sure I can't cause any more trouble," she finished shakily in a distracted tone.

He bolted away from her with unsettling swiftness. Had

he been anyone other than who he was, Neely would have thought he hadn't heard her explanation, but she knew very little got by Aidan, whether he appeared to be paying attention or not.

"It will require some thought—your predicament, I mean," he said gravely, avoiding her gaze. "Please, make yourself comfortable. I'll bring the car to the front of the house in a few minutes. I don't use it often, so the engine will need some time to warm up."

Neely nodded, feeling both relief and disappointment at the prospect of being separated from him.

"Thank you," she said.

Aidan left the room.

Neely waited, then raised herself out of the chair, supporting her weight with one hand and clutching the empty snifter in the other. Her legs were still trembling, and the small injury she'd done to her shin earlier stung like crazy, but the brandy had definitely restored her. And none of those things were of any consequence at all in comparison to the emotions and yearnings Aidan Tremayne brought out in her.

She crossed to Aidan's desk and set the snifter down.

There was a music box sitting just to the left of the blotter, and Neely automatically reached for it, wanting to think of something else, if only for a moment, to shift her thoughts from the master of that spooky old house.

Besides, she had a collection of such boxes tucked away in a rented storage unit, along with most of her other belongings. The small mechanisms and delicate tunes had always appealed to her.

This one was clearly antique, perhaps dating back to the early nineteenth century. The case was carved of the finest rosewood, and there were tiny forest animals etched into its top.

Neely lifted the lid, and the tinkling notes of an old tune rose from inside. She trembled, and her heart lurched painfully.

It was the same melody she'd heard in her dream.

With a little cry Neely closed the music box and stepped back.

"Is something wrong?" an unfamiliar male voice inquired.

Neely whirled, one shock compounding with another. She had never seen the man standing behind her; he was enormous, imposing, and, she supposed, handsome, with his rich chestnut hair and discerning violet eyes. She clasped one hand to her chest and made an inarticulate sound.

"I've frightened you." With a calm, easy smile the man bowed his head. "I apologize."

Neely was still shaken, but she was beginning to regain her equilibrium. She would work out the music box thing later, she decided. As for the man's sudden appearance, well, that was easily explained. The Tremayne house was large, and Aidan hadn't said he was alone there. She had simply assumed that.

"My name is Valerian. Yours?"

"Neely," she said, still breathing fast. Could this man be the same one who had chased her into the woods? No— she'd been watching too much television and reading too many thrillers, that was all. This guy was hardly the sort to go rambling through the trees in the dead of night, and it was impossible to imagine him behind the wheel of a Blazer. "Neely Wallace."

"A pleasure," he said, taking Neely's hand, which she didn't recall extending, and barely brushing the knuckles with his lips.

A shiver went through her, part pleasure and part primal fear. She felt light-headed, almost as if she'd been hypnotized. She wrenched back her hand just as Aidan entered the room again, bringing the scents of fresh air and snow with him.

He looked at Valerian but spoke to Neely.

"The car is ready," he said. His tone was terse.

Neely nodded and scrambled into her coat, eager to be away. And, if she was to be honest, eager to be alone with Aidan again.

A white English sports car, a Triumph Spitfire with a canvas top and plenty of chrome, waited in front of the house. Aidan opened the passenger door for Neely before going around to the driver's side and sliding behind the wheel.

"What's going on around here?" she demanded, surprising even herself with the bluntness of the question. It seemed her troubled subconscious mind had decided to make a move on its own, bypassing the usual channels. "Aidan, I had a very strange, very vivid dream last night, about you. We danced, you and I, to an old-fashioned tune, one I'm certain I've never heard before. Tonight I lifted the lid of that music box on your desk, and out came that very same song."

Aidan shifted the expensive car into gear and stepped on the accelerator. The machine navigated the snowy driveway with ease. "Coincidence," he said, but he didn't so much as glance in her direction.

"No," Neely insisted. She was certain of that one conviction, if nothing else. "I couldn't remember the dream—it drove me crazy all day long—but when I heard that tune, everything came back to me. You and I were dancing. And— and I'm not sure now that it really *was* a dream. What's going on here, Aidan?" She paused to gather her courage. "Am I imagining the attraction between us?" she asked in a small but determined voice.

He shifted again, and the car fishtailed slightly but quickly regained its traction. "No," he said, with succinct reluctance, and in spite of all the danger she was in, Neely felt a rush of wild, flamboyant joy. She wanted Aidan to kiss her again, the way he had in the dream or delusion, whatever it had been, but he didn't even glance in her direction. "We're playing for very high stakes, here—much higher than you can possibly imagine. You must keep yourself safe, inasmuch as you can, and most of all you have to trust me."

She sighed and settled back in the leather seat, clasping her hands in her lap and memorizing his profile. "Well," she said. "That was certainly cryptic. Why do I get the feeling you don't intend to explain?"

At last he looked at her, and even though he kept his distance, Neely had the oddest sensation that she'd just been soundly kissed. The incident left her dizzy and wanting Aidan with an embarrassing desperation.

"I will explain everything when I can," he said kindly.

Neely touched her fingertips to her lips, which were still tingling from a kiss that hadn't happened.

Aidan lifted one corner of his mouth in a teasing and damnably mysterious smile. "I can do other things as well," he said, leaving her even more mystified than before. "One of these nights I'll show you."

Neely blushed and barely kept herself from blurting out that she wanted him to show her all his tricks, then and there.

They had reached the highway, and Aidan made a right turn, chuckling to himself as if he'd heard her thoughts. She squirmed as the small, sleek car shot toward the Lakeview Trailer Court and Motel.

Neely looked around, forcing herself to think of something besides the inexplicable need Aidan had managed to stir in her.

There was no sign of the Blazer; the only other vehicle they encountered was a county snowplow.

Aidan turned onto the gravel road that wound through the trailer court and came to a stop at Neely's door.

She felt as awkward as a teenage wallflower at the biggest dance of the year. She wanted Aidan to touch her and at the same time was terrified that he would. She opened the car door hastily and climbed out. "Good night," she said cheerfully. "And thank you."

He left the car, walked Neely to her door, and waited patiently until she was inside. "Good night," he said formally, although something mischievous smoldered in his eyes all the while, as she closed the door.

It was only after Aidan had driven away, the taillights

of his car blinking red in an otherwise white night, that she realized she'd never told him which trailer was hers.

"Hunt with me," Valerian pleaded as Aidan tossed his car keys into a china dish on the bookshelf behind his desk. His attention was focused on the music box.

"I've already fed," he replied, picking up the little rose-wood case and lifting the lid.

"Then feed again," Valerian said.

At last Aidan lifted his gaze. "Why? You know I abhor it."

Valerian sighed. "Yes," he agreed. "But a surplus may heighten your powers. It is more important than ever that you be strong, Aidan."

Now it was Aidan who sighed. "Another dire warning," he said, returning the box to its place. "What would you have me do? Become a hedonist as well as a heretic, like you?"

The other vampire slammed his hands down hard on the top of Aidan's desk, making the music box and several other items jump. "Spare me the moral discourse," Valerian rasped, his eyes seeming to burn like Saint Elmo's fire as he glared at Aidan from under his heavy brows. "Others have seen Lisette. She is beginning to circulate."

Aidan shoved a hand through his hair. "Perhaps the thing to do is confront her," he said.

Valerian shook his head. "In your present state, that would be disastrous. Lisette is the queen of all vampires, the first female ever created. Even after a long sleep, her powers will be formidable."

Aidan's mind touched on Neely, on her softness and warmth. He had to protect her, and the best way to do that was to leave twentieth-century Connecticut entirely. "All right," he conceded raggedly, "I'll put myself in your hands, Valerian. We'll feed together, and I'll at least listen to your counsel. I want one promise from you first, however."

The elder vampire did not speak but simply raised one eyebrow in silent question.

"You must give me your sacred vow that you will not come back for the woman."

Valerian made an exasperated sound. "I presume you mean Neely Wallace."

"You presume correctly. I saw the way you looked at her, and I know what you were thinking. I want your word that you'll leave her alone."

Valerian laughed, but there was no mirth in the sound and certainly no joy. He raised one large hand as if to swear an oath. "I will not feed on the waitress," he said. There was a pause. "Just remember, Aidan. I cannot speak for the others."

"They won't bother Neely unless you call their attention to her."

"I could say the same thing to you, my friend." With that, Valerian raised both his arms high in the air and made a sweeping and wholly theatrical gesture.

Chapter

5

Valerian was not without sympathy for Aidan, and a number of other emotions in the bargain. Indeed, he loved the younger vampire jealously, and with a devotion and tenderness that transcended all earthly meanings of the term.

Which was not to say he did not consider the poor fiend to be wholly misguided. While he himself had been a vampire for nearly six centuries, and a happy one for the most part, Valerian also cherished certain recollections of humanity. There was the warmth of spring sunlight on winter-pale flesh, for instance, the oddly pleasurable sensation of an explosive sneeze, the sweet ache that followed in the wake of unrestrained laughter, the solace of tears. Now, as they sat in the rear of a dingy London pub, pretending to consume ale and kidney pie, savoring those last precious moments before they would be forced underground, Valerian reached out to touch his companion's arm.

Aidan, who had been staring morosely into space ever since they'd left the battlefield where they'd fed last, started slightly.

"Do you really hate it so much?" Valerian asked in a low and, for him, somewhat fragile voice. He could not credit Aidan's aversions; in all his wide experience he had never encountered another vampire who did not relish what he was.

Aidan forced a smile; he was a handsome lad, and he stirred things in Valerian's being that were probably better left alone, but he lacked the sensual abandon of most immortal creatures. "Yes," he said. He was pleasantly flushed from their recent feast, but there was a look of anguish in his eyes, of torment that far exceeded any felt by the dying soldiers they'd seen that night. "Yes, I hate it. I despise it. Hell itself cannot be worse than feeling this vile compulsion!"

Had anyone else made such a statement, Valerian would have asked archly why they had troubled to become a creature of the night in the first place, but this was Aidan. Aidan, the one blood-drinker he knew who had not made the transition willingly. He sighed, turning his plain wooden cup idly in one hand. "What would you have me do? What is it you want?"

There was a quickening in Aidan; he sat a little straighter in his chair, and his blue eyes glittered with something more than the temporary fever caused by feeding. "You are the oldest vampire in our circle, except for Lisette," he said quietly, "and among the most self-serving. If there is a remedy for this wretched curse, you either know what it is or how to find out."

Valerian looked away for a moment, toward one of two small, filthy windows. A subtle grayness permeated the black of night; dawn was near, and they must take refuge very soon, or the sun would catch them abroad. "I heard a legend once," he said in a ragged, distracted whisper. "Mind you, it was only a story, I'm sure of that—"

Aidan rose and seemed to loom over him. "Tell me!" he demanded.

Again Valerian sighed. "There is no time," he replied, hoping he'd disguised his relief in feigned regret. "It's almost morning." He rose and looked Aidan squarely in the eye. "Come. I know a place where we can rest safely."

He reached out, clasped Aidan's arm, and gripped it hard when the other vampire moved to pull away. In the space of a wink they were inside a crypt in a country churchyard, far from busy, suspicious London.

"Damn you!" Aidan cried, lunging toward Valerian with

his hands out, as if to choke the life from him. Which was, of course, a macabre joke, since he was neither truly alive nor truly dead. "Tell me what you know of this legend!"

Valerian raised his arms, erecting a mental barrier between them, like a wall of glass. He smiled at Aidan's frustration and then yawned copiously. "I am too weary to tell tales," he said. "We will speak of it when the eventide comes again."

With that, Valerian turned to a stone slab, brushed away the bones and dust and the debris of a coffin that had rested there, and stretched out with a sensual sigh. He saw Aidan hesitate, then slowly, reluctantly recede, until his back touched the crypt's heavy door. He slipped into a crouch, his arms folded across his knees.

"Until evening," Aidan said. There was a warning in his tone, though his words were weighted with fatigue.

Valerian smiled again and slowly closed his eyes. Unlike younger, less sophisticated vampires, he was not totally lost to sleep; he often dreamed and sometimes projected his awareness to other places, leaving his physical self behind.

Such journeys were unquestionably dangerous, for the silver cord that anchored the spirit to the form could be severed in any number of ways. If that happened, the two could never be rejoined, and the traveler would be forced to contend with whatever fate awaited him in the next world.

The mere contemplation of such an event was a terror to sensible vampires, for even they could not see beyond the Veil to determine the true shapes of heaven and hell.

Far down in the deepest regions of his comalike rest, Valerian shuddered at the visions of eternal torment that had been impressed on his mind so long before, while he lived and breathed as a human animal. Since he had been born in medieval England, the images Valerian carried of the damned were especially horrible.

Still, he was an adventurous vampire, interminably curious, and he loved to explore the dusty little corners and pockets of time that generally went unnoticed in the great intertwining schemes of history.

And there was a secret.

Valerian loved secrets, and mysteries, and conundrums of all sorts, shapes, and sizes. All the better that only he and a handful of other old ones knew. By concentrating very hard, Valerian could cast his consciousness into the most remote folds and burrows of eternity, venturing back and back in time, passing beyond his mortal life and even his birth as a human being.

It was perilous work, utterly debilitating, often leaving him too exhausted to hunt for days afterward. Even so, Valerian could not resist occasional forays through the void, each time venturing closer to the Beginning.

That particular day he had an added impetus, bittersweet and compelling; he sought the oldest, most closely guarded secrets of the vampire, for only in finding those could he learn what Aidan so desperately wanted to know.

At nightfall Aidan stirred, opened his eyes, and raised himself slowly out of his crouch against the wall and into an upright position. Valerian still lay on his slab in the middle of the crypt, though he was awake, and he looked shrunken somehow. Even gaunt.

His flesh was a ghastly shade of gray, and there were great shadows beneath his eyes. He raised one hand weakly, to summon Aidan to his side, and even though there were no tears, it was plain that he was weeping deep down in the essence of himself.

Aidan clasped Valerian's upraised hand in both of his; they were not friends, but they were of the same brotherhood, they trod on common ground.

"What is it?" Aidan whispered. "What have you done?"

"I went back—to search—" He paused, made a strangling sound low in his throat. "Blood. I—need—blood." The plea rasped in Valerian's throat like a saw severing hardwood. He clutched Aidan's fingers so tightly that it seemed the bones would snap, brittle as twigs, drawing Aidan downward to hear, "Bring me blood."

Aware of an inexplicable urgency, and very little else,

Aidan did not pause to question the gruesome request. He went to the door of the crypt, stopped to look backward once, and then willed himself to a time and place in London he'd often visited before.

He returned within minutes, burgeoning with the blood of a back-street thief and murderer. By instinct, or perhaps by some subliminal instruction from the still-stricken Valerian, he transfused the life-giving fluid into the other vampire by puncturing the papery neck with his fangs. The process left Aidan temporarily weakened, clutching the edges of the slab to keep from falling, and only partially restored Valerian.

The elder vampire sighed and slipped into a light, fitful slumber. His skin, which had looked as fragile as ancient parchment before, took on the faintest tinge of color, and his frame seemed to fill out slightly, having fewer hollows and sharp angles.

Now that the crisis had passed, whatever it had been, Aidan was wild with impatience. He paced at the foot of Valerian's slab, feeling confined and restless to the very core of his soul. The mere memory of his strange communion with the other vampire sickened him, and yet he could not deny, even to himself, that there had been some sort of fusion of their two spirits.

After a while Valerian stirred and opened his eyes. He seemed stronger, but his whisper was labored and raw. "Leave me, Aidan. I must rest."

It was all Aidan could do not to grasp his companion's lapels and wrench him upright, so desperate was his need. "You promised to tell me what you learned!" he blurted. "You *promised!*"

"And I will keep my vow," Valerian answered, grating out each word. "I cannot—speak of it now. Have pity, Aidan."

"Just tell me this," Aidan pressed, moving to Valerian's side, clasping his cold hand. "Is there hope? Can I be unmade, become a man again?"

The answer gurgled on Valerian's tongue, as though he

were choking on the blood Aidan had given him. "It is too—dangerous," he gasped. With that he lost consciousness again.

Aidan was torn between a desire to stay and look after a fallen comrade and an almost uncontrollable urge to flee, to be as far from this place and this horror as possible.

He wanted Neely, wanted her to comfort him, to hold him tightly in her arms. He craved her humanity and her warmth, her very womanhood, but it was just that yearning that forestalled him.

Yes, he loved her, he knew that now, had begun to accept the realization. But he could not allow himself to forget that he was a beast, at least in part, and his need for blood was as great as that of any other vampire. He couldn't be certain, for all that his soul had already joined itself to hers, that his terrible thirst would not cause him to fling himself on her in a fit of passion.

The prospect of awakening from a frenzy, of finding Neely limp and lifeless in his arms, was worse than any punishment a demon could devise.

Frantically Aidan formed Maeve's image in his mind.

Neely had just finished the breakfast shift at the café when an ancient station wagon rattled into the parking lot, came to a shrill, steamy stop by the front window, and emitted a tall, gum-chewing blonde. The woman was wearing frayed jeans, an equally worn denim jacket, a tank top with a picture of a motorcycle on the front, and the kind of open, friendly smile that turns strangers into friends.

"Hi," she said, taking a seat at the counter and reaching out to pluck a menu from behind a chrome napkin holder. "My name's Doris Craig. I'm flitter-flat, down-and-out busted, and that old car of mine isn't gonna go much farther. You the manager here?"

Neely untied her apron, glancing past Doris's right shoulder, which bore a tiny tattoo of a bumblebee, to the loaded-down beater parked out front. But for its relatively modern vintage, the vehicle might have belonged to the Jode family of *Grapes of Wrath* fame, there was so much stuff tied on top and stuffed inside.

"No," she answered. "My brother manages the whole place. I just work here."

Doris closed the menu resolutely and gave Neely another of her guileless, openhearted smiles. "You aren't thinkin' of quittin' or anything, are you? If you are, I'd sure like to have your job."

Ben hadn't said he was looking for more help, but he hadn't said he wasn't, either. Neely poured a cup of hot, fresh coffee and set it down in front of Doris. "I think of quitting for the last three hours of every shift," she confessed with a grin, tapping her name tag with one finger. "I'm Neely Wallace. Glad to meet you."

Doris nodded cordially. "If you're not plannin' to quit," she said, blue eyes twinkling, "is there any chance of your gettin' fired?"

Neely laughed. "Sorry—like I said, the boss is my brother, and he's pretty well stuck with me. I'll be happy to send him over to talk to you, though. In the meantime, what'll you have?"

Doris pried two crumpled dollar bills from the pocket of her jeans and smoothed them out on the counter. "Soup and milk, if this will cover it," she said. While her circumstances were obviously desperate, there wasn't a trace of self-pity in either her voice or her manner, and Neely couldn't help being struck by such uncommon courage.

She nodded and went back to the kitchen, passing the teenager who was taking over for the afternoon and early evening shift. Heather was no unchained melody of ambition, but she showed up on time and did her job well enough, which meant she probably wouldn't be creating a vacancy anytime soon.

In the back Neely dished up a bowlful of vegetable-beef soup and grabbed a basket of soda crackers in individual wrappers. She set the food down in front of Doris, along with a spoon, and proceeded to the milk machine.

She was just putting the glass on the counter when the

little bell over the door jingled and Ben came in. He'd been shoveling snow from the walk over at the motel, and his cheeks were red from the cold.

It seemed providential to Neely, his showing up at the perfect moment like that. "Ben, this is Doris Craig," she said. "Doris, my brother, Ben Wallace. Doris is looking for work."

Ben's ever-ready smile flashed instantly; he took off his plaid coat and came over to greet Doris, one hand extended. Neely poured him a cup of coffee, then grabbed her purse, said good-bye to Heather, and hurried out.

As far as she could tell, glancing back through the frosty café window, Ben hadn't even noticed that she was gone.

Neely was deep in thought as she crossed the parking lot. Maybe the fates were trying to tell her something, sending Doris along when they had. Perhaps it was time she got on with her life; she was only marking time in Bright River, and she could no longer overlook the fact that she represented a very real danger to her brother and nephew.

Because of her distraction, Neely all but collided with the dun-colored rental car that was parked just on the other side of the hedge, motor running. There was a whirring sound, and the window on the passenger side disappeared into the door. Senator Dallas Hargrove himself leaned across the front seat and said, "Get in, Neely."

In spite of all the senator had been a party to, and all she had done to ensure his intense dislike for all eternity, Neely still couldn't believe he would actually hurt her. She'd seen him with his wife, Elaine, who suffered from a degenerative muscular disease, and knew there was no violence in him. She drew a deep breath, let it out in a rush, and got into the car.

The senator was handsome, with well-cut blond hair and a square jaw, but there had never been an attraction between them. "That was pretty stupid," he said, steering the car onto Route 7 and away from Bright River. "For all you know, I might be planning to knock you over the head and dump you in some lake."

Neely relaxed against the seat and closed her eyes for a

moment. She was so tired all of a sudden, so full of a longing she couldn't begin to understand. "You've made some terrific mistakes in your life, Senator," she said, "but you're not a murderer. Not a direct one, at least."

She could feel his tension; he was like tightly coiled wire, ready to come unwound. Still, she wasn't afraid.

"What do you mean, 'not a direct one'?" he demanded.

"We both know you've fixed it so that certain drug dealers can bring their wares into the country without the usual inconveniences," Neely answered with a sigh. "What do you think is happening to that garbage after it hits the streets? Real people are using it—kids, pregnant mothers, people who get behind the wheels of semi-trucks and school buses."

"If I didn't cooperate, someone else would." Hargrove's knuckles tightened on the steering wheel, relaxed again.

Neely reflected that her decision to get into the car with the senator might have been a bit rash after all. "That's a load of horse crap," she replied calmly. "Let's not waste our time debating the subject, since we'll never agree. What are you doing in Bright River? You can't be stumping for votes, since this isn't your district."

He turned the car off the highway onto a bumpy, unplowed road that snaked in behind a large Christmas tree farm. He stopped the car beside a weathered old mill spanning a narrow, silvery brook. His blue eyes were tormented as he looked at Neely. "Look, I came here to warn you. The people I deal with know you tried to bring the FBI down on their operation, and they want you dead. You've got to get out of here as fast as you can."

Neely regarded him in pensive silence for a time, her arms folded. "There's something I don't understand," she finally said. "I gave the government hard evidence of your involvement in a major crime syndicate. If your man on the inside hadn't managed to turn the tide—at least, that's what I *think* must have happened—you would have lost everything and gone to prison, maybe for the rest of your life. Why are you trying so hard to save me? How come you don't hate me and want me dead, like those hoods you've been hanging around with?"

Hargrove gave a despairing rush of a sigh and leaned forward, letting his forehead rest against the steering wheel. "I'm not a killer, Neely—I never meant for things to turn out this way. I needed money—there were so many debts— and then I was in too deep to get out."

"Debts? For Elaine's medical care, you mean? Come on. Thanks to the long-suffering taxpayer, you have a more than respectable salary and excellent health insurance."

The senator sat up straight, gazing out at the snow-laced mill wheel. The weathered building supporting it seemed about to cave in on itself. "There were all those special treatments, in Europe and Mexico," he said. "None of them worked, of course."

Impulsively Neely reached across the seat to touch his arm. She liked Elaine Hargrove, a brave and smiling person, liked the man the senator became whenever he was in his wife's presence.

"It wasn't just the treatments, though," Hargrove confessed wearily. "When Elaine was first diagnosed, I went a little crazy. I don't know what it was—the fear, the stress—I can't say. In any case, I was involved with a woman for a while, and then there were some gambling debts. . . ."

Neely had known about the woman, but the gambling was a new element. She closed her eyes for a few moments while she assimilated everything. "And I thought *I* was in trouble," she said.

"We're both in trouble," Hargrove replied. "Don't forget that for a moment, Neely. Get your things together and get out of here before they come after you!"

She nodded slowly. Although Neely wanted fiercely to live, just as she always had, it wasn't self-preservation that pushed her over the line, causing her to make the decision she'd been putting off. It was the knowledge that Ben and Danny would be in terrible danger as long as she stuck around.

From out of nowhere, like a careening vehicle, came the

thought that she might never see Aidan Tremayne again. She tried to sidestep the realization, but it crashed into her full force, and she gave a soft cry of despair on impact.

Hargrove had turned the car around and was on the way back to the highway again before she could speak.

"You've got to turn yourself in," she said. "Sure, the sky will fall in, and there will be hell to pay, but at least you'll be alive—and free of those awful people."

The senator was shaking his head even before she'd finished the sentence. "No," he told her. "The publicity, the scandal, would be torture for Elaine. She'd never survive it!"

Sadly Neely thought of the once-vibrant Elaine Hargrove. She'd been a famous television journalist, still active and vocal about her opinions even after her sudden immersion into political life. Then, just two years before, she'd started feeling tired and having episodes of unusual awkwardness. The diagnosis was grim, the prognosis, terrible. Elaine had been going downhill, physically at least, from the very first. Neely looked out the window for a few seconds, struggling with emotions of her own—horror, pity, and, yes, God forgive her, a certain savage gratitude that *she* hadn't been the one to be struck down that way.

"I think your wife is a whole lot stronger than you give her credit for," she said.

"She's had to endure enough suffering as it is," Hargrove said. "Once it's all over, and she's—she's at peace, then I'll go to the authorities with the truth." The rental car bumped onto the highway and fishtailed slightly on the ice-coated asphalt. The senator's attention was fixed on Neely. "I'll do anything to protect Elaine," he told her. "Anything."

Neely understood. "You've done your duty by warning me," she replied, "and now I'm on my own. Does that about cover it?"

Hargrove nodded. They rounded a bend, and the café sign came into view, a symbol of everything ordinary. Just then Neely would have paid practically any price to have a mundane life again, uncomplicated by desperate politicians, vengeful drug dealers, and her unremitting fascination with Aidan Tremayne.

They came to a stop in front of Neely's trailer, and Hargrove looked around nervously. Then he reached into the inside pocket of his jacket and took out an envelope. "Here—take this cash and get as far away as you can, as quickly as possible."

Neely didn't want to accept the money, knowing only too well where it had come from, but her choices were limited. She'd put aside a little over the past few years, but it was mostly in long-term CDs, and she wouldn't be able to get to it without drawing unwanted attention to herself.

"Thanks," she said without checking the contents of the envelope or looking directly at the senator. She opened the car door and got out, and even before the sound of the engine had died away, Neely was packing a suitcase.

When that was done, she borrowed Ben's truck and went to town to pick Danny up in front of the school. He beamed when he saw her and broke away from his friends, who were boarding a bus.

"Hi," he said, flinging himself onto the springy leather seat beside her. "What's the deal?" Danny paused and frowned. "I don't have to go to the dentist again, do I?"

Neely shook her head and smiled, but at the same time she fought back tears. "No, you're done with dentistry for a while, kid. I do have news, though, and frankly I'm a little worried about how you're going to take it."

Danny's freckles stood out against his pale skin. "Those bad dudes are after you, aren't they?"

Neely drove down Main Street, past the drugstore, the Sweetie-Freeze drive-in, the library, and the bank. She was going to miss this town, but not as much as she'd miss Danny and Ben. She frowned. "What do you know about anybody being after me?"

"I heard you and Dad talking once."

Neely eyed the sheriff's office as they passed and wished she could solve the problem by stopping in and reporting the situation, but she knew that wouldn't work. If the FBI hadn't come through for her, she could hardly expect protection from an aging, overweight sheriff with one part-time deputy. No, her only real hope was to get her copies of the evidence against Dallas Hargrove and the others and turn it over to the media. The trick would be in staying alive long enough to pull it off.

She reached across the seat and ruffled Danny's soft brown hair. "I should have known I couldn't keep something like this from a super-detective like you."

There were tears in Danny's eyes. "You'll come back sometime, won't you?"

Neely was possessed of a sudden and rather ill-advised fit of optimism. Incredible as the prospect seemed, she had to make herself believe she was going to survive this mess—if she didn't, the terror of it all would immobilize her. "You bet," she sniffled. "Once the good guys get their licks in, everything will be okay again. In the meantime, I want you to promise me two things—that you'll say a prayer for me every single night, and that you'll look after your dad."

Danny offered a high five, and Neely completed the gesture. Now all she had to do was tell Ben good-bye, grab her suitcase, and hit the road. She wished she could see Aidan once more as well, but time was short. Besides, she hardly knew the man.

Five hours later Neely was headed north in the car she'd bought from Doris Craig. Saying good-bye to Ben hadn't been easy, but he'd urged her to disappear as quickly as possible, pressing all the money from the restaurant till into the pocket of her peacoat.

She'd turned her trailer and her job over to Doris and set out in Doris's old clunker of a car, making only one brief stop before leaving Bright River to ring Aidan Tremayne's doorbell. She'd hoped to bid him farewell, but he evidently wasn't at home.

Neely scribbled a note on the back of an expired registration found in the glove box of Doris's car, stuck the paper in the frame of Aidan's front door, and fled.

Twilight was gathering by the time the town of Bright River fell away behind her.

Maeve was visiting the Havermails at their estate in the English countryside, circa 1895. She was embroiled in a game of croquet, played by the light of thousands of colorful paper lanterns, when Aidan materialized at her elbow.

With a little cry Maeve started and accidentally tapped the croquet ball wide of the wire hoop she'd been aiming for. "Great Scot, Aidan," she hissed, "I hate it when you do that!"

He clasped her arm, heedless of the staring guests, and yanked her toward the shrubbery. "It's Valerian—he's found some way to change a vampire into a man," he told her.

Maeve stared at him, letting her wooden mallet topple forgotten onto the grass. "What?"

Aidan began to pace, unable to stand still because of the torturous agitation the knowledge had roused in him. "He's ill—I gave him blood—he sent me away without telling me—"

"Aidan, *stop*," Maeve pleaded, reaching out and clasping his shoulders in her extraordinarily white and graceful hands. "What in the world are you talking about? There is no way to change a vampire into a man—is there?"

"Yes," Aidan said. Now he couldn't contain his joy. Dear God, the very thought of it—breathing, having a heartbeat, living by daylight, loving Neely freely and fathering her children, and, when the time came, dying. In peace. "Yes! He says it's dangerous, but—"

"Would you truly become a mortal again, even if such a thing were possible?" Maeve whispered, plainly stricken.

He paused before answering, looking deep into his sister's eyes. He loved her with the whole of his being, and it was torment to think of such a chasm opening between them, but the bright, shining prospect of redemption blinded him to everything but itself.

"Yes," he whispered. "Oh, God in heaven, *yes*."

Maeve lifted her chin, but her lower lip was trembling.

"You would leave me, Aidan? You want so much to be a mortal that you would turn your back on your own sister, for all eternity? Such a thing would make enemies of us." She stopped and with visible effort took control of her emotions. She even managed to smile. "I don't know why I'm worrying," she said, her voice brittle and bright. "Vampires are vampires, darling. They cannot be men just for wishing, any more than they can be angels. Come—I want you to meet the Havemails."

Aidan allowed Maeve to loop her arm through his and escort him across the lawn and into one of the estate's many fragrant gardens, where the mistress of the great house held court. Mrs. Havermail, like her husband and her two children, who gave new weight and substance to the term *brat*, was a creature of the night, and she showed her fangs and made a soft hissing sound as the newest guest approached.

Chapter

6

Doris's rattletrap of a car seemed to stagger along the inter-state, coughing, flinging itself forward in a wild, smoky burst of fumes and fervor, nearly stalling, then shuddering with the effort to begin the whole process all over again. A little after midnight Neely pulled into the parking lot of a tacky motel and, with no small amount of trepidation, turned off the engine. If the motor wouldn't start in the morning, she told herself wearily, she would abandon the heap with no real regrets and step onto a bus.

Maybe that would be better anyway, she thought, taking her purse and overnight case and heading for the front of-fice. A neon sign burned dimly in the window, announcing a vacancy.

The clerk was a taciturn Yankee woman, clad in a che-nille bathrobe and furry slippers that looked as though they might be developing mange, and she was none too pleased to be awakened.

Neely signed the register with a false name, purposely illegible, and paid cash. She was given a key with a red plastic tag emblazoned with a 6.

The room was small and smelled vaguely of mildew and stale cigarette smoke, but Neely was far too tired and dis-traught to care about amenities. As long as the sheets and the bathroom were clean, she could overlook the rest.

After carefully putting the chain lock on the door, she undressed, put on a nightgown, brushed her teeth and splashed her face with warm water, then toppled into bed. She was exhausted, both emotionally and physically, and unconsciousness offered a welcome respite from reality.

Lying in the darkness, she found herself longing for Aidan. The desire was not merely sexual, though there could be no denying, at least in the privacy of her own mind, that she wanted him with a wild, primitive, even violent sort of ardor. No, there was much more to her yearning; it was complex, a living thing rooted in the very core of her spirit, spreading graceful vines into her mind and heart and even into the deepest recesses of her unconscious.

Despite her loneliness, life had never seemed sweeter or more precious to Neely. There were so many things she wanted to see and feel and do—not the least of which was to give herself to Aidan—and now she was probably going to die.

Neely turned onto her stomach, buried her face in the musty pillow, and wept, softly at first. Soon, however, her sniffles turned to unrestrained howls as she grieved for a future that might well be denied her.

In the charcoal-smudged hours just before dawn, something awakened Neely, a feeling rather than a sound. She lifted her head from the pillow, squinted into the darkness, felt a twinge at the realization that she was not at home in her trailer, but on the road, and running.

She groped for her watch, which was lying on the nightstand, and peered at the numbers.

3:20 A.M.

With a sigh, Neely rolled onto her back and, in the next second let out a low, croaky cry.

A cloaked form towered at the foot of the bed.

"Oh, God," Neely whimpered. She didn't want to think the shadowy shape belonged to one of the senator's business associates or some serial rapist, but the possibilities had to be considered.

She had just made up her mind to fight the intruder with everything she had when a familiar voice spoke.

"Don't be afraid."

Neely snapped on the bedside lamp and gasped. She blinked hard, but when she looked again, Aidan Tremayne was still standing there, smiling at her.

She was at once wildly relieved and totally mystified. Had she conjured an image of him somehow, by entertaining all those scandalous sexual fantasies just after she went to bed?

Neely scrambled to the foot of the mattress, tugged at his cloak to assure herself that it had substance, and then hurtled back to the other end.

"It *is* you," she said in a tone that was almost accusing.

"Quite so," he replied gently, folding his arms.

Neely swallowed hard. She was at once terrified, sensing in her deepest being that Aidan had not entered her room by ordinary means, and at the same time wanting him to hold and caress and finally take her.

"Damn it, what's going on here?" she cried impatiently.

Aidan raised both hands, palms out, in a conciliatory, calming gesture. "I'm about to tell you the absolute and un-varnished truth. After that, you'll understand why I've been somewhat . . . secretive. First, though, I believe I'd best keep a promise I made not so long ago."

"What promise?" Neely whispered, but she knew. She knew, and her body, suddenly shameless after a lifetime of relative modesty, was already burning.

Aidan arched one eyebrow to show he wasn't buying her attempt at ingenuousness. "Among my other talents, my darling, I can read minds. You want me to make love to you—is that not so?"

Neely gulped. "What if it is?" she finally managed.

He smiled. "Not good enough, Neely," he scolded. "If you want me to give you pleasure, you will have to say so, straight out. Whatever my other sins, I do not take women against their wishes."

Neely stared at him, fascinated, her whole body thrum-ming with the need of him and his intimate attentions. "I—I want you," she said.

Aidan did not move from his place at the foot of the bed,

and yet Neely felt herself being pressed gently back onto the pillows. After that came light, tantalizing kisses, unseen lips grazing her mouth, nibbling at her earlobe and the side of her neck, tracing pathways of passion across the rounded tops of her breasts.

She moaned, overwhelmed by her need, too caught up in the sensations that were being evoked inside her to question the strange detachment of Aidan's lovemaking. Even as her nightshirt was gently removed, and her slender body lay bared to whatever magic he was working upon it, she could dimly see that he was still standing some distance away.

Impossible—he was touching her, kissing her, teasing her, everywhere. Wasn't he?

He told her to part her legs for him, and she did, though she could not have said whether the command had been spoken aloud or had simply come sauntering into her mind on its own.

Neely felt his hand, nimble-fingered and firm, brush the nest of curls hiding the physical center of her wanting. Incredibly she felt his touch in her soul as well, and the tension building there was even more tumultuous than the sweet, frightening eruption rising in her body.

She arched her back to welcome him and whispered, "Yes! Oh, yes . . ." as he uncovered the hidden nubbin of flesh and gently toyed with it. "Please," she whimpered, having lost all semblance of pride, tumbling toward a spiritual release of cataclysmic proportions even as an equally powerful physical climax loomed just ahead, waiting to consume her.

"Tell me what you want," Aidan said.

"I want *you*!" she cried out, not caring if anyone heard. "Oh, God, Aidan, I need you . . . the real you . . . inside me!"

Both her breasts were being suckled at once, and she felt strong, warm hands slide beneath her bottom to raise her high for the final conquering. She even felt him enter her with a hard, delicious thrust that made her cry out in ecstacy. Still, even through the fog of this all-encompassing passion, she could see that Aidan had not moved to join her on the bed, that he was watching her pleasure with a shimmer of tears in his eyes.

The crescendos were so violent, her body and her soul being satisfied in the same joyously terrifying moments, that Neely shouted aloud as she came, in involuntary triumph, lost in the glorious dual releases.

It was a very long time before she could speak or move, so completely, so thoroughly, had she been loved. But the moment arrived, finally, when the words that had been clamoring in her mind took shape on her lips.

"Why, Aidan?" she whispered. "Why did you make love to me that way, without actually touching me?"

He turned away from her briefly, and even though he held his head high, Neely knew he was overcome by emotion. Then he faced her again.

"I did not trust myself," he confessed hoarsely.

Neely managed to raise herself onto her elbows, but she was still in a state of bliss and hadn't the energy to demand answers to all the obvious questions. "What do you mean, you didn't trust yourself?"

Aidan averted his gaze for a moment, then looked directly into her eyes again. "My passion for you is fathomless," he said. "It is wolflike, a thing of the darkness. I could not be certain of maintaining control."

She yawned, beginning to drift. "Most people lose control when they make love, Aidan," she observed. "That's the idea."

One corner of his inviting mouth lifted in a sad, rueful attempt at a smile. "Yes," he said. "But I am not a person. I am a vampire."

Neely sat bolt upright, as wide awake as if she'd just had an intravenous dose of pure caffeine. "Did you just say that you're a vampire?" she asked, sounding ridiculously cordial. A strange excitement rushed through her, along with a whisper of primitive fear.

At long last Aidan rounded the bed and sat down on its edge. "I'm afraid so," he said.

It was remarkable, incredible, his claiming to be a supernatural creature, but it made an odd kind of sense, too. After all, he'd disappeared that night, in the parking lot outside the Lakeview Café, in quite literally the blink of an eye. Furthermore, he'd just made love to her in a very extraordinary way, a way no normal man would have done.

Yes. There was surely some kind of magic at work.

He must have seen the beginnings of belief in her eyes, for his smile was less forlorn than the one that had preceded it, less weary.

"Let me see your teeth," Neely said impulsively. She was still a little afraid, but she was fascinated, too, and wildly curious.

Indulgently Aidan permitted her to lift his upper lip and peer at one shining, sharp incisor. It was obviously no ordinary tooth, so she checked its counterpart.

"Good grief," she whispered, marveling. She knew her eyes were wide with wonder as she drew back to look at him, and she felt a shiver of fear as she began the arduous process of letting herself accept the remarkable possibility that Aidan had spoken the truth. "Were you afraid you would bite me?" she asked, unconsciously laying her hands on his broad shoulders. "Is that why you didn't lie down with me?"

"That's a rather simplistic way of putting it," Aidan said, with a glint of humor in his eyes, "but yes. I was afraid of hurting you."

Neely frowned. "What about your own pleasure? Did you feel what we were doing?"

Aidan looked away, clearly embarrassed, but then met Neely's gaze again. "Holding you in my arms, entering you physically, would have been better, but yes, I took a certain amount of satisfaction from the experience."

Neely rolled her eyes. "You make it sound as if I gave you a back rub."

He smiled. "There are releases that are felt in the emotions, Neely," he said gently. "It was that way for me."

On an impulse she couldn't have explained had her very life depended on it, Neely put her arms around Aidan's neck and planted a light kiss on his cheek. His flesh felt cool and smooth beneath her lips, strangely like fine marble, and yet pliant, too. He flinched and started to move away, but Neely did not release her hold on him.

"If I trust you," she said quietly, "why can't you trust yourself? Lie down with me, Aidan. Sleep in my arms."

"I can't," he replied, and she heard unremitting anguish in his voice, felt it in his magnificent body.

Perhaps it was the ancient, elemental attraction she felt toward Aidan that made her behave so boldly in the instant that followed; Neely didn't try to analyze the decision. Still naked from his lovemaking, she raised herself onto her knees and brushed her left breast lightly across his lips which felt strangely warm and soft against her flesh. It was the only way she could think of to offer him her trust, as well as the intimate comfort he so clearly needed.

With a moan Aidan took her nipple into his mouth and suckled greedily, and Neely entangled her fingers in his dark hair and tilted her head back, feeling fresh ecstacy rise within her as she nurtured this man—this creature—that she had come to love.

"See," she told him softly as he moved to her other breast and took pleasure there, too, "you needn't be afraid—not of me, not of yourself."

He eased her backward onto the mattress and would surely have taken her, but just when Neely was ready, body and spirit, to receive him, he stopped, held himself utterly motionless, and listened with the intensity of some wild, exotic beast.

"Aidan," Neely pleaded softly.

But he raised himself from her, his attention so focused on some sound or feeling that he did not even seem aware of her presence.

"What is it?" she asked.

He gathered her into his arms and enfolded her warm nakedness within the whispering smoothness of his cloak. "I'll explain later," he promised, and then he bent and kissed Neely on the mouth. A drumming sound filled her ears, and it seemed that she was propelled outward into a dark universe, even while she lay helpless in Aidan's arms. She was made of thought alone, not flesh, and then she knew nothing.

Nothing at all.

Aidan laid the unconscious Neely gently on his bed in the house in the woods of Connecticut. The sound of her pursuers' approaching that faraway motel room still echoed in his head; by now the two men would be inside, ransacking the place, wondering how their quarry had managed to escape them.

He bent, kissed Neely tenderly on the forehead, and fought the awesome need to complete the dangerous process she had begun by taking him to her breast. The courage and sweet generosity of the gesture were beyond comprehension; he did not think he would ever fully understand why she had chosen to give him that singular joy.

"Sleep well," he whispered, tucking the blankets around her. Then he touched her cheek and whispered a command that would anchor her to the bed as effectively as the heaviest chains, for that was the only way he could think of to keep her safe. Then he vanished.

Aidan found the thugs in Neely's motel room, just as he had expected. They relished their criminality, he thought with disgust, and from what images he could glean from the recesses of their diseased minds, they hadn't even had particularly difficult childhoods. He filled the doorway, making no effort at all to hide what he was, or to be subtle about his powers.

They whirled to face him, and one of them cried out.

Aidan wanted to kill them, yearned to drain them of every glimmering red, droplet of blood, and then toss their husks aside to rot. This development unnerved him, for he was always coldly dispassionate about his victims, and what he felt now was a fiery and utterly ruthless appetite.

He crossed the room on the impetuousness of that

thought, grasped a throat in either hand, and pressed his struggling captives to the wall.

"You may want to rethink this whole matter," he instructed politely. "It's a dangerous business, you see, involving forces and creatures you can't begin to grasp with those pitiful little snot-wads you fancy to be brains."

The thugs stared at him, mute with confusion. They were strong in a bullish sort of way and must have wondered why a lone man could render them powerless so easily.

"What the hell are you?" one of them managed to croak out.

Aidan showed his fangs then, although he personally thought it was a touch melodramatic—more Valerian's style than his own.

"Jesus Christ," murmured the first thug, while his partner fainted.

Aidan sighed. It was nearly dawn, and there was no time to go back to the Havermails and explain his sudden disappearance to Maeve, nor could he return to Neely. No, he must go to Valerian, who still lay stricken in that dusty crypt well outside of London, and it was imperative that he bring blood to give the other vampire sustenance.

Aidan eyed the two criminals before him, one awake and one unconscious. The bloodlust he'd felt earlier had turned to the purest disgust; he would have preferred to drink from rats. Regrettably, though, there was no real choice.

He fed on the larger one first, bringing him as close to death as he dared, and then lifted the smaller man and drank again.

The usual delirium of joy came over him, but it was nothing compared to what he'd felt when Neely had lain naked before him and cried out at the pleasure of his caresses.

But he could not think of her now.

Aidan blinked, and when he opened his eyes, he was in the crypt with Valerian. The sun had already risen by the time he arrived, although its light could not reach through the stone walls or the metal door, but the inevitable fatigue threatened to swallow his consciousness.

"Aidan," Valerian whispered in a hoarse, fitful murmur of joy, and groped for his hand. "Quickly—"

Aidan bent and, once again, found Valerian's throat. Black weariness clawed at him, pulled him downward, toward the filthy, bone-littered floor. He struggled back to the waiting vein and willed the blood to flow into Valerian, and it was still pouring forth when he collapsed.

Far away, yet near as the next heartbeat, Neely stirred in her soft, unfamiliar bed but did not climb toward wakefulness. She knew, on some level, that it was better to stay asleep, to wander in dark dreams. When she opened her eyes, after all, she would have to make sense of all that had happened to her in recent hours, and that was going to be virtually impossible.

Maeve found Aidan insensate on the floor of the crypt, his back to the high stone slab, his fine clothes speckled with blood. Ignoring Valerian, who stirred above their heads, she shook her brother and called his name in a frantic whisper.

He was empty and wasted, and Maeve knew he would perish if she did not save him. She ripped away the fitted cuff of her frilly shirtwaist and pressed the inside of her wrist to his lips. He resisted weakly, then drank.

After a few moments Aidan revived, opening his eyes. "Maeve," he said, giving the name the shape and substance of a sob.

She smoothed his lovely dark hair back from his wan face. "There now, you'll be fine after this. It's night, and you're strong enough to feed properly."

"Valerian," he said. "Is he all right?"

Maeve remembered the other vampire, her mentor and erstwhile friend, and rose slowly to her feet. Seeing Valerian's sunken cheeks and shadowed eyes, she clutched his hand and demanded, "What have you done?"

"Atlantis," he said. "Atlantis—"

Aidan scrambled up beside Maeve, fairly shouldering

her aside to peer down into Valerian's tormented face. "What are you saying?" he rasped. "What about Atlantis?"

"That's—where it—began," Valerian managed. "The mystery lies on the lost continent—"

"Enough!" Maeve interrupted, her temper flaring. Having fed amply, she was by far the strongest of the trio, and she could afford to issue orders. "There will be no more talk of mysteries and lost continents! Can't you see that he's dying, Aidan? Don't you realize that you nearly perished yourself?"

Despair and frustration howled within Aidan like a spiritual storm. He grabbed at the bloody front of Valerian's shirt and wrenched the other vampire upward with the last of his strength. *"Tell me!"* he cried, and when Valerian remained silent, clearly too enervated to speak, Aidan wailed with all the forlorn grief of an animal caught in a trap.

Maeve whirled on him, her blue eyes, mirror-images of his own, flashing with pain. She raised one hand, fingers spread, and pressed it to his face. He felt her horrific power surge through him, like a double dose of lightning, and then he swooned.

When he awakened, he was lying on a wide-planked table, stripped to the waist. He turned his head—it felt as though a speeding locomotive had crashed into each temple at full throttle—and saw Valerian lying next to him.

"Maeve?" Aidan lifted his head. The room was dark and dank, and it had the oppressive feel of a dungeon.

"She's out hunting," answered a small, sweet voice.

Aidan relaxed for a moment, getting his bearings. Candlelight flickered over the ancient, moss-streaked walls, where rusted iron rings were bolted. "What is this place?"

A horrible parody of a child appeared at his side, a little girl with brown-gold ringlets, impossibly pale skin, and dark circles around her eyes. Her delicate fangs glinted in the candlelight.

"It's Havermail Castle," she said.

Ah, yes, Aidan recalled, despairing. The august home of Maeve's hideous friends, the Havermails—a mommy vampire, a papa vampire, and two absolutely vicious baby vampires.

He shuddered and tried to sit up, only to find himself too weak to rise.

The child laid a clammy hand on his bare chest. "You're not supposed to move," she said, and while this announcement was delivered ingenuously, it also reverberated with warning. "Neither is Mr. Valerian. You're to be our guests, until Maeve says otherwise."

"What's your name?" Aidan gasped the question, appalled at his weakness. As a mortal man, he had loved children and been able to communicate intelligently with them.

"I'm Benecia," the monster said. "And my sister is Canaan. She's gone out to hunt with Mummy, and when they come back, it will be my turn."

Valerian stirred next to Aidan, but it was plain that he was still in a stupor.

"How long have you been a vampire?" Aidan inquired of Benecia. This was a ludicrous conversation, in an even more ludicrous setting, but he was certain he would go mad if he tried to keep silent.

"Oh, a long time," Benecia replied sunnily. "Almost as long as Valerian, in fact—about five hundred and forty years."

Aidan stared at her, appalled that even a blood-drinking fiend would stoop to turning a child into a vampire. Surely hell itself could not boast of a crueler demon. "How did it happen?"

Benecia giggled, and the sound echoed eerily off the wet stone walls that had absorbed so much misery over so many centuries. "Papa was a scholar, and he joined a secret society. They met only in darkness, and he thought that was very curious, but nonetheless he was flattered to be invited, and he attended the meetings religiously. Finally he was initiated—the members made him into an immortal, like themselves. He came straight home and made Mama into a vampire, and she in turn transformed Canaan and me because she couldn't bear to be parted from us."

Aidan whispered a profanity because he did not dare to pray.

Valerian reached out and grasped his arm before he could express his opinion further, however, effectively silencing him.

Alas, Benecia was already offended. "I don't like you," she told Aidan in a sweetly vicious tone. "I don't like you at all."

"My friend is comparatively young, for a vampire," Valerian put in quickly, and with good nature aplenty. "Be patient with him, Benecia. Remember what it was to be foolish and impulsive."

Benecia's eyes were narrowed, and her searing gaze had not wavered from Aidan's face. "I'm much older than you are, and much stronger, and much smarter," she said with icy confidence. "Mind your tongue, fledgling, or I'll dangle you from a high window by your feet!"

Valerian laughed, though Aidan heard tension plainly in the sound. "Now, now, darling—is that any way to speak to a guest? Aidan is your aunt Maeve's favorite creature in all the earth. She will expect you to be pleasant to him."

Benecia subsided, but only after a snakelike hiss and a rather chilling display of her fangs. She turned and flounced away, a small horror in her pink ruffled dress; then a door slammed somewhere, and Aidan knew he and Valerian were alone.

Furthermore, Valerian was in a towering fury, the state of his health notwithstanding. "You are truly remarkable, Mr. Tremayne, for your arrogant stupidity!"

Aidan was in no mood for a dressing-down. He'd been through enough as it was, what with all the high drama of recent nights. "I will not be threatened by a child!"

"That *child* was old when Shakespeare penned his sonnets," Valerian raged. "She can summon more power in a blink of her eyes than you've ever dreamed of attaining! Were she not mortally afraid of her beloved auntie Maeve, your head would probably be bouncing off an outside wall by now!"

Aidan gave a ragged sigh. He still had the psychic equivalent of a headache. "If Benecia is so terribly powerful," he began, "why is she afraid of Maeve?"

Valerian's chuckle was raspy, void of all humor, and hollow. "Do you know so little about your own sister, Aidan?" he scolded. "Maeve has special gifts—she lacks your aversion to the finer points of vampirism, you know—and it is said that she will someday replace Lisette as queen of the nightwalkers."

The thought made Aidan sick. He recalled Maeve as a human girl, warm and pretty and full of laughter and innocent mischief, and he came as near to weeping as a vampire is able. "You did it," he remembered as hatred pooled in his breast. "You made her into a monster, Valerian."

There was grief in the other vampire's voice, as well as resignation. "She pleaded with me," Valerian said. "She offered me her throat, and I was hungry."

Aidan had heard the story before, but even now, after two centuries, he couldn't fully accept the reality. "You might have resisted her. There were others about who could have slaked your thirst."

Valerian was growing weak again; Aidan could sense it because, for better or worse, their two beings were connected somehow, had been ever since that first sharing of blood. "We've been over this before," he answered wearily. "There is no changing it. I've been conscious for at least five minutes, Aidan. How is it that you have yet to hound me about what I learned of Atlantis?"

As incredible as it seemed, Aidan *had* forgotten about the miraculous secret that might be his salvation. His mind had been filled with thoughts of Maeve and of Neely. He rolled onto his side and reached over to clasp Valerian's arm, which was bare like his own. "Did you go there?"

Valerian shook his head slowly. "No, I tried, but I hadn't the strength. I caught glimpses of it, though, and heard the music—"

"But you discovered something."

"Yes," Valerian murmured. "Vampirism began on Atlantis, with a series of medical experiments."

"How do you know this?" Aidan demanded, tightening his grasp on Valerian's cold flesh.

"I'm not sure. The knowledge was just—there. Please, Aidan—I grow weary. Let me rest."

"Not until you tell me how to change myself back into a man!"

There was a long, horrible silence. Then Valerian answered, "You cannot. There is an antidote, but you would have to venture back even farther than I did to find it, and you are not strong enough. Resign yourself, once and for all, Aidan. You are, and shall remain, a vampire."

Chapter

7

It took a long time to awaken, and Neely managed the task in stages, grappling her way from one level of consciousness to the next. The struggle required all the will she could summon, for the lethargy that pressed down on her was oddly blissful, a sweet sleep, peaceful and all-encompassing.

At last she persuaded her eyelids to rise.

She was lying in a strange, beautiful bed, an enormous four-poster of mahogany or some other dark wood. The canopy overhead was trimmed in exquisite ecru tatting, the sheets were the softest linen, and the coverlet was made of worn blue velvet.

Aidan's bed.

Neely remembered everything in a breathtaking rush—fleeing Bright River in Doris's old car, renting the motel room, waking to find Aidan standing at the foot of her bed. It all flooded back, the unbelievable lovemaking, his convincing claim that he was a vampire, all of it.

She gasped, stiffening beneath the covers. Aidan had wrapped her in his cape, and by some incomprehensible magic he had brought her here.

That was it.

Aidan must be a magician, and a very good one at that.

She began to make a case for her theory, in the courtroom of her mind. Yes, she was in his house in Connecticut, not a mile from the Lakeview Truck Stop, and she had no memory of making the trip; those were undeniable facts. But

Aidan could have hypnotized her, or given her drugs, and planted the other recollections in her consciousness like seeds.

She would just get up, she decided, get herself dressed, and leave. Aidan Tremayne might be the most attractive man she'd ever met, and he'd certainly captured her heart, not to mention turning her inside out sexually, but that didn't mean she was going to let him kidnap her and play crazy games with her psyche.

Brave talk, she said to herself. The truth was, if Aidan came to her at that moment, she would let him—let him? she would *beg* him to—make love to her all over again.

She drew a deep breath and released it slowly in an effort to calm the dark, sweet excitement the memory of their strange intimacy stirred in her. In a more rational moment she faced another facet of her attraction to Aidan Tremayne, and that was plain, simple fear.

The man was probably just a very good magician, as she'd decided earlier, but suppose he'd been telling the truth? Suppose he really was a vampire, for God's sake?

Neely was confused and irritated, and besides that she figured her bladder was going to burst at any moment.

She moved to toss back the covers and sit up, but it was as if she were pinned to the mattress by some benign force. She ran a rather frantic mental check of her muscles and found them all in good working order. "Damn," she said and attempted to rise onto her elbows.

It was as if the ceiling had collapsed onto her, though there was no pain.

"Aidan!"

The name echoed in the large, empty room.

Neely waited, working up another burst of energy, fighting the urge to slip back into sleep. "Aidan!" she called again. "You get in here and help me out of this bed, damn it! I have to pee!"

There was no response at all, except for the hollow reverberations of her own voice.

Neely summoned all her will, which was formidable,

and managed to make an inch of progress toward the side of the mattress. She waited, then moved again.

After ten minutes Neely was perspiring so heavily that the sheets clung to her skin. She reached the edge of the bed, spent a minor eternity gathering her strength, and then lunged again.

She landed on the cool hardwood floor with a thump and lay there dazed for an interval, exulting because she'd made it, yet so drained by the effort that she wasn't sure she could stand up.

The insistent complaint of her bladder forced her to try; she reached her knees, gripped the antique bedside table for support, and raised herself shakily to her feet. She stood there, trembling and drawing deep breaths, until she dared attempt a step.

To Neely's surprise, walking was easy. She went into the adjoining bathroom, which was fitted out in the costliest Italian marble, used the facilities, then draped an afghan around herself to keep warm and set about exploring the enormous bedchamber.

There were high casement windows on both sides of the suite, with built-in seats overlooking the snowy garden and the front yard, and the bureaus, closet, and armoires contained a wide assortment of men's clothing. The room boasted its own fireplace, fronted in priceless hand-painted tiles, and here and there an exquisite Persian rug graced the gleaming wooden floors.

Neely ventured out into the hallway. She was hungry, and a little reassurance from her mysterious host wouldn't have done any harm, either.

"Aidan?"

No answer.

She opened the double doors of the room across the hallway from Aidan's and found another suite, almost as big and grand as the one she'd just left. Here the closets and bureaus were empty, however, and Neely's hope of finding something to wear was dashed. She returned to the master chamber long enough to drop the afghan and put on one of

Aidan's tailored white shirts, then ventured into the hallway and headed toward the rear stairs.

At the bottom of these was a kitchen, large and immaculate. The shelves of the cupboards and the pantry were bare even of dust, and there wasn't a plate or a glass or a butter knife to be seen.

Did vampires eat? Neely wondered. She immediately checked the silly thought. This whole setup was getting weirder and weirder.

Neely shifted her concentration away from her grumbling stomach and examined the rest of the massive house. In the movies it would have been filled with cobwebs and dust and spiders, she supposed, but instead the place was as tidy as a nun's dresser drawer. The massive crystal chandeliers glistened, the rugs and floors felt clean under Neely's bare feet, and the walls were decorated with fine original art. In Aidan's study, the only part of the house she had been in before, there were stacks of paper on the large table he used as a desk, and books lined the walls from floor to ceiling, on every side.

Neely gravitated to the music box she had discovered on her last visit, wound the brass key on its underside, and lifted the lid.

Sweet yet unbearably sad music flowed from the tiny, precise mechanism, arousing emotions so deep Neely could not even begin to identify them. She felt hot tears sting her eyes as she whirled round and round in a solitary dance, caught up in the sorcery of the tune, clutching the little chest in both hands. As she moved, twilight gathered at the tall, deeply set windows, and heavy flakes of snow waltzed past the glass.

"What a will you must have," Aidan said, startling Neely so badly that she stumbled and nearly dropped the music box.

He was standing in the doorway leading to the entryway, wearing a black overcoat, trousers, a white shirt, and a tie. Snowflakes glistened in his ebony hair and on the shoulders of his coat.

Neely stared at him, unable, for the moment, to speak. The impact of his presence was overwhelming; her soul trembled, her heart pounded. She didn't know whether to laugh or cry, whether to fling herself upon him in rage or seduce him on the spot.

Aidan's fine mouth tilted upward at one side as he indulged in a weary grin. "I guess I should have brought your suitcase when I carried you away from that dreadful motel," he said, pulling leather gloves from his hands and shoving them into the pockets of his coat. "Though you do look quite charming in my shirt. Tell me—how did you manage to get out of bed?"

She raised her chin. "No force can stop a woman who needs to go to the bathroom," she said.

Aidan laughed. "I see." He removed his coat and hung it from a brass coat tree.

"There's nothing to eat in this place," Neely said, her voice shaking a little.

"Oh, but there is," Aidan replied, disappearing into the entryway and returning momentarily with three cartons of Chinese take-out and a plastic fork wrapped in paper napkins. He smiled when she snatched everything from his hands and sat cross-legged on the hearth rug to rip open the boxes. Then he crouched beside her and said gently, "You're not a prisoner here, Neely, and you won't be mistreated. Please don't be afraid."

She gulped down a mouthful of fried rice. " 'Don't be afraid'?" she echoed, somewhat bitterly. "I'd be some sort of idiot if I weren't."

He smiled at her reasoning, touched her hair briefly, then drew his hand back. In the next moment an expression of infinite sorrow filled his eyes.

"I can't bear it," he whispered hoarsely, "knowing that you fear me."

Neely set aside the food, for even though her body still craved sustenance, her emotions had taken full control. She could not stop herself from touching Aidan, from laying her hands on either side of his face.

For one long moment they simply gazed at each other, exchanging some silent, mystical form of comfort. Then Neely said, "How did I get here, Aidan? Did you hypnotize me or something like that?"

He shook his head. "Nothing so ordinary, I'm afraid," he told her. "I really am a vampire, Neely, just as I said. And you were in rather grave danger last night, I might add. It was foolish of you to set out on your own like that."

She looked away because she wanted him so much, wanted to become one with him right there on the hearth rug, and out of the corner of her eye she saw him stand and distance himself from her.

"What kind of danger?" she asked, a little testily. She suspected Aidan had looked into her mind and seen her insatiable passion for him. His withdrawal struck her with the force of a blow.

"Two blighters came round to kill you," Aidan answered from the vicinity of his desk. He sounded distracted, like an ordinary man recounting the events of his day while flipping through the mail at the same time. "There's no reason to worry, though—I dealt with them."

So that was why he had suddenly stopped and thrust himself away the night before, when he'd been about to make love to her in the normal way. He'd heard someone approaching the room.

Neely allowed herself a slight shudder and took up her dinner again. "I'll bet you came as something of a surprise—especially if you let them see your teeth."

Aidan chuckled. "Yes, I daresay they weren't expecting to encounter me."

"Of course, it isn't over," Neely said with a sigh, reaching for one of the other cartons of Chinese food. "They're not going to give up quite so easily."

"Neither am I," Aidan remarked.

Neely could no longer resist looking at him, and when she did, she saw that he was watching her with a mixture of bewilderment and delight.

"What a hot-blooded little creature you are," he reflected.

Neely blushed. "What makes you say that?"

He laughed. "A few moments ago you wanted to make love on the hearth."

She didn't deny the thought; she couldn't. "I'm not normally so—amorous," she said.

"I should hope not," Aidan teased.

Her eyes flew to his face. She felt fury first, but the tender mirth she saw in his gaze stole her momentum, and she could not be angry with him.

"Have there been other men in your life, Neely?"

She was at once insulted and pleased by the question. "You claim you can read minds. Why don't you just look inside my head and find out for yourself?"

"Because it would be an intrusion," he said with a slight and very appealing shrug.

Neely sighed. "Fair enough," she replied. "The answer is, just one. He broke my heart, my first year in college." She decided that turnabout was fair play. "What about you, Aidan? How many women have you taken to your bed?"

His jaw tightened, and he looked exasperated. Then he murmured something that sounded like "This modern age!" A moment after that, however, he replied, "There were a number of tavern wenches in my youth—"

" 'Tavern wenches'?" Neely interrupted, struck by this old-fashioned turn of phrase.

Aidan was clearly growing impatient again. With quicksilver speed he changed the subject. "I will find you something more appropriate to wear," he said in a cool and formal tone. "Maeve must have left a few things behind—"

Maeve. Neely was troubled by the name, but she had enough to assimilate without pursuing yet another subject.

By the time Aidan returned, carrying a bundle of clothing with him, Neely had finished eating and stashed the leftovers in the big, hitherto empty refrigerator humming away in the kitchen. She was perched on a window seat, knees drawn up, the tails of Aidan's shirt tucked modestly beneath her, watching the snow fall.

"There's still some sweet and sour pork left . . ."

He smiled. "Vampires don't eat, Neely. Not in the same way humans do."

She rolled her eyes, accepting the folded cotton garment he held out to her. "Please," she said. "You're no ordinary guy, I'll grant you that, but you can't really be a vampire. Can you?"

Aidan's laugh seemed to burst from his throat, rich and sensual and warm.

Neely slid out of the window seat and went to stand behind a high-back leather chair, her imagination running wild all of a sudden. "You don't actually drink blood?"

Again she saw that peculiar, fathomless look of mourning in his eyes. "Yes," he said miserably. "I despise it—I hate everything about being a vampire—but without blood I would die, and I am not quite prepared to do that."

She felt conflicting desires—to take him into her arms and to run away, as far and as fast as she could. She squinted, a habit she'd acquired in college, when she was trying to work out something that both intrigued and puzzled her.

"Show me your coffin," she challenged.

Aidan arched one dark eyebrow. "I beg your pardon?" he replied, looking and sounding genuinely bewildered.

"If you're a vampire," Neely said, trying to make reason of the unreasonable, "you have to sleep in a coffin."

He sighed, and his expression shifted to exasperation. "I most certainly do not sleep in a casket," he said, plainly insulted. "This is not the second feature of a drive-in movie we're talking about here, it's reality. I drink blood, I sleep during the day, and I can indeed be killed by having a stake thrust through my heart. And that, my darling, is the extent of my resemblance to a Hollywood vampire!"

She frowned, trying to remember if she'd ever encountered Aidan before sunset and failing to recollect a single instance. "Calm down," she said. She ran her tongue over her lips in a gesture of distraction rather than nervousness. "If you hate being a—a vampire so much, then why did you become one? Assuming, of course, that you really *are* a supernatural creature."

Aidan sagged into the chair behind his worktable with a great sigh, and that was when Neely noticed that he looked gaunt. There were faint smudges under his eyes, like bruises, and his skin was pale as marble. "You are impossible!" he muttered.

Neely smiled. "True," she claimed and promptly determined to show more appreciation. After all, no matter what Aidan was, or claimed to be, he had saved her from crooks who had almost certainly been ordered to assassinate her. And she still needed a place to hide.

Thinking it was a good time to take her leave, at least temporarily, she slipped out of the study. In the downstairs bathroom she exchanged the borrowed shirt for the graceful blue caftan Aidan had found for her. When she returned, he was standing at one of the windows, staring out at the dark, snowy forest edging the yard.

He turned to face her as she stood uncertainly in the arched doorway.

"I must go out for a while," he said solemnly. "Do not admit anyone to the house before I return." While Neely stared at him, trying to assimilate the news that he meant to abandon her, he lifted a fragile necklace over his head and placed it around her neck. A delicately shaped golden rosebud dangled from the chain.

"What is this?"

Aidan chuckled grimly. "Not the equivalent of a silver bullet or a crucifix, if that's what you're thinking. My sister and the others know it belongs to me, and that you would not have it in your possession except by my favor."

Curiouser and curiouser, Neely thought. She should be glad Aidan was leaving, she supposed, but instead she had to fight an urge to drop to her knees and fling her arms around his legs to make him stay. "What—what if those men come after me again? The ones who tried to break into my motel room."

Aidan made a gentle move in her direction, then drew

111

himself back with a sharp, alarming motion. "They won't," he said. Raising his hands over his head, he slipped into a corner of the room and dissolved into the shadows.

Neely just stood there for a few seconds after he disappeared, staring, immobilized with shock. Then she broke her paralysis and hurtled across the room to the place where Aidan had been only a heartbeat before.

There was no trace of him, nor was there a door or a window near enough to accommodate such a dramatic exit. Murmuring, Neely knelt and felt the wainscotting with both hands, searching for a secret panel.

Nothing.

With a shiver Neely got to her feet. She was going to have to ask Aidan to show her how to do that particular trick—it might come in handy if those hired thugs ever caught up to her again.

Her glance strayed to the telephone on Aidan's table. She wanted to call Ben and let him know that she was all right, but she didn't dare. Dallas Hargrove's drug-dealing associates might have her brother's line tapped, and if they traced a call to this house, she was as good as dead.

With a groan Neely raised moist palms to her temples and rubbed. It would have been a relief to tell someone all that was happening to her, but who'd believe it?

Restless, Neely made a fire on the hearth and began examining Aidan's vast collection of books. A set of thick volumes, bound in Moroccan leather, drew her attention, and she reached for the first one on the left.

The thing was huge, and heavy, and Neely dropped into Aidan's desk chair before lifting the cover.

The paper was fine parchment, substantial and smooth, and the first few pages were blank. Neely flipped carefully through them until she came to one that bore an inscription in fading black ink. *This being the Record and Journal of Aidan Tremayne, Vampyre. Begun March 5, 1793.*

Neely felt something tickle the inside of her spine. She stared at the writing for a long time, then moved on to the next page. Here she found a pen-and-ink drawing that practically stopped her heart; Aidan's laughing, handsome face looked back at her from the parchment, while a beautiful young woman, his female counterpart, peered smiling over his broad shoulder. Both subjects wore clothing typical of the eighteenth century.

For a while Neely just sat there, stunned.

Surely the man in the drawing could not be Aidan—the sketches had obviously been done generations before—no, it had to be one of his ancestors. Still, the image reached out to her somehow, and the laughing eyes pleaded with her to believe.

Just believe.

Shaken, she turned her attention to the woman, one of the loveliest creatures she had ever seen. The resemblance between the two was so strong that Neely knew they were brother and sister, or perhaps cousins. . . .

Neely swayed and closed her eyes. Some primal instinct insisted that this laughing young man in the drawing was indeed Aidan Tremayne—her Aidan.

Impossible.

Believe.

Neely took a deep breath and held it for a moment. Then, with a shaking hand, she turned another page and began to decipher the neatly written but quaint script, with its antique spellings and randomly capitalized words. "I, Aidan Tremayne," she translated, "set Down this Tale for the Sake of my own Sanity, and as a Warning to all those who come after. . . ."

Soon Neely was so absorbed that she was unaware of the passage of time. She devoured page after page, spellbound by the young Irishman's account of his meeting with Lisette, the mysterious woman who had stopped for him in a carriage one evening, along a muddy road, and quickly captured his soul. Even though this other, earlier Aidan—he could not be the one she'd held, the one she loved, could he?—was a shameless hedonist, mostly concerned with sex, music, and good ale, Neely felt pangs of despair and, yes, jealousy, as she read. She did not want another female to figure into the story at all.

When she came to the part where Lisette pounced on young Aidan and sank her fangs deep into his throat to virtually inhale his blood, Neely felt her own face go white and cold as window glass in winter. It was fiction, of course, a brilliantly conceived and quite horrible fantasy, but it seemed so *real*, the action so immediate and vital, that Neely almost became a part of the scenes herself.

The account only became more incredible. The boy Aidan had died in the bed of a flea-ridden eighteenth-century inn above a tavern, and yet he had *not* died. The innkeeper, his son, and a local priest had declared him dead, and he'd tried desperately to communicate somehow that he was alive, but to no avail. The men had taken the body, never dreaming that a spirit still occupied it, to the undertaker's establishment. He'd been abandoned there in that dreadful place, and forgotten.

Tears blurred Neely's vision as she read of Lisette's return, and how she had raised Aidan up as a monster, a *vampire*, by tapping into his jugular vein again, this time giving blood instead of taking it.

While she was fascinated and curious to a morbid degree, Neely found that she could not go on from there, not yet. She was deeply shaken, as if she'd witnessed the occurrences personally, in every gruesome detail. She felt true and abiding hatred for the heartless Lisette, along with an unholy resentment that the woman had lain with Aidan, had given him pleasure, and taken the same from him.

For a long interval she just sat, dazed by the intensity and variety of her emotions, staring into the fire but seeing instead the nightmare images so carefully outlined in the journal. How could anyone, even a vampire, do such a terrible thing to another, to condemn him, as Lisette had condemned Aidan, to an eternal nightmare?

"Neely?"

She started and guiltily slammed the volume closed.

Aidan was standing only a few feet away—she hadn't

heard him come in—and he carried her suitcase, the one she'd been forced to leave behind at the motel the night before.

She felt such overwhelming love, just looking at him, that she could not get her breath to speak.

"I thought you might like to have some of your own clothes," he said innocently, sounding almost shy. His gaze dropped to the heavy book in her lap, and she saw both resignation and relief in his bearing. "You've found my histories, I see."

Looking up, Neely noticed that his skin, deathly pale before, was now healthy in color. A wild suspicion played in her mind; she chased it out and dropped her gaze to the suitcase in his hand. "Where did that come from? I thought we left it."

"We did. I went back."

Neely's eyes shot back to his face. "You couldn't have. It's too far."

Instead of replying, Aidan simply raised one of his aristocratic eyebrows.

She bolted out of the chair and grabbed for the case. "I have to let my brother know I'm all right," she blurted, desperate for any distraction from the threatening truth, the reality that was becoming too complex and too pervasive to be ignored or denied. "When the police visit that room and find no sign of yours truly, Ben will hear about it on the news. He'll be frantic. He might even think I'm dead."

Aidan folded his arms. "If you telephone Ben, we may soon have more of the senator's friends to deal with. That's all well and good, provided I'm here when they arrive, but what if you're alone, Neely? What if I'm hunting, or asleep?"

A chill, colder than the center of a snowman's heart, touched her stomach and seeped into her soul. " 'Hunting or asleep'? For God's sake, Aidan—you're really scaring me now. This vampire game has gone far enough!"

He took the book gently from her hands, laid it aside. "I was hoping I wouldn't have to resort to parlor tricks to convince you," he said in a quiet and damnably reasonable tone.

"That's my story you were reading, Neely. The image in the drawing is mine, the girl is my twin sister, Maeve—"

"No!" She put her hands over her ears.

Aidan grasped her wrists, lowered them, pressed them to her sides. "You *will* listen," he said in a desperate whisper. "You know it's true—somewhere inside, *you know it's true.*"

Neely uttered a sudden, wailing sob, because he was right. As incomprehensible as it all was, as much as she wanted to turn away from the evidence, she could no longer do that. It was no dream, and no one had given her drugs or induced any kind of hypnotic trance. All the strange things that had happened since she first met Aidan had actually, truly *happened.*

Aidan touched her elbows and then her shoulders, tentatively. After that, though, instead of taking her into his arms as she yearned for him to do, he retreated a few steps. "I'm sorry, Neely," he said gruffly. "I should have left you alone—"

"But you didn't!" she cried. She looked up at him, wiping angrily at her wet cheeks. "I'm fascinated, I'm entranced, God help me, I think I'm in love—with someone who isn't even human! Tell me, Aidan—where do I go from here? What do I do now?"

He flinched, as if she'd hurled bricks at his broad back instead of words. He did not face her as he replied raggedly, "I could walk away, and you would get over what you're feeling now. But that wouldn't change the fact that there are more of those cretins out there, waiting for a chance to cut your throat!"

Neely moved to face Aidan and glared up into his face. She was wild with confusion, shock, and pain, and she spoke without thinking. "You could make me into a vampire, like you."

Aidan seemed to loom over her, taller for his fury. "Don't ever say that!" he cried. "You're asking to be damned, to be a fiend who feeds on the blood of living creatures! You're asking God Himself to turn against you, and for all eternity!" His anguish lay naked and vivid in the words, and Neely's first real comprehension of its extent took her breath away.

She approached him, laying her hands gently on his face. "Aidan—" she whispered, longing to comfort him, knowing there was no way to do that.

He wrenched free of her and moved away. "Didn't you hear me, Neely?" he growled, reminding her of a wolf that had just chewed off its own paw in a desperate effort to save itself from the metal teeth of a trap. "I am cursed for all time, and to care for me is to blaspheme against Creation itself!"

She was shaking her head again. "No, Aidan—no." It couldn't be a sin to love, could it? But, yes. The act of adoring something evil did not transform it into good, but instead poisoned what was holy.

They both stood still, the silence ringing around them like the deafening toll of some horrid death bell, for the longest time. Then, unable to bear it, Neely muttered, "My brother—"

Aidan moved to his desk, keeping his back to her. "Write him a letter, then, and explain as best you can. Just remember that he will have to live with your words until the end of his days."

Neely nodded distractedly, well aware of Aidan's meaning. She could tell Ben only that she was in hiding—it would be an outright lie to say she was safe, and there was no plausible way to describe the terrible truth.

She went upstairs to the room where she had awakened hours before, switched on a lamp, and sat down at a small desk to stare, unseeing, at a blank piece of paper.

Aidan paced his study, too restless to work on his journals, not daring to follow Neely upstairs and continue their conversation. He had fed sparsely that night, and he had yet to look in on the still-ailing Valerian, who was his only hope of finding redemption and, with it, peace. Maeve, adore her though he did, was embroiled as usual in adventures of her own and could not be depended upon to look after wounded ones.

He rubbed his temples with a thumb and forefinger, slouched back against the edge of his desk, and sighed. Then, with the utmost reluctance, he took himself to the dungeon of Havermail Castle.

Valerian still lay prone and ill, his long frame covering the length of a trestle table. In the flickering lights of the candles Aidan saw a small, snarling creature spring out of the shadows and attach itself to Valerian's throat.

Horror rocked Aidan as he realized that this abomination, this greedy fiend, wore the person of a child. He plunged forward and tore the small, wiry body away from Valerian's neck as though it were a leech. The little girl—this had to be Canaan, Benecia's sister—twisted in Aidan's grasp, baring her lethal fangs and making a vicious sound low in her throat, like a starved she-wolf.

Valerian moaned and rolled onto his side. "Stop," he pleaded. "Please—*stop*!"

Remarkably, the hellion went still, but when she raised her sherry-colored gaze to Aidan's face, he saw the most abject hatred there that he had ever encountered. Coming from a being who looked for all the world like a sweet and warm-blooded five-year-old, the experience was particularly chilling.

"She was merely trying to help me," Valerian said gently.

"Shall I leave you alone with this one, Valerian?" the fiend-child inquired, in a voice as delicate as the chimes of an exquisite little clock. "I do not favor him, you know."

Valerian gestured affectionately toward the door. "I am quite safe with Aidan," he insisted. "Go now, please, and tell your mama and papa that we have a guest."

Aidan's gaze sliced to his friend's face. He had no real desire to socialize with the elder Havermails; they were innately horrible creatures, like their daughters. When Canaan had swept from the room, he bit out, "Honestly, Valerian, I can't think what you and Maeve see in this family of monsters!"

"We see ourselves," Valerian answered quietly.

The words left Aidan stricken, for no weapon could wound as deeply and as savagely as the truth.

"This is what we *are*, Aidan," the elder vampire insisted in an urgent whisper.

"No," Aidan rasped, shaking his head, trying to pull free of Valerian's grasp. "*No!* You went back, almost to Atlantis— so will I. I will find the antidote for this curse or die seeking it!"

Incredibly, Valerian smiled. "What a passionate specimen you are. Come with me, my friend, and let me show you other realities." He paused, patting Aidan's hand fondly. "You might have been a stage actor, with your flair for the dramatic. Together we could write plays that would outshine the words of the Bard himself. We could—"

"Damn it, Valerian, you're dreaming!" Aidan broke in sharply. He hadn't meant his tone to be harsh, but it was, cruelly so, and the momentum carried him farther. "I want nothing from you, do you hear me, *nothing*, except for the secret that would restore the life that was stolen from me!"

Valerian turned his head to one side, and it seemed that he was caving in on himself again. He looked much as he had that first terrible night in the crypt, when he had come so close to perishing. His suffering was tangible; it swelled in the room, choking Aidan, crushing him.

Because of their bond, Aidan felt Valerian's pain as keenly as if it were his own. And maybe, since he had caused it, it was. With a cry, Aidan let his forehead fall to Valerian's concave chest. "I cannot offer you the devotion you want from me," he whispered in agony. "*I cannot!*"

Slowly, and with tenderness, Valerian raised a trembling hand to the back of Aidan's head and entwined cold fingers in his hair. "Yes," he said brokenly. "I know."

Just then, a nearby door swung open with a *thunk*, and Aubrey Havermail swept in, accompanied by his small, demonic daughter. He smirked as he watched Aidan step back from Valerian's side, dazed by despair.

"Such a touching, tender scene," Aubrey drawled.

119

Chapter

"We were just about to sit down to dinner," Aubrey Havermail went on after a brief, charged interval of silence had passed. "Won't you join us?"

Under other circumstances, Aidan might have laughed at the idea of vampires taking a meal in the human way, but he sensed that his host was in deadly earnest. When Valerian reached out to grasp Aidan's hand and squeeze, silently urging him to accept, Aidan inclined his head in polite assent.

"We'll just go on ahead, then," Havermail went on, when it was clear that Aidan didn't mean to leave the dungeon before he had a private word with Valerian. "Come, darling." He took Canaan's tiny, snow-white hand. "I'm sure our guest will be able to find his way on his own."

When the pair had gone, Valerian raised himself onto one elbow and regarded Aidan with sunken, shadowed eyes. "Is there any way," he began, "that I can dissuade you from attempting to uncover the secret that would make you mortal again?"

Aidan shook his head. "No," he said.

"I thought not," the stricken vampire replied in a rasp of despair. He struggled for a time, grappling visibly with some fathomless fatigue, and finally went on. "My advice to you, as you already know, is to turn from this foolish pursuit and never look back. Clearly, though, you are not wise enough to heed my counsel—in which case, I offer you what little information I have to give."

Aidan leaned closer to his companion; had he been a man, he would have been holding his breath. "I beg of you, Valerian—tell me."

Valerian closed his eyes for a moment and was taken by an almost imperceptible fit of trembling. Then he met Aidan's gaze and said, "You must learn to *listen*, my friend, if you are to survive! Do you not recall what the other child, Benecia, said before, when you asked how an entire family had become vampires? *She stated that her father had joined a secret society.* I've been thinking about it ever since and exploring this dreary castle with my mind whenever I could manage the effort, and I've come to a conclusion. Benecia spoke of one of the oldest fraternities on earth, Aidan—the Brotherhood of the Vampyre. This fellowship can trace its origins back to Atlantis itself!"

Now it was Aidan who trembled, for the implications of Valerian's words were, to him, profound. The Brotherhood, an organization Aidan had heard of only once before, when Maeve had mentioned it in passing, might well possess some clue to the secret of his own redemption—if not the means itself.

"Thank you," Aidan said, his voice hoarse. He enclosed one of Valerian's large, elegant hands between his own. "I will come back to speak with you before I go."

Valerian held him fast when he tried to walk away. "What of that mortal woman you became involved with? Have you set her free, Aidan?"

"She was never my prisoner."

"You are hedging!"

Aidan forced himself to meet Valerian's gaze. "Neely is living in my house. I cannot take the time to explain everything now; suffice it to say that I can neither hold her nor let her go."

Valerian stared bleakly up at Aidan, saying nothing.

"You have fed?" Aidan inquired quietly. At Valerian's nod, he went on. "Are you recovering your strength?"

At this, the elder vampire turned his face away from Aidan and remained stubbornly silent.

Reluctantly Aidan left Valerian's side, left the dim candle-glow of the dungeon for the torch-lit passageway beyond. Instinct led him up a curving flight of stone stairs, worn to slippery smoothness by centuries of use, through a dusty corridor, and into the castle's great hall.

There was every probability that all manner of knights, nobles, ladies, and wenches had dined and celebrated in this yawning chamber in some distant century. Now, however, the place was empty, except for the four Havermails, who sat around a long wooden table next to an enormous fireplace, their empty plates and glasses making clinking sounds, their horribly beautiful faces bathed in the crimson glow from the hearth.

Aubrey, head of this ghoulish family, rose from his chair when Aidan approached. "Our guest has arrived. We wondered at the delay."

Aidan reminded himself that this posturing creature he so despised might be the very one who could solve his dilemma. "I hope I did not inconvenience you," he said evenly. "I was concerned for my friend."

Benecia looked up at him with large, malevolent eyes, her tarnished-gold ringlets capturing the firelight. "Valerian is not your friend," she said. "No vampire is, truly, for you are not one of us. Why do you pretend?"

"That is quite enough," Aubrey interceded. He was a slender, finely built man, obviously a product of generations of aristocracy. "Do join us, Mr. Tremayne."

Aidan was, for the first time in recent memory, mildly embarrassed. He took the only empty chair at the table, situated between Mrs. Havermail—Maeve had introduced her as Roxanne during his last visit—and Canaan, who looked as fragile as a kitten and was clearly about as well-mannered as a white shark in frenzy.

Roxanne gave a trilling laugh that tripped down Aidan's backbone, leaving patterns of frost as it passed. She had rich, dark hair, uncomfortably reminiscent of Lisette's, perfect bone structure, and practically no color at all to her skin. "Please don't be alarmed by our strange custom of sitting down at table together, Mr. Tremayne," she said. "It is the one semblance of family life that remains to us."

Aidan nodded, his eyes moving from one lovely monster to another. Despite differences in size and in human age, all the Havermails were no doubt equals in their powers and experience as vampires. Roxanne's reasoning made a grisly sort of sense; while seated around a table, they could *pretend* to be flesh and blood again.

And that was something Aidan understood.

"Do you miss being mortal?" he inquired, just to make conversation.

Roxanne's chuckle was wicked enough to curdle a saint's blood. "Miss being mortal?" she echoed. "Dear me, Aidan—I feel that I know you well enough to address you informally, since dear Maeve has spoken of you so often—why would anyone *miss* head colds and bunions and broken hearts?"

"And having to die," Benecia put in.

Canaan wrinkled her delicate, freckle-spattered nose. "And sitting in the schoolroom hour after hour, learning dull lessons."

Aubrey called the group back to order by raising both hands, palms out, making a silly smirk, and turning his head slightly to one side. "Here, now. Let's not be rude."

Rude, Aidan thought. Amazing. These were beings who surely stalked their mortal counterparts by night, drained them of their life's blood, and slept off the kill by day in perfect contentment. And Havermail was concerned about their table manners?

"I don't like you," announced Canaan, as her sister had before, regarding Aidan with cheerful disdain.

"I feel much the same way about you," Aidan replied cordially.

The other Havermails were amused by his audacity and cackled among themselves, putting Aidan in mind of the three crones in *Macbeth*. *Double, double, toil and trouble,* he thought, *fire burn and cauldron bubble.*

Roxanne startled everyone by picking up a silver spoon and setting it clattering against the side of a crystal goblet.

"Canaan, Benecia—you will atone for your poor manners by entertaining. Canaan, you may recite. Benecia, you will sing."

Inwardly Aidan groaned. Was this atonement, or was it free rein to torture a hapless captive?

"Jolly good idea," said Aubrey Havermail, leaping up from his chair with such suddenness that he overturned his empty wineglass. "To the main drawing room, then, where we shall find the pipe organ."

Aidan smiled, already in acute pain, and followed the family of vampires across the great hall and into another, smaller chamber. There was indeed an organ, along with tarnished candelabras and dingy chandeliers, all dripping cobwebs, and rugs so long neglected that wisps of dust floated up from them as they were trod upon.

Canaan took her place next to the organ, while Roxanne sat down at the discolored keyboard. Aubrey sank into a leather chair and drew Benecia onto his knee, just as a human father might have done. Aidan perched gingerly on the arm of a settee, trying to comprehend the fact that his sister deliberately spent time with these beasts.

The younger daughter, not even three feet tall, clasped her tiny white hands together and held forth, reciting Shakespeare's poem, "Venus and Adonis," with chilling precision. "I know 'The Rape of Lucrece,' as well," Canaan said, upon finishing.

"Sit down, dear," Roxanne told her fondly.

Aidan held himself still, though he wanted to fidget and, even more, to flee.

Benecia slipped off her father's lap and sashayed forward to stand in front of the small company. She and her mother conferred, in whispers, and then Roxanne struck an introduction on the stained organ keys, and Benecia began to sing.

The lyrics were Latin—something quite ordinary, concerning bluebirds and meadows and sparkling streams—but it was the child-vampire's voice that struck Aidan. It seemed

125

to move in the chamber like the eddies, swirls, and under-tows of some vast, invisible river.

When the performance was over, when the last quaver-ing note had fallen away into silence, Aidan remembered to clap. This drew a look of scathing reprimand from Canaan, whom he had neglected to acknowledge in quite so formal a fashion.

Roxanne rose from the organ bench and gathered her children close. "Come, darlings—there are still several hours left in which to hunt," she said in the same tones a human mother might use to summon her brood to the station wagon for a trip to the nearest shopping mall. "Say good-bye to Mr. Tremayne."

Benecia and Canaan stood primly before Aidan and curt-sied in unison. Then they chorused, "Good night, Papa," kissed Aubrey on either of his waxen cheeks, and scampered out, their mother following.

"Am I keeping you from anything?" Aidan asked when he and Havermail were alone in that odd room. The place might have come from the pages of a Dickens novel, he thought; all it really lacked was a spoiled cake being nibbled on by rats, and a demented old woman in a rotted wedding dress.

Aubrey sat back in his chair as Aidan went to stand next to the fireplace, where an old clock stood on a mantel be-neath a drapery of spider weavings.

"No," Havermail replied, studying his guest thought-fully. "I fed some hours ago and have no desire to gorge myself, as my wife and daughters often do. Tell me, Mr. Tremayne—what is it you want from me?"

Aidan thrust his hand through his hair, fingers splayed. "According to your elder daughter, you became a vampire some five hundred and forty years ago, when you joined a select fellowship and undertook their initiation."

Havermail's countenance darkened, and his mouth pursed for a moment. Clearly the lovely, vicious Benecia had spoken out of turn. "What is your interest in the Brother-hood?" he asked after a long and somewhat awkward silence. "It cannot be that you seek immortality, since you are already a vampire."

Aidan framed his words carefully, setting them out like so many fine porcelain plates. "I seek—mortality. In short, I want to be a man again."

After staring for several moments, Havermail burst out laughing. "You cannot be serious!" he howled when he'd recovered just a little.

"I have never been more sincere about anything," Aidan replied evenly. "I was robbed. I want the forty-odd additional years of life that were my due."

Aubrey stood, all vestiges of mirth gone from his expression. "Who made you a blood-drinker?"

Aidan hesitated. "A powerful female called Lisette."

Havermail made a sputtering sound and moved one hand as if to make the sign of the cross over his chest, before stopping himself. An old habit, evidently, that had died hard. "Powerful, indeed," he murmured. "All sensible vampires fear Lisette, Tremayne. Why should I risk incurring her wrath?"

"You needn't risk anything," Aidan snapped, barely keeping himself from grasping Aubrey by the lapels of his cutaway coat and lifting him onto his toes. "I want to know about the Brotherhood, that's all. Is it true that the fellowship has existed since before the fall of Atlantis?"

Aubrey looked patently uncomfortable. "Yes," he said, "but that is all I will tell you without permission from the elders." He moved to the fireplace with that quick, gliding motion typical of vampires, took a poker from its place on the hearth, and jabbed at the burning logs until sparks rose toward the chimney in a crackling shower. "Leave this house, Tremayne. Go on about your business, whatever it is. If the Brotherhood wishes to grant you admittance, you will be contacted."

Desperation filled Aidan, along with a certain fragile elation. The Brotherhood existed, and he would be given audience only on the approval—perhaps the whim—of these mysterious elders.

Still, the fellowship might well possess the knowledge he needed, the secret that would set him free. He must bide his time and be patient. He started toward the doorway. "I will be back again tomorrow night to look in on Valerian," he said in passing. "Thank you for a most interesting evening."

Down in the dungeon, Aidan was surprised to find Valerian sitting up and looking a bit more chipper. He was wearing a snow-white shirt, buttoned halfway up his chest, dark trousers, and boots.

"I've decided to go back to Connecticut with you," he announced.

Aidan stopped cold, felt the smile freeze on his mouth, and let it fall away. "What?"

"I'm bored with this place, and you plainly need a guiding hand, given your reckless ways." He was rolling down his sleeves, fastening cuff links made from Roman coins. "Don't worry, Aidan. I won't corner your lovely mortal and bite her neck. I only want to help you."

Aidan sighed. "I suppose there is no persuading you to stay here?"

Valerian smiled fondly. "It would be easier to make a bat love daylight," he said.

And so it was that when Aidan returned to his house outside of Bright River, Valerian was with him.

Not surprisingly, considering the many recent upheavals in her life, Neely hadn't been able to sleep. She had taken a long, hot bath in Aidan's tile-lined tub, dressed in jeans and a sweatshirt taken from the suitcase he'd recovered for her, and finished off what was left of the Chinese leftovers she'd stashed in the refrigerator. Then she'd meandered back to Aidan's study, taken up the first volume of his journal again, and tumbled headfirst into the story.

She'd read, spellbound, of Aidan's early adventures as a vampire. Early on, he'd traveled to the north of England by night, intending to visit his twin sister in her convent school. He'd stopped at an inn along the way and there been approached by an imposing vampire who called himself Valerian—

"His lucky night," a masculine voice commented.

Neely jumped in her chair and had to grab at the book to keep it from toppling to the floor. Before her stood the towering, graceful creature she'd met once before, the night the man driving the Blazer had chased her into the woods. The night she'd found the music box.

"Yes," he said drolly, with a slight bow. "It is I—Valerian—in person. So to speak."

Neely tried to melt into the chair cushions, her eyes rounded, her heart flailing with the purest sort of terror. "Stay away from me," she whispered, holding out the rose medallion Aidan had given her, hoping it had some power to ward off intruders.

Valerian laughed. "What? No garlic? Such is the shameful state of vampire lore in this modern and wholly unromantic age!"

Just then, when she thought panic would surely consume her, Neely caught sight of Aidan. He smiled at her but spoke sharply to the intimidating Valerian.

"I meant what I said. Leave her alone."

Valerian yawned. "Of course I will obey your every wish," he said convivially. "It's almost dawn, in case you haven't noticed. What assurance can you offer that this delicious gamine will not drive stakes through our hearts as we slumber?"

"None," Aidan answered wearily, "except that the task would be a nasty one, and she's probably not up to it. Stop your teasing and retire, Valerian. I want a word alone with Neely."

The great vampire sighed in a long-suffering way, raised his arms over his head, and disappeared without a trace.

Neely stared at the space Valerian had just vacated, blinked, and then passed a hand slowly back and forth in the vacuum, certain her eyes had deceived her.

Gently Aidan took the book from her and set it aside. Then he bent to kiss her forehead. "I know what you're thinking, but you mustn't tax yourself with conundrums about smoke and mirrors," he advised. "What you just saw was neither a trick nor an illusion. Vanishing is elementary vampire stuff."

"Elementary vampire stuff," Neely repeated. By that point she was almost completely overwhelmed, through no fault of her own, and that irritated her. She flushed and looked up at Aidan with defiance in her eyes. "Tell me, Aidan—what else can vampires do?"

He sat down on the hassock, next to her feet, and folded his graceful hands. He looked forlornly amused as he regarded her. "They can travel through time—back to the point of their own death as a human being, though not forward past the present. The future is as much a mystery to them—us—as it is to you. They are able to communicate mentally with other creatures like themselves, across great distances, and move so rapidly that they cannot be seen."

Neely eased past Aidan and stood, her hands on her hips, her mind filled with dangerous puzzles. "Can they—can you—reproduce?"

Aidan sighed and rose to his feet. "Not the way mortals do. But rest assured, vampires are quite capable of making love."

Neely felt the familiar heat, along with a measure of fear and a storm of loneliness that rushed through her spirit like a wailing wind. "I know," she said, remembering.

He reached out and touched the base of her throat with the tip of a cool index finger. "You know far less than you think you do," he said, not unkindly. "We're greedy, violent creatures, quite fond of pleasure—which explains the typical penchant for immortality."

"Vampires marry, then?"

"They sometimes mate, though it's rare," Aidan clarified, and although one corner of his mouth was raised in the slightest smile, he looked sad. "For the most part, Neely, we nightwalkers tend to keep to ourselves. We mistrust even our own kind, and especially other sorts of fiends." He glanced uneasily toward the window, where dawn was beginning to thin the darkness.

Neely took hold of his arm when he would have turned from her. "You—you mean there are other things"—she paused to blush—"*monsters*—walking around among regular people?"

"Yes," Aidan answered, sounding mildly impatient now. "There are werewolves and ghosts, angels and fairies—lots of 'things.' And then there are the other dimensions, overlaying this one. Were you truly so vain as to believe that humanity has the universe all to itself?"

The question required no reply.

"I don't want you to leave me," Neely blurted out when he moved to pull away. "Please, Aidan—I want to go wherever you're going."

He laid his hands lightly on her shoulders and looked deep into her eyes. "I cannot allow that," he said gently. "Go upstairs and try to rest. I will come to you through your dreams if I can."

She had to be content with that, for it was almost morning; any minute the sun would spill over the horizon and flood the world with light.

Aidan traced the outline of her jaw with one finger, then raised his arms and disappeared.

Neely lingered for a time, trying once again, and wholly in vain, to make sense of what she had just experienced. Her insomnia left her, she was infinitely weary all of a sudden, and felt as if she could sleep for a century.

After returning the first volume of Aidan's journal to the shelf, she slowly climbed the stairs, entered the bedchamber, took off everything but her T-shirt, and tumbled into bed.

Soon after she closed her eyes, Neely found herself floating serenely on the dark inner waters of her mind. She allowed her consciousness to drift, too weary to anchor it in reality.

*   *   *

Aidan was in his lair, at least physically, crouching against the wall as he always did, but that day he left the husk of himself behind and sought Neely. He was inexperienced at such travel, unlike Valerian; he could not feel the sunshine or the wind, and he could see only dimly. With practice, he knew, his senses would sharpen.

He found Neely easily, saw her as the dimmest of shadows, sprawled in the middle of the large bed he had never actually slept in, her arms and legs askew.

He thought her name, and she stirred, uttering a soft, despairing sound that made him yearn to console her. All the while, Aidan was aware that he should not be testing the limits of his powers in this way, without first taking instruction from Valerian or Maeve. He was in danger because of his wandering, but there was a much greater peril to be considered now—Neely's. As fiercely as he wanted to protect her, she was at risk, for Lisette and perhaps even Valerian would not hesitate to use her, should the opportunity arise.

Valerian was given to dalliances; he would drink from her, toy with her for a time, as cats do with rubber balls and cloth mice, and then toss her aside when his fickle interest waned.

Lisette, and a few others who had reason to hate Aidan, would delight in destroying Neely or, worse yet, turning her into a fiend.

Imagining Neely as a vampire made Aidan cry out softly, in anguished despair. He had to let her go, he thought, to walk away and not look back, to forget her and pray that she would go unnoticed by his enemies.

But could he do that? Did he have the strength, needing the woman as he did? The comfort and affection and love she gave him were as necessary to him as the blood he was condemned to drink, and her whispered gasps of passion engendered in him an ecstasy he had never felt before.

Yes, he admitted to himself, at last, he loved Neely Wallace, fully and completely, as he had never loved anyone else before, in all his two centuries of existence, but he had no right to such tender sentiments. No right on earth, or in heaven.

It was torture, the wanting, the needing and, worst of all, the knowing.

Aidan caused the covers to slide slowly downward, to the foot of the bed, and Neely groped for the pillow next to her and sighed his name.

With that simple, innocent sound the last vestige of Aidan's already tenuous self-control faded. Easily, using only the mental power at which all vampires are adept, he arranged her on her back and removed the T-shirt, drawing it off over her head.

Neely didn't open her eyes, but she was aware of his presence, and she welcomed him, crooning softly and arching her wondrous, supple body once, as if to entice him.

Still, Aidan cherished this fragile, independent creature too much to press his advantage. *May I touch you, Neely?* he asked, exerting no other power now beyond being mentally present in that room. *May I give you pleasure?*

A fine sheen of perspiration glistened on her skin, and the tips of her lush breasts shaped themselves into buds. "Yes," she whispered. "Oh, yes."

"...yes..."

Neely had never had a more sensual, more downright delicious dream. It seemed that Aidan was lying with her in that huge bed, naked and warm and gloriously passionate.

She felt his hands stroking her, moving over the length of her, learning the curves and hollows of her body, taking their time. When it seemed that her every pore was open to him, he narrowed his caresses to her breasts, weighing them in his palms, fondling them with a gentle reverence that made her want to weep, chafing their nipples with the sides of his thumbs.

She wanted *this* to be real, this tender, fiery loving. *Oh, please*, she wished in silence, *let all the rest of it, the vampires and the men who want to murder me, let those things be the dream.*

Neely cried out in nearly unbearable pleasure when Aidan moistened one nipple with his tongue, then began to suckle. She tried to put her arms around him, but there was nothing to hold, for he was a phantom lover.

Neither waking nor sleeping, Neely responded without restraint as Aidan pressed her breasts together and somehow teased and tasted the straining tips of both. Her body began to undulate, and she felt her hair clinging to her face in moist tendrils. Again she reached for Aidan, again she failed to find him, though he was undeniably *there*, loving her more fully than she'd ever been loved.

She clawed and clutched at the bedclothes as he continued to worship her, rose high off the mattress with a cry of primitive surrender when he burrowed through the silken delta between her legs and nibbled greedily at the very core of her femininity. At the same time he continued to enjoy not one breast, but both, and then—then he added the final element to her conquering. He thrust inside her, hard and hot, while still subjecting her to all the other sensations, too.

Neely was not inexperienced—she'd been deeply in love once before, after all—but she'd never felt anything like this before Aidan. He, and only he, was touching her, and yet all her erogenous zones were being attended at once. She thought the pleasure would surely kill her, and didn't care one whit if she died, if only she could have the promised satisfaction first.

Her release was savage in its intensity, seeming to draw her up onto her elbows, the rounding of her heels, the crown of her head, where she hung suspended, uttering one ragged shout of ecstasy after another. Aidan plied her senses mercilessly, the whole time refusing to allow her to fall after scaling only one peak. No, he took her to another pinnacle, and then another, still higher, and when he finally allowed her to rest, she was mute with exhaustion. She curled up in a corner of her own heart and slept a fathomless sleep.

When she awakened, it was late afternoon. Somewhere deep inside her a chord still resonated with the last sweet music of Aidan's caresses. Neely smiled, stretched, reached for him . . .

And remembered.

She had only dreamed that Aidan had made love to her.

Tears blurred Neely's vision as she turned onto her side and gazed toward the row of windows on the other side of the room. Winter would soon arrive in earnest, and the first faint shadows of twilight were already gathering. She lay there, watching the daylight fade, mourning for the dream world where she and Aidan had become one.

An hour passed, and part of another. When the room was bruised with darkness, Aidan came to her. She saw him, felt him with her outstretched hand, and his weight pressed into the edge of the mattress, gloriously real.

"Aidan."

"Yes, my love."

She reached up, smoothed the sleek, raven-dark hair at his temple with her palm. "I had the loveliest, most scandalous dream."

He smiled that sad, poignant, beautiful smile again, the one that never failed to pierce her heart. "Did you?"

Chapter

9

As he sat beside Neely on the bed, looking down at her and remembering her responses to his purely mental lovemaking, Aidan again acknowledged the most difficult and treacherous reality of all. She was safe from human enemies while in his house, but in the gravest of danger from immortal predators. Valerian would see her as a plaything, Lisette, as a tool of revenge—even Maeve, in her reckless sisterly and somewhat possessive affection, represented a threat to Neely.

Besides, whatever loyalty Maeve and Valerian might feel toward him, they were vampires, first and always, and as such they could not be trusted with a mortal.

Aidan felt starved and enervated himself, for he had expended tremendous energy pleasuring Neely, and he knew better than anyone what a temptation she offered. Even though he was certain now that he could make love to her, with his body as well as his mind, without fear of doing her harm, he was still terrified for her.

He stood, then retreated a pace. "I'll return in a little while," he said gruffly. "While I'm gone, I want you to remember—to go over every hour, every moment of your past—until you think of some place where you might hide from the senator and his friends until I can deal with them."

She sat up, regarded him with round eyes, unconsciously covering herself with the sheets. "You were really here, making love to me, weren't you? It was some sort of—of vampire magic, like before—and like the night we danced."

Aidan could not look at her, could not bear to reply. He'd done a vile, damnable thing, tainting her delicate purity with his own foul passions. By loving her, he might well have condemned her to a fate that was quite literally worse than death.

"Aidan," she persisted.

"Yes," he admitted, fairly sobbing the word. "Damn it, *yes*, it was real!"

She left the bed, the top sheet wrapped around her slender figure and trailing behind her like a bride's train, and came to him.

"Are you still afraid?" she asked. Her voice was like balm to his tormented spirit, a drop of water on the tongue of a sinner suffering in hell.

"Oh, yes," Aidan ground out, visibly forcing himself to look at her. "Not of bedding you, my lass—I know now that the love I feel for you is far greater than any lust for blood—but there are other dangers."

She stood on tiptoe and kissed him with a tenderness that broke his heart.

"Then let us have whatever time together that we can," she said. "Come, Aidan, and lie with me."

He had never wanted anything so much, with the possible exception of his lost mortality, but he forced himself to draw back from her, knowing that every moment they spent together made her doom more likely.

"There are things I must do," Aidan said, leaving her alone again.

Neely took a quick shower and donned yesterday's jeans and one of Aidan's sweaters, then dashed down the stairs. In a moment of panic, she considered bolting out the front door and running—just running—until she collapsed. The problem was, there was nowhere to run to, and there was certainly no place to hide.

Anyway, she couldn't tolerate the thought of being separated from Aidan—she would rather become a blood-drinker herself than to lose him.

She stood in the dark entryway, breathing deeply, until she'd calmed herself a little. Then she marched resolutely into the kitchen. A bowl of fresh fruit and a loaf of French bread had materialized on the counter; Neely wondered, with grim amusement, if Aidan had conjured the food for her.

Vampire magic, she thought, gazing at the stuff, and doubted that she'd ever feel like eating again.

Although Valerian was ambulatory, he was still too weak to hunt in his usual flamboyant fashion. For exactly that reason—and because Aidan did feel a degree of compassion for the older vampire—he wasn't about to leave his charge alone with Neely.

Instead, at Valerian's suggestion, they visited a bar on a back street in a modern American city, where the local deviants gathered. Here, in the Last Ditch Tavern, drug dealers congregated, along with pornographers of every description, and others who preyed upon the uncertain, the weak, and the naive.

It was a crowded dive, too warm and too dark, filled with shrillness and smoke, harsh music with indecipherable lyrics, and the intangible specters of lust and hatred and fear.

Aidan despised the Last Ditch instantly, but Valerian surveyed the place as though it were a superb gourmet restaurant. The elder vampire nudged Aidan and pointed to a lonely figure seated at a corner table. He spoke mentally, since it would have been futile to address anyone in the ordinary way in the midst of such chaos.

That pale, skinny creature, there in the shadows, Valerian said. *He's a serial killer, specializing in teenage prostitutes. Likes to make them suffer a little before he finally snuffs them out.*

Aidan regarded the quarry with revulsion. *Scum*, he replied.

Precisely, Valerian answered, beginning to weave his way through the howling, oblivious crowd toward his prey—

who undoubtedly, and quite mistakenly, considered himself to be the predator.

Aidan followed, albeit reluctantly, reflecting as he went that there were indeed many kinds of monsters abroad, and relatively few of them were supernatural. *Are there other vampires here?* he inquired of Valerian's broad back.

No, came the sharp retort, rapid-fire, *and you'd damn well better learn to sense their presence on your own.*

We're the only immortals, then? Aidan asked, feeling only mild chagrin. He hated being a vampire and saw no reason to polish the attendant skills.

Valerian turned his head and pinioned Aidan with a brief glare. *There are two warlocks at the bar. Go ahead and look at them. They've been watching us since we came in.*

Aidan tried to resist, but he could not. He glanced toward the long bar, with its brass rails and milling crowd, and immediately spotted the male witches. They stood out in a subtle way, being taller and handsomer and of brighter countenance than most humans. One lifted his glass to Aidan in an elegant salute and smiled benignly.

Valerian was already closing in on his quarry, the sullen killer sitting alone and feeling sorry for himself. *Don't be fooled by their friendliness,* he warned as a hasty aside, already concentrating palpably on his imminent feeding. *The warlock's blood is poison to us, as I've told you many times before. They envy our powers and use their own to thwart us whenever they can.*

Aidan shifted his attention to the measly specimen Valerian had chosen to feed upon. The elegant vampire smiled his most charming smile, pulled back a chair, and sat down at the table.

"Hello, Udell," he said to the pockmarked boy.

Aidan sat, too, although he could hardly tolerate the psychic stench that rose from the lad's diseased soul. To his amazement, Udell smiled at the beast who would consume and perhaps kill him.

"How'd you know my name?" he shouted over the perverse celebrations and the grating music.

Valerian looked as handsome as an archangel as he set-tled back in his chair and regarded the monster with appar-ent fondness. "By magic," he said.

Watching the interchange, Aidan felt sickened, even though he had no pity at all for the hapless Udell. He'd already glanced into the little worm's mind and seen his favorite forms of amusement firsthand. No, it was Valerian's blithe amorality that troubled Aidan now, that hardened hazy suspicions into fact. Here was a creature who, in the final analysis, would indulge his own dark appetites, wherever the opportunity arose. Whether the victim was good or evil, male or female, old or young, might not matter at all.

Suddenly Valerian's gaze sliced to Aidan's face. *It isn't true, what you're thinking,* he told him, in the same silent way they'd communicated before. *I am capable of love and the purest devotion, just as you are.*

Aidan looked away, uncomfortable. *Just get on with it,* he replied. One of the warlocks was moving through the throng toward them, smiling. *I don't want to stay here any longer than I must.*

Valerian held out a hand to Udell, who took it, smiling foolishly, like an old maid who has finally been asked to dance. Together, vampire and witless victim disappeared, blending into the grinding, sweating mass of humanity choking the dance floor.

Great, Aidan thought, watching the warlock. *Now I get to make small talk with somebody who wants to turn me into a toad.*

The warlock laughed. He was attractive, with soft brown hair, impish hazel eyes, and a quick grin. "I want to do noth-ing of the sort," he said, holding out his hand. "My name is Cain."

"Figures," Aidan replied, ignoring the gesture. He looked toward the other ghoul, still standing at the bar, and arched one eyebrow. "Is that your brother, Abel?"

All the mirth had drained from Cain's manner. "Not funny." He grabbed a wooden chair, wrenched it around, and straddled the seat, his sinewy arms folded across the back. "You cannot possibly be so naive as you seem," he declared. "Do you know what goes on in this bar?"

"Every sort of depravity, I would imagine," Aidan answered coolly. "Look, I'm not out to make friends or bridge any philosophical gaps between your kind and mine, all right? I'm here to feed, and for no other purpose."

Cain's smile returned. He turned his head slowly and pulled down on the collar of his expensive sweater with one hand to bare his throat in invitation.

Aidan wondered if it was possible for a vampire to vomit. "Thanks, anyway," he said, rising from his chair. He scanned the crowd, looking for Valerian, enjoying a brief fantasy in which he drove a spike through that particular vampire's heart with a croquet mallet.

That night Aidan made a point of selecting a female victim, a very disturbed creature who had left her children with an abusive biker boyfriend to come to the Last Ditch for an evening's diversion. Minutes before Aidan approached her, she had sucked the week's grocery money up her nose through a rolled-up dollar bill. Her name was Fay, and she was more than neglectful, she was a sociopath, untroubled by the dimmest flicker of conscience.

They danced for a while, moving against each other, and then he led her through the hallway at the rear, past the rest rooms, and into the alley.

It certainly wasn't a sexual encounter, but when Aidan bit into Fay's narrow throat to drink, he felt the usual jubilation—and an almost paralyzing rush of guilt.

He left the woman half-conscious, but very much alive, huddled beside an overflowing trash bin, and went in search of Valerian. At first, seeing no sign of the other vampire only annoyed Aidan, but then, when a single, grim possibility struck him, he was alarmed.

Neely was alone, unguarded. And Valerian surely saw her not only as a tempting delicacy, but as a rival.

There, on a snowy street corner, Aidan raised his arms over his head, clasped his hands together as if to pray, and vanished.

*   *   *

Neely had found Aidan's car keys after an impulsive search. She was bending over his desk, hastily penning a note, when there was a rippling stir in the air. Catching her breath, she looked up to see Valerian standing only a few feet away.

She laid one hand to her heart, willing it to slow down to its regular pace, and managed a shaky smile. "I was just going to the market," she said, feeling foolish even as she uttered the words.

Valerian folded his arms and tilted his magnificent head to one side. He had a mane of chestnut-colored hair and mischievous violet eyes, and he grinned as he regarded her, as if he were mildly puzzled.

Neely reminded herself that this was a vampire she was dealing with—an ancient and very accomplished one, according to Aidan's journals. She took a step backward. "Where is Aidan?"

Valerian sighed. "He's occupied with other matters just now. You shouldn't go out. It's very dangerous."

She put her hands on her hips, figuring bravado was a better bet than sniveling cowardice, though it was the latter she was inclined toward. "Don't look now," she said tartly, "but I'm not exactly safe and sound as it is."

He chuckled, his arms still folded and his expression still curious. "It's hopeless—loving Aidan Tremayne the way you do, I mean. He can never be a husband to you in any fashion you would even begin to understand."

Neely's temper, an unwary and impulsive force in its own right, flared with all the fury of the fires that burned at the center of the earth. She forgot all about Valerian's supernatural talents and went to stand directly in front of him, looking straight into his eyes. "You want him for yourself," she accused quietly. "You want him for a lover."

Valerian's eyes flashed, and he seemed to grow taller, fiercer, and much more dangerous. "You cannot possibly comprehend my feelings for Aidan, with your pitiful mortal brain," he growled. "*I am a vampire*, and my affections transcend such trivial concepts as sexuality! Do you think you can categorize me into your narrow human view of what a lover should be? Well, you are wrong!" He paused and, to Neely's enormous relief, made a visible effort to restrain his temper. "Once Aidan comes to terms with who and what he is—"

"No," Neely interrupted quietly, almost gently, shaking her head. "You're the one who needs to get in touch with reality, Valerian. Be careful, or your delusions will destroy you."

The legendary vampire actually looked crestfallen, as well as enraged, just for the merest flicker of a moment. He turned aside and shoved a hand through his thick hair. "To be a creature of the night," he said in a hoarse voice, "is to feel every emotion that mortals feel, a hundredfold, a thousandfold, be it an admirable one or not. In the immortal world, gender has no real bearing on matters of the heart—it is the individual, the object of one's love, who matters."

Neely hugged herself and turned away, hoping Valerian would not sense what she was feeling just then—pity. She reached into the pocket of her coat and jingled Aidan's car keys with her fingers, in a nervous and singularly impotent gesture. She wasn't going anywhere now, that much was clear.

"Perhaps we're both fooling ourselves," she reflected miserably. "I'm as guilty of it as you are."

Before Valerian could offer a response—maybe he had never meant to anyway—Aidan arrived. His appearance wasn't subtle, but violent, and the very force of his rage seemed to shake the room like an earthquake.

"What are you doing here?" he demanded, seeming to tower over the gigantic Valerian, like a mountain about to spew lava.

Neely shrank back, taking refuge behind Aidan's desk.

"Calm yourself," Valerian said good-naturedly, laying his hands on Aidan's shoulders. "I was finished before you left the woman."

Aidan flung Valerian's arms aside while Neely sagged

into the desk chair, stricken. She had no claim to Aidan's fidelity—and certainly no sane person would expect loyalty—but she was wounded all the same.

"Damn you," Aidan spat at Valerian, as fierce and ferocious as an angry panther, "get out—leave us!"

Even though she'd witnessed the phenomenon before, it still left Neely shaken, the way Valerian just dissipated into the air like so much smoke. Unconsciously she had raised both hands to her face, and now she gazed at Aidan through splayed fingers, unable to speak.

He crossed the room, then stood just on the other side of the desk, looking down at her with an unreadable expression. His words startled Neely further, for she had expected, hoped for, some explanation. Some impassioned defense.

"Well?" he asked impatiently. "Have you thought of a place to hide?"

Neely felt shattering despair at the idea of leaving him, even though she'd been telling herself earlier in the evening she must do just that. Like Valerian, she had been whistling in the dark, making-believe that she and Aidan could ever have any sort of sane relationship. "I really have to go, then?"

Aidan nodded, looked away. She saw her own anguish reflected in his countenance, mirror-perfect. "Yes," he said raggedly. "Involving you in my life was an unconscionable thing to do, Neely. My enemies—good God, even my friends—are infinitely more dangerous to you than any human criminal could ever be."

She wanted to go to him, to clasp his arm and rest her head against the outer length of his shoulder, but she held herself back. "Valerian, Lisette, the others—yes, I can believe they might do me harm. But you, Aidan?"

He whirled on her, imperious in his pain, taller and fiercer for it. "No," he said in a bitter hiss. "But I am not a man—I have no literal, physical heart, no lungs to breathe with, no stomach to fill. I cannot give you children or walk with you in the light of the sun. My passion for you is an unholy thing—" Here he held his hands up, white and strong and elegant, as if offering some monstrous display. "Don't you understand that I am, first and foremost, a beast, cursed by man and by God?"

Neely felt herself go pale, and she wanted to faint from sheer grief, but she would not let it happen. "It's impossible, isn't it?" she mourned with quiet dignity.

Aidan's eyes were bleak indeed as he regarded her. "I made love to you with my mind, Neely," he said despondently, "not my hands, my mouth, my body. I am a monster, and I beg you not to forget that, even if I should. Although I would not hurt you, ever, I endanger you simply by the fact of loving you. Now, is there a place you can go to hide?"

Glumly Neely nodded. "Yes," she said. "There's a cottage on the coast, up in Maine. It belongs to a college friend of mine, Wendy Browning. She's in London now, studying drama."

"Very well," Aidan agreed reluctantly. "I will take you there."

Neely shook her head. "I don't want to be beamed anywhere," she replied. "It's too hard on my nerves. If you would just lend me your car, or I could rent one under another name—"

Aidan stood still, visibly debating the idea in his mind. "You will take mine," he finally conceded. He arched one dark eyebrow and smiled slightly, his gaze fixed on the pocket of Neely's coat, which she'd forgotten she was wearing. "You were going to, anyway, weren't you?"

"I didn't know what I was going to do." The words were fragile, and several splintered and broke as Neely uttered them.

He moved, as if to approach her, then visibly held himself in check. He went the long way around to reach the desk, giving Neely a wide berth, and took a handful of cash from the one drawer. "Here," he said. "Take this."

"Will—will I see you again?" Neely hated herself for asking, but she had to know. She had enough on her mind without wondering about that, too.

"Yes," Aidan answered, albeit reluctantly. "I have certain hopes for myself, for us, though I can't discuss them with you now. And wonderfully independent Yankee that you are, I think you'll need my help to completely resolve your problem with the senator and his buddies."

It was incredible, Neely thought, the exultation she felt at being told she wasn't seeing Aidan Tremayne for the last time. She was, logically speaking, in no position to be exulted about anything. "I'll make a map—so you can find the cottage," she offered, perhaps too eagerly, and with a sniffle.

Aidan smiled, very sadly. "No need, my love. There is no place, time, or dimension where you could hide from me. Your beautiful, brave spirit shines as brightly as if it were the last star in the universe."

Neely sniffled again and wiped her eyes with the back of one hand. "You know, if you ever get tired of the plasma business, I think you could make it big as a poet."

He chuckled, but the sound was hollow and desolate. "Go," he said.

Neely went, taking his car, the money he'd given her, and her toothbrush.

When Neely had gone, Valerian reappeared. Undoubtedly he'd folded himself into some nook or corner and watched the whole melodrama with acute interest.

"If you know what's good for you," he told Aidan, going to the liquor cabinet to pour a brandy he could not drink, "and for that fetching little creature who just left, you'll never go near her again."

Aidan was standing at the parlor window. He'd seen the sleek white car move into the driveway, watched until its foggy-red taillights had disappeared into the snowy gloom. "I have never known what was good for me," he answered. "That's why I ended up in this fix."

"What are you going to do now?"

Aidan sighed, but he did not turn around to face the other vampire. "Two things: make myself available to the Brotherhood, should they decide to pay me a call—and find Lisette."

The brandy glass clattered to the floor and broke, and Aidan felt a certain triumph in the knowledge that he'd startled the great Valerian. That wasn't an easy thing to do.

"Are you mad?" Valerian demanded.

"You know I am," Aidan answered.

"How will you find her?"

"Easily. I mean to put myself directly in her path."

Valerian's voice trembled with rage. He gripped Aidan's arm and wrenched him about so that they faced each other. "She will destroy you!"

"Maybe," Aidan agreed, lifting his shoulders in a distracted shrug. "I mean to find out, as soon as possible."

"It's this girl," Valerian cried, waving his arms wide in a gesture of fury, "this Neely Wallace, who has brought all this grief and trouble down on our heads! I should have destroyed her long ago!"

Aidan narrowed his eyes as he looked into Valerian's strained features. "You have that power," he agreed. "No one can dispute that. But if you harm Neely, my friend, you will have to destroy me as well. For if you do not, I will plague you with every step you take, until the last trumpet sounds!"

Valerian's expression was one of grief and subsiding fury. "Doesn't it matter, that I care for you?"

"No," Aidan answered. "Your kind of caring is perversion to me. There is a bond between us, because of the blood communion, but I cannot give you anything more than loyalty and friendship. The sooner you accept that, Valerian, the sooner we can go on to other things."

The elder vampire did not reply but instead turned his back to Aidan without a word and made himself into a shifting wisp of smoke.

Aidan sat down in a leather chair near the fire, closed his eyes, and mentally followed Neely's progress through the town of Bright River and northward, toward New Hampshire and, beyond that, Maine.

Neely stopped at an all-night café just before dawn and put a call through to her brother. She had not been watching television or even reading newspapers, but she knew her disappearance from that tacky motel room several days before had probably drawn some media attention. Although she'd finally written a note, which Aidan had delivered by some means she hadn't asked him to explain, she wanted to reassure Ben and Danny that she was still alive and well.

"Hello," her brother said, sounding alert even at that unholy hour of the morning. He was an ambitious sort and had probably been up long enough to shower and make coffee.

"Ben," Neely whispered, hunching close to the pay phone, which was situated in a narrow hallway, next to the café's rest rooms. "It's me. I can't talk long, in case someone traces the call, but I wanted to tell you that I'm okay, and that I love you and Danny—"

"Neely." Ben sighed the name; it resonated with sadness and relief. "Thank God. I thought maybe they'd gotten you, those bastards from the Capitol."

"Not yet," Neely said. She smiled grimly, glad her brother didn't know what *else* might be stalking her. "Look, don't worry about me, Ben, because I've got at least one very powerful friend. Gotta go now."

"I love you," Ben said in parting, understanding as always. "Take care."

With that, Neely hung up. Tears stung her eyes as she turned around and nearly collided with a smiling truck driver, who was waiting to use the phone. He was tall and good-looking, and the name "Trent" was stitched on the pocket of his shirt in red thread.

Neely was hungry, but she was afraid to linger too long in one spot, just in case Senator Hargrove's henchmen were following her. She found a McDonald's, bought a breakfast sandwich and some orange juice at the drive-through window, and headed back out onto the freeway.

Spain

Lisette was feeling stronger with every fall of twilight, every fevered feeding. Her favorite victims were innocents; their blood gave her the most energy and the greatest euphoria, and she always pressed them as close to death as she dared.

She slept in a hidden crypt by day, a safe nook tucked away in the cellar of the villa she'd bought generations ago. Every fifty years or so, she'd willed the place to herself, along with the fortune that had been hers ever since she'd arrived in Europe, many centuries before, and married a very rich mortal. She was feared and revered by all but a few very foolish vampires; she had everything.

Almost.

Seated on the stone railing of the terrace outside her bedchamber, gazing out at the star-dappled water, Lisette thought of the one scalawag in all her long history who had managed to break her heart.

Aidan Tremayne.

She smiled a fragile smile, remembering. She'd given him immortality, the ungrateful wretch, and taught him to stalk and kill, to navigate through time and space, to protect himself from other immortals and veil his presence from humans and lesser vampires. In return for her kindness, he had betrayed her.

Lisette sighed and tossed her head, so that her rich dark hair tumbled back over one alabaster-smooth shoulder. She wore a Grecian dress, strictly for the sake of drama. Her mistake, she reflected, had been in making Aidan into the splendid fiend he was. Instead she should have used him until he bored her, like the multitude of handsome young mortals who had preceded him, and then consumed his life force and discarded him.

"Fool," she said to herself in a bitter whisper. A soft breeze carried the word out over a warm Spanish sea.

Lisette stepped up onto the terrace railing and stood there, her arms spread wide, her white gown flowing and billowing wonderfully around her slender figure. For a century and a half she had lain dormant in her hidden tomb, rising only when she knew she would perish if she did not feed, languishing in her despondency, too distraught to function.

Then, during one of her brief, slightly frantic forays into the world of humans, she'd caught a glimpse of another female vampire, Maeve Tremayne. Maeve was Aidan's twin, and her resemblance to him had stirred some sudden and harsh violence deep in Lisette's being.

From that night onward, Lisette had forced herself to rise and feed. She had been practicing her powers and regaining her former strength for months. Soon she would be immune to the light of the sun as she had once been, able to track errant vampires to their lairs.

She was still queen of the blood-drinkers, among the oldest on earth, and she intended to show them all that she had no intention of abdicating. After that she would deal vengeance to her enemies, one by one.

Valerian would be first, that despicable traitor. After him, Maeve, who, Lisette was convinced, secretly aspired to reign over the nightwalkers herself. And when Maeve and Valerian were nothing but smoldering piles of ash, shifting in the sunlight, Lisette vowed, she would turn her full attention on Aidan.

By the time she was through meting out her myriad punishments, the very fires of hell would look good to him.

"Lisette."

The voices came from behind her, speaking in chorus and startling her so that she nearly toppled off the high terrace onto the rocky shore below. The fall would not have done her bodily injury, of course, but her dignity might have been hopelessly wounded.

She turned slowly and looked down into the white, upturned faces of her visitors.

Canaan and Benecia Havermail stood before her, wearing identical dresses of yellow satin. Lisette was glad they would never grow to adult size, for their natures were at least as vicious as her own, and she would not relish the competition.

"What do you want?" she snapped, irritated.

Again the child-fiends spoke in eerily perfect unison, their fangs glinting in the starlight as they chattered. "We've come about Mr. Tremayne. He's been to Havermail Castle, you know, inquiring about the Brotherhood."

Lisette floated down from the railing to stand before the horrid little pair. "What does Aidan want with the Brotherhood?" She raised a hand when they both started to talk again. "Only one of you need answer."

Benecia, after a triumphant glance at her younger sister, went on alone. "He desires to be mortal again," she said. At this oddity she giggled, and so did Canaan.

Lisette, however, was not amused. She turned away from her visitors and grasped the terrace railing in both hands. No vampire, to her knowledge, had ever made such a transition, but Aidan was just brazen enough, just fanciful enough, to try.

Perhaps she would be forced to resolve the matter sooner than she'd planned.

Chapter
10

Neely drove until midafternoon, when she simply could go no farther. She rented a room somewhere in New Hampshire, this time choosing one of the large chain motels, and secured all the locks carefully before collapsing onto the bed. After an hour or so she awakened just long enough to remove her coat and kick off her shoes, then sank back into an exhausted sleep.

When she opened her eyes, feeling as if she'd just risen from the depths of a coma, there was no light except for the red numerals on the clock radio on the lamp table.

3:47 A.M.

Neely would have been glad to sleep another twelve hours, at least, but she didn't dare linger in one place for too long. Although she was fairly certain no one was following her, she couldn't afford to depend on luck.

She stumbled into the bathroom, showered, and put yesterday's clothes back on. Later, she promised herself, she would buy jeans, sweaters, underwear, and the like. For now she was traveling light.

At 4:14, Neely left the motel room. She was starved, but the fast-food places weren't open yet, and the idea of wandering into a big, well-lit truck stop for oatmeal and toast made her feel too vulnerable. In the end she stopped at a convenience store for high-octane coffee and a sweet roll.

As she had the day before, Neely drove until she was blind with fatigue. Then she stopped at a shopping mall, entered a crowded discount store, and bought the clothing she needed, along with a hot dog and a bag of popcorn. That afternoon she checked into a motor court beside a frozen lake. She propped a chair under the doorknob, since the locks didn't look all that secure. After devouring her scanty supper, she bathed and toppled into bed.

Sleep didn't come as readily this time, even though Neely was every bit as tired as she had been the night before. She switched on the television set, turned to one of the cable networks, and settled in to watch a tabloid program.

"This is Melody Ling," a sharply dressed reporter was saying, "reporting from Washington, D.C., where Mrs. Elaine Hargrove, wife of the prominent senator, is allegedly recovering satisfactorily from emergency surgery."

Neely sat bolt upright against the musty pillows at her back, staring at the screen, willing Ling to say more. Unfortunately the piece was over.

She grabbed up the remote, then sought and found the twenty-four-hour news channel. She'd had the car radio on all day while she traveled, but she'd heard nothing about the Hargroves.

Neely watched three segments—a scandal concerning the sale of arms to some hormonal Third-World country, a piece on distraught dairy farmers, and the latest tidbit out of Buckingham Palace. Then, finally, Senator Dallas Hargrove appeared on the screen, striding out of a well-known Washington hospital, looking harried and impatient.

Although Hargrove was definitely a skunk and a moral lightweight, Neely thought, it was impossible not to feel sorry for him just then. Reporters barred his way, the portable lights deepened the lines and shadows in his face, and microphones stabbed at him like drawn lances.

"Senator Hargrove, can you tell us anything about Mrs. Hargrove's accident?"

"Is she resting comfortably?"

"Will she recover?"

"Was she driving when the accident occurred?"

The senator stopped and held up both hands in a bid for

order. "Elaine—Mrs. Hargrove—is conscious," he said tersely. "We have every hope that she will survive. And no, my wife suffers from a chronic illness and does not drive. She was riding with our chauffeur when the limousine was forced off the road by a reckless driver."

"Has an arrest been made?" a reporter called out, but Hargrove was plainly finished with the interview. He forced his way through a throng of newspeople and got into the backseat of a waiting car.

The camera switched to an anchorwoman in the network newsroom, where the scanty details of Elaine Hargrove's accident were reviewed. She had been on her way to a luncheon, where she was to be presented with an award of some sort, when, according to the chauffeur, another car had come up behind them and crashed hard into the bumper. The driver, already traveling at a fairly high speed, had been startled and lost control of the wheel. The limo had sideswiped a concrete abutment and then swerved into the path of an oncoming semi-truck.

No one else had been injured besides Elaine Hargrove.

Chilled, Neely hobbled in and took another bath, soaking in the hottest water she could stand. When she got out of the tub, however, and wrapped herself in a rough towel, she was still as cold as ever.

Obviously the senator had run afoul of his drug-dealing friends, and they'd made a cruel example out of Elaine. Hargrove would be desperate to appease the mob now, which meant he would make no further efforts to protect Neely.

All thoughts of sleep deserted her, even though she was half sick with weariness. She was on her own, and if she wanted to stay alive, she'd better move fast.

She tore the tags from her new clothes and wrenched on panties and a bra, stiff jeans, and a starchy sweatshirt. Then she groped for the telephone and dialed New York information.

Ten frustrating minutes later, Neely was speaking to someone in Melody Ling's department at the television network. Ms. Ling was still out on assignment, and it would probably be impossible to reach her before morning.

Neely slammed down the receiver, snatched up her few belongings, and rushed out to the car.

She tried twice more to get through to Ling, the following morning and the one after that, and was unsuccessful both times. Finally, in the midst of a blizzard, she reached Timber Cove, a tiny town on the winter-bleak coast of Maine. Wendy Browning's summer cottage was five miles north, and after buying a few supplies in a small grocery store, Neely took refuge there.

The front door key was under one of the legs of the picnic table out on the snow-mounded deck, as always. Neely had been a guest in the cottage many times, and before flying off to London, Wendy had told her she was welcome to use the place whenever she wished.

She let herself in, turned up the gas heater, and lifted the telephone receiver to her ear. There was a dial tone.

Neely carried in her bags of clothing and her groceries, set a pot of coffee to brewing, and stood at the glass doors leading to the deck, looking out at the rocky, snow-streaked shore.

When she had had a cup of coffee to warm herself, she put on her coat and trekked outside, through the grayness of late morning on a stormy day, to the woodshed. There she knelt in a corner and raised a loose floorboard with both hands.

Underneath lay a fat manila envelope, wrapped in plastic, just exactly where Neely had left it.

She carried the packet back to the house, opened it, and saw that all the documents and recordings were still there. Trembling slightly, Neely returned to the telephone and dialed Melody Ling's number.

This time she got lucky.

Aidan found Maeve easily, for once. She was at her house in London, in her beloved nineteenth century, entertaining a drawing room full of guests. A string quartet played Mozart in one corner, while elegantly dressed visitors mingled, some sipping champagne and nibbling clam puffs, others only pretending.

It was an interesting mix of vampires and humans, jaded writers and artists who probably knew full well that they were socializing with fiends. In Aidan's experience the right-brain types found such things stimulating.

"Darling." Maeve swept toward him, her crisp satin dress rustling as she moved, both hands extended. Her dark blue eyes were alight with surprise and pleasure, both swiftly displaced by worry. "What a lovely—surprise. Aidan—?"

He kissed her cheek and smiled wanly, but that was the extent of his effort to appear normal. He had not fed for three days, he'd been so grieved over the parting with Neely, and he was faint with the lack of nourishment.

Maeve frowned, still holding his hands, and he felt some of her abundant strength flow into him. She pulled him through the strange crowd and out onto a stone terrace with high iron railings.

The wind was bitingly cold, but it did little to revive Aidan.

"What's happened?" Maeve demanded. "Honestly, Aidan, if this has something to do with that wretched woman—"

He looked directly into his sister's angry eyes. "It has everything to do with Neely," he said. "I love her. I'd rather perish than lose her, and I would sell my soul, if indeed I have one at all, to live with her as a man."

Maeve's face tightened, and for a moment her fury pulsed between them, but then she let her forehead fall against his shoulder and wept disconsolately.

Aidan held her in a gentle embrace. "I'm sorry," he whispered raggedly.

She looked up at him, after a long time, her beautiful eyes glimmering with tears. Aidan was heartbroken to see his sister in such a state.

"There is no turning you aside from this course, is

there?" Maeve asked, lifting her chin. "You'll either succeed in your foolish enterprise or perish in the attempt."

Aidan laid his hand gently against her cheek. "Anything is better than being what I am, darling," he said. "Even eternal damnation."

Her alabaster skin grew even paler, and she clutched at the satin lapels of his dinner jacket. "Don't say that!" she pleaded in an agonized whisper. "To think of you burning forever and ever—oh, Aidan, I can't bear it!"

"Shhh," Aidan said, laying his hands on her glowing shoulders and giving her just the slightest shake. "Then don't think of that."

"How will I know what's happened to you?" Maeve pleaded. "How will I know whether you're alive or—or dead?"

He kissed her forehead. "Wait until you hear the first rumors," he told her with a sad smile. "Then visit my house in Connecticut. If I've managed to make the transition, I'll leave a bouquet of white roses on that round table in the entryway, as a sort of signal."

Maeve studied his face for a long moment, then nodded. "You haven't fed. Surely you know you cannot hope even to survive if you do not guard your strength."

Aidan let his hands fall to his sides, though he still studied his sister with affection. He wanted to remember her always, whether he writhed in hell or was allowed to live out his allotted number of years as a man.

"The hunger makes it possible to think more clearly, Maeve," he said. "You know that."

She touched his cheek, and her lips moved, but no sound came from her.

"Good-bye," he said.

Valerian crashed Maeve's party half an hour after Aidan left, looking distracted and a little frantic. He grabbed her hand and pulled her out onto the same terrace where she'd stood with her brother, her heart broken at her feet.

"Have you seen that idiot sibling of yours?" Valerian demanded.

Maeve bridled, but not because Valerian had called Aidan an idiot—she quite agreed, just now, that the description suited. "Who do you think you are, dragging me away from my guests like this and speaking so familiarly?"

He paused, then shamed her with a languorous smile.

Maeve looked away, remembering things she would rather have forgotten. Valerian had taught her much more than how to travel through time and read minds during their long association. "That's over," she said.

"Perhaps," Valerian agreed. Then he grew impatient again. "Tell me—have you seen Aidan?"

"Yes," Maeve said, leaning back against the terrace railing and studying her mentor in the cold light of the stars. "He was here earlier, to bid me farewell."

"What?"

She nodded, and when she spoke, her voice was lined with tiny fractures. "He would rather die than be what we are, Valerian—he would choose oblivion, even hellfire, over the life of a vampire. He despises himself, and us."

Valerian gave an explosive sigh and shoved one hand through his mane of rich brown hair. "I should never have left him alone," the magnificent monster fretted. "It's just that he exasperates me so, and he has no compunction whatsoever about breaking my heart—"

"You don't have a heart," Maeve snapped, annoyed. As usual, Valerian was thinking only of himself. "And why *did* you leave Aidan alone?"

"He was moping about over that woman, and I needed to hunt, to rebuild my strength," Valerian said, flinging his hands out wide in a gesture of angry resignation. "I spent a few nights indulging myself—I admit that—and when I returned to Connecticut to look in on Aidan, he was gone."

Despair swelled up inside Maeve. "He's not coming back, Valerian. The sooner we both give up and accept that, the better it will be."

"You don't understand!" Valerian cried. "Somehow he's

learned to veil his whereabouts from me. Maeve, without me he has no defense against Lisette!"

"Some defense you offer," Maeve accused. "She despises you almost as much as she does Aidan. Leave my brother alone, Valerian—let him work this out for himself."

"Damn it, Maeve, do you have any idea what she'll do to him?"

Maeve closed her eyes. "I have to believe he'll escape her," she said. "I cannot think otherwise and still go on living." With that, she turned and would have gone back into the house to rejoin her guests, but Valerian forcibly stopped her, gripping her shoulders and wrenching her around to face him.

"Perhaps you are willing to let Lisette play vile games with Aidan until she finally decides to kill him, but I am not. And I am more powerful than you are, Maeve—don't forget that."

She trembled, this female vampire who was afraid of nothing, save seeing her brother suffer. "What do you want?"

"Look deep inside yourself," Valerian ordered, his voice low and hypnotic, but urgent, too. "There you will see Aidan's reflection. Tell me where to find him, Maeve."

Maeve began to shiver. "He's standing on a terrace—like this one—" She gave a small, involuntary cry and raised curled fingers to her mouth. "Oh, Valerian, Aidan has gone to Lisette's villa, on the coast of Spain!"

Valerian released her so swiftly that she sank to the tiled floor of the terrace, too weakened by horror to rise. He held out his cloak and spun around, and before he'd completed a single turn, he'd vanished.

Maeve sat dazed on the tiles for a few minutes, sobbing inwardly, longing to rush to Aidan's rescue, as Valerian had, and knowing that her brother would never forgive her if she did. As rash and ill-advised as Aidan's decision had been, no one, not even Valerian himself, would be able to sway him from it.

*   *   *

"You *are* the adventurous type."

Aidan whirled, though he knew the voice behind him wasn't Lisette's, and saw a youth leaning against the stone wall of the villa, his arms folded. He was dressed all in black, like a cat burglar, and wore a cocky grin. By Aidan's guess, the lad was no older than seventeen.

"Who are you?"

The sleek young vampire pushed himself away from the wall with one foot. "The name is Tobias—Aidan. You ought to be more alert, you know. It's nothing but luck that Lisette is hunting elsewhere tonight."

"Yes," Aidan said, "it's luck, all right. Bad luck." He tugged at the cuffs of his dinner jacket. "What do you want—Tobias?"

"Not a thing. I'm here because of what *you* want. Or, at least, what you told Aubrey Havermail you wanted—a chat with a representative of the Brotherhood."

Aidan was taken aback, but he smiled and offered his hand. "Aren't you a little young to be part of such an august group?"

Tobias gave a slow grin. "I guess that depends on how you define the word *young.* I was among the first vampires created." The sudden stunned expression on Aidan's face seemed to please him. "Come. Even we old ones don't enjoy tangling with the likes of Lisette. She can be such a bitch."

In the next instant everything went dark, and Aidan heard a rushing sound. When he was conscious again, he found himself standing with Tobias in a natural tunnel, beside an underground river. There was no light, but that didn't matter, of course, for a vampire's vision is at its best in the blackest gloom.

"Where are we?"

Tobias sighed. "You don't need to know that," he answered with cordial impatience. He sighed again. "I'm afraid Aubrey was quite right about you. You're not much of a vampire."

"No," Aidan said evenly. "I'm not."

"He says you want to be changed back into a man." The

words echoed in the dank chamber, hollow with disbelief. "Is that true?"

"Absolutely," Aidan answered. He felt a thrumming excitement deep inside, as well as a certain well-founded terror. "I did not willingly become a vampire. I was forced."

"You are not the first," Tobias pointed out, clearly unmoved.

"Perhaps not," Aidan agreed mildly. "But I am a weak link in the chain. You saw for yourself, back there on Lisette's terrace, how easy it is to catch me unawares. Suppose I fall into the hands of those who are enemies to all vampires—the Warrior Angel, for example. What's his name again? Ah, yes. Nemesis. What if I were to be captured by Nemesis and forced to tell all I know about blood-drinkers such as yourself? The Dark Kingdom would crumble then, wouldn't it, like a castle of sand?"

"I have only to destroy you, here and now, to prevent such a tragedy," Tobias said coolly. Aidan was aware of the creature's tension, however; he was like a string on an instrument, pulled tight and ready to snap.

Aidan smiled. "I am an insignificant vampire," he admitted, "but there are those who would miss me, and even dare to avenge my destruction."

"Valerian," Tobias said despairingly. "And Maeve."

"You know them, then," Aidan chimed, in a pleased tone that was meant to be irritating.

"They are rebellious and cause the elders a great deal of consternation."

Aidan made a *tsk-tsk* sound, well aware that he was on proverbial thin ice. "I don't know what vampirism is coming to," he said. "Do you?"

Tobias glared. "This way," he growled. Then he turned and moved along the stream's edge, headed into the very heart of the darkness, and Aidan followed.

Eventually they reached a large, torch-lit cave, where ancient scenes and symbols had been painted onto the walls, among the earlier sketches and scrawls of prehistoric man.

Aidan would have been fascinated if his business in that place hadn't been so crucial.

The vampires assembled themselves from particles of dust in the air around Aidan, it seemed to him, the oldest blood-drinkers on earth, some fresh-faced like Tobias, others with flowing silver beards and skin as crinkled and weathered as aged leather.

"This one would be mortal again," Tobias announced to the gathering, his bewilderment plain in his voice. "He says he was made against his will."

The elders murmured among themselves as they walked around Aidan, examining him, but their language was unfamiliar.

Aidan kept his shoulders straight and looked each one, in turn, directly in the eye. He caught the name "Nemesis" in the conversational drift, and knew Tobias had reported his threat.

They might well destroy him now, Aidan thought. He was mildly surprised to realize that he didn't care; having met Neely, and been reminded of what he was missing, he knew he would rather perish by the most horrible of means than live for all eternity knowing she could never be his.

If he could not be restored to his humanity, if he could not love Neely freely, and without fear, he wanted only destruction.

At long last the circling ceased. One of the elders leaned close to Aidan and rasped in English, "Do you follow Nemesis?"

Aidan showed his fangs, in a rather impudent and theatrical way. "I am no angel," he pointed out in the next moment.

The ancient vampire's glacial blue eyes narrowed, and he made an angry gesture with one age-gnarled hand. "Confine this unmannerly whelp where he can do no harm to himself or the rest of us. We will decide his fate later."

Vampires closed in on either side of Aidan, taking his arms, and he struggled, but in vain. Still, he did not regret the course he'd taken, for he was willing to risk anything, undergo any ordeal, in order to be with Neely.

Aidan was dragged to a barred chamber and flung inside. His fine clothes were torn away without ceremony or apology, and he was given a monk's robe, made of some coarse brown cloth. He put the garment on, for the sake of his own dignity, and when his jailers had left him, he tried the bars.

They were immovable.

"I trust you're happy now," a familiar voice said.

He turned to see Tobias standing just behind him, inside the cell, and scowled. "Overjoyed," he replied.

Tobias shook his head, clearly amazed. "Such infernal audacity."

"There's nothing worse than a smart-ass vampire," Aidan agreed.

Tobias laughed outright at that. "If you say so. You're the first blood-drinker ever to ask for transformation—did you know that? That's why you're not staked out in some desert somewhere, waiting for the sun to cook you by degrees, you understand. Because you're an oddity."

Aidan was careful not to let his trepidation show, although to be forced to endure the cruel ministrations of the sun was among the worst fears of nearly every vampire. "Have they destroyed others that way?" he asked.

"Oh, yes. Over the centuries certain rebellious ones have had to be . . . dealt with," Tobias answered. "We learned that particular trick from Nemesis."

An involuntary chill passed through Aidan at the mention of the Warrior Angel, and Tobias chuckled, recognizing it for what it was. There was no mercy in Nemesis, despite his ties with the Kingdom of Heaven; he had been conducting a personal vendetta against blood-drinkers for thousands of years.

"Is there a way?" Aidan whispered, his voice hoarse. "Is it possible to go back to what I was?"

For the first time since their arrival in that pit, there was a glimmer of compassion in Tobias's deceptively youthful face. "Some of the oldest ones wanted to try, for the sake of learning, but it was always forbidden. After all, those who failed would logically be brought before the Throne of Judgment. If Nemesis is as he is, can you imagine what his Master must be like?"

Aidan squeezed his eyes shut for a moment and nodded. "Yes—yes, I can imagine. And I'd rather face even Him than go on as I have been since Lisette changed me!"

"Then you are either a vampire of uncommon courage or a mad one! Which is it?"

He sighed, ran a hand through his hair. "I don't know," Aidan said. "I honestly don't know."

"Why do you want the transformation so much?"

Aidan knew he could not hide Neely's image from this ancient vampire, and he did not try. "I love a human woman."

"You must care a great deal," Tobias marveled, "to take such a risk as the one confronting you now." Having offered this observation, he watched Aidan in troubled silence for a few seconds, then vanished.

Aidan slept, dreamed fitful dreams of Neely, and awakened believing they were together. His despair at the discovery that he was still alone, and a prisoner in the bargain, was a crueler burden than any he had ever borne.

Twenty-four hours later, when Aidan was half-mad with thirst, he was given three enormous rats, scrabbling inside a picnic basket.

Aidan broke their necks, one by one, and tossed their blood-filled bodies through the bars.

When another twenty-four hours had passed, he was in a fever, crouched against a wall of his cell, his mind loose inside his skull, hot with delirium.

A form appeared before him, wavering and slender.

"Go away," he moaned, turning his head.

"So stubborn," a feminine voice scolded, and the sound of it was like cool water pouring gently over his parched spirit.

"Neely," he rasped.

She laughed at him. "No, silly." He felt her cold lips nuzzle the burning flesh of his throat, started when her fangs punctured it. Blood flowed into Aidan, reviving, sustaining blood, and he was helpless to resist. He drank, all his dried and empty veins leaping greedily to life, and when at last it was over and he could focus his gaze, he saw Roxanne Havermail kneeling beside him.

She ran her fingers through his dirty hair, and he felt the sticky pressure of her lips where she kissed him on the forehead, undoubtedly leaving a smudge of blood.

"How did you get in here?" Aidan rasped, resisting the urge to push her away.

Roxanne smiled, then touched his mouth tentatively with her own. "What does that matter? I am well able to escape and I will take you with me." She laid her hand to his face, and he felt its hardness and its chill. "Close your eyes, darling. Think of candlelight, and soft music, and—"

Aidan lost consciousness, mesmerized by her words, her tone, her caress.

When he awakened, he was lying on silk sheets, stripped of the rough robe his captors had provided, and Roxanne was washing him tenderly with warm, perfumed water.

He tried to sit up, found himself too weak. Obviously the one feeding had not been enough to restore his full powers. Instead it had merely drawn him back from the brink of either blessed oblivion or the unbridled wrath of God.

Roxanne bent and kissed his bloodless chest.

"No," he said.

She drew back, looked at him with wide amber eyes, then narrowed ones. "What did you say?"

Vampire sex, a cataclysmic and usually violent joining of two immortal bodies, was not without a certain appeal at that point, but Aidan wasn't about to indulge. His love for Neely, however hopeless, wouldn't permit it.

"You heard me," he told Roxanne. "Nothing is going to happen between us—Mrs. Havermail."

Roxanne sighed and continued to bathe him. "Honor among fiends," she said. "Tiresome. Plain tiresome."

Valerian, Aidan thought. *Help me.*

Chapter

—❦11❦—

Melody Ling, the television reporter, agreed to a rendezvous, but only after a little fast talking on Neely's part. Although Neely refused to identify herself directly, she had to do some pretty heavy name-dropping in order to establish credibility—*and* hint that someone inside the FBI had obstructed justice. The site of the proposed meeting, an isolated, long-unused wooden bridge in the woods of central Maine, was chosen by mutual consent, during half a dozen fragmented calls from as many different telephones.

Neely left Aidan's car parked in the small garage behind Wendy Browning's beach cottage and took the bus to the village, stopping off on the way to purchase a long red wig and big sunglasses. Of course she was taking an enormous chance, trusting a total stranger to meet her alone in an out-of-the-way place, but it seemed like a better bet than heading for New York and strolling into network headquarters with the packet of proof under one arm.

When the bus stopped in snowy Danfield Crossing, Neely remained in her seat, toward the back, watching everyone else get off. Once she was fairly sure no one was lurking outside, waiting for her, she made her way up the aisle, her purse under one elbow, carrying a disreputable old duffel bag she'd found in the shed behind Wendy's cottage.

There was no need to ask directions to the old bridge; Neely and Ben and their father had fished for brook trout there, years ago, and the place shimmered brightly in her memory. After a quick glance around, she set off for the woods, not following the county road, but keeping to the narrow, hard-packed trails left by cross-country skiers.

Melody Ling was waiting patiently behind the wheel of a rental car, looking intent in the chilly afternoon sunlight. Her dark hair was moussed, her makeup too heavy and artful for the occasion, and she seemed poised to go on camera immediately. None of which mattered to Neely.

Seeing her mysterious contact come trundling out of the woods beside the road must have been disconcerting, but Ling didn't flinch. She opened the car door and stepped out onto the icy road in high heels.

Neely glanced around nervously, but no gun-toting criminals or FBI men burst out of the bushes, and it was still too early in the day for vampires.

She approached Ling and held out the manila packet, which was still wrapped in plastic. "Here's the evidence we talked about," she said, considering a preamble unnecessary.

Ling took the offering. "You'll grant me an exclusive interview, once everything has gone down?"

Neely nodded. "I'll be in touch," she said. She smiled. "Good luck—and thanks."

The reporter nodded back, got into her car, and left.

Neely immediately returned to the village, by way of the woods. She bought a fish sandwich and a diet soda in a convenience store and hitched a ride back to the coast with a trucker who wore a T-shirt with a picture of his three toothless children on the front.

It had all gone so well, she reflected, settling into the passenger seat of the big rig to watch the night scenery go by.

So amazingly well.

"What happened to him?" Valerian demanded, arriving in the guest wing of Havermail Castle with an unceremonious crash.

Roxanne turned from Aidan's bedside, one hand to her throat in a gesture of gracious alarm. She was a vile strumpet, without a shred of loyalty to adorn her nature, and Valerian despised her.

She simpered. "Mr. Tremayne actually dared to challenge the Brotherhood," she marveled. "Was that your idea?"

Valerian approached the bed and peered down into Aidan's sleeping face. The basement chamber was completely dark, since the windows were sealed, and tallow candles provided an eery, wavering light. Gently the elder vampire laid a hand to a pale but well-sculpted shoulder.

"Aidan," he said, despairing, ignoring the female.

"He's weak," Roxanne said with a saintly sigh, "but he'll recover with proper care."

Valerian was at last able to lift his eyes from Aidan's still features to Roxanne's chillingly perfect ones. "He was a captive, and you rescued him." The statement was meant as a question, and it held no note of praise.

Roxanne nodded. "In a manner of speaking. The Brotherhood had thought to break Aidan by punishment, and they failed. No one tried to stop me when I went to him."

"What punishment?" Valerian rasped, furious. He held tightly to his anger, knowing he would give way to utter despair if he loosened his grip for even a moment.

"Poor Aidan. He was confined in a small space and subsequently starved." Roxanne spoke matter-of-factly, making her way around to the opposite side of the bed and taking one of Aidan's limp hands into her own. She ran the pad of her thumb thoughtfully over the protruding knuckles. "It was his own fault that he nearly perished for want of feeding—he refused the rats they offered."

In that moment Valerian felt such contempt, not only for Roxanne, but also for the Brotherhood, that he could barely contain it. "Rats," he rasped. "They gave him *rats*?"

Roxanne shrugged. "It's not such a terrible shame. Most of us have subsisted on vermin at one time or another," she said. "If anything destroys our Aidan, Valerian, it will be his own stubborn refusal to follow the rules."

Valerian sensed that dawn was nearing; they would all

be safe from sunlight in this dark cellar chamber, but he did not want to sink into the near-coma of sleep in that place. He didn't trust any of the Havermails, including the children.

He wrapped Aidan's inert form carefully in the bedclothes and lifted him into his arms.

"What do you think you're doing?" Roxanne cried, incensed. "I found Aidan, and *I* fed him and brought him home. He's mine!"

Valerian held out one hand, fingers splayed, and pressed it to Roxanne's morbidly beautiful face. "Sleep," he said in a sort of crooning drawl, and she dropped to the floor with a thumping sound.

The fiend would succumb to her vampire slumber, there on the cold stones, and awaken just a little the worse for wear when night came again. Only her dress and her temper would be ruffled.

Valerian lowered his magnificent head, until his forehead touched Aidan's fevered one, and together they vanished.

Aidan dreamed that he was a Viking, that he'd died bravely in battle, and his comrades had arranged his body in the curving belly of a dragon ship. He was covered with straw, which someone set ablaze with a torch, and the small, flaming craft was pushed out onto the still blue sea. It burned brightly, a majestic pyre, and Aidan burned with it, but he felt no pain, only joy and the most poignant sense of freedom. . . .

When he opened his eyes, realized that he'd only been dreaming, that he was still trapped in the immortal, marble-cold body of a fiend, the disappointment was crushing.

He was lying on a flat surface, in a dark place that he didn't recognize, and he was so thirsty that he felt raw inside. "Neely," he whispered, the word scraping painfully from his throat.

Then he saw Valerian looming over him, his face twisted with anguish. He started to say something, this enigmatic ghoul with the looks and countenance of a favored angel, then stopped himself. Instead Valerian bent, gently plunged his fangs through the skin of Aidan's neck, and gave him blood.

Aidan moaned in a combination of ecstacy and revulsion; he wanted to resist this macabre salvation, but his will to survive, which seemed a wholly separate entity at the time, refused to surrender itself. He felt Valerian's tears on his flesh but decided fitfully that he must have imagined that.

"Where—what is this place?" he managed as the new blood surged through him, vital and warm, as intoxicating as the finest brandy on a cold night.

"Never mind that," Valerian answered shortly, his voice gruff. "Your thoughts are generally written in neon letters five feet high. If you don't mind, I'd prefer that every other vampire between here and the gates of Hades wasn't able to pinpoint us by reading them."

Aidan chuckled, but the indulgence cost him dearly. "You saved me," he said. "Shall I thank you for that, Valerian, or call you cursed?"

"Neither. I didn't truly save you, except from the wiles of that witches' spawn, Roxanne Havermail."

Aidan's laugh was soblike. "Thank you for protecting my virtue," he said. "You'll understand if I consider the gesture a little dubious."

Valerian scowled down at him, but the expression didn't hold. He gave a throaty chuckle, wholly involuntary, and then turned away—ostensibly to compose himself. When he met Aidan's gaze again, his manner was as coldly remote as that of the Grim Reaper. "Fool!" he spat. "Do you realize how close you came to being destroyed?"

"Not close enough, evidently," Aidan reflected, looking past Valerian to the ceiling, which was lined with dusty beams. "What can you tell me of Neely? Is she safe and well?"

Valerian's jawline tightened for a moment, then he bit out, "I wouldn't know. I have only one use for humans, and the fascinating Miss Wallace's association with you puts her off limits. For the moment."

" 'For the moment,' is it?" Aidan asked, reaching up, clasping the front of Valerian's flowing linen shirt in one fist.

Valerian slapped Aidan's hand away. "What an arrogant pup you are," he snarled, "issuing challenges to me—*me!*" He paused to thump his own chest angrily. "If I desired the delectable Neely, I would have her, and no force on earth could stand in my way, including—*especially not*—you!"

Aidan's strength, so temporal, was waning again, but he found enough to press the argument. "Get a grasp on your emotions," he said. "I grow impatient with your constant histrionics."

The great vampire gave a snarling shriek of frustration and rage and disappeared completely.

Inwardly Aidan sighed. He'd probably just offended the only friend he had, besides Maeve, but fruitless acts of impulse seemed to be a part of his nature of late.

He'd failed miserably with the Brotherhood, he reflected, absorbing the knowledge like a series of painful blows. He'd found out nothing and had managed to infuriate the elders in the process. It probably wouldn't be long before they came for him, he supposed, and dispensed their vampire justice.

Valerian had obviously been right in refusing to tell him where they were. Aidan's mental state was such that he probably would have broadcast the information for any passing ogre to pick up on.

Neely shrieked and sent the magazine she'd been reading fluttering into the air like some ungainly bird. Valerian stood between her and the television set, glorious in the usual fine evening clothes, his arms folded, his big head tilted to one side.

"Are you quite through?" he inquired scathingly, retrieving the magazine and setting it neatly on the coffee table.

Neely's gasps slowly slackened into regular breaths. She

gave one violent hiccough, in a spasm of residual terror, and Valerian rolled his violet eyes disdainfully.

"Well, you scared me!" Neely said, more angry, all of a sudden, than afraid. Then even the anger faded away, and she got awkwardly to her bare feet, pulling Wendy's pink robe close around her, like chenille armor. "This is about Aidan, isn't it? What's happened to him?"

Valerian looked down his perfect nose at her for a long interval, then answered, "*You* have happened to him, more's the pity. He loves you, and that foolhardy affection may well cost him his very existence."

"Where is he?"

"I wouldn't dream of telling you that," Valerian said sharply. "Like all humans, and some vampires as well, unfortunately, you have a billboard for a mind—complete with loudspeakers and sweeping searchlights. Suffice it to say that Aidan needs comforting very much just now. Besides, you are probably the only being in the world who can cause him to see reason at this point."

"You'll take me to him, then?" Neely's heart was wedged into her throat. She clutched the lapels of the borrowed bathrobe in one trembling hand.

Valerian nodded grudgingly. "Put on some decent clothes."

Neely turned and hurried into the cottage's closet-size bedroom, where she hastily donned jeans, sneakers, a pink bulky sweater, and her coat. Back in the living room, she looked up into Valerian's face with wide eyes. "Is this going to be a Superman sort of thing? I mean, are you planning to tuck me under one arm and just—fly?"

Valerian only shook his head, came a step closer, and swirled his cape around Neely like some whispering, perfumed cocoon. She fainted, only to revive seconds later and find herself in a place so dark she thought she had gone stone blind.

"Just a moment," Valerian barked impatiently, as if she'd complained aloud. A match was struck, a tallow candle lit.

Neely was taken aback to find herself inside a crypt, an

old one, judging by the looks of the disintegrating caskets and random bones lying about.

In the center of it all, on a high Roman couch upholstered in ugly maroon velvet, lay Aidan, as white and still as a corpse.

"He will awaken soon," Valerian said, his voice passing Neely's ear from behind, like a fall breeze moving through dry leaves. "If you love Aidan, then make him see that there can be no future for the two of you. Should you fail to reach him, he will continue on his present course, careening toward destruction. He will be executed, Neely, as an example to all vampires—staked out in the sun and left to die in the most horrible agony imaginable. Do you want that for him?"

Neely forgot her surroundings and stumbled forward, her white-knuckled hands clasped together. She would rather suffer the death Valerian had just described herself, she thought, than see Aidan endure such torture.

She touched her beloved's still face. "Aidan?"

He opened his eyes, and she felt a sweet seizing in her heart as he looked at her, apparently dismissed her as an illusion, and then realized she was truly there. "Neely," he said and groped for her hand.

She pressed her palm to his, and their fingers interlocked. "What's happened?" she whispered.

Aidan stared up at her, mute, clearly bursting with a sorrow he could not begin to articulate.

She kissed him lightly on the forehead, and then on the mouth, and felt his fever sear her own skin. She laid her head against his chest then, but heard no heartbeat thumping away beneath her ear, no breath flowing in and out of his lungs.

He entangled his fingers in her short hair, holding her close. They were simply *together* in those moments; it was as simple, and as complicated, as that.

After a long interval had passed, Neely raised her head and looked into Aidan's soul, her vision glittery and blurred, as though she were seeing the world through melted diamonds. She could not leave him now when he was so broken, but deep inside Neely knew Valerian was right. By loving Aidan, by dreaming an impossible dream, she could only destroy him.

And that was unthinkable.

Resigned, heartbroken, Neely climbed onto the Roman couch with Aidan, stretched out beside him, held him close in her arms. Soon enough, they would be parted, for all of time—alpha to omega, world without end, amen.

Amen.

For now, though, nothing would put them asunder.

Valerian's grief howled within him, like a storm wind, but he dared not release it there in the crypt, however oblivious Aidan and Neely might seem. Brashly, too driven by pain to think, Valerian fled to an earlier century, the eighteenth, and hid himself in an isolated lair. It was little more than a mouse's nest, really, a hollow place in the wall of an ancient abbey, mortared over so long ago that there was no demarcation between the old stonework and the new.

Now he curled up in that space, as fragile as an unborn chick still cosseted in its shell, and he wept.

It wasn't as though Aidan hadn't warned him, more than once, that there was no hope. Still, Valerian had heard what he wanted to hear and forgotten the rest. But now he had seen the true state of matters between Aidan and Neely, and he could no longer ignore the evidence.

Somehow, even without the sacred exchange of blood, the pair had forged that most intimate and unbreakable of all bonds.

Valerian sobbed like a stricken child, his anguish as deep and unbridled as his devotion. What he felt for Aidan was indescribably sensual, and yet it transcended gender and completely overshadowed the simple animal gratification humans know. No, it was communion with the other vampire that Valerian craved, something far more profound than mere sex, for he loved Aidan as he had never loved another creature.

Save one.

He threw back his head and cried out in torment, the sound as shrill as the cry of a wolf on a clear winter's night. When that wail had died away, he loosed another, hoarser this time, and full of despair. Finally, when he could weep no more, when he had purged himself of all emotion, Valerian closed his eyes and slept.

Twelve hours later he awakened and wafted through the cracks and chinks in the old abbey wall like so much pale smoke.

Inside the crypt where he had left Aidan and the woman, Valerian assembled himself again.

Neely was asleep, curled up against Aidan's side like a kitten. Her pale skin was flushed from some dream, and Valerian could hear her heart beating, and he wanted so desperately to drink of her warmth and vitality.

He must not indulge, he told himself. It would be a poisoned victory and, thus, a defeat.

Aidan opened his eyes and spoke to his friend, but with his mind instead of his voice. *Take her away from this place,* he pleaded. *If you ever cared for me, Valerian, put Neely back where you found her and make sure she's safe. Now, before she awakens.*

Valerian nodded, but he could not answer, not even silently. He laid his hand over Neely's face, and her breathing deepened, and she was pulled by her own inner forces into that shadowed place well below simple sleep. That done, Valerian lifted her into his arms and thought grimly of the little cottage on the coast of Maine.

The television set was still on when Neely opened her eyes to find herself lying chilled and cramped on the couch in the cottage living room, an open magazine spread under her cheek. She was wearing her nightshirt and Wendy's chenille robe, and there was a blizzard blowing up outside.

Neely tossed the magazine aside, and her fingers were smudged with ink after she rubbed her cheek. She rolled onto her back and stared up at the ceiling, mourning. It had all seemed so real—Valerian, practically giving her a heart attack by appearing from out of nowhere, in all his intimidating splendor. Aidan, lying helpless and sick in that terrible place.

It couldn't have been a dream.

They'd been so close, she and Aidan, so connected, as they lay innocently in each other's arms, their souls fused. She would have given him her very blood, had he asked, and willingly, as a mother gives breast milk to an infant. Such sharing could not have been a travesty, for in those precious hours they were as one being, with but one heart and a single soul, and all their veins were interconnected.

Neely was too numb and too stricken to weep. She rolled off the sofa and raised herself drunkenly to her feet. She went to the thermostat, sent heat booming through the vents with a dusty *whoosh*. Then, shoving her fingers through her sleep-rumpled hair, she made her way into the kitchen and put coffee on to perk. Maybe a jolt of caffeine would get her confused brain back on track, and she would be able to untangle dreams from reality.

Valerian had definitely paid her a visit the night before, she assured herself later as she sipped hot coffee at the window and watched the snowstorm obliterate the ocean from view. She had put on jeans and a sweater, and he had taken her to Aidan. . . .

Neely hurried into her bedroom and opened her dresser drawers, one by one.

The pink sweater was neatly folded and tucked away in one section, the jeans in another.

She unfolded the jeans, felt a whisper of relief when she saw that the denim was embedded with white dust. She made a face and, conversely, held the garment close against her chest, glad of the proof it offered.

She *had* been with Aidan the night before, and for a moment she was joyous.

Then Neely remembered what Valerian had said: Other vampires viewed Aidan as a threat. They might well tie him down in the night and leave him for the brutal sun to find with the morning. He would suffer horribly, devoured by the same light that nurtured virtually every other living thing on earth, and the fault for this would lie, at least partially, with Neely herself.

Desperate for some distraction from her thoughts, she went into the living room and switched on the TV again. The news channel came up immediately.

There was no word of a scandal involving Senator Hargrove and his friends in the drug cartel, and Neely's uneasiness, already considerable, grew significantly. Once before, she'd tried to right a wrong, to stop a gross misuse of authority, and her contact inside the FBI had betrayed her trust. Suppose Melody Ling did the same thing?

Neely glanced at the telephone, but she was afraid to try contacting the network from the cabin. Technology being what it was, the call could probably be traced right back through the circuits to the cottage, and she certainly wasn't ready for that.

She dressed, put on her warm coat and some rubber snow boots she'd found on the floor of the laundry room, and took the keys to Aidan's Spitfire from the hook beside the back door. She might have worn the wig and sunglasses again, but she'd dropped them into a trash bin the previous night, just before catching a ride back to Timber Cove with the good-natured trucker.

Snow had been falling all night, and it was deep enough to make the tires of the sports car spin helplessly in the driveway. The sky was clear by then, however, a soft blue dusted with wispy clouds, and the sun shone brightly.

Neely fetched a wide shovel from the shed and worked industriously to clear a path to the road, which had, fortunately, been plowed and sanded. She went back inside the cottage for her purse and keys, and when she did, she found herself paralyzed by what should have been a very ordinary sound.

The telephone was ringing.

Neely had not given the number to anyone, and she hadn't even contacted Wendy in London to let her know the cottage was in use. No one—besides Valerian and Aidan, who had no use for telephones anyway—was supposed to know she was there.

She hesitated, her hand poised over the receiver. The jangling continued, and Neely thought frantically. Had she given the number to Ben, or to Melody Ling, and simply forgotten? No. A person didn't let things like that slip her mind, not when her very life depended on secrecy.

Finally Neely snatched up the receiver, to end the terrible ringing if nothing else, and said, "Hello?" She hoped she sounded like a man, annoyed at the disturbance.

"Neely?"

Her blood turned to small, jagged shards of ice, piercing her veins in a thousand tender places. The voice was feminine and vaguely familiar, but Neely couldn't match it with a face or a name.

"Neely, are you there?"

She closed her eyes and let out a long breath. She'd already given herself away by staying on the line so long, even though she hadn't admitted to her identity. "Who is this?" she asked.

"My name is Lisa Nelson—I'm Senator Hargrove's personal secretary—"

What a fool I've been, Neely lamented silently, *actually telling myself they wouldn't track me down*. Before she could say anything, think of a lie to tell, or even just hang up, Lisa went on.

"Senator Hargrove asked me to tell you that some mutual friends are on their way to pick you up for the services."

"What services?" Neely asked, glancing accusingly at the blank screen of the television set. The remark had to be a warning; if Elaine Hargrove had succumbed to her illness or her recent injuries, there would have been some mention of it on the news.

"He just said, well, that there's going to be a funeral. Didn't some mutual friend of yours pass away?"

Neely's heart was pounding. She was glad Mrs. Hargrove was still alive and, at the same time, painfully aware that her own days—maybe even her hours and minutes—

were numbered. "Right," she said. "Thanks, Lisa." With that, Neely hung up with a crash, flung her few belongings back into her suitcase, and ran for the car.

She'd traveled a considerable distance before she realized that she was headed toward Washington, D.C. She'd chosen an out-of-the-way place to take refuge before, by going to live with Ben and Danny in Bright River; now she would try hiding in plain sight.

Too afraid to check into another motel, Neely drove until she was blind with exhaustion, then pulled into a rest area and slept with the car doors locked, slumped over the steering wheel like a drunk. She chose to have breakfast in a tavern, hoping to throw off any pursuers, and gulped down German sausage and a diet cola while the morning drinkers nursed their beer.

There were two bikers at the pool table, big and hairy, with every visible part of their anatomies tatooed, but they didn't bother Neely. They just poked coins into the jukebox and sang along with various artists in off-key voices. Nobody in the place, least of all Neely, was stupid enough to protest.

There was a television set behind the bar, but the proprietor had tuned it to a game show, and he didn't look like the type who would switch to the news channel just because somebody asked. Neely paid for her food, used the rest room, and started out again.

Aidan's car radio picked up nothing but static for the next few hours, so Neely bought a newspaper when she stopped for gas, along with a plain seltzer. Normally she would have been hungry again by then, but she was scared and upset, and the sausage she'd consumed at the tavern that morning was still roiling in her stomach.

The store's parking lot was empty, except for a few teenagers, so Neely took time to scan the newspaper. There was nothing about Senator Hargrove's shady doings, but in the upper right-hand corner of page five she found an interesting item.

MYSTERIOUS BLAST DESTROYS BEACH COTTAGE NEAR TIMBER

COVE, the headline read. Neely folded the paper, then folded it again, and braced the article against the steering wheel. Sometime during the night, the eager reporter had written, an explosion had leveled the Browning cottage on Blackberry Road. It was not known if there had been any casualties, but investigators were sifting through the wreckage.

Neely pushed open the car door, ran behind the store's giant garbage bin, and was still retching long after her stomach was empty. If Senator Hargrove hadn't warned her, however indirectly, she would have been blown to smoldering fragments, perhaps in her sleep.

She went into the public rest room when the bout of sickness was over, rinsed her mouth, and splashed cold water on her face until she figured she'd recovered her senses. Maybe, she thought, leaning shakily against a graffiti-scarred wall, she should rethink the idea of returning to Washington. It might be smarter to find a circus, climb into the tiger cage, and juggle a couple of raw pot roasts until the cats noticed.

Chapter

—❧12❧—

Even separated from Neely by time and distance, Aidan felt her turmoil in his own spirit. He knew she was in the gravest danger, and yet his weakness pinned him to the couch in that lonely crypt, far more effectively than any physical bond could have done. He struggled, but the effort was fruitless.

"Valerian!" he shouted into the dry darkness of the tomb. He waited, listening as the echo of his voice slowly faded away, but the other vampire did not appear. Aidan's pride would not let him call out again.

He closed his eyes, tried to calm himself. In his mind, he saw Neely standing next to a garbage bin, behind some roadside shop, retching. He watched her hurry into the women's room, tasted the rusty water she used to rinse her mouth, felt the cool relief as she splashed her face. Then he frowned, trying to make sense of a sudden vision of Neely venturing inside a tiger cage at a circus, juggling ugly chunks of raw meat.

The ludicrous image disappeared; Neely was behind the wheel of a car—he recognized the interior as his own Spitfire. He felt her quick, shallow breaths as if he'd drawn them himself, and the warm moisture of tears on her cheeks.

She was afraid and confused, and not being able to go to her was among the greatest agonies Aidan had ever suffered.

Neely, he thought, his soul reaching for hers. She didn't

consciously hear him, he knew, but she sniffled and squared her shoulders.

"Okay, Wallace," she said aloud. "No more panic. It's time for some straight thinking."

Atta girl, Aidan encouraged, still seeing the world through her eyes and picking up her emotions and physical sensations.

"I can't go to the police, and certainly not to the FBI. I don't know if Melody Ling is going to break the story or if she's going to cave in to pressure and pretend it never happened." With one hand she mussed her pixie hair in frustration, and Aidan felt the softness between his own fingers, and the tugging wiggle of her scalp. She sighed—he shared that, too—and his eyes filled with tears because he had been deprived of such simple, sweet nuances of humanity for so long. "If I go back to Bright River, then Ben and Danny will be in danger again. Which leaves my original plan—I'll take the proverbial bull by the horns and head straight for Washington. I'll confront Dallas Hargrove, either in his office or in the Capitol Building, and if the mob shoots me, they might just have to do it on the floor of the Senate." With that, she started the car engine, shifted deftly into first gear, and guided the Spitfire back onto the slush-covered highway.

No, Aidan protested, but it was to no avail, of course, for Neely apparently wasn't aware that he was with her, even though he was conscious of her every pulse. He noted the electrical activity of her brain, along with other subliminal processes, like digestion and the manufacture of all sorts of chemicals and hormones. He warmed his own frozen soul at the silver spark of divinity shining at the core of her, the mysterious gift that was given to all mortals with the first tentative *tha-thump* of their hearts.

Aidan rode with Neely for an hour or so, but the effort sapped him, and he withdrew. He had been foolish, he realized now, to squander his strength so recklessly by seeking out Lisette and the Brotherhood the way he had. Now, when his powers might have made a positive difference, he was all but depleted.

He began to drift, now fully conscious, now only half aware. He slept, finally, and awakened to a ravenous hunger and a sense of terrible urgency.

He had to rise, feed, and go to Neely, and the fact that those things might well be impossible had no real bearing on anything. Aidan was fresh out of choices.

He shook his head, fighting the disorientation, the infernal weakness.

After a painful struggle Aidan managed to raise himself onto one elbow. The effort left him grimacing, bruised with exhaustion, but he refused to lie down again. He used all his will to rise to a sitting position and then to stand, knees trembling, beside the couch. The piece of furniture, so absurdly out of place in that old crypt, was high and curved at one end. Aidan gripped that part for support.

He needed blood, a lot of it, and fast.

Aidan thought frantically. The tightly mortared stone walls of the crypt admitted neither the light of the sun nor that of the moon, but he knew it was night simply because he was conscious. What he did *not* know was whether the dawn was hours away, or just seconds, for he carried no watch. How much time had he lost to delirium?

Should he miscalculate and be caught abroad at sunrise, the result would be an interminable and hideous death. That possibility was terrible enough, but there was a very real danger that this cruel passage would be only the beginning of his suffering. If there was indeed such a place as Hell, beyond the mysterious veil that separated the known from the unknown, Aidan would surely be condemned to everlasting torment.

Remembering Neely, Aidan sought and found a forgotten reservoir of courage within himself. He began to pace, stiff-legged, from one end of the crypt to the other, forcing his woodlike limbs to function.

He wanted to tune in to Neely again, to find out where she was, and how she was, and what she was feeling, but he didn't dare waste energy. Before he attempted anything else, Aidan reminded himself, he must feed.

All three floors of Senator Dallas Hargrove's elegant Georgetown house were brightly lit, even though it was nearly three in the morning when Neely arrived. She'd driven for thirteen hours, on and off, and she was hungry, drained of all but the last quivering dregs of energy, and badly in need of a hot bath. For all of that, just the knowledge that she'd reached her destination gave her a second wind.

She glanced around, saw designer Christmas wreaths on some of the doors. Getting out of Aidan's car, Neely felt a stab of chagrin. Had Thanksgiving gotten by her somehow, when she wasn't looking?

She didn't even know the date, she realized, with a sense of quiet shock. She just hoped Ben and Danny had roasted a turkey for the occasion, and maybe invited Doris, the new waitress, to dinner.

Staunchly Neely moved up the front walk, climbed the brick steps, and rang the bell. The senator himself answered the door, and when he saw Neely, he swore and made a move to block her way, but she was too quick. She pressed past Hargrove and stood facing him in that spacious entry hall, with its parquet floors, cherrywood grandfather clock, and marble-topped credenza.

"You must be suicidal!" the senator snapped. He had taken off his jacket at some point and opened his shirt, and his tie hung in a long loop, like a noose about to be jerked tight. There were shadows under his eyes, his cheeks were gaunt, and it was anybody's guess how long it had been since he'd shaved. "Damn it, Neely—I did everything I could to warn you—it's a miracle you're alive—"

Neely didn't retreat, even though Hargrove's stance was intimidating because of his superior size and strength. "I'm tired of running," she said. "I won't be tracked and hounded like some pitiful creature wanted for its hide!"

After regarding her in stricken silence for several moments, the senator groaned. "No, Neely, you won't be hunted anymore," he said. "You won't be hunted because they've *found* you, you little fool!"

At this, four large men in dark, high-quality suits appeared, one from the room on the right side of the hall, two from the left, and another from the curved staircase. Neely dived for the door, but she was tired and her reflexes were poor.

The smallest of the thugs caught her easily, pulling her arms back, hooking his own beneath her elbows.

Neely struggled and screamed, but the man held her easily. One of the others came over and slapped her hard across the face, and the coppery taste of blood covered her tongue.

"There's no need for violence," Hargrove protested, but his tone was weak, like his character.

Neely stomped on her captor's instep with one heel, and he howled in pain and released her. In a movie the trick might have worked, she thought fancifully as the other three bad guys rushed forward. In real life, however, two of the trio of stooges held her, while the third one brought a syringe from the pocket of his coat.

"For God's sake," Hargrove pleaded, as ineffectually as before. Neely wondered how he'd ever attained high office in the first place, let alone held on to his seat in the Senate and married a topflight person like Elaine. "I see no reason to—"

Neely struggled, making an inarticulate sound as she tried to avoid the needle. She felt a minute puncture in the side of her neck, then a stinging sensation as the drug, whatever it was, entered her system. After that, reality dissolved into a colorless, shifting mass of nothingness.

When Neely came to her senses, she was surprised and alarmed to find herself lying on the hard, bare floor of a pickup truck or a van, her arms tied behind her back, her feet bound at the ankles. Her throat felt raw and dry.

Senator Hargrove lay beside her, also tied.

He glared at her. "I hope you're happy now," he whispered.

Neely didn't answer immediately; her thoughts were still pretty incoherent. Her head ached, and so did her right hip and knee. She saw a metal roof a few feet overhead and decided the vehicle was probably a van.

"They're going to kill us," Hargrove said in a stage whisper.

Neely tried to sit up and failed miserably. The floor of the van was as hard and cold as marble and, worse, it was corrugated, making a new bruise every time they went over a bump.

"And you thought they were such nice guys," Neely drawled, shifting in a restless effort to make herself more comfortable.

"Shut up," snapped her former employer.

She tilted her head back, caught glimpses of shadowy hulks in the passenger and driver's seats. It was still dark, and snow swirled against the dark windshield, while the wipers went *thumpety-thump, thumpety-thump.*

"You aren't going to get away with this," she called out cheerfully, toward the front. "I turned all the proof over to a television reporter, and she's going to make household names of the lot of you. Who knows? Maybe they'll show your trial on cable. . . ." Neely was well aware that she was ranting like an idiot, but she didn't give a damn. Her only other option was screaming in hysteria.

The driver crumpled a paper bag in one meaty hand and tossed it over his shoulder. His aim turned out to be pretty good; the wad struck Neely on the chin, and she caught a whiff of stale french fries. "Put a sock in it," he said in classic Brooklynese.

Neely didn't stop talking, she couldn't, but she lowered her voice and directed her comments to the senator. For once in his life, she thought, he was going to have to actually *listen* to an unhappy voter.

"I can't believe you ever got involved with these people!" she hissed.

Hargrove closed his eyes for a moment. He looked sick, and Neely scooted back a ways, until she felt the cold steel of the wheel-well against her bottom. "I had to," he said. "Elaine—needed so many things—"

"Do me a favor and don't blame this on your wife, all right?" Neely interrupted furiously. "I know the lady, and I can't imagine her cooperating with a drug cartel for any reason or any amount of money!"

"Keep it down back there," grunted the guy in the passenger seat. He sounded as though he needed adenoid surgery.

Neely bit her lower lip to keep herself from talking back. These creeps were for real, and if she made them mad enough, they might just pull over to the side of the road and blow her brains out with an illegal handgun.

Hargrove gave a low, strangled sob, and his face contorted into a mask of grief.

Neely felt sorry for him, but there was no way to lend comfort. Her hands were tied behind her back, and, besides, she wasn't sure she wanted to touch the senator anyway. "I heard about the accident," she said moderately. "How is Elaine?"

He made a broken sound, deep in his throat, and it was terrible to hear. "She—she isn't going to make it," he managed.

Neely ran the tip of her tongue over her lips and tasted dried blood. Perhaps because she was half out of her mind with fear, she wondered what Aidan and Valerian and the others liked so much about the stuff. The flavor was salty and metallic.

"I'm sorry," she said gently. "About Elaine, I mean."

Hargrove nodded. "It's selfish of me, I know," he confessed in a miserable rasp, "but I'm almost glad. She would be destroyed if she knew what I've done."

Neely followed the old rule of saying nothing when she couldn't say something nice. She wanted to console the senator, yes, but she also ached to condemn him.

The van bounced violently over what must have been a cattle-guard, and then Neely heard branches scraping the vehicle's sides. They were in the countryside somewhere, maybe deep in a wood, but she had no idea where because she didn't know how long she'd been knocked out.

"I have to go to the bathroom," she called out.

Hargrove sighed. "Don't try any stupid tricks, Neely," he whispered. "This is no time to be a hero!"

"It's no trick," Neely replied. "I really have to go."

The driver cursed—more fluent Brooklynese—but he wrenched the van over to one side of the road, and it jolted to a stop. "I told ya we shoulda just shot 'em both dead," he muttered to his partner. "Next thing you know, this broad is gonna wanna pick up a frozen yogurt someplace."

"Keep goin'," the other thug replied. "She can just hold it."

"I can't *hold it!*" Neely protested.

"Look, lady, I ain't gonna fall for any of that TV stuff and untie your hands so's you can go to the john in some blackberry thicket, awright? Only other option is, I go out there, too, and pull your pants down for you. You want that?"

"No," Neely snapped. "Of course I don't."

"Then shut up."

"I wouldn't mind pullin' down the lady's pants, Sally," volunteered the driver.

"Ain't you been payin' attention, Vinnie? You can catch bad diseases doin' stuff like that. And don't use my name again!"

"Right, Sally," grumbled Vinnie.

They went over a particularly large bump, and Neely's head thumped hard against the floor. She closed her eyes and fought a wave of dizzy nausea with all her strength of spirit. This was no time to pass out, even if she did find oblivion more appealing than reality.

The van soon ground to a stop, and the front doors slammed almost simultaneously. On Hargrove's side there was a click as a latch was lifted, a grinding rush as the panel was shoved aside.

Vinnie and Sally showed no inclination toward gentleness or mercy as they wrenched their captives out onto the snowy ground, the senator first, then Neely. She pressed her thighs together, desperate to relieve herself.

They were propelled forward, toward a shadowy, box-like house, passing an ancient clothesline and a mossy, snow-dusted cement birdbath. Time and neglect had tilted the structure to one side, and it reminded Neely of a tomb-stone.

The way things were going, she thought, it might turn out to be her own.

Vinnie, who was at least eighty pounds overweight and probably on the fast track to a triple bypass, lumbered up a set of creaky wooden steps and produced a jangle of keys from the pocket of his pants. Maybe he was a slob, and he'd certainly made poor career choices, but he dressed well.

They entered a room, and the lights blared on, revealing a kitchen with a sagging floor and one of those old refrig-erators with the motor on top, among other things. To the left, at the end of a long, narrow hallway, Neely saw the glimmer of white porcelain.

"Please," she said.

Surprisingly, Sally gripped her by the back of the neck and marched her toward the bathroom. "I never nabbed no-body that was more trouble than you," he griped. He wrenched the ropes off her wrists and flung her through the doorway. "Don't try nothin' stupid, neither. That window over the toilet is painted shut, and even if you broke it, you wouldn't even get across the yard before I caught you. You got it?"

"Got it," Neely said with a sigh. She went into the bath-room, switched on the light, and quickly attended to her business. While she was doing that, she scanned the small cubicle for a weapon, such as an old-fashioned razor or maybe a plunger with a thick handle. There was nothing visible except for a scrub brush that had been stuck bristles first into a rusty coffee can.

Neely flushed, fastened her jeans, and washed her hands at the stained sink. When she came out, Sally was waiting. He didn't bind her wrists again immediately but instead gripped her elbow and double-timed her into what had probably been a living room at one time.

There was a piano with a warped keyboard on one side of the room, a wood stove on the other. On the wall over a filthy, rat-chewed sofa was a maudlin portrait of some martyred saint, suffering big time.

Aidan, Neely thought.

The distinctness of the answer startled her so much that she jerked, as if someone had touched her with something hot. *Hang on, love. I'm on my way.*

Such relief swept through Neely at the clarity of the thought, and the knowledge that it had not been her own, that she swayed on her feet.

Vinnie thrust her into a chair and wrenched her hands back, to be tied again. The senator was beside her in another chair, also bound. He looked strangely detached, as if he'd managed to move out of his body and watch the evening's events from a distance.

Inwardly Neely sighed. Given all the things Dallas Hargrove had done, it wasn't surprising that he was a master of denial. No intelligent person could have betrayed so many trusts, public and private, without practicing a great deal of self-delusion.

Calmer now—although her senses told her Aidan was nowhere near, she *had* heard his voice—Neely watched as Sally built a fire in the stove to take the chill off the room, with its wavy, linoleum-covered floor. Vinnie wandered over to the opposite side of the room and opened a battered old cabinet that looked as if it might contain a Murphy bed.

Instead there was a big-screen TV set inside.

Vinnie switched it on, tuned it to the news channel, and cursed. Melody Ling's carefully madeup face loomed on the screen; she was standing in front of the Capitol Building in Washington.

Neely listened with gratitude and relief. Quietly, professionally, the journalist blew the lid off the whole scandal, listing crimes and naming names.

Senator Hargrove was still in a stupor; he didn't look up

or react at all to the mention of his part in the complicated, ugly matter. Officers of both the DEA and the Bureau wanted to talk to the politician, Ling said; the head of an eastern crime syndicate and two FBI agents had already been arrested.

As if as an afterthought, she went on. "Added to this tragic perversion of justice is the fact that Elaine Hargrove died tonight at Washington Hospital. She never regained consciousness, following a recent automobile accident, and was surrounded by friends and family at the end—except, of course, for her husband, Senator Dallas Hargrove. . . ."

The senator emitted a wolflike howl of grief that tore at Neely's heart. *Godspeed, Elaine,* she thought sadly. She had sincerely admired the other woman's professionalism and courage, and nothing could change that.

Vinnie and Sally were in a panic. "Did you hear that?" one of them demanded of the other—Neely wasn't paying enough attention to notice which. "They brought down the Boss, for God's sake!"

The voices became distorted, seeming to pulse and echo through a tunnel.

"I say we kill 'em both!"

"The hell with that! You wanna stay here and play wise guy, you do it, but I'm getting out."

The senator began to sob, but for once he probably wasn't worried about his own hide. He'd just learned that his wife was dead, he had not been with her at the moment she'd most needed him, and in spite of all the terrible things he'd done, Neely sincerely pitied him.

Chapter
13

Vinnie and Sally were still arguing under the painting of the martyred saint when Aidan materialized in a corner of the room.

Neely grinned, being both glad to see him and fairly used to his theatrical entrances and exits. He was wearing the uniform of a Nazi officer, of all things, and he slapped one gloved palm with a riding crop as he stood glowering at the two crooks from Brooklyn.

"Holy shit," said Vinnie.

"Where did *he* come from?" Sally asked.

Aidan gave Neely a sidelong glance and a wink, though no one else seemed to notice the gesture. "So," he began, the word properly guttural and Germanic. He took the greatest care to show his teeth. "You have taken these people captive."

Sally was blathering by then. "God," he moaned, "it's that guy Max kept talking about, the one that drank his blood!"

"You don't believe that crap, do you?" Vinnie asked his partner, but there was a distinct lack of conviction in his tone. Aidan was backing the two of them slowly across the torn linoleum floor.

Senator Hargrove came out of his daze just long enough to mutter, "Who the hell is that?"

Neely didn't answer but instead glanced nervously toward the windows, then around the room, searching for a clock. If dawn happened to be imminent, the rescue would be spoiled, to say the least.

Aidan tossed the riding crop aside when he was face to face with Vinnie and Sally, who were now cowering against the wall.

Neely braced herself, suddenly terrified of what he might do. She loved Aidan Tremayne with her whole soul, but that would certainly change if she witnessed the true reality of vampirism.

As if hearing her thoughts, Aidan looked back at her over one shoulder, favored her with a half-grin, and turned again to his prey. Raising both hands, he pressed a palm to either man's face, and a strange energy seemed to move through his body, along his arms, and into the crooks.

When Aidan drew back, graceful and cool, but visibly weakened, Vinnie and Sally glided to the floor, both staring stupidly at nothing.

"What did you do to them?" Neely whispered. He hadn't bitten their necks, but the night was still young. She hoped.

Aidan turned, straightening his tunic. "Not much, really. They're just taking a little nap—one that will last three or four weeks. They'll remember you one day, it's true, but given the recollection of tonight, they won't be anxious to look you up to reminisce."

In the chair beside Neely's, Senator Hargrove sat with his head lolling. He moaned something incoherent.

Aidan untied Neely but regarded the senator with a pensive expression. "What about him?" he asked, frowning.

Neely was rubbing her sore wrists and, at the same time, heading in the direction of the bathroom. She gave Vinnie and Sally a wide berth, even though they looked about as dangerous as a pair of carrots. "Don't do anything till I get back," she called to Aidan.

When she returned, he was pacing.

Ah, Neely thought whimsically, *the vampire I love.*

"What's with the Nazi threads?" she asked.

Aidan shrugged, stopping his pacing to lay another thoughtful frown on the senator. "I had to wear something," he answered distractedly, "and this was what came to hand. This is the infamous Senator Hargrove, is it not?"

"You know who he is." Neely sighed, folding her arms. "You're psychic, along with all your other talents."

Aidan walked around the senator's chair once, pondering the slumped figure. "He's not all bad, you know," he reflected, as though reading an in-depth dossier. "Just weak."

Neely nodded, then looked again toward the window. "Yes," she agreed. She explained about Dallas Hargrove's great, destructive love for Elaine. "On top of everything else," she finished, "Mrs. Hargrove died tonight, and he wasn't able to be with her. My guess is, he's probably having the kind of breakdown a guy doesn't come back from. So maybe he doesn't need prison, too."

Aidan paused, silently considering, and Neely would have given anything to read his thoughts. Was he thirsty, for instance?

"He's gone," the vampire said finally. "The senator has retreated so far inside himself that he may never find his way out."

"What if the prosecution needs him to testify?"

Aidan untied Hargrove and draped the man's inert frame over his shoulders, fireman-style. "Their tough luck, I guess. Come now, I'll load your friend here into the van for you, but you'll have to get yourself back to Washington because the sun will be up in about forty-five minutes." He nodded toward Vinnie and Sally, who were still sitting on the floor, staring vacantly into the distance. "The fat one has the keys—they're in the inside pocket of his jacket."

Neely approached the men gingerly, fully expecting them to jump at her, but they didn't even seem to see her.

"Even if you're right, and they don't come looking for me when their memories return, I still won't be completely off the hook," she said, fishing a key ring from the appointed pocket and withdrawing quickly. "I'll still have to deal with their bosses, won't I? Am I going to have to be part of the Witness Protection Program or something?"

"Yes," Aidan answered, hauling Senator Hargrove's limp person toward the back door. "The Aidan Tremayne Witness Protection Program." He looked very solemn for a moment. "Frankly, my love, these thugs are the least of our problems. They're far easier to deal with, after all, than some other creatures abroad on this earth."

Neely rushed after him, but she didn't offer a reply to his remark, though it had reminded her of the grim truth. She would probably have to give Aidan up one day soon, in order to protect him from the outraged indignation of his own kind, among others, but she wanted to pretend, for a little while at least, that it wasn't so.

Aidan gave her a wry look over one shoulder, turning so that he could see around the senator's rear end. He'd obviously been reading her mind again. "Come, now," he scolded gently. "You're not going to give up so easily as all that, are you? Where's that Yankee persistence I've heard so much about?"

"I used up a lot of it tonight," Neely answered, but she managed a smile.

They trudged through the deep snow in the backyard, passing the clothesline and the leaning birdbath. The van was parked behind a looming, weathered shed.

The snow had stopped, but there was no moon. Still, Neely could see Aidan as clearly as if he were giving off some inner light all his own. He put the senator in the back of the van, taking care not to hurt him, and closed the door.

Aidan and Neely stood facing each other in the cold chill, Neely's breath making a white cloud between them.

"Thanks," Neely said. Again she noticed that he seemed enervated, as though the evening's events had been unusually taxing for him.

Aidan leaned forward and kissed her forehead. "Anytime," he answered with tender irony. "Can you find your way back? You just follow this road west until it intersects with the main highway, then turn left. After that, there will be plenty of signs to point the way."

Neely started to speak, but her voice came out as a croak,

and she had to begin again. "What about Senator Hargrove? What am I supposed to do with him, Aidan?"

"Take him to the emergency room at the first hospital you see. He'll be looked after."

Neely glanced toward the van. It had seemed so sinister before, but now she saw that it had a few dents in the fender and green fuzzy dice hanging from the rearview mirror. It looked, well, innocuous.

"Is the senator going to be some kind of vegetable?"

"I can't answer that," Aidan answered with a weary sigh. "I don't think you'll ever have anything to fear from him, though—my guess is, he never really wanted to see you harmed in the first place."

Neely recalled the times the senator had warned her, both directly and indirectly, and nodded in agreement. She would feel pity for him after that night but never fear. She worked up a faltering smile and jangled the keys. "I'll be in Bright River, at my brother's place," she said. She wanted to ask if she was ever going to see Aidan after that night, but she was too afraid of the answer. "Thanks again."

Aidan lifted his hand in farewell. "Take care," he said, and then he simply faded away, boots, swastika and all.

Neely stared at the place where he'd stood until a moment before and wondered if she was in any better shape mentally than Vinnie and Sally and the senator. Then she climbed resolutely into the van, started up the engine, and ground the gearshift into reverse.

Aidan barely reached the sanctity of his lair behind the Bright River house before he collapsed. He slept sprawled on the dirt floor of the old mine shaft, and when he awakened, he was sick with weakness.

He had been lying on his stomach, but when he sensed another presence, he rolled quickly onto his back.

Tobias was crouching beside him, grinning his ancient, teenage grin. "You seem to be feeling poorly," he observed. He ran his eyes over Aidan's dusty tunic, cobweb-laced breeches, and smudged boots. "Can't say I care much for your taste in clothes, old fellow."

Aidan struggled to raise himself to a sitting position, found that he could manage no more. If Tobias had come to destroy him—and he might well do just that, being an elder and therefore exceedingly powerful—then he, Aidan, was done for.

"What do you want?"

Tobias stood gracefully. His garments looked medieval— he wore leggings, a long tunic, and leather shoes that curled at the toes. "You didn't think you were finished with the Brotherhood just because Roxanne Havermail carried you off to her castle, did you? Come, now, Aidan, this isn't a fairy tale, and there may well be no happy ending."

"If you're trying to be witty," Aidan replied, groaning a little, "you're only half successful. Get to the point."

Tobias laughed. "Such audacity. That, you know, is both your greatest blessing and your worst curse, Aidan. I suggest you curb the trait if you want the tribunal to decide in your favor."

Aidan got slowly to his feet, swayed, but was steadied by Tobias's quick grasp on his shoulders. "What tribunal is this?"

"You might say it's the vampire version of the Supreme Court," Tobias answered. "They're interested in you and want to know what makes you tick, so to speak."

"Am I to be tried for some crime?" Aidan felt no fear, so none showed in his manner or his words. He was through running; he had to confront his personal demons and be done with it, for better or for worse.

Tobias shrugged. "Not really, though the tribunal does want to determine firsthand whether or not you're a threat to the rest of us. Suppose you turned traitor, for instance, and somehow made contact with Nemesis? We might all be destroyed then."

Nemesis, Aidan recalled foggily, was the Warrior Angel so feared by lesser supernatural beings. "I, too, am a vampire," he reasoned. "If I were to go to Nemesis, it would surely be the end for me." He sighed, ran a hand through his hair. "Or worse yet, the beginning."

"The elders are worried that you might sacrifice yourself in some fit of heroism or despondency. You must admit, Aidan, that you are a very reckless vampire at times."

Aidan sighed, then gave a half-hearted grin. "All right," he said wryly. "I'll go peaceably."

Tobias spread his hands. "You don't have much choice, it seems to me." He ran his gaze over Aidan's stolen Nazi uniform. "You'd better change first, though. Some things are too disgusting even for vampires."

Aidan blinked, and when he opened his eyes, he was standing in the cold bedroom of his great house, the room where Neely had once slept, so warm and womanly. Tobias was right beside him and sat down in the window seat with a sigh.

"I do want one assurance before I submit to questioning," Aidan said, taking jeans and a heavy sweater from his bureau. He strolled into the adjoining bathroom to change.

"And what is that?" Tobias inquired companionably, as if he didn't already have the upper hand.

"I'm concerned about my sister, Maeve. And Valerian. They have no part in my discontent with vampirism, and I don't want the Brotherhood bothering them."

Tobias rose from his seat with another sigh, this one philosophical and slightly martyred. "The elders have no quarrel with them, for the time being at least."

"But you know exactly where they are at all times," Aidan deduced.

"Of course we do," Tobias answered. "Maeve has taken to her loom and hunts only enough to keep up her strength. As for Valerian, well, he's curled up in the wall of an old abbey, whimpering over his wounds."

Aidan felt a stab; he didn't need to ask what injury Valerian had suffered, because he knew only too well. "He's strong," he murmured. "He'll recover."

"I have no doubt of that," Tobias answered, "but it may be a hundred years or so before Valerian is truly himself again. Vampires can lie dormant, except for an occasional feeding, for centuries—but of course, you know that."

"Yes," Aidan answered distractedly, thinking of Lisette and feeling a chill grasp his psyche. "I know. But Valerian is different. He'll sulk awhile, but once he realizes that the world is going right on without him, he'll come back. He won't be able to bear the thought that he might be missing something."

"I hope you're right," Tobias said, without evident conviction one way or the other. "Let us go now, Aidan. The tribunal awaits."

Aidan remembered the cell he hadn't been able to escape on his own, the hunger, the filthy rats he'd been given as sustenance. A part of him wanted to feel the upcoming confrontation, but he accompanied Tobias without struggle.

Although Ben and Danny were ecstatic at Neely's return, the hole her leaving had left had already knitted itself closed again. Ben was in love with Doris, as were half the regular customers at the café, evidently, and business was thriving.

"All that trouble," Ben had asked, the night Neely arrived in Aidan's sports car. "It's over?"

Neely had nodded. "I can't explain it, Ben, but my part in the Hargrove thing is history. I wouldn't have come back here if I didn't know it was settled."

Ben had taken her into his arms then and hugged her.

At first Neely had slept a lot, and taken a great many hot baths, and helped out by cleaning motel rooms and occasionally waiting tables with Doris. She yearned for Aidan even as she tried to forget he'd ever existed, but there was no putting him out of her mind. Waking and sleeping, he haunted her.

She took to breaking and entering, letting herself into Aidan's house through a window off the mud room, and spent night after night reading the chronicles he'd written. In truth, of course, she was waiting for him to return—but he didn't.

His sister did appear, however, two nights after Christmas, when Neely was sitting by Aidan's hearth and gazing at the flames.

Her heart wedged itself into her throat and hammered there, for Neely knew from the drawings in the first journal that this was the legendary Maeve. Aidan's twin was stunningly beautiful, with her rich ebony hair and dark blue eyes, and she was also a vampire. An accomplished one, if Aidan's written accounts meant anything.

This is it, Neely thought with a strange sense of calm resignation. *She's going to drink my blood and leave me flat as an old tube of toothpaste.*

Maeve laughed, obviously sharing her brother's ability to read minds.

"Are all vampires telepathic?" Neely heard herself ask.

"More or less," Maeve answered. She went to the desk, picked up the music box, and listened thoughtfully as it played its quaint familiar tune.

The ditty left Neely stricken with love and longing for Aidan. She had not been able to bring herself to lift the lid of the small box and wind the key, for fear she would fall apart.

"Do you know where Aidan is?" Maeve asked, quite cordially. She was dressed in a simple muslin gown, and she sat down on a nearby settee, folding her arms and regarding Neely pensively.

Neely gulped, then shook her head. "No," she replied honestly. "I wish I did."

Maeve fiddled with the brocade upholstery on the arm of the settee, not looking at Neely. "He's been taken before the elders of the Brotherhood," she mused, revealing none of what she was feeling. Her blue gaze rose, linked with Neely's. "They may destroy him."

Neely sank back in her chair and closed her eyes. She'd never felt so helpless before, not even when she'd been tied up in the back of Vinnie and Sally's van and slated for a mob-style execution. Somehow she'd known she would survive.

This was different; Neely couldn't return the favor and

rescue Aidan, as he had done for her. She had none of his powers.

"I see you're wondering how you might be of help to my brother," Maeve went on. "There is a way, Neely."

Neely leaned forward, still afraid, but curious, too. It wasn't every day, after all, that one sat and chatted with a lady vampire. "What?"

"You could become one of us," Maeve said bluntly. "Then perhaps Aidan could forget this nonsense about being human again."

Maeve's pronouncement brought about an emotional earthquake, and almost a minute must have passed before Neely was able to reply.

She shook her head. "Not that," she said. "I love Aidan more than I've ever loved anybody, but I won't sell my soul even for him. And he wouldn't ask it of me."

"You're right," Maeve said coolly. "He would be furious at first, but he loves you desperately. Can you honestly say it holds no appeal for you, the immortality of being a vampire? The power?"

Again Neely shook her head. "All I want to be is a woman, a plain, ordinary woman." She paused, waited a heartbeat, then dared to ask, "Aidan really wants to be human again?"

"He'd do anything to accomplish it," Maeve answered in a rush of confounded annoyance. She arched one eyebrow, studying Neely, paying a little too much attention to the pulse point at the base of her throat. "I don't have to give you a choice, you know. I can make you into a vampire without your consent."

Neely thought of the early entries in Aidan's journals, the despair and anger he'd felt. "That was what was done to your brother," she answered evenly, fingering the golden rosebud on the pendant Aidan had given her. "He despises the one who changed him, and he would be outraged if it happened to me as well. Do you want Aidan to hate you, Maeve?"

The impossibly blue eyes widened at the sight of the

pendant, then were averted. "I adore him," she said brokenly. "I became a vampire so that Aidan and I would not be separated. Now he wants to change back."

Neely folded her hands in her lap and spent a few seconds gathering her courage, which, it seemed to her, was mostly bluster. Since that was all she had to work with, she proceeded. "Is that possible, for a vampire to be turned back into a human being?"

Maeve stared into space for a long time, then shrugged. "To my knowledge, no one has ever done it. But there are secrets and rituals only the elders know."

Neely bit her lower lip and offered a silent prayer, not for her safety, but for Aidan's redemption.

Abruptly Maeve rose from her seat and stood glaring down at Neely, her expression imperious and completely chilling. "You cannot stay here," she announced. "If I found you, so might the others."

Neely shivered as horrible images from books and movies flooded her mind. "What quarrel do any of you have with me?" she dared, setting aside the last volume of Aidan's journal, the one that mentioned his love for her, and getting shakily to her feet.

"You are a threat to all of us," Maeve answered. "Vampires and humans do not normally mix, beyond the obvious feedings and an occasional brushing of shoulders."

"But what could I possibly do to you?" Neely pressed.

"You have already done it," Maeve said, and her words rang with an infinite and eternal sorrow. "You have taken Aidan's heart and made him into a weak link. He might betray us all, not intentionally, of course, but simply because he's lost a large part of his reason."

Neely put a chair between herself and Aidan's twin, although she knew only too well that no such puny effort would save her if Maeve decided to follow through on her original idea and make this troublesome human into a vampire.

"My crime, then," she whispered, "is that I love your brother with my whole heart. As you do, Maeve." Neely watched as the majestic creature of the night turned her straight, slender back, apparently struggling to contain some emotion. "We aren't enemies, you and I. We're on the same side."

When Maeve turned to face Neely again, there were tears glittering in her sapphire eyes. "What will become of him?" she murmured. "Of all of us?"

Neely actually wanted to touch Maeve, to comfort her, but of course she didn't dare make any such move. To do so would be like petting a wild tigress. "I don't know," she said honestly. "But there is one thing you can count on. I truly love Aidan, and I will never purposely hurt him."

Maeve assessed Neely in silence for a long time, probably weighing her words. In the end she evidently found them true. "I have promised not to interfere in this other madness of Aidan's, this transformation he so foolishly seeks. But there is one thing I can do, and that is protect the woman he loves more than his own soul."

Neely waited, having no idea how to respond. For all she knew, making her, Neely, into some immortal, blood-drinking monster was Maeve's idea of protecting her. Or perhaps the beautiful vampire would simply kill her, angering Aidan but at the same time saving him and a lot of the mysterious "others" mentioned earlier.

As it happened, Maeve stepped back to the desk, found a pen and paper, and scribbled something. "Come to this address, in London, as soon as you can. It is perhaps your only hope, to be under my protection."

Neely swallowed. "London?" she echoed.

"Yes," Maeve snapped, shoving the scrap of paper at her. "And be quick about it. The housekeeper will let you in. You do have money?"

Neely nodded. Dallas Hargrove had given her a healthy sum in cash, and so had Aidan. She'd spent very little. "Is that where Aidan is? In London?"

"Would that he were," Maeve said with a bitter sigh. Having so spoken, she raised both her arms, as Neely had seen both Aidan and Valerian do, and vanished.

"London?" Neely muttered to the empty room.

The next day, after saying good-bye to Danny and Ben and Doris, who had begun to assemble themselves into a tight family unit, Neely got into Aidan's car and drove to New York City. She carried only her passport, a toothbrush, and her wad of cash; she was getting very good at traveling light.

Another day passed, and then Neely flew out of JFK Airport, aboard a 747 bound for Heathrow. She sagged numbly in her seat, now sleeping, now staring out the window at the clouds blanketing the Atlantic. She held one shimmering, fragile hope close to her heart: that she would see Aidan again soon.

The flight was interminable, and when the plane finally landed, there was still Customs to be gotten through. Neely managed the task, practically dead on her feet. Outside, in the gray, slushy twilight of an English winter, she found a cab right away.

Neely gave the driver the address Maeve had written for her and ignored the gregarious cabbie's whistle of exclamation.

"Pretty fancy real estate, that," he said.

Neely wasn't up to chatting, but as it turned out, that hadn't been a problem. The driver had talked nonstop from Heathrow to the quiet, elegant neighborhood that was her destination.

He brought the old cab to a lurching stop in front of one of the most impressive mansions Neely had ever seen, Washington and New York included. The place was three stories high, made of gray stone, and surrounded by a high iron fence.

Even as Neely sat still in that tattered backseat, wondering how she was ever going to get inside the place and what she would do when she got there, a figure came hurrying out to open the gate.

Neely paid the driver, stepped out onto the sidewalk, and was immediately grateful for the bracing bite of the wind. The cab sped away, leaving its former passenger to stand there with her hands in her pockets, gaping.

"Miss Wallace?" the figure asked, clattering a key in a great lock and then swinging open the gate.

Neely blinked. She'd been expecting Frankenstein's monster, but Maeve's housekeeper was instead a plump, genial woman with rosy cheeks and bright, mischievous brown eyes.

"Yes," Neely answered.

The housekeeper beckoned. "Well, come along then," she prompted, with good-natured impatience. "No sense in our standing out here, freezing our bums off, now is there?"

In spite of herself, Neely laughed, drawn by the woman's ordinary kindness.

"No sense at all," she agreed.

Neely made little note of the inside of the house that first night, for she was too tired and too distracted. She simply followed the housekeeper, whose name, to Neely's delight, was Mrs. Fullywub.

"Call me Mrs. F.," the woman ordered benignly, depositing Neely in a guest suite on the second floor. "I'll bring up some tea and scones shortly. There's a robe and nightgown, folded all neat and tidy on the bench in the water closet—through that door." She pointed a pudgy finger. "A hot bath can resurrect the dead, I always say."

Neely made no answer, since none seemed to be needed. She took off her peacoat, looking around at the unbelievably sumptuous room in a state of mild shock. There was a fireplace, with glistening brass andirons, and a bed that probably dated from the reign of Elizabeth I. The couches and chairs were upholstered in mint-green silk, to match the spread and pillow shams, and there was a Chippendale desk in one corner.

It was like stepping into a layout in a high-tone decorating magazine, but Neely was too far gone to appreciate her surroundings. She soaked in the guest bath, which was roughly the size of a Scottish loch, then put on the waiting nightgown and robe. She brushed her teeth, stumbled back into the bedroom, and collapsed.

Mrs. F. brought tea and scones, which Neely ignored, and built a fire on the pristine hearth. Soon shadows danced on the high, molded ceiling, taking the shapes of vampires and angels.

Chapter

—❈14❈—

In the morning Mrs. F. brought Neely breakfast in bed—
orange juice, oatmeal, buttered wheat toast, and a slice of
melon. Tucked under the housekeeper's right arm were two
newspapers, which turned out to be the London *Times* and
yesterday's *USA Today*. Neely might have enjoyed the small
irony, not to mention the luxury, under other circumstances.

"Thank you very much," she said after forcing herself to
take a sip of the orange juice, for her fearful yearning for
Aidan was a shrill, relentless thing that left no room for food.
"But you needn't wait on me after this. I can look after myself."

Mrs. F. beamed, looking bright-eyed and matronly with
her salt-and-pepper hair arranged in a loose but tidy bun.
She wore a flowered dress, along with a pristine white cob-
bler's apron. Neely wondered if Mrs. F. knew that the lady
of the house was a vampire.

"Nonsense," said the good woman, in her brisk and
lively accent. "You've great dark circles under your eyes,
you have, and if you don't mind my saying so, miss, it's
apparent that you could do with a little seeing to. Besides,
there's the jet lag to consider. You'll enjoy your visit more if
you give your mind and body time to adjust to the changes."

For a moment Neely wanted to weep. She couldn't remember the last time anyone had treated her with such tenderness, except for Aidan, of course, and that made the
experience bittersweet.

She blinked back tears of terror that Aidan would be hurt or destroyed by forces she couldn't begin to understand, let alone combat, but there was an element of self-pity in her sorrow as well. She *was* exhausted, not to mention confused, scared, and more than a little heart-sore, and she could use some time to heal, gather her scattered thoughts, and make plans for the future.

After a few moments of inner struggle, she managed to compose herself.

Neely pretended to nibble at her toast as Mrs. F. toddled over to the hearth and stirred a cheery fire from ashes and embers. "Have you been working for—?" She stopped. How was she supposed to refer to Mrs. F.'s employer—as Maeve? Miss Tremayne? That woman with the fangs? She redirected. "Have you been here long?"

"A few years," Mrs. F. replied. "Madam isn't around much, so it's quite an easy job, really. Which is good, since my knees aren't what they used to be. The heavy cleaning is done by a service, once every fortnight, regular as teatime. I putter, for the most part—dusting, answering the telephone, the like of all that. Once in a while, the Madam decides on a party, and then there's a flurry, I don't mind saying."

Neely smiled, though she still felt as if she'd been broken to bits and glued back together with some of the pieces missing. This gregarious, talkative woman knew nothing of Maeve's other life, and wouldn't believe the truth in any case. Who could blame her?

"How did you come to be acquainted with the Madam?" Mrs. F. inquired, catching Neely off guard.

No longer pretending to an appetite, she set the tray aside. "I'm a friend of her brother's," she said.

Mrs. F. looked disapprovingly at Neely's untouched breakfast but refrained from comment. In the next instant her face was alight. "Oh, you're one of Mr. Aidan's lot. Now, there's a lovely gentleman for you. As handsome a rascal as the Lord ever turned from His hand, he is. Makes me blush with his teasing, and me twice his age."

Neely thought of Aidan's birthdate—the spring of 1760—and sighed wistfully. She didn't know if she'd ever come to understand the mystery that was Aidan Tremayne; she just hoped she'd get the chance to try. "You're younger than you think, Mrs. F.," she told the other woman.

The housekeeper took the tray and left, and Neely immediately reached for her newspapers. At that point she was in dire need of a distraction, a way to avoid further thoughts of the dangers Aidan faced.

USA Today said nothing about the Hargroves—Elaine's funeral and the senator's subsequent "nervous breakdown," which had rendered him temporarily unfit to stand trial, were old news. The London *Times*, however, contained an update on Dallas Hargrove's condition, tucked away in a corner of page 14.

The senator had contracted pneumonia, and while everything possible was being done for him in the way of medical treatment, he did not seem to be responding. Neely suspected that he'd simply decided to die; without Elaine, without his freedom and his reputation, he might well feel that he had nothing left to live for.

Feeling even sadder than before, Neely refolded both papers, set them on the bedside table, and tossed back the covers. A yellow-gray fog was curling at the mullioned windows, and there was a distinct chill in the air, even with the fire popping in the grate.

"Vampire weather," Neely mused fancifully.

Soon enough she realized that even though she was weary to the point of collapse, inactivity would be the worst thing for her. Perhaps if she just kept moving, she reasoned whimsically, then disaster would not be able to overtake her.

Half an hour later, bathed and clad in a gray cashmere pants and sweater set that probably belonged to Maeve, she ventured out of her room. She would explore the house first, then call her friend, Wendy Browning, who was in London studying theater arts, and make arrangements to meet. Maybe that afternoon, if she felt up to it, Neely would go shopping for clothes. As it was, she had only the outfit she'd worn on the plane, and she couldn't go raiding closets and bureaus for more of Maeve's things.

Neely found the stairway leading to the third floor and climbed it. Here, instead of a nursery or servants' quarters, as many such houses would have had, there was one great, drafty room.

Neely's footsteps echoed off the walls of that lonely chamber as she approached the object that dominated it—a huge old-fashioned loom. Someone, Maeve surely, had been weaving a tapestry in delicate pastels and deep earth colors, though all that was visible was the hem of a pale, gauzy dress, a carpet of brown and crimson maple leaves, and a fallen rose, shedding its ivory petals.

A chill tickled Neely's spine, and she hugged herself. *Aidan*, she mourned silently. *Where are you?*

Tilting her head back, she saw that huge skylights had been cut into the roof, and the fog brushed against the glass like an affectionate cat.

There was a stack of completed tapestries on a table next to a far wall, but Neely didn't approach. She felt as if she'd seen a private part of Maeve's life as it was, and besides, this was a place of sorrow. Suddenly that huge room seemed as barren of life and hope as a cemetery.

She turned and hurried out of the attic studio.

On the second floor were a number of bedrooms and baths, along with a sitting room that overlooked the sumptuous garden at the rear of the house. Neely proceeded to the first floor, where she found an old-fashioned and purely elegant drawing room, a combination library and study, a formal dining area, the kitchen, of course, and a gallery.

Neely was even more drawn by the paintings on the walls of the gallery than she had been by the curious tapestry in Maeve's attic room. These works, at least, had purposely been put on display, and because of that, Neely could look without feeling that she was prying.

The morning dawdled by, it seemed, and promptly at one o'clock Mrs. F. served a luncheon of deviled eggs, fruit compote, and salad in the kitchen. Neely forced herself to eat a little, then went off to the study to call Wendy Browning.

An answering machine clicked on. "Hi, this is Wendy. Jason and I are probably in class, acting our brains out. Leave a message, and one of us will call you back at the first opportunity. In the meantime, break a leg. Bye."

Neely grinned as she left her name and the number where she could be reached. The thought of seeing Wendy again lifted her spirits, though she wasn't looking forward to explaining why her friend's seaside cottage in Maine had been blown to splinters. This might just be one of those rare incidences where it truly was better to lie, or at least go on pretending she didn't know what had happened.

Feeling restless as the gloomy day wore on and twilight approached—Neely realized that she was both dreading the coming of darkness and looking forward to it because it might bring Aidan to her side—she called for a cab. While she waited for the car to arrive, she reflected on her own mixed emotions.

True enough, Aidan could appear. On the other hand, so could Maeve or Valerian or other vampires she wouldn't even recognize. The cab appeared before she'd worked out the problem in her mind, and Neely put on her coat and rushed down the walk and through the gate to meet it.

It was time for a little therapeutic shopping.

She avoided the posh places, like Harrod's, the designer shops, and the trendy boutiques, and spent the remainder of the afternoon in a fascinating establishment called Tea and Sympathy, which dealt in secondhand clothing. It was up-scale stuff but definitely used.

In that hectic, cheerful, crowded atmosphere, Neely felt wonderfully safe and ordinary; she was even able to forget, at least during that brief, shining interval, that vampires were real creatures and that she'd fallen hopelessly in love with one.

She bought a black skirt that had supposedly once belonged to the princess, along with several pairs of equally royal-looking woolen slacks, some sweaters in soft colors, and a black, sparkly dancing dress. On the way home she had the cabdriver stop at a neighborhood shop, where she purchased a supply of underwear, some pantyhose, and three soft cotton nightgowns.

Later, Neely settled into the guest suite, back at Maeve's house. Mrs. F. brought tea and "biscuits," which were really cookies, and built up the fire. Neely couldn't ignore her hunger any longer, so she sipped from a bone china cup, ate exactly one biscuit, and reviewed the day's loot. Briefly she entertained a wry, bereft hope that someday she would have steady access to her own wardrobe again, instead of having to rush out and buy things everywhere she went.

Wendy called just before dinner, and she and Neely made plans to meet for lunch the next day, near the theater academy.

"Anything exciting going on?" Neely inquired, winding an index finger nervously in the telephone cord. She imagined herself blurting out the gist of her own situation. *Guess what? I'm in love with a vampire.*

Wendy's voice was bubbly and cheerful, like always. "Well, the police in Timber Cove did call to say my cabin in Maine had been reduced to ashes. I'll have it rebuilt with the insurance check. What are you doing in London, anyway?"

Neely suppressed an urge to tell all.

Of course, she didn't talk about Aidan, or his mysterious mission, or the other vampires who threatened to demolish any whisper of a chance that they could ever be happy together. "You've read about the big scandal stateside, involving Senator Hargrove and the drug cartel, haven't you?"

Wendy laughed. "All I read is *Variety* these days, and Shakespeare." She paused, and there was a worried note in her voice when she went on. "Sounds like pretty dangerous stuff. Are you okay, Neely?"

Her friend's concern warmed Neely, reassured her that there were still regular people in the world, affectionate, funny people who didn't believe in the Undead.

"I'm terrific," Neely lied, feeling her hard-won facade starting to slip. "I'll explain it all tomorrow."

"Great," Wendy responded. "Now remember, twelve-thirty at Willy-Nilly's."

"I'll remember," Neely promised. But a nervous tremor struck her as she hung up the receiver, there in Maeve's august study, a new and very frightening feeling came over her—the absolute conviction that someone was watching her.

Now, she thought with bravado, *if I can just make it to tomorrow.*

This time the Brotherhood did not mistreat Aidan physically, though his mental powers and his emotional strength were both severely tested.

He was given an austere chamber in the cellar of a remote hunting lodge in Scotland and allowed to come and go as he pleased, feed in his own way, and wear his own clothes.

Each night, however, as soon as he'd fed, Aidan was expected to present himself in the lodge's main hall, where he sat in a great carved chair of medieval oak, facing the five members of the tribunal.

The elders lined a long wooden table, sometimes just staring at Aidan, but mostly they interrogated him. They asked seemingly limitless questions about every corner and facet of his life, explored his most private thoughts and beliefs with their probing minds. Since there was nothing Aidan could do to stop them, for his puny powers were laughable beside theirs, he endured the inspection as patiently as he was able.

The experience was intensely painful on a psychic level, and the Brotherhood made no particular effort to be merciful. They saw Aidan as a potential threat to themselves and all other vampires, and half of them argued openly and heatedly for an immediate execution. That, the angry ones claimed, would settle the problem once and for all.

Others, however—Tobias among them—spoke for simple justice. Tremayne had not, after all, committed any crime, and surely he should not be destroyed on the mere speculation that he *might* betray the others. Besides, if he passed through the ancient purging process—even in his suffering, Aidan was jubilant to learn that such a process existed at all—his memory of life among blood-drinkers would vanish, along with all the powers and demands of vampirism.

The group seemed to be deadlocked, and there came a time when Aidan's impatience and fear and unceasing mental pain made him reckless. He finally demanded some answers of his own.

"Tell me," he dared, believing he had nothing to lose, on the twelfth night of the inquisition, "which of you would make a vampire of a mortal man, if that man did not ask you to do so?"

The five members of the court turned to each other and communicated for several minutes. He did not hear what they were saying because they veiled their words by some mysterious means of their own. There was much Aidan didn't know about vampires, for all his two hundred years among them, because he'd spent most of that time rebelling against his fate.

Finally the archaic creature on the far right stroked his white beard and muttered, "There is no ordinance among us forbidding the making of new vampires, be the mortals involved willing or unwilling. I personally would like to witness the results of such an experiment as we speak of here, however, and for that reason I vote that we allow it."

Aidan started to speak, but the elder cut him off with a look and a warning. "The process is extremely painful, and most dangerous. It is possible, for example, that the silver cord connecting your spirit to your physical being will be severed during the transformation. If this happens, you will be neither vampire nor mortal, and it may be that such a fate is even worse than the Judgment of Heaven."

There was a hush in the great chamber, for this was an

eventuality inherently feared by every vampire, warlock, shade, and specter.

Aidan rose slowly from his chair, gripping the armrests, weakened by the ordeal and all that had gone before it. He did not dare to think of Neely, though her image was safely hidden in his heart, sustaining him, giving him courage, making it possible to bear the pain of the Brotherhood's unmerciful poking and prodding.

"How?" he whispered. "How is it done?"

"Be seated," ordered one of the elders, obviously stunned by such audacity on the part of a mere fledgling.

"I will not," Aidan answered, standing squarely now. He was trembling inwardly, and there was an echo in his brain—*difficult . . . painful . . . dangerous*. He didn't care about those things; what was important was that the transformation was *possible*. Besides, the name nestled in his heart made him bold. "I have cooperated with you. I have answered your questions and opened my mind, my very spirit, for your inspection. Now you must tell me how to become a man again!"

More murmuring ensued, then another member of the vampire court stood and rounded the table. He wore coarse, monklike robes that rustled when he walked, and had long, flowing red hair and fierce features.

"In early times on Atlantis," he said ponderously, "great medical experiments were carried out. Scientists discovered a means of immortality, through a change in the chemistry of the blood, and we, the first vampires, were created by a special system of transfusion. We thought, in the beginning, that our—appetites—could be satisfied intravenously. Soon, however, we learned that it was not so. We had to drink the blood of living beings or perish of a terrible starvation.

"Some chose this fate, rather than prey upon mancreatures, while others allowed the sunlight to burn them to ashes. Most of us, however, chose to go on, for it was eternal life we sought in the first place."

Aidan listened, and waited, with all his being.

"We escaped the Catastrophe because of our unique

powers and brought some of the knowledge with us. Alas, much was lost. There is an antidote for what is to you a curse, and to us a blessing. One receives a transfusion, after the blood has been treated with several chemicals and herbs. The experiments were interrupted by the great Disaster that befell our beloved continent, but some things are known. For one, the procedure is an enervating ordeal, probably as painful as being staked out to burn."

Aidan did not flinch. No suffering could be worse than what he already felt. He loved a human woman and dared not be close to her, and he drank blood to survive. He clung to life with an involuntary fervor, and yet he called himself monster—abomination—devil.

"I don't care," he said hoarsely after a long and echoing silence. "I will risk anything—suffer any torment—to be a man again!"

The vampire who had been speaking—none of them, besides Tobias, had deigned to give Aidan their names—uttered a sigh and turned to stare at his comrades for a long moment. Then he looked upon Aidan again.

"Be aware, fledgling, that should this mad enterprise succeed, you will indeed be wholly human. You will live an undetermined number of years, you will grow old and sick, and *you will die*. With the transformation you will lose all the special powers you possess now and, gradually, all memory of those abilities as well. In time you won't even believe in us any longer."

Aidan said nothing.

"You must also remember," the older vampire went on, seeming stunned and bewildered by Aidan's determination, "that when you perish, as all men must perish, you will then face eternity—either oblivion or the wrath of a God we all rightly fear."

Aidan nodded. Hidden away, in a secret fold of his being, was the hope that with the transformation would come some sort of absolution. All sensible creatures, good and evil, trembled at even the mention of God, but was He not known for forgiveness and mercy, as well as damnation and fiery rage?

"I'll take my chances," Aidan said.

The elder sighed again, heavily. "Very well. Such a thing cannot be undertaken lightly, however, and we must debate the matter further among ourselves. We will send Tobias when we have reached a decision."

"Thank you," Aidan replied with cool dignity. He wanted to scream with frustration and impatience, but of course, to give free rein to such emotions would be foolhardy. He rose again from the chair, turned, and walked out of the hall without once looking back.

Outside, in the rich black-velvet embrace of the night, he allowed Neely's cherished image to rise from his spirit into his mind.

He wondered how he had come to love her, while no other woman had touched his heart in all his two centuries of living, and knew that there was no real answer. Why did any man or immortal fall in love with another? It was a timeless mystery that would probably never be solved, and in any case, he didn't care. All that mattered to him was the shining, eternal reality that his soul was somehow linked with Neely's, and that as long as he existed as a conscious being, in whatever form, inhabiting whatever part of the vast universe, he would love, adore, *worship* this one woman.

He had forgotten that intense thoughts of Neely would either draw her to his side or carry him to hers, and thus he was surprised to find himself in the elegant bathroom adjoining one of Maeve's guest rooms. Neely sat in the tub up to her chin in soap bubbles.

She gave a little squawk when she saw him, and for a moment he thought she was going to slide right under the water. "What are you doing here?" she sputtered, sending suds skittering with her breath. For all her shock at seeing him, there was a light in her dark sprite's eyes that said she was glad of his appearance.

Aidan shrugged. "I might ask the same thing of you, love," he answered somewhat gruffly. His adoration of her swelled inside him, like another being trying to burst through his skin. It was a sweet agony, and he wondered that he'd never dreamed, in two hundred years, that it was even possible to cherish one woman so thoroughly, so hopelessly.

He saw her love for him in her wonderful eyes and knew it for an emotion as elemental as his own. Such joy, such beauty—what an irony that it might well be doomed.

"Maeve invited me here," she explained in an uncertain voice. "In case you're wondering, I came by plane. Look Ma, no magic."

Aidan chuckled, and the sound held both marvel and despair. At no time had he ever yearned more desperately to be a man again than he did in those moments. If he had been he would have taken off his clothes, climbed into that big bathtub, and made love to Neely until there was nothing left for either of them to give to the other, but he was not a man. He was a fiend, and he was afraid that if she saw his body, pale and statuelike in its hardness, she would be repulsed.

He leaned against the framework of the bathroom door with an indolent impudence that was wholly feigned, his arms folded, one eyebrow slightly elevated. "I didn't know you and Maeve were acquainted."

"We're not, really," Neely answered, making nervous waves under the water by flapping her hands back and forth. "She claimed this would be a safe place for me to stay—I guess it's the old trick of hiding in the open—lest any of your vampire friends decide they want me instead of a V-8. There is, of course, a glaring possibility that she just wants to kill me personally, so she knows the job has been done right."

Aidan shoved splayed fingers through his hair. "Maeve won't do you any harm," he said with quiet certainty.

"Don't be so sure," Neely responded, and very quickly, too. "She worships the ground you walk on, and she also thinks I'm the worst thing that could have happened, not only to you, but to the whole vampire community." She drew a deep breath and let it out again, sending more soap-suds tumbling, and looked at Aidan warily out of the side of her eye as she reached for a sponge on the tiled shelf bordering the tub. "Did you ever like being a vampire, Aidan? Even for a moment?"

He sat down on the lid of the commode, resting his fore-arms on his knees and leaning toward Neely. She was watching him now, with a fragile hope in her eyes. "There was never a time when I didn't want to be a man, if that's what you mean," he answered. "I did enjoy making love to you, and I will always cherish the memory of the night we danced on a carpet of stars."

Tears glimmered along her dense lashes. "Can you—can you make love to me again—this time in the regular way?"

Aidan felt his heart splinter and fall into assorted pieces. "It's possible—mechanically, if you'll excuse the expression—but—"

"But what?" She sounded impatient. Irritated. "You said yourself that you're not afraid of—of biting my neck any-more, and we almost made love once, if you'll remember. Is it that you don't want me, Aidan? Is it because I don't look and feel like a vampire?"

"No," he said, his voice gravelly with the frustration of wanting her so much and, at the same time, struggling to keep himself from indulging. "It's because I do look and feel like a vampire."

She stared at him, her gamine eyes even rounder than usual. "I don't care," she said. She raised one toe out of the water and poked at the spigot with it. "What if I said the whole idea turns me on a little? Hell, call me kinky, it turns me on *a lot!*"

He averted his gaze, for although he knew this woman thoroughly, her frankness still surprised him. His last ex-perience with love had happened in the eighteenth century, after all, when young ladies of Neely's quality and station would have burned at the stake before admitting to such an attraction.

"Neely," he reasoned finally, making himself meet her

eyes again. "Even though I would never willingly hurt you, I am much stronger than you are, and I want you in a way that is almost frenzied. In my passion I might not be gentle."

"What if I say I'm willing to risk it?" she asked in a tremulous tone.

Aidan felt conflicting urges to laugh and cry. "Then I would reply that you are a damnably stubborn, if very beautiful, woman."

Neely just looked at him, full of defiance, silently daring him to take her.

In spite of himself, in spite of the ordeal he faced and all his misgivings, Aidan laughed. An instant later he had composed his features into a solemn expression.

Then he simply held out one hand to her.

She blushed furiously, and the very splendor of her made his soul ache within him. She rose, dripping soapsuds and water, and their fingers intertwined.

In order to lighten the moment a little, Aidan glanced at the tub and mentally pulled the plug. A gurgling sound ensued, but Neely wouldn't be distracted by showmanship; she wanted, plainly and simply, to be taken to bed.

Even the prospect filled Aidan with ecstacy, but now that he had made the decision to express his love to Neely in the most intimate way possible, he would not be hurried.

He stepped back to allow her to pass into the bedroom before him, and she did so regally, with all the haughty dignity of some beautiful pagan queen. Her skin was still wet and shiny from her bath; it would be slippery to the touch.

Once Neely was standing beside the bed, however, she lost some of her aplomb. She was, for all her bluster, a virtual innocent where such matters were concerned—even if she'd been with a thousand men, she would have been pure, for her spirit was the sterling sort, rare as golden pearls— and Aidan thought his adoration for her would be his undoing, so intense was it.

He went to her instead of touching her mentally from across the room, as he might have done had he not been so thoroughly bewitched. And when he stood face to face with her, so close that he could literally feel the beat of her heart in his own senses, she reached out and began lifting his heavy fisherman's sweater up, revealing his midsection, then his chest. Finally she pulled the garment off over his head and tossed it aside.

Aidan braced himself for her horror when she saw the alabaster whiteness of his chest, but it never came. Instead there was a sort of reverent tenderness in her eyes as she touched him, spreading her soft palms over musculature as hard as the finest marble.

She looked up at him in loving surprise. "Oh, Aidan," she whispered. "You're so beautiful—it's like touching one of Michelangelo's sculptures."

He was unbearably moved by her acceptance—he was the Beast being transformed by the Beauty's tenderness—and he feared for a moment that he would break down and weep. But then Neely opened his trousers and boldly stroked him. Aidan's senses, all of them, were infinitely keener than any mortal's, and he groaned in ecstatic misery as she grew even more brazen and closed her strong fingers around his staff. When she teased the tip with the pad of her thumb, he thought he would go wild with the need of her, but he took care to remember that she was flesh and blood, that the bones and tissue beneath her moist, supple skin were fragile. He drew her close against him and kissed her, softening his lips by a trick of the mind, and knew a stunning joy when she whimpered in pleasure and fell onto the bed, pulling him with her, as eager and wild as a female panther in her season.

Aidan kissed her deeply, once, twice, a third time, but his control was tenuous indeed, for he felt as though he'd dreamed of this woman, yearned for her, since the foundation of the world.

He tasted her breasts, frantically, and delighted in her cries of pleasure as he nipped at their hard, sweet little peaks.

"Take me," Neely pleaded finally. "Oh, Aidan, take me, or I'll die—"

He found the musky, warm entrance to her body and prodded gently with his rod, as much to warn her of its size and its hardness as to tease her into wanting him even more.

"Now, then," Aidan said gruffly as he glided slowly, carefully into Neely's tight depths, "we can't have you passing on for want of something I would so willingly give you—"

She clutched at his shoulders, spread her fingers over his chest, stroked his buttocks in fevered urging. "Aidan," she whimpered. "Do it to me—really do it to me—"

He began to move upon her, and her magic encompassed him, and her sweet sorcery tormented him, and he was a man again, not a fiend. His tears—tears born of a joy so fierce he feared he could not contain it—fell softly on her cheekbones and sparkled like diamonds in her hair.

Neely arched beneath him, pleading, in stark Anglo-Saxon terms, for what he and he alone could give her. And when she came, Aidan climaxed as well, and lost his mind in a maelstrom of light and sound and pleasure so intense that it seemed, for a few moments at least, that he had been pardoned and admitted to Heaven after all.

"I love you," she whispered breathlessly when their lovemaking was over and they lay still, their limbs entangled.

Aidan kissed her forehead, wanting to hold the truth at bay as long as he could. "And I love you," he answered. "Whatever happens, Neely, I want you to remember that."

Her fingers traced a pattern on his chest, and she gave a combination sigh and moan, since they were still joined and he was still steely. The tip of his staff rested against that very sensitive place deep within her, the one scientists had only just given a name to, though lovers had known of it forever.

"Can I—can you—?" Neely paused, and gave an involuntary shiver of rising pleasure. "Can we make a baby together, Aidan? Is that possible?"

Aidan felt a grief as expansive as his earlier jubilation. "No," he said raggedly, grateful that he could not plant an abomination such as himself in the receptive, nurturing flesh of a mortal woman.

She stirred again, her body deliciously soft under his, and spoke shyly, breathlessly. "I—I think I need you again—" He rotated his hips, and she gasped and clutched at his shoulders. Soon the maiden had turned into a demanding little wench once more, and Aidan marveled at the way she abandoned herself to pleasure and at the same time gave it with such generosity.

Aidan loved Neely again and again that night, until she was exhausted, her lush body flexing with climaxes even in sleep. He withdrew from her gently, kissed both her plump, well-suckled breasts, and rose from the bed. For a time he stood there in the moonlight, admiring her, worshiping her, lusting after her even though she had satisfied him over and over.

He sat in a chair near the bed and watched over Neely, a guardian angel from the wrong side of the universe. Aidan did not leave Neely's side until just before dawn, when he took himself off to the dark chamber in Maeve's cellar.

There he crouched against the wall, lowered his head, and slept.

Far away in his lair, within the crumbling ruins of the abbey, Valerian stirred uneasily in his own comalike slumber. She had found him, he could feel her presence stretching over his prone form like a smothering fog.

Lisette, he thought, despairing.

Valerian heard her laughter. *So you remember me, do you?* she trilled, her voice seeming to come from within his skull. *Isn't that touching.*

Having been dormant for several weeks, swallowed whole by his despair, Valerian was feeble. His strength was gone; he had no means of self-defense.

What do you want with me? he asked. *We were never lovers. Never friends.*

You poisoned Aidan's mind against me, Lisette's voice answered, burrowing deeper into Valerian's head like some hard-shelled parasite. *You loved him. Deny it if you dare!*

Valerian's sigh was not physical; it came from the very

depths of his spirit. *I deny nothing, least of all my affection for, Aidan. I would have died for him.*

How very dramatic. As it happens, my darling, you shall both die. Horribly.

Do what you will to me, Valerian responded, *but leave Aidan be. You've already robbed him of the one thing he held most dear, his humanity. How can you ask more?*

The whole of the supernatural world seemed to quake with the ferocity of Lisette's fury. Her final words reverberated through Valerian's wasted soul. *I ask. And I will not be denied.*

Chapter

15

Neely awakened bemused, hardly daring to believe that Aidan had truly visited her the night before, fearing that she might have dreamed the entire encounter. Whether real or strictly fantasy, however, the experience had left her with a vibrant sense of well-being, and she was already up when Mrs. F. knocked at the door of the suite and entered with a tray.

The housekeeper took in the princess's skirt and the soft blue sweater Neely wore with it, and smiled. "Very nice," she confirmed. "Are you going out again today, then?"

Neely nodded. She wanted to visit at least one museum before her lunch date with Wendy Browning and Wendy's boyfriend, Jason.

Mrs. F. set down the tray and glanced toward the windows, where a gray mist was shifting and flowing, a cloud come to earth. "Well, it's typical London weather we're having, and that's for certain. Have a care that you dress warmly, miss, because an English wind will go straight to your marrow and take hold there, if you let it."

"I'll be very careful," Neely promised, feeling at once mellow and energetic. She knew a fresh, fragile new hope that things would be all right, though she couldn't imagine how.

By the time Neely left the house for a waiting cab, having fortified herself with one of Mrs. F.'s substantial breakfasts, the wind was mixed with icy slush, and the charcoal skies promised snow. The trip into the heart of the city was harrowing because of the narrow, perilously slick roads, and Neely felt lucky to be alive when she finally stepped out onto the sidewalk in front of a famous art museum.

She paid the driver hastily, rushed up salted stone steps, and, inside the building, paused to rub her reddened ears with her palms in an attempt to restore circulation.

"Good morning," a gracious gray-haired woman said from behind a podium. "We ask all our visitors to sign our guest book."

Neely nodded, handed over the price of admittance, and signed with a flourish. When she stepped into the museum itself, she was stricken by a kind of delighted reverence. It had been a long while since Neely had visited such a place.

She viewed sculpture and paintings of various sorts, along with furniture from the medieval period and pottery from the time of the Romans. Neely indulged herself that day, reading every sign and studying each piece closely, and before she knew it the morning was gone.

She had about twenty minutes to find Willy-Nilly's, the club where she and Wendy and Jason were to meet for lunch, but even so, Neely didn't rush. There were still some tapestries she wanted to see.

The first three were pretty prosaic—plump, cherry-cheeked maidens with flowing hair and crowns of flowers, frolicking with unicorns, angels, or fairies—but the fourth creation all but wrenched Neely forward onto the balls of her feet.

She stared up at the eight-by-twelve-foot hand-loomed tapestry in amazed fascination. It showed a beautiful, dark-haired woman—plainly Maeve Tremayne—enfolded in the flowing cape of a handsome vampire—plainly Valerian. There was a castle or an old monastery in the background, along with an oak forest so realistically wrought that delicate veins were visible in the leaves on the trees.

Neely raised one hand to her mouth, both fascinated and repulsed. She studied Maeve's face, creamy white with the merest hint of pink in her cheeks, and saw joy in the wide blue eyes, as well as a touch of fear.

The tapestry was a cruel reminder that there was much to be resolved before Aidan and Neely could hope to share a life; it left her stricken and supplanted her lingering satisfaction with the old, familiar terror.

"Isn't it magnificent?" asked a woman standing beside Neely, startling her anew. Neely was flustered and would have babbled if she could have spoken at all, which she couldn't. She bit her lower lip and nodded instead.

The woman, wearing a severe brown dress, pearls, and a name tag that identified her as Mrs. Baxter, an employee of the museum, smiled, showing large grayish teeth that arched high into mauve-colored gums. "This tapestry is close to two centuries old, you know. We've taken great pains to preserve it."

Neely finally found a fragment of her voice. "It's—it's—"

"It's quite horrible," said Mrs. Baxter cheerfully. "But the weaving itself reveals an almost supernatural talent, don't you think?" She paused, studying the ominous work of art solemnly. "One would almost believe in vampires, when looking upon such a piece."

"Almost," Neely agreed, shaken. She knew from Aidan's journals that it had been Valerian who had transformed Maeve from a woman to a vampire, and that Maeve had wanted to be changed. Still, it was jarring to see a near-perfect rendering of the actual event, as if the moment were frozen in time, existing, always, as an unutterably tragic truth.

It was knowing that the art depicted a very real event—that the travesty had happened before and would happen again, no doubt—that nearly crushed Neely's spirit on the spot.

She made her way out into the museum lobby, fearing she would either vomit or faint, her program rolled tightly in one sweaty hand, and found a fountain. After several sips of tepid water, she felt a little better and, by means of grim resolve, set out to find Willy-Nilly's.

She had to keep functioning, stay in touch with the ordinary world, give herself time to assimilate facts she had been taught since infancy to regard as fables.

A blizzard greeted her at the threshold of the museum's outer door, and Neely was actually grateful for its biting chill. She drew the shocking cold into her lungs and was a bit less light-headed.

There were no cabs, but fortunately the combination club and restaurant she sought was only a few blocks away. By the time Neely rushed down a set of stone steps to a basement establishment swelling with music, she was numb.

Wendy was there, however, smiling her brilliant smile, her long auburn hair gleaming under the fluorescent lights. Wearing a funky black chiffon dress, a flowered vest, and high-top shoes from some thrift store, she looked delightfully theatrical.

They embraced, and Wendy's dark blue eyes shone as she introduced her tall, handsome actor-student-bartender boyfriend, Jason Wilkins.

Neely felt sane again, and real. She knew the sensation might be temporary, but she grasped it and held on tightly.

Over mugs of dark amber beer and orders of fish and chips served on newspaper and sprinkled with malt vinegar, Wendy and Neely chatted, being sure to include Jason in their conversation. Wendy described her life in London, then propped one elbow on the table, cupped her chin in her hand, and demanded, "Okay, so what was this you mentioned on the telephone, about the senator and some drug cartel?"

Neely drew a deep breath, then told the story, beginning with her first suspicions, a year after going to work as Senator Hargrove's assistant, that something shady was happening. She told of copying files, letters, and memos, and finally turning everything over to the FBI.

Wendy's eyes were bigger than ever. "They didn't help you?"

"I approached the wrong people the first time. The evidence I gave them probably went no further than the office shredder."

"Did you contact the police?" Jason asked.

Neely shook her head. "No. After the debacle with the Bureau, I was afraid to trust anyone else. I hid the duplicates I'd made of everything—" She paused, blushed, then met Wendy's gaze. "I drove to your cottage up in Maine and hid the papers under a floorboard in the shed. Then I took a bus to Bright River, Connecticut, where my brother lives. I wanted to lay low for a while, for obvious reasons."

"Maybe it wasn't smart to go straight to Ben that way," Wendy observed. If she'd caught the connection between Neely's purloined evidence, the cartel's determination to silence her, and the explosion that had leveled the cottage, she didn't let on. "I mean, that would be the first place they'd look."

"I know." Neely sighed. "I wasn't thinking straight—I was so scared and confused." She would leave the most astounding part of the story—falling wildly in love with a true vampire—for another time. Say, some future incarnation, when such phenomena might be commonplace.

With regret Wendy glanced at her watch. "As fascinating as this is," she told Neely, "Jason and I have a class in ten minutes." She nodded toward the narrow windows that afforded a view of passing feet and deepening snow. "Have you noticed that we're having the storm of the century? You'd better stay in the city tonight—public transportation will be hell."

Neely nodded distractedly; a little snow was the least of her problems.

"I'd invite you to stay at my flat, but all I've got is a fold-out couch," Wendy said, rising from her chair. Jason helped her into her coat before donning his own, and Neely felt a stab of envy. Jason and Wendy were living ordinary lives, sharing days as well as nights. They would probably grow old together, unlike Neely and Aidan; only Neely would age. Aidan was immortal, for all practical intents and purposes, though he was not invulnerable.

Neely said good-bye and promised to call soon, and then her friends were gone, and she felt as if she'd been abandoned in an empty universe.

All her carefully cultivated bravado deserted her.

She toyed with the remains of her french fries for a while, then left the restaurant to brave the frigid streets. She rented the last available room in a shabbily elegant old hotel across the street—apparently quite a few Londoners had decided not to risk the commute—and called Mrs. F. to let her know she wouldn't be returning that night.

The doting housekeeper warned her to keep her feet warm and put extra lemon in her afternoon tea, and Neely promised to follow instructions.

After hanging up, she ventured as far as the gift shop in the hotel's gilt-trimmed lobby, where she purchased several newspapers, that week's issue of *Time*, and a paperback romance novel. Back in her room she ordered hot tea and biscuits from room service and settled in to wait out the storm.

The air in Valerian's cramped hiding place fairly throbbed with Lisette's presence. He felt her energy and her boundless hatred, but he was half-starved now, and far too ill to do battle with such a powerful creature.

She became visible at twilight, curled up beside him, as if they were twins sharing a stony womb. He looked at her bleakly, too spent to speak aloud or with his mind.

It made everything infinitely worse, the fact that Lisette was so beautiful. Valerian had always cherished beauty, whether he found it in a woman-creature or a male, and the reminder that sometimes pure evil was lovely to look upon was like a fresh wound to him.

Lisette laughed, curling a finger playfully under Valerian's chin, where the flesh was paper-thin and dry as fine ash. "So you think me evil?" she chimed in a merry voice. "How very hypocritical of you, Valerian—you, who have always sought pleasure wherever it was to be found."

Slowly, and at great cost, Valerian shook his head. "No," he croaked. "I have no taste for innocence."

She smiled, but her aquamarine eyes were hard with anger. "So very noble," she taunted. "Wasn't the lovely Maeve Tremayne an innocent when you found her? And what of your many and varied lovers, Valerian? Were they all vampires when you seduced them, or were some of them hapless humans who had no idea what sort of fiend they were consorting with?"

Valerian closed his eyes for a moment. "Stop," he rasped. "You will gain nothing by torturing me."

"I will gain everything," Lisette snapped. "And the torture has only begun." With that, she glared at the outer wall of Valerian's narrow lair, and the stones themselves seemed to explode, bursting outward into the purple-gray chill of a winter evening, scrabbling onto the ground.

Briefly Valerian yearned for life, and for mercy, but these frail wishes were soon swamped by his despair. What good was there in saving himself, even if he had been able? What right had he, who had fouled what was holy, to live forever?

He did not move but remained curled up inside the crumbling wall.

Lisette scrambled over him, being purposely ungraceful, he was sure, and stood in the soft, powdery snow, the night wind playing in her coppery hair. With a murmur of irritation she reached into the chasm and clasped Valerian in both hands, using her legendary strength to wrench him out like a baby torn too soon from its mother's belly.

He was fragile, like something broken, and lay helpless in her arms, his head against her cold breast. For a time she just stood there, cradling him, crooning some demented lullaby, but then she began to glide over the ground.

They must have traveled that way, a hideous pair abroad on a winter's night, for the greater part of fifteen minutes. Then Valerian recognized the unsanctified ground beyond the outer walls of the abbey, the forgotten place where heretics and murderers had been buried. The weeds and the soft ground had long since swallowed up all but one of two of the few crude markers that had been there in the first place, but Valerian was aware of the moldering skeletons and half mummified corpses beneath the earth, and he shuddered.

Lisette laid him in the center of that desolate place, and he still had no strength to resist. She spread his arms and legs wide of his wasted body and pinned him there, with a mental command, a bond stronger than any steel manacle. He felt the first faint stirrings of fear.

She smiled down at him when she'd completed her work, her arms folded. "Aidan will sense your despair and come to save you like the fool he is. And when he does, I will destroy him."

Valerian moaned, blocking Aidan's image from his mind with the last shreds of his strength. If he didn't cry out to Aidan, didn't think of him, the other vampire might not be drawn into the trap.

Lisette knew Valerian's efforts and laughed, flinging her head back in a fit of mirth. "You're all idiots," she said after the terrible, shrill sound of her amusement had faded away into the night. "Since when do vampires behave like besotted humans, rescuing each other, pretending to honor and chivalry? Where is your white charger, Valerian?"

Valerian didn't reply. He was losing consciousness; he could feel his spirit seeping into the cold ground, curling like smoke around the bones of the long-dead and eternally unforgiven. As terrible as the experience was, he knew he would long to be as insensate as those corpses when morning came and the sun found him. The hot rays would consume his flesh like a rain of acid, but slowly. Long after his physical body was nothing but a smoldering shell, he would still be imprisoned inside himself, and he would feel agony until his thoughts were snuffed out like the flame of a candle.

And after that he might find himself in Dante's version of Hell, on the threshold of an eternity of suffering.

He groaned aloud at the prospect, and Lisette laughed again, then shrieked into the night sky, "Let all vampires see, and remember, what it means to betray me!"

In the next moment a soft, cool snow began to fall. Flakes

covered Valerian's closed eyes, the hollows in his gaunt face and body, and suddenly, vividly, he recalled being a human boy, no older than eight. He remembered the drawing of breath and the steady thump of his heartbeat; he heard his own laughter, felt it in his throat, felt the warm, pliant muscles in his legs as he ran, in just such a snowfall as this.

For the merest fragment of time, Valerian was innocent again. He was free and whole, and the greatest powers of heaven looked upon him with benevolence.

Just before he swooned, a smile touched his mouth.

Aidan awakened in Maeve's cellar, well-rested from a day of slumber and determined to avoid Neely for as long as he possibly could. He knew the Brotherhood was keeping an account of his whereabouts and his actions, allowing him an illusion of freedom while the members decided his fate among themselves, and the last thing he wanted was to draw their attention to the woman he loved.

His soul still hummed with the joy Neely had brought him by offering herself in passion and in trust.

In a blink he transported himself to his room on the second floor of the mansion. He seldom used the chamber, but there were fresh clothes in the wardrobe, and he felt like sprucing himself up. He would hunt in nineteenth-century London, perhaps among the riffraff along the waterfront, and then look in on Valerian. Surely the other vampire would be over his sulk by now, and they could talk. Aidan was eager to tell his friend that it was possible to be mortal again; he wondered if other vampires would step forward and ask to be changed, if he succeeded in making the transformation.

Aidan whistled as he put on his most elegant evening clothes—black trousers with a glistening silk stripe down either leg, a cutaway coat with tails, a ruffled white shirt of the finest linen, a narrow string tie, and a top hat. He wore spats over shiny shoes and completed his ensemble with a long cape lined in gold.

He looked down at himself, decided he looked like a

proper vampire, raised his arms above his head, and disintegrated into a wispy vapor.

I'm going to miss doing that, Aidan admitted silently when he reassembled himself in a filthy, rat-infested alleyway behind a combination brothel and opium den within a stone's throw of London's waterfront.

Snatches of fog curled around him, around empty crates and whiskey barrels and piles of garbage, like dancers in a spectral ballet troupe. Aidan sighed and waited; there was a corpse sitting upright, just a few doors down, crouched against a brick wall with its head resting on its updrawn knees.

He shuddered in distaste and tried to ignore the thing, but that was difficult. Out of the corner of his eye he saw the ghost rise from the body, heard it wail in despairing protest.

Suddenly it flew at Aidan, a bluish-gray blob of wavering light, keening and shrieking. The creature was—or had been until about half an hour before—a seagoing lad, barely fifteen years of age. He'd been robbed of the few pence he possessed, then stabbed under the ribs with a fisherman's knife.

"Go on," Aidan told it, speaking kindly but in a tone that would brook no argument. "There is nothing for you here. Look around you for the Light, and follow where it leads." He was no more certain that there was an afterlife than the shade itself was, he supposed. He said the words because he had heard his mother say them to a dying man when he, Aidan, was a small boy. The unlucky fellow had gotten in the way of a runaway coach, and his legs, pelvis, and rib cage had been crushed beneath the horses' hooves and the wheels, but he'd taken comfort from a tavern maid's pretty assurances and passed on peacefully.

Aidan was just about to move along when a great, loud hoyden of a woman burst through a rear doorway, dragging a gawky, half-starved child along with her. Gripping the young girl's hair—she was twelve, Aidan saw, by glancing briefly into her mind—the drunken harridan flung her victim hard against the brick wall.

The child sobbed, almost hysterical, as helpless as an animal with one limb in a trap. She'd stolen from the kitchen, a piece of bread, a crumbling morsel of moldy cheese, and the woman had caught her.

"Now I'll box your ears for you!" the drudge shrilled. "See if you dare steal from Dorcus Moody again, you workhouse brat!"

Aidan stepped out of the shadows, resplendent in his gentleman's clothes, and both the old witch and the child stared at him, obviously confounded.

"What is your name?" he asked the girl gently.

Mistress Moody did not move, for Aidan had frozen her in place.

"Effie," came the whispered response.

"You took the cheese and bread for your mother," Aidan said, having already discerned the fact.

Effie nodded.

"She's sick."

The child nodded again. "We got throwed out of the workhouse—my brother made trouble when one of the blokes as looked out for us there tried to put his hand down me dress."

Aidan gestured for Effie to wait, slipped inside the tavern's gloomy kitchen, and gathered up two loaves of bread, a block of cheese, and a joint of venison. After dropping the loot into a cloth sack, he brought it outside and silently offered it to the girl.

Dorcus Moody was still facing the wall with one meaty hand raised to slap, eyes staring, muscles as rigid as if rigor mortis had set in.

Effie snatched the bag of food, turned on her bare feet, which were blue with cold and encrusted with the filth of the street, and ran, without giving Aidan, Mistress Moody, or the sailor's corpse a second look.

Aidan walked around Dorcus Moody's hulking frame

and smiled into her senseless face. She had a wart beside her nose, and a thin trail of spittle trickled down her chin.

"May I have this dance?" Aidan asked with a slight bow. He put his hands on her, as if for a waltz, then bent his head to her jugular vein and drank.

He left her beside the dead sailor, staring witlessly into space, her pulse thready but regular. She was a vile creature, was Mistress Moody, Aidan observed to himself as he walked away, but her blood was as potent as a fine Madeira.

He turned, there in the gloom of the alley, and took his hat off to her. "May you live to nourish another vampire, Gentle Dorcus," he said.

She made a soft, whimpering sound, low in her throat.

The image struck Aidan from out of nowhere as he left the alley; he saw Valerian, staked to the ground in some snowy cemetery, awaiting the dawn.

Aidan muttered a curse, then focused all his powers into one single thought. *Valerian!*

The reply was faint, but it formed instantly in Aidan's mind. *Stay away. I beg you, stay away!*

Aidan was on the point of ignoring the injunction and seeking Valerian out in the same way he would have sought Maeve, or Neely, when someone on the fringe of a passing mob of drunken swabs bumped into him, hard.

"I wouldn't if I were you," Tobias said good-naturedly. "You could never save Valerian alone."

Tobias was right, but Aidan could not turn his back, even though the scale was balanced between himself and Valerian, and all debts had been canceled. Yes, the other vampire had cared for him when he was ill, nourished him, even brought Neely to his side, but Aidan had saved Valerian once, too, after the attempt to travel too far back in time.

"I can't leave him to burn," Aidan answered.

"Suppose I told you that you have one chance to become a man again, and that you must take that opportunity now, this moment, or lose it for all of eternity?" Tobias asked in a reasonable tone. He, too, wore evening clothes, and the two of them strolled down the street together, an odd sight indeed in that grim, desolate part of London.

Aidan thought of Neely, of all his dreams. He wanted to come to her as a man, not a monster. He wanted to lie beside her in a real bed, make love to her as often as possible, and work in the sunlight every day, until his skin glistened with sweat and his muscles ached. He wanted to vote and attend PTA meetings and drink beer on the beach and complain about taxes.

For all of that, he still could not desert Valerian. Aidan knew only too well that, if their positions were reversed, the older vampire would try to help him.

"I guess I'd say I have rotten luck, and you and the Brotherhood have lousy timing," Aidan finally replied. "So long, Tobias."

With that, he did his vanishing number, and almost immediately found himself standing on the ruined wall of an old abbey. His cape floated in the wind, in true vampire tradition, and Aidan felt a certain bitter amusement. Damned if Valerian hadn't found a way to screw up his plans after all, even if it had been an inadvertent move.

Aidan focused his powers into a single invisible beam and found Valerian almost immediately. He was on the hillside, well beyond the outermost wall of the abbey, and he was helpless.

"Damn," Aidan said. He closed his eyes, opened them again, and found Valerian spread-eagle at his feet.

The other vampire seemed delirious, drifting in and out of consciousness, and when he saw Aidan crouched beside him, he moaned. "I told you," he rasped, "to stay away. She's—she's here—waiting."

"Lisette," Aidan said. "Yes, I figured as much."

Just then, a weird, shrill music filled the cold night air, and Aidan raised his eyes from his stricken friend to see Lisette pirouetting gracefully atop a crude stone slab.

Valerian began to weep. "Why, Aidan—why did you come? I could have borne anything but what she will do to you—"

"Stop whining," Aidan instructed him lightly. He discerned the mental bonds that held his friend, tried them with his mind, and found them strong. "If there's one thing I truly despise, it's a sniveling vampire."

Lisette ceased her hideous dance and held out her arms to Aidan. She seemed to waver in her white, shroudlike robe, a specter with substance.

"Come waltz with me, my precious."

Aidan approached her. He supposed he should have been scared, but he was well beyond that, well beyond cold terror and even outright panic. A strange calm possessed him. If he was never to be a man again, never to hold Neely in his arms, then he wanted to perish.

"Release Valerian. You have no quarrel with him."

Lisette pouted prettily, and Aidan recalled an innocent time when he had believed her to be a flesh-and-blood woman and had taken unabashed pleasure in her embrace. "I do have a quarrel with him," she insisted. "He plotted to be your companion for all of eternity!"

"He's since found me uncooperative. Let him go, Lisette."

She pirouetted again on top of the gravestone, her auburn tresses blackened by the gloom, moving like living strands woven of the night itself. She laughed, and the sound was silvery, sparkling, and brimming with madness.

"Foolish boy," she scolded. "Valerian is going to die screaming with the sunrise, and so are you, my sweet darling."

It was not an idle threat, but Aidan was still calm. If his existence was to end this way, then so be it. No doubt, from a cosmic point of view, his fate was a just one. "I thought you wanted to dance with me," he said evenly.

Lisette descended to stand facing Aidan in the snow. There was a mischievous glint in her cool blue eyes. "Do you imagine for a moment, Aidan Tremayne, that I don't know when I'm being patronized?"

He simply held out his arms as he had long ago, when

they had danced on summer grass, under bright stars, and he had not yet guessed what horror he courted.

She batted her thick eyelashes coquettishly, then drifted into Aidan's embrace. He began to turn around and around, and her shroudlike gown billowed out around them, as did his cape, and after a while Lisette began to hum softly.

He thought, once or twice, of the spectacle they all made—he and Lisette, a pair of monsters, waltzing in a moonlit graveyard, Valerian staked out on the ground like some hapless character in an old Western. Aidan might have laughed, had he dared, but dawn was already approaching, a faint grayish glow shimmered along the horizon.

"You were such a delightful creature in the beginning," Lisette fretted, running the tip of an index finger from Aidan's throat to the top of his cummberbund. "I should never have changed you, though. That was my fatal mistake."

Privately Aidan agreed, although he was glad he'd stayed alive long enough to know Neely. That wouldn't have happened, of course, if he'd lived out his normal span of years. "Did you create others?" he asked on a sudden hunch. "Valerian, for instance?"

She sighed and tossed a disparaging glance in the other vampire's direction. "That insufferable pest? I should say not. I don't know how he was made, much less why, and I don't care if he screams in hell from now until the end of eternity."

"Why do you hate him so much?"

"Because he dared to love you."

"Do you hate yourself as well, then?"

Lisette stopped cold and stared up at Aidan, her face rigid. "I do not love you."

"I think you do."

She was silent for a time, utterly motionless, her expression unreadable. "It changes nothing!" she screamed in sudden, wild fury. At the same moment a border of golden light formed between earth and sky.

It was almost morning.

Chapter
❧16❧

An unearthly shriek rent the air, and Aidan didn't know if Lisette had made the sound, or Valerian, or even he himself. Full sunrise was minutes, perhaps only moments, away, and already he felt as though a miniature fire blazed in every pore. Pain seared his eyes, and he stumbled slightly, blinded.

Neely, he thought, involuntarily unleashing all the power of his love for her, of the dreams he'd cherished, and the hopes. The soul-cry was not offered in an effort to save himself—it was surely too late for that—but because he could not bear to leave her.

Whatever his intentions, the name sent him plummeting through time and space, and he landed with a hard thump on a carpeted floor.

He rolled, still unable to see, as the morning sunlight licked at him like the very flames of hell.

"Aidan!" Neely cried, and he was aware that she'd dropped to her knees beside him. "Aidan, what is it?"

"The light," he managed; it was all he could do to speak without screaming.

She bounded away for a moment; he heard a rushing *whoosh* as she yanked the drapery cord to cover the offending window, and he actually chuckled, impressed by her quick thinking, even though he was suffering the purest agony he'd ever imagined.

Neely returned to him, and he felt her hands against him, pushing. He was sheltered beneath something then, and the pain lessened ever so slightly. Still, he could see nothing but the blazing light of the fire that was consuming him.

Aidan lay gasping, realized that the cooling touch of darkness surrounded him, eased the pain. "Where—what is this place?" he whispered.

"You're under my bed at the Majestic Arms Hotel," she answered breathlessly; he could tell she was rushing about, doing something. "Nice of you to pop in."

He made a groaning sound. "This is no time for morbid humor," he said.

She dropped to the floor and crawled under the bed frame to lie beside him. The mischief was gone from her voice; she sounded fragile, worried, and very sad. "Are you going to die?"

"Probably not, thanks to you," Aidan answered. "For someone who hasn't been trained to administer emergency aid to vampires, Neely, you did rather well." He sensed that she wanted to touch him but hesitated because she feared causing him further discomfort.

"I untucked the blankets and sheets from the mattress and arranged them so the light couldn't get in," she said earnestly. She was about to cry, Aidan thought, and he was at once touched that she cared so deeply and fearful that he would find her sorrow even more torturous than the sunlight.

"Very good." He sighed the words. "It feels as if—I'm going to lose consciousness for a time. There may be changes—please don't be frightened. . . ."

A sheen of tears glistened in her eyes. "Is there anything more I can do?"

"Yes. You can stand guard, so to speak, and make sure I'm not exposed to the sunlight."

She was silent for a few moments and made no move to leave his side. In fact, she cuddled close and cautiously put an arm around him. "There's a storm outside, you know," she finally said. "A blizzard, actually. The sun is mostly hidden."

Aidan was slipping, though he didn't know whether

death and judgment awaited him or an ordinary, healing sleep. "A stroke of good fortune, that," he mumbled, "though the light always gets through—no matter what." He opened his eyes, but Neely was only a faint shadow beside him; his vampire vision, ordinarily sharper than a cat's, was gone.

In the next moment oblivion closed around him like dark, cool water.

Aidan might only be resting, and he might be dead of his injuries. Neely had no way of knowing, since the usual signs of life—a heartbeat and breath—didn't apply in this case. Being careful to let in as little light as possible, she slipped from beneath the bed and got to her feet.

The room was gloomy, since she'd closed the drapes and turned out the lights, but it was a poor substitute for the kind of deep, encompassing darkness Aidan needed.

Neely put the DO NOT DISTURB sign on the door and locked the room from the inside, just to be extra careful. Then she snatched all the towels from the bathroom racks and draped them over the sides of the bed, along with the heavy blankets, sheets, and bedspread, in an effort to shelter Aidan as completely as possible. When that was done, she crawled underneath the bed again, on the side opposite the window, and lay beside him, trying by an effort of sheer will to transfer her own strength to him.

The telephone rang once, but Neely ignored it, leaving the improvised lair only when she needed to use the bathroom or get a drink of water. Since she didn't want to leave Aidan, and was even less willing to call room service, Neely breakfasted on half a candy bar, found adrift in the bottom of her purse, and reminded herself there were worse things than an empty stomach.

Like seeing Aidan die, for instance.

Maybe it was the jet lag Mrs. F. had spoken of, but after a while Neely nodded off into a half-sleep and drifted along the moving surface of dreams yet to be dreamed and hopes yet to be recognized.

*   *   *

Maeve awakened at sunset, in the corner of what had once been the abbey's wine cellar, and saw that Tobias was already conscious. Perhaps he had never slept at all; he was a very old vampire, despite his youthful appearance, and she had heard that some of the old ones did not require rest or even very much blood.

She shifted her gaze toward Valerian's prone form. His skin was lumpy and gray, as if bubbles had arisen beneath. He was utterly motionless, and Maeve sensed no vitality in him, no power. "Is he dead?"

Actually she was much more interested in finding out what had happened to her twin, her beloved Aidan, but caution guided her words. She was not used to these elder vampires, did not know enough of their ways and habits to predict the things they might do. This was not the time for a faux pas.

"Perhaps we were too late."

Tobias laid one hand lightly on Valerian's disfigured forehead. "He wanders somewhere far from here," he mused, "keeping his distance from the pain."

Maeve shuddered, the memory of the nightmare unspooling itself in her mind in the course of seconds. She had sensed Aidan's distress, being so attuned to him, and raced from her den, where she'd been about to settle down for the day, to find her brother on the hillside behind the old abbey.

If she lived to be a thousand, Maeve reflected, she would never forget the terror of reaching his side, only moments before the sunrise. Seeing Lisette, she'd screamed in fear and rage.

Maeve had heard, or perhaps only felt, Aidan's cry. *Neely.* In the next instant, he was gone, utterly vanished, and then Lisette had fled as well.

"Come," a voice had commanded from behind her. "Quickly!"

Maeve had whirled, seen the stranger crouched beside Valerian's inert body, watched mutely as he lifted the fallen one into strong arms. She'd felt the first acid sting of the sunlight then, and hurried to the other vampire's side.

The next thing she remembered was the blissful, chilly safety of the wine cellar. There she had learned that Valerian's rescuer, and perhaps hers as well, was called Tobias, and that he was an ancient one, a member of the Brotherhood.

"What of Aidan?" she whispered now as the night stirred around them. Indeed, she could withhold the question no longer. "Where is he?"

Tobias arched an eyebrow. "Don't you know? The two of you are twins, are you not? Linked by some unseen and unbreakable cord?"

Maeve's eyes burned, but she told herself that was only a residual effect of her close call with the sunrise. "It used to be that way," she said woodenly. "Before—"

"Before the woman?"

Maeve looked away. "Yes. Her name is Neely, and Aidan is a fool for her."

"I know," Tobias said easily. "He was never meant for this life in the first place, in my opinion. He thinks too much like a mortal."

"Yes," Maeve agreed sadly. Eternity yawned ahead of her like a great void, and she knew some of Valerian's fathomless despair, though she had been slightly contemptuous of it before. She had become a vampire to keep from losing Aidan, but now it appeared that it had all been for naught. Even if he had escaped Lisette and found safety somewhere, he was bent on either destroying himself completely or becoming human again. The very fact that she couldn't locate him in her mind meant he was veiling himself from her.

"Tell me, please. Where is my brother?"

Tobias sighed. "London, I believe. It was a near miss for him, and he's blinded—though that condition is probably temporary—but the woman is looking after him."

Maeve's relief was so great that she nearly swooned under the force of it. "What will happen now?"

The other vampire shrugged. "Nothing has been decided, really. There are those in the Brotherhood who want to agree to the experiment, merely for the sake of learning. Others feel that rebellious vampires should simply be destroyed, for the protection of all, and as an example to those who would digress from our code."

"I see," Maeve whispered. So there *was* a way to be mortal once more, and Aidan had found it. Inwardly she grappled with the staggering realities of what her brother meant to attempt.

"In either case, Maeve," Tobias said kindly, "there is nothing you can really do besides accept whatever course he chooses."

"And Lisette?"

Tobias sighed. "I must go now," he said, nodding toward Valerian, "and hunt for this one, since he cannot hunt for himself. As for Lisette's whereabouts, I know not, but she has surely taken refuge in some lair. She will not return for a while."

"Why not?" Maeve asked. She had never feared another vampire, had in fact grown stronger herself with every night's feeding, exercising her powers, learning, practicing, but she knew Lisette was a dangerous adversary.

"She wants no truck with the Brotherhood," Tobias said. "And now, adieu."

With that he was gone, and Maeve was alone with the cobwebs, the rats and spiders, and Valerian's insensate hulk. She ventured to his side, touched his warped, discolored skin, and remembered a time when she had loved him. Even after she'd come to despise Valerian, she'd thought him beautiful.

"Come back," she said softly.

One of Valerian's eyelids twitched, just slightly, but he did not look at her or speak.

She stroked his singed hair, half burned away now, but once so glorious and thick. "You mustn't leave me, Valerian," she whispered. "I've lost Aidan—I can't spare you as well."

The wounded vampire did not stir.

Maeve watched him for a long time, remembering. Soon her own hunger drove her out of the hiding place to hunt.

Night came, finally, and Neely crawled out from under the bed and sat cross-legged on the carpet, biting her nails and waiting for Aidan to rouse. She didn't think about what she would do if he was dead—weren't vampires supposed to be immortal?—but she did consider his need for blood.

She even thought of offering him some of her own, though she hoped it wouldn't come to that.

Ten minutes passed, and there was no ruffling of the edges of the blankets. Neely gathered her courage, lifted the covers, and peeked.

Aidan was gone.

Neely was relieved—surely this meant he was alive—but she was annoyed, too. Why, if it hadn't been for her, that vampire would be nothing but a mysterious pile of ashes waiting to be vacuumed up by the maid, and how had he repaid the favor? By vanishing without so much as a good-bye or a thank-you!

She dropped to her knees and peered under the bed again, just to make sure. There was nothing there, not even a dustbunny.

Soon Neely became restless, her emotions in a tangle, and the half candy bar had long since worn off. She showered, dressed, brushed her teeth, and put the bed back into a semblance of order, so the maid wouldn't speculate, then went out for some fresh air and food.

The night was dark and cold, and, though the storm had abated a little, the great city was still essentially paralyzed. Neely called Mrs. F. again, from a corner pub. She was safe and sound, she told the housekeeper, and taking plenty of extra lemon in her tea.

After eating, and warming herself with said tea, Neely braved the sidewalks again. A part of her wanted to go back to the hotel room and wait for Aidan there, but she discarded the idea. When the time was right, she would see him again.

She bought a ticket to a foreign movie and whiled away a couple of hours in the dark theater, but she never really saw the film itself. She was busy thinking about what it meant to be a vampire, not just to drink blood, but to be a creature of darkness, never stirring into the daylight.

Tears brimmed along Neely's lashes. She was a day person; if she ever traded her flesh and blood for immortality, she would always yearn to see the sun, even as she lived in terror of its rays.

She was pondering this when suddenly the empty seat beside hers was filled.

Wild hope stirred Neely's heart, but in an instant she knew that her visitor was Maeve, not Aidan. The vampire was clad in a hooded cloak of dazzling dark blue velvet, and she brought along with her an ambience all her own, one rife with tension.

"Where is Aidan?" she asked moderately.

"I don't know," Neely answered in a mild state of shock. She'd bought popcorn, but so far she had just held the carton in her lap and played idly with the kernels. She told Maeve about Aidan's sudden appearance the night before, his condition, and her own clumsy efforts to help him.

Maeve was silent for a few moments, probably absorbing the images and emotions Neely's account would stir in a sister's heart. "I see," she said finally.

The remark sounded ambiguous to Neely, but she wasn't foolish enough to say so.

"It was wise, your leaving my house, although I wouldn't have recommended it," Maeve announced presently. "Perhaps this is the safest place for you after all, in the very heart of London, among the throngs."

The theater was more than half empty—not much of a throng—but again Neely kept the opinion to herself. "Am I really in such terrible danger?" she asked.

Maeve looked at her in silence for several seconds, then answered gravely, "Yes, you are. After this I recommend that you stay in at night, however. These are, after all, the hours when vampires stalk their prey."

Neely suppressed a chill. She was well aware that Maeve Tremayne could turn vicious at any moment, like a once-wild wolf thought to be a pet, and tear her apart. "Is there anything you'd like me to say to Aidan if I see him before you do?"

The beautiful creature stiffened, her face glowing pale as alabaster inside the graceful hood of her cloak.

A heartbeat too late, Neely realized her mistake.

Maeve leaned close, so close that Neely squirmed, and whispered, "Aidan and I took root in the same womb. We grew together, each of our hearts beating in perfect unison with that of the other. No one will ever, *ever* displace me in his affections."

"I don't want to be his sister," Neely pointed out, wincing inwardly at her own bravado, especially since it came on the heels of a blunder. Some instinct told her, however, that since she was in for a penny, she might as well be in for a pound. Maeve wasn't the sort to respect any person less forceful than herself.

"No? And what would you be to him, if you are not willing to become a vampire?"

Neely was defiant, angry that the most basic, the most cherished, of her emotions should be questioned. "I love Aidan. He is a part of me, and I am a part of him. And if he succeeds in making the change, I will be his wife—more than that, his mate, for all of eternity if I have anything to say about it—and I will bear his children."

Maeve was silent for an uncomfortably long time. "Tell Aidan not to forget the white roses," she said in a very sad tone, and then she vanished again.

Neely gave up trying to watch the second feature, tossed her popcorn into a trash bin in the lobby, and walked out into the snowy street. Even at that late hour the traffic was still tangled and angry. Accompanied by the sound of honking horns and insults shouted between cars, she hurried back to the hotel.

It was something of a disappointment to find that Aidan had not returned, a conclusion Neely didn't fully accept until she'd looked under the bed as well as behind the shower curtain and inside the closet.

Unable to sleep, too proud to keep a vigil, Neely opened her romance novel and began to read. She visualized the hero as Aidan and the heroine as herself, and for a brief, tenuous time the story kept her distracted from her own problems.

The return of Aidan's vision was gradual—the patrons of the Last Ditch Tavern were mere shadows, shifting and swaying—but his other senses compensated quite nicely. He circulated, catching a scent here, picking up a snatch of conversation there.

That night, feeding, and feeding well, was a matter of survival.

Finally he selected his prey, a young thug named Tommy Cook, who made his living snatching purses and holding up the occasional convenience store. Tommy's mind was a greasy, unpleasant place, but Aidan planted an idea there, and it soon bore fruit.

Cook wandered into the gloomy hallway leading to the rest rooms, stopped in front of the cigarette machine, and fumbled in the pockets of his jeans for change.

Aidan closed in, rendered Tommy unconscious with a strategic tap at his nape, and caught him before he slumped to the floor. Though several people passed while Aidan was taking the pint or so of nourishment he needed, no one looked twice, let alone interfered.

Tommy's blood was powerful stuff, like potent wine. Although Aidan hated it, just as he always had, he felt a sweet, dizzying ecstasy, unlike anything he'd experienced before. A moment after he'd hauled Tommy to a chair at a corner table and left him there to sleep it off, however, it was as though someone had just injected him with a syringe full of raw sunlight. He was on fire, but this time his insides burned, not his flesh.

Aidan's knees buckled; he fought to remain upright.

Tommy, stuporous before, was now smiling up at him,

his dark, impudent eyes flashing with triumph. Aidan's vision sharpened, dulled, and sharpened again, in sickeningly rapid sequence, and he gripped the table edge to keep from falling.

"What is it, Vampire?" Tommy drawled. "Are you ill?"

Warlock, Aidan thought. Too late, he remembered Valerian's injunction to beware of other supernatural creatures when he ventured into such cesspools of consciousness as the Last Ditch Tavern.

Tommy laughed. "Yes," he said.

The pain rose up around Aidan now, as well as within him, like a smothering vapor. He turned, staggered, fell.

The warlock's taunting laughter echoing in his brain, Aidan struggled back to his feet. Mostly by groping, for the vivid world of the night was branded into his injured eyes one moment, hopelessly black the next, he found a side door and thrust himself over the threshold.

He gasped, then fell unconscious into a new, powdery snow.

"Look," said Canaan Havermail, giggling as she pointed a small, chubby finger. "He's a snow angel."

"Do hush!" Benecia hissed as she knelt beside Aidan Tremayne's inert frame and turned him over onto his back. It always made her impatient when Canaan behaved childishly, for she had lived quite four centuries as a vampire, and that was enough to mature anyone. She brushed the soft snow from his scarred but still handsome face and felt a broken yearning in her heart, long since withered and atrophied though it was. She was fond of Aidan, though she hadn't admitted the fact to anyone else, but she could never have him for a lover. In his eyes she was not an adult female with powers equal to and even exceeding his own. Instead he saw her as a monstrous mockery of a child. "We've got to take him to Mother or Aunt Maeve. I believe he's been poisoned."

Canaan sighed, irritated to have the night's adventures interrupted by duty, especially when it was still early. "Oh, bother. What do you suppose it was that got him—a warlock?"

"Probably," Benecia said, speaking tenderly as she lifted Aidan's upper body into her plump, dimpled little arms. "Are you coming with me, or must I do this alone?"

Canaan tapped one delicately shod foot, her head tilted to one side. "If I help you, might we have a tea party?"

"Yes," Benecia agreed wearily.

"With our dolls?"

"With our dolls!" the elder sister snapped. In the next instant she turned herself and Aidan into a wafting mist.

The trio arrived at Havermail Castle seconds later, only to find that both Aubrey and Roxanne were still out hunting.

Canaan wanted to dump Aidan in the dungeon and indulge in the promised tea party, but Benecia wasn't about to let him out of her sight. Thus it happened that the three of them gathered around a low, square monument to a long-dead contemporary, in the oldest part of the castle's cemetery. Aidan slumped in his chair, still unconscious, while Canaan arranged her dolls in little chairs around the improvised table. Her china tea set, complete with miniature silver spoons, was carefully arranged.

"Have some tea, Benecia dear," Canaan urged, her voice chiming with delicate malice. "Don't you think your friend would like a cup?"

Benecia rolled her eyes. "Does he look thirsty to you?"

Canaan pretended to pour, then handed her sister a fragile cup filled with nothing. "You needn't be so tiresome," she scolded. She might have had the body of a little girl, but there was something of the fussbudget spinster in her as well. "It's not as if I'm asking you to do anything terrible."

The elder sister suppressed a sigh and pretended to sip from the cup. Their mother, Roxanne, liked to play the same silly game with plates and glasses and silverware, as if they were all still human and required the sustenance of food and drink.

Aidan moaned and moved his head slightly.

"There, see!" Canaan cried. "He *does* want tea!"

Benecia set her cup and saucer down with a clink and rushed to his side. "Good heavens, Canaan, get a hobby. He doesn't want tea, you ninny—he's dying!"

"Poppycock," said Canaan in a crisp tone. "Vampires don't die."

Before Benecia could respond to the contrary, they were surrounded by dark, shifting forms. She and Canaan huddled close together, trembling slightly, for they did not recognize these creatures.

"Look," Canaan whispered. "We have guests for our party."

"Who are you?" Benecia demanded of the robed figures, pretending to possess courage that had long since deserted her. "What do you want?"

A fierce-looking vampire stepped forward, his hair and beard as red as fire. He resembled a Viking, with his hard features and strong build.

He did not trouble to answer Benecia's questions but instead bent and draped Aidan's lifeless arm over his massive shoulders, then lifted him to his feet.

"Wait!" Benecia cried, rushing forward, grabbing at the sleeve of the vampire's tunic. "Where are you taking him?"

Still, the Viking offered no reply. Supporting Aidan against his side, he disappeared into the darkness, and the others filed after him.

Canaan gripped Benecia's arm when she would have followed. "Let them go," she said quietly. "We'll find another plaything."

Benecia was trembling. "I wanted *him*."

"Don't fuss," said Canaan, shaking a finger in her sister's face. "He's gone, and as far as I'm concerned, it's good riddance." Purposefully she refilled Benecia's cup with emptiness, and there was nothing to do but drink of it.

Lisette crouched in a corner of her lair, deep in the bowels of the villa on the coast of Spain, whimpering. Her hands and arms were piteously scarred, and her face misshapen, disfigured. Her once beautiful hair now hung in hanks and wisps, and her scalp was black and crumbling.

She tossed her head from side to side, wailing in her grief. She had been such a fool to dally with Aidan those extra minutes, caught up in the old fascination, forgetting her own vulnerability to the glaring sun. Now he'd escaped her vengeance, as had that miserable specimen, Valerian, and she found the knowledge virtually unbearable.

Lisette collapsed onto her side, too aggrieved to stand, and curled herself into a tight little ball. Inside she was shrieking, but all that came from her parched throat now were soft, squeaking mewls.

Her body was an unbearable place to be, and she left it to wander in happier places, knowing all the while that she would return, stronger and more beautiful than ever. And when she did, both Valerian and Aidan would know the depth and breadth of her wrath.

Neely awakened with a start, sending her book tumbling to the floor. "Aidan?" she whispered, even though she knew he wasn't with her in the hotel room. In fact, she had a feeling that he was in terrible trouble.

She rushed to the window and pushed aside the curtain. Dawn was still several hours away, but the snow had stopped, and there were cabs and buses moving along the streets.

Neely gathered up her belongings, put on her coat, and took the elevator to the lobby, where she settled her bill in cash. Flagging down a cab took longer than she would have liked, and she was numb with cold by the time one stopped for her. She sat shivering in the back seat, her teeth chattering as she gave the driver Maeve's address.

The going was slow, given the state of the roads, but roughly forty-five minutes later, Neely found herself standing outside the high iron gates in front of the mansion. The cab scooted away, and she pressed anxiously at the button that would alert Mrs. F. to her presence.

A considerable interval went by before the housekeeper

came bustling out, wearing galoshes, her nightdress, and a huge woolen overcoat. "You might have telephoned ahead," she scolded, fumbling with the lock and key on the other side. "At least that way you wouldn't have had to stand out here like a lost soul!"

"I'm sorry for waking you," Neely said, hugging herself, feeling very much a lost soul. Mrs. F. opened the gate, and she slipped through. "I came on an impulse, and I didn't think to call first. Is Miss Tremayne around?"

"Well, now, that she is, miss," said Mrs. F., hustling Neely up the walk and through the gaping front door. In the entry hall she set about brushing the snow from Neely's coat. "It happens that she's up in the studio, on the third floor, hard at her weaving. Why, she's working that loom as if all that mattered in this universe hung in the balance."

Chapter
—❦17❦—

Although Valerian's body was all but ruined, some essential part of him crouched inside the husk, a small spark of consciousness able to recognize itself and, however laboriously, to reason.

Fact by fact, Valerian pieced together what had happened to him. It had all begun with his love for Aidan, an emotion born long before, on that night when they'd met for the first time, in an eighteenth-century inn. Aidan had been new to blood-drinking then, bitter and afraid, wanting only to say farewell to his sister before seeking a way to destroy himself—actually believing it would be so easy to find peace and oblivion.

Soon after, Valerian had met the beautiful Maeve, still warmly human then, and been tempted to his limits. Maeve, after all, had been a female version of Aidan, and for that Valerian had adored her. When she learned what had happened to her beloved twin—convincing her of the truth had been no small task—Maeve had demanded a transformation of her own.

She and Aidan had argued violently, because Aidan despised what he was from the first and could not fathom why his sister would willingly choose such a fate. Maeve had wanted to be close to her brother for eternity, but there were other reasons for her aspirations as well.

Valerian had recognized in her a fierce hunger for immortality, for the singular powers Aidan so reluctantly demonstrated, and from the very first he had taken note of her wild and adventurous nature. She was greedy for life, like Valerian himself, wanting to test every sense, explore every emotion.

After the shouting match, which took place in the moonlit orchard of the convent where Maeve had been raised since the age of seven, Aidan had vanished in a rage. Some things never changed; Aidan was forever acting on impulse and then living to regret whatever he'd done.

Maeve had turned to Valerian and begged him to make her into an immortal, and heaven forgive him, he'd done it. He'd taken her blood and then restored it to her, changed.

It still bruised him to remember how Aidan had hated him for that.

For a time Valerian and Maeve had traveled together. He'd taught her to hunt, to sense the presence of other vampires or such enemies as angels and warlocks, and to hide herself from the sun. They had been lovers, as well, in that unique mental way of nightwalkers that was so much more profound than the frantic, messy couplings of humans.

Eventually, however, Maeve had caught Valerian playing similar games with a fledgling vampire named Pamela. After that, they had not been truly intimate again, though they had finally established a bristly truce. For the most part, Maeve and Valerian had avoided each other, but their common weakness for Aidan often caused their paths to cross.

The glow of awareness inside Valerian's devastated hulk began to gather strength, though the process was torturous and awkward, rather like trying to gather scattered buttons with bandages swelling one's fingers.

His fundamental fascination with Aidan Tremayne had never truly left him. Perhaps, he reflected, Maeve had known that all the while, known the real reason for her appeal to Valerian.

Of course, Valerian had not been the only one obsessed with Tremayne; Lisette, Aidan's creator, had regarded the lad as her own plaything. Had Aidan's angry spurning not wounded the vampire queen to the point that she'd sought dormancy, open warfare between Lisette and Valerian would probably have erupted immediately.

He'd been such a self-pitying fool, he thought now, to curl up in a hole like a wounded rat and let his strength seep away into the rubble around and beneath him. If it hadn't been for that very embarrassing mistake, he would still be a powerful vampire, and not this little flash of sensibility trapped inside a drying corpse.

It came to him then that perhaps, just perhaps, he wasn't imprisoned after all. Suppose he could transmit himself to other places and times, as he'd done so often in dreams?

Valerian gathered his being together into a small, whirling nebula of light and remembered Aidan fiercely. If any bond still linked them, he wanted to travel along it, hand over hand, until he found his friend.

His friend.

That was all that would ever be between him and Aidan, and Valerian found surprising peace in accepting the bittersweet truth. In the next instant he felt himself spinning through space, through dark, mindless oblivion, and then crashing against something hard.

That something was the stone wall of a crypt or cellar.

For a few moments Valerian was disoriented. He collected and calmed himself. There was a creature huddled before him, and he recognized it, though just barely.

Lisette raised her head, aware of Valerian even though his presence was purely mental. She was a hag, charred and almost hairless, incomprehensibly ugly, and she shrieked and raised her hands, as if to hide herself from his view.

You've failed, Valerian told her. *Plainly, I am not destroyed.*

If you've come for vengeance, then take it! Lisette responded in torment. *I have no spirit for battle.*

I will have my revenge, Lisette—you may be assured of that. For now, however, I have more important things to attend to.

With her thoughts, not her melted, misshapen hands, Lisette clutched at Valerian. *Does he live? Does Aidan live? Tell me!*

I don't know, Valerian answered, *but hear this, Queen of the Vampires: If you've harmed him—and I swear this by all that is unholy—your suffering will be without end.*

Lisette snarled and batted at the ball of light that was Valerian with one blackened claw. It was the movement of an animal, cornered and vicious. *You dare to threaten me? You are an even greater fool than Aidan!*

Valerian offered no reply; he was impatient to move on, to find the vampire he had originally sought. It didn't trouble him that he'd willed himself to Aidan's side and ended up facing Lisette instead. That was probably just some sort of psychic short circuit.

Once again Valerian focused all his energies on finding Aidan. On this second attempt he was successful.

Aidan was in a cavern, far beneath the surface of the earth, a dank place echoing with the sound of water dripping. He lay naked, except for a loincloth, on a table formed of natural stone, his still, pale form surrounded by robed members of the Brotherhood. The light of a few torches flickered eerily through the chamber, dancing with shadows.

The redheaded Viking whirled, sensing Valerian's arrival, and called out, "Who is it?"

There would be no eluding these, the oldest and most formidable vampires on earth. Valerian volunteered his name readily.

"Leave this place," ordered one of the elders with an impatient wave. "We have important rites to perform."

I want to stay, Valerian responded. He could not speak audibly as they did, for he had no body, and thus no throat muscles or voice box to form the words.

For a few moments there was utter silence, except for the incessant *plunk-plunk-plunk* of water droplets striking stone.

"What is your business here?" one of the other elders demanded. They were being remarkably patient, but Valerian took nothing for granted.

The wounds Aidan suffered, he suffered because of me, Valerian said. *I was Lisette's prisoner, tied down to be burned alive in the sunlight, and he tried to help me.*

The Viking gestured toward Aidan with a meaty, hair-covered hand. "Would you have us stand about yammering with you while he perishes? He, too, was injured by the sun, but that is the least of his problems. The Vampire Tremayne drank the blood of the warlock, and he is filled with poison."

Valerian would have sworn it was impossible to feel more pain than he already had—until now, that was. Through a new and excruciating baptism in despair, he learned that he had not even begun to suffer. He receded into a corner, pulsing with private anguish, to watch the proceedings. *Damn you, Aidan,* he told the inert being on the slab of stone, furious in his grief, *I warned you about warlocks. I warned you!*

Just then Tobias appeared, sparing not so much as a glance for Valerian. He took Aidan's limp hand into his own, but his question was addressed to his companions. "Are we ready?"

One of the others sighed heavily. "Yes."

While Valerian watched, helpless, yearning as he never had for his lost right to petition favor from heaven, the mysterious ceremony began. A golden chalice was taken from a blue velvet bag, along with a gleaming knife with a whisper-thin blade.

The Viking was the first to grasp the knife, slice deeply into his own wrist, and allow some of the blood to drip into the chalice. After that, the others did the same, one by one. Then, when the cup brimmed with crimson nectar, Tobias took a small vial of distilled herbs from his tunic pocket and added the contents to the cup.

That done, he lifted Aidan's head and held the chalice to his lips.

Nothing happened at first—Valerian was certain Aidan had already perished. Then Tobias muttered some quiet urging. Aidan began to drink, though in the vampire way, drawing the liquid through his fangs instead of over his tongue to be swallowed.

Valerian drew nearer—he could not help himself—and hovered just behind Tobias's right shoulder. Aidan had taken all the chalice held, and there were crimson specks of blood on his mouth. Before Valerian's eyes, he turned the blue-gray color of death.

What will happen to him? Valerian demanded. Tobias was not truly his friend, for vampires did not generally form such maudlin attachments, but the elder had been Valerian's rescuer not so long ago. There must be a shred of pity or understanding somewhere inside the ancient creature.

Tobias heaved a mental sigh. *I do not know—we had to act quickly to counteract the effect of the warlock's poison. Even if our efforts have succeeded, Aidan must endure other ordeals and move through passages none of us can imagine.*

Valerian wanted to take the potion and walk through the Valley of the Shadow at Aidan's side, though he did not form the desire into words, even in his mind.

The wise vampire, so deceptively youthful in appearance, read the emotion and responded, *Come, Valerian. Would you truly give up all that you are, all that you have, even now, to be a man again? To live a few brief years and then perish? I think you are neither so noble, nor so stupid.*

Valerian recognized the truth in Tobias's words and was shamed by it. He drifted into the shadows again and fretfully kept his vigil.

Aidan wandered, as if in a dream, back and back, through foggy drifts of time and memory. He did not suffer, and yet he was suffering itself, pain and struggle embodied. While on some level he knew exactly what was happening— his body was lying in a cavern, with the blood of the oldest vampires on earth sustaining it—other elements of the experience were more nebulous. This other self, this mental energy gone traipsing on its own, was as much his true being as the form on the stone slab.

He saw himself, long ago, lying in the undertaker's back room, undead and yet certainly not alive, either. He felt the horror again, and the helplessness, and cursed Lisette from the core of his soul.

Aidan did not expect to travel farther; he'd always understood that such a feat was impossible, except to the most accomplished and reckless vampires, like Valerian. To his surprise, he heard a whistling sound, shrill and harsh, and felt himself plunging through wisps of moonglow and sharp, splintered stars.

His stopping was a collision, not an arrival, and it was several moments before he recovered his equilibrium. He was in a pit, dark and cold, echoing with the screams and rustlings of beings he could not see.

This, then, was hell, or its anteroom. Aidan stifled a wail of his own, for his despair was crushing, unbearable, and worst of all, almost surely eternal.

In desperation he dared what no vampire would and cried out from his heart, *God of Light, have mercy on me—I was condemned on the whim of another, and not by my own choice!*

Silence. Even the moaning of the lost souls haunting the darkness was stilled.

Aidan waited.

Valerian remained in the cavern as long as he could, keeping watch, but he soon discovered that this separate, mental self could not long survive apart from the body. He returned, or rather was wrenched back, to that lonely, moldering place, and there he waited. There, almost against his will, he began to heal.

Neely did not trouble Maeve at her weaving, but instead took a bath, put on one of the nightgowns she'd left behind, in the guest suite, and collapsed into bed. She slept deeply, dreamlessly, and awakened to a foggy morning and a ringing telephone.

The jangling stopped and presently there was a tap at Neely's door. "For you, miss," Mrs. F. called breathlessly from the other side. "Your friend Miss Browning, I think."

Neely sat up and reached for the receiver on the bedside table. "Hello?" she mumbled, rumpling her hair with one hand and feeling as befogged as London itself. Beneath that murky layer was the terrible longing for Aidan, and the un-faceable fear that something was dreadfully wrong.

"Hi, Neel," chimed Wendy. "I hope you enjoyed the bliz-zard. We gave it in your honor, you know."

Neely laughed, though the sound scraped at her throat and made swallowing difficult. "Thanks a whole lot," she said. "Next time, how about a hurricane?"

"Done," Wendy agreed cheerfully. "Listen, we're doing a sort of showcase thing at the academy tonight—scenes from different classic plays—and I'd like you to be there. I do a mean Lady Macbeth."

"Is there any other kind?"

Wendy's smile was transmitted over the wire, warming her voice. "Such a wit. Will you be there? We could have dinner afterward."

What Neely really wanted to do was hibernate and wait for Aidan to reappear, but she forced herself to accept the invitation. She made a mental note of the time and address, rose, and dressed in slacks and a sweater.

If she remained in her room, watching the fog shift in front of the windows, she knew she would go insane. So she went to the kitchen, where Mrs. F. was dutifully assembling a tray, and insisted on eating there.

Neely and the housekeeper chatted, though Aidan's name certainly didn't come up, and neither did Maeve's.

After clearing away her dishes, Neely went to the down-stairs gallery, though she'd been there before, feeling drawn by the art. Mrs. F. chose that room to dust, probably for want of company.

Neely inspected each painting again, marveling. Some were portraits—Maeve, Aidan, Valerian—but most were landscapes. Intuitively she knew these green rolling hills and harsh rocky cliffs overlooking tempestuous blue-gray seas were glimpses of Ireland. Her practiced eye told her that all but a few of the works had been done by one artist.

She dragged a wooden stool over and climbed onto it to peer at a signature. "Tremayne," she muttered. Neely turned, still poised on the stool, to look at Mrs. F., thinking of the beautiful tapestry she'd seen at the museum. "Did Maeve do these?" she asked.

Mrs. F. laughed as she orbited a lampshade with her fluttering feather duster. "Oh, no, miss. Those are old paintings, for the most part—look closely and you'll see that they're done on wood instead of canvas. Priceless, they are, and not just because they were painted by an ancestor of the Madam."

Neely swallowed, feeling strangely moved. She touched one of the paintings tentatively, with just the tips of her fingers. Somehow she knew the truth even before Mrs. F. cleared up all vestiges of the mystery.

"The artist's name was Aidan Tremayne," she said proudly. "Just like our own Aidan he was, dark and handsome and full of charm, if the stories are to be believed."

Just like our own Aidan, Neely repeated to herself, and then she smiled. Very like our own Aidan indeed, she thought. She had not known that Aidan painted—there wasn't a word about it in his journals—but she should have guessed because of the sketch of him and Maeve on the first page of the original volume, far away in that Connecticut study.

"It's where all their money comes from, you know," Mrs. F. confided in a whisper, her feather duster shedding sparkling particles of dust. "They've sold a painting from time to time, and Mr. Tremayne is very good with investments—another family trait."

Neely turned her face to hide her smile, which might have been a bit secretive and perhaps even a touch smug. "Fascinating people," she said. The compulsion to explain that Maeve and Aidan were immortal, that they were in fact their own ancestors, was almost overwhelming, but of course Neely kept the information to herself. It would be a betrayal of trust, and besides, the housekeeper wouldn't believe a word.

Neely lingered a while, to be polite, and went on her way only after Mrs. F., settled in with a cup of tea to look at her favorite morning program on "the telly." Neely was drawn to the third floor, the very place she'd avoided the night before, when she'd known Maeve was there. It was a contradiction, of course, but Neely's life had been fraught with such things since Halloween. That was what she got, she supposed, for hanging out with vampires.

Reaching the studio's high, arched door, which was made of glowing English oak and beautifully carved with tiny birds and acorns, Neely paused and knocked softly, even though she knew Maeve would not be inside. Although the day was cloudy, and the atmosphere gun-metal gray, the sun was shining as brilliantly as ever beyond the earth's shroud of fog. Maeve, like all the other vampires, would be sleeping in some dark and hidden place.

Neely turned the brass handle on the door and stepped inside the great drafty room. She wondered if Maeve had woven the tapestry of herself and Valerian in this room, the one that was on display at the museum in the center of London. The house, like the tapestry and those paintings downstairs in the gallery, was old, and so was the loom.

She approached it cautiously, as though it might spring suddenly to life and chastise her, then touched its rough-hewn wooden frame in wonder. How beautiful and spare it was in its rustic simplicity. It was so plain, that loom, and yet it could mirror the visions of an artist in fine detail.

Neely walked around to look at the emerging tapestry again. There was the hem of the gauzy dress, the toe of one black slipper, the leaves, the ivory rose with its scattered petals. Something about this incomplete scene gave Neely a sense of deep sorrow, almost of mourning, and she had to turn away from it.

She moved to the windows, which stretched from floor to ceiling, their diamond-shaped panes lined with lead. The fog had gone, but now there were fat, soft flakes of snow drifting down, draping the metal gate out front, trimming the square tops of the old-fashioned lampposts, disguising cars and other evidence of the modern age.

It might have been 1894, Neely reflected fancifully, as she stood there looking out, or even 1794. She imagined, for a moment, that she could travel through time, as the vampires described in Aidan's journals did, and the idea sent a chill skittering up her spine.

Neely bit her lip as she turned away from the windows. Between getting herself mixed up with Aidan and his crowd and playing chase with the drug cartel back in the States, she'd had all the adventure she needed for one lifetime. She wanted what Aidan did—for him to be a man again, so that they could both live in the sunshine. She wanted to make love to him and to bear his children.

The possibility seemed remote, impossible, and yet Neely clung to it with all the tenacity of her being. She loved Aidan too deeply to give up now, even in the face of incomprehensible odds.

Still, Neely was used to taking action, and waiting was not her strong suit. She needed to be busy, building a life somewhere, carving out a place where she and Aidan could begin again.

He would find her, she thought as she left the studio, closing the door quietly behind her. Aidan would come to her when he could, and she would be waiting for him with an open heart.

One tear slipped down Neely's cheek as she descended to the second floor, for despite her faith in her love for Aidan and his for her, she knew that their happiness would be won only after a fiery battle.

In the guest suite she found her passport, opened it, and wondered at the innocence of the face in the photograph.

After the lonely, whispering darkness came the fire. Aidan felt its heat pulsing all around him, and yet he was oddly detached, untouched by the flames. He was silent now, for he had offered his prayer, and there was nothing left to say.

Then, suddenly, the flames became a living presence, not God Himself, but Someone. Definitely an individual, thinking Someone.

Vampyre, a silent voice boomed. *By what name are you called?*

Aidan quaked. Now it would happen, now he would tumble into the bowels of hell, to be consumed, and not consumed. So be it, he decided. At least he wouldn't be a blood-drinking monster anymore, preying on humans, passing himself off to the dying as an Angel of Mercy.

I am Aidan Tremayne, he answered at length. Then some spark of his old arrogance prompted him to ask, *Who are you?*

There was a thunderous hush, followed by amusement. *I am the Warrior Angel, Nemesis*, the voice replied. *Do you know that you are damned?*

Aidan was awe-stricken now, beyond fear into an emotion so profound that he could not call it by name. *Yes*, he replied when he could recall his own language and once again shape its words in his mind.

You have asked for absolution, Nemesis replied. *What right have you, a vampyre, a fiend and a demon, to expect the mercy of Heaven?*

None, Aidan answered. *But what right have they, those humans your Master so cherishes, to their redemption? And yet the choice between Heaven and Hell is their birthright, is it not?*

Nemesis was silent for a time, considering. *You are bold, Vampyre*, he said.

At this point, what else would serve me? was Aidan's response.

Again the Warrior Angel, dreaded from one end of Creation to the other, was amused. *True enough. What is it that you would have me do?*

There was no other course but to brazen it out. *None are to be snatched from His fingers*, Aidan challenged. *So say the holy words. But I am the exception, for my soul was stolen, not given willingly.*

Another pause, long and thoughtful, dangerously charged. *I will consider*, Nemesis replied.

* * *

Neely put on her black dancing dress, borrowed an evening cape from Maeve's closet, with Mrs. F.'s permission, and took a cab to the address Wendy had given her. The theater academy was in London's West End, and the ride was a long one.

She arrived just five minutes before curtain time, clutching a bouquet of yellow roses she'd sent out for earlier, but her thoughts were with Aidan, of course, and the need of him was raw within her.

Tomorrow or the day after—as soon as she could get a seat on a plane—Neely would return to the United States. The danger from the drug cartel was past, and she was determined to live constructively while she waited for Aidan to return to her.

When he was ready, he would find her.

She went into the theater, took her assigned seat, and was, for a time, lost in the performances of her friends, Wendy and Jason, and their talented classmates. Between scenes, however, Neely's mind groped for images of Aidan and clung to them.

She figured she was going to need some therapy once this whole thing was over, one way or the other, though God only knew how she would explain her obsession with vampires. Any normal shrink was certain to see that as a neurosis, plain and simple, and classify Aidan and the others as unconscious archetypes.

Once the evening's presentation was over, Neely met Wendy and Jason in the lobby, near one of the stage doors. She handed Wendy the roses and gave her a congratulatory hug, then embraced Jason as well.

They had supper three blocks away, in an elegant club where the music was soft and smoky. Neely surprised herself by actually choking down a reasonable amount of food.

When Jason left the table for a few minutes to speak with friends, Wendy gently squeezed her friend's hand. "What's wrong, Neel? I've never seen you look so miserable."

Neely wished she could confide the whole truth, but of course that was impossible. Even the artistic, talented

Wendy, with her fertile imagination, would not be able to take in the undiluted facts of the situation. How could Neely explain that she was hopelessly in love with a vampire?

"I guess I'm just tired. I've been through a lot in the last few months."

Wendy nodded sympathetically, her blue eyes wide with compassion. At least she knew about Neely's adventures with the drug cartel. "You certainly have," she agreed. "What you need is a good rest. You should go somewhere warm, where the sun shines, and think things through."

Neely sighed in agreement. "I don't know where I'll wind up, just yet," she answered, "but I feel ready to leave London now and make a lasting niche for myself somewhere. I'll be in touch with you as soon as I get my bearings."

Wendy patted her hand. "You'll be all right, Neely. You're the bravest, most resilient person I know."

"Thanks," Neely said. She knew her friend had meant the compliment, but at the same time she couldn't really take it in. The days and nights ahead looked bleak to her, for as badly as she wanted to, she could not ignore the possibility that Aidan might never return to her.

She finished out the evening, cried all the way home in the cab, and spent much of the night composing a letter to Aidan. She wrote that she loved him, that she would always love him, that she would wait for him, even into the next lifetime, if that proved necessary.

Neely left the letter on the mantelpiece in the gallery the next morning, beneath one of Aidan's paintings, said goodbye to Mrs. F. and set out in another cab for the airport.

Chapter

—❧18❧—

For four days and three nights, Aidan lay upon his slab, motionless and pale as death. Valerian came, in spirit, to watch over him and stayed as long as his limited energy would allow, before scurrying back to his own ruined and unwelcoming body to regroup. The old ones returned every twenty-four hours, always at nightfall, to fill the golden chalice from their wrists as they had on that first occasion, and add their concoction of herbs. The only sign of life Aidan ever showed was when he opened his lips to draw from the cup.

Each night, as Valerian kept his helpless vigil, a new fissure traced itself over his heart. He would gladly have taken the beloved one's place on that cold bed of stone, borne all his pain, argued his case for him in that other world, the mystical one, where some part of Aidan surely wandered. None of these courses were open to Valerian, however, all he could do was wait.

When the fourth sunset came, Valerian was there in the cavern even before the elders appeared. It was as if he were the heart of some giant unseen entity, pumping fear, like blood, into veins and limbs and organs beyond his awareness.

He drew near Aidan, but it seemed that a wall of cold surrounded the still form, now as rigid and gray as a cadaver. Valerian withdrew again, scorning his vampire powers for the first time since his making. *Smoke and mirrors*, he thought furiously. *What good are my tricks and secrets if Aidan does not live?*

The others arrived, one by one, solemn in their dignity, wearing it as tangibly as their robes. They made a circle around Aidan, then, in a single motion, lifted him up in their hands.

Valerian was jolted out of his angry reverie; he rushed back to Aidan, shimmering above his bare middle like a firefly.

Wait, he demanded of Tobias, seeing no sign of the chalice. Something had changed; the ritual had taken a new turn. *What are you doing? Where are you taking him?*

Tobias sighed, and his effort at patience was lost on Valerian for the moment because he was too frantic to recognize it. The older vampire responded in the language of the mind, though there was never any question that the others could hear and understand.

We can do no more for the fledgling, Tobias said. *The sunlight must now be his final judge.*

Valerian felt horror batter against him, then surround and absorb him. *What?*

We will lay him out in a place once holy to mortals. If he survives the full rising of the sun, the transformation will be complete. If he cannot be changed, and we have failed in our efforts, he will be destroyed.

Valerian became a scream, since he could not utter one without his body. *No!*

It is done, Tobias responded.

In the next instant they were gone. All of them—Tobias, the other elders, Aidan.

Valerian's strength was already waning—his body claimed much of it, being determined to renew itself—but he used all his will to follow the elders and their unconscious burden.

The small, hideous company reassembled itself in the center of a circle of ancient pillars, not far from Stonehenge. Moonlight splashed the ruined monument to some long-forgotten deity and turned the crusted snow to iridescent silver.

Aidan made no sound or movement as the elders laid him in the exact center of the ring of giant stones and stepped back, each one fading slowly, slowly, until they'd all vanished.

Valerian shrieked soundlessly, wild in his frustration and fear. He could not bear it, seeing Aidan left to await the sunrise and suffer the terrible cruelties reserved just for vampires, but there was nothing he could do.

Still, Valerian lingered as long as he was able, and when he saw dawn trim the distant horizon in golden lace, he tried to form himself into some kind of shield, to cover and protect his friend. Alas, he was made of nothingness, and he could offer no protection.

He was wrenched back to his own faraway body, just as the light tumbled and spilled over the snowy hills and into the circle of stones where Aidan lay.

Neely sat numbly on the postage-stamp-size terrace outside her hotel room in Phoenix, sipping iced tea and staring at the shifting patterns of turquoise light playing over the pool below. The sun was dazzlingly bright, and its warmth teased the very marrow of her bones.

She sighed, reached for her ice tea, and took another sip. She didn't know a soul in Arizona, and Ben had made it plain when she telephoned him, on her first night back in the country, that he thought she needed looking after—at least for a while.

Neely didn't want anyone fussing over her, for in those freaky times when the numbness wore off, she was hypersensitive to pain, and the very currents in the air bruised her. During these periods, the slightest sound seemed deafening and hammered against her senses until she trembled.

She needed to think. That was what she'd told her brother. She had money, now that the drug people weren't tracking her anymore and she could tap her personal funds. She wanted to wait, and later, if necessary, do her grieving, in peace and privacy. Before she could go on and begin making some sort of life for herself and Aidan, however, she must finish putting herself back together and smoothing away the rough places where the breaks were mended.

As soon as possible, Neely planned to find herself a job as an assistant to some executive, rent an apartment, buy a car, make new friends. She wasn't planning to sit on the sidelines while she waited for Aidan, though she certainly didn't intend to date other men, either, for Neely knew one thing: For the rest of her natural days and, most probably, throughout eternity as well, she would love no one but Aidan Tremayne.

Neely closed her eyes, leaned back in the chaise lounge, and sighed, letting the sun caress her winter-whitened skin. It frightened her that sometimes she could almost convince herself that she'd imagined the whole fantastic experience— encountering Aidan for the first time, sleeping beside him under a hotel-room bed in London, Valerian and the paintings and the tapestries and Maeve's grand mansion. The memories always returned, vivid and sharp, and wore well in her mind like a bright picture on a bar of novelty soap, one that would never wash away.

The last thing she wanted was to forget.

Often she awakened in the night, thinking Aidan was there beside her, and weeping when she found herself alone. She tried hard to accept reality: Aidan was a vampire, with all the attendant gifts. If he had not perished in that strange experiment of his, or been grievously injured, he would find her.

Neely waited, suspended, swinging back and forth between one emotion and its opposite, reminding herself to eat and sleep and even breathe.

She would hold on, though—she was determined to do that.

The first thing Aidan was conscious of was light. Dazzling, fiery light. He waited for the glare to consume him, but instead it played sweetly over his skin like some intangible ointment. He slowly opened his eyes, saw nothing but the luminous glow, and closed them again.

The next sensation he recognized was cold. Saints in heaven, he was lying in snow, bare as a pauper's purse, and freezing his ass off in the bargain.

He raised his eyelids once more, only to be driven back a second time into the comforting darkness.

Aidan tried to lift his hands after that, but they were heavy at his sides. Where was he? In Hell? It would be some joke, he reflected, if the place turned out to be an ice pit instead of an everlasting pyre.

"Great Scot, Martha," a male voice boomed from somewhere above him. "He's quite naked, isn't he? And him out here in the weather and all. Might be he's a Druid or something like that."

Someone crouched beside Aidan. He felt a woman's hand come to rest on his shoulder, strong and blessedly warm. "Druid or none, he's in a bad way. Run and get the woolen blanket from the car, Walter, and we'll wrap him up snug in that. Then we'll try to lift the poor man between us."

He felt the blanket go round him, and the awkward angels wrested him onto his feet. He could neither see nor speak, but as he stumbled along between his rescuers, a momentous realization came upon him.

He was *breathing*.

Aidan's spirit soared even higher when he explored his chest and found a living heart beating there. "Neely," he whispered as tears slipped down his half-frozen face. "Neely."

When he awakened again, he was in the hospital, and the numbness of hypothermia had worn off, leaving a raw, scraping pain in its place.

Aidan exulted in that pain, however, for it was more proof that he'd been given a second chance.

He was a man.

He lifted one of his hands to his mouth, with no small amount of struggle, and felt his teeth. His fangs were gone, leaving an ordinary pair of incisors in their places.

Aidan tried to sit up, only to be gently pressed back to the bed again.

"There, now," a woman, probably a nurse, said gently, "just rest and don't be trying to rise. You came very near to meeting your Maker, you know."

He felt tears gather in his lashes, hot and wet. *You can't imagine how near*, he thought. He'd been forgiven, it seemed, or at least given an opportunity to redeem himself. He meant to make full use of whatever time was left to him.

"Thank you," he whispered as the pain took hold and started to drag him under again. The nurse thought he'd been speaking to her and assured him that she was just doing her job.

In the days to come, Aidan tried to keep track of time, but the task proved impossible, since he was conscious only in bits and snatches. During those brief intervals, he reveled in the steady beat of his heart, the ragged but regular meter of his breathing, the ache in the back of his hand, where an intravenous needle was lodged. Even the need to relieve himself in a cold steel urn brought by a nurse was cause to celebrate.

When he found the strength to lift his eyelids for the first time, he saw gray-green walls, uninspired hospital art, a tiny television set that seemed to huddle in a corner of the room, near the ceiling. His bed was the crank-up sort, an iron monstrosity that might well have been a relic of some war.

A moment passed before Aidan realized that it was night, and he was seeing clearly. The knowledge frightened him; he thought for a moment that he'd only dreamed of being a mortal.

Then he saw the vampire, standing motionless and majestic at the foot of the bed. Aidan did not recognize the creature, and that only increased his alarm. He drew back against the pillows and held his breath.

The stranger raised a stately hand. Like his face, it glowed white in the darkness, illuminating him, so that he appeared to have swallowed the moon itself. "Do not be afraid, Mortal," the creature said, sounding mildly exasperated. "I have not come to change you, but only to bring a message from the Brotherhood."

Aidan's heart had risen to his throat and was pounding there. He was frightened, and yet the mere existence of his pulse caused him almost incomprehensible joy. "What is this message?" he managed to ask, and as vulnerable as he was, there was a note of challenge in his voice.

The vampire chuckled. "Tobias was right," he said. "You are certainly brave to the point of idiocy, Aidan Tremayne." He took several items from inside his coat, then rounded the bed to lay them on the stand and look down into Aidan's defiant eyes. "I've brought you a passport, credit cards, some money. You have lost your powers as a vampire, of course, so you will have to make a place for yourself in the world of humankind now."

Aidan glanced at the leather packet on the bedside stand. He'd had no use for identification and money before, but they were quite necessary to mortals. "Did Maeve ask you to help me—or Valerian?"

"Neither," the fiend replied, moving away to stand at the window, looking out. "No one knows where that pair has gotten themselves off to, as a matter of fact. The Brotherhood simply felt that matters should be brought full circle—your mortal life was taken from you, now it is restored. In these modern times it is difficult to function without passports and the like."

Aidan was silent for a moment, absorbing the knowledge that Maeve and Valerian had both disappeared. He felt his limitations as a man sorely—he could do nothing to help his sister or his friend—and then he accepted the new reality.

"How long?" he asked. "Am I going to live a day—a decade—another fifty years?"

The vampire smiled, then shrugged. "How long would you have lived before, if your life had not been interrupted? Only those beyond the Veil of Mystery possess such knowledge." He sighed, tugged at the sleeves of his elegant coat, and approached the bed again. "I must go soon and feed." He laid one of his cold alabaster hands to Aidan's head.

"You will forget what you were, in time, and, someday, even laugh at those who believe in such creatures as vampires and warlocks."

Aidan caught at the corpse-like hand with his own warm fingers, tried in vain to throw it away. "Wait—there is a woman—I want—I *have*—to find her—"

"You will always be Aidan Tremayne," the monster said. "Although your mind will soon dismiss her image, your heart will remember forever."

"But—"

"It is done," decreed the vampire quietly. And then he was gone, and Aidan tumbled into sleep, as if he'd been pushed over the edge of an abyss.

The next morning he ate solid food for the first time in more than two centuries and wondered why he was so excited over milk toast and weak tea. Wild, macabre images played chase in his mind; he told the pretty nurse he'd dreamed a vampire came to his room the night before, and she smiled and shook her head and pronounced the human brain a strange organ indeed.

Aidan had to agree, at least privately, for he held another picture in his mind, that of a lovely woman with short hair and large pixie eyes. He knew the gamine's name was Neely, but that was the sum total of what he remembered about her. It was miraculous, considering that he'd had to take his own identity from the packet of identification that had turned up on his bedside table one night while he slept.

He grew strong in the days to come, and his mind manufactured a complicated and quite viable history for him. Soon Aidan believed the assortment of facts and actually thought he remembered the corresponding experiences.

He was alone in the world, having been born to his Irish parents very late in life. He had money, a grand house outside of Bright River, Connecticut, and an impressive career as an artist.

Certain mysteries remained, however. Aidan still did not know where he'd been before he was discovered lying in the middle of that ancient circle of stones, naked as a newborn, or how he'd gotten there in the first place. The police were equally baffled, but after an initial interest and a barrage of questions in his hospital room, they'd stopped coming round. No doubt they'd written the patient off as a head case, and Aidan had to admit there were ample grounds for the idea.

He left the hospital in borrowed garb, bought himself new clothes, luggage, and toiletries, none of which he seemed to possess, spent one night in a London hotel, took a cab to the airport, and then flew to the United States.

In New York he rented a car and drove the rest of the way to Bright River.

Upon arriving in that small Connecticut town, he went immediately to the big house in the country. He didn't remember the place being so gloomy, he thought, as he went from room to room, flinging back the heavy draperies to let in the sunlight.

The snow was melting, and spring wasn't far off. He opened a few windows and doors to let in some fresh air.

Aidan wandered into the kitchen, humming. His breakfast, a muffin and a cup of coffee he'd grabbed at the airport, had long since worn off.

He opened one cupboard after another, amazed to find that there wasn't so much as a can of chili or a box of salt on the shelves. There were no plates, no cups, no knives, forks, or spoons.

Puzzled, he shrugged his shoulders, found a leather jacket in one of the closets, and left the house. There was a truck stop just down the road; Aidan was sure he remembered eating there once or twice.

He set out on foot, his hands jammed into the pockets of his coat, reassuring himself as he walked. Although the doctors in London had insisted that the gaps in his memory would surely close someday, he was still troubled.

For one thing, there was that name that haunted him, and the sweet face and figure that went with it. *Neely.* Who was she? She had touched his life, he was certain of that, but he couldn't remember where he'd known her, or when.

On the most basic level of his consciousness, a driving, urgent need to find the mysterious woman raged like a river at flood tide.

Aidan reached the truck stop, a noisy, cheerful place where the jukebox played too loudly, and felt better for having people around him. He took a seat at the counter and reached for a menu.

A friendly waitress—her name tag read "Doris"—took his order right away. While Aidan was sipping his coffee, a boy rushed in, waving a sheet of pink paper and beaming. He was about seven, Aidan guessed, and he had freckles and one missing tooth.

"Look, Doris!" the child cried, scrambling onto one of the stools, right next to Aidan. The lad glanced up at him, smiled with what could only be amiable recognition, nodded a greeting, and then turned his quicksilver attention back to Doris. "There's a letter from Aunt Neely!"

Aidan's heart somersaulted at the mention of the familiar name. It was unusual, after all, and it followed that he'd known her here in Bright River.

"What does she say, Danny?" Doris asked, grinning as she set a dinner of chicken-fried steak, mashed potatoes, and green beans in front of Aidan. She winked at him before turning her full attention on the boy.

Danny still clutched the letter in one grubby hand, and it was all Aidan could do not to reach out and snatch it away from him. "She isn't in Phoenix anymore—she's in Colorado," the kid announced importantly. "She was working in an office for a while, but now she's got a job in a steak house. Aunt Neely was bored sitting behind a desk. She says she's got all kinds of—all kinds of—" He paused and consulted the paper. "Nervous energy," he finished.

Aidan felt warm inside, and oddly amused, and he could explain neither emotion. He stuck his fork into his food, but his ravenous appetite was gone.

"And look at this great stamp!" Danny said, slapping a pink envelope down on the countertop.

Aidan strained, saw the return address: 1320 Tamarack

Road, Pine Hill, Colorado. "I used to collect stamps when I was a lad," he commented casually.

Danny beamed at him. "I must have a thousand of them. Aunt Neely sends them to me all the time. I've got a whole boxful from England."

England. That produced another vague recollection, more a feeling than an image. He'd been so certain that he'd met the elusive Neely in Bright River, but the mention of the country he'd just left touched a resonant chord in his spirit.

1320 Tamarack Road, he repeated to himself. *Pine Hill, Colorado.*

"This Aunt Neely of yours must be a pretty interesting lady," Aidan commented when Doris had given Danny a cup of hot chocolate and bustled off to wait on some new arrivals.

Danny's eyes were alight. "She is. She used to work for a real senator. He was a crook, and she almost got killed because she told the FBI what he was doing, but she's okay now."

Aidan frowned, for the child's words stimulated still another memory that wouldn't quite come into focus.

He finished his meal, returned to his huge, echoing house, and wandered restlessly from room to room.

In the morning, after a virtually sleepless night, Aidan called the car rental company and asked them to pick up the vehicle he'd driven from New York. Then he went out to the garage where his white Triumph Spitfire awaited him.

He smiled when the engine caught on the first try, and sped into Bright River. His first stop was the supermarket, where he purchased staples—milk and butter and bread—along with tea and potatoes, both fresh and frozen vegetables, and a thick steak. Passing a florist's shop, he suddenly stopped, grocery bags in his arms, oddly stricken by an enormous bunch of white roses on display in the window.

Aidan felt yet another tug at his deeper mind, and this one was patently uncomfortable. The flowers had some significance, he was certain, but that was all he knew.

Walking slowly, Aidan took the bags of food to the car

and set them on the passenger seat. Then he returned to the florist's window and stood there, looking at the roses, trying to work out why they stirred him so.

He swallowed, fighting an unaccountable desire to weep.

A gray-haired woman put her head outside the door of the shop and called, smiling, "Hello, there, Mr. Tremayne. Aren't those the finest roses you've ever seen? I buy them direct from a nice man upstate—he raises them in his own greenhouse. They smell wonderful, too, unlike those poor anemic things they sell in the supermarkets these days."

Since the woman had called Aidan by name, he probably knew her, but her identity eluded him. He smiled and went into the shop, drawn there by some curious force buried in his subconscious.

The scent of the roses was delicate, but it seemed to fill the small shop, overshadowing the perfumes rising from bright splashes of colorful flowers grouped in buckets and pots and vases.

Aidan selected eight of the roses, which were still tightly budded, and put money on the cluttered counter.

"Good day, Mrs. Crider," he heard himself say as he left the shop with the strange purchase. So he *had* known the woman's name, after all, though he still had no recollection of meeting her before.

How odd, he thought.

At home Aidan found a crystal vase in a cabinet in one of the bedrooms and put the roses in water even before bringing the groceries in from the car. He set the flowers on the marble top of the round antique table in his entry hall and then stood staring at them for a long time, his arms folded. He wondered why the sight satisfied him so much, and at the same time stirred in him a seemingly fathomless sense of loss.

He supposed he was probably a little crazy, which wasn't really surprising, considering that he'd been found naked in the middle of an English snowstorm, lying inside a circle of stones like some kind of sacrifice.

He'd get over it, he assured himself, turning from the

roses and heading outside for the bags he'd wedged into the passenger seat of his car. One of the few things he knew for certain was that he was a resilient sort, not easily broken.

Still, the scent of those flowers haunted him, and he kept going back to them, wondering and trying to remember.

Something else troubled him, though, even more than the roses did. It was the name Neely and the newfound knowledge that she lived in a place called Pine Hill, far away in Colorado.

After a steak dinner, which he devoured, Aidan retired to his study. The place was crammed with books, some of which he remembered reading and many that he didn't. The paintings on the walls were only vaguely familiar, though he knew he'd done them with his own hands.

He sighed, took an atlas from the shelf, and flipped through until he located a map of the United States. Bewildered, fascinated, *driven*, he sought and found Colorado, then traced the distance between that place and Connecticut with the tip of one finger.

Once again Aidan whispered the name of his private ghost: "Neely." Once again he searched his mind for something more than the fading image, but it was no use. Nothing came to him, except for a sensation of sweet sadness, and a yearning so keen that it brought tears to his eyes.

Suddenly Aidan was seized with a terror that he would forget the face, and even the name, as he had forgotten so many scattered details of his past.

He rummaged for paper, scrounged up a pencil, and bent over his desk, in such a hurry to sketch the features wavering in his thoughts that he wouldn't even take the time to sit down. He finished in a few strokes, wrote "Neely" beneath the rendering of the beautiful young woman with large, inquisitive eyes and short dark hair, and gave himself up to the sweeping relief of having captured her likeness before she vanished from his mind's eye.

Aidan sat looking at the drawing for a long time, memorizing every line and curve.

*   *   *

Neely huddled in the big leather chair facing her thera-pist's desk, her blue-jeaned legs curled beneath her. She bit her lower lip, silently reminding herself that she wouldn't be able to come to terms with the events of the past few months unless she talked about them. Still, getting started was hard.

"You work at the Steak-and-Saddle Restaurant, don't you?" Dr. Jane Fredricks prompted kindly, reviewing Neely's information sheet.

Neely nodded, grateful for the gentle push. "I wait tables there. I like being busy all the time—that way, I don't think so much—and since I work the night shift, I'm always with other people when it's dark."

"You're afraid of the dark?" the doctor asked.

Neely bit her lip again, then forced herself to go on. "Not exactly," she said. "I'm afraid of—of vampires. Except for one, I mean, and—oh, hell." She bit down hard on her right thumbnail.

Dr. Fredricks didn't grab the telephone and shout for help, or even gasp in surprise. "Vampires," she repeated, with no inflection at all, making a note on Neely's chart.

Neely's voice trembled. "Yes."

Dr. Fredricks met her gaze directly. "Go on," she said.

Neely stared at her for a moment. "I suppose you're go-ing to say there aren't any such things as vampires," she finally blurted out, "but there are. As crazy as it sounds, they really exist."

"I'm not questioning that," the doctor pointed out calmly. "You needn't convince me of anything, Neely—you're not on trial for a crime, you know. You needn't justify what you believe. Just talk."

Tears welled in Neely's eyes, blurring her vision, and she snatched a tissue from a box on the edge of Dr. Fredricks's desk to dry them. "I met my first vampire on Halloween night," she began, sniffling. "Isn't that fitting? Of course, I didn't *know* Aidan was a vampire then—I just thought he was, well, a little different—"

Dr. Fredricks nodded encouragingly.

Neely spilled the whole story, over the next forty-five minutes, and even though nothing was resolved at the end, she felt better for having told another human being what had happened to her.

"Are you going to lock me up in a rubber room?" she asked, toying with the pile of crumpled tissues in her lap.

The doctor laughed. "No, of course not."

Neely leaned forward in her chair. "Surely you don't believe there really are vampires?" she marveled.

"It doesn't matter what I believe," reasoned Dr. Fredricks. "We're here to talk about you. Can you come back next Tuesday?"

Chapter
—❧19❧—

Neely was just reaching for the handle of the front door at the Steak-and-Saddle when, through the glass, she saw chaos erupt. The fire alarm and the inside sprinkler system went off simultaneously, and patrons and staff alike shrieked and scurried in all directions. Water roared from the ceiling and spattered on the floor, the counter, the people, everything.

Neely stepped back from the entrance just in time to avoid being trampled, and even then she was nearly knocked into the flowerbed.

Duke Fuller, the owner of the restaurant, came out laughing, soaked from the top of his balding head to the soles of his expensive cowboy boots. Duke had a way of taking things in his stride, a trait that made most people like him right away.

"Go on, take the night off," he said, waving a huge hand at Neely as she stepped over the bricks bordering the petunia patch. "I got an idea Coach Riley's boys were behind this—they're feelin' their oats because of that basketball game they won—and I'm damn well gonna make 'em clean up the mess."

Some of the customers stayed to help, but Neely had been feeling drained since her session with Dr. Fredricks that afternoon, and she had cramps in the bargain. So she turned around, got back into the used Mustang she'd bought after arriving in Denver by plane, and drove home.

1320 Tamarack Road was a humble place, a one-bedroom

cottage with linoleum floors and plumbing noisy enough to disturb the dead, but it was solid and real, and Neely liked it. Besides, she spent very little time there, since she worked all night and, having developed chronic insomnia, sat reading in the library most of every day.

She hoped she'd be able to sleep, now that she'd told Dr. Fredricks the secret she hadn't been able to give voice to before. The effects of her problem were beginning to show; she had bruise-like shadows under her eyes, she was too thin, and she cried so easily that it was embarrassing.

Every day, every night, she told herself that Aidan would come back to her, and still there was no sign of him, and no word. Had he perished in the attempt to become mortal again? Or had he simply lost interest in her?

Neely hung her coat in the tiny closet just inside her front door and kicked off her crepe-soled waitress shoes as she moved across the living room. She flipped on the television set as she passed to the kitchen, which was really just three cabinets and a sink shoved into an alcove, and the frenzied cacophony of some commercial tumbled into the quiet.

The refrigerator yielded the remains of a carton of cottage cheese; Neely got a spoon and went back to the living room. There, she curled up in the ancient easy chair, still in her polyester uniform and her pantyhose, to eat and watch the news channel.

Neely kept expecting to miss politics, all of a sudden, to yearn for the excitement, the prestige, and the intrigue of being in the center of things. All she missed, however, all she ever yearned for, was the sight of Aidan Tremayne, and the sound of his voice. She could adjust to the rest, even the outlandish truth of what he was.

She sighed, spooning a small heap of cottage cheese onto her tongue even though, as usual, she had no appetite. It was downright crazy to be this miserable, she thought, chewing and then forcing herself to swallow—and over a missing monster, no less—but she couldn't seem to lift herself out of the doldrums.

Neely took another bite, then could bear no more and

set the thin plastic carton aside, atop last week's issue of *TV Guide.* She got out of her chair, crossed the cool, smooth floor to the television set, and switched channels until she found one showing classic movies.

When a forties-style Count Dracula appeared on the screen, resplendent in his high-colored black silk cape, Neely made a soft, abrupt sound that might have been either a chuckle or a sob. The Count had very white skin, and his hair came to a dramatic widow's peak on his forehead, but of course it was his overlong and extremely pointed incisors that marked him as the dreaded vampire.

Neely reached out for the old-fashioned channel knob— the TV, like the rest of the furniture, had come with the house—but she couldn't quite complete the move. She stepped backward, away from the set, filled with a strange tangle of emotions—panic, joy, fascination, a fierce desire to deny that any such creature could ever have existed.

She went into the bedroom and exchanged her uniform and pantyhose for warm flannel pajamas, figuring that, by the time she returned, either the movie would be over or she would have found the fortitude to turn to something else.

Instead Neely moved like a sleepwalker, sank numbly to the floor in front of her chair, and sat watching as if she'd been hypnotized. She knew she should get up, go to bed, read a book, take a bath, do anything besides just sitting there obsessed, but she couldn't gather the strength to move. Her gaze slid to the telephone on the other side of the room; she wondered if she was finally going to collapse under the strain. Maybe she should call Dr. Fredricks, right now. . . .

And say what? *I'm so sorry to bother you, Doctor, but it seems I'm watching an old vampire movie—a hokey one, at that— and I can't bring myself to miss a moment.*

Neely caught her right thumbnail between her teeth and bit. The movie went on, darkness gathered at the windows, and still she sat there, mesmerized.

A sudden burst of light, barely glimpsed out of the corner of her right eye, made Neely jump and cry out.

Valerian himself was standing in front of the couch,

gaunt and even somewhat scarred, but for all of that, just as magnificent as ever. Instead of his usual dashing evening garb, he wore medieval garments, leggings, soft leather shoes, and a tunic of rough brown wool. A mean-looking sword dangled from a scabbard on his belt.

Watching the screen image of Count Dracula, the vampire laughed aloud.

Neely's inertia finally left her, she scrambled to her feet and looked around for a weapon, but all she found was the cottage cheese.

Valerian's gaze sliced to hers. "What will you do," he drawled, "stab me through the heart with a teaspoon?"

Neely's own heart seemed to bounce spasmodically between her breastbone and her spine. Valerian had been cordial enough in the past, but she had never deluded herself, for so much as a moment, that he was her friend.

"What do you want?" she asked.

Valerian sighed, one hand fiddling with the fancy molded steel handle of his sword. "It would take more time than I have to tell you that, my lady," he said sadly.

Neely collapsed into the easy chair, since she couldn't stand any longer. Now that the first rush of fear had subsided a little, she wanted to ask about Aidan. At the same time she was afraid—what if Valerian answered that the experiment had failed and Aidan was dead? What if he said his friend was alive and well but had decided not to go to all the trouble of loving a mortal woman after all?

"He loves you still," Valerian said; clearly, he found her thoughts as easy to read as one of those big billboards out by the freeway. His voice seemed to echo the combined sorrows of the ages, deep and profound and eternal.

Neely raised one hand to her throat. "He survived, then."

Valerian's great shoulders seemed to sag beneath his tunic; he was the very image of weary despair. "After a fashion, yes. He's a mere man—good-looking, but really quite ordinary, when you consider what he once was. All eternity would not be time enough to work out the puzzle of why Aidan, or anyone, would make such a sacrifice."

A shout of joy rose in Neely, but she stopped it in the middle of her chest. She wasn't about to put her most private feelings on display for the likes of Valerian, but there was another reason for her reticence as well. Aidan had become a man again, as he'd dreamed of doing, but he'd apparently made no attempt to find her.

Even without his supernatural powers, it shouldn't have been that hard to track her down, she thought, heartbroken. True, she hadn't left a forwarding address on file at the Bright River post office or anything so obvious as that, but Aidan could have reached her through Ben if he'd half tried.

Neely's older brother was a stubborn man, and he probably wouldn't have told Aidan where to find her, but he would surely have acted as an intermediary and passed on any messages.

"Aidan doesn't remember you," Valerian said, mind reading again. "Not completely, at least. He clings to a few scattered images, as I understand it, but in time even those will fade. The Brotherhood thought it better if he could not recall too much of his old life."

Fury and relief warred in Neely's soul, fury because someone had come between her and Aidan, relief because he'd *wanted* to remember her.

She sat up a little straighter. "Is that why you came here? To tell me everything is over between Aidan and me? I won't accept that, Valerian—I won't believe it unless I hear it from him personally."

He looked miserable to her, though that could have been an act. Valerian had loved Aidan—he probably loved him still—and it was unlikely that he had Neely's best interests at heart. Or those of any human, for that matter.

"Be that as it may," he responded in a deep voice. "It must be ended. No mortal can be allowed to go about with knowledge of the sacred things. It is dangerous."

"Sacred?" Neely snapped, driven by impulse, as usual,

rather than good sense. "What an odd word to use, in reference to creatures who drink blood to sustain themselves!"

Valerian's countenance seemed to darken, and he towered like some mountain thrust suddenly up from level ground; he was a black cloud, roiling and huge, ready to erupt with lightning and thunder. "I will not debate semantics with a mortal!" he roared.

"No problem," Neely assured him hastily.

The vampire took a few moments to compose himself, visibly smoothing his ruffled dignity. Then, imperiously, he announced, "For the sake of all who walk the night and take the communion of blood, this foolishness must be ended at once." He paused, rubbing his chin with one hand and regarding Neely thoughtfully. "I would be well within my rights to feed upon you. However, I have decided that sparing you shall be my last tribute to Aidan."

Neely let out her breath in a rush, only then discovering that she'd been holding it in her lungs and sinuses. In the next instant Valerian was standing close to her, though she hadn't seen him move.

He raised one hand, laid it to her forehead, like a clergyman offering a blessing.

"No vampires," he whispered. "There are no vampires, and there never were. You will forget, and any mortals who knew of your love for Aidan will give up all memory of it as well. . . ."

Neely fought the barrage of thoughts as long as she could, but Valerian's mind was much stronger than her own; soon her consciousness was swamped in inky darkness.

The following Tuesday, Neely arrived at Dr. Fredricks's office right on time, settled into the big chair, and waited expectantly.

"I believe we were discussing vampires last week," the psychologist said, closing Neely's chart and settling back to regard her patient.

Neely laughed. "Vampires? You're joking, right?"

The doctor frowned. "Joking?"

Neely thought back and remembered telling Dr. Fredricks about her job in Senator Hargrove's office and the subsequent adventures with the mob, in detail, but that was all. "I—I talked about vampires?" she asked in a small voice. She felt the color drain from her face.

Dr. Fredricks smiled reassuringly, opened the folder on her desk, and read back the outlandish story Neely had evidently told her the week before.

Neely shook her head, frantic to deny what she did not remember. She blurted out the short version of her adventures with Senator Dallas Hargrove and his criminal associates, in a flash flood of wild, eager words.

The psychologist digested the account in respectful silence, then said gently, "Neely, you've obviously undergone quite a series of traumas in the past year. Is it any wonder that you invented a flock of vampires—a sort of theater company of the mind—to help you sort through it all?"

The reasoning seemed sound, but Neely still had absolutely no recollection of talking about vampires. She hadn't even thought of the creatures since last Halloween, in fact, when her nephew, Danny, had worn wax fangs and a plastic cape to go out trick-or-treating.

"I guess that could be it," she said tremulously.

Dr. Fredricks seemed to be on some private roll. "Often," she said confidently, "the human mind will create personal myths in order to cope with some struggle in the unconscious. Generally these little dramas are played out in our dreams, but in some cases we feel called upon to produce something more flamboyant."

From what the doctor had read from her chart, Neely thought uneasily, her own presentation had boasted a cast of thousands. She'd actually mentioned names, if the psychologist's account was to be believed—*Maeve. Valerian. Tobias.*

She sank back in her chair, shaking. "Could I have a glass of water, please?"

*   *   *

After a week of driving west, thinking all the while that he must have lost his mind as well as large parts of his memory, Aidan crossed the Colorado border. He stopped at a motel that night, wolfed down a bagful of fast food while watching the Comedy Channel on cable TV, showered, and slept like a mastodon entombed in a glacier.

The next morning he bought a road map of the state, located Pine Hill, and pointed himself and his Spitfire in that direction. He had no idea what he was going to do when he arrived in the small mountain town, beyond finding the elusive Neely. Maybe when he looked into those big, luminous eyes of hers, he would remember whatever it was that had happened between them and understand the fascination that tormented him so much.

He arrived in Pine Hill in the middle of a sunny, late-winter afternoon. It was an ordinary place in itself, like a hundred other small towns all over the West, but the scenery was spectacular. The mountains were capped with snow, the landscape densely carpeted in blue-green trees that marched on and on, as far as he could see.

Aidan drove into a filling station parking lot, took the folded sketch from the inside pocket of his jacket, and spread it over the steering wheel to study it for what must have been the hundredth time.

With one index finger he traced the outline of her cheek, the lips that almost smiled—but not quite—the hair he somehow knew was soft and glossy.

For a time Aidan just sat there, engaged in a peculiar mixture of mourning and celebration. Then he folded the sketch and tucked it back into his pocket, as carefully as if it were a map that would lead him to some incomparable treasure.

He frowned as he drove back onto the slushy gray asphalt of the highway. It was just as likely that this was some sort of fool's errand. After all, if whatever had passed between him and this woman had been right and good and real, why weren't they together? Why had he blocked every detail besides her face and her first name from his mind?

Aidan passed a construction sign announcing the building of a condominium complex, shifted into reverse, and backed up to read it again. There was the usual builder's hype, but someone had tacked on a HELP WANTED notice, and that was what had captured Aidan's true interest.

He had a wallet full of money, and much more stashed away in various trust funds and bank accounts, so it wasn't the prospect of a paycheck that attracted him. He felt a craving, in the very depths of his muscles, to work at hard, physical labor, to sweat and pound and carry things under the bright light of the sun.

To put off driving to 1320 Tamarack Road, wanting to savor the prospect a while longer, Aidan located the construction company's temporary office instead. Within an hour he had been hired as a day laborer—he was to start in the morning and arrive with his own tools—and he felt as though he'd just found a part of himself that had long been missing.

He rented a motel room, hastened to the hardware store for a hammer, a tool belt, a handsaw, and a measuring tape, along with a few things the salesman recommended, then bought work clothes and boots at the mercantile. That done, Aidan consumed another of the fast-food lunches he seemed to love—just where he'd acquired the taste was one of many things he didn't quite remember—and continued his search for the woman of mystery.

Neely was waiting tables at the Steak-and-Saddle that night when, through the restaurant's wide front windows, she saw the small white sports car swing into the parking lot and come to a flourishing stop near the door.

She tightened her grasp on the handle of the coffeepot she carried, wondering why the sight of a simple automobile should shake her so. First, she'd babbled out some crazy story about vampires to her doctor, and promptly forgotten the whole thing, and now she was freaking out over traffic.

She'd better get a hold of herself.

Neely poured coffee for her customers and took the pot

back to the burner without glancing at the door, even though she felt the rush of cool air when it opened. She was on her way to table 4, carrying two pieces of lemon meringue pie, when she saw the dark-haired man.

He was a stranger, and yet Neely felt a deep connection with him, an almost savage wrenching. It was nothing new; no, this was something ancient, something predating the moon and stars.

He smiled, inclined his head slightly, and said, "Hello, Neely."

The pie plates clattered to the floor. Neely didn't know this man, and yet she did. She knew everything about him, and nothing at all. She had a vague recollection of thrashing on a bed while he loved her, though that was impossible, of course, since they had never met.

She bolted back to the kitchen for a wet cloth, and when she returned, the newcomer was crouched on the floor, gathering up the plates and broken pieces of pie. He took the cloth from her and wiped the tiles.

"Do I know you?" Neely whispered, blushing and painfully conscious of the fact that practically everyone in the restaurant was staring at them with amused interest. His face seemed as familiar to her as her own, so maybe she'd just conveniently forgotten him, the way she'd forgotten telling Dr. Fredricks about those damn vampires.

He shrugged as he rose gracefully to his full height. "Maybe. My name is Aidan Tremayne."

Again Neely felt an inner earthquake; again she had no idea why. "Neely Wallace," she answered. She was flustered all over again. "How did you know my first name?" she demanded.

Tremayne regarded her in wry silence for a moment, then nodded toward the shamble of plates and pies and cleaning cloth in her hands. "Perhaps you'd better tend to business, Miss Wallace. I wouldn't want to be the cause of your getting the sack."

Neely bustled away in a quiet panic, gallantly pretending that all was well. She disposed of the spilled food and dirty dishes, washed and dried her hands, and made a second attempt to carry pie to the people at table 4. She succeeded that time, and everyone in the restaurant cheered.

Neely's cheeks were crimson when she rounded the counter and made herself wait on Aidan Tremayne, who sat at the far end, watching her with laughter in his indigo-colored eyes. "What will you have?" she said, tapping her pencil against the top of her order pad.

He smiled. "I'll take the special," he said, closing the menu. "For now."

Neely narrowed her gaze. She wasn't angry, exactly—as a waitress, she met more than her share of smart guys, and most of them didn't mean any harm. No, it was her own overwhelming attraction to this stranger, the way he'd made her pulse flutter erotically, that troubled her.

"Before I get you the liver and onions," she said in a low voice, "I want you to tell me how you knew my name."

He leaned toward her. "I'm psychic," he whispered.

After that a tour bus arrived, and a crowd poured into the restaurant, and Neely was too busy to pay any more attention to Aidan Whoever.

Tremayne, supplied a voice in her harried heart.

The next day Neely worked the afternoon and early evening shift again, and Aidan came into the restaurant for supper, in the company of half a dozen workers from the construction site just up the mountainside. He was freshly showered and wearing clean but casual clothes, and Neely felt a sting of annoyance because he didn't seem to notice her, even when she asked for his order.

"Who's that?" Angie, another waitress, inquired with interest, her warm-syrup eyes bright with speculation as she looked at Aidan.

Neely glared at the other woman. "He's just some construction worker," she snapped, reaching for a steak platter and a cheeseburger in a basket.

Angie popped her gum in good-natured defiance. "Yum," she growled under her breath. "I think I need some remodeling."

Neely stormed away to deliver her order.

She didn't see Aidan again until Sunday, her day off. She'd been to the supermarket and was carrying in groceries when the expensive sports car purred to a stop behind her dented Mustang.

Neely let the wooden screen door slam behind her when she went into the living room, but she felt a contradictory little lurch of pleasure in her middle when she came outside for another bag of groceries. Aidan was still there, leaning against his Triumph, his arms folded across his chest.

"I've come a long way to find you, Neely," he said quietly. "And I won't be easy to put off."

She felt as though she'd been riding a roller coaster and had stepped off before the thing came alongside the platform. She would have dropped the second shopping bag, but Aidan reached out and caught it just as it slipped from her arms.

"How did you know my name?" This time she wasn't going to let him sidestep the question.

"I own a house in Bright River, Connecticut," he said. "I think I must have seen you there."

Neely saw the confusion and bewilderment in those ink-blue eyes, and it stopped her, put a cap on her rising temper. "My brother, Ben, manages a café and motel outside Bright River," she said lamely. "I worked for him for a while, waiting tables and cleaning rooms."

The relief she saw in Aidan's face was too sincere to be false. Something very weird was going on here.

"That must have been where we met," he said. Then he carried the groceries up the walk, onto the porch, and past the green-painted screen door. "Nice place."

Neely felt herself flush again. Suddenly she was embarrassed by the chipped linoleum floors, the television set with foil flags on its antenna, and the cheap, ugly curtains made of dime-store fabric.

Aidan set the bag on the counter, beside the one Neely had brought in a minute earlier, looked back at her over one well-made shoulder, and grinned.

"You're not thinking I'm some kind of lecher, I hope," he said. "I'm a gentleman, Neely, and you've nothing to fear from me. Why don't you stop looking like a deer that wants to bolt into the nearest thicket?"

She smiled and relaxed a little. "Where are you from originally?" she asked, still keeping her distance as she took off her peacoat and hung it up. "You sound English."

"Perish the thought!" he said with drama and yet another nuclear-powered grin. "I'm Irish, though I've spent most of my adult life in the United States."

Neely wanted to know everything there was to know about Aidan Tremayne. She also wanted never to have met him, because he did things to her senses that made her deliciously uncomfortable.

He stayed for dinner.

Neely guessed she still would have had a chance if she'd just let things go at that, but Aidan asked her to go for a ride in his fancy car, with the top down and the moonlight playing over them both like liquid silver, and she couldn't resist.

On a high point overlooking all of Pine Hill, he parked the car, leaned over, and kissed her. His lips moved lightly against hers at first, almost mischievously, and yet Neely felt as if someone had just threaded her onto a live wire, like a bead onto a necklace. Things awakened inside her and collided in a mad rush to find their right places.

"I've never known you," Aidan said huskily, when the kiss finally ended. "And yet I've *always* known you. Can you explain that to me, Neely?"

She thought—as best she could, that is, given the helter-skelter state of her emotions. "Maybe we were together in a past life," she offered.

Aidan smiled. "Maybe," he agreed without real conviction, and then he kissed her once more.

"I want to see you again," he said a few moments later.

Neely could only nod.

After that she and Aidan were together for at least a part of every day. He rented an apartment on the other side of town, and she helped him furnish it. He chose gracious things, antiques and folk art and one very good painting, and Neely wondered what kind of work he'd done before taking up construction.

"I was a painter," he said when she finally worked up the nerve to ask him. They'd eaten roast chicken, corn on the cob, and salad at her place, and he was helping her take down the horrible living room curtains so she could replace them with the snappy white eyelet ones she'd just bought.

Neely felt afraid, as if she were trying to cross an expanse of wafer-thin ice spanning a deep and frigid river. Caring too much would be the equivalent of falling through; she couldn't afford to love this good-looking, bewildering man because he was just passing by, like the other men who'd come to Pine Hill to build condominiums.

"Did something happen?"

Aidan looked at her curiously, raising one dark eyebrow in that ponderous way he had. "What do you mean, 'did something happen'?"

Neely shrugged, crumpling the new curtains because she was holding them too tightly. "Last time I looked, you were working on a construction site," she said, and though she tried to offer the statement lightly, it came out sounding momentous.

He grinned. "Nothing dramatic. I just got tired of painting. I'm a sensualist, I guess," he said. "I enjoy the feeling of sunlight on my skin, and the way my muscles move underneath." His blue gaze seemed to caress her for a moment, making her flesh tingle beneath her clothes. "I like everything about being a man."

Neely turned quickly away. Ever since that first time Aidan had kissed her, she'd been sizzling like so much water spilled onto a hot griddle. Some primitive sense warned that he had the power to hurt her as no other man ever could, and Neely's emotions were fragile as it was.

If she waited long enough, maybe he'd go away, and she wouldn't have to take the dangerous chance of loving him.

Chapter

—❧20❧—

Twilight gathered behind the mountaintops, then spilled down over the throngs of evergreen trees, shrouding them in pale apricot, and after that lavender, and finally a velvety purple. Neely and Aidan watched the spectacle from the window in the dining room of his apartment, where they sat at the round oak table, each gripping the other's hand.

Neely's emotions were very close to the surface, and the glorious sunset brought tears to her eyes. She moved to rise from her chair, but Aidan held her in place by gentle force.

"Neely," he said quietly. "Don't run away. It's time we talked."

She wanted to look anywhere but at Aidan, but she couldn't; his gaze seemed to hold hers fast. "About what?"

"You know 'about what,' " Aidan sighed with a touch of exasperation.

Neely bit her lower lip for a moment. "You're leaving," she blurted out. "You've been in Pine Hill for six weeks, the construction job is about to end, and—"

"Yes," Aidan said. His dark blue eyes reflected the faint smile that touched his mouth. "I'm leaving."

She sniffled and straightened her shoulders. "Okay, good," she said. "So long." She tried again to stand, intending to bolt, but Aidan wouldn't release her hand. She sat trembling for a few moments, refusing to look at him, but then the compulsion grew too strong. "What do you want?" she snapped.

He said nothing, sensing somehow that there was more she needed to say, silently insisting that she come out with it.

Neely shoved her fingers through her hair. "I know we—we haven't made love or anything, but—well—I thought something was happening between us. There's a lot of electricity, or so it seemed to me. Now you're just going to leave."

"There's a great deal you don't know about me, Neely," Aidan said sadly, staring not at her but through the window, glazed with light on the inside now, dark beyond. "And a great deal I don't know about myself."

She narrowed her eyes and sniffled again, then dashed the back of her free hand—Aidan still held the other—across her wet cheek. "I know you're an artist, that you have a house in Connecticut, that you were born in Ireland but raised in the United States—"

He silenced her with an infinitely tender glance. "All those things are true," he said, running his finger lightly over her knuckles. "At least, they *seem* true. But there are some serious gaps in my memory. You know about my adventures in England, for instance—how I woke up in the hospital, only to be told that I'd been found naked as a flounder in that old pile of stones. What the devil was I up to before that, Neely? How did I get there? Am I some kind of madman? What *else* have I done that I've conveniently forgotten?"

Neely slipped out of her chair, still holding Aidan's hand, and settled on his lap. From the moment she'd met him, she'd wanted him, with every breath she drew and every beat of her heart, but there had been a certain courtly, old-fashioned restraint in his manner. "I don't know," she assured him softly. "I've got a few ghosts of my own, remember—all that babble to my doctor about vampires, for one thing." He smiled at that but didn't interrupt, and Neely went on earnestly. "There are a lot of mysteries in this life, Aidan Tremayne, but there are also a few things I'm absolutely certain of, and here they are: You are a fine, sweet, gentle man, good to the core of your soul, and I love you."

Aidan touched her trembling lower lip with the tip of an index finger. "Suppose you're wrong?" The pain of his own uncertainty was clearly audible in his voice. "Oh, Neely, what if I'm some sort of maniac?"

She rested her forehead against his. "I'll take my chances." She pulled in a deep breath, let it out in a rush, and sat back to look into his eyes. "Is that why you haven't made love to me, Aidan? Because you're afraid you're really a modern-day Jack the Ripper and the fact has simply slipped your mind?"

He chuckled, but there was anguish in the sound. "No, it isn't that—I know I could never hurt you, under any circumstances." Aidan actually looked shy, and she would have sworn there was a blush under that spring suntan of his. "The truth is, I seem to be rather behind the times when it comes to sex. I feel as if I've been searching for you for a thousand years, and when we make love, it's going to be a sacred event."

Neely's tough, scarred heart softened, then melted entirely. "Well, then," she said with sniffly briskness and a pinch of sarcasm, "it makes perfect sense that you're planning to leave, doesn't it?"

Aidan gave her a brief, nibbling kiss, the kind that always drove her crazy and left her aching for hours afterward.

"It does," he affirmed, a few sweetly torturous moments later, "when you consider that I'm asking you to go with me, as my wife."

It seemed that the floor buckled a little just then, and Neely tightened her arm around Aidan's neck, afraid she would tumble from his lap. "You want to marry me?"

Aidan grinned, looking damnably Irish and outrageously handsome. "Do I ever," he replied.

Neely was in a state of blessed shock. All her life she'd been waiting for a man like Aidan, one who could make her heart sing, and help her to be her best self, and she'd been disappointed more than once. In short, Aidan Tremayne seemed too good to be true. "You haven't even said you love me," she pointed out.

He took her chin in his hand and then kissed her, with slow, deliberate heat and a skill that incited a riot of sensation inside her, then drew back. "Haven't I?" he whispered. "Funny, that's what I thought I was saying when I told you I've been searching for you for a thousand years. I do love you, Neely. Very, very much."

She buried her face in his neck and held him tightly for a long time, overwhelmed with happiness, struggling to assimilate it somehow.

At long last he stood, holding Neely close and looking down into her eyes. "Here, now," he said gruffly. "I'd best take you home, Miss Wallace, before I break my own rule and carry you straight off to bed."

There was nowhere Neely would rather be that night than in Aidan Tremayne's bed, for her senses had been humming with anticipation since the first time he'd kissed her, weeks before. "You know what they say about rules," she ventured tentatively.

Aidan ran the pad of his thumb over her moist lower lip. "This is one I don't mean to break," he said. He held her a little closer, though, and went on. "It's a gypsy's life I'm offering you, Neely. You'll never want for anything, but I've no idea when or where we'll settle. I want to see everything, be everywhere—to dance on mountaintops and make love to you on star-washed beaches—"

She stood on tiptoe to kiss him. "Such a romantic," she said with a happy sigh. "Tell me, though—what about that big fancy house of yours, back in Connecticut?"

He sighed again, resting his strong, work-callused hands on her shoulders. "There's nothing there that I want, Neely—it's as if the place belonged in some other man's life, not my own. I'm thinking of signing it over to one of the universities or perhaps some charitable organization." He frowned pensively. "Would that bother you?"

Neely shook her head. "I think it's a wonderful idea,"

she said. For now, Aidan was all she needed or wanted; she would take all future days and moments one by one. "Let's get ourselves married, Mr. Tremayne."

He laughed, hooked his thumbs through the loops at the back of Neely's jeans, and hoisted her against him for one deliciously frustrating moment. "The sooner, the better," he answered.

Aidan found Neely's jacket and politely escorted her outside to his car. "Time you were tucked up in your own bed, fast asleep," he said when she was settled in the passenger seat and he was behind the wheel.

Neely blushed and kept her attention focused on the windshield, which had become a star-spangled mural. "Kindly stop reminding me that I'm going to be all by myself."

Aidan grinned, starting the Spitfire's powerful engine and deftly working the gearshift. "We'll be together soon enough," he assured her. "Be patient."

Neely was anything but patient.

That night she tossed and turned, catching only fleeting minutes of sleep. She felt like a complicated clock, wound so tightly that her inner springs were about to burst out in every direction.

The following day Neely gave notice at the Steak-and-Saddle, and Duke jokingly told her to go ahead and clear out, because he didn't want her underfoot for another two weeks.

She was so grateful that she flung her arms around the older man's neck and gave him a resounding kiss on the cheek.

She and Aidan applied for their marriage license later that morning at the courthouse, and then they went shopping for their new home.

Neely referred to their house on wheels as a recreational vehicle, while Aidan called it a "caravan." It was a sleek, shiny marvel, complete with its own bathroom, a queen-size bed, and a small kitchen. There were so many options that

Neely expected to spend at least a week immersed in the owner's manual.

Of course, it would be some week far in the future, when the novelty of being a gypsy bride had worn off.

Aidan didn't seem to mind trading in the sports car; he took an object from the glove box, dropped it into his jacket pocket, patted the vehicle's gleaming hood, and walked away. He and Neely were rambling down the road in their RV when he took one hand off the wheel and extended a small box to Neely.

"There were only two things in the Connecticut house that I wanted," he said. "Here they are."

Neely's hands trembled as she accepted an exquisite old music box, surely an antique. When she opened it, a few slow, poignant notes drifted out, then there was silence. She started to rewind the key, hungry to hear more, and that was when she saw the ring glimmering in the worn velvet lining of the lid.

Aidan had pulled the large vehicle off to the side of the road and sat watching her with his heart in his eyes. "According to these strange memories of mine, that ring has been in the Tremayne family for almost a century."

It was a simple piece of jewelry, a wide gold band with a large marquis diamond set at an angle. Inside that magnificent, multifaceted stone glimmered the sunlight of a hundred summers and the sparkle of as many stars.

"It's so beautiful," Neely whispered, slipping the ring onto her finger. It was only slightly too big.

"It can't begin to compete with you," Aidan replied.

That evening Neely found it even more difficult than usual to say good night to Aidan. Yes, she wanted him to make love to her, but even more than that, she longed to sleep in his arms, naked and trusting.

Neely spent the next day cleaning her rented house and packing up the few personal belongings she'd brought with her when she left Connecticut. She found a store selling antique clothing and jewelry in the next town and bought a lovely old dress of ivory and silk, made sometime in the twenties, along with an ornate sterling silver broach, studded with marcasite.

She hung the dress on her tiny back porch to air through the afternoon and evening, then mended a few tiny tears in the fabric while watching television. Even with everything she had to do, it seemed to Neely that time was passing with all the speed of a snail stuck in neutral.

She was lying on the lumpy sofa in her living room, legs sticking straight up in the air and waving her feet back and forth to dry the polish on her toenails, when the jingling of the telephone made her start. She grappled for the receiver and nearly fell off the sofa in the process.

"Hello?"

Her brother Ben's voice echoed warmly in her ear. "Hello, Sis. So, how does it feel to be almost married?"

"You tell me," Neely responded with a grin. The relationship between Ben and Doris had developed into a grand passion, and the two of them were planning a summer wedding.

Ben laughed. "Sweetheart, if you're as happy as I am, then you're doing just fine."

Joyous tears blurred Neely's vision. "How's Danny? Is he glad about having Doris in the family?"

"He's crazy about her." Ben was quiet for a moment. "Neely, you're really sure this is what you want to do, aren't you? I mean, getting married is a pretty big step."

Neely lifted the hem of her T-shirt to dry her cheeks. "I know it sounds strange, but I've never been more certain of anything in my life. I was born to love this man, Ben, and he was born to love me."

"All the same," Ben said grudgingly, "if he mistreats you, I'll take out his teeth. You tell him that for me."

Neely smiled. "Okay, big brother," she said obediently. "I'll tell him, but you don't need to worry your bushy-bearded head, because Aidan Tremayne is a gentleman."

After that, Neely talked to Danny for a few minutes, and then to Doris. When the phone call was over, and everyone had congratulated everyone else, she went into her room to admire her wedding dress, which hung on the outside of her closet door.

The moonlight lent the gown a special sort of magic, catching in the pearl buttons rimmed with tiny crystals, making the exquisite, hand-worked lace seem almost new again.

Neely fell asleep admiring it.

Aidan slept with the peaceful abandon only a mortal is capable of, dark hair rumpled, one arm flung up over his head.

Valerian watched him in silence, knowing he shouldn't linger, but not quite able to tear himself away. A thousand times the dark angel had wanted to reach out his hand and restore Aidan's memory of all he had been before, and he wanted that now, as keenly as ever. He even went so far as to brush his fingers lightly over Aidan's forehead, causing him to stir in his sleep, but in the end Valerian drew back.

Rare vampire tears glittered in his eyes. *We could have owned the stars*, he told the sleeping one.

Aidan rolled onto his side, still deeply asleep, and murmured a single word. And with that one word he broke Valerian's heart.

"Neely," he said.

Suddenly a burst of strangely dark light filled the room. Valerian raised his eyes and felt the most abject horror he had ever known, for Lisette stood on the opposite side of the bed, majestic and evil, plainly restored to all her former powers. Her once-scarred skin was unmarked, her auburn hair was as lush and gleaming as ever, her blue-green eyes bright with triumph, fury, and madness.

She looked upon the sleeping Aidan for a long moment, as if to devour every line and fiber of him, and then raised her eyes to Valerian's face again.

Lisette laughed softly, musically, and Aidan stirred on the mattress, unaware that his soul was about to be stolen for a second time.

"Did you think, Valerian, that I would let him go so easily as all that?" Her face became hard and horrible for a moment; no doubt, she was considering the events of recent months. "Aidan is mine—my creation, my treasure. I will not give him up."

At last Valerian found his voice. "You must," he said hoarsely. "If you have any mercy in you, any decency—"

She laughed again, but it was a silent laughter, much like the unspoken language vampires and other immortals use to communicate with each other, and Aidan did not seem to hear it.

'Mercy,' is it? 'Decency'! Oh, but that's amusing! What good are such fatuous concepts to me, Lisette, the Queen of all vampyres?

Valerian closed his eyes briefly, searching his mind and his soul for a solution, finding none except to plead Aidan's case and, if necessary, to fight Lisette to the death. He held little hope of success either way, however, for the queen was not one to listen to reason, and she had plainly regained her powers, perhaps even garnered new ones through the peculiar graces of suffering.

Think what Aidan has been through, he reasoned, touching the forehead of the sleeping vampire-turned-mortal. *Imagine what he risked, what he endured, to be a man again, to find his way in the mortal world. How can you—even you—take that from him? Great Zeus, Lisette—if you must have a plaything, take me.*

Lisette glared, plainly displeased, and folded her white arms over the even whiter, flowing fabric of her Grecian gown. *You?* she scoffed. *Do you think me a fool, Valerian? You are as elusive as quicksilver—the moment I turned my back, you would be off dallying with some fledgling. No, I don't want you— you're far too troublesome as it is.*

Slowly Valerian rounded the bed, forced himself between Lisette and the still oblivious Aidan. He loomed above the older and more powerful vampire, the first female blood-drinker ever made, and called upon all the showmanship and bravado he possessed.

Go from here, he commanded. *This one you shall not have.*

Lisette was clearly undaunted. The sorceress drew herself up, and Valerian felt her powers focus on his midsection just before she sent him hurtling backward over Aidan's bed to crash silently against the opposite wall.

Valerian recovered quickly and moved to stand and resist her further, but she struck him again with another of her purely mental blows, and he felt himself paralyzed, not just physically but spiritually as well. He watched helplessly as Lisette stepped close to the bed again, knelt, and reverently smoothed Aidan's dark hair.

Valerian struggled to shout a warning to the sleeping mortal, but he could not force a sound past his throat. He had, he realized, vastly underestimated Lisette's powers.

I will make you love me, the vampire queen told Aidan. *I will show you the stars, and we will not be parted again. No power on earth, or in heaven, shall ever separate us.*

Inwardly Valerian shrieked in protest, and his helplessness was in those moments the greatest burden he had ever been made to bear, either as a vampire or as a human man.

No power . . . Lisette vowed again as she bent, fangs plainly in view, to give Aidan the fatal kiss, the one that would damn him for the second time, and for always.

Aidan made a soft, sleepy sound, innocent as a child as he wandered in his dreams, and Valerian could make no move to save him. The only response he could manage, in fact, was the sheen of tears that blurred his vision.

Please! he cried out silently to any benevolent being who might be nearby. *In the name of justice—this cannot happen!*

It appeared there was no hope, for Lisette moistened a patch of skin on Aidan's neck, using her tongue, her eyes raised to meet Valerian's. She was enjoying his torment, the damnable, whoring witch, and he swore that even if it cost him his own existence, if it took a hundred years or a thousand, he would avenge the events of this night.

Lisette's long vampire teeth glimmered, pearly in the dim moonlight, and she moved to lunge, to bury her fangs in Aidan's sleep-warmed flesh.

Valerian managed an anguished groan, but he still could not move. Still, the fog in his mind began to clear at last, and he was able to send a single name, in itself a plea for help, echoing into the universe.

Maeve.

In the next instant, just when Lisette's fangs would have broken Aidan's skin and begun to draw upon the healthy blood flowing through the veins and arteries beneath, the chamber seemed to burst with blinding, silvery light.

Valerian's heart surged with hope, though he knew this was not Maeve, or Tobias, or any of the vampires of his acquaintance. No, this was a holy being, sanctioned by Heaven itself, and as such it would surely destroy Valerian.

If Aidan could be saved, he didn't care.

The being of light seemed to push the walls out with its power; Valerian was sure the room, indeed the building itself, would explode into splinters. He soon realized, however, that the temporal world was not affected by this phenomenon—even if Aidan had been awake, he would not have seen or heard anything out of the ordinary.

Humans.

Slowly the entity took on shape and splendor, and Valerian realized that the newcomer was an angel. It was male and dressed, oddly enough, in the garb of a Spartan warrior.

Lisette had raised herself from Aidan's bedside, abandoning her prospective feast, staring in horror. *Nemesis,* she whispered fearfully.

The spirit laughed. *No one so important, Vampyre. I am Jafar, and I am an ordinary enough creature—what mortals call a guardian angel.* He looked fondly upon Aidan, who had begun to toss and turn upon his modern pallet. *This one is my particular charge, and I am sworn to protect his soul with all the powers of Heaven.*

Jafar had not yet spared a glance for Valerian, who was recovering now that Lisette's powers had slackened so dramatically, but Valerian watched the angel in stricken fascination. In all his existence he had never seen a being so magnificently beautiful.

What must Nemesis, one of the greatest angels in creation, be like?

Lisette had backed herself against the wall of Aidan's very ordinary bedroom, her eyes wide with terror.

Go from this place, Jafar told her. *And do not come near my ward again, for if you do such a foolish thing, I will be permitted to destroy you.*

Lisette made a mewling sound, one that could be heard only in the spirit, like all that had transpired that night, and vanished.

The angel bent over Aidan with a tenderness that was heartbreaking to see and carefully straightened his blankets, the way a mortal father might do for an exhausted child.

With the return of Valerian's physical powers came a serious fear that Jafar would turn his angel-strength upon him.

The splendid creature knew he was there—there had never been any question of that—but his regard, when he finally looked at Valerian, was remarkably gentle. *You did an uncommonly generous thing by summoning me back to the mortal's side with your cry of despair, but now you must keep away from him.*

Valerian nodded, though he wasn't at all certain he could comply with such an order, even if it came from the most wonderfully frightening being he had ever encountered. He found that he could move, and rose slowly to his feet.

He looked at Aidan, memorizing his features and frame, and then met the angel's gaze once more.

I hope you'll be more efficient in the future, he said, and as he vanished, he heard the seraphim laugh.

Come the morning, Valerian knew, Aidan would awaken and marvel over the strange dreams he'd had.

Vampires and angels, indeed, he would think, perhaps with a chuckle.

On Saturday morning Neely and Aidan were married in the big gazebo in the center of the town park, with a justice of the peace officiating. Neely's friends from the restaurant came to share their joy, as did Aidan's buddies from the construction job.

316

Neely felt beautiful in her antique dress, and the whole ceremony passed in a glorious haze. When the judge reached the I-now-pronounce-you-husband-and-wife part, and Aidan kissed her, she almost fainted with the joy of it.

Duke held a reception for the bride and groom at the restaurant, complete with wedding cake, supermarket champagne, and lots of rice and birdseed.

"I'll look after that car of yours," Duke said when Neely went to him to thank him and say good-bye. He was an old-timer, and it was hard for him to express emotion.

Neely stretched to kiss Duke's freshly shaven cheek. "When somebody comes through who looks like he needs a dented Mustang," she said with a misty smile, "you just hand him the keys and tell him to drive it in good health."

Duke smiled. "You've got a generous heart, little lady. I always knew that. I know somethin' else, too."

Neely had never been happier, but she felt sad, too, saying good-bye to such a good friend. "What?" she sniffled, still smiling brightly.

The big man planted a shy kiss on her forehead. "That joy will follow you everywhere you go, from now on," he answered. "You stop in and say howdy to old Duke if you're in this neck of the woods again, you hear?"

"You can count on it," Neely answered softly.

A few minutes later she and Aidan left the reception and drove away in their brand-new "caravan," a couple of very proper gypsies.

Aidan, who had bought a suit and tie for the occasion, looked comfortable behind the wheel of the RV—perhaps too comfortable. He pulled off his tie and tossed it over one shoulder, then quickly unfastened the top three buttons of his shirt.

"Forgive me if I sound like a bumper sticker, Mrs. Tremayne," he said cheerfully, keeping his eyes on the open road ahead, "but today is the first day of the rest of our lives."

Neely scrambled into the back of the RV to exchange her wedding dress for a pair of jeans, a lavender T-shirt, and sneakers. "That's very profound," she responded, trying to keep her voice light. The truth was, she was thinking about the patch of strong masculine chest she'd glimpsed when Aidan opened his shirt, and wondering when the honeymoon would begin.

"What are you doing back there?"

Neely rejoined her husband in the front of the RV, plopping into the passenger seat and giving him a sultry look as she fastened her seat belt in place. "What do you think I was doing?" she teased. "Sipping champagne from my shoe? Sprinkling the bed with perfume?"

A slow blush moved up Aidan's neck and glowed along his jawline. He gave her a sidelong glance and a high-voltage grin. "I wouldn't put it past you, you hot-blooded little vixen. You've been after my virtue from the first."

Neely felt her own cheeks glow, and she sagged deeper into the seat with a soft but long-suffering sigh. "Now what are we going to wait for? Our golden anniversary?"

Aidan laughed, and the sound was rich and masculine, causing Neely to want her husband that much more. "That or the first wide spot in the road," he teased. "Whichever turns up soonest. Great Scot, woman, did you think I was going to fling you into the sheets the moment we stepped over the threshold and have my way with you, right there in the steak-house parking lot?"

This time Neely laughed, too; but her blush deepened, and she reached across to give her husband a playful slap on the arm. Then she squirmed in her seat and said, "Are we there yet?"

An hour later Aidan brought the RV to a stop at the edge of a sun-splashed meadow. Then he came around to open Neely's door and help her out.

She had looked forward to being alone with her husband, yearned for it, in fact, but now that the time had arrived, Neely suddenly felt shy. "Here?" she whispered.

Aidan laid a hand to either side of her face and kissed her lightly, and much too briefly. "Here," he confirmed.

"Look at the way the sun slants between those trees over there. There's something cathedral-like about the place."

He was right, but Neely suspected the reverence they both felt came from their own hearts, rather than from the landscape around them.

"It's beautiful," Neely agreed.

Aidan eased past her, into the RV, and returned in a few moments carrying blankets, a chilled bottle of very good champagne, and two fluted glasses. Slipping one arm around Neely's waist, he escorted her toward the trees where the light fell so gracefully onto the fragrant grass.

He put the champagne and glasses aside to spread the blankets over the soft ground, then beckoned to Neely. "Come over here, Mrs. Tremayne."

She went to him happily, and he took her into his arms and held her close. He kissed her thoroughly, as he had so many times before, but this time he would not be leaving her to merely imagine his lovemaking.

After a while, when Neely was half-dazed with wanting her husband, Aidan began stripping away her clothes. He worked very slowly, tossing aside her T-shirt first, caressing and admiring her for a long time before unclasping her bra and disposing of that, too.

Her breasts stood bare and proud, their tips hardening in the spring breeze, and when Aidan bent with a groan to touch one morsel with his tongue, Neely cried out in hoarse joy and pressed him close.

They sank to the ground one limb at a time, like some graceful four-legged creature, and Aidan continued to enjoy Neely's full breasts. She kicked off her sneakers and tore at the zipper of her jeans, and Aidan chuckled against her nipple and stilled her frantic hand with his own. He made her wait.

Finally, though, each was bared to the other.

Aidan stroked Neely's thighs lightly and made teasing circles on her belly with his fingers.

"No longer, Aidan," she whispered franticly, slipping

both arms around his neck. "I've waited too long, and I want you so much—"

"And I want you," he said, his mouth falling to hers. Their tongues battled, then mated. With a groan Aidan mounted Neely, easing her legs apart with one knee.

She cried out and arched her back as he glided inside her and settled deep for a moment, claiming her, letting her body get used to his.

He chuckled as he nibbled at her lips. "Little vixen," he teased. She struggled beneath him, wanting to thrash and writhe, but he held her firmly in place.

Neely made a sound that was half passion and half frustration. "Aidan," she pleaded, "make love to me—please—or I swear it's going to happen on its own!"

Aidan raised himself onto his elbows, withdrew from her, then made a steady, smooth lunge into her warmth again.

That was all it took. Neely's body was so primed for Aidan's conquering that one stroke brought on a raging, cataclysmic climax. Eyes unfocused, she jerked helplessly beneath him while a low, lingering wail of pleasure poured from her throat.

Aidan held Neely while she responded, lodged far within her, and murmured gentle, senseless words against her ear. She'd been still, dazed and sated, for some time before he moaned and stiffened and spilled his warm seed inside her.

For a long time they lay there, arms and legs entwined, bodies joined, and their breaths might have been one breath, their heartbeats a single steady meter.

"I'm sorry," Neely said when she could finally speak.

Aidan raised his head and looked at her with incredulous, ink-blue eyes. "What did you say?"

"I was so eager. It happened so fast." Tears started in her lashes because she wanted Aidan to be pleased, the way she was, and she thought she'd failed.

He kissed the moisture away, aroused her all over again simply by caressing her eyelids with the tip of his tongue.

"No, darling," he whispered tenderly, "this day has been an eternity in the making." He slid lower, brushed his lips over her collarbone and the soft rounding of her breasts. "And the best part is," he added presently, "that this is only the beginning."

Neely spread her hands over Aidan's muscled back then, and a sob escaped her, a hoarse, splendid sound born of jubilation, not sorrow. Their souls spoke a silent, private language, and their bodies needed no words at all.

When they had spent still more of their passion, they drank champagne from their wedding glasses and, with laughing reluctance, began to dress each other. When it became a game, however, and the players started kissing places before they covered them, the clothes came off again.

"We're going to catch pneumonia, lying out here in the breeze in the altogether," Aidan said some time later.

"You're right." Neely sat up and started reaching for scattered garments and pulling them on. She was ridiculously happy, and she couldn't help humming a little under her breath. "I'm glad we didn't wait for our golden anniversary."

Aidan, who had dressed more quickly, pulled Neely to her feet and kissed her as they collided. "I could never have lasted past the silver one," he teased.

Once they'd put away the blankets and glasses and the champagne, Aidan got behind the wheel and started the engine.

"Well, Mrs. Tremayne, where do we go now? South to Mexico, or north to Canada?"

Neely considered, smoothing her hopelessly crumpled T-shirt and straightening her seat belt. "Surprise me," she said.

Late that night Aidan and Neely stopped in a moonlit RV park, at the edge of a southbound highway. There they grilled hamburgers on their tiny stove, crowded into their minuscule shower stall together, and finally made feverish love on the fold-out bed.

Aidan slept when it was over, but Neely lay curled

against his side, watching the stars through the skylight in the roof of the motor home as they did their intricate, shining dance around the moon. If anybody had ever told her she was going to be this happy, she reflected, she would have thought the notion was insane.

After the sky patterns had shifted several times, Neely rose, pulled an oversized T-shirt over her head, and crept to the drawer where she kept her most treasured belongings. Inside were school pictures of Danny, a necklace that had belonged to her mother, and the antique music box that Aidan had given her the night he proposed.

Holding the box close to her heart, Neely made her way to the door, opened it quietly, and stepped out into the silver-spangled night. She needed to be in the open spaces, at least for a few minutes, because the RV was simply too small to contain all the love and gratitude she felt.

Standing on the metal step, Neely wound the key on the bottom of the rosewood box, then lifted the lid. Sweet, oddly familiar music flowed into the night, and Neely danced in the damp and scented grass, turning round and round, like the stars overhead.

When she had spent her energy, she stopped the music and went back inside to crawl into bed next to her husband.

Aidan slept without reservation, sprawled every which way, with one arm flung back over his head. "Hmmm?" he said.

Neely smiled, kissed the pulsepoint at the base of his throat, and thought briefly of a wondrously handsome, elegant vampire who had once visited her dreams.

How odd, she thought as she toppled into sweet sleep, that she should think of him now.

For All Eternity

For Wendy—again, always, just because.
You're still the best thing that ever
happened to me.
I love you, Sweetheart.

"We are shaped and fashioned by what we love."
—*Goethe*

Chapter

❦ 1 ❧

Bright River, Connecticut
The present

Vampires are not supposed to cry.

So Maeve Tremayne told herself, in any case, that day in midsummer, as she stood in the echoing entry hall of her brother's house, gazing through a sheen of tears at the bouquet of dead roses he'd left for her.

The pale, shriveled petals lay scattered across the dusty marble tabletop, their curled edges the color of tea. Clearly Aidan had been away for some time.

Maeve took a certain bittersweet solace in this confirmation that her twin had not forgotten his promise to let her know whether his grand and foolhardy experiment had met with defeat or triumph.

The message of the roses was unmistakable: Aidan had surrendered his immortality to become a man again.

Maeve reached for a papery white petal, turning it slowly in her long, pale fingers. Aidan had never known a moment's happiness as a vampire, she reflected, in an effort to console herself. He had, after all, been changed against his will by a vindictive lover, the legendary Lisette.

For more than two centuries Aidan had despaired of his wondrous powers, instead of glorying in them, as Maeve had in her own. Even now it amazed her that her brother hadn't appreciated the extent of his gifts; vampires could travel through time and space at will, manipulate objects and human beings by mental tricks, disguise their presence from any lesser creature and most equals, and think with the entire brain, rather than just a small portion, as mortals did.

Oh, yes, vampires were far superior to those pitiful creatures, with their fragile organs and brittle bones. Immortals were able to see and hear as well or better than the average alleycat, and except under very bizarre circumstances, they need not fear the specter of death that awaited all humans.

Maeve shuddered, remembering the nightmare scene that had taken place only a few months before in an isolated graveyard on a hilltop behind an ancient abbey. Aidan had nearly died the most horrible of vampire deaths, a hellish, fiery ordeal triggered by the light of the sun.

Damn Aidan and his fatuous nobility, she thought. He'd gone willingly into Lisette's trap in an effort to rescue another nightwalker, his friend Valerian. If it hadn't been for Maeve herself, and for Tobias, one of the oldest vampires on earth, Aidan would have perished, screaming and writhing in the snow.

Maeve gathered petals in both hands and pressed them to her face. She caught their faint scent and tucked it away among her memories to recall at another time.

"Aidan," she whispered brokenly. "Oh, Aidan."

She was alone in the vastness of creation now, Maeve told herself, parting her hands and letting the rose petals rain gracefully down upon the tabletop. She had only enemies and acquaintances, but no friends.

Vampires were not particularly social creatures, since they feared certain angels and warlocks, as well as seemingly blundering humans who were in truth ruthless hunters, out to destroy them. Moreover, blood-drinkers mistrusted each other, and with good reason, for they tended to be greedy and unprincipled, unabashedly devoted to their own best interests.

Maeve sighed and wandered into Aidan's study, where he had worked so many nights on those damnable journals and sketches of his. He had always fed early, if possible, and then returned to this great, ponderous, lonely house to pretend he was a mortal, with a piddly life span of seventy-six years or so. It still mystified her that he'd admired them so, these awkward beings who were almost completely oblivious to the marvelous powers evolving in the secret depths of their own spirits.

She took the first volume of Aidan's many bound journals down from the shelf and felt a stab of grief when she saw the sketch of herself and her brother on the initial page. She recalled their human beginnings, in eighteenth-century Ireland, when they'd been born to a bawdy but very beautiful tavern wench, with a rich English merchant for a sire.

Alexander Tremayne had taken good care of his byblows, Maeve had to confess, considering that he had another family, a legitimate one, back in Liverpool. His great sin, the one Maeve would always despise him for, had been in separating the twins when they were just seven years old.

Just prior to that fateful parting, Aidan and Maeve's flighty, superstitious mother had taken them to an old gypsy fortune-teller. The crone had studied their small palms and then rasped, "Cursed! Cursed for all eternity, and beyond!"

At that, the ancient creature had risen from the steps of her colorful wagon and tottered inside. Moments later she had returned with duplicate medals, rosebuds shaped of gold and suspended from sturdy chains. With great ceremony she had hung a pendant around each child's neck.

"These cannot save your souls," she'd said, "but they will remind you to uphold the qualities of mercy and faith, no matter what befalls you. From those will come your strength and your power."

Maeve had kept the gypsy's gift ever since, taken comfort from it after she was sent away from her mother and brother.

From an upstairs room in an Irish tavern, Maeve had gone to a nunnery, where she'd been taught to sew, weave, and embroider, as well as to read and write. Aidan had been sent to an expensive school for boys, far away in England, and he, too, had kept his pendant close.

The two children had soon discovered an eerie ability to communicate via images held in their minds, and that contact had been Maeve's consolation during dark, lonely hours.

Then, when Aidan had reached young manhood, he'd met Lisette, the most powerful of all female vampires, and had mistaken her for a mortal woman. In the end Lisette had murdered Aidan, and then restored him as a nightwalker by giving him back his own blood, altered.

When Maeve had discovered the truth, through the offices of an exasperating, impudent, and unbelievably handsome immortal called Valerian, she was shattered. From then on, she knew, all eternity would lie between herself and Aidan, for he would live forever, while she was destined to grow old and die.

Valerian had graciously explained the benefits of becoming a vampire, as well as the obvious drawbacks.

On the one hand, an immortal could do virtually anything he or she wished, on the strength of a single clearly focused thought. The world, even the universe, was their playground. But on the other, Valerian had said with a shiver, there was no doubt that if the fundamentals of religion were true, all vampires would surely be damned. There would be no help for them, and certainly no mercy; if they were judged before the courts of heaven, they'd be cast into the Great Pit as well.

Raised in a convent, Maeve had heard plenty about hell and been taught to fear it with her whole soul, but she was also irrepressibly adventurous. Moreover, she could not bear for Aidan to leave her behind, and, in the last analysis, the consumption of blood seemed a small price to pay for the privileges vampires knew.

After all, she wouldn't have to kill her victims if she didn't choose to, and even in her innocence she knew there were plenty of scoundrels in the world to take nourishment from. She needn't pick on anyone with an honest heart.

When all these matters had been carefully reviewed, Maeve made her decision and asked Valerian to make her a vampire, since she knew Aidan would never consent to do it himself. At first, Valerian had refused, but he'd been attracted to Maeve, too, and she'd used the fact to her advantage.

Eventually Valerian had changed her, and it was not at all the unpleasant experience Aidan had described. In fact, Maeve had known unbounded ecstasy that night.

Aidan had been enraged when he discovered that his sister had followed in his footsteps; he'd called her all sorts of a fool and cursed Valerian to rot under a desert sun, and then he'd simply vanished.

For a time Maeve had been Valerian's lover, as well as his apprentice. He had introduced her to the pleasures of vampire sex, a mostly mental pursuit vastly superior to the comical wrestling humans seemed to enjoy with such abandon. Since Maeve had been a virgin when Valerian transformed her, she'd been spared the indignity of sweating and straining and thrashing under some man's thrusting hips the way mortal women did.

Valerian had introduced her to many other things besides the intense delights of mating, of course. She'd learned all the nightstalker's tricks and learned them well. One night, when she caught Valerian playing vampire games with a beautiful fledgling named Pamela, Maeve had decided to strike out on her own.

She'd done well, too, eventually reconciling with a still-vexed Aidan and hurling herself into one wonderful adventure after another.

Now, as Maeve stood in the deserted room that had once been her brother's favorite retreat, holding the golden rose pendant between two fingers, she struggled to accept another reality, another turning in the road.

She must leave Aidan to his humanity, though the temptation to seek him out was almost irresistible. It was to be hoped that he'd made a happy life for himself.

Maeve figured she would never know; Aidan was dead to her, and she to him, and there could be no returning to their old bonds.

There was nothing to do now but feed and retire to the

attic studio of her home in London, where she liked to go when she was sad or injured. There she would sit at her loom, letting her thoughts drift while she worked the shuttle, allowing her deeper mind to dictate the image that would appear, as if by magic, on the resultant tapestry.

Gettysburg, Pennsylvania
July 14, 1863

When Calder Holbrook slept—a rare event in itself—his dreams were haunted by the bone-jarring thunder of cannon fire and the screams of schoolboys-turned-soldier. Not a moment passed, sleeping or waking, when he didn't want to lay down his surgical instruments and go home to Philadelphia, but he couldn't leave the wounded. The color of their tattered uniforms meant nothing to him, though some of the other doctors refused to treat "the enemy."

That particular summer night was hot, weighted with the metallic scent of blood and the more pungent stenches of urine and vomit. After operating for twenty hours straight, Calder had stretched out gratefully on the soft, cool grass covering an old grave, there in the sideyard of the small clapboard church, and plunged headlong into a fitful slumber. In the early hours, well before dawn, something awakened him, something far more subtle than the cries and moans of the injured boys inside, sprawled end to end on the pews.

Aching with despair and fatigue, Calder lifted himself onto an elbow and scanned the churchyard. There were so many wounded, such an impossible number, that they spilled out on the crude sanctuary to lie in neat rows on the grass. Even so, this was only one of many improvised hospitals, all overburdened, overwhelmed.

Some of the patients shivered or sobbed in their inadequate bedrolls—if they were lucky enough to have a blanket in the first place. Some moaned, and some had suffered only minor injuries and were just marking time, waiting to be sent home or to rejoin the Union troops at the front. The Confederates, of course, would be marched to some prison camp, or hauled there in whatever rickety wagon could be spared.

Calder came back from his musings and squinted. Something was different; he had an eerie, fluttery feeling in the pit of his stomach, made up partly of excitement and partly of fear. He dragged himself upright, his back against the cool marble headstone, ran blood-stained fingers through his dark hair, and strained his tired eyes.

And then he saw her.

She was a creature made of moonlight, moving so gracefully between the rows of fallen soldiers that she seemed to float. Her gown was pale, sewn of some shimmering, gauzy fabric, and her ebony hair tumbled down her back in a lush cascade.

Calder rubbed his eyes, then the back of his neck, mystified, certain that he must be hallucinating, or at least dreaming. This was not one of the good women of the town, who had been assisting so tirelessly with the injured of both sides since the terrible battle earlier in the month; none of them would have worn something so impractical as a white frock into the midst of such filth and overwhelming gore.

An angel, then? Calder wondered. Some of the stricken boys had spoken of a beautiful guardian spirit who came in the night and gave nurture and comfort to those who were the nearest to death. Of course, they'd been seeing what they wanted to see, being so far from their mothers, wives, and sweethearts.

Calder narrowed his eyes again, trusting neither his vision nor his reason. The woman did not vanish, as he had expected, but instead knelt beside a sorely wounded lad and drew him against her bosom with such tenderness that Calder's throat tightened over a wrenching cry.

Her glorious hair, seemingly spun from the night itself, was like a veil, hiding the lad's head and shoulders from view.

Calder finally gathered enough of his senses to scramble awkwardly to his feet. "You, there," he said in a low but forceful voice. "What are you doing?"

The creature raised her head, her exquisite face pale and glowing like an alabaster statue in the silvery wash of the moon. The boy lay in her arms, his head back in utter abandon, an expression of sublime jubilation plain in his features. Even from that distance, Calder knew the soldier was dead.

The doctor scrambled to his feet, swayed slightly from weariness and hunger, and started toward the woman. She laid the boy on the ground with infinite gentleness, bent to kiss his forehead, and then rose gracefully to her full height. Just as Calder drew near enough to see her clearly, she raised her arms and clasped her hands together, high above her head. She favored the physician with one brief, pitying smile, and vanished like so much vapor.

Calder gaped, shaken, terrified that he was at last and indeed losing his mind, and oddly joyous, all of a piece. After a moment or so he composed himself and crouched beside the boy the woman had held so lovingly, searching with practiced fingers for a pulse.

There was none, as he had expected, but Calder felt the familiar mixture of rage and grief all the same. The soldier had obviously been trying to grow a beard, and he'd produced peach fuzz instead. His features were more those of a child than a man.

Damn this war, Calder thought bitterly, and damn the politicians on both sides for sending mere children into the fray. He was about to straighten the boy's head, and cover him so that the overworked orderlies would know to carry him away in the morning, when he noticed the odd marks at the base of the lad's throat—two neat puncture wounds, just over two inches apart.

"What the hell?" Calder whispered.

Tom Sugarheel, an earnest but largely incompetent fellow who had been dragged out of some second-rate medical college and pressed into government service, suddenly appeared, squatting at Calder's side. "That'll be one less to bawl and snuffle for his mama," the other man said.

Calder reminded himself that he was here to attend the sick and injured, not to kill, then glared at Sugarheel. It galled him to ask an opinion of this oaf, but sometimes even idiots possessed insights that escaped other minds. "Look at these marks," he said, pointing to the boy's throat. "Have you seen anything like this before?"

Sugarheel shrugged, reaching into the torn, bloodstained pocket of the dead lad's dark blue tunic. "Not as I recollect." He found a small tintype, probably intended for the soldier's mother or young bride, and ran a dirty thumb over the cracked glass while he pondered the already fading throat wounds. "Looks almost like something a snake would do."

"You're the only snake in the immediate vicinity," Calder pointed out impatiently, snatching the photograph in its blood-speckled leather case from Sugarheel's grubby grasp. "Rustle up a couple of orderlies, and don't touch this boy's personal belongings again."

Sugarheel's expression was wry and defiant. "Most of these lads carry a paper with the name of their folks and such. I just wanted to make sure his kin got any valuables he might have."

Calder felt a crushing weariness, deeper than physical exhaustion, something that lamed the spirit. "That's the chaplain's duty, not yours. Make no mistake, *Doctor*—if I catch you stealing, be it from the quick or from the dead, I'll cut you open like a bloated cow and fill your guts with kerosene. Is that clear enough, or were there too many syllables for you?"

Hatred replaced the amusement in Sugarheel's narrow, pockmarked face, but he didn't respond. Instead he got to his feet and ambled off to fetch the requested orderly.

Calder rose a moment later, after silently bidding the fallen soldier Godspeed, and stumbled back to the soft mound, hoping to sleep again, knowing with despairing certainty that he would not.

Maeve reached her new lair, a long-abandoned wine cellar in an old villa in nineteenth-century Italy, just moments before the light of the morning sun came flooding over the low hills to blaze in the olive groves and vineyards and dance, sparkling, on the sea. The inevitable sleep overtook her, and she sank into utter unconsciousness. All levels of her mind were blank, as usual, empty of the random images and fragmentary dreams some vampires experienced.

When she awakened, however, hours later, at the precise moment of sunset, a man had taken up residence in her thoughts—a *mortal* man, no less. He was very handsome, in a patrician sort of way, with dark hair, good teeth, and broad shoulders, but Maeve still resented the intrusion. Why, she wondered pettishly, should she find herself pondering the likes of a beleaguered army surgeon like Calder Holbrook?

Maeve rose from her improvised bed of dusty crates and smoothed her hair, feeling even more irritated at the realization that she'd taken the trouble to ferret out his name before leaving the Civil War field hospital for more pleasant surroundings. She had no particular fascination with human beings—beyond feeding on them when the need arose, that is.

In a flash, much of the doctor's history flooded, unbidden, into Maeve's mind. Calder Holbrook was the second son of a wealthy Philadelphia banker. He'd graduated from Harvard Medical School with honors and taken further training in Europe. He'd been married once, to a selfish socialite who had deserted her husband and their small daughter to run away with a lover. Holbrook had endured this betrayal with admirable equanimity, but when his beloved child had perished of spinal meningitis a year later, he'd turned bitter and cold, devoting himself to his work. His father had begged him to spend the war years in Europe, advancing his studies, but Holbrook had accepted a commission and left his comfortable life in Philadelphia without so much as a backward glance. . . .

Maeve put her palms to her temples and closed her eyes, trying to stop the onslaught of images and emotions, wanting to know nothing more about Dr. Calder Holbrook. All the same, she was well aware that she would see him again, whether she wished it so or not.

Exasperated, Maeve formed a picture of her grand house

in London, with myriad comforts of the twentieth century, and centered all her inner forces on the desire to be there. In an instant she found herself standing in her own lush suite of rooms.

Moving rapidly, as if to shake persistent images of a doctor from her mind, thoughts of a man as sorely wounded as any of his patients, Maeve exchanged her white dress for a comfortable gown of red velvet. It was a simple creation, really, loosely fitted at the waist, with wide sleeves tapering into cuffs that buttoned with jet. After brushing her hair, she left her private apartments, walked along the wide hallway, and climbed the attic stairs to her studio.

She must feed soon. Maeve was not one for starving herself, knowing as she did that her powers, rare even among vampires, as well as her unflagging strength, came from the blood she took each night. Besides, she looked forward to the sweeping, thunderous joy that always overtook her during that intimate communion.

When she opened the door to the studio, however, and saw her loom awaiting her there, Maeve was drawn to it. During those early, wildly painful nights when she'd first known that her brother had either ceased to exist or somehow been restored to all the faults and frailties of humanity, weaving had been her only solace. She had not seen Valerian during that time—for all she knew or cared, her former lover and mentor was rotting in some crypt with a stake through his heart—nor had she encountered her acquaintances, the Havermails, or any of the members of the Brotherhood. Indeed, Maeve had taken care to avoid all other vampires, fearing they would sense her unusual vulnerability and close in on her like so many frenzied sharks.

Maeve had no illusions about blood-drinkers; except for Valerian's odd fascination with Aidan, and the deep bond that had once existed between her brother and herself, she had never known one to harbor true affection for another.

The pull of the loom was strong, stronger even than the unholy thirst.

She found the long box that contained her many spools

of colored floss, then seated herself on the stool facing the primitive mechanism. Soon the shuttle was making its comfortingly familiar, rhythmic sound, and Maeve lost track of time, sublimating even the ravenous hunger she felt.

When a form suddenly towered opposite her, she cried out, startled. In the next instant, she was furious, for Maeve had not been caught off guard in such a fashion in nearly two centuries.

Valerian was examining the growing tapestry, a frown creasing his handsome brow. The scars from his graveyard encounter with Lisette, the one from which Aidan had so nobly attempted to save him, were now almost fully healed. His lush mane of chestnut hair had grown back, thicker than ever. The old mischief flashed in his blue eyes, though this was tempered by a certain quiet sorrow.

"You really ought to be more vigilant, my dear," the seasoned vampire said, leaving off his former thoughtful inspection of the half-finished tapestry to round the loom and stand at Maeve's side. "Suppose I had been Lisette, or some wandering warlock?"

Maeve was embarrassed, and that made her angry, for her besetting sin had always been pride. "Had you been Lisette," she said, seething, "or 'some wandering warlock,' instead of your pompous and arrogant self, you probably would have had the decency to knock at the door."

Valerian arched one eyebrow and studied her with a wry expression, though the sadness in his gaze did not lessen. He had suffered, and in spite of herself, Maeve felt a twinge of pity for him.

"I see no reason to continue this nonsensical debate," he said. "The point is, I am here."

"You'll pardon me if I don't touch my forehead to the floor three times or kill the fatted calf," Maeve retorted with slightly more charity in her tone.

Valerian laughed, but despair rang in the sound, as well as mirth. "What a relief to find that you haven't changed—you're still the same saucy, peevish chit I transformed these many years ago."

Maeve narrowed her dark blue eyes. When Valerian reminded her of her making, it was usually an indication that he wanted something. "Next you'll be pointing out that you taught me everything I know," she accused.

"Didn't I?" he asked lightly.

"No!" Maeve cried. "I can't count the number of times you nearly got me burned, beheaded, or staked through the heart in my sleep." She paused, calming herself slightly. "Come, Valerian—no more hedging. What do you want?"

He sighed dramatically—pure affectation, since vampires do not breathe. "I'm surprised you haven't asked about Aidan," he said softly.

Maeve felt dizzy, as if she'd taken a blow. "I know he gave up his immortality," she replied. "Nothing matters beyond that."

"Oh, no?"

Maeve lifted her eyes, met Valerian's penetrating and somewhat hypnotic gaze. "He is well?" she asked, quickly and in a low voice. At the other vampire's slight hesitation, she whispered in a furious rush, "*Damn* you, Valerian, *is he well?*"

Valerian engaged in a slow scowl. "He and that Neely creature are married now, and they're expecting a child." He stopped for a moment, bristling with distaste. "They're actually living in a *motorhome*," he went on, "like a pair of latter-day gypsies!"

Maeve laughed, amused at Valerian's snobbery, but the sound was a bitter one because she had realized the danger. Her expression turned deadly serious. "You've been following Aidan about, haven't you? You idiot—you've probably set half the ghouls in creation on his trail!"

The accusation made Valerian draw himself up in an imperial swell of annoyance. As usual, he wore tailored evening clothes and a cape, and in one hand he held a very expensive top hat. The attire served to accentuate his natural majesty of countenance.

"I veiled myself," Valerian said scathingly, glowering down his nose at a thoroughly undaunted Maeve. "No other vampire, not you or even Lisette herself, would have sensed my presence." He seemed to deflate a little then, though the change was nearly imperceptible, and Maeve could not be certain whether she'd seen or just imagined it. He examined his perfectly manicured and buffed fingernails. "The truth is, I was bored to distraction within a week," he finally allowed in a moderate tone of voice. "I'd forgotten what mundane lives humans lead."

Maeve was frowning and, being unusually adept at such things, even for a vampire, Valerian read her thoughts. He smiled gently and reached out to raise her chin with an index finger.

"There, now," he said. "Don't be worrying about your foolish brother, my sweet. Only Lisette has reason to quarrel with our Aidan, and I've stolen all memory of him from her mind."

"However did you manage?" Maeve asked, surprised. "Don't tell me you actually approached her again, after she staked you out in that graveyard to be destroyed by the sun!"

"It was easy," Valerian scoffed. "When her plan backfired and she herself was nearly caught by the light of day, she was badly disfigured. Being a vain creature, Lisette has secreted herself away. Most nights she does not even rise to feed."

Maeve left the stool and went to the tall leaded windows that looked out over London. "Lisette is dormant?" she asked casually, knowing all the while that she wasn't deceiving Valerian; that was virtually impossible.

"For the most part," Valerian replied, moving silently and swiftly to her side and pretending an interest in the lights of the city.

"So that's why you've come," Maeve said. "You hope to destroy her, and you want my help."

Valerian didn't reply immediately. When he did speak some moments later, his voice was oddly hoarse and grim with determination. "Lisette is a scourge on mortals and immortals alike," he said. "When she rallies—and believe me,

Maeve, she *will* find her old strength—she will be more dangerous, more unreasoningly greedy, than ever before. I have seen her return from one of her monumental sulks innumerable times. She goes on rampages, feeding on innocents, changing most of her victims into vampires, and killing those who are too weak to make the transition. It must not be permitted to happen again."

"Why do you want me to help? There are others who are older and more powerful."

"You know very well why I want you," Valerian replied tersely. "Lisette is the undisputed queen of all vampires, and you, my difficult darling, are her logical successor."

Chapter

Maeve was particularly hungry and rather weak, having missed her feeding that night, and she was impatient with Valerian and his penchant for high drama. She turned to look up at him, there by the towering windows in the studio of her London house, and folded her arms. "Suppose I tell you I have no desire to be the vampire queen? What if I simply want to go on living strictly for myself, the way I always have?"

Valerian's smile was almost—but not quite—a smirk. Even he would not have dared that, for he knew better than anyone that she was his equal, in power and in skill. "I would not believe a word of it—there is something of your heroic brother in you. Besides, you have no choice in the matter, darling. It seems to be fated."

"Fated," Maeve scoffed quietly, but she felt troubled on some deep level of her being. "Nothing is fated for vampires—we are not a natural creation, remember. We have no place in the grand scheme of things."

"Alas," Valerian said, with another of his theatrical sighs, "you are right, my darling, but you are wrong, as well. Some thousand years after the first vampires came into being on Atlantis, other supernatural creatures waged war against our kind. Blood-drinkers were forced into hiding, and still we were nearly destroyed. Then, in meditation, one of the elders saw a vision—a battle between Lisette and a new queen,

blessed—if that's the proper word—with powers more formidable than any vampire has ever possessed."

"What does that have to do with me?" Maeve snapped,
fearing sorely that greatness would be thrust upon her,
whether she desired it or not. She liked her existence just
the way it was, though she would have preferred to be
spared the grief Aidan had caused her, of course. "There are
other strong female vampires, you know. Your friend Pamela, for instance. And then there is Dimity—"

"Do not waste my time," Valerian snapped, interrupting
Maeve with an imperious wave of one hand. "Pamela loves
her own pleasure too much, and it is rumored that Dimity
consorts with angels. There is no one but you, Maeve. You
must help me destroy Lisette before she regains her former
strength and wreaks havoc on the natural and supernatural
worlds alike."

Maeve was honestly baffled. "Why do you care?" she
asked. "Pardon my saying so, Valerian, but you aren't
known for your generosity and self-sacrifice—especially on
behalf of human beings."

Valerian turned his head for a moment, but Maeve saw
nearly fathomless grief in his magnificent profile all the
same. *Saints in heaven*, she thought, *he misses Aidan even more
than I do.*

"I've changed," he said finally. He looked at her again
then, with a mischievous, slanted, and slightly haunted grin.
"Somewhat."

Maeve felt a small rush of affection for her old friend
and erstwhile adversary but offered no response to his statement. Instead, after a few poignant moments had passed,
she sighed and said, "I must feed—the sun will be up soon."

"You'll think about what I've said?" Valerian asked.

Maeve gave a reluctant nod and watched with grudging
admiration as the other vampire drew back, swirled his expensive cape, and vanished into a shifting vapor. She'd
never known another nightwalker with Valerian's flair for
showmanship.

Maeve's temptation to return to the American Civil War,

and thus to Dr. Calder Holbrook, was monumental. As an exercise in self-discipline, and because she would be damned and double-damned before stooping to consort with a mortal the way Aidan had, Maeve turned her thoughts in another direction.

She blinked and found herself in her suite, on the floor below. The housekeeper, Mrs. Fullywub, a chronic insomniac, was there, neatly folding the jumble of silky lingerie in one of the bureau drawers.

The pleasant woman started at Maeve's appearance. "Dear me," she fussed, "I wish you wouldn't do that. I don't believe I'll ever get used to it."

Maeve smiled, went into her walk-in closet, which had been a dressing room in earlier times, and selected a pair of tight blue jeans, a black leather jacket with studs, and a tank top that resembled a man's undershirt. Scuffed boots completed the ensemble.

Mrs. Fullywub shook her gray head. "Don't tell me you're going about with one of those American motorcycle gangs now," she said. "They're mostly bad company, those people."

Maeve changed hastily. "For my purposes," she answered, "bad company suits best."

"I suppose you're right." The housekeeper sighed with motherly regret. "Still, I hope you'll pay close attention to whatever is going on around you. You remember what happened to your brother, when he mistook a warlock for one of us poor, hapless mortals."

Maeve sprayed mousse on her hair and combed it through with splayed fingers, giving the formerly smooth tresses a wild, spiky look. She ignored the mirror above the dressing table, since it would not reflect her image anyway. "I'm nothing like Aidan," she said, somewhat testily. "And you needn't worry about me."

"You're more like him than you think," Mrs. Fullywub insisted, "and not a moment goes by that I don't fret for your safety. You have powerful enemies, don't forget."

Maeve raised her hands over her head, palms touching,

fingers interlocked. "Good night," she said, and disappeared.

Moments later Maeve reassembled in a place Valerian had introduced her to long before, a bar called the Last Ditch. The term suited the filthy dive; "hell" would have been a more apt name, but that one was taken.

Smoke filled the crowded bar, tinting the air a greasy blue, and the singular smells of unwashed humanity were more pungent than ever. Maeve twitched her nose, revolted, engaging in a brief and wholly idle wish that vampire senses were not quite so keen.

She noted a warlock near the jukebox and nodded to let him know she was aware of his presence. He returned the courtesy and added a smile and a jaunty salute.

Go to hell, Maeve told him. It was easier, with all the noise of the bar, to speak mentally.

The warlock's smile enlarged a little. *If I get there before you*, he replied, *I'll save you a seat.*

Maeve shuddered slightly in spite of herself. Long ago, in the eighteenth-century nunnery where she'd spent most of her childhood, the good sisters had taught her to fear the devil's hearth to the very center of her being. It was a fixation that she, like Valerian, who had been human in medieval times, had never quite been able to shake.

She said nothing more to the warlock, but instead scanned the crowd for a deserving victim.

She passed over the ones who were merely misguided, and those who suffered from some hidden wound of the mind or spirit, looking for someone who relished evil and practiced it willingly.

She was in luck, for there was a noted politician present, though he'd taken care to keep a low profile. He sat at a corner table, pawing a vacuous young girl who wore too much makeup and too few clothes.

Maeve made a low, purring sound in her throat and sashayed toward the senator's table, slim, rounded hips swaying, thumbs hooked saucily in the pockets of her leather jacket. "Dance?" she said.

The girl stuck out her lower lip, and tears brimmed in her eyes as the politician clambered to his feet, upsetting his chair in his eagerness to accept Maeve's invitation. Seconds later he was in her arms, and they were moving slowly to the music, swirls of smoke eddying around them, drifting even closer to the deep shadows next to the bandstand.

The senator never stood a chance.

"Don't you think you're cutting it a bit close?" Tobias demanded when Maeve popped into her special chamber underneath the London house, soon after her feeding. "The sun will be up in five minutes."

"What are you doing here?" Maeve countered, pulling off her jacket and tossing it aside. "Don't you have a satin-lined coffin waiting for you someplace?"

Tobias shook his head. He looked young, with his slender frame and eternally boyish features, but in fact he was a founding member of the Brotherhood of the Vampyre. He had been among the first blood-drinkers created, long ago on the lost continent, during a series of medical experiments.

"Such a bold creature," he said. "You remind me of your brother, Maeve—you seem to have no sense of what is appropriate, and that fact may well be your undoing."

Maeve tossed her hair, wishing she could brush out the sticky mousse, but there was no time. Soon the consuming need to sleep would drag her down into the darkest depths of her own mind. "It's beginning to get on my nerves," she confided, sitting down on the row of crates to kick off her motorcycle boots, "the way everybody keeps comparing me to Aidan."

Tobias, apparently in no hurry to return to his own lair, wherever it was, leaned against the dank brick walls and folded his arms. He was clad in a plain tunic, colorless leggings, and soft leather shoes. "It's natural, I think—you are his twin, after all."

Maeve tried to be polite to her uninvited guest, though she could not quite bring herself to smile. She'd just dumped a state senator in a crumpled heap behind the Last Ditch, seriously anemic but alive, and his blood had left her feeling a little ill.

"I *was* his twin," she corrected her elder. After that she paused and then made an effort to be polite. "Please forgive my tart manner, Tobias—it must be the costume."

Tobias took in her tough-chick getup with quiet amusement. "Indeed," he agreed. His expression turned serious in the next instant, however, and he went on. "Word has reached the Brotherhood that Valerian has been attempting to incite some kind of rebellion against Lisette. Is this true?"

Maeve felt uncomfortable; for all her quarrels with Valerian, she was no snitch. Besides, she owed the other vampire a debt, since he'd given her immortality in the first place. "What if it is?" she asked moderately. Even respectfully.

Tobias might have sighed then, had he been human, or even a little inclined toward feigning their singular traits. Instead, he just looked resigned and weary. "Valerian has been a nuisance since his making," he said. "Still, I personally find him entertaining, and therefore I tend to overlook his . . . foibles." The elder paused, regarding Maeve with a searching stare for a long moment before continuing. "Did he ask you to lead some kind of campaign against Lisette, as we suspect?"

Maeve hesitated, then remembered that it would be absolutely useless to lie to an elder. Her thoughts were probably as clear to him as if they were goods on display in a shop window. "Yes. For some reason I cannot quite grasp, Valerian sees me as the next queen. But don't worry—I'm not interested in a political career." Exhaustion swamped her, tugged at her consciousness, and she marveled because Tobias seemed unaffected by the vampire's need to lie dormant during the daylight hours. "I hope you're—not planning to—sleep here," she struggled to say. "I have a—reputation to consider—you know."

He bent over her. "You must not confront Lisette," he said clearly. "She is more powerful than you can ever imagine, and we will all suffer if she is angered. Besides, it is not ours to protect humans—that is the task of angels."

"Angels," Maeve repeated softly. And then she drifted into the dreamless place where vampires slumber.

Gettysburg, 1863

The battle had ended days before, Calder reflected as he moved among the wounded. The little church on the outskirts of town still brimmed with them, as did the whole of Gettysburg, and the graveyard had long since been filled. In many ways the aftermath was worse than the fighting itself, for there were no surges of adrenaline now, no stirring drumbeats and certainly no talk of glory. This carnage around him, the crushed or sundered limbs, the blinded eyes and deafened ears, the putrid infections and the dysentery, *this* was the true nature of war.

A boy dying of gangrene clutched at Calder's wrinkled shirt as he passed, grinding out a single word. "Doctor—"

Calder braced himself, knowing the child-soldier was about to plead for something to kill the pain, and there was nothing. The supply of morphine, inadequate in the first place, had been exhausted long before. "Yes, son," he said gruffly. "What is it?"

"I reckon the Lady will come for me tonight, as she came for those others I heard about," the lad said. Instead of desperation, Calder saw hope in the youthful face, along with agony. "She'll take me home to heaven."

Several moments passed before Calder's suddenly constricted throat opened up again so he could speak. A week had passed since he'd seen the beautiful specter, and every moment of that time he'd been telling himself she'd been a figment of his imagination. "The Lady," he said, somewhat stupidly.

The boy released his hold on Calder's shirt. "You ever see her?"

Calder sighed. He was on the verge of collapse as it was,

and he didn't have the strength to lie. "I thought I did," he admitted. "What's your name, lad?"

"Phillips, sir. Private Michael Phillips, Twentieth Maine. I fell when the Rebs tried to take Little Round Top." Again the boy grasped at Calder, this time closing grubby fingers around his wrist. "You get them to take me outside and lay me in the sweet grass," he rasped. "They say she won't come inside the church—that's mighty strange, for an angel, don't you figure?—and I want her to take me."

Tears stung Calder's eyes, and he looked away for a moment. Damn, but it still galled him that he couldn't save them all, every last one, instead of just a few lucky ones here and there. After all this time in medicine, first as a civilian and then as an Army surgeon, he continued to find the reality nearly unbearable. "You seem to know a lot about this Lady," he said.

"She's about all anybody talks about," Phillips replied weakly. It was plain that he was barely holding on, and the stench of his infection came near to choking Calder. "Will you get me outside, Doctor, so's she can find me?"

Calder raised a hand and signaled for a pair of orderlies. They were actually ambulatory patients, these ready helpers, one of them hailing from Richmond, Virginia, the other from somewhere in the New Hampshire countryside. For them, the fighting was over; one would be sent home, with a permanently lame leg to remind him continually of his brush with glory, and one to a prison camp.

"This is Private Michael Phillips." Calder performed the introductions with proper dignity, once the orderlies had reached him. "He wants to see the blue sky when he looks up. Get a stretcher and find a place for him outside."

"Yes, sir," said the boy from Richmond.

As gently as they could, the Yankee and the Confederate shifted Phillips onto a canvas stretcher stiff with dried blood and hauled him through the open doorway and down the steps. Calder followed as far as the church porch and stood watching them, gripping the rail.

He should have been thinking about home, he supposed,

or about those peaceful, idyllic days before war had torn the nation into two bleeding parts. Instead his mind was full of the mysterious woman he'd seen moving among the fallen soldiers that night a week before. Had she been real? he wondered yet again. After all he hadn't been the only one to see her—she was the hope and comfort of many of the wounded, and their description of her matched the vision Calder himself had glimpsed.

His hands tightened over the railing until the knuckles ached. The reasoning, scientific part of him said she could not be an angel or a ghost as the others believed. No, as beautiful and real as the Lady was, she was merely a projection of all their tormented brains—his, those of the other doctors and orderlies, and, most of all, those of the patients themselves. The power generated by such grief and suffering had to be formidable.

Calder watched as Phillips was carefully laid out on the grass, in a space left by a boy who'd passed on that morning, and found himself wishing with his whole heart that the Lady was real. Just then, he very much needed to believe in some benevolent force, however strange and inexplicable.

He got through the rest of that day by rote, and at sunset a messenger rode in, painted with dust and so weary he could barely sit his horse, bringing word that four doctors would arrive within the week to relieve Calder and the others.

The news filled him with both relief and despair. He was mentally and physically exhausted; soon he would be of little or no use to the fallen soldiers around him. Still, he hated to leave them, and, even more, he feared that he would never see the Lady again.

That night, while Calder sat waiting, his back to a birch tree, she returned. It was about two in the morning, he reckoned, though he did not take out his pocket watch, and she went straight to Phillips.

Calder was fascinated, stricken by her beauty and her magic, unable to move from his post by the tree and approach her as he'd hoped to do. Instead, he simply watched, powerless and silent, while she smoothed back the dying child's rumpled, dirty hair and spoke softly to him.

As Calder looked on, the lad raised his arms to her, like a babe reaching for its mother. She drew him close and held him tenderly, and for a moment Calder believed she truly was an angel.

She rocked the boy against her bosom for a sweet, seemingly endless interval, then bared his fragile neck and buried her face there. Phillips shuddered in her arms and then went still, with that same trusting abandon in his bearing that Calder had seen in the other soldier, the one she'd taken on her last visit. The Lady seemed to nuzzle him, and when she lifted her head, her gaze met Calder's.

He felt some kind of quaking, deep in his being, but even then he knew it stemmed from excitement, not fear. He willed her to come to him, and she did, drifting along with steps so smooth that she appeared to be floating.

When she stood only a few feet from him, her dark tresses tossing in the slow summer breeze, her pale skin bathed in moonlight, he believed in whatever she was, believed with the whole of his spirit.

"Who are you?" he managed to whisper after a long time. His voice was a raspy sound, scraping painfully at his throat.

She drew nearer, knelt beside him, and touched his hair. At first he thought she wasn't going to speak, because she was just a vision, after all, and therefore without a voice. Then she smiled, and Calder felt a pinch in his defeated heart as she said, "What does it matter who—or what—I am?"

"It matters," he confirmed.

"Perhaps it does," she said. She removed the pendant she was wearing, an exquisitely wrought golden rose on a long chain, and put it around Calder's neck. "Very well, then. I am quite real, and this shall be your proof."

"You truly are an angel," Calder marveled hoarsely.

She laughed softly. "No," she said. "My name is Maeve, and I am quite another kind of specter." She searched his eyes for a long moment, an expression of infinite sadness in her face, and then lightly kissed his mouth.

He felt a surge of sensation, both physical and emotional, and was completely lost to her in the space of a single heart-beat. He groaned and closed his eyes, and when he opened them again, she was gone.

Calder was paralyzed for a time, full of confusion and wonder and a peculiar, spiraling joy, but when he could move, he groped for the pendant. It was there around his neck, real and solid to the touch.

"Maeve," he repeated, in a whisper, as though the name itself had the power to work magic in a world sorely in need of just that. "Maeve."

Maeve was distracted as she worked at her loom that same night, her mind full of Calder Holbrook. She had been foolish to approach him and worse, to speak to him and leave her precious pendant, like some smitten maiden in a troubador's song.

She felt a surge of emotion that would have caused her to blush, had she been human. For all practical intents and purposes, she thought, she *was* a virgin. While she and Valerian had often engaged in torrid bouts of mental sex after her making, no man had ever touched her before that. Now, no man ever would.

The idea was oddly painful, and that made Maeve furious with herself. She had, after all, vowed never to become involved with a mortal, and she wasn't the least bit like the legendary Lisette, who enjoyed bedding human lads at the height of their physical prowess.

Maeve murmured a curse, trying to shake the images that suddenly filled her mind, images of herself, coupling with Calder Holbrook. The effort was futile.

"It would be dangerous," she said aloud, at once irritated and dizzy with desire, working her shuttle so forcefully that it was in danger of snapping. "Such a thing must never be allowed to happen!"

But Maeve still felt the hot, powerful yearning, stronger

even than the need for blood. Knowing that at the height of her savage passion she might well lose control and actually kill her lover did nothing to ease the wanting.

She had always been so pragmatic, oblivious to the charms of humans—beyond drawing sustenance from them, of course. What was happening to her?

"Whatever it is," a voice intruded, "you'd better put a stop to it before you end up mortal, living in a motor-home and making babies."

Valerian. For once Maeve was glad to see him.

"Thank you for announcing yourself," she said coldly. "And for rifling through my thoughts like a pile of rummage in a market stall!"

Her visitor was dressed in unusually ordinary clothes, for him. He wore blue jeans and a sweatshirt with a picture of a wolf on the front.

"Tsk-tsk," he scolded. "You have much greater problems than my abrupt entrances. Lisette is prowling, Maeve. It is happening."

The news wrenched Maeve out of her self-absorption without delay. "What do you mean, she's 'prowling'?"

"Just that. Lisette is not merely taking blood, as the rest of us do, she's creating new vampires. Indiscriminately. And they are ugly, mindless creatures, with no more discretion than army ants."

Maeve abandoned all pretense of working at her weaving, and slipped off her stool to approach Valerian. "Does the Brotherhood know of this?"

Valerian's expression conveyed both amusement and well-controlled fury. "They chose to ignore it."

Maeve recalled her visit from Tobias. "Then perhaps you should follow their lead, Valerian. I've already been instructed not to interfere with Lisette."

For a moment it seemed that Valerian would explode with frustration. "Don't you see what will happen if she isn't stopped?" he demanded when he'd composed himself again. "The world will be overrun with these monsters, and if that's allowed to continue, there will soon be no humans to sustain us." He gripped Maeve's shoulders in strong hands and looked deep into her eyes. "But it will never come to that, Maeve," he went on, "because Nemesis will be forced to step in. He will mobilize armies of angels and destroy not just Lisette, but every vampire on earth. He's been itching to do just that for centuries, and this may be all the excuse he needs. Remember—as a warrior, it is his charge to protect the mortals his Master so cherishes!"

Maeve felt cold. "Surely the Brotherhood has considered—"

"Please!" Valerian scoffed furiously. "What has happened to your brain, Maeve—are you thinking with only a tiny portion as mortals do? The Brotherhood is a group of doddering old fools who have long since lost touch with the true state of affairs."

Maeve raised the fingertips of her right hand to her mouth, taken aback. Valerian's words had been bold, even for him. "Be careful," she warned after a moment of recovery. "It may not be Lisette our Brothers rise against, but you. As it is, they think you're rash and hot-headed, and they've warned me not to listen to your wild ideas."

Valerian's brow furrowed as he frowned. "Since when does anyone—the Brotherhood included—tell the illustrious Maeve Tremayne what to think and whose words to heed?"

She did not reply, for Valerian's question had struck its mark. Maeve valued her right to choose her own path and make decisions for herself above everything but her singular vampire powers.

The older blood-drinker smiled now and cupped his hands on either side of her face. "All I ask," he said quietly, "is that you look at what Lisette is doing. Once you've seen, you can make your own judgment."

Maeve started to argue, but the words stopped in her throat. Instead she simply nodded.

Valerian wrapped his arms around her, and the embrace became a nebula, spinning faster and faster. Maeve clung to the front of his shirt with both hands and devoutly hoped he knew what he was doing.

When the whirling stopped and they were still, Maeve was ruffled, and she pushed herself out of Valerian's arms with slightly more force than necessary.

"Why do you always have to be such a show-off?" she demanded. "Why can't you just will yourself from one place to another, the way the rest of us do?"

Valerian's eyes laughed, though his mouth was solemn. He raised a long finger to his lips. "Shhh," he whispered.

Maeve looked about and realized they were in a hospital, and judging by the high-tech equipment, she determined the time was the late twentieth century.

A nurse rounded the corner and stopped cold in the dimly lit corridor, clutching a medical chart to her chest. She was staring at Valerian and Maeve with her mouth open.

"You don't see us," Valerian said cordially, approaching the poor startled creature, who was now as immobile as a small animal blinded by a bright light. He rested the back of one hand against her forehead and repeated his words, this time gently, like a parent comforting a distraught child.

The young nurse stiffened for a moment, as if a charge had gone through her slender form, then proceeded down the hall, her conscious mind clear of impossible creatures knitted of shadows.

Valerian watched her go, a sort of affectionate concentration evident in his handsome face, and then gestured for Maeve to follow him. She did and found herself in a cold, sterile room with metal cabinets lining the walls. There was a human in attendance, but Valerian rendered him unconscious with a touch to the nape of the neck.

Barely a moment later a metal drawer slid open, seemingly of its own power. Maeve watched in disbelief as a bluish-gray corpse sat up and swung down from its storage place as nimbly as an athlete, though the body was that of a very old man.

The sight made Maeve shudder, though she'd seen many macabre things in her time; the thing was a vampire, and yet it seemed unaware of itself, unaware that two other blood-drinkers were nearby. It crept slowly toward the sleeping mortal, fangs glinting horribly in the fluorescent night.

"Do something," Maeve whispered, for the moment too repulsed to move.

Valerian stood still, his arms folded, his manner thoughtful and unhurried. "There—a specimen of Lisette's work," he said. "And this is only the beginning of the nightmare."

Chapter

3

The hospital morgue was utterly still.

Maeve started as the living corpse reached the mortal attendant, who was catatonic with terror, and closed waxen fingers over his shoulders.

After casting a contemptuous glance at Valerian, who was watching the process with a mixture of clinical interest and smugness, Maeve finally shook off her own morbid fascination and stepped forward.

She had never, since the night of her making, consumed the blood of an innocent, and she would not stand by and watch while another vampire did so.

"Stop," she said clearly, her voice charged with warning.

The freak looked at her stupidly, clearly confounded, but its hold on the mortal did not slacken. Its face was all the more hideous, it seemed to Maeve, for the ragged vestiges of humanity that still showed in its features.

Maeve knew that reasoning would not reach the creature, nor would the threat of greater powers, for it was conscious of nothing but its own mindless, unceasing hunger. Feeling a strange, disconsolate pity even as she moved to destroy, she reached out and closed her fingers over the creature's clammy throat.

"Be careful," Valerian coached dispassionately, sounding a little like a university professor overseeing a flock of mediocre students. "Its bite may be venomous. We don't know much about these aberrations, you know."

"Thank you so much for your input," Maeve replied, her gaze never shifting from her prey. She gave the ghoul a hard shake, and its grasp on the human, now blathering, was broken. The mortal scrambled to safety, making a low and wholly pitiful whimpering sound as he went.

Maeve did not pause to watch the attendant's flight, but instead concentrated on forcing the lesser vampire onto a shining steel autopsy table. She hissed an order, and Valerian finally troubled himself to stir, handing her a pair of scissors.

Maeve subdued the demon when it struggled, dared to murmur a prayer for its true soul, and drove the long, narrow blades of the scissors through the beast's chest wall and straight into a heart that had long since stopped beating.

The monster would not rise again.

A clamor stirred in the outer hallway; clearly the terrified attendant had been carrying tales about the strange and fearful goings-on in that eerie way station for the dead.

Valerian sighed. "We'd best get out of here," he said. "In a few seconds a horde of panicky mortals will come bursting through the doorway, and I would rather not deal with the poor wretches at the moment."

Maeve glared at him, even as she raised her hands over her head for a swift departure.

To Maeve's frustration, when she reassembled herself in the center of an ancient stone formation in the English countryside, the place where rumor had it that Aidan had been found, months before, Valerian was already there.

"Well," he began, in that imperious tone that came so naturally to him, "do you believe me now?"

Maeve was still shaken and not a little disgruntled, for she had felt a potential strength stirring in the being she had destroyed, a primitive agility that would be terrible if it were even properly channeled.

Still, she did not want Valerian to be right.

About anything.

"Any vampire could have made that—that thing," she said. "We have no proof that Lisette was responsible."

Valerian gave a raspy, tormented cry, full of profound exasperation. "Very well," he snapped. "Let us suppose, for a moment, that Lisette is not the culprit. The fact would remain that we are dealing with a renegade of some sort—one that must be stopped."

Maeve felt a chill, even though the night was warm, and a painful sense of desolation settled behind her heart, leeching her strength. She missed Aidan more sorely in those moments than she ever had, and yearned for his counsel.

She spoke patiently. "It could have been a random episode, an act of passion or revenge. We have no reason to believe it will be repeated."

Valerian gazed deeply into her eyes. "You are fooling yourself," he told her, touching a deep, well-hidden nerve with his words. He knew her so well and often taught her things about herself that she would rather have ignored. "This is no time to bury your head in the sand, Maeve—the existence of all vampires may depend on the choices you make."

She turned from him, let her forehead rest against one of the cool, towering stones that had witnessed her brother's transformation, from blood-drinker to mortal. Weariness swept over her, and for the first time in over two hundred years she wanted to retreat, as Valerian and others had done through the centuries, to lie dormant in some hidden tomb until the challenges facing her now had passed.

"Perhaps," she finally said after a long while, still not looking at Valerian, "vampires should not be saved. It could be that our time has ended—"

Valerian gripped her shoulders and wrenched her around to face him. "You cannot stand back and allow this to happen," he growled, showing his fine white teeth, including the sharp incisors that were only slightly longer than their counterparts. "The rest of us have sacrificed much—indeed, our very souls—for our immortality and our singular powers. Do you think that would be the end, if we all perished, that we would lie peacefully in our graves, oblivious to the universe around us? You must know that we would be sent into the pit, multitudes of us, to suffer agony for all eternity. Will you condemn us to such a fate, Maeve? We who have been your friends—your lovers?"

Maeve felt a stab of conscience, a certain annoyance, and no small amount of fear. "I have had only one lover," she was compelled to point out, even though the fact had no relevancy to the dilemma she faced.

Valerian narrowed his magnificent, mesmerizing eyes. "Vampires are not creatures of conscience or charity," he admitted softly, "but we are living beings who feel sadness and pain, as well as pleasure—and far more keenly than mortals do. Will you not fight for us? Will you not defend us, your sisters and brothers?"

"Why me?" Maeve cried in an agony almost as great as the one she'd endured when Aidan abandoned her. "Why not you? Or Tobias?"

The vampire laid his hands on either side of her face. "Deep inside, in the center of your mind and heart, you know the answer, Maeve," he said, his voice soft and grave. "Some unconscious consensus of the species has appointed you to take up the sword in our behalf."

Maeve was silent for a time, considering. She hesitated so long, in fact, that the first pinkish-gold light of dawn was tracing the horizon before she replied. "I will find out what is happening, but that is all I am willing to promise."

Valerian, to her weary annoyance, was smiling as she locked her hands together high over her head and vanished.

Calder Holbrook sat glumly in his father's august study, an overfull snifter of brandy close at hand, gazing out one of the windows overlooking the formal rose garden that had been his mother's pride. In one hand he fingered the necklace the Lady had given him, as though it were a rosary instead of a simple pendant on a chain.

Only a few feet away, in the carefully cultivated soil of the garden, the roses conducted a silent riot of color, their reds and pinks and yellows gaudy and rich in the afternoon sunlight. It seemed ironic to Calder that such shameless beauty could exist in a world where young boys played soldier, blowing each other to shreds at the behest of politicians and merchants and bankers.

"You needn't go back, you know." The voice came from the broad archway behind Calder, the doorway leading into the main part of the house, and, though it was unexpected, it did not startle him.

He did not turn to face his father, but instead closed his fingers tightly around the strange, simple pendant. His inner organs seemed to stiffen as he bolstered himself against this quiet, ruthless man who had sired him.

"Do not suggest buying my way out of the Army again," he warned. "I volunteered and I will serve my time."

Calder could imagine Bernard Holbrook's rage, as fathomless and cold as a well lined in slippery stones. "When will I understand you?" Bernard asked, and the clink of crystal meeting crystal echoed in the muggy, ponderous room as he poured a drink of his own.

Calder sighed but did not turn his attention from the lush roses, which seemed to frolic even in the still air, like trollops in gaudy dresses. "Perhaps never," he replied. "We are too different from each other."

"Nonsense," blustered Bernard, who preferred not to entertain realities that weren't to his liking. William, Bernard's elder son and Calder's half brother, looked and thought like their father and was a fawning sycophant in the bargain, but that apparently did not satisfy the old man. "Nonsense," Bernard said again. "You are flesh of my flesh, bone of my bone. We are more alike than you want to believe."

Suppressing a shudder at such a prospect, Calder dropped the pendant into the pocket of his starched linen shirt—he had long since tossed aside his suit coat—and summoned up a somewhat brittle smile. "Think what you wish, Father—as you always do."

Bernard was a portly man, with a wealth of white hair, a ruddy complexion, and shrewd blue eyes that were often narrowed to slits in concentration. Whatever his other faults, and they were many, his mental powers were formidable, and he could discern much that would escape a lesser mind.

"Surely you won't try to convince me that you—even you, with your curious ideas of mercy—actually *want* to go back to another of those damnable field hospitals. Good God, Calder, the places have got to be horrible beyond comprehension."

Calder's broad shoulders sagged slightly. "They are," he confessed in a tone that betrayed more than he would have revealed by choice. He rubbed his temples with a thumb and forefinger, remembering the incessant screaming, the sound of saws gnawing at bone, the vile, smothering stenches.

Bernard took a pensive sip of his brandy, looking out at his late wife's roses as though in fascination. Calder knew the expression was deceptive; he would have wagered the last decade of his life that the older man didn't even see the blossoms. Finally, when he was damn good and ready, he spoke again.

"Why, then, do you insist on going back?" he asked, and for a moment the question seemed reasonable to Calder, and he did not know how to answer. "Well?" Bernard prompted when an interval had passed. "Is it because you want so badly to spite me?"

Calder sprang from his chair, invigorated by a sudden rush of fury, and turned his back on the man who had sired him to gaze up at the woman in the portrait displayed above the mantelpiece. "Damn it, Father," he bit out after several seconds when he did not trust himself to speak, "when are you going to realize that the sun and the planets do not revolve around you?"

"When," Bernard countered quietly, "are you going to realize that in throwing your life away like this you injure yourself far more grievously than you could ever hurt me?"

Slowly Calder turned to face the other man. "I am not 'throwing my life away,' " he said coldly in measured tones. "I am a *doctor*, Father. Is there a more logical place for me to be than in the midst of suffering and pain?"

"Yes," Bernard said with a patient sigh. "You could be

a society doctor, like many of your schoolmates, and treat rich ladies with the vapors."

Again Calder felt such contempt that he dared not speak. Instead he moved close enough to the place where he'd been sitting to retrieve his half-finished brandy. He tossed back the contents of his snifter and felt the fire spread through his veins, the sudden, almost painful slackening of the muscles in his neck and shoulders.

"Calder," Bernard went ruthlessly on, his voice level and sensible like that of a snake charmer. "Listen to reason. I have friends who can arrange an honorable discharge. You can spend the rest of the war in Europe if that's what you want, learning those new surgical techniques you're forever yammering about."

Calder closed his eyes, shaken and shamed. A part of him wanted to do as his father urged, to flee the carnage plaguing his own continent and lose himself in the knowledge he craved, to pretend there was no unnecessary pain in the world, no savagery.

"No one would blame you," Bernard pressed, probably sensing his advantage.

Calder came back to himself in a flash of conviction and hurled his empty snifter against the polished black marble of the fireplace. The crystal shattered into thousands of glittering shards, and he wondered if that was not how God must see His creation: as broken, shining bits of something originally meant to be beautiful. "*I* would blame me," he said softly.

Bernard sighed again. "Would that your sainted mother, God rest her soul, had taken her stubbornness to the grave with her," he said, "rather than leaving it in your keeping."

Calder said nothing. He was, in fact, already looking toward the doorway, yearning to be away.

As had ever been, Bernard did not seem to know when to quit. "If you will not put the war behind you for your own sake," he said, "then do so for mine. I need you here, under this roof."

"You have William," Calder replied, unmoved.

Bernard offered no comment on that statement; he could not fault his elder son without faulting himself, for they shared the same thoughts and feelings and opinions. "Why in the name of heaven do you hate me so much?" he asked. "You have never been abused, and you have lacked for nothing. I saw that you had the finest possible education, even when you insisted on wasting that marvelous mind of yours on ordinary medicine. Tell me—I think I deserve to know— why is it that you have chafed and strained against me from the time you learned to grip the rail of your baby bed and hold yourself upright?"

Calder raised his eyes to the lovely, guileless face in the portrait over the mantel, the face of his mother. Somewhere deep in his mind her sweet voice echoed, shaping the words of some silly lullaby.

Finally he turned to Bernard. "I don't hate you," he said. "I cannot spare the energy hatred demands."

"But you do not love me, either. You never have."

"Wrong," Calder said in a low, insolent voice. "She loved you once"—he gestured toward the painting that dominated the room—"and so did I. Until I saw that you were destroying her with your polite cruelties and gentle betrayals."

Bernard threw up his hands, then let them slap to his sides in frustration. His face was redder than usual, and the white line edging his mouth gave evidence that he was shocked as well as infuriated.

"Great Scot," he whispered. "After all this time, are you telling me that you have scorned my every effort to be a father to you because of a few fancy women?"

"She thought you loved her," Calder said, looking up at his mother's face, feeling again the terrible helplessness and despair he'd known as a small child. She'd wept over her errant husband, the beautiful, naive Marie Calder Holbrook, until Calder had thought his own heart would break. And in the end her abiding grief had caused her death.

"Marie was weak," came a third voice from the inner doorway.

Calder's gaze shot to his half brother, who was fifteen

years his senior. William might have been a comfort to Marie, even a friend, for he'd been quite near her own age; instead, he had tormented her for taking his dead mother's place in that yawning tomb of a house.

A charge moved in the room, a silent crackling, nearly visible for its sheer strength.

"Do not tempt me to do you harm, brother," Calder said to William. "The pleasure of the prospect is very nearly more than I can resist."

William, who would look exactly like Bernard in another thirty years, started to speak and then wisely restrained himself.

Calder pushed past him to enter the wide hallway just beyond.

Bernard shouted his name, but Calder did not turn back. Instead he kept walking, his strides long, until he was far from the great house and the others who lived beneath its heavy slate roof.

Benecia and Canaan Havermail were having one of their ludicrous tea parties when Maeve appeared in the ancient graveyard behind their family castle.

Benecia, a gold-haired wisp of a girl, and Canaan, her younger sister, who was dark of coloring, appeared at first glance to be children. They were in fact vampires, with some four centuries of grisly escapades behind them, and all the more terrible for their doll-like beauty.

Seeing Maeve, Canaan clapped her tiny, porcelain-white hands. Her nails were delicate pink ovals, microscopic in size and smooth as the interior of a sea shell.

"You've come to have tea with us!" she cried in childish delight.

Maeve felt a pang, looking upon this exquisite monstrosity, and wondered again if she hadn't been right, during her last encounter with Valerian, when she'd suggested that it might be better to let all vampires perish.

"Sit down," Benecia trilled, drawing back a dusty chair.

Her golden sausage curls bounced in her eagerness to welcome the unexpected guest.

Maeve took in the scene without speaking or moving. The tea table was a dusty monument, smudged with moss and draped with the weavings of spiders, but it was the other guests that gave her pause.

The sisters had disinterred two corpses and a skeleton, no doubt from graves in other parts of the cemetery, and arranged them around the tombstone-table in a hideous parody of a favorite human tradition. One body, mummified by some strange subterranean process to a hard brown thing, mouth open wide as if to scream, had been neatly broken at the waist so that it would sit like a proper guest. The other was a gray, dirty thing, with rags hanging from its frame, its bony, long-dead fingers curled around a pretty china cup. The skeleton was perhaps the least ludicrous of the party, for it was clean of grave-dust, and no atrophied muscles clung to its ivory smoothness.

Maeve shook her head, marveling, not bothering to decline the invitation to join in the festivities. Before she could speak, a fourth creature lumbered into view, and she gave a little cry of amazement when she recognized what it was.

The grayish corpse, only recently dead, had been changed, like the poor creature Maeve had destroyed in the hospital morgue, into a low-grade vampire.

"Where did you find this beast?" Maeve demanded of the ancient children as the blood-drinker went from one horrible guest to another. It bared its long fangs as it wrenched one after the other to its mouth, then tossed each aside in blind frustration when there was no blood to drink.

Benecia, the elder of the two most terrifying fiends in the lot, batted her enormous china blue eyes in feigned innocence. "We stumbled across him when we were out feeding," she said in a sweet voice underlaid with vicious determination. "He's perfectly dreadful, isn't he?"

Canaan had plagued the wretched thing into chasing her, and she giggled with all the merriment of a human child frolicking with a kitten. In that moment Maeve understood her brother Aidan's revulsion for the ways of vampires as she never had before.

"We've named him Charlie," Benecia said cheerfully.

Maeve tried again. "Where did you find him?" A suspicion dawned in her mind, ugly and totally feasible. "Or did you make this abomination yourselves?"

Canaan stopped her happy dance to stare at Maeve, and Benecia was still as well.

"Tell me," Maeve ordered.

Hatred flashed in Benecia's cornflower-blue eyes, with their thick, fringelike lashes. She answered in a respectful tone, though her words were flip.

"Of course we didn't make him ourselves, Auntie Maeve," she said with acid goodwill. "We only *drink* from mortals, we don't change them."

The corpse had stopped scrambling after Canaan to stare at Maeve, round-eyed and slavering. She suppressed a shudder.

"Then where did he come from?" she insisted.

"We told you," wailed Canaan, stamping one impossibly small, velvet-slippered foot. "We *found* him. He was wandering outside All Souls' Cathedral in London."

"Were there others like him?" Maeve asked distractedly. With the formidable power of her mind, she reached into the skull of the pitiful creature before her and found no consciousness there, no vestige of a mortal soul.

Benecia shrugged, then bustled to put the tattered fragments of humanity Charlie had disturbed back into their chairs. "*If* there are more, we didn't see them."

Canaan was glaring at Maeve, her small arms folded across the ruffled bodice of her pink taffeta dress. "Mummy's still hunting, if you wished to see her."

"Get me a sharp stick," Maeve ordered, drawing the hapless, unresisting creature toward her by the strength of her thoughts.

"You're going to stake him?" Benecia and Canaan cried in eerie unison, their voices ringing with mingled horror and eager anticipation.

"Just do as I tell you," Maeve snapped, mentally pressing poor Charlie to the rocky ground.

Canaan brought a piece of half-rotted wood that had probably served as a marker for one of the graves, in some long-ago time.

Maeve centered the stake over the beast's cold chest with one hand and took up a rock with the other. Destroying the other creature had been relatively easy, if horrible, but this instance proved more difficult. When she pounded the wooden point past skin and tissue and bone, however atrophied, the thing shrieked in rage and pain. Maeve felt sick as she struck wood and stone together, over and over, until the screaming ceased and the monster was truly dead.

When she looked up from her task, Benecia and Canaan were looking on, faces white as moonglow, eyes gleaming with pleasure. They reminded Maeve of wolves held at bay by firelight, yearning to spring, to tear and plunder with sharp teeth.

"Be gone!" Maeve cried in disgust, trembling slightly as she rose to her feet. She did not wish to be other than what she was, a practicing vampire, even after what she had just experienced, but she did long for a confidante, a mate, a kindred spirit who would lessen the horror.

Yet again, her thoughts strayed to Calder Holbrook, the American doctor. There was something in him, some combination of talents and foibles, that grasped at her heart and would not let go.

Instead of seeking him, however, Maeve focused her attention on Valerian, leaving Charlie's still body to the ravenous hunger of the dawn.

She found her erstwhile mentor in a harem, clad only in a loincloth and a blue silk turban trimmed in pearls and sporting a magnificent emerald for a clasp. The scantily clad dancing girls surrounding Valerian scattered with little cries when Maeve took shape in their midst.

"I might have known you'd be someplace like this," Maeve huffed, looking around her in contempt while Valerian raised himself gracefully to his feet and dismissed the dancers with a clap of his hands and a few indulgent, smoky words.

Valerian chuckled, folding his beautifully sculpted arms over an equally well-shaped chest, and arched one eyebrow. "Are you jealous?" he drawled.

The very suggestion made Maeve dizzy with fury. "Most certainly not," she snapped.

Valerian removed his turban and set it carefully aside, then, with a sweeping gesture of his hands, magically clothed himself in his usual formal garb, cape included. He'd been on a Dracula kick for some time now, and Maeve wished he'd get over it.

He smiled at her thoughts. "If you'd like," he said, "I could dress as a sultan. I rather like the way I look in that jeweled turban."

Maeve sighed. "You would," she muttered. "Listen to me, Valerian—I encountered another of those creatures tonight. Benecia and Canaan found it wandering around All Souls' and brought it to one of their infernal tea parties."

Valerian winced. "What reprehensible creatures they are." A mischievous look shimmered in his eyes. "Have you ever noticed what a tacky lot vampires can be?"

"I wouldn't talk if I were you," Maeve replied, tossing a telling glance toward the discarded turban. She put her hands on her hips to let Valerian know she would countenance no more nonsense. "We must do something," she said.

The other vampire spread his hands in a gesture of helplessness. "I seem to remember telling you exactly that," he said, as if saddened that modern manners had degenerated to a pitiable state.

"You might well have been wrong in suspecting Lisette," Maeve insisted. "All the same, the situation bears looking into. Where do you suggest we start?"

"We?" Valerian echoed, giving the word a rich and resonant tone.

"Damn you, Valerian, do not try my patience. It has already reached the breaking point!"

He swept his cloak around her in a patronizing gesture

and crooned his answer into her ear. "Relax, darling," he said. "Valerian will protect you."

Maeve was still kicking and struggling when the two of them landed in a tumbling heap on the stone sidewalk outside London's All Souls' Cathedral. Maeve quickly discerned that it was the late twentieth century, and her fury at Valerian was tempered with a great sadness rooted in the fact that, in this time and place at least, Calder Holbrook did not exist. Except, perhaps, as a pile of moldering remains as ugly as the guests at Benecia and Canaan's tea party.

Valerian got to his feet first and offered a hand to Maeve. She slapped it away and stood under her own power, ignoring the curious glances of the few passers-by abroad at that hour.

Valerian started after one of the stragglers, in fact, and Maeve was forced to pull him back by his cloak.

"I haven't fed," he complained. It was a wonder to Maeve how he could look and sound imperious even when he whined.

"You should have thought of that before you squandered half the night playing sultan," Maeve snapped, dusting off her long dress and hooded velvet cape. She needed sustenance herself, but she could delay it for a while.

"Come," Valerian said, suddenly serious, taking her hand. "Let us see what other fiends wander the earth besides ourselves."

Chapter

4

Maeve was rapidly becoming an obsession.

Calder thought of her constantly, the woman he knew only by her given name. He wondered who and where and, indeed, *what* she was, and agonized over the distinct possibility that he would never see her again. Despite years of scientific training and a purely practical turn of mind, he felt certain she was not a mortal woman.

He fingered the pendant she'd left in his keeping; he wore it around his neck now, as faithfully as small children and elderly women wore religious medals. No, the mysterious Maeve was not an ordinary human, but she had not been born in Calder's imagination, either, as he had once feared. She was quite real, as real as this talisman she'd given him.

He stretched in his hammock, which he'd suspended between two birch trees behind the summerhouse on his father's estate, out of sight of the great house. Hands cupped behind his head, Calder reflected that it would be a mercy if he could just return to his work—the local hospitals were overflowing with wounded soldiers and victims of the current typhoid epidemic—but he had already pushed his normally sturdy body beyond its considerable limits. If he did not rest, he risked physical collapse, a state that would put him completely at his father's mercy.

Despite the leaden heat of that summer afternoon, Calder shivered. He would get through his confinement, and that horrific war awaiting him just beyond the gates of the magnificent house like a sleek and violent beast, simply by living from one moment to the next.

And perhaps, if he'd done anything right in his life, anything deserving of reward, he would see Maeve again and begin to learn her secrets.

Maeve looked up at the shadowy spires of the great cathedral with trepidation. It would be morning soon, she had not fed, and just being in that place brought all her fears of divine punishment surging to the fore.

"Where do we begin?" she asked in an unusually small voice.

Valerian was silent for a moment, thinking, then replied, "Lisette has to have some place to hide these revolting creations of hers during daylight. Surely they can't tolerate the sun any more than we can. If I were her, I would keep them in the old tombs beneath the cathedral—there's a nice irony in that, if she hasn't gone too mad to notice it."

Maeve glanced nervously toward the sky. She'd had a brush with the dawn herself once and wasn't anxious to repeat the experience. "Let's hurry," she said, tugging Valerian toward the nearest entrance to the great church.

Valerian balked, suddenly tense. "Not so fast," he rasped. "I sense something. Lisette may be lying in wait for us."

Deliberately Maeve calmed herself. Valerian might be right; it would be like Lisette to bait them. Narrowing the blazing light of her consciousness to a pinpoint of concentration, she assessed the general atmosphere; yes, there was danger, but the vampire queen was nowhere about.

"Something else," Maeve said thoughtfully. "It's waiting for us in the tombs."

Valerian nodded. "Forewarned is forearmed," he said and proceeded toward the entrance.

With a trick of his facile mind, he sprung the lock on the heavy wooden door, shaped from oak trees that had probably towered in some dark northern forest well before his human birth. They entered, hesitated in the shadows, sensing the lurking danger.

Together the vampires proceeded through passageways and corridors until they found the inner door leading down filthy stone steps to the catacombs. The lock was forged of iron, rusted through, and the key had been lost so long that even the oldest priest would have no recollection of it.

Again, Valerian maneuvered the mechanism by his own brand of sorcery, but the task was more difficult this time. He was clearly tiring; like Maeve, he had not fed, and as the dawn neared, the deep sleep of all vampires surely tugged at the underside of his consciousness. For all that, he was insufferably bold.

"Do you think we don't know you're there?" he called irritably, his voice echoing through the dark, dank chamber where only the moldering dead and the scurrying rats belonged.

Maeve braced herself as the door swung open on hinges that shrieked in protest. This was not just one thing lying in wait for them, but many, and the danger was immense. Still, she felt angry challenge, rather than fear, and made ready for any sort of battle.

"Come," Valerian snapped. "Show yourselves."

Although the enormous chamber was utterly void of light, Maeve saw clearly and knew Valerian did as well, for vampires functioned best in darkness. There was nothing to see, except for crypts and tombs and marble monuments of the sort Benecia and Canaan used for tables at their infamous tea parties.

The cavernous, dusty place, with its great curtains of spiderwebs, seemed suddenly to echo with tension, and Maeve focused all her being on the powers she'd honed since the night of her making.

A humming silence throbbed and rushed throughout the chamber, encircling Maeve and Valerian like invisible floodwaters, and in the next instant the attack began.

Their assailants were not the lumbering, corpselike vam-

pires they'd encountered before, but great, raucous creatures, ravenlike beasts the size of humans.

Valerian had set himself to fight and began to flail
against the things, when Maeve reached out to stop him,
touching her fingers lightly to his forearm.

"Illusions," she said.

In that instant the fluttering, noisy onslaught ceased.

"Of course," Valerian confirmed in a rather sheepish
tone. "Warlocks. How many?"

Maeve considered briefly. "Ten or twelve."

Valerian sighed. "Damn." He turned away from Maeve,
and she pressed her own back to his, preparing for the true
battle. "If we end up in hell together," he went on, "please
accept my apology for getting you admitted."

A soft, mocking laugh escaped Maeve. "Your apology,"
she marveled. "A rare gift indeed. And what a comfort it
will be during an eternity of suffering."

The warlocks came at them then, from behind tombs and
out of crypts, shrieking and clawing and assaulting both
Maeve and Valerian with their greatest weapons, their
minds.

Back to back, the two vampires fought for their lives,
both well aware that if the warlocks overcame them, they
would not leave them to recover on the cool stone floor of
the mausoleum. No, if they lost the battle, Valerian and
Maeve would be taken to some very public place and left
there to smolder in the sun, as a gruesome warning to all
other vampires.

Once, Valerian slipped to his knees—Maeve felt him
slide gracefully down the length of her back and thighs—
but he fought just as valiantly as a knight defending his
queen.

"We should have fed first!" he sputtered.

Like her friend, Maeve fought on two fronts; she flailed
her arms and kicked mightily, at the same time forming a
mental shield to protect her mind from the assault of many
others.

"Yes, yes," she answered Valerian impatiently. "I know. You *told* me so!"

It had been a mistake, shifting even a small part of her concentration from the warlocks to Valerian. One of the enemy got through at that precise moment; Maeve felt a tear in her consciousness, followed by a dizzying sickness.

In the next instant blunt teeth sank themselves into the side of her neck, and agony flashed from the wound into every part of Maeve's body.

"Be ye cursed, Vampire!" one of the would-be slayers shrilled.

Maeve had not experienced physical pain of this magnitude before, even while mortal, and the force of it stunned her, weakened her knees. She swayed, but felt Valerian surge upward to stand back to back with her again, to virtually support her with his own strength.

Hold on, he told her mentally.

In the next moment the attack suddenly ceased, and the abruptness of it was somehow like an added blow. Valerian whirled and took Maeve into his arms, holding her up.

One of the warlocks came slowly toward them, pushing back the hood of his black cloak to reveal the handsome, ingenuous face that was so typical of his breed.

"It grows late," he said with a smile. Neither he nor his companions were human practitioners of the old religion; they, like the vampires, had been born of some ancient curse, some misbegotten magic, and they too were immortal. "Soon the dawn will come."

"What is your business with us?" Valerian demanded, his embrace tightening around Maeve.

The warlock's dazzling smile intensified, and he spread his arms, in their drapery of black, wide of his body. "We wanted only to get your attention, Vampire—obviously, we could have destroyed you both if we'd wished it so." He paused, splaying his fingers and touching the tips together in a prayerlike fashion. All in all, he made a disturbing caricature of a holy man, with his reverent stance and flowing robes. "Hold your arguments," he told Valerian, thus proving that he was perceptive as well as theatrical. "There is no time. Carry our message to the Brotherhood of the Vampyre."

Maeve felt adrift in a deeper darkness than she'd ever known before; she could barely comprehend the warlock's words and would have fallen if Valerian hadn't been supporting her.

"There is a renegade among you," the creature went on calmly, "the female, Lisette. She makes vampires indiscriminately; mindless, bumbling ghouls who wander the earth murdering children."

Maeve could not be sure whether she actually heard Valerian's reply or only sensed it. Dawn was close; the need to sleep was pulling her downward, as was the injury.

"Since when do you mourn slaughtered humans, Warlock, be they children or the oldest of the old?"

"Your assessment is quite right—we don't give the proverbial damn about mortals, except for the amusement they provide. But the Warrior Angel cherishes them, as does his Master. Even now, Nemesis implores the highest courts of heaven to let him wage war on *all* unnatural creatures, not only vampires, but werewolves and witches and faeries and warlocks—all of us. He's been waiting centuries—nay, eons—for an excuse to wipe the earth clean of all immortals except his own angels, and your Lisette may well have given it to him!"

Valerian was weary, too; Maeve heard it in his voice, felt it in his large frame. "What do you want of us?" he asked.

"That is simple," the warlock replied. "Stop the female, Lisette, immediately. If you do not, then our kind will declare war upon yours, in the hope that by destroying every last one of you, we can win mercy from Nemesis. Do not forget, Vampire, that we have an advantage over you—we can venture out into the daylight."

A vision entered Maeve's fevered mind; she saw black-cloaked figures moving through sunshine from one vampire lair to another, while the blood-drinkers lay helpless, systematically driving stakes through their hearts.

Valerian was undaunted, or at least he appeared so to Maeve. "Do not threaten us," he retorted. "We are not without superior powers of our own, and if you are wise you will remember that."

There was a general rustling, and Maeve fought the darkness even as she saw the first faint tinge of dawn shining beneath the ancient oaken door.

"They're gone." These two words, spoken by Valerian, were the last things Maeve heard before she sank into utter oblivion.

The warlocks vanished as quickly as they had appeared, for, although their leader had boasted of their ability to move about in the light of day, they were essentially creatures of darkness, like vampires.

Valerian had no time to consider them further, however, for dawn was imminent and he could already feel its molten fingers groping for him and for Maeve. He swept her up into his arms and hastened into the blackest regions of the crypt, found a chamber with a door, and dodged inside.

The sleep took him before he could set Maeve down, or even assess their surroundings—all Valerian knew, as he lost consciousness, was that he had found a place where the light would not penetrate.

Maeve awakened on a cold stone floor scattered with bones and crumbling mortar from the ancient walls, her head in Valerian's lap. The wound to her neck, inflicted by a warlock during the battle the preceding night, had already begun to heal, but she was weak with the need for blood.

Valerian woke up just as she was raising herself from his thighs. "So," he said and shrugged. "We shall live to hunt another night. Frankly I wasn't entirely sure the warlocks wouldn't come back while we were sleeping, armed with stakes and mallets."

Maeve's head spun; she wondered if she had the strength to hunt. "Think, Valerian," she said, somewhat peevish in her discomfort. "They want us to carry the message to the Brotherhood. Destroying us now would have defeated their purpose."

The magnificent vampire thrust himself to his feet and pulled a shaky Maeve after him. "We are not the only blood-drinkers who could spread the word," he pointed out with weary reason. "Come, let's find nourishment before we perish."

Fortunately for both Maeve and Valerian, All Souls' Cathedral was in an area of London that had degenerated into crowded squalor, teeming with small-time hoods, drug dealers, and pimps.

Spotting a smarmy-looking man in a cheap striped suit, leaning against a lamppost, Maeve raised the collar of her cloak higher, in order to hide the mark on her neck, and elbowed Valerian aside.

"You're on your own," she said. "This one is mine."

Valerian shuddered. "Yuk," he said.

"Beggars can't be choosers," Maeve retorted and sashayed toward the pimp. She saw, in the recesses of the man's mind, that he made a habit of picking up scared runaways, in bus and subway stations, winning their confidence and then introducing them to prostitution.

As she approached, she felt an inexplicable need to see Calder Holbrook again; he was proof that decency and honor still existed in the world.

For now, however, Maeve had to play a part, for if she did not feed, she would perish.

She formed her mouth into a saucy smile, and the pimp straightened and looked her over with a practiced eye.

"You ain't no workin' girl," he said in a thick cockney accent.

Maeve laid her hands on his shoulders—he was wearing a worn drum major's coat, burgundy velvet with gold piping—and looked deeply into his eyes, his mind, his spirit. By the mental equivalent of flipping a switch, she shut down his brain.

He followed her mutely into the nearest alleyway, and there Maeve drank. For the first time since her making, she was tempted to take her victim beyond the point of death, and the realization worried her. While she felt none of her brother Aidan's sentimentality toward humankind—indeed, she was contemptuous of such attitudes—Maeve was not vicious; she took blood only to sustain her powers and remain immortal.

Restored and strengthened, Maeve left the procurer sitting in the alleyway, vacant and staring, with the seed of a moral awakening sprouting in his brain. Come the bright light of morning, this particular deviant would forsake the life of sin, move in with his poor mother in Manchester, and spend the rest of his days clerking in a series of small shops.

Valerian was waiting impatiently on the sidewalk when she reached it, pacing back and forth, his cape flowing behind him. His color was high, which meant that he, too, had fed.

"It's about time you came back," he snapped, stopping in the center of the walk, arms folded, glaring down at Maeve. He was, typically, completely unaware of what a spectacle he made, with his imposing size, his cape, and his haughty manner. Nor did he seem aware of the flow of pedestrian traffic moving around him.

"You shouldn't have waited," Maeve said, refusing to be intimidated. Valerian might be able to dominate other vampires, but she was different.

"We have to speak to the Brotherhood," he told her huffily. "Or has it slipped your mind that the warlocks are threatening to make war on all of us?"

"Of course it hasn't," Maeve replied pleasantly but in a firm tone. "It's just that there is something else I want to do first." She glanced at the starry sky with its tracings of clouds, for this was the vampire's way of measuring time. "I'll meet you at the stone monument where Aidan disappeared—two hours before sunrise."

"Maeve—" Valerian protested.

She did not give him time to finish speaking before she interlocked her fingers above her head and vanished, for there was a sort of sustenance her spirit needed as badly as her body needed the blood of mortals.

Maeve returned to the nineteenth century, her favorite for all its trials and shortcomings, and found herself on the steps of a summerhouse behind the Holbrook mansion in Philadelphia. There was a soft, warm rain falling, and Calder was standing with his back to her, his hands gripping the rail that encompassed the open structure.

He sensed her presence immediately, although Maeve had not made even the intimation of a sound, and whirled to face her.

He said her name as though it were holy, and in that moment Maeve did what she had sworn she would never do. She lost her heart to a mortal.

The realization left her stricken, for, even now, in the face of a love she knew was unceasing and eternal, she did not want to become human again, as Aidan had done for his beloved Neely.

For Maeve, then, this grandest and most powerful of all emotions was a sentence to loneliness without end. Overcome, she turned, there on the steps that glimmered with rain, and would have vanished if Calder had not grasped her shoulders from behind.

"Don't go," he pleaded hoarsely. "Please—stay. Just for a few minutes—just long enough to tell me who you are."

She faced him then, for she hadn't the heart to disappear from his embrace, and looked up at him, knowing that all her suffering was visible in her eyes. "Who do you think I am, Calder Holbrook?" she asked gently.

He had stepped out from under the summerhouse roof, and the rain wet his dark hair and turned his fine linen shirt transparent against his skin. "An illusion? An angel? Or perhaps a beautiful devil?" he mused gruffly. "I don't know, God help me. Nothing in my medical training, or in all my life before that, could have prepared me for this. All I know is that I think of you, and nothing and no one else, through every day and every night." He paused, pushed back his dripping hair in a gesture that was touchingly boyish, and then whispered, "Tell me what is happening here, before I go mad. I beg of you—*help me understand.*"

She wanted to weep. The truth was a crushing burden, and she knew he would not believe her. As a doctor, a man of science, Calder would find even the existence of blood-drinkers impossible to accept.

Nevertheless, she could not deny him an answer, or anything else for that matter, because he was too precious to her. "I am a vampire," she said, her voice soft but matter-of-fact.

Calder stared at her, and she saw that the color had drained from his strong face. "A drinker of blood?" he marveled, and the words were hardly more than bursts of breath.

Maeve nodded, while parts of her spirit trembled and collapsed beneath the weight of Calder's horror. "Vampires are immortal," she explained, all the while wishing she'd never let herself begin to care for a human being. "Without blood, however, we would perish in a way far more terrible than even you, with all your knowledge of battlefields, could ever imagine. We must avoid daylight at all costs, and we have special powers—the ability to travel through time, for instance."

Calder seemed unaware of the rain, which was coming down much harder now. "What do you mean, you can travel through time?"

She felt a stirring of hope because Calder had not bolted in revulsion or terror, but she was far too wise to let herself think he believed her. He was probably humoring her, as he might a mad person.

Only then did it strike Maeve that Calder's mind was closed to her; she could not divine his thoughts or feelings.

"I just came from the late twentieth century," she said, amazed, prodding gently with her thoughts and meeting with an impenetrable block.

To her surprise, Calder clasped her hand, led her into the summerhouse, and sat her down on a wrought-iron bench tucked into the cool folds of shadows. "Tell me—what sort of world exists—in that other place and time, I mean? Do they still make war? What advances have been made in medicine?"

For a long moment Maeve was too taken aback by his ready belief to speak. Then she whispered, "You don't think I'm insane or a liar?"

"You are not a mortal woman," Calder answered. "That much was clear from the moment I first saw you." He was wearing the pendant she'd given him during their last encounter, and he held it out for her to see. "It was only this medal, solid proof of your existence, that kept me from having myself admitted to the nearest asylum," he said. "Now—please—tell me about medicine and warfare in your century."

Maeve checked the sky, only too aware of her commitment to meet Valerian at the stone monument in the English countryside. When she gazed into Calder's eyes again, however, she wondered if she would ever be able to look away. "There have been tremendous advances in medicine—they can cure or control a lot of diseases that are fatal in your time. It is possible to immunize children against measles and diphtheria and many of the other illnesses that almost always end in death here. Surgeons are performing successful organ transplants there, and the infant mortality rate is a fraction of yours.

"War is very much a part of the modern world unfortunately. There are weapons capable of destroying the earth, and while the largest and most powerful nations are trying hard to get along, there are a number of small, fanatical factions that are not so willing to cooperate."

Calder absorbed her words for a long interval, one of his hands clasping hers. "Can you take me there?" he asked, finally, catching Maeve off guard with the last question she would have expected him to ask.

She shook her head regretfully. "Mortals cannot travel through time as yet, though you do have the propensity for it locked away somewhere in your brain. It is an ability that must evolve over many, many generations."

He looked so disappointed that Maeve's heart ached, but a moment later his countenance brightened again. "Can you bring me things from the future, Maeve—like medicine, or books about surgery and diagnosis?"

Maeve considered, knowing she should leave this man's side, once and for all, and never return and, at the same time, feeling infinitely grateful for an excuse to see him again. "I suppose there would be no harm in that. There's just one thing, however—it isn't wise to change the course of history, because one can never predict all the ramifications of even the simplest act. You could use the things you discover in twentieth-century books, but you must not teach them to others." She stood, unable to ignore the hour any longer, and Calder rose with her. She put her hands on the warm, supple flesh of his face. "I cannot stay any longer—there are matters that must be attended to."

"Will you be back?"

Maeve felt a pang, for she could not discern whether he wanted to see her again because he cared for her just a little, or because he wanted the books and wonder drugs she could bring from the future. "Yes," she said. "If I can return, I will."

Calder bent his head then and touched Maeve's lips with his own, and as brief and innocent as it was, the contact rocked her to the very center of her being.

Her gaze flew to his, searching for the revulsion she so dreaded, seeking Calder's horrified reaction to kissing a cold mouth. Instead of those things, however, she saw a certain reverence, unmasked affection, and, yes, a disturbing sort of curiosity—that of a scientist studying a unique specimen.

Filled with sadness and bliss, she reached up and touched his lips with three fingers.

"Good-bye," she said.

One moment Maeve was there, standing before him, pale and ethereally beautiful in the darkness, and the next she was gone.

Calder felt a bleakness unequaled in his memory; he wanted to be with Maeve, now and forever, but that was clearly impossible. He would wait, he told himself, as patiently as he could, and one night soon she would return to him.

He stood in the rain for a long time, remembering. Then he dropped the pendant down inside his wet shirt, to hide it from the curious gazes of his father and half brother in the same way he had always hidden his heart from the world.

Until Maeve.

The pattering shower turned to a downpour, but still Calder remained where he was, marveling, telling himself that Maeve could not exist, could not be what he knew she was. An immortal.

Finally Calder broke his stunned inertia and strode toward the house, where he was met by Prudence, the family's longtime housekeeper.

"Lord have mercy," that good woman fussed, seeing Calder's wet clothes and distracted expression. "I thought you had better sense than to be runnin' around in a cold rain! You want to die of the pneumonia, you foolish chile?"

Calder paid no attention to Prudence's ire, for the affection between them was old and deep. "Send Perkins around for the carriage," he said, entering the big kitchen and heading straight for the rear stairway. "Tell him we're going to the Army hospital on Union Street."

Prudence followed her erstwhile charge as far as the newel post, her sizable body quivering with disapproval. The glow of the gaslights flickered over her beautiful coffee-colored skin, and her jaw was set at a stubborn angle. "You ain't goin' to no hospital at this hour," she ranted. "I swear this war of Mr. Lincoln's done somethin' to your brain. . . ."

The war had "done something" to Calder's brain, all right, and it had nearly broken his spirit and his physical strength in the bargain. Now, however, knowing there was a future, a time when miracles would occur in the realm of medical science, gave him new hope.

"Tell Perkins to bring along a slicker," he called back over one shoulder as he gained the upper hallway. "It might be a long night, and this rain isn't likely to let up."

"Mr. Calder!" Prudence bellowed after him. "You get back here—you hear me? You ain't well!"

Calder opened the door to his room, already stripping off his wet shirt when he crossed the threshold, thinking to himself that, contrary to Prudence's assessment, he was feeling better than he had in years.

Chapter

5

Maeve passed the following day not in her favorite lair beneath the London house, as usual, but in a dusty crevice behind the foundation of the Union Hospital. She'd known Calder was going there after their meeting in the summerhouse, and she had wanted to be near him.

Normally Maeve's slumber was untroubled by dreams, be they pleasant or unpleasant, but that time was different. The wards and even the passages of the old hospital were filled with the wounded and the dying. They were only boys, these soldiers, most of them so young that they'd never been away from home at all before marching off to battle.

Maeve did not hear their screams of physical pain, for suffering, however intense, is a temporal thing, meaning little in the face of eternity. No, it was their soul-cries Maeve discerned, the agonized protests of their spirits.

When she awakened at sunset, she was instantly aware of her mistake in coming to that particular place. With so many mortals in torment, it was only logical that the premises would be crawling with angels.

A surge of terror moved through Maeve as she raised herself, dusted off her clothes, and pressed her back against the wall of the foundation. What had possessed her to make such a dangerous error in judgment?

She listened, and waited. Now, with all her senses on the alert, she could feel the presences of companion angels, hundreds of them. Fortunately—and this fact, she thought, might well save her from certain destruction—they were not warriors, these winged messengers from heaven, but comforters. Their full attention was fixed on their charges.

For all of that, Maeve was trembling when she closed her eyes and willed herself away from that hospital and far into the future, where other challenges awaited her.

She fed on a mean drunk, who'd been on his way home from the pub with every intention of beating his wife for his own sins, as well as a bevy of imagined infidelities, and left him whimpering on a heap of trash.

Maeve found Valerian at the circle of stones, sitting patiently on a fallen pillar and blowing a haunting, airy tune on a small pipe.

"Well, then," the great vampire said with good-natured sarcasm, "you have at last decided to honor me with an appearance." He bowed deeply. "Welcome."

Maeve was still agitated by the foolish carelessness she had exhibited back in Calder's Pennsylvania. She'd never made such a mistake before, since the night of her making.

Valerian climbed gracefully down from his perch and approached. For the first time since her arrival, Maeve noticed that he was dressed as a seventeenth-century gentleman. He wore a waistcoat of the finest silk, along with kid-skin breeches, leggings, and buckle-shoes. His hair was tied back with a dark ribbon and lightly powdered.

"Going to a costume party?" Maeve asked with the merest hint of disdain in her voice.

Valerian smiled indulgently, using only one side of his sensual mouth, and dropped the musical pipe into a pocket of his coat. "I was indeed attending a festivity, of sorts, but since this is the way the French aristocracy always dressed during those glorious pre-Revolutionary days, I did not stand out from the other guests."

Maeve sighed. Valerian would always stand out from the other guests, no matter how carefully he chose his clothing, in her opinion, but to say so would only inflate his already monumental ego, and she wasn't about to do that.

"Where is the lecture?" she asked instead, sounding

weary and dispirited even to herself. "Surely you expected me before this?"

Valerian shrugged. "I kept myself occupied in your absence," he said. "What were you doing—mooning over that mortal of yours? What is his attraction, Maeve—is it the fact that he spends most of his days drenched in blood?"

Maeve was instantly angry, though in truth, had she been in Valerian's place, she might have offered much the same question. She whirled away from the other vampire, restraining her temper, and then, after a few moments, turned back to face him again. "Calder is accustomed to blood," she admitted softly. "He's a doctor, a scientist, and it isn't revolting to him, the way it is to most mortals. Indeed, I imagine he knows, on some level, what a magical substance blood really is."

Valerian arched one eyebrow. "After all your grumblings about Aidan and his penchant for that human woman, Neely Wallace, I would never have expected this of you. You're smitten with a mortal, just as your brother was." He paused and touched her face lightly with curled fingers. "Nothing can come of this affection of yours, Maeve. Not, that is, unless you're willing to make the fascinating Dr. Holbrook into a blood-drinker."

Maeve gave her head a quick and slightly wild shake. "I won't risk that—you know how many vampires come to despise their makers. An eternity of Calder's hatred would be worse than Dante's version of hell."

"Do you hate me?" he asked with uncommon gentleness.

She looked at him for a long moment, then shook her head.

Valerian made a soft sound of exclamation. "Ah, well, that is a relief." He raised an eyebrow. "Still, the situation is dire indeed. I needn't tell you what a rare instance it is when a nightwalker puts the welfare of another before its own wants and pleasures—particularly when that other is mortal."

Trembling, Maeve nonetheless drew herself up and glared at Valerian in her most aristocratic fashion. "Enough talk of my personal affairs," she said, her voice icy with authority. "What of Lisette? Have you learned anything new? Has she made more of her deviant vampires?"

Valerian's smile was slow and insolent, and he had the audacity to touch the tip of Maeve's nose with a forefinger. "All vampires are deviant, my darling—don't ever forget that. Now, to the business at hand. Lisette is ranging far and wide, but from what I can discern, she has made her vampires only in this time period. Still, we must find her, before she strews the beasts throughout history. Surely you know without my telling you how the warlocks, not to mention Nemesis and his army of angels, would react to *that*."

"We'll start by approaching the Brotherhood," Maeve said in a tone that invited no disagreement. "Then, with or without their approval, we will hunt Lisette down and destroy her."

Valerian affected a sigh; it was one of his favorite forms of expression, especially when he was feeling martyred. "At last," he said. "You have grasped what I was trying to tell you all along—that both the mortal and immortal worlds are in desperate trouble."

Maeve could not disagree. The warlocks would not stand idly by while Lisette filled the earth with zombie-like vampires, and Nemesis was surely lobbying the highest courts of heaven for permission to make war. Should the battle actually break out, it would make the ancient tales of Armageddon sound like cheerful whimsy.

"I must change into something more fitting for an audience with the Brotherhood," Maeve said, looking down at her dusty gown and cloak and then focusing a critical gaze on Valerian's garb. "Although no costume could possibly be more in character for you, I do hope you aren't planning to approach the Vampyre Court dressed as a French aristocrat."

Valerian sighed again, and all the sufferings of the ages echoed in the sound. He splayed the fingers of one hand over the place where his heart should have been. "You wound me," he said, but there was a broad grin on his face. At Maeve's scowl he gave another sigh. "Very well," he agreed. "I'll meet you in the south garden on the Havermail estate. The Brotherhood's headquarters isn't far from there."

Maeve frowned. "Why not go directly to the secret chamber?"

"You don't just pop into the place," Valerian replied indignantly, tugging at one elaborately trimmed cuff and then the other. "These are the oldest vampires on earth, and we must use a degree of protocol."

"We could bypass them completely and handle the problem ourselves, I suppose," Maeve mused, resting her hands on her hips.

"Perish the thought!" Valerian said, and for once in his immortal life, he sounded sincere. "They'd never tolerate such disrespect!" There was a pause, then he leaned toward Maeve and peered into her eyes, narrowing his own. "You have fed, haven't you? You'll need your strength to deal with the old ones."

Maeve simply gave her companion a scathing look, raised her arms, and vanished.

She materialized in her suite in the London house, where she shed her rumpled, dust-splotched garments, washed her alabaster skin, and brushed dust and tiny stones from her hair. Finally Maeve donned a beautiful dress, made of shimmering red silk, with Irish lace trimming the cuffs and yoke, along with a matching cape.

Moments later she stood in the Havermails' south garden, where a long-forgotten marble fountain presided, nearly hidden under blackberry vines and wild roses. The statue in the center had once been lovely, an exquisite sculpture of a young Greek boy with a vessel in his arms, but now it was spotted with moss and bird scat, and a knee and elbow had been chipped away.

"Couldn't you have found a more dismal place for us to meet?" Maeve snapped when Valerian joined her in the garden. He stood upon a low stone fence, practically invisible for the brambles and scrub brush that had grown up around it.

He looked like the conductor of a great orchestra, or perhaps a movie vampire, in his rustling black cape and impeccably tailored tuxedo. "The whole of the Havermail estate is dismal," he said irritably. "They wouldn't have it any other way. Now, might we stop this quibbling, please—at least long enough to deal with the difficulties at hand?"

Maeve felt a degree of chagrin, though she would not have admitted as much. Because of her past relationship with Valerian, and the pain he had caused her with his cavalier ways, she invariably sought to rankle him. He was right, however—this was no time for childish jibes. There were true perils that must be overcome.

"Take me to the Brotherhood," she said quietly.

Valerian closed his cape around her, and, momentarily at least, she put aside her own powers and surrendered to his.

With dizzying quickness the two of them disintegrated, shot through space like a single beam of light, and reclaimed their normal forms inside a cave far beneath the surface of the earth.

"This is the place where Aidan became human again," Maeve said in a stricken whisper. She saw clearly in the dense blackness, and took note of the paintings of animals and primitive gods and goddesses on the walls.

"Yes," Valerian said hoarsely. He, too, seemed shaken. "The resurrection ritual was carried out here, in the central chamber." He took Maeve's hand and began leading her along the edge of an icy subterranean stream.

"If you've having any thoughts about becoming mortal so that you can live happily—not ever after, as in the fairy tales, but merely for the length of a heartheat—you'd best reconsider. The Brotherhood has decided that no more vampires will be allowed to cross over after this—they've destroyed all written records of the rite and cleansed their minds of any memory of the chemical formula."

There were more paintings on the walls along both sides of the stream, and Maeve marveled at their pure definition and richness of color. The artists had been dead in the neighborhood of thirty thousand years, at her best guess, and yet their handiwork looked as fresh as if it had been completed that morning.

"I wasn't thinking of becoming mortal," Maeve bristled a few seconds after the fact. "I've told you before, I'm not interested in giving up my powers to sit and darn stockings in some man's parlor."

"Things have changed a bit since your time as a mortal, Maeve," Valerian pointed out dryly as they proceeded along the narrow path. "Modern women don't mend stockings, to my knowledge, much less gather or wash them. They work at their own careers and guard their independence."

"I would not wish to live in the twentieth century were I human again," Maeve said, sounding just a bit defensive even in her own ears. "I prefer the nineteenth, as you know. It's more gracious and elegant."

"And Calder Holbrook is there," Valerian said.

Before Maeve had to answer, a brilliant wall of sunlight appeared ahead, and both she and Valerian stopped, keeping to the shadows. Maeve stared in wonder and no little fear, for she had not looked upon such light in two hundred years and, had she stepped into it, it would have consumed her in invisible flames.

"Don't be afraid," Valerian said quietly, squeezing Maeve's hand. "It's only an illusion—the Brotherhood's way of guarding the innermost cave."

"What makes you so certain it's an illusion?" Maeve snapped. "There could be a crevice on the surface. . . ."

"Think," Valerian scolded with gentle exasperation. "The sun set less than an hour ago. How could that be daylight?"

Maeve felt foolish for the second time since she'd awakened in Calder's hospital and realized that it was full of angels, a vampire's most dangerous enemies, and her impatience with herself made her prickly.

"Do they know we're here?" she asked in a peevish tone.

Valerian glanced back at her over one broad shoulder. "Don't be a ninny," he said. "Of course they know. We'll wait here until they send someone out to meet us."

Maeve gazed upon the false sunlight, both fascinated

and repelled. She did not miss the limitations of human life, the aches and pains and superficial joys that were always so quickly gone. She sometimes yearned for bright spring days, however, for azure skies, and fields of wildflowers and sweet grass rippling beneath a golden sun. . . .

Only moments had passed before Tobias appeared, walking straight through the light, smiling and unharmed. He was one of the elders, a member of the ancient Brotherhood, and yet he looked no more than seventeen years old, with his slender, ladlike figure and youthful features.

"This way," he said. "The others await you."

Valerian started toward the light, but Maeve drew back, afraid. Illusion or no illusion, sunshine was a terror to all vampires, as agonizing as the flames of hell itself, and she was wary.

"Did you see this—this barrier of sunlight, when you were here before?" she whispered to Valerian.

"No," he said, sounding mildly impatient. "What's the matter with you, Maeve? I've already told you the light isn't real—Tobias probably projected it from his mind."

"He's right," said the latter, standing only a few feet away now. "I manufactured the barricade in my imagination. Isn't it splendid?"

Maeve would not have described it so charitably, but of course she wasn't about to voice her observation aloud. "Lead the way," she said, determined to bring her fear under control. If she and Valerian were to succeed in their quest and stop Lisette, then she, Maeve, would have to face many more challenges. This was no time to allow her courage to fail.

She stood at Valerian's side, instead of cowering behind him, as she had done for the space of several humiliating moments. "That's a marvelous trick," she said, swallowing the desire to turn and flee. "Will you show me how to do it?"

Tobias shrugged. "Perhaps," he said. Then he turned and strolled back through the shimmering golden curtain.

Maeve rushed past Valerian, in a burst of bravado, and

hurled herself through the barrier. Even though she knew the veil was an illusion, she was still surprised that there was no burning as she passed, and she was dizzy with terrified relief to find herself safe.

Valerian was next to her in an instant, a half-smile curving his mouth.

Annoyed at his smugness, Maeve drew herself up and then turned to look back at the golden curtain. It dissolved into a magical fog of shining dust and finally vanished entirely.

Maeve was impressed, and her mind was busy as she and Valerian followed Tobias through the twists and turns of the natural passageway alongside the stream. If Tobias could do such magnificent things as make walls of sunlight appear, then she, too, must possess at least the seed of that ability. . . .

What wonders might she be able to perform if only she knew the trick?

She was still pursuing that intriguing idea when suddenly the passageway widened into a cathedral-size chamber, filled with the light of burning torches. The stream meandered off in another direction, into the depths of the earth.

The Brotherhood was gathered, and they were an imposing lot, seated along the length of a long, exquisitely carved table as they were. They did not wear black capes or somber hooded robes, as Maeve had expected, but instead were clad in garb typical of various periods of human history.

The spokesman, a giant with a red beard and piercing blue eyes, seemed to be a Viking. As Tobias took a seat behind the table, the vampire with the fiery hair stood and rounded one end to face Valerian and Maeve squarely.

He merely nodded at Valerian, but studied Maeve with such concentration in his features that she began to grow uncomfortable. "You are the one," he said at last. "The one spoken of in our legends."

Maeve said nothing, for she was still not at all certain that she was "the one," nor was she sure she wanted to be.

"Our next queen," Valerian said smoothly with a grand nod in Maeve's direction. His eyes twinkled as he registered her carefully concealed irritation.

Still, though she was simmering with denials, Maeve did not speak.

Valerian, as usual, was not at a loss for words. "We've come about another matter," he said formally, taking in the other members of the vampire counsel with a polite sweep of his eyes. "As you probably know, Lisette, in her madness, is making an undue number of blood-drinkers. They are substandard creatures, insensible and indiscriminate."

Maeve was listening, but she was also looking around the enormous cavern and wondering what thoughts had been in her brother Aidan's mind when he was here, undergoing the terrible transformation from vampire to mortal. Surely he had been afraid and, at the same time, full of hope.

The Viking brought her attention back to the matter at hand with surprising ease. "We despair of what Lisette is doing, of course," he said. "But we are weary, and we do not wish to govern any longer."

Valerian leaned slightly forward, as he always did when he was trying to make a point. "You cannot abdicate your authority now!" he hissed furiously. "Don't you understand? The warlocks are ready to wage war against all vampires if Lisette is not stopped, and even at this moment Nemesis impugns the highest authorities in the heavenly realm to let him unleash his angels upon all of us! If this happens, the suffering, both human and immortal, will be incalculable!"

The Viking spread his hands as if to say he could offer no solution, and turned to walk away.

Impulsively Valerian reached out and grasped the ancient vampire's shoulder in an effort to make him listen.

The old one whirled, icy blue eyes shining with fire. "It is your battle, Arrogant One," he said, and then his gaze shifted to Maeve with all the sharpness of a fine-edged sword. "And yours. As for us, we want only to rest. Eternity has gone on too long for us as it is!"

Maeve shrank back a little, startled, as Valerian obviously was, that any living thing would actually yearn for death. Perhaps, she thought, she would feel that way herself after a few thousand years, but at the moment the idea made her shudder inwardly.

"If you refuse to help us," she said with dignity, "at least promise that you will not hinder us, either." Her gaze sought and found Tobias's face. "So be it," Maeve finished, when no member of the Brotherhood spoke up.

She wanted to go to Calder, to have what might be her last look at him before she found Lisette and engaged her in battle, but she brought her emotions under stern control.

The old ones stood and bowed—except for Tobias, who regarded her with an expression of curious concern.

Maeve turned and walked regally to the center of the chamber, well aware that only one choice was left to her.

For the sake of all other vampires, for her own sake and that of Calder and of Aidan, the two mortals in all creation that she loved, she must take charge, with Valerian, and find a way to stop Lisette. If she failed, the most savage and terrible war since the expulsion of Lucifer would break out.

Perhaps even then it was too late.

She regarded each of the old ones in turn, then clasped her hands together and vanished.

A moment later she was far away, as she had wished to be. A cool night breeze ruffled the heather of a Scottish moor, and in the distance Maeve heard the crashing of the surf against rocks that had been part of some earlier earth.

Valerian was beside her, but before either of them could speak, Tobias arrived.

His voice was infinitely sad. "They plan to destroy themselves," he said, speaking, of course, of his friends in the Brotherhood. "They are so tired, and this modern time is foreign and confusing to them. They do not wish to survive."

Maeve caught hold of Tobias's sleeve; he was wearing a flowing white shirt, reminiscent of a pirate captain's, along with leggings and soft leather shoes. "What about you, Tobias? Do you want to die, too?"

He shook his head. "No, but I, too, am weary. I will lie dormant, for a century or so, and recover my strength. I'm afraid the battle does indeed fall to you, my friends."

Valerian made an angry sound, but Maeve had tender feelings towards Tobias. He had saved all their lives, once upon a time, her own, Aidan's, and especially Valerian's, and she owed him a tremendous debt.

"Rest easy," she said gently, taking his upper arms in her hands. "And when you awaken, please seek us out."

Tobias nodded, looking out of his young face with ancient eyes, and then he disappeared.

"Who would have thought they'd abandon us like this?" Valerian demanded when they were alone. "Great Zeus, Maeve—where do we begin?"

Again Maeve thought of Calder, and of Aidan and Neely, and her beloved housekeeper, Mrs. Fullywub. All their lives depended upon her, and upon Valerian, and Maeve would perish herself before she let any harm come to them.

"At the beginning, of course," she said with a bright carelessness she most certainly did not feel. "We must find Lisette and confront her."

Valerian was pacing back and forth in a patch of moonlit heather. He had been the instigator of the campaign against the queen, and now he was plainly terrified.

Which only went to prove that he was as smart as Maeve had always believed him to be.

"I last saw her the night before Aidan and Neely were married," he said.

Maeve was stunned; Valerian had not mentioned that encounter with Aidan, let alone with Lisette. *"What?"*

He stopped his pacing and tilted his magnificent head back, silhouetted against the bright, enormous moon. "I wanted to see Aidan once more, to say good-bye to him, so to speak, though of course he didn't know I was there. He was sleeping." Valerian's voice became choked and raspy.

"He was so beautiful, and I loved him so much. And then she appeared—Lisette, I mean. She planned to make Aidan into a vampire all over again."

Maeve hugged herself, seeing the horrible vision in her mind's eye. Such an occurrence would have utterly destroyed Aidan—he would almost certainly have laid himself down in some open place and waited for the sun to rise and devour him.

"Lisette was strong," Valerian went on, his voice still sounding strangled, when Maeve didn't speak. "I tried to fight her, but she overcame me easily."

"What happened?" Maeve managed to ask after a long silence had stretched between them.

Valerian was weeping quietly at the memory, and Maeve wanted to touch him, to offer some small comfort, but she restrained herself. "She was about to change Aidan, Lisette was. I cannot describe the agony I felt watching that, unable to help him . . ."

"Go on," Maeve urged.

"It seems that all mortals do indeed have an angel assigned to them," he finally said, after regaining his composure, "though I must say I wondered where the creature was when Lisette met Aidan the first time and changed him against his will."

"You saw an angel?"

Valerian nodded. "Yes—it was a spectacular being, full of light and power. Lisette fled in terror."

"Why didn't you tell me this before?" Maeve demanded, though her tone was still quiet and even.

"You were upset about Aidan's transformation as it was. Since the knowledge wouldn't have done you any good, I decided to make the accounting another time, when you were stronger."

Maeve turned her back to Valerian, arms folded, and stood regarding the gigantic moon for some minutes, dealing with a riot of conflicting thoughts and emotions. Finally she faced him again. "Aidan is gone from me," she said. "And the important thing is that he is safe, for the time being at least, and happy. The only point that should concern you and me is that Lisette has regained her strength, and is perhaps more powerful than ever because of her madness."

"Together," Valerian said, with a brazen confidence that was typical of him, "we have the power to destroy Lisette."

"I hope you're right," Maeve reflected. Lisette's age made her a formidable enemy, for with the passing of centuries came unpredictable abilities, traits that were not common to all vampires, but often wholly unique. It was rumored that one member of the Brotherhood, for instance, could walk freely in the light of day, and Maeve had heard of vampires who did not need to drink blood, and even of some who could travel between dimensions as well as centuries. The possibilities were disturbingly infinite.

Valerian was in full control of his dignity again. "What choice do we have," he reasoned, "but to try?"

"None," Maeve answered. "Do you know where Lisette is?"

He shook his head. "Others have told me that she strikes at random, and that she is able to veil herself from ordinary vampires."

"But we are not ordinary vampires," Maeve reminded him.

Valerian smiled. "No, my darling, we are not." He paused, and his countenance darkened again. "Still, we have expended considerable energy this night. In my opinion, it would be unwise to face Lisette now, though we might certainly seek her out."

Maeve nodded in agreement. "We will concentrate on her majesty, then," she said with quiet sarcasm, "and see where our thoughts take us."

"Yes," Valerian said. "But remember—be cautious. This is no time to show off."

Maeve gave the other vampire a wry look even as she raised her hands high and interlocked her fingers. "You're a fine one to lecture me about showing off," she said, but as she vanished, she was glad to know Valerian was with her.

Chapter

—❦6❦—

Valerian assembled himself a split second before Maeve managed the same feat, and he immediately uttered a curse.

Maeve looked around anxiously, getting her bearings. They were in the common room of an elite boy's school, she soon realized, tucked away in the quiet of the English countryside. One of the instructors, recently human but now a walking corpse, with bluish-gray skin and protruding eyes, came snarling from the shadows.

Flanking him were two smaller vampires, with fangs bared. Before their making, they had been ordinary schoolboys.

"Children," Maeve whispered in stunned despair. "Valerian, she's changed mere *children.*"

"Have a care. Lisette may still be here somewhere," Valerian replied in a taut voice, "and there could well be other creatures like these prowling about." He stopped, strengthening his resolve, and then went on. "We'll have to destroy them, Maeve."

"I know that," she murmured as the erstwhile teacher and his now-vicious pupils encircled them.

"Great Zeus," Valerian muttered, "they're too stupid to know they're no match for us. Look at them—circling like sharks around a shipwreck."

Maeve shuddered. She had not anticipated having to kill child-vampires, and the prospect filled her with grief and fury. When she could, she would settle this grim debt with

Lisette, but in the meantime there could be no question of her duty.

The schoolmaster lunged at Valerian with an earsplitting, unearthly shriek, and Valerian's responding shout of anger was far more terrifying.

"Bloody wretch!" he cried, after flinging the lesser creature hard against the nearest wall.

The two boys were staring hungrily at Maeve and making dreadful, slavering sounds. She felt no pity for these monsters, for they were beyond such tender emotions now, but she did despair for the parents and siblings who had loved them. They would never know, of course, what had really happened on this horrible night.

Valerian had, by this time, overcome his attacker and forced him down onto the cluttered surface of an antique mahogany desk, one hand clamped around the beast's throat. With another swearword, this one only murmured, he raised a sterling letter opener and plunged it into the other vampire's heart.

"Handy item, that," Valerian remarked, jerking the blade out of the creature's chest wall again and staring at it. It was bloody. "Do you suppose it's the equivalent of a silver bullet?"

Maeve had her hands full, what with two agile boy-fiends hurling themselves at her, and she snapped, "Oh, for heaven's sake, Valerian, will you stop babbling about the letter opener and help me?"

"Since heaven does nothing for my sake," Valerian replied, catching one of Maeve's assailants by the back of his collar and curving one arm around to stab him, all in a single swift motion, "I will do nothing for heaven's."

Maeve was distracted, though only for a moment, but in that time the other creature was upon her, biting and clawing, fierce as a winter-starved wolf. She flung him off and, since Valerian did not offer the sleek blade he'd used on the others, grabbed a decorative sword from its place on the wall and pinioned her mindless enemy in one ferocious thrust.

The corpse was now truly dead. Maeve withdrew the

sword and watched as the thing's knees folded, and it toppled to the floor.

"We'd better see if there are others," Valerian said gently, putting an arm around her shoulders and turning her
away from the scene. As they left the common room, he
warned, "Remember—be on your guard, my friend. Lisette
may still be about, veiling herself from our awareness."

There were no more victims, as it happened. Apparently
the carnage of that night had been meant as a message—
perhaps even a challenge.

Maeve and Valerian proceeded carefully through the
school, room by room. They found a great many sleeping
boys, warm and blessedly human, and several teachers, also
unharmed. There was no sign of Lisette, but that meant
nothing; she was the most treacherous of creatures and
might loom up before them at any moment.

Eventually they returned to the common room where
they collected the bodies of the vampires they'd destroyed
earlier. The things were already shriveling, their flesh crumbling to dry, gray dust; the morning sun would reduce them
to fine grains that would blow away in the first brisk wind.

"How will their disappearances be explained?" Maeve
asked when she and Valerian had laid the unholy and now
harmless trio out on the green grass bordering a rose garden.

Valerian shrugged. "Who cares?" he asked. "Let them
broadcast the horror on every television and radio station in
the world. Let the local police wonder. Such things make no
difference to us."

"I care," Maeve insisted, nodding toward the school
buildings. "One of those children is bound to stumble across
these things and be marked forever by the discovery."

The great vampire lifted one eyebrow. "There it is
again," he said in a tone of playful warning, "that Aidan-
like tendency to worry too much about the affairs of mortals."

"Valerian, these are *children* we're discussing here. Surely
even you have some shred of compassion for them."

He affected one of his sighs. "Very well—if we burn

them, there'll be no trace of their bodies or clothes by sunrise. Wait here."

"I wasn't going anywhere," Maeve said peevishly. It had been a hellish night for her, and she wanted only to find a safe lair somewhere near Calder and sleep.

Valerian entered the nearest building through a pair of French doors, returning momentarily with lighter fluid and matches. With uncanny calm, he doused the horrid evidence of Lisette's rampage and lit the dead creatures afire.

Within seconds there was nothing left of the vampires themselves or of their clothes, except for a few curling ashes. Neither the police nor the teaching staff nor the children would be able to discern that bodies had been burned here.

Maeve turned away, scanning the star-spangled sky, trying to take comfort from its constancy and beauty but instead feeling weary, and sick at heart over the events of that night. At last Maeve spoke aloud, but she was not addressing Valerian. "Where are you, Lisette?" she whispered, her voice taut with rage. "Show yourself."

There was a great rustling sound, like the wings of many enormous birds, and a sudden, high wind scattered the last few ashes over the grass and the flower beds.

"You might have consulted me," Valerian hissed angrily through the din, "before you issued a challenge!"

Lisette was at first a swirling blackness before them, an unreasoning hurricane of fury, bending the rosebushes close to the ground with her force. Then she solidified into a dark angel, at once breathtakingly beautiful and horribly unnatural. Her long auburn hair moved softly, as the furious wind died down, and she looked at Maeve with glittering, curious eyes.

"Who are you?" she demanded, holding herself with all the regality befitting her position as the oldest and most powerful female vampire on earth. "You resemble Aidan Tremayne."

What Maeve felt was not fear, exactly, but an excited sort of awareness. She was an equal to this creature, she sensed that, but at the same time she must be alert to every nuance, every shift of Lisette's body and mind.

"I am—or was—his twin sister," Maeve allowed. She took a step toward Lisette, and Valerian grasped her arm, tried in vain to pull her back.

Lisette laughed, and the sound was high and musical and utterly chilling. "Do you imagine that you can protect her from me, Valerian?" she demanded. "When last we met, at Aidan's bedside, I dealt with you as easily as one of these schoolboys." She gestured toward the still-dark and silent buildings. "Or have you acquired an angel to guard you, like Aidan?"

Maeve interceded before Valerian could reply, certain that he would have chosen brash and foolish words to do so. "I don't need Valerian or anyone else to look after me," she said. She narrowed her eyes, studying the vampire queen's perfect features and cloud-white skin. "I think I know the answer to this question, Lisette," she said, "but I'm going to ask it anyway. Did you change this schoolmaster and the two students?"

Lisette laughed again, and the sound must have soured the sweet dreams of a hundred boys, turning them to nightmares. "Yes," she said defiantly after a brief interval of studying Maeve, sizing her up. "I made the others, too."

"Why?" Maeve wanted to know. "It makes no sense."

Suddenly a storm raged around Lisette again, a tempest of her own making. "Do not try my patience!" she shouted. "I am the queen of all blood-drinkers, and I answer to no one, mortal or immortal!"

Maeve took another step forward. "You must stop this," she said, even though she knew there was no hope of persuading this most daunting of all vampires to show mercy. "The warlocks have threatened open warfare on all of the dark kingdom if you persist in creating these unreasoning creatures, and it is said that Nemesis will unleash his armies of angels at any moment."

For the merest flicker of an instant, Lisette looked uncertain, even afraid. Then she drew herself up and lifted her arms from her sides, and the breeze caught her voluminous black sleeves and made them look like wings.

"Stop me if you can," she said. She looked Maeve up and down with mad, beautiful eyes. "I look forward to the challenge."

With that, the legendary Lisette glanced toward the lightening sky, laughed again, and vanished into nothingness.

Valerian spat an exclamation, gripped Maeve by the arms, and turned her to face him. "Do you know how lucky you are that she didn't bind you to the ground and leave you to broil in the light of tomorrow's sun?" he rasped. "How could you be so stupid, so rash?"

Maeve drew back out of the other vampire's grasp, straightening her sleeves. "She tried," she said. "She tried to overcome me—I felt it—and I resisted her."

For a long moment Valerian searched Maeve's face, his own expression solemn. Then, finally, he smiled and said, "I was right. You *are* fated to be the new queen."

Maeve was in no mood for Valerian's self-congratulations and I-told-you-so's. She knew the full extent of the ordeal she faced now, for she had felt the first tentative tugs of Lisette's power, and she was afraid.

"I must go—I will need to feed and fortify myself before I do battle with the likes of Lisette," she said.

Valerian clasped her hands and looked deeply into her eyes. "We're all depending on you, Maeve," he said hoarsely. "And there is little time to lose."

Maeve only nodded. Then, after one last sad glance at the school buildings, she interlocked her fingers over her head and vanished.

She gathered herself into solid form briefly in London's Fleet Street, just long enough to purloin three newly published medical textbooks and a selection of drug samples from a surgeon's office.

She ended her journey in the wine cellar beneath Calder's family home in nineteenth-century Philadelphia, with the booty held close in her arms. After a few minutes of searching, she found a long-forgotten hidden passageway that probably dated back to the American Revolution and took refuge there.

The place was cold and dank, populated by spiders and skittering mice, but it would shelter Maeve from the coming sunrise and the bumbling discoveries of mortals, and it was close to Calder. Close enough, in fact, that she could feel the strong, steady beat of his heart in her own spirit. She set her treasures on top of an old whisky barrel and stretched out on the floor to let the vampire sleep overtake her.

At sunset Maeve awakened immediately, and she knew Calder was there, somewhere in the reaches of the great house towering above her, but she did not go to him straight away. First, she went to one of the scores of field hospitals near a battleground and fed, taking nourishment from dying soldiers and giving comfort and ecstasy in return.

She stopped to reclaim the medical books and drug samples before centering her thoughts on Calder and transporting herself to his presence.

He was standing at one of the windows in his spacious bedroom, the lace curtains billowing on either side of him as a rain-scented breeze blew in. While Maeve watched him, marveling at the perfection and strength of his strong arms, his powerful legs, and broad shoulders, she felt again that most treacherous of emotions—unconditional, unreasoning love.

"Calder." Even his name was sweet on her tongue, like the chocolates her father's solicitor had often brought when visiting her, as a human child, in that faraway convent.

He turned, his expression bleak, and silently held his arms out to her. It was an entreaty, as well as an offer of comfort, of sanctuary.

She thrust the things she carried into a leather chair and moved into Calder's embrace.

"What is it?" she whispered.

"I had pushed my emotions away," Calder answered, his breath brushing her temple, "into the farthest recesses of my soul, and you made me face them again. You brought them back, Maeve, and some of them hurt like hell."

She drew back a little way and looked up into his wonderful eyes. "So, then," she said softly, "you too were only pretending to live. Inside, where no one could see, you were really dead."

He nodded, pulled her close again very gently, and kissed her forehead, her temple, the hollow beneath her ear. "It's rather like freezing a hand or a foot—the numbness masks the pain for a time, but the healing process is agonizing."

Maeve felt a rising excitement as Calder held and caressed her, and that surprised her, even though she'd had tender feelings toward him from the first. As a rule, vampires mated only with other vampires, and then it was always a detached, mental sort of intercourse.

Now, to her amazement, Maeve wanted a different kind of loving. She wanted to lie naked in Calder's bed while he touched and kissed her everywhere, and then give herself to him just as a mortal woman would.

She was instantly terrified, for, although such things had happened before—Lisette, for instance, had made love with Aidan while he was still a mortal—it was wildly dangerous. Other vampires Maeve had heard of, male and female alike, had become frenzied in lovemaking with humans, and had quite literally torn their lovers apart. She moved to pull away, but Calder did not release her.

"What are you afraid of?" he asked huskily. "Tell me."

"Myself," Maeve whispered, lowering her eyes. "I'm afraid of myself and—and of the revulsion you might feel if you touch me. I'm—I'm not like the women you've known, Calder—"

He curved a finger under her chin and lifted it so that she had to look at him. "I'm feeling a lot of things toward you right now, God help me, and revulsion isn't one of them." He bent his head slightly and touched his lips to hers. In the next moment, instead of withdrawing in disgust as she'd feared he might, he intensified the kiss, deepened it until Maeve's entire body was throbbing with sensation.

Nothing, not even her wild exploits with Valerian in the

early years following her transformation, had prepared her for this onslaught of passion and pounding, relentless pleasure. As a vampire, Maeve felt everything a human woman would have, multiplied a hundred-fold.

It was terrifying.

Again she pushed away from Calder. He waited without speaking, letting his eyes ask the questions.

Maeve hugged herself. "Suppose I'm not—suppose I *can't* make love the way you expect? I'm not a woman, Calder, I'm a vampire."

He smiled that heartbreakingly gentle smile of his. "I have no expectations, Maeve, and I'm not about to make judgments. Have you ever been intimate with a man before?"

She shook her head. "I was a virgin when Valerian changed me into an immortal." She looked away again, then forced herself to meet Calder's tender but steady gaze. "Vampires mate—even physically sometimes—but most often their lovemaking is mental. For all I know, I won't be able to respond the way a woman would."

Calder reached out and traced the outline of her jaw with one curved finger. "If that kiss was anything to go by, my love, you'll have no trouble responding. Tell me the truth—you're afraid of hurting me, aren't you?"

She felt the unvampirelike tears spring to her eyes even before they blurred her vision. "Yes—Calder, I'm far stronger than you are, simply because of what I am. I could lose control."

"You love me, don't you? As I love you?"

Maeve couldn't speak; she merely nodded. No man had ever told her he loved her before, and no vampire, either—except, of course, for Aidan. That was a different sort of love, since he was her brother.

Calder stroked her dark, silken hair with his hands, and she felt his gentleness seep into her, through her skin, where it melted the last of her resolve. "You would never do me harm," he said. "Never."

She went into his arms again and gripped the front of

his fine linen shirt in her fingers, just to hold him close. "Kiss me again," she whispered, and he did.

This contact was even more electrifying than the first, and Maeve was dazed by the extent of her yearning—it was a primitive and elemental thing, older than stardust. To prevent an intrusion by Valerian, or any other immortal, she cast a mental shield around that quiet room. After that, Maeve and Calder might as well have been alone on the planet.

When Maeve was bedazzled by kisses, and certain she could bear no more of the ecstasy they gave her, he withdrew gently and began removing her clothes. As those garments fell away, so did all Maeve's private heartaches and horrors. Nothing else existed except for the two of them, that room, and the passion they felt for each other.

By the time Maeve stood naked before Calder, and his clothes had joined hers, she had forgotten that she wasn't a flesh-and-blood woman, but an immortal.

Calder arranged her in the center of his bed and then lay beside her, admiring her, caressing her, murmuring soft words that made her long to be joined to him.

She knew a moment of fear when Calder bent his head to her breast, but as he tongued her nipple and took it into his mouth to suckle, all her self-doubts were lost in a pleasure so fierce, so keen, that it was nearly painful.

For a long while Calder simply loved Maeve, introducing her to a new universe of sensation. Then, when she was clearly ready, indeed nearly delirious with the wanting of him, he parted her legs with a gentle motion of one hand and mounted her.

Again she was afraid and was certain she would die if she could not take this man inside her in the same way a mortal woman would do.

He touched an index finger to her full lips to quiet her and whispered, "Shhh. It's all right." Then, slowly, cautiously, Calder entered Maeve's body in a single, gliding stroke.

There was no problem in receiving him, only in restraining her passion, which escalated to a feverish pitch as he began to move upon her. She cried out and clutched at his shoulders with her hands, and then, fearing to cause him pain, spread her fingers over his back.

"Move with me, Maeve," Calder said in a tender rasp. "It will be even better for both of us if you do."

She was breathless, even though she had had no need of her lungs in more than two hundred years, and she felt certain that if she'd had an actual, living heart, it would have burst in her chest. Obediently, with all the trust she had to offer, she began to return his thrusts.

The ecstasy was intolerable, consuming, and she shouted with it, aware even in her fever that it was an animal sound, wild, untempered by any constraint of humanity, but she could not keep herself silent. The noises she made, the small groans and whimpers and pleas, as well as the lusty cries, were all part of what was happening, interwoven with the loving itself.

Nor was Calder silent, as he approached some soul-sundering completion of his own. He moaned Maeve's name and, just when her body and indeed her soul exploded in a burst of glorious, brutal passion, he stiffened upon her and rasped some senseless plea to heaven.

Maeve continued to react helplessly beneath him for some time, her body seemingly independent of her mind, trembling and flexing in a downward spiral of pure joy. Even while this was happening, however, she watched Calder's face and feared that she'd killed him, for his eyes rolled back, and he was still and rigid as his warm seed emptied into her.

He finally collapsed beside Maeve, his head resting on her bosom, and she wept with relief because he was breathing, and she could feel his heartbeat through her own flesh.

She wound a finger in his soft, glossy hair as he slept. At last she understood why her brother had been willing to risk the very fires of hell to be with the woman he loved, to exchange his immortality for a short span of human years.

It wasn't just the physical joining—it was the vast universe of emotion that underlaid that need to be of one body, of one flesh, with the man she loved.

Dawn was beginning to light the sky when Maeve gently removed herself from beneath the weight of Calder's sprawling arms and legs and climbed out of bed. She dressed without waking him, knowing he would find the books and medicines she had brought for him, and bent over him to lay a kiss as soft as a fairy's whisper on his forehead.

Then, regretting the necessity of leaving as she had never regretted anything, Maeve took herself to her favorite lair, the one beneath the London house, and stretched out on the stone slab that awaited her there.

She had only moments to think, before the day-sleep of all blood-drinkers captured her and dragged her under, but it was long enough. She had done something irrevocable this night, something that might bring doom, but she had no remorse.

If she perished that very night and spent the rest of eternity among the damned, the glories Calder had fostered in her spirit, the joys he had taught her in his bed, would sustain her throughout.

Calder awakened slowly, groping toward the surface of consciousness, fairly drowning in the deep sense of well-being his lovemaking with Maeve had engendered in him. In the next instant he wondered if he'd imagined the entire encounter.

"You have a woman in here last night?" Prudence boomed, sending the door crashing inward with a motion of one large hip. She was carrying a breakfast tray, and her round face was full of wary disapproval. "I heard plenty of carryin' on, and me way down on the second floor, too. It's a wonder your daddy didn't march right in here with a horsewhip!"

Calder raised himself to a sitting position, the sheets covering him to the waist, and grinned groggily at the beloved housekeeper. "You've been in this house a lot of years, Pru," he teased. "You must know by now that my daddy is no moral giant himself. Any crusade he might mount on the side of virtue would probably collapse under the weight of its own hypocrisy."

Prudence set the tray down in Calder's lap with unnecessary force. "I don't see why you can't talk in plain and simple words like anybody else!" she fussed.

He chuckled as he lifted the silver lid of a serving plate and saw his favorite fried potatoes and onions beneath it, along with several strips of bacon and some toasted bread. "And here I thought you were my greatest admirer."

The housekeeper stopped herself from smiling, but just barely. "Go on with you," she huffed, waving a scornful hand at Calder. She lingered a few moments, perhaps hoping he would say more about his night visitor, but, of course, he did not. At long last Prudence heaved a great and martyrly sigh and left the room.

Calder's banter with the housekeeper had been mostly superficial; inwardly he was reliving the events of the night, pondering them in his heart, wondering if he wasn't insane.

He might have believed that if Maeve's pendant didn't still rest against his bare chest.

Just as he was finishing his breakfast—for the first time in weeks he ate ravenously—Calder noticed a stack of books and other, less recognizable items in a nearby chair. Excitement possessed him—Maeve had remembered her promise to bring medical texts back from the latter part of the next century.

He nearly sent his tray flying in his eagerness to bound out of the bed and cross the room. Reaching the chair, he simply stood there, naked and transfixed by the books and by the strange medicines. They were pressed into tablets, these drugs, and packaged with stiff paper on one side and some hard, clear substance he didn't recognize on the other.

Calder felt wonder as he studied those strange packets and no small amount of frustration with his own lack of knowledge. In the end he was able to identify only one of the compounds—morphine, the painkiller that was in such tragically short supply on the warfront.

Reverently he picked up one of the books and opened it to the copyright page. The publisher was William B. Finley and Sons, and the publication date was 1993.

1993.

Even though he knew the volume was real—it had weight and substance in his hands—Calder was still shaken. It had been—*would be?*—printed one hundred and thirty years in the future. He dressed, never taking his eyes off the book for more than a few moments, and kept it open on the washstand while he shaved. Unable to restrain his curiosity and his desire to learn, Calder stopped now and then to read a sentence or two.

By the time he was through grooming himself, he'd cut his chin and right cheek with the razor, but he didn't care, for he was in a state of quiet ecstasy. Maeve had brought him not just one medical book, but several, along with some of the miraculous concoctions of twentieth-century chemists, and he was greedy for their wisdom.

Bending close to his mirror, Calder touched one of the spots where he'd nicked himself, then stared curiously at the bead of blood on his fingertip. As he did so, he thought of Maeve, and of her wonderful powers, and began to speculate. . . .

Chapter

7

Maeve ached to go to Calder, to warm herself by the gentle fire burning in his soul, but her practical instincts warned her to be wary. It would be only too easy to bring him to the attention of other fiends—most notably, Lisette, though Maeve was by no means certain she could trust even Valerian.

Instead she fed in the seamiest part of London, near the docks, and tried to content herself with the fact that she and Calder were at least in the same century. Because she was building her strength and attempting to hone her skills, she took blood often. As always, Maeve was careful to prey only upon the deliberately evil, not on the merely misguided.

On her third night among seagoing rats, of both the two-legged and four-legged varieties, Maeve encountered another vampire—one she had only heard of before, but never actually met.

The female was from the fourteenth century, like Valerian, and that made her old. She was, despite her great age, as beautiful as an angel, with waist-length blond hair, enormous eyes the color of spring violets, and a sweet, heart-shaped mouth.

She took shape at the end of an alleyway as Maeve was leaving another victim to sleep off his blood loss, and she was a vision in a blue velvet gown trimmed in exquisite handmade lace.

"You are Maeve Tremayne," she said in a voice like the merest brush of fingers over the strings of a harp.

Maeve gave a cordial, if guarded, nod, for she recognized Dimity from Valerian's description, and she recalled that the beautiful vampire was rumored to consort with angels. In some quarters of the dark realm, this was considered mildly suspicious behavior; in others, it was outright treason.

"Dimity," she said by way of acknowledgment and greeting.

The other nightwalker tilted gracefully to one side, in order to peer around Maeve and have a look at the victim. "You chose well," Dimity said thoughtfully. "This one is so foul-natured that even the devil would not wish to keep him company."

Again Maeve nodded. She had, of course, assessed the man before feeding from the vein in his throat. "Do you have some business with me?"

Dimity smiled, clasped the rich velvet of her skirts in both hands, and executed a half-curtsy. "Yes, indeed, my queen," she said, and though she was plainly teasing, there was a note of awe in her voice as well.

"Save your curtsies," Maeve said, approaching Dimity. She was cautious and full of amazement, for the other vampire seemed to glow with some inner light, the way creatures of heaven did. It was possible that this ethereal beauty was not a blood-drinker at all, but an angel. "I am not yet queen. Perhaps I never will be."

Dimity's delicate mouth curved again, into another, softer smile. "Oh, but you will," she said with certainty. "And you are wrong in what you're thinking about me. I am a vampire like you." She stepped forward and linked her arm with Maeve's. "Come," she said, her expression serious now. "We must talk."

Dimity led Maeve along the street, into another alleyway, and far back into the complexity of that London slum. Finally they came to a pair of cellar doors, beneath a place that seemed to be a second-rate mortuary, and even though Maeve was used to death, she shuddered.

The other vampire's laugh chimed like music, and she raised the heavy wooden doors as most immortals would—by a trick of her mind.

Dimity started down the stone steps, glancing back at Maeve over one shoulder. "Does it trouble you to know the dead rest here?" she asked, indicating the mortuary with a slight motion of her glorious head. "Who would understand better than you, the queen of nightwalkers, that they are mere husks, incapable of harm?"

Maeve didn't speak, though she was well aware that that didn't matter. Dimity could discern at least the shadow of her thoughts, as Maeve could hers. Dimity wanted to tender a warning, and it didn't take a genius to guess what it was.

For Maeve's part, she was recalling her brother Aidan's account of his making as a vampire, in the eighteenth century, when he'd lain in such a place as that morgue, cold as a corpse and unable to move the tiniest muscle. Those who had attended him had believed him dead, and though he had struggled to convey the fact that he was, despite all outward indications, very much alive, they had prepared him for burial.

Maeve, being Aidan's twin, as close to him as his heartbeat and his breath, had felt the ordeal herself, even as it occurred, and even, after all that time, she had not forgotten the inexplicable, smothering terror. When Aidan had given an account of the experience, some weeks later, she had relived it with him. For that reason Maeve longed to be far away from this disturbingly familiar place.

Dimity continued into the cellar and then into another chamber, below that, a place lighted by the glow of scores of candles and quite comfortably furnished. There was an elegant Roman couch, where Dimity undoubtedly slept during the day beyond the reach of the sunlight, along with several comfortable settees and velvet-upholstered chairs.

There was even a painting on the wall, and it brought a sad smile to Maeve's lips, for it was a portrait of two elegant vampires, waltzing together. She knew without looking at the signature that this was Aidan's work, done many decades ago, when he was struggling to come to terms with what he was.

"Did you know my brother?" Maeve asked, her voice unusually thick.

"Only by reputation," Dimity answered, taking a seat in one of the beautifully upholstered chairs, kicking off her delicate velvet slippers and wriggling her toes. "He became a legend, understandably, when he traded vampirism for mortality." She winced prettily at the thought. "Can you imagine it?"

"No," Maeve admitted readily. The image of Calder nearly came to her mind, but she managed to keep it hidden. Or so she hoped. "But the life of a blood-drinker was torment to Aidan. He'd reached the point where he was ready to perish—even to risk the Judgment—rather than go on as he was."

"And he loved a mortal woman."

Again Maeve struggled to suppress thoughts of Calder, but this time she wasn't quite so certain of her success. "Yes," she said, staring at the portrait.

"And now you love a mortal man," Dimity pressed.

Maeve turned her back on the painting with rather a lot of difficulty, since it represented a connection with her lost brother, however indirect.

Dimity laughed and raised a finger to stop Maeve from speaking. "Do not worry," she said. "Your human lover is safe from me. Like you, I feed only upon the lowest of the low. Child molesters are my particular favorite, though I enjoy the sort of ham-fisted, drunken louts who like to beat their wives as well."

Only moderately reassured—for vampires were not, as a rule, creatures of their word—Maeve took a seat on a settee. "You are very good at veiling your thoughts," she said, "but I have discerned that you want to warn me about something. Please, tell me, although I believe I know."

Dimity arched one pale gold eyebrow. "You _are_ powerful," she said. "I am an old vampire, and shielding my mind is one of my most distinctive skills."

Maeve leaned forward slightly. "Please."

Dimity folded her hands gracefully in her lap, and the candlelight flickered and danced in her fair hair. "I am acquainted with certain angels," she said after a few moments of deliberate silence. "They tell me that war is imminent—vampires will be purged from the earth, along with warlocks and werewolves—all immortals, in fact, except for those who belong in the ranks of Nemesis's army."

Maeve was not surprised, but she felt a tremor of terror all the same. "Because of Lisette?" she asked, although she knew the answer.

Dimity nodded.

Maeve thought frantically of Calder in this century and Aidan in the next. Even she, with all her gifts and powers, could not be in two places at once and protect both of them at the same time. "Where will this war be fought?" she asked.

"In all times and dimensions," Dimity replied. "Although every effort will be made to preserve mortals—as you know, the angels bear them unceasing affection—many will be wounded or killed in the fray."

Rising from the settee, Maeve went back to the painting, touched it gently with the palm of her right hand, and spoke very quietly. "Can it be stopped?"

"Yes," Dimity said doubtfully, and that single word flooded Maeve with relief. "But only if Lisette is destroyed within a fortnight. At the end of that time Nemesis will be given free rein."

Maeve turned to face Dimity again. Before, the threat of war had been only rumor, but now she had to accept it as fact. She knew with all the certainty of her being that Dimity was telling the terrible, unvarnished truth.

"How do you know these things?" Maeve did not wait for a reply. "Is it true what they say—that you keep company with angels?"

Dimity smiled, unruffled. "The answer to the second question is also the answer to the first—I do have a special friend from that quarter. His name is Gideon, and he is indeed an angel. He told me."

Maeve had been shaken by Dimity's earlier warning, but she was also curious. "How can such a thing happen? I have always been told that angels are the most fearsome of all our enemies."

The golden-haired vampire raised one shoulder in a shrug. "Nothing is absolute," she said. "Gideon, like many angels, despises the vile creatures you and I feed upon, especially since the women and children who suffer are so often their particular charges. Angels, however, are not free to wreak vengeance, no matter how justified it may be—as you have seen, even Nemesis, the greatest of all warriors, must have the sanction of the highest realms before he can make war."

"That is probably as it should be," Maeve observed quietly. "If it were not so, you and I and a great many other beings would have been destroyed long ago."

Dimity's expression was one of mild agreement. "Perhaps."

A thought struck Maeve. "Would they take our side against Nemesis, these sympathetic angels?"

"Never," Dimity answered with gentle certainty. "They are loyal to heaven, first and always. When the line is drawn, they will stand with the uncounted legions who are their brothers and sisters."

Maeve might have sighed then, had she been human. "They couldn't save us anyway," she said.

Dimity shook her head. "No, it is true, they could not. Even if each of Nemesis's warriors stood touching another angel on all sides, over the face of the whole earth and upon the surfaces of all the seas, there would not be room for even a fraction of their true number."

The image practically overwhelmed Maeve, and the most dreadful thing was that she knew she hadn't even begun to picture the full size of the opposing army. If such a conflict came about, Calder and Aidan would both be wiped out in their separate centuries, and if that happened, even Maeve herself would yearn for death.

No, more than death. Oblivion.

"I have to stop her," she whispered, thinking aloud, feeling the truth of the situation for the first time. It was like some acid, eating away the marrow of her bones, working its way slowly, relentlessly, toward her soul. "I cannot allow this to happen."

Dimity's hand came to rest on Maeve's shoulder; until then, she had not been aware that the other vampire had risen and crossed the candlelit chamber to stand beside her.

Maeve raised her gaze to the shadowy ceiling. "Perhaps they are to be envied after all," she said in a hoarse whisper.

Again Dimity lifted an eyebrow. "And perhaps not. Remember, we don't know what actually becomes of them, after they shed those weak and pitiful bodies of theirs."

Standing, gathering her strength and her resolve for all that faced her, Maeve allowed a touch of sarcasm to creep into her voice. "Couldn't your friend Gideon enlighten you about that?"

Dimity was unruffled. "He knows the truth, of course, but to speak of it is forbidden—especially to us."

Maeve started toward the door, which was a high archway of stone. One would never have guessed, from the ringing silence of that place, that busy, raucous London lay above it. "Thank you for the warning," she said, pausing at the bottom step to look back. "I trust I will see you again?"

"I am your servant," Dimity said with another nod and a twinkle in her purple eyes. Then she sat down, calmly took an embroidery basket from a table next to her chair, and brought out her stitchery.

For a long moment Maeve hesitated. Then, knowing she had no choice, she turned and climbed the stairs, toward the ugliness and the glory, the love and the treachery, that awaited her.

She half expected Valerian to be there, on the surface, pacing impatiently, but there was no sign of him. Both disappointed and relieved, she stood in the passing crush of

sailors and prostitutes, missionaries and thieves, staring up
at the starry heavens and wondering why this terrifying, impossible task had fallen to her.

Maeve awakened with sudden violence, like a sub-
merged buoy rushing to the surface, at sunset of the following day. She was filled with the sense of being watched, and
looked wildly about for Valerian or Tobias, but she was
alone in the chamber beneath her London house.

Her second thought was of Calder and all the horrors he
would see and suffer if angels actually made war on vampires and other creatures. She had to protect him; she would
not be able to think clearly, to track and destroy Lisette, if
Calder wasn't at least reasonably safe.

She went upstairs, by normal means, drawing no more
attention from her nineteenth-century servants than she ever
had. Just then, a little sympathetic notice would have been
welcome, and Maeve found herself missing Mrs. Fullywub,
her housekeeper in the nineteen-nineties, who hadn't been
born yet. Mrs. F. knew when and how to fuss over her mistress.

After grooming herself and donning a simple gown of
royal-blue sateen, Maeve immediately took herself across the
ocean to Pennsylvania.

She materialized just inside the great double doorway of
the Holbrook mansion's main parlor and immediately regretted her impulsive entrance. Calder was there, standing
next to the fire and brooding, but so was another man, thin-
ner and shorter than Calder, perhaps a decade older. This
second person was looking right at Maeve when she took
shape, and his glass fell to the floor with a clink, spreading
whiskey over the Persian rug.

The dropping of the glass made Calder turn, and when
he looked at Maeve, the light in his eyes stopped all other
thoughts. He came toward her, took her hands in his, and
bent to kiss her gently on one cheek.

"My darling," was all he said, but those two words

might have been an epic love poem, given the effect they had on Maeve.

"Who the devil are you?" the other man demanded, breaking the spell and causing Calder and Maeve to draw apart slightly. "And where did you come from?"

"Maeve," Calder said, his voice weighted with quiet irony, "may I introduce my half brother, William."

She smiled at William, even though he was bad-tempered and petulant, and gently closed down a major part of his brain. He sagged to the floor in a faint, and Calder, ever the doctor, was about to stoop to the other man's aid when Maeve stopped him.

"Your brother is neither ill nor injured," she said. "He will be all right in a few minutes, though he'll never have more than the foggiest memory of meeting me."

"He's my *half* brother," Calder stressed, smiling. "William is a mean-spirited little jellyfish, quite deserving of whatever ill fate might befall him, but tonight I actually pity him. He has met you, only to forget the experience in the next instant. How sad that is."

Maeve remembered the reason for her mission, and the smile faded from her lips. "You must come with me, Calder—now, without asking questions."

She had not expected him to balk—Maeve was used to getting her own way—but Calder did resist, however gently. "I can't leave my patients," he said. "Or, for that matter, the experiments I've been performing in the laboratory at Union Hospital."

Maeve was exasperated. "I have no time to explain this to you now," she said imperiously. "After I have fed—"

"I'm not going anywhere," Calder interrupted stubbornly. He looked puzzled as well as recalcitrant. "What is this all about, Maeve? You've never behaved this way before."

She might have left him there, to face his fate, except that she loved him too much. While Nemesis could not attack for nearly two weeks, the warlocks were under no such compunction, and neither was Lisette, who might think it a great joke to make Calder into one of her witless monsters. It was absolutely vital that he be hidden away somewhere, at least until she'd had a chance to decide on a precise course of action.

Being in no mood to argue, Maeve laid a hand to Calder's forehead and caught his strong, solid frame in her arms when he sagged against her, temporarily unconscious. She saw William Holbrook raise himself from the floor and gape in horrified amazement as both she and Calder vanished into thin air, but she didn't worry, knowing he would forget.

Within moments, of course, the two of them were in Maeve's London house. It was still the nineteenth century, for mortals had yet to develop the faculties for traveling between time periods, and Calder had not yet regained his wits.

She laid him on the bed in her suite, smoothed his hair, and felt a mixture of sympathy and amusement as she imagined his reactions when he realized he was in England and not Pennsylvania. Unfortunately she needed to feed, and that meant there was no time to wait for him to come around and try to cushion the shock a little.

Maeve bent, kissed Calder's forehead, and disappeared from the room as quickly as she had arrived there moments before.

Soon she was on the waterfront, stalking the night's prey. She fed once, twice, a third time, feeling her powers grow with each infusion of fresh, vital blood. All the while, she waited for Lisette and wondered where Valerian was.

Several nights had passed since she had seen him and, under normal circumstances, Maeve would not only have been unconcerned by this, but relieved in the bargain. Valerian was a hopeless hedonist, totally devoted to his own pleasures and interests. Therefore it was not unusual for *years* to pass between their encounters, not to mention a few scant turns of the moon, while he indulged one or more of his complicated fantasies in some far-off and very exotic place.

This was different, however, for Valerian was well aware

of the danger and urgency of the situation—indeed, he had been the one to bring it to Maeve's notice—so it seemed unlikely that he would have gone off on one of his tangents. . . .

Maeve slipped into an alleyway, closed her eyes, and concentrated on Valerian. Within a moment an image formed in her mind: She saw the other vampire in the depths of some sort of pit.

The image came clearer as she focused her thoughts . . . the pit was an abandoned coal mine, somewhere in Wales. Slowly the story unfolded in her mind.

Three nights past, Valerian had been set upon by warlocks, outnumbered by the sneaking blackguards. They'd beaten him, torn his flesh with their talons and their teeth, and carelessly cast him aside, to be consumed by the next day's sunlight. Somehow, the legendary vampire had dragged himself to that forgotten mine, and found sanctuary in the cool darkness.

Heartsore, Maeve went to Valerian immediately, in that rat-infested hole in the stony, unforgiving Welsh ground, and gathered him up into her arms. He felt as light as a child, and she did not know, or care, whether that was because of his weakness or her increased strength.

Holding him, in quite the same way she had held Calder earlier, Maeve took her mentor to London, and the chamber beneath her house. There, she laid him on the stone slab where she so often slept, then took a blade from the pocket of her skirt and drew it across her wrist.

When the blood flowed, she held her flesh to Valerian's mouth, and slowly, tentatively, he took sustenance from her.

"What in the name of God—?"

Maeve started at the sound of that voice, for she had not sensed anyone's approach, and she was genuinely shocked when she looked up from Valerian's prone form and saw Calder standing only a few feet away. He was holding a lamp high over his head, and his face was white with horror.

"Calder," she said, stricken. But she did not take her wrist from Valerian's lips.

"What devilment is this?" Calder demanded. "First you bring me to this place against my will, and now I find you—I find you—" He stepped closer, his physician's curiosity beginning to take precedence over his shock. "What in hell *are* you doing?"

"This is my friend, Valerian," Maeve said evenly. "He is a vampire, like me, and as you can see, he has been sorely wounded. Blood is the only thing that will restore him, though I think it may already be too late."

Calder set the lamp down on a ledge nearby and took Valerian's right wrist into his hand, searching for a pulse. Of course, he didn't find one. He raised questioning eyes to Maeve's face. "What happened to him?"

"He was attacked by warlocks," Maeve answered, almost defiantly, because she knew only too well how outrageous the story would sound to a mortal. She sensed that Valerian had taken all the blood he could assimilate in his weakened condition, and she withdrew her hand and turned it palm up so that Calder could see it clearly in the light of the lamp.

He watched, obviously stunned, as the wound in Maeve's wrist closed before his eyes, leaving only a trace of a scar. That, too, would disappear with the passing of another sunset.

She waited while Calder absorbed the things he had just seen, and tried to deal with them in his mortal, if formidable, mind. No doubt the events of this night had been too much for him to take in.

When he met Maeve's eyes, however, she took heart, for the pallor had left his face, and he was breathing at a normal rate instead of in fast, shallow gasps.

"Is there anything I can do to help?" he asked.

Even though Calder was visibly calmer, Maeve was still taken aback by his question. In his place most mortals—even the bravest—would have been thinking mostly of escape, of their own survival. "Valerian is not human," she said after a long pause. "He is a vampire. We are different anatomically from you."

Calder's gaze touched her, gently and with remembrance. "Not so different," he said softly.

Even in that dark place, with tragedy present, Maeve felt a tender stirring inside. Calder had done more than make love to her a few nights before—he had changed the shape and substance of her soul.

It was Calder who was the first to speak again. "Let's have a look," he said, stepping closer to the slab were Valerian lay and handing the lamp to Maeve. "Hold this for me, please. Although I suspect *you* can see in the dark, I can't."

Maeve accepted the lantern and did as Calder had asked.

Without taking his gaze from the unconscious Valerian, Calder pulled off his rumpled suit coat and tossed it aside. "The next time you kidnap me, madam," he said to Maeve, still not looking at her, "I hope you will do me the favor of letting me fetch my medical bag first."

"Instruments will do no good," Maeve said, feeling an overwhelming sadness as she looked down at Valerian. Although he often annoyed and even enraged her, she bore certain tender sentiments toward him, and it did her injury that he had been the first real casualty of the coming war. "I told you before. Vampires don't have what you doctors call vital signs—we have hearts that do not beat and lungs that do not breathe."

"Hmmmm," said Calder, obviously not listening. He had opened Valerian's shirt and was examining the wounds thereupon. "Remarkable," he reflected, excitement rising in his voice. "He's healing so rapidly that I can see it happening—just as you did!"

Maeve closed her eyes for a moment as relief rushed through her. So they hadn't killed Valerian after all, those rampaging warlocks. He was coming back, getting stronger—his healing faculties were indeed remarkable, as Calder had termed them. Even for a vampire.

"You really thought he was going to die?" Calder asked, lifting one of Valerian's eyelids with a practiced thumb and peering into the glassy depths. "I thought members of your—species were immortal."

Valerian stirred slightly and made a muttering sound.

The word "species" had roused Maeve's temper just a little, but she stopped herself from indulging it. After all, it was true that vampires and mortals were not of the same genus. "Vampires can be destroyed," she said quietly, laying a hand on Valerian's forehead to soothe him as he struggled to regain consciousness. "Some of the lore is true, you see. A stake through the heart will finish us, and so will fire and the light of the sun." Her voice caught. "The blood of a warlock is a lethal poison, often fatal for us, and Valerian's wounds tell me he was infused with the stuff."

Calder shuddered. "What else?"

Maeve shrugged, but she felt despondent. Now he would begin to feel repulsed by her, and by the world she lived in. Calder had seen too many of the realities of life as a vampire. "There is nothing else, as far as I know."

Valerian had at last gained the surface of awareness, and with a shake of his head, he raised himself onto his elbows and narrowed his eyes at Calder.

Calder stared back at him, with interest but not fear.

"Who the deuce is this?" Valerian demanded, in the booming and imperious voice of old. His gaze shifted, flashing with accusation and ill temper, to Maeve. "Are you mad, bringing a mortal here?"

"Incredible," Calder muttered, surely seeing, as Maeve did, that the last of Valerian's wounds had knit themselves together.

"Explain!" Valerian thundered, turning to Maeve again.

Maeve would not be intimidated—especially by Valerian. "Your manners are insufferable," she said, and although her tone was lower than Valerian's had been and much more moderate, it carried an unmistakable warning. "Kindly remember that I am not required to explain anything to you."

Valerian subsided a little, but he still looked petulant.

"This is the mortal lover," he said with a theatrical sigh of realization. "I should have known from the first."

Calder watched Valerian with amazed fascination and said nothing.

Maeve had long since set the lantern aside, but now she grasped its curved handle and handed it to Calder. More misgivings stirred in her as she considered the possible meanings for the doctor's fascination—the most alarming of which was that Calder might see her, and Valerian, as specimens to be studied. "We have things to do," she said to Valerian. "Are you well enough to wage war?"

Chapter

Calder followed Maeve and her strange friend slowly up the winding stone staircase that led to the main part of the house. The place was as dark as a deep well, and if not for the flimsy light of the lantern he carried, he would have been completely blind.

Maeve and the other vampire were silent, and yet Calder knew they were communicating; he could feel their unspoken words flowing like a river, just beyond the edge of his understanding, rapid and urgent and angry.

He supposed at least some of the discussion concerned him, but at that point Calder didn't care. He was still struggling to come to terms with what had happened to him during the course of that evening.

He'd been standing in his father's parlor, he clearly remembered that, thinking about the war that was tearing his country apart, and William had been there, too, hectoring him about something. Then Maeve had appeared, in that dramatic way of hers, and Calder had been so glad to see her that he hadn't really thought beyond his joy.

After that she had transported him here, to this vast, elegant and vaguely spooky house, where he suspected she meant to hold him prisoner.

Calder objected to that on principle, even though he was sure she believed she was protecting him from some mysterious peril. He wasn't an inanimate object, and he wouldn't be swept up and whisked off to faraway places on Maeve's whim.

Yes, he decided, as they gained the main floor of the dark, empty house, Maeve would have to take him back to his real life straightaway. He had patients to look after, wards full of them, thanks to the war, and then there were the medical books she'd brought him from the twentieth century. Practically every spare moment had been spent poring over those volumes, though free time was rare in his life, and on some level of his being he'd been sorting and assimilating the knowledge the whole time, waking and sleeping.

Maeve's friend turned his leonine head to glare at Calder in brazen assessment. For the first time since the three of them had left the cellar, the vampire spoke in audible language. "I say he'll be nothing but trouble," he told Maeve. "Furthermore, as you might expect, I'm long overdue for a feeding."

Maeve glided between them, and Calder's feelings about that were immediate and mixed. On the one hand, he was insulted that any female should think he needed physical protection, and conversely, he was relieved because he knew Valerian would probably have devoured him had Maeve not been there to intervene.

"Lay a hand on him," she said evenly, her backbone rigid, "and I will kill you for it, Valerian. I swear that by the heart that beats in my brother's breast."

There was a short, thunderous silence, during which the two vampires glared at each other in unspoken challenge.

Then, with a contemptuous sweep of his eyes and a dismissive and patently arrogant gesture of one hand, Valerian subsided. "He's probably anemic anyway," he said. An instant later he simply vanished, leaving not so much as a wisp of vapor in his wake.

Calder immediately turned Maeve to face him. "Time for some explanations, my love," he said, his hands still resting on her shoulders. "First of all, why did you bring me here?"

The expression in her eyes, which were alight with fierce pride, implored him to understand, to trust. "You are in the gravest of danger—we all are. I must keep you safe, within these walls, until it is past. For the time being, I can say no more than that."

Calder drew in a great breath, thrust it out again in a raspy, exasperated sigh. "You didn't seem to think I was particularly safe a moment ago, when you stepped between me and your friend."

"You weren't," she conceded. "You needn't worry, however—Valerian won't do you any harm now. He knows I meant what I said about killing him."

Calder shook his head, and a grim chuckle escaped him. "I've never been defended by a woman before—at least, not in that way. It's going to take some getting used to."

Maeve straightened her shoulders and raised her chin a degree. "I am not a woman," she reminded him. "I am a vampire, and whether you like it or not, I am far stronger than you."

In truth, Calder didn't know whether he "liked it or not"—he was attempting to digest an already complicated reality. "I want to go back to my own life, Maeve. The change was too abrupt, and there are things there that need doing."

She shook her head, and an infinite sorrow showed in her wide eyes. "I can't oblige, my darling," she said. She raised one cool, graceful hand and laid it against his cheek. "I love you so that it grieves me to refuse you anything, but I cannot do what you ask. You will simply have to occupy yourself here and trust me until I can take the time to explain fully."

They were in the kitchen, and, despite the strangeness of the situation, Calder was suddenly hungry. He went to a wooden icebox, worked the brass latch, and opened the door. There was a platter of cold chicken inside.

He was devouring his second piece when he spoke again. "All right," he said, amused at himself because he sounded as though he thought he had a choice in the matter, which he plainly did not. "I do indeed love you, Maeve Tremayne, and I will trust you. All the same, I am a man, with a life and responsibilities, and you cannot simply pick me up and haul me from continent to continent the way a child drags a rag doll from one room to another. You have twenty-four hours to convince me that I belong here, and at the end of that time I want to go back. I will book passage on a ship if you refuse to take me there by means of your hocus-pocus. Agreed?"

She regarded him with those sorrowful eyes, taking a long time before she replied. "I can promise you nothing, Calder, except that I will perish myself before I will see harm come to you." She came a step nearer, and this time it was she who laid her hands on his shoulders. "I must go. Amuse yourself as best you can—there will be plenty of food because the servants are all human—but please don't venture outside this house, no matter what the temptation."

Calder lifted a drumstick and started to wave it in protest, but in the space of an instant Maeve was gone, and he was alone in that enormous, echoing kitchen. Even with the gaslights burning, the place seemed bleak and dark without her.

He sat down at a long trestle table, where there were benches instead of chairs, and tried to steady himself, to catch up with reality. Calder might have thought he was hallucinating, but the experience was undeniably solid, and the proof of that was all around him.

After an interval of gathering his strength, as well as yearning for a double shot of brandy, he raised himself to his feet. If he couldn't get an explanation from Maeve, then perhaps he could find one by exploring.

Calder found the brandy he wanted in a cabinet in the main parlor and poured a generous portion into a cut-glass snifter. Then, carrying the drink in one hand and a small kerosene lamp in the other, he set out on his private expedition.

The first floor alone was vast. There was a ballroom with floors of gray marble, three massive chandeliers, and mirrors for walls, as well as formidable library, a gallery, two parlors, servants' quarters, and various nooks and crannies where perfectly ordinary things were stored. On the second level of the house was Maeve's bedchamber, where Calder had awakened earlier in the evening, completely bewildered and suffering from the headache of a lifetime. He'd wondered wildly where he was and how he'd come to be there, connected it all to Maeve, and then gone in search of her.

That was when he'd found her in the cellar, with one seemingly fragile wrist pressed to Valerian's lips.

Calder decided to think about that later, and continued his tour of the house.

It was on the third floor, in a huge chamber with high slanted ceilings and towering mullioned windows, that Calder found what he believed to be the heart of Maeve's home. There, in that solitary place, stood an ancient weaver's loom, with a half-finished tapestry spilling from one end.

The light of the moon flowed unobstructed through the great arched windows, and Calder set aside the lamp, having no need of it. He examined the loom first, and then the weaving itself.

It showed a woman's delicate slippered feet, the skirts of her gauzy dress, a scattering of pale rose petals and autumn leaves on the ground. Behind the figure of the woman was a low stone wall, but Calder could make out nothing more because the rest of the image had not yet been woven.

He stood for a long time, looking at the partial scene, feeling a strange urgency to understand. He knew the work was Maeve's and that it was important to her, but the meaning of the thing, like so much of her life, was a mystery.

Calder finally turned away from the tapestry and crossed the bare wooden floor to the windows. Beyond them lay London, a scattered tangle of light and darkness, good and evil, joy and sorrow.

London.

He took out the watch his mother had given him, one long-ago Christmas, flipped open the case, and narrowed his eyes to read the numerals. The watch had stopped, and he was too distracted and too tired to work out the difference between American time and British; it was enough just to comprehend that he'd been taken from that place to this one in minutes or even moments.

It was incredible.

Terrifying.

Fabulous.

Calder finished the brandy and turned the snifter thoughtfully in one hand. What would it be like to possess such powers? To travel through time and space so easily as ordinary mortals moved from their front parlors to the post office or the grocer's?

Was it possible to go backward in time, as well as forward? To the terrible period preceding his daughter Amalie's death, for instance? Could that tragedy be undone somehow, or even prevented?

Uncomfortable with the turn his thoughts had taken, Calder reined in his imagination, picked up the lamp he had set down just inside the door of Maeve's private refuge, and left the room.

The brandy was taking effect, and he was weary. He returned to the second floor, entered one of the guest suites, and collapsed, fully clothed, on the bed.

Calder immediately tumbled headlong into a fathomless sleep, but after a little while he began to dream of Amalie. He saw the five-year-old chasing butterflies in a sun-spangled meadow, her laughter riding softly on the breeze.

He called to his child, shouted her name over and over again, but she couldn't hear him. It was as though an invisible wall stood between them, transparent, eternal and utterly insurmountable.

Calder sat bolt upright, prodded awake by a stabbing sense of grief, and felt the wetness of tears on his face. "Amalie," he whispered hoarsely.

"Your child?" Maeve's soft voice did not startle him, even though he hadn't known she was there. She stepped out of the shadows to lay a cool hand on his forehead.

Calder nodded, full of a misery that was at once ancient and brand-new, and even though he suspected that Maeve knew all about Amalie, despite her question, he answered readily. "She was five."

Maeve sat down on the bed beside him and gathered him close in her arms. He realized in that moment of bittersweet tenderness that she was everything to him—goddess and lover and comforter—and the weight of the love he bore her was terrifying.

"What happened?" she asked, although she knew all the secrets of his heart, and although dawn, her most vicious enemy, was already tingeing the darkness with the first faint strains of apricot and crimson. Calder was well aware that Maeve had tendered the question only because she knew he needed to answer it, and he loved her all the more for her charity of spirit.

"My wife, Theresa, fell in love with an old friend of mine and left Amalie and me behind. Secretly I blessed the bastard for stealing the woman before she drove me mad with her sniveling and her petty concerns, but Amalie was a child, hardly more than a baby, and she missed her mother." A memory came back to haunt Calder then; he saw Amalie standing at one of the windows on either side of the door of the town house they'd rented in Philadelphia, her face pressed to the glass, waiting for Theresa to come back. "She was listless, Amalie was, as though her spirit was dying. She fell sick about the time of the first snow, and by Christmas she was consumed by fever. She developed spinal meningitis, and when the new year came, she was gone."

Maeve pressed her dry cheek against his damp, beard-roughened one. She didn't speak—indeed, there was no need for that, for Calder knew her feelings as though they were his own.

He put his hands on either side of her smooth and unbearably beautiful face. "Go now," he said. "The sun will be up soon."

She turned her head slightly, kissed the palm of his right hand, and nodded. Then, without another word, she rose and left the room, her movements graceful and unhurried, and when she was gone, Calder believed for a few moments that she wasn't real at all, that he had only dreamed her.

Valerian lay in bed beside Isabella, a saucy mortal who was one of his favorite companions, and marveled.

It was morning. All his instincts told him this was so, even though the light could not reach into that hidden place, tucked away beneath the oldest part of Madrid.

He waited for the trancelike sleep to suck him under, just as it had at dawn every morning for nearly six hundred years, but nothing happened. He was wide awake, full of energy and ideas and questions.

Could he stand daylight, for instance? He considered testing the theory, then decided not to push his luck. This was no time for impulsive moves.

Wait until Maeve heard about this, he thought, settling back against the pillows with a self-satisfied smile. Even she, with all her power, had never managed such a feat.

Isabella stirred, rustling the sheets, and opened one of her lovely dark eyes to peer up at him. She knew Valerian was not made of flesh and blood as she was, though he had never, in the course of their long association, explained the exact specifics. They had met often, always at night and always in places where the rays of the sun could not reach. In the past, however, Valerian had invariably awakened her well before dawn and escorted her back to the world she knew.

She reached out and made a twirling motion on his belly with the lip of one index finger. "It is morning," she observed in soft Spanish. "And you have not sent me away."

Valerian wanted to shout with joy, but at the same time he was frustrated because he couldn't tell another vampire about the miracle. Not until nightfall, at least, for all but a select few were asleep in their lairs.

"*Sí,*" Valerian responded with a smug smile. "It is morning, and you are still here." When night came, he would stand with Maeve against the warlocks and the unpredictable Lisette, but for now he would remain where he was—

442

safe in the bowels of the great Spanish city, under layers of brick cobblestones, dirt, and rocks.

She smiled mischievously. "You do not wish me to hurry away?"

"No," he said, turning onto his side to look deeply into her eyes. He could almost hear her warm, rich, vital blood coursing beneath the flawless surface of her flesh, and he felt a wounding thirst. He bent his head, kissing her throat, and she gave a crooning whimper, never guessing how she tempted him. Her pulse throbbed beneath his lips, a sweet torment, and Valerian relished it, as he always relished the forbidden.

Perhaps just a taste . . .

"Valerian." The feminine voice jolted him; he whirled to see Lisette standing at the foot of the rumpled bed. She looked like a beautiful witch, fresh from the pages of a storybook, in her high-necked satin gown, with her rich auburn hair tumbling almost to her waist. "Did you think you were the only vampire who could be abroad while the sun was up?"

"Go," Valerian whispered to Isabella in a hoarse voice, all but shoving her from the bed.

Lisette watched with amusement as the naked woman scrambled for her clothes, trembling and casting quick, frightened glances in Valerian's direction.

Miraculously Lisette allowed Isabella to escape, but when she turned her attention on Valerian again, he saw the hatred in her eyes and remembered the last time he'd seen the other vampire.

They had stood face to face on either side of Aidan Tremayne's bed, while he slept, unknowing and vulnerable, between them. At that time Aidan had been newly human—he had risked everything, even his immortal soul, to be changed back into a man—and Lisette had meant to transform him again, to rob Aidan of his hard-won humanity. The idea had been all the more ironic for the fact that she had been the one to condemn Aidan to a life he hated in the first place.

Valerian had moved to defend Aidan, one of only two mortals he had ever loved with honor and purity of heart, but Lisette had been much stronger and rendered him virtually powerless. Had it not been for the intercession of another, she would have succeeded in making Aidan into a vampire again.

It was the ease with which she'd overcome him that Valerian recalled most vividly at that moment. He was indeed afraid, but he wasn't foolish enough to show that. He would deal with Lisette in the same way an old snake charmer in India had taught his students to deal with cobras—by keeping calm and making no sudden moves.

"We meet again," he said, rising slowly from the bed, making no effort to hide his nakedness. He reached for his clothes—doeskin breeches and a loose silk shirt with no buttons—and donned the trousers unhurriedly.

Lisette was watching him with a troubled, curious expression. "I will not destroy you immediately," she mused aloud. "I have uses for you, as it happens."

"I'm delighted to hear it," Valerian responded in the most cordial of tones, pulling the shirt on over his head. "Did you know there may be a war because of you and those damned brainless creatures you've been making?"

"War? With whom?"

Valerian pretended to sigh. "None other than Nemesis himself, I'm afraid. Then there are the warlocks—"

"I don't care about angels or warlocks!" Lisette interrupted, spitting like a cat.

"That's because you're quite mad," Valerian answered as pleasantly as if he'd been chatting with a pretty prospect in some elegant vampire's drawing room. He ran the fingers of both hands through his love-mussed hair and smiled indulgently. "You really ought to put yourself out of all this misery, poor darling. I'd be happy to oblige by driving a stake through your shriveled little heart."

Lisette glowered at him for a long, tense moment, then erupted in a burst of musical laughter. It was not a melodious sound, of course, but something better equated with a funeral dirge. "Great Zeus," she said. "You've never lacked for balls, Valerian, I'll say that for you, even if you *are* the most self-indulgent, arrogant, and impulsive vampire on the face of the earth."

He executed a mocking half-bow. "At your service," he said. Then, in the desperate hope that his other powers had gotten stronger when the mysterious change had occurred that made him able to function during the daylight hours, he fixed his thoughts and energies on a place far away.

It was rather like flinging himself at a rock wall with all his strength, he discovered in the next instant, when the impact of Lisette's opposing wishes slammed into him from every direction.

Valerian slipped to one knee, dazed by the intangible blow she'd struck, but soon raised himself back to his feet.

"No more of your foolish tricks," Lisette scolded coyly, almost crooning the words. She came to stand before Valerian and wound a lock of his hair around one index finger. "You are a splendid creature. How sad I will be to destroy you." Her whole countenance darkened as her mood and expression changed. "Make no mistake, Valerian. This time no one will save your miserable hide. This time you will perish, as you should have months ago, when I bound you to the earth in that old cemetery behind that beloved abbey of yours to await the sunrise."

Valerian did not allow himself the shudder that threatened as he entertained *that* memory. Lisette had caught him in a state of great weakness, and staked him out in a neglected graveyard. Aidan, still a vampire then, had been her real prey; Valerian had been little more than bait. Had it not been for Maeve's timely arrival, and that of Tobias, both he and Aidan would have been roasted like pigs at Easter.

"If you think you can draw Maeve into a trap by holding me prisoner," he said in tones of contemptuous reason, "you are misguided as well as mad. She has no great love for me, and even if she bore me the utmost tenderness, she is entirely too cunning to fall for such a silly trick."

Lisette looked and sounded disturbingly sane, which

was, no doubt, only another indication that her mind was as diseased as her spirit. "You are right—Maeve Tremayne loves another, a mortal, and most devotedly, too. She came to help you after your little episode with the warlocks, however, and she will appear again."

For once Valerian was not thinking of his own difficult position, but of the singular vulnerability of Maeve's cherished mortal. He still didn't really care what happened to Dr. Calder Holbrook, late of Philadelphia and Gettysburg, but Maeve's happiness mattered to him. In fact, it mattered far more than he would ever have guessed.

"Tread carefully, Lisette," he warned in his soft, smooth snake-charmer's voice. "Maeve is no ordinary vampire." He smiled in his most irritating fashion. "Don't say I didn't warn you, darling. Your day is over. You're out of your league with her."

"Enough," Lisette snarled, raising her arms from her sides. In the next instant Valerian lost all conscious awareness.

"Damn that vampire," Maeve murmured, tapping one foot. "Where is he?" She'd tried focusing her mind on Valerian, a technique that had always worked before, but this time no image came into her head, no whispered warning or cry for help.

"Aren't all vampires damned?" Calder asked dryly. They were in Maeve's front parlor, where gaslights flickered and popped, and night was thick at the windows.

"That isn't funny," Maeve snapped, pacing now.

Calder leaned against the huge mahogany desk that served Maeve in that century and the succeeding one as well, his arms folded across his chest. He needed a shave, and his dark hair was rumpled from repeated combings with his fingers.

"Twenty-four hours have passed, my love," he said with gentle solemnity. "As delightful as I find your company—and rare though it is—I still want to go home."

Maeve looked at him and ached. "I'm sorry, that's impossible."

What he said next rocked her to the center of her being. "Then make me a vampire, Maeve," he suggested quietly. "Give me the powers you enjoy, and the immortality."

She stood still, staring at him, stunned and brimming with conflicting emotions. On the one hand, she wanted to make Calder a blood-drinker, like herself, and keep him at her side forever. On the other, she recollected only too well how Aidan had hated Lisette for changing him. In Calder's case, after all, the alteration would be irrevocable.

"I couldn't bear it if you despised me," she whispered.

Calder approached her, looking honestly puzzled, and laid his hands lightly on her shoulders. "I could never do that," he said. He sounded sincere, but he didn't really understand what he was facing.

"Before, when you said all vampires were damned," she began miserably, "you were very close to the truth. Becoming an immortal means wagering your soul against an eternity in a fiery hell, Calder. It means that you can never walk in the sunlight again, and that many years would pass before you could get through even a single night without taking blood. In fact, my darling, being a vampire means living forever—and forever is a very long time."

He bent his head and touched his mouth to hers. "Would you watch me get old and die instead?" he asked, after giving her a kiss so gentle that it nearly broke her heart. "Damn it, I don't care how long eternity is—and I don't mind the other things, either—not if I can be with you."

She studied him uncertainly, weighing his words in her mind. She had never changed a human into a vampire before, and the decision was not one she could make easily—especially when someone she loved so desperately was involved.

She recalled his great love for his lost daughter and felt a new level of sadness. "There would never be any children," she said. "Vampires mate, but they do not reproduce."

Calder curved a finger under her chin, and Maeve tried to probe his thoughts, but as before, she had no success. The love she bore this man seemed to function as a barrier between his mind and her own.

"I would have liked having another child," he said quietly. "I won't deny that. But given the choice between marriage to a mortal woman and all that entails, and the adventure of living with you, there is no contest. I love you Maeve, and it's you I want."

His words warmed Maeve's heart and at the same time wrung it painfully. For the first time in her two centuries as a vampire, she missed mortality and all its sweet, if temporal, joys.

"I must go," she told him after a moment of struggling with her emotions. "Please, darling—trust me, and do as I ask. Stay here until I come back."

He nibbled at her lips, tempting her to stay, and she decided to punish him with a very special kind of pleasure. "All right," he conceded, with a heavy sigh. "I'll wait. But don't be long, because I want to make love to you."

She smiled mysteriously and straightened his collar. "When I return tomorrow night, I will show you more of my magic."

A twinkle lit his eyes, though there was frustration there as well, and sorrow. "What sort of magic?"

Maeve ran her fingers lightly down his chest and made a circle around his belt buckle. "You'll see," she said. Then she stood on tiptoe, kissed the slight cleft in Calder's chin, and vanished.

Chapter

9

Maeve did not like leaving Calder unguarded, for even in that house, where few vampires and even fewer warlocks would dare to venture uninvited, he was a target. Still, the day of Nemesis's revenge was drawing nearer with each passing moment, and her instincts told her that skirmishes between vampires and warlocks were breaking out all over the planet. On top of that, every night when the moon rose there were more of Lisette's creatures to contend with.

Powerful as she and Valerian were, Maeve reasoned, they wouldn't be able to handle the entire situation alone. They might go after Lisette personally, but other vampires and even warlocks, if they could be enlisted, would have to be sent out to battle the corpselike wretches she continued to create.

Maeve fed twice, within the space of an hour, near the London docks, and still there was no sign of Valerian. Her irritation with him began to turn to concern. Normally, of course, she would have been able to track the other vampire's thoughts, or at least pick up on his whereabouts, but things were far from normal.

She hurried distractedly along a crowded roadside, pondering. Likely as not, Valerian was simply being his usual thoughtless and undependable self, playing sultan in a harem or pretending to be a gunslinger in some saloon in the American West. She was probably worrying needlessly.

Still, Maeve couldn't shake the uneasy feeling that Valerian was in trouble again. After all, the last time he'd disappeared, she'd found him lying at the bottom of a mine shaft, half dead of a warlock attack.

One way or the other, she must find the unpredictable vampire or tackle the job of destroying Lisette on her own.

"I wouldn't if I were you," a feminine voice said.

Maeve turned her head and saw that Dimity had fallen into step beside her. She was carrying a dulcimer, and Maeve could hear the faint hum of the strings in the night breeze.

"You wouldn't go after Lisette if you were me?" Maeve retorted with grim impatience. "Well, then, can you offer a better suggestion? In less than two weeks Nemesis and his legions of angels will be turned loose, and the situation with the warlocks and Lisette's vampires gets worse every night."

"You'll need Valerian's help—as well as mine and that of every other vampire you can manage to recruit."

"I can't find Valerian," Maeve said in frustration. Drunken sailors, men who hadn't been within a furlong of a bathtub in months, were stopping in the street to stare at Dimity and Maeve, their eyes glittering with lust and speculation. "Concentrate, Dimity. See if you can pick up an image or something. I've tried, but there's nothing."

Dimity stepped into an alleyway, and, of course, Maeve followed. While she watched, the angelic blond vampire closed her blue eyes and fixed her thoughts on Valerian.

More sailors gathered at the mouth of the alley, leering, plainly getting ideas. Neither Maeve nor Dimity paid them any attention for, as mortals, they were no threat.

"I see a dark-haired woman with beautiful brown eyes," Dimity said after several moments. "She's in Spain—Madrid, I think. I'm sorry, that's all I can determine."

"Isabella," Maeve murmured. Usually she didn't keep track of Valerian's many and varied playmates, but she knew about this particular mortal because he had told her once in a moment of candor. The woman was a simple soul, he'd said, though beautiful and possessed of a fiery spirit; she worked in a cantina, serving wine and ale.

Dimity cast a glance toward the growing crowd of sailors, and her sweet mouth formed a smile. "It would seem that we have admirers, you and I," she said.

Maeve curled her lip in contempt. "You can have the lot of them," she replied. "I'm going to find Isabella and ask if she's seen Valerian. In the meantime, I would appreciate your help."

"Anything," Dimity answered as the little cluster of men started toward them. She smoothed her hair and skirts, as though intending to waltz with each one in turn, instead of feeding on their life-blood and then tossing them aside like chicken bones.

"Spread the word to as many vampires as you can that there will be a ball at my house tomorrow night, immediately after sunset."

Dimity inclined her lovely head in agreement. "As you wish," she said.

Maeve hesitated for a few moments, watching as the first misguided sailor reached out a grubby fist to grab a handful of Dimity's silky blond hair.

The magnificent vampire made a snarling sound and tore into her would-be assailant like a tigress. The man screamed, probably more from terror than pain, and his companions turned to scramble toward the relative safety of the street.

It did them no good, trying to flee, Maeve noted with a certain grim satisfaction. Dimity had worked some mental trick, thickening the air around them until it was like invisible quicksand, and though they ran, their efforts took them nowhere. They had surely planned a savage rape, but they had expected to be the hunters, not the prey.

By Maeve's reckoning, having to deal with Dimity was no less than the blackguards deserved; she clasped her hands together and vanished without giving the matter another thought.

She found Isabella alone in the back room at the cantina, polishing copper mugs. The woman started violently at

Maeve's sudden appearance, crossed herself, and murmured a rapid petition to the Holy Mother.

"Don't be afraid," Maeve said in unhesitating Spanish. One of the talents she'd acquired upon becoming a vampire was an ability to learn languages and indeed memorize the histories of whole societies, simply by paging through books on those subjects. "I mean you no harm. I'm Valerian's friend and I want to know if you've seen him."

Tears brimmed in Isabella's dark, thickly lashed eyes. Maeve could glean no real information from the woman's brain because the poor creature's emotions were in absolute chaos.

"He was killed by a witch!" Isabella sobbed after several false starts and so much blubbering that Maeve wanted to shake her. "We were—together, Valerian and I. *She* came—" Again the mortal paused and made the sign of the cross with a swift, practiced motion of one hand. "She appeared out of nowhere, just as you did. Valerian told me to go quickly— *Madre de Dios*, I ran for my life—and I did not look back." Isabella stopped to draw in a great, snuffling breath, then lifted her apron to her face and wailed, "He is dead! I know he is dead!"

"Stop it!" Maeve said firmly, her mind already racing. It wasn't hard to figure out who the "witch" had been. The question was, what had Lisette done with Valerian? "I want you to take me to the place where all this happened. Right now."

Isabella mopped her face, now puffy and tear-streaked, on the apron. "I c-cannot," she said balefully, interspersing her words with hiccoughs. "It was a secret. Valerian worked some spell to take me there."

"But you must know where it is, if Valerian sent you away on your own when the witch came," Maeve insisted, speaking more moderately this time. She was worried about Valerian, of course, but beneath her fear ran an undercurrent of pure annoyance. If the vain creature hadn't been so oc- cupied with his pleasures, he might have sensed trouble in time to protect himself. Instead, he'd quite literally been caught with his pants down.

If Valerian managed to survive this latest escapade, Maeve thought furiously, she would probably kill him herself.

"It was dark," Isabella said, shaking her head. "I was afraid. I remember only that it was the oldest part of the city, and that there was a cemetery nearby, a forgotten place where all the stones were crumbling."

Maeve gave a soft exclamation of frustration, composed herself, and spoke again. "If you see Valerian before I do, please tell him that Maeve Tremayne is looking for him. This is important, Isabella, so make certain it doesn't slip your mind."

"I will remember," Isabella said with an indignant sniffle. "This is not the sort of experience one forgets."

Maeve smiled. "I suppose not," she agreed. Once again she vanished, arriving moments later in the heart of Los Cementerio de Los Santos y Los Angels, the graveyard Isabella had mentioned.

A cool wind tossed Maeve's dark hair as she stepped up onto one of the ancient, sinking crypts and scanned her surroundings. *Valerian!* she called in the silent language that could be heard in other times as well as other places, but, as before, there was no answer.

She was concentrating on finding the love nest where Lisette had surprised Valerian—it was almost surely underground—when the sound of hoarse, wordless whispers began all around her. The noise came from behind every crypt, every broken headstone, growing louder and louder.

Maeve kept her composure, even when the warlocks began to appear, one by one, seeming to take shape from the shadows themselves. They wore hooded cloaks that hid their faces and rustled as they made a large circle around her, these ancient and deadly enemies.

She might have fled, for she had the power to transport herself anywhere in the known universe, but her pride would not allow it. Besides, instinct would have taken her straight to Calder, and the warlocks would surely follow.

"What do you want?" she shouted, in order to be heard over the incessant, thunderous whispering.

It stopped, that grating sound, as suddenly as it had begun. One of the warlocks stepped forward to look up at Maeve, who stood regally atop the old headstone, like a queen on a dais.

The creature pushed back his hood, revealing a head of brown hair and a face as fetching as any angel's. The beast looked human, even to the discerning eye of a vampire.

He inclined his head in a polite gesture of greeting and actually smiled. "Allow me to introduce myself, Your Majesty," he said, and to Maeve's surprise there wasn't so much as a hint of derision in his tone or expression. "My name is Dathan, and I speak for the covens."

Maeve did not ask how many covens; she knew this being was a leader among his kind, with much power. "I am no one's queen," she said coolly. "There is no need to address me so formally." She narrowed her blue eyes and folded her arms. "But perhaps you were mocking me?"

"Never," Dathan replied with watchful geniality. His hair and eyes were brown, and his face had a look of impossible innocence. It was as if he were really an altar boy, turned warlock only an instant before by the spell of some evil magician. "A counsel was held, and we have decided to ask for an alliance between vampires and warlocks—albeit a temporary one."

Maeve was suspicious, and she could discern little from the friend's mind because he was uncommonly powerful in his own right. "An alliance? Why should we trust you, we who do not trust our own kind?"

"Our mutual survival depends upon it," Dathan reasoned. "There are already warrior angels moving among the mortals—scouts and spies preparing the way for war. Need I tell you, gracious queen, that we cannot win against such enemies?"

Precisely because her courage was flagging a little, Maeve raised her chin. "I am well aware of that," she said.

"Our only hope lies in destroying the vampire called Lisette," Dathan went on moderately. "We left this task to you and your heedless friend, Valerian, and—please excuse my directness—we have not been pleased with the results."

Maeve's considerable pride was nettled. "Perhaps if Valerian had not been set upon by warlocks, poisoned and then left for dead, we might have succeeded sooner." The large, rustling circle of cloaked figures drew tighter as each one stepped forward a pace. "I warn you"—she paused and then raised her voice so that it would carry—"*all of you*—that I will be taken only at great cost to you. The first to fall will be your leader, Dathan."

There was an angry murmuring in the ranks, but Dathan silenced his followers almost immediately, simply by raising one hand into the air.

"I have told you, my queen," he said to Maeve a moment later, "we mean you no harm. We want only to ally ourselves with you, with all reasonable vampires, until the danger is past."

Maeve raised an eyebrow. "And then?"

Dathan smiled his endearing, altar-boy smile. "Should we be fortunate enough to survive, I'm certain our separate factions will return to their old enmity. Our differences are deep-seated, after all, and our feud is so ancient that no one seems to remember how it began. It is time for a meeting between vampires and warlocks."

"I will consider your proposal," she conceded warily. She swept the circle of cloaked creatures up in a single eloquent glance. "Come alone to my house in London, at midnight tomorrow, and I will give you my decision."

The warlocks began to mutter and stir again, and Maeve knew the consensus of the crowd would have been to take their chances and make an attempt at tearing her apart, had Dathan not been there.

"Enough," that warlock said sharply, and his eyes glittered with fury as he assessed his minions. "Go now and do not trouble this or any other vampire before the agreed time has come!"

They vanished, moving noisily into the night, like a pack of crows flapping their wings, but Dathan lingered.

He reached up to offer Maeve his hand, and after only the briefest hesitation, she accepted it and let him help her down from her perch on the headstone of some long-dead and probably forgotten Spaniard.

"Until midnight tomorrow," Dathan said smoothly. Then he lifted Maeve's hand to his lips, brushed her knuckles with the lightest of kisses, turned, and walked away to become a part of the darkness that claimed his soul.

And her own, Maeve thought glumly. Again Calder's image filled her mind, and again she despaired because he had no glimmer of what it meant to be an immortal.

She would return to him, she decided, for the night was almost over and she had no choice but to seek shelter. She was discouraged that she had made no more progress in finding Valerian.

Perhaps, just as the mortal, Isabella, had said, that august vampire had finally met his end. It wasn't impossible that he'd gotten himself destroyed, considering the foolish risks he undertook in his constant pursuit of pleasurable adventure. And that would certainly account for the fact that she was unable to link her mind with his as she had always done before.

Glumly Maeve lifted her hands above her head and took herself home to London and to Calder.

She found him in the library, surrounded by stacks of books and voluminous notes. He started when she appeared before him, and a heavy tome tumbled to the floor.

He rose, his grin revealing irritation as well as genuine welcome. "I wish you wouldn't just pop in out of nowhere like that. It's unnerving."

"What would you have me do?" Maeve inquired, short-tempered because she could not find Valerian and because a devastating war was imminent. "Arrange for someone to blow a trumpet announcing my arrival?"

Calder sighed. "We can't go on like this, Maeve. I'm a doctor, and back home the hospitals are brimming with wounded soldiers. I cannot hide here any longer, no matter how much danger I might be in."

Had she been a mortal woman, Maeve might have given way to tears at that moment, so great was the pressure she was under. The paradoxical nature of their situation threatened to tear her apart; she loved Calder entirely too much to hold him prisoner in that house and too much to let him go out and face perils he couldn't begin to comprehend.

He saw that she was wavering. "Make me a vampire," he said quietly.

She stared up into his eyes, searching his very soul, seeking some shred of understanding. The dawn was near; she could not tarry much longer or she would be badly burned, perhaps even devoured, by the first apricot-gold light of the sun.

"Why?" she whispered, tormented. "Why do you want this?"

Calder didn't hesitate; she knew he'd given the matter a great deal of thought. He'd had a lot of solitude since coming to Maeve's house, after all. "I want the power," he said plainly. His thumbs moved on her shoulders, caressing, reassuring her. "Even more, I want to be with you always. I want to sleep when you sleep, and for your battles to be my battles, too."

Maeve rested her forehead against his strong shoulder for a few moments before gazing up at him again. He looked gaunt, tormented, and more earnest than she'd ever seen him. "You don't know what you're saying," she told him sadly after a few moments had passed. "There is going to be a war, and Valerian is missing, and tomorrow night I must meet with the leader of the warlocks—"

"I'm no stranger to war," Calder broke in. He'd sensed the coming of the sun, too, and taking Maeve's elbow, he began escorting her through the house, toward the cellar door. "I've been up to my elbows in bleeding, dying soldiers for three years. As for Valerian—"

"Never mind him," Maeve said impatiently. "I know your American war is a terrible one: I would not presume to minimize the suffering or the significance of such a thing. But the conflict I'm speaking of would destroy the world as you know it, Calder. Though the battles would take place between angels and those who move in darkness, like vampires and warlocks, human beings would necessarily be caught up in the fray. It would make your war of states look like a playground scuffle between children."

They had gained the cellar, and Calder moved unerringly toward the door of the hidden chamber, the place that had once been a secret from all mortals, even those who had lived and worked in Maeve's house for years. "If this apocalypse comes about," he said reasonably, "then I'll not escape it anyway. I might as well be at your side, with at least a chance of being some help to you."

Maeve lighted a candle, for Calder's sake. She, as always, could see plainly in the dense darkness. "That is a noble, if foolish, argument," she said wearily, seating herself on the edge of the stone slab where she would sleep in the same way a mortal woman might sit on the side of a bed. "There are still other considerations, however." Her words were coming more slowly now, and they were slightly slurred. "Once you make this decision, you will never be able to undo it and go back to being a man. You might come to hate me for changing you."

Calder laid her down, as gently as if she were a tired child, and took one of her hands into both his own. "That's what you really fear, isn't it? That I'll grow discontented with the life of a vampire and then despise you for making me into a nightwalker in the first place. It won't happen, Maeve. I'm not an impulsive man. I've thought this through. For our sakes, yours and mine, and that of a great many suffering mortals, I want to be changed."

Maeve could no longer keep her eyes open. She tightened her fingers around Calder's for a moment, then sank into the fathomless sleep that awaited her.

* * *

Calder sat with Maeve for a long time, until the candle flickered wildly and guttered out, in fact. During that bittersweet interval, he held her seemingly lifeless hand and wept for all that might have been, all that would never be.

Then, partly by groping and partly by memory, he found his way back to the main part of the cellar, where thin London sunlight came in through narrow windows at the ceiling level.

Leaving Maeve would be the hardest thing he had ever done, but if he could not be what she was, if he could not serve and protect her, and share her life to the fullest extent, then leave her he would. He'd book passage on a ship— even though he had no money, his family's credit was good in virtually any part of the world—and God help him, once he left, he'd never look back.

But what agony he would feel, remembering her, missing her, cherishing her. He had not dreamed, even in the poetic passion of his youth, that it was possible to love another as deeply as he loved Maeve.

Still, he was a doctor, first and foremost, and to him life was a sacred thing. To waste that most precious of all gifts was the greatest sin a mortal could commit. And this was no life he was living now; he was cowering, like some hunted creature, while the minutes and hours allotted to him were passing by, unused.

In the meantime, patients were suffering and dying. *His* patients.

He would wait no longer; he must *do* something, he must stop the waste.

Having spent several days in the Tremayne house, Calder had gotten to know the servants a little. They all regarded him with bafflement and no small amount of fear, and he thought he detected a smidgeon of pity as well. Obviously they were not used to having members of the household underfoot during the daylight hours, either.

"I'll need the carriage, if there is one," Calder said to the butler, Pillings, a beanpole of a man who said as little as possible but always made sure the newspapers were brought in and the fires lighted.

"You'll want to shave and change your clothing, sir," Pillings replied. "I believe Mr. Aidan Tremayne's garments would fit you. And I daresay he wouldn't mind making you the loan of a razor as well."

Calder knew Pillings was referring to Maeve's brother, the vampire of legend, the only blood-drinker in history to have turned mortal again. It was a safe bet, however, that Pillings didn't know Tremayne in quite the same context as that.

"Thank you," Calder said, looking ruefully down at his own rumpled garments. "I came away from home rather quickly, not to mention unexpectedly, and had no chance to pack a valise before I left."

"Quite," said Pillings in a noncommittal tone, giving a little bow before starting up the main staircase. "I will see that the appropriate items are brought to your rooms, sir."

Half an hour later Calder was freshly groomed, and a sleek black carriage drawn by four matching gray horses awaited his bidding. The driver greeted him by touching the handle of his driving whip to the brim of his hat, and Pillings insisted on opening the door for Calder and lifting down the portable step inside.

"The offices of the London-New York Bank, please," Calder said to the driver before climbing into the carriage.

The driver nodded and touched his hat.

"The mistress won't like this, you know," Pillings confided at last, so tall that he could look straight in through the carriage window. One of his temples was throbbing, and Calder deduced from the man's state of controlled agitation that he'd been wanting to protest the idea from the first and had only now worked up the courage to do so. "She gave express orders, she did, that you were not to leave the house for any reason."

Calder hoped his smile was reassuring, and that it didn't reflect the annoyance he felt at being cosseted and caged like some exotic bird, or the terrible, clawing grief that bruised his heart. "Don't fret, Pillings. I'll be happy to bear the brunt of Miss Tremayne's fury—if indeed she ever finds out that we conspired to ignore her instructions."

At that, the driver cracked his whip in the moist, cool air, and the carriage moved forward, wheels rattling over the cobblestones, leather fittings creaking.

Reaching the bank, Calder arranged for a transfer of funds from one of his own accounts in Philadelphia. Even there, an ocean away from his own country, the Holbrook name was influential enough that strangers would advance pound notes against it.

Leaving that establishment, he went to the wharf, where he booked passage on a ship leaving for New York the following morning. If he and Maeve could not agree on a course of action when they spoke that evening, he fully intended to be aboard the vessel.

After that Calder visited a shop where men's clothing was sold ready-made, and purchased enough garments for the journey, which would take ten days to two weeks. Provided, of course, that Maeve didn't give in and change him into an immortal, as he wanted her to do.

Eventually Calder returned to the Tremayne house, where he was greeted with no little relief by Pillings. He enjoyed a lengthy luncheon in the library, while Pillings and the footman carried his purchases upstairs and stowed them away in his rooms.

When he'd finished his meal, Calder paced, impatient. It would be hours before Maeve awakened, and even then he might not see her. She was an unpredictable creature and might start off on one of her adventures without bothering to speak with him first.

The thought filled him with frustration and loneliness. Every moment, every hour away from her side, was like a wound to his spirit.

He could go to the chamber belowstairs and wait there, holding her hand, until she opened those beautiful, impossibly blue eyes of hers, but he was afraid of drawing attention to her. Calder knew little about vampires, but he had gleaned, both from things Maeve had said and from an obscure book on the subject that he'd found on one of the library shelves, the worrisome fact that a blood-drinker was never more vulnerable than when it lay sleeping.

At that point Maeve was utterly unable to defend herself. He could not risk having one of the servants follow him, or worse, some supernatural being. He had no idea who—or what—might be watching with interest the events taking place in this household.

The thought only deepened his wish to be a vampire himself, to share Maeve's fate, be it damnation or an eternity of walking the earth. He didn't care, as long as he could be with her.

At sunset, while Calder was having tea beside the fire in the sitting room off his bedchamber, Maeve appeared before him, her form seeming to knit itself from the very ether.

She took in the boxes of new clothes with a sweep of her eyes, then stood frowning down at him, her arms folded.

Calder rose from his chair, out of good manners, yes, but also because he'd felt like an errant schoolboy sitting down, looking up at her, awaiting his fate. "What have you decided?" he asked quietly.

He saw an infinite sorrow in her eyes and knew her answer before she spoke. "I will not be the one to damn you, Calder. I cannot sever the invisible cords that bind you to your Creator."

He did not attempt to argue, for he could see that she'd made up her mind. He was sick at his soul—his very heart seemed to crumble within his chest—and he would not allow himself to think of being parted from her, inevitable though it was, because he could not bear the knowledge.

"Tonight," she said before Calder found the strength to speak, "you will see other vampires firsthand. I will show you what dreadful creatures they can be."

Calder was shattered, but he was also intrigued, for he was first and foremost a scientist, and he was more than curious, he was greedy for whatever knowledge of vampires he could garner. "How?" he asked simply.

Maeve smiled, but her eyes were liquid with mourning, for she knew he would not stay and await her brief appearances, warming himself on the hearth like a lapdog. "There will be a vampire ball," she said. "Right here, in this house, this very night. Will you be my escort, Dr. Calder Holbrook?"

Chapter

❧10❧

Maeve's guests began arriving at approximately ten-thirty that night. Most were vampires, ruddy from recent feedings, but Calder noticed a surprising number of mortals, too. These brave, or perhaps reckless, souls were artists mostly, and writers; curious people, like himself, fascinated by the nightwalkers.

All were ushered into the great ballroom, where gaslights flickered softly, their glow dancing golden in the polished mirrors that lined the walls. At the far end, on a dais, a small orchestra played Mozart.

Glancing at the butler, Pillings, who was unruffled by this grand and innately horrible affair, Calder realized that he'd been wrong, thinking the other man didn't know that there was something very different about the mistress of this house. Pillings obviously understood that the majority of that night's visitors were not human.

"Why didn't you tell me you knew?" Calder said in a low voice after making his way to the butler's side.

Pilling's manner was smooth and rather smug. "Because I couldn't be certain that *you* did, sir."

Calder smiled, though he felt raw inside, and broken. Maeve had made her decision; she would not turn him into a vampire, and since she wanted him to stay in London, where she could protect him, she probably wouldn't agree to transport him home by means of her strange magic, either.

All of which meant that he would be traveling back to America by ship and leaving Maeve behind forever.

The prospect of being parted from her filled Calder with a grief the like of which he had not felt since those torturous days, weeks, and months following his daughter's death. All the same, there was no question of staying. He would have died for Maeve but, ironic as it was, he could not live for her—not if it meant enduring an insipid, sheltered existence. As it was, he felt like a tame mouse, caged, running round and round inside a wheel.

Just then Maeve came to his side. She looked magnificent in a voluminous gown of purple velvet, the skirt decorated with crystal beads that glimmered like frost over clean snow. She might have been mortal, except for the pale, extraordinary perfection of her skin and the restrained energy she exuded with every movement.

Calder looked down into her eyes and felt himself tumble, then free-fall, headlong into her very soul, where he would doubtless be a prisoner forever, even if he never saw her again. "How can I leave you?" he whispered raggedly.

Maeve laid one slender, elegant hand to his cheek, and her touch sent a charge through his system. Then, silently, she linked her arm with his and led him the length of the ballroom and out through a set of French doors. They stood then on a terrace, under a glittering arbor of stars.

"Perhaps it's better if you go away," she said coolly, but Calder wasn't fooled. He heard the sorrow in her voice and felt it throbbing in her soul, the counterpart of his own mourning. "Better if you have no memory of me, or of what we've shared together—"

"Wait a minute," Calder snapped, unable to hide the note of desperation that reverberated through his whole being. "What do you mean, 'if I have no memory of you'? Surely you can't—" He paused, realizing that Maeve could do virtually anything she wished. "You wouldn't—take that, the most precious gift I've ever been given!"

She looked away for a moment, then faced him squarely again. "One night soon, when I can bear it," she began evenly, "I will return to the precise instant when you first saw me, outside that church at Gettysburg. I will adjust that moment, make myself invisible to you, and all that came after will be undone."

Calder felt his eyes go wide. "No!" he protested in a hoarse cry.

Maeve nodded sadly. "I should have done it days ago."

He shoved one hand through his hair and turned away to stand at the stone railing of the terrace, looking out over the rooftops of London. "I can't endure it," he said.

He felt her hands come to rest on his shoulders. "It's for the best, darling," she said.

Calder whirled, putting his arms around her slender waist, pulling her close to him. "What about you?" he demanded, and although he sounded angry, what he really felt was wild, raging despair. "Will you remember?"

She regarded him for a long moment. "Briefly," she replied. "Then, after a while, our time together will seem like a lovely dream, the kind that comes just as one is waking from a pleasant sleep."

"You can't do this," Calder rasped. "You can't!"

Maeve's gaze was steady. She tugged at the chain around his neck, brought the pendant from beneath his collar, lifted the necklace over his head, and dropped it into her bodice. "I can, my darling," she said gently. "And I will. For your sake, as well as my own. Perhaps, by the grace of the One who cherishes all mortals, you will be protected from the evils that surround you now." She took his hand. "Come now—let us dance together while we can. Then I will take you home to Philadelphia and your wounded soldiers."

He swallowed hard, knowing it would be useless to argue the point, that night at least, and finally nodded. Even so, he could not, would not accept Maeve's decision without a fight.

Inside, among the pallorous, beautiful ghouls, they danced, two lovers doomed to be parted so completely that soon, too soon, they would not even remember each other.

Midway through the evening a family of vampires arrived. Maeve explained that they were the Havermails, Avery and Roxanne and their offspring, Canaan and Benecia. The smaller pair were, in some ways, the most chilling of all the fiends Calder had seen that night, for although their eyes were ancient, they were trapped forever in the bodies of little girls.

Calder shuddered in Maeve's embrace as they waltzed.

"And you were aggrieved that we'd never have children," Maeve jested. Although she was plainly teasing him and her eyes were mirthful, Calder knew her sorrow was as fathomless as his own.

At eleven-thirty Maeve called a halt to the dancing and stood on the dais, in front of the orchestra, to address her guests.

Her voice was at once gentle and full of authority. She told the crowd about a vampire called Lisette, who had been creating blood-drinkers at random. They were mindless inferior creatures, she said, and because of them the angels were ready to make war on all night-walkers, not only vampires, but every supernatural being.

Calder listened in fascination as Maeve went on to say that the warlocks were outraged over this situation. Either the vampires would have to join forces with their age-old enemies, to destroy Lisette and defeat her growing army of ghouls, or the warlocks would make war on all blood-drinkers. Their hope was that, by wiping out vampires, the warlocks could appease the warrior angels and their commander, Nemesis, and thus avert their own destruction.

A stir rose in the gathering, and then one of the macabre child-vampires stepped forward. She was small and blond; Benecia Havermail, Maeve had called her.

"Where is Valerian?" she asked in a clear voice. "Can we not depend on him to lead us? He is the oldest and most cunning vampire of us all."

Maeve seemed to grow before Calder's weary eyes, to loom taller and more imposing. She was terrifying to see, in her beauty and her power, and yet he knew he'd never loved her more than he did at that moment, when he first realized that she truly was royalty.

"Valerian has disappeared," she answered without hesitation. "And even you, Benecia, should know better than to expect leadership from him. Furthermore, he is *not* the oldest blood-drinker—Lisette and the members of the Brotherhood of the Vampyre are ancient compared to him."

Benecia subsided a little, though she didn't look happy about it. Calder imagined encountering such a creature on a dark sidewalk some evening, in the thin light of a gas-powered street lamp, and shivered.

"Tonight," Maeve went on, "Dathan, a warlock, will come to this house. He seeks a pact between our kind and his, a temporary truce. His suggestion is that we band together, blood-drinker and warlock, long enough to destroy our common enemy."

An elegant-looking male vampire with dark hair and eyes stepped forward. Like the other guests, he wore formal clothes, but there was an air of refinement about him that went deeper than appearances. "Are you suggesting that we trust those creatures?" he asked of Maeve. "Warlocks have been our greatest foes from the beginning. What is our assurance that they won't turn on us, that this isn't some sort of trick?"

Murmurs of agreement rose from the crowd, but Maeve silenced the lot with a single sweep of her eyes.

"Your question is a reasonable one, Artemus," she said to the elegant male, "but this is a desperate time and it calls for desperate measures. Keep in mind, all of you, that we have more fearsome enemies than warlocks—angels. And they will descend on us in legions, these beings, unless we stop Lisette and destroy her minions. It will take all our strength to accomplish such a task, and that of the warlocks as well."

Calder was mesmerized, having forgotten his own despair for the moment. Maeve had spoken of the approaching cataclysm and stressed that all their circumstances were dire indeed, but he had not guessed the true scope of the situation. Incongruous though it seemed, the matter was one of life and death for immortals.

Roxanne Havermail stepped forward, to stand next to Artemus. She, too, was beautiful, but, like her daughters, she made Calder's skin crawl. "If Lisette is sent to face the Judgment, there will be no queen. Is that not so?"

A collective groan followed her words.

Roxanne bristled. "Well, if there's going to be an election or something, I think I should be considered." She cast an accusing glance in Maeve's direction. "I am eminently suited to be queen, it seems to me, since I've been around much longer than certain upstarts I could mention."

"Yes," muttered a short, squat male vampire in a bottle-green waistcoat, breeches, and a ruffled shirt, who stood within range of Calder's hearing. "Roxanne has been around, all right. Around the block."

The female's gaze sliced to her critic's face in an instant; she had heard him plainly, even though a considerable distance lay between them. "You may keep your fusty old opinions to your fusty old self, Clarence Doormeyer," she said, and Doormeyer actually quailed.

Having dispensed with her detractor, Roxanne turned back to Maeve, hands resting on her hips. "Well? Will I be queen or not?"

"There will be no dominion for you to reign over," Maeve responded reasonably, "if we do not stop Lisette in time to appease Nemesis and his armies."

"We have something to say about who is queen, it seems to me," put in a male dressed in the garb of a seagoing brigand. The remark started another uproar.

Maeve raised both her hands in a graceful command that there be silence. There was. "Such matters need not be decided now," she said.

Roxanne went back to stand beside her vampire husband, looking disgruntled and unhappy. Apparently she'd expected a coronation on the spot.

"What will I tell the warlock, Dathan, when he comes to me tonight to ask for our decision?" Maeve went on, and even though she didn't raise her voice, there was a note of steel in it that brooked no further nonsense. "Do we stand together against this threat, or do we scatter like frightened hens and perish at the hands of angels?"

For a moment the room seemed to rock with a sort of silent thunder. Then Artemus spoke again.

"I say we have nothing to lose by allying ourselves with Dathan's followers, and our very lives to gain. What other choice do we have? Shall we allow angels to take us, and find out firsthand what special hells their Master has set aside for the doubly damned?"

Silence reigned again, then Canaan Havermail spoke up in her sweet, horrid, piping voice. "Suppose it's all a lie?" she offered, glaring at Maeve. "Why should we trust this one? Perhaps she is weak, like her brother." Her unholy eyes sought and found Calder in the crowd, and he felt his spirit shrink before the magnitude of her evil. "Here is the proof. Maeve Tremayne consorts with mortals!"

Maeve's fury, though contained, was nearly tangible. Calder feared that she would explode and that when she did, the mirrored walls would shatter and the marble floor would undulate with the force of it.

"Look around you, Canaan. There are any number of mortals here," she said. "I am not alone in finding them diverting."

Diverting. The word sliced into Calder, sharp as a scalpel. Was that what he was to Maeve—a plaything, a curiosity, a diversion? He pushed the feeling aside to consider later.

Just then, the doors to the terrace burst open, as though they'd been struck by some great, silent wind, and all heads turned.

Calder felt his heart pound in a combination of excitement and fear.

In the next instant a creature as lovely as any angel of the highest realms appeared in the opening. She was female, with flowing golden hair, eyes the color of bluebells, and a sweetness of countenance that was truly remarkable.

Calder glanced at Maeve and saw that she was watching

him, a pensive expression on her face. It gave him hope, though precious little, to think she might be jealous of his attentions.

"It's Dimity," someone whispered close behind Calder. With reluctance he shifted his gaze from Maeve, who was more poignantly beautiful to him than any angel could ever be, to watch this new drama unfold.

Dimity did not speak, but instead stepped aside to make room for a second entrant. This creature was male, and he seemed to blaze with some fire of the soul. He was so tall that he had to lean down as he stepped through the doorway from the terrace, and when he lifted his head again, Calder saw that his eyes were as black as polished onyx. His hair was fair, like Dimity's, and he wore medieval garb, leggings and a tunic. He carried a magnificent sword with a jeweled hilt.

Calder was drawn toward him, and the wild thought crossed his mind that this was the legendary Arthur, King of Camelot, founder of the Knights of the Round Table. He soon realized, however, that everyone else in the room, with the exception of Maeve and the vision called Dimity, had retreated.

"Do not be afraid," the lovely female said in a voice as soft as a summer shower. "Gideon has not come to do harm to any of you, but to relay a message."

Calder saw Maeve move to approach the giant, Gideon, and he followed, wanting to be at her side whether the outcome of the confrontation be good or ill.

"What are you?" he asked baldly. Gideon's person shone so brightly that Calder had to squint.

Gideon smiled. "I am a Comforter," he said. "A Guardian." His wondrous features became solemn. "What are you doing here, Mortal, with these blood-drinkers?"

Calder stepped a little closer to Maeve. An angel. God in heaven, this creature was an *angel*, albeit without wings, robes, harps, or halos. The experience was remarkable, even after encountering vampires. He tried to answer, but no words came to his mind, and no sound to his lips.

Dimity linked her arm with the angel's. "Do not try the poor human, Gideon," she said in a tone of good-natured scolding. "He has the gift of free will, just like the rest of us."

Calder found his voice; he had to answer, for his own sake and for Maeve's. "I'm here because I love Maeve Tremayne."

"You must indeed love her," Gideon replied. "More than your own soul, in fact."

"Yes," Calder answered.

Maeve laid a hand on his arm in an unspoken command that he be silent. "What is your business with us?" she asked Gideon.

"I've come to warn you all," he said in a clear voice, "for I feared that you would not believe Dimity if I sent her in my stead." The angel paused, perhaps formulating his thoughts, perhaps translating them into words lesser beings like humans and vampires could understand.

"Why would you, an angel, an *enemy*, want to help us?" Benecia Havermail demanded.

It was Dimity who answered. "You heard what Gideon said. He is a Comforter and a Guardian—it is his task to look after one particular mortal. That mortal, a child, has been sorely abused by people who should nurture and protect him. I, and some other vampires, feed on the likes of that little one's tormentors, and certain of the angels appreciate that. They, you see, are not permitted to take vengeance on human beings, no matter how grievous the offense."

Finally Gideon spoke up. "Mind you, one and all, that I have no sympathy with those among you who feed on the blood of innocents." He laid one great hand to the hilt of his sword, and Calder saw his muscles tighten as he gripped it. "Such vampires should be shown no more mercy than their victims have known!"

"What message do you bring?" Maeve asked, and although there was no fear in her voice, Calder had seen her glance quickly at a small timepiece hidden beneath a ruffle on the bodice of her gown.

"Listen well, one and all," Gideon began, and though he spoke quietly, the words reached into every corner of that enormous room. "I come at the order of my commander, Nemesis. He bid me tell you that if the renegade vampire, Lisette, is not stopped, he will destroy each and every one of you, with pleasure, and that even the darkest corners and crevices of hell itself will not hide you from his wrath."

Calder felt a communal shudder move through the room, and he was afraid himself, but his fascination had not lessened. Had anyone told him that such creatures as these actually existed, he would have dismissed that person as mad. Now, here he stood, watching as the light and the darkness confronted each other.

Having spoken, the great angel turned and walked away, bending low again as he passed through the doorway onto the terrace, and, after a quick nod to Maeve, Dimity followed him. The doors closed with a crash behind them.

A moment later Maeve's ballroom erupted with the terrified chatter of vampires who faced an enemy they could not hope to defeat.

"Silence!" Maeve shouted, and, reluctantly, the others obeyed her, though it seemed to Calder that the air fairly crackled with the force of their fear, outrage, and frustration. "What else must happen before you are convinced that our only hope is to rally our forces, join ourselves with the warlocks, and bring Lisette down like the rabid animal she is?"

No one spoke or even moved. Even Pillings, or perhaps *especially* Pillings, stood motionless and stricken, watching Maeve.

"If you stand with us, come forward," she said, stepping up onto the dais again and indicating an area in front of it. "If you do not, leave now."

Still, for what seemed like the longest time, no one moved. Then all the mortals, except for Pillings and Calder himself, headed toward the door, followed by a few sullen vampires. The others gathered, as Maeve had bid them to do, looking up at her with expressions that ranged all the way from fearful reluctance to unbounded admiration.

Calder watched in wonder as she dispatched groups of vampires to other parts of the world, where they were to do all in their power to find and destroy Lisette's creations. When the long-case clock in the entryway chimed twelve times, however, she left her followers and strode toward the front door.

Calder was right behind her, even though he knew instinctively that she didn't want him there.

Reaching the massive door, she swung it open, and on the step stood another visitor. He wore a black cloak and pushed back the garment's yawning hood to reveal a head of shining brown hair and an innocent, boyish face.

This, Calder knew, was Dathan, the warlock Maeve had spoken of earlier, and the newcomer greeted her with a single word.

"Well?"

"We will join forces with you," Maeve said in a cool, reserved tone. It was plain that she didn't relish the prospect of dealing with warlocks any more than her colleagues did, despite the fact that she had offered the suggestion herself.

Dathan inclined his head in a cordial nod. "Very well," he said. "All that remains is for you and I to plan our strategy."

Maeve looked back at Calder over one slender shoulder, and he saw a fathomless grief in her eyes. "Yes," she answered distractedly. "That is all that remains."

Calder felt a chasm open between them, a vast, eternal one, and some part of him died in that instant.

Dathan spoke again, and his words wrenched Maeve's attention back from Calder. "We have word of your friend, Valerian."

At that, Calder turned away, for there was no love lost between him and Valerian, and he frankly didn't care what predicament that vampire might be in. His mind was full of the terrible, splendid things he'd seen and heard that night, while at one and the same time his heart was breaking.

In his rooms he gathered his things together and began packing them neatly into the trunk he'd purchased that day.

He wanted to weep, but that release, which would have been so welcome, was denied him by his own long-standing habit of stoicism.

Although he waited, Maeve did not come to him that night.

Maeve spent the remainder of the dark hours with Dathan, laying plans to find and destroy Lisette. She did not allow herself to think of Calder, indeed, she could not afford the indulgence, for there were so many things to be decided.

According to Dathan, Valerian was alive, though he was indeed a captive. Lisette almost certainly planned to use him as a weapon or a pawn, and for the moment there was nothing Maeve could do about that.

Just minutes before sunrise, she went to Calder's rooms and found him sprawled across his bed in his clothes, sleeping as deeply as a child. Maeve lay down beside him, wrapped her arms around him, and thought of the great house in Philadelphia.

In moments they were there, on Calder's bed, and he was still asleep, though his rest was fitful now and probably haunted by dreams.

Maeve kissed his forehead and then, with only seconds to spare, vanished, assembling herself inside a small space a dozen feet beneath the surface of the earth. There she settled, in that gravelike place, into the vampire sleep.

Calder awakened suddenly, his body drenched in sweat, and sat bolt upright. He was stunned to find himself in his own bedroom in the Philadelphia house, bathed in the light of a late-summer sun.

He blinked, terrified that his time in London, and Maeve, and the vampire ball, were all just fragments of some feverish dream. He was still trying to discern between reality and illusion when the door of his room flew open and William burst in.

"Where the hell have you been?" his brother snarled,

storming over to the side of the bed and gripping Calder's shirtfront in clenched fists.

Calder threw William's hands off and stood up. "What the devil do you care?" he countered, just as furiously. He groped for the pendant Maeve had given him and found it gone.

William paled, but with fury not fear. He knew, in some part of his withered little soul, that Calder would never do him actual physical harm, because it would have been a violation of his personal code of honor.

"It's Father," William said. "He's taken sick, and the doctor says he's dying. He's been asking for you, though I can't think why he'd make the effort. He must know, as I do, that you don't give a damn about him now any more than you ever have!"

Calder had believed himself to be utterly without sentiment where his father was concerned, but this news shook him, distracted him from the mysteries Maeve had brought into his life. "Is he here, or did you have him taken to the hospital?" he snapped, already halfway to the door.

"Father would never set foot in a hospital," William snapped. "Besides, there isn't a bed to be had because of this damn war. You ought to know that better than anyone."

Calder ignored his half brother, wrenched open the door, and strode down the hallway to his father's bedroom. He found the old man sitting up, though he looked smaller, as the dying often do, as if his body were crumbling in upon itself.

Bernard held out one hand imploringly and croaked Calder's name.

Calder realized, with shattering suddenness, that the little boy who had loved and idolized his father still lived, tucked away in some part of his psyche. His own caring struck him with the force of a meteor, and tears sprang to his eyes.

"Papa," he said, clasping the offered hand in both his own and brushing his lips once across the knuckles. He started to pull away. "I'll get my bag—"

"No," Bernard protested. "Don't—go. I want you to listen. I'm sorry, Calder, so sorry—for all the things I did and—all the things I should have done—and didn't. I loved you, and—I loved your mother. But I didn't have your strength—none of us did. Not your mother—not Theresa or Amalie—not William. You were always so—impatient, so in-intolerant."

Calder's shoulders heaved as grief assailed him for the second time in twenty-four hours. A sob tore itself from his throat. He could not speak.

"Rest, Papa," William said from the other side of the bed. It seemed to Calder that his half brother's voice came through a pipe or tunnel, from somewhere far off. "Don't try to talk."

"I've made my peace with you, William," Bernard said quite clearly. "Go now, and let me do the same with your brother."

Calder sat down on the edge of Bernard's deathbed, still too overcome to utter any of the words that crowded his heart and throbbed in his throat.

His father spread one surprisingly strong hand behind his son's head and pressed him close, into his shoulder. "Forgive me," he pleaded again. "Forgive me for not being the man you are."

In the next moment Calder felt the old man's spirit leave his body like warm vapor rising into the air. It was as simple, and as complex, as that, and having witnessed the phenomenon a hundred times before did nothing to lessen its impact.

He drew back, looked into the familiar face, and saw empty, staring eyes. Gently, with practiced fingers, Calder lowered his father's eyelids.

Regret filled him, regret that he had waited so long to face and accept the love he'd always borne for this man. He sat there for a long while, keeping a lonely vigil, and only when Prudence came in, sometime later, did Calder stand and move to the window where he stood staring out at the sunlit courtyard below.

"He's gone," he said quietly.

Prudence wept and wailed and began to pray, and it seemed to Calder that, for all her noisy suffering, she was better off than he was. She knew how to release her emotions, at least, while he'd carried his own around like the carcass of an albatross.

It was really no wonder, Calder thought numbly, that he'd lost everything and everyone who had ever mattered to him. He did not know how to love.

Chapter

—✵11✵—

"You made his life miserable, you know," William said in a wooden voice as he and Calder stood in the formal parlor that afternoon. The undertaker and his assistant were upstairs, in their father's room, preparing the old man for viewing and subsequent burial.

Calder was still dazed, by his experiences in London with Maeve, by the death of his sire, and by the realization that he had indeed loved Bernard Holbrook, faults and all, despite his own utter conviction to the contrary. He squeezed the bridge of his nose between his thumb and index finger. "Spare me the discourse on my shortcomings as a son," he said wearily, looking out the window. "I'm well aware, believe me, that I might have been a little more tolerant."

" 'A little more tolerant'?" William repeated furiously. The last time Calder had glanced in his direction, his half brother had been standing next to the mantel, brooding over a glass of bourbon. "You crucified him daily with your damnable contempt, your self-righteous assumption that he didn't want to be better than he was. The man craved your respect and affection, God help him, every day of your life, and you withheld those very things!"

Calder closed his eyes tightly, for nothing possessed the power to wound quite so deeply as the truth. While he regretted some of the choices he'd made, and bitterly, he'd dance with the devil before apologizing to William.

"Are you through?" he inquired with biting politeness.

He heard the musical explosion of glass shattering against stone and turned at last to see that William had flung his drink onto the hearth. "No, *God damn you*, I am not through! My father is dead, and his suffering was compounded by your arrogance and insensitivity!"

"What do you expect me to do?" Calder asked reasonably, his voice as cold as his manner. "Resurrect him? Turn back the clock to the time he was driving my mother to despair, perhaps, and decide that it was all right for him to break her heart with his women? Declare that, after all, 'boys will be boys'?"

William's handsome if faintly ineffectual face went ruddy with anger. "You bastard! I want you to say you're sorry."

"Apologize to you?" Calder rubbed his chin, which was stubbly with a day's beard-growth. "Never. I've done you no wrong, William."

William's features contorted. "Haven't you? That's my father lying up there with embalming fluid in his veins! If it hadn't been for you, he might still be alive!"

"I won't take the blame for his death," Calder replied. "He came down with pneumonia and couldn't rally his strength. I had no part in that."

"You *robbed* him of his strength!" William insisted, and Calder began to fear that if his half brother did not contain his temper, he would burst a blood vessel. "Papa expended all of it, worrying that you had finally vanished forever. He might have used that fervor to cling to life!"

Calder shook his head and sighed, too weary and too stricken to be diplomatic. "Damn it, William, open your eyes—you just accused Father of wasting energy, yet your hatred for me and your petty jealousy are eating you alive!"

William turned away then, lowered his head onto the arm he'd braced against the mantel, and gave a choked sob.

Calder started toward him, realized there was nothing he could say that would give the other man comfort, and stopped himself. Nothing less than his younger brother's complete humiliation would satisfy William, and Calder wasn't willing to supply that.

Prudence rushed in just then, eyes swollen from weeping, carrying a broom and dustpan. She glared accusingly at Calder and William in turn, and bent to sweep up the shards of glass littering the hearth. "Land sakes," she huffed. "A body'd think you two could keep civil tongues in your heads at a time like this, but no—here you are, bellowin' at each other—and with a dead man in the house, too."

William lifted his head, seething with abhorrence, and flung a scalding stare in Calder's direction, at the same time straightening his perfectly tailored coat. If he'd heard Prudence's admonition, or even taken note of her presence, he gave no indication. "You've destroyed this entire family," he said. "How I wish your whore of a mother had died before ever giving birth to you."

Calder took a step toward his brother, his voice deceptively quiet. "I know you're suffering, William, and I'll abide your insults because of that. If you value your hide, however, you will not refer to my mother again, except in the politest of terms. Do you understand me?"

Prudence stepped between the two of them, her great, warm girth quivering with outrage, a dustpan full of broken crystal in one hand and a broom in the other. "If I has to take a buggy whip to the both of you so's you'll behave respectful-like, that's just what I'll do! This ain't no time to be workin' out your brother troubles."

Despite Prudence's words, which made a great deal of sense, Calder still wanted to slam his fist into William's smug, haughty face, and he expected that his half brother was thinking similar thoughts about him. He breathed deeply, purposely relaxed his hands, and turned away, intending to return to the window and his private musings.

William made that impossible by spitting defiantly, "Stay out of this, old woman. This is my house now, and I'll speak to this bitch's whelp in any way I choose."

Calder crossed the space that separated him from his sibling in two strides. Ignoring Prudence's fluttering fury, he grasped the lapels of William's suit coat and hoisted him onto the balls of his feet. "Nothing will appease you but an opportunity to draw my blood, it would seem," he hissed. "Well, then, so be it." He flung his brother free, and William scrambled, his face purple with anger, to keep from losing his balance. "We'll settle this out back," Calder finished.

William nodded, spun on his heel, and headed for the door. Calder was right behind him, but Prudence waylaid him by gripping his elbow, with surprising strength, in one large black hand.

"That man up there didn't deserve to have his only sons brawlin' in the backyard like a pair of drunken field hands, no matter what his failin's might have been!"

Calder's head felt light, and he saw the familiar parlor and the woman who had comforted him from childhood through a shifting haze of red. "On the contrary," he rasped, "my father pitted William and me against each other from the first." He wrenched his elbow free of Prudence's grasp. "This is *exactly* what dear Papa always wanted, to see the two of us fight like roosters until one left the other bleeding in the dust. And you know it as well as I do."

Great tears welled in Prudence's eyes. "Don't do this," she pleaded. "William's hurtin' something terrible, him bein' so close to your papa, and he ain't right in the head."

Calder shoved splayed fingers through his rumpled hair. "I'm sorry, Pru," he said gruffly. "I would do anything in the world for you, anything except run from my brother."

He heard Prudence weeping as he moved along the hallway leading to the rear of the house and the yard beyond it.

William was standing in front of the summerhouse, waiting, his jaw hard with conviction, his eyes flashing. He'd already taken off his coat, draping it neatly over the back of a wrought-iron bench, and was in the process of rolling up his sleeves.

"I half expected you to disappear again, little brother," he taunted.

Calder wore no coat, and no gold links bound his cuffs

to his wrists. He pushed up his sleeves, one at a time, ashamed of the wicked joy he felt at the prospect of doubling up his fists and pummeling William into a whimpering pulp. "You knew better," he said with a grim smile. "Of course, you can still save your worthless ass by taking back every rotten thing you've ever said about my mother. If you don't, I'm going to stuff parts of you down every gopher hole on this property."

William faltered slightly, but he didn't relent. On the contrary, he poured salt into raw, gaping wounds. "Did you know she ran away with another man, the night she died, your sainted mama, just the way your wife did years later?"

Calder felt cold and sick, as though some evil creature, some dragon of the invisible realms, had opened its mouth and spewed forth its vile, frigid breath. "Enough," he said, all but strangling on that single word.

His half brother smiled, resting his pale clerk's hands on his hips. "Oh, no, Calder," he said. "That wasn't nearly enough. You're going to hear the truth about your mother, the beautiful Marie, at long last. She was leaving Papa the night she died in that carriage accident, running away with a lover, just the way your wife left you. And, like Theresa, Marie was abandoning her child as well. She didn't want you, Calder."

Calder laughed, actually laughed, though bile scalded the back of his throat and he really believed, in that moment, that he could kill his half brother without compunction. "You're lying, about all of it," he said. "My mother died of a fever. And she would never have abandoned me—never. If you're looking for a way to make my blood boil, brother, you'll have to do better than that."

William made a contemptuous sound. "Fool. They brought Marie home after the accident, and she never re-gained consciousness. Papa only told you she was suffering from a fever to save your precious feelings—ask old Dr. Blanchard if you don't believe me. She'd broken every frag-ile bone in her body in the wreck, and they carried her here to die. The truth was, she'd been whoring with some second cousin of hers. They'd conceived a bastard, Marie and her sweetheart—she lost the poor little creature, of course, only hours before she passed on." He sighed philosophically. "That was for the best, no doubt."

Calder's knees felt weak. In his mind he heard Marie Holbrook's lilting voice singing a lullaby, felt her hands tucking the blankets in around him, knew again the brush of her lips across his forehead. "You're a liar," he said.

William went on as though Calder hadn't spoken. "Personally I've always wondered if *you* weren't the by-blow of one of Marie's many admirers," he said. "Papa was in his late forties when you came along, remember, and he hadn't sired a second child by my mother or, to my knowledge, any of the paramours that came later."

Because William's assertions challenged some of his most basic beliefs about himself, because he sensed a grain of truth in them, Calder was shattered. "Suppose you're right," he said in a low, raw tone of voice. "Let's assume my mother was indeed a tramp, and I was sired by one of her lovers. Why did you wait until now to say these things, when you've obviously hated me for so many years?"

William indulged in a slow smile, even though he had to know he was about to take a trouncing from a younger, stronger man. "Papa wanted to pretend you were his. You were everything he would have asked for in a son, you see. Isn't that ironic? You, Calder, were the prodigal, always running off to some far country, or landing yourself in the middle of this damnable war. You tormented him, and he loved you for it, *cherished* you for it." He paused, took a deep breath, and tilted his head back to search the azure sky for a few moments. "Obviously I couldn't tell you the truth. I would have been disinherited for my trouble."

Calder ran a hand over his face. The fight had not even begun, and William had already defeated him, already broken him. "Can you prove any of this?"

"Of course I can—if I hadn't, you would be able to discount everything I've said on grounds of petty jealousy and spite. I have letters addressed to the lovely Marie, as well as some she'd written herself but never had a chance to post."

"I want to see them," Calder said. He was reeling inwardly, fighting for balance. He turned and moved away, toward the house.

William would not leave matters at that. Instead he came after Calder, grabbed him by one shoulder, whirled him around so that they stood face to face.

"You've already won," Calder said grimly, shoving a hand through his hair again. "What more do you want?"

William didn't bother to answer, he just flung his right fist at Calder, who saw the blow coming and blocked it by raising one arm. He was baffled, for a few moments at least, by his brother's insistence on provoking him, for *this* was truly a fight William couldn't win. Then, in a blaze of revelation, Calder realized that William *wanted* the pain, needed it to expunge demons of his own.

Closing his hand, Calder brought his knuckles up hard under William's chin. The punch connected; William's teeth slammed together, and a tiny bubble of blood appeared at the corner of his mouth.

"Is that enough?" Calder demanded, clenching his teeth. He almost missed the uncontainable anger he'd felt only minutes before; now he was numb. There was no fury inside him, no joy or sorrow. Nothing. "Or do I have to beat you senseless?"

William threw another punch, and this one was more accurate. He caught Calder square in the center of his solar plexus, forcing the air from his lungs.

Adrenaline surged through Calder's system, though his emotions were as dead as the man who had sired him. He hurtled into William headfirst, as he'd done many times as a boy, when his brother had tormented him until he lost control. The difference was, William was no longer bigger and stronger than Calder.

The conflict continued from there, fairly equal at first, and Calder reveled in it. He got as much pleasure, in fact, from taking punches as he did from throwing them. While the battle raged, he did not have to think about the impossible, fantastical situation with Maeve, the loss of a father he had not known he loved, and now this second, and somehow more wrenching, forfeiture of a mother he had adored.

Finally, his own face bloody and his knuckles bruised, Calder sent William to the ground with a right cross, and William did not rise. He half lay, half sat, one shoulder braced against the edge of a garden bench, breathing hard and deep. His eyes were blackened and nearly swollen shut, and yet there was an expression of redemptive bliss on his face that made Calder want to tie into him all over again.

He turned and stumbled toward the house.

The undertaker and his helpers had brought Bernard's body downstairs by that time; he was to lie in state until the next morning, when there would be a formal ceremony, followed, of course, by burial.

Capshaw, the mortician, assessed Calder's rumpled, grass-stained clothes and bleeding face with undisguised disdain. He and the old man had played poker together, among other things, and there had been a certain grudging friendship between them.

"You haven't changed," the undertaker said, reaching into the fancy mahogany coffin his helpers had brought in to straighten Bernard's ascot.

Calder forced himself to the side of the long library table that had been moved into the parlor to support the casket and the sizable man reposing inside. He curled his fingers around the side of the coffin, heedless of the small bloodstains he left on the white satin lining, and stared down into the pale, still face of his father.

Or the man he had always believed was his father.

"Was my mother leaving him, the night she died?" he asked, mindful of the words only after they had left his mouth. It was a question Capshaw might well have the answer to, since he was close to the family and had probably prepared Marie Holbrook's broken body for the grave.

The undertaker cleared his throat. "This is no time to be discussing—"

Calder raised his eyes, locked his gaze with the other man's. "Damn you, *just tell me*," he rasped.

"Yes." Capshaw sighed the word, sending it out of his mouth on a rush of air. "Yes, Marie was leaving Bernard. And don't devil me about it, Calder, because that's all I'm going to say. Perhaps you don't have any respect for the dead—perhaps you've become hardened to it, seeing so much destruction on the battlefields—but I do. Bernard was a good friend to me, and I won't see his death turned into a parlor theatrical!"

Calder studied his father's cold, marblelike face, as if expecting to see some answer written there. Then he turned and moved away, walking slowly, like a man entranced, toward the main staircase.

He took refuge not in his room, but in the nursery where he had slept and played as a child. It had been kept much as it was, in the hope, Calder supposed, that there would be other children after the disastrous loss of Amalie.

One of her dolls was still seated in a miniature rocker next to the fireplace, as if waiting for the little girl to come back and claim it. Calder touched the toy as reverently as if it were some holy object, a belonging of Saint Paul or even Christ, then wrenched his hand back.

He'd lost everything, he realized. His life with Maeve—soon, even the memory of her would be gone, thanks to her macabre magic—his child, his father, his illusions that there had been one person in his life—Marie—who had loved him selflessly, even his own identity. Calder no longer knew who he was.

It would have been a mercy if he'd been able to weep then, or curse the heavens, but he was still without feeling. His was a dead soul, entombed in living flesh.

Presently Calder returned to his own room.

He wasn't surprised to find a packet of letters resting on his bedside table, tied with faded ribbon. Beneath them were a few miscellaneous pages of expensive vellum, still faintly scented with his mother's perfume, their edges crumbling with age.

He left them long enough to go to the washstand and cleanse the blood and dirt from his face and hands. Then he carried the letters to a chair near the window and hunched there, stretching out his long legs, to read.

The loose pages told him all he needed to know; Marie Holbrook had indeed been leaving her husband for a lover, and she made no mention of her son.

Doubtless, he'd been nothing more to her than an inconvenience, despite the soft lullabies he remembered, the gentle nurturing, the tender words. Had Marie lived, then he, Calder, would have been as bereft as his own child was, years later, when Theresa abandoned her.

He laid the letters aside, closing his eyes, willing Maeve to come to him, willing her to be real.

In her cool, dark burrow, deep beneath the surface of the ground, Maeve stirred in her vampire sleep, but she did not awaken until sunset. She was aware of Calder's desperate summons the moment she opened her eyes, but she paused before going to him. She and all blood-drinkers were at war, and she could no longer follow every whim.

Lisette was clever, and she would like nothing better than to take Maeve prisoner. The ancient vampire was mad, but she wasn't stupid; she surely knew that the rebellion would fall apart without its central players, and she had already taken Valerian.

So Maeve waited, there in her hidden pit, until full consciousness returned. She felt a terrible thirst and knew that it must be slaked first thing. She could not risk weakness now, any more than she dared take impulsive chances.

She assembled herself in a faraway field hospital and fed on a dying soldier, obliterating his agony and his fear, making his passing one of ecstasy. Like the others, he mistook her for an angel of mercy, and blessed her, and Maeve wondered who the true monsters were—creatures like herself, or the mortals who orchestrated war.

After that, Maeve's head was clear, and she felt strong.

Before setting out to search for Valerian, and thus, Lisette, she took herself to Calder's room in the family mansion.

He was slouched in a chair, unshaven, his hair and clothes mussed, drunker than a lord. Maeve went to his side, sensing the presence of death in the house, as well as rage and sorrow and, worst of all, hopelessness.

She touched his hair. "Calder."

He opened his eyes and looked at her, and even in that very disheveled state he was so beautiful to Maeve that she wondered how she could ever wipe out all memory of the love that had grown between them. She only knew that she must.

He groped for her, drew her down onto his lap. "I was beginning to think even you were a lie," he murmured, burying his battered face in her hair, which fell loose around the shoulders of her blue woolen cape.

"Tell me what's happened," Maeve said gently, placing light kisses on each of his bruised cheekbones. "Please."

Calder released the story in agonized increments, telling how he'd adored his mother, and believed in her, and found out only today that she'd deceived him, that her devotion had been nothing more than pretty pretense. He produced the crumbling pages, penned by her own hand, and Maeve felt his grief move in her spirit, like a child in a womb, as she read the telling words.

She thought, too, of her own mortal mother, a laughing, beautiful, and completely scatterbrained tavern maid. She'd lived in the eighteenth century, had Callie O'Toole, and gotten herself pregnant during a flirtation with a wealthy English merchant named Tremayne. Maeve and her twin brother, Aidan, had been the result of that liaison.

Maeve tilted Calder's head gently back and examined his wounds. "I could find out," she said, the idea coming to her only as she voiced it.

"Find out what?" Calder asked. He was more sober now, more focused.

She smoothed his hair. "About your mother. I could go back to that night, Calder. I cannot change history, that's entirely too dangerous, but I can find out whether she really meant to leave you. The question is, can you deal with the truth?"

He considered for a moment, his arms around her waist, drawing her closer. "There's no need of that, Maeve. I'm a grown man—I'll learn to accept that I've mourned a fantasy mother all these years. God knows, I've had enough practice at learning to accept unpleasant realities."

Maeve knew that he was right, but she also knew that emotions weren't governed by logic. Understanding what had happened to him, accepting it, would not spare Calder the pain of disillusionment. And there was always the chance that his suffering was based on a lie.

She rose from his lap and stood straight and tall. "When did it happen, your mother's accident?"

Calder murmured a date, his reactions slowed by the liquor he'd consumed earlier, then thrust himself to his feet, groping for her. "Maeve, wait—"

She closed her eyes and concentrated, ignoring Calder's protests, and when she opened them, she was standing on a sidewalk in front of that same house, but it was nearly thirty years earlier.

A storm was brewing; the wind was high and the sky dark. Maeve wrapped her cloak more closely around her, even though she did not feel the chill. She focused on the woman she sought, and was transported inside the great house, into a nursery.

There candlelight flickered, and a low fire burned on the hearth. A slender dark-haired woman sat on the side of a child's small bed, her narrow shoulders slumped. She was dressed in traveling garb, a simple dress, bonnet, and cloak, and as Maeve drew nearer, she realized that Marie Holbrook was weeping.

It was the sight of the child, however, that stunned Maeve to the core of her being. This was Calder, her love, the one man she would have considered spending all eternity with, as a little boy.

He was sound asleep, his dark hair tumbled over his

forehead, his thick lashes brushing cheeks still plump with youth and innocence.

As Maeve watched, Marie bent and kissed the boy Calder's forehead lightly. He stirred and murmured something, but did not awaken.

"My baby," Marie whispered brokenly. She rose from the edge of the mattress with reluctance, and Maeve saw her in profile, saw the gleam of tears on her cheek, catching the light of the struggling fire. "Good-bye."

No, Maeve thought, closing her eyes for a moment. *Don't let it have happened this way, please.*

Lightning blazed beyond the leaded windows of Calder's room, and thunder threatened to burst the sky, but still he did not awaken.

Marie turned, half-blinded by obvious grief, unaware of Maeve's presence because Maeve had willed it so.

Maeve was confused; the woman didn't appear to be leaving her child willingly, and yet she did not bundle him up and carry him away with her, as a thousand, nay a million, other women would have done in a like situation.

She followed Marie into the hallway, where a young, thin, eager-looking lad awaited. Maeve guessed accurately that this was William, the difficult half brother Calder had mentioned, and she felt a surge of fury even before the youth spoke.

He flung himself away from the wainscoted wall to stand behind Marie, and his very being seemed to bristle with hatred. "Leaving so soon, Marie? Why don't you take your brat with you?"

She whirled, the fiery Marie, and slapped William hard across the face. "You know," she whispered. "Damn you, *you know* why I have to leave him—because no matter where we went, your father would hunt us down and tear Calder from my arms. I would die before I'd see that happen!"

Strangely prophetic words, Maeve thought sadly, watching from a little distance away. Marie Holbrook would indeed die, and soon; her accident was probably only minutes away.

It was a mercy, then, that the doomed woman had been forced to abandon her child. If she hadn't, Calder would surely have been killed, too, or at least crippled.

Maeve was still dealing with the mental images that idea produced when suddenly William grabbed at Marie, wild-eyed, shaking with some unholy passion. "Why did you waste yourself on that old man?" he rasped, speaking, no doubt, of his own father. "What do you see in this lover, this cousin of yours? Don't you understand that *I* can love you as no one else ever could?"

Marie struggled in the youth's grasp, her eyes bright with fury, despair, and fear. "William, let me go! This instant!"

At that moment a door closed heavily downstairs, and then a younger Bernard Holbrook started up the stairs. His handsome face was contorted with angry confusion.

"What in the name of hell and all its demons is going on here?" he demanded.

Marie was still fighting to free herself, and it was all Maeve could do to keep from interceding. No matter what transpired this night, she must not meddle, for the ramifications would creep into the years ahead like vines, dividing and dividing again, changing the future in myriad unpredictable ways.

William raised his voice to an unnaturally high, thin pitch, and his fingers bit into Marie's shoulders as he tightened his grip on her. "She was leaving you, Papa!" he cried. "Your *wife* was running away, but I stopped her!"

The expression on the elder Holbrook's face was one of wounded bewilderment. "Release your stepmother, William," he ordered, hurrying up the stairs. "Have you taken leave of your senses?"

"*Bitch,*" William whispered, and then he flung Marie from him. She struggled to regain her balance, a look of startled horror on her face, and then tumbled not down the stairs, but over the railing that edged the uppermost landing. She did not scream as she fell, and there was no sound after her body struck the marble floor below, except for William's rapid breathing and the tick of the long-case clock on the first landing.

Bernard broke the silence first, with a choked sigh. "Good God," he cried, scrambling, groping his way back down the stairs, like a man blinded. "Marie! Oh, dear God help us, *Marie!*"

Chapter

—❦12❦—

"Oh, Marie," Bernard Holbrook whispered brokenly, kneeling beside his wife's motionless body, there on the marble floor of the entryway. He took her limp hand and smoothed the knuckles with a circular motion of his thumb. "Marie—"

Maeve followed, still invisible to both William and his father, as the former moved slowly down the stairs. Above, in the nursery, the youthful Calder slept, heedless of the fact that his life had just been altered forever.

"Will she die?" William rasped when at last he'd reached his father and the stepmother he had clearly both loved and despised.

"I hope not," Bernard said in an agonized whisper. "Dear God in heaven, I hope not." Tears gleamed in his eyes. "All the servants are out, so you'll have to go for help. Get Dr. Blanchard, quickly!"

William lingered, clenching and unclenching his fists, his collar wet with perspiration. "But what if she dies?" he asked. "They'll say I killed her. I'll hang or spend the rest of my life in prison—"

Bernard stroked Marie's pale forehead with a tender motion as she stirred and murmured, trapped beneath a crushing burden of pain. The older man spoke with quiet determination. "I know you didn't mean for this to happen, William. And you are, after all, my son. I will do whatever I must to protect you."

William's look was hot with contempt and totally void of pity as he glared down at the unconscious Marie. "She was nothing but a whore," he said. "She even tried to lure me to her bed—"

The elder Holbrook closed his eyes tightly for a moment, and a crimson flush climbed his neck to throb in his face. "Enough," he growled. "Get the doctor before I change my mind and hang you myself!"

At last William turned and hurried toward the door, but the expression on his face was hard with a hatred terrible to see, even for a vampire.

Maeve drew nearer, soothing Marie's internal suffering as much as she could by means of her thoughts, but she dared not show herself.

Bernard was weeping quietly, pressing Marie's small hand to his mouth. "Oh, darling," he pleaded. "Forgive me."

Marie stirred again and moaned softly. "Calder," she said in the merest shadow of a whisper. "Help him—William will—kill him—"

A ragged sob escaped Bernard. "No, my darling—I promise you, Calder will be safe. Please, Marie—were you truly leaving me?"

"Yes," Marie said. Her eyes were open now, though there was a faraway light in them, as though she looked beyond Bernard, beyond the walls of that grand house, beyond the stormy night sky. She felt no pain, for Maeve had mentally deadened those places inside Marie that measured suffering.

"Why?" Bernard said, although he must have known.

"I wanted—needed your love—you wouldn't give it." Marie's gaze shifted, then locked with Maeve's. The vampire saw quiet acknowledgment in the woman's eyes.

It didn't surprise Maeve that Marie could see her, while she was invisible to both William and Bernard. The dying could often discern shapes where the living saw only thin shadows, or nothing at all.

After that, Marie closed her eyes and lapsed into the enfolding warmth of a coma, one from which she would never recover.

Bernard kept his vigil at his wife's side, smoothing her hair now and then, or stroking the curve of her cheek. Presently William and the doctor burst into the foyer, along with two men they must have recruited along the way.

The doctor, a diminutive man with a balding pate and blue eyes as fierce as those of a Viking, dropped to one knee to examine Marie. In a soft voice he said, "You'd best prepare yourself for a loss."

Marie was carefully placed on a long panel of mahogany, the extension piece from the huge table in the dining room, and carried upstairs to her deathbed by the two strangers.

When those men had gone, and Dr. Blanchard had joined William and Bernard in the study, Maeve was present, too, a part of the night, listening and watching.

It was there, in Bernard Holbrook's august study, that the story of the carriage accident was concocted. A wrecked coach would be easy enough to produce, they agreed grimly, and from that night forward they would all swear that Marie Holbrook had met with tragedy as she fled her unhappy marriage.

Maeve's feelings were mixed as she left the study for the nursery upstairs, where the boy who would become the man she loved more than life itself lay sleeping. He was beautiful, that child, with his mother's coloring and his father's strength of features, and she stood watching him as long as she dared.

Gazing at him, Maeve mourned her lost humanity bitterly, if briefly. This sleeping child was the mirror image of the little ones she would never be able to give Calder, despite the staggering depth and breadth of her love for him.

It would be difficult to go back to that future time, where her cherished one awaited her now as a grown man, and tell him the whole truth. He was bound to be furious with William for causing Marie's death, even though the act had been committed more by negligence than intent, and he would hate his dead father all over again, for engineering and then perpetuating a lie to protect his elder son.

Maeve crept close to the bed, brushed the slumbering child's tousled hair with the lightest pass of her fingertips, indulged in the futile wish that she could somehow spare him the suffering he faced, and then took herself ahead in time.

Calder was keeping a vigil in the main parlor, where his father lay in state, a pale, solemn figure grand even in death.

"What happened?" Calder asked when Maeve appeared at his side.

She took his hand and drew him away from the casket and the husk of a man inside, toward the glow of the fire. There was no other light in the room, but for that and the shimmer of the summer moon.

She said the most important thing first, and she said it gently. "Your mother didn't want to leave you, Calder—it broke her heart, in fact. All the same, she couldn't stay with your father, and she knew there was no place she might take you where Bernard wouldn't find you. She wanted to spare you the trauma of being pulled from her arms by some sheriff or detective and taken away again."

Calder closed his eyes, absorbing what Maeve had told him. Then he laid his hands on her shoulders and said hoarsely, "There's more."

She nodded and then, slowly, as tenderly as she could, she explained how Marie had really met her death that night—how William had flung her from him, in a fit of thwarted passion, and she'd fallen over the rail at the top of the staircase. How Bernard had staged a carriage wreck and told everyone that Marie had sustained her fatal injuries in the accident.

Calder's face, already bruised and abraded from the altercation with William earlier in the rear garden, tightened with rage as he listened. Maeve began to fear that he would go straight to William's room, drag his brother from his bed, and kill him with his bare hands.

Maeve's worry did not stem from the possibility that

William Holbrook might be the next to lie in a coffin in that very parlor; it was the knowledge that Calder would be hanged for the act that troubled her.

"Let me take you back to England," she pleaded softly when the sorrowful tale had been told and a few moments of silence had passed. "You'll be away from this place, these people—"

Calder turned from her abruptly and strode toward the center of the house, and Maeve went after him, forgetting to use her vampire powers, hurrying as a mortal woman would.

Instead of climbing the stairs, however, Calder turned up the gaslights in the massive foyer and stood on the exact spot where Marie's shattered body had struck the hard, cold floor. As he looked up at the rail of the highest landing, Maeve knew he was imagining the whole terrible scenario, assimilating the fear his mother must have felt as she fell, the blinding pain that would have assailed her at impact.

"Calder." Maeve said his name quietly, laying calming hands on his broad, tension-corded shoulders. "Let it be over now. Forgive your father and brother and go on."

He whirled, his face as cold and hard as the polished marble beneath his feet. "Forgive them? That would mean saying they were right in what they did!"

Maeve shook her head, very human tears gathering in her eyes because looking upon Calder's torment was far worse than bearing her own had ever been. What treacherous business it was, this loving another being so completely, so hopelessly.

"No, darling—that isn't the case at all. Forgiving won't change what Bernard and William did—it's not something you'd be doing for them, but for yourself. Don't you see? You'd be rolling back the stone that keeps you inside your tomb."

Calder's smile was rueful and bitter, utterly void of tenderness or mirth. "That sounds like an angel's reasoning to me," he said. "Have you been consorting with Gideon, like Dimity?"

She rested her forehead against his shoulder for a moment, coping with the inner tumult of loving this man, then looked up at him, her hands resting on his chest. Beneath her right palm his heart thumped, pumping the substance that sustained them both, though in very different ways, of course.

"Whether spoken by a devil or an angel, the truth is the truth," she said wearily. "Hating your father and brother will serve no purpose but to sap your strength. Now—will you come away with me? Please?"

He averted his gaze for a long moment, then looked directly at Maeve again. "I can't," he said in a voice gruff with desire and regret. "Unless I can share your life—every part of it—then it's better if I stay here. When I was in London, I was hardly more than a house pet. I can't live that way."

Maeve knew he was right, and she nodded woodenly. Although leaving Calder behind was torture, she had no choice—there was a war being fought in her world, as well as his. The night was passing, and she had yet to find Valerian or confront Lisette. "I love you," she said, desperate to retain some link between them.

He leaned forward and kissed the top of her head. "I know," he said. "And I certainly love you. But it appears that we're a star-crossed pair if ever there was one. Even Romeo and Juliet can't equal the tragedy of our romance."

Maeve's heart splintered within her. She wanted to deny his words, wanted it with everything in her, but she couldn't. Again, he was right. "I'll make you forget me soon," she said raggedly. "But just now, during this terrible time, I need for you to love me consciously, willingly."

"It's all right," Calder said. "Kiss me good-bye, darling, and go on about your deadly business."

She shook her head again, stepping back. The temptation to give in to her own selfish desires and make Calder into a blood-drinker, like herself, was overwhelming. She couldn't afford to forget, even for a moment, that if she transformed this man, she would also seal his eternal damnation. From the moment of change, his soul would belong to darkness.

"I don't trust myself to kiss you," she said, feeling as though she would shatter into pieces, crushed between her passion for Calder and the purity of the love she bore him.

He laid his hands to either side of her face, his thumbs stroking her cheekbones. Then he offered a familiar plea. "Make me a vampire, Maeve. Make me like you. Can't you see that there's nothing here for me anymore? That there is no reason for me to go on living as a mortal?"

Maeve's temper flared. "There is every reason!" she cried. "You're a doctor, and there are human beings suffering in hospitals, on battlefields—"

He silenced her by moving the pad of one thumb across her mouth. "I would be able to relieve far more of that suffering if I had powers like yours," he said gently. "As it is, I can do very little, except watch my patients die in agony, or worse, survive, in the kind of pain that can only produce madness."

She hesitated, wavering, swayed by Calder's argument and by the fact that she wanted him near her, now more than ever. Then, however, her prior convictions won out. What were a few score years spent as a mortal, compared to an eternity of hellfire?

"Good-bye," she said, and then she raised her hands high, closed her eyes, and vanished.

The warlock, Dathan, was pacing when Maeve met him at the agreed place, the stone monument in the English countryside that had figured so prominently in her experiences. Aidan had died to the life of a vampire and been resurrected here as a mortal man, and she and Valerian had met within the druids' circle many times, to argue and confer.

"Where have you been?" the warlock demanded, the night wind catching his dark cloak and causing it to flow behind him.

"I had business to attend to," Maeve said stiffly. "And kindly remember that I don't have to account to you—about anything."

Dathan's strangely beautiful countenance softened, but

only slightly. His eyes were still feral and sharp, missing no physical nuance of emotion or intent, no matter how minor. "We will not serve our purposes by arguing," he said finally. "My forces, because they can move about in daylight, have destroyed a vast number of Lisette's vampires with stakes and fire. She herself still eludes us, however."

"We'll find Lisette when she wants us to find her," Maeve said with weary certainty. "What of Valerian? Is there news of him?"

Dathan looked impatient for a moment, as though he'd rather not trouble himself with the likes of that particular, and undeniably controversial, vampire. Then he sighed like a suffering saint and said, "She's taken him to a place we cannot reach."

Maeve stiffened. "Back in time," she mused aloud as the realization struck her. "Back to a period before my death as a human, so that I cannot reach him."

Dathan nodded. "We warlocks cannot travel between decades and centuries, the way you blood-drinkers do, so we can be of no assistance in this matter. Far better if we simply put all thought of the unfortunate Valerian behind us and concentrate on the business at hand. Time is slipping away, remember. The forces of Nemesis will be on us soon."

Turning away, Maeve stepped up onto the curve of a fallen pillar and stood gazing at the dark plain that stretched away to the horizon. She knew well that time was sorely limited, and that the effort to destroy Lisette would neither stand nor fall because of Valerian. Still, he was the one who had given Maeve the dubious yet cherished gift of immortality. It had been he who had shown her her new powers and taught her to use them. He who had loved her once, in his own way, and introduced her to passion.

No matter what came of it, she decided, gazing up at a star-splattered sky, she could not abandon Valerian. She would have to find a way to help him.

When she turned to face Dathan again, she saw that he had divined her thoughts, and he was coldly furious.

"Come," he said in a charged but otherwise even voice.

"Let us seek the troublesome Lisette and move to destroy her."

Maeve assessed the sky. "It will be morning soon. I cannot tarry much longer."

Dathan looked violently impatient. "Then shift yourself to the other side of the world, where the light won't reach."

His reasoning was simple, and it wasn't as though the option hadn't occurred to Maeve many times since her making as a vampire. Some blood-drinkers, however, had experimented with the technique and never been seen again.

"It would be logical," she reflected, "for Lisette to do that. It's evident that she can move about during the day, from what Isabella said about Lisette's sudden appearance in her and Valerian's love-nest that morning. But I doubt our queen has progressed to such a point that she can endure the full glare of the sun."

"Exactly," Dathan said. "Let us go there—to China—and search for her."

Maeve turned, looked down into the warlock's handsome face in surprise. "You can do that? Travel so far, simply by the power of your mind?"

"Of course we can," he replied with exaggerated politeness. "Did you think we had no magical powers?"

Maeve went to stand facing him, on the stony, much-trampled ground. The druid stones were obviously a popular meeting point for humans, too, though only the most intrepid would venture there at night. "Let us see what powers you have," she challenged coolly. "Just as dawn arrives, we'll take a little journey together."

They waited, side by side, cloaked in silence and private musings, until the first glow of pink and apricot rimmed the horizon. Then, like a fledgling swimmer plunging into deep water, Maeve thrust herself into the unknown, the darkness on the opposite side of the globe.

At first, dazed by the swiftness of the trip and the energy it required, Maeve could not discern where she was. She knew only that Dathan was beside her, and that he supported her with a chivalrous arm around her waist.

After a few moments Maeve's head cleared. She had not been stricken by the distance, she knew, but by the avoidance of the vampire sleep that would normally have claimed her just then.

"Fascinating!" Dathan remarked, looking down into a moon-washed pit, where dozens of life-size bronze soldiers marched in formation, accompanied by life-size horses and chariots. The excavation had clearly been abandoned for some time, and Maeve knew intuitively that there were hundreds, perhaps thousands, more of these ancient sculptures buried all over China.

Maeve marveled, but not at the industry of a long-dead civilization. No, it was her own ability to resist that all-encompassing sleep that amazed her. It was probably these reflections, she would conclude later, that prevented her from sensing the impending attack.

They came out from behind every soldier, those terrible, blood-drinking corpses Lisette had made, making a shrill sound that was part shriek and part groan.

Dathan muttered an exclamation and tensed beside Maeve, and she knew that if he'd had a sword, he would have drawn it.

"Great Zeus," he rasped, "there are hundreds of them!"

Maeve nodded, a half-smile forming on her lips at the prospect of challenge. "It would be my guess," she said, "that we have found more than this army of blathering creatures."

"What?" Dathan demanded, bracing himself as the creatures scrambled out of the pit and began lumbering toward them.

"Lisette is here," Maeve said calmly.

In the next instant a geyser of blue-gold light exploded in the center of the pit full of statues, and as the glow solidified into a female shape, looming some twenty feet off the ground, even the mindless army stopped and stared.

Maeve applauded. "Very impressive," she called as the shape became Lisette, dramatic and horrible in a gauzy gown that caught the night wind.

"Are you insane?" Dathan hissed, as the bluish light of Lisette's countenance played over both their faces.

"Perhaps," Maeve said, taking a step forward to stand at the precipice of the pit. "If you can summon your warlocks, you'd better do it now. Otherwise, you and I are doomed to a terrible end that might well have a beginning but no finish."

Dathan shuddered, the way a mortal would have, and whispered back, "Don't be naive. I don't have to send for my armies—I brought them with me."

Maeve did not look over her shoulder; indeed, she did not shift her gaze from Lisette's shimmering form. Still, she could feel the warlocks now, gathering in the darkness behind her and Dathan.

Their presence, while reassuring, was by no means a reprieve from Lisette's vengeance, however. She was possessed of spectacular powers—that much was obvious—and her army of brainless marvels would fight tirelessly at her command, not out of any such unvampire-like trait as loyalty, of course, but because she controlled them so completely.

"You are bold, Maeve Tremayne," Lisette said in an ear-splitting and yet strangely sweet voice, looming there in the darkness like the angel of death.

Oddly, Maeve thought of a movie she had seen once, during one of her reluctant visits to the twentieth century—a tale containing an alleged wizard, who had projected a terrifying image to frighten visitors away. All the time he'd been hiding behind a curtain, pulling levers and twisting dials, a nervous, fretful little man with no magical powers at all.

"Yes," Maeve agreed. "Some would even say brazen. Show me your true self, Vampire. I am not misled by this theatrical trick of yours, though I must say it's memorable."

The creature that Lisette wanted them to believe was herself undulated with furious, beautiful light, and a continuous shriek of rage filled the night, loud enough, piercing enough, to shatter the very stars themselves.

Suddenly the banshee-like cry shaped itself into words. "Kill them!" Lisette screamed, and her troops, mesmerized only a moment before, began their stumbling, awkward advance again.

Battle erupted all around Maeve and Dathan, but they were in the eye of the storm, at least temporarily, for the warlocks came out of the night to meet the vampires and engage them in bitter combat.

Unearthly shrieks rent the air as warlocks were cut down by the vampires' superior strength and, conversely, blood-drinkers were infused with the poisonous blood of their enemies.

Maeve concentrated on Lisette, whose image still hovered above them, shining and huge, and her thoughts transported her to a niche in a sheer cliff overlooking the battleground.

There Maeve found the vampire queen, no bigger or more daunting than she was herself. Lisette looked disconcerted for a moment, but then, with a scream of madness and outrage, she flung herself at Maeve.

They fought, the two vampires, snarling like panthers battling over a kill on some African steppe, tearing at each other. Maeve felt herself weakening, felt the vampire sleep threatening her, and redoubled her efforts, knowing that if she did not win this battle she would be left in the open to face the ravages of the morning sun.

Just when Maeve believed she could not continue, that the disastrous sleep would swallow her, however, Lisette turned to vapor and vanished.

Maeve collapsed against a wall of the shallow cave. She was alone, and gravely weakened, and if she did not feed and rest in a dark, safe place, she would be lost. She tried to transport herself back to her lair in England, but the effort failed. She clutched her middle and slid helplessly down the side of the cave to the ground.

She heard the battle going on and on outside. Evidently, when Lisette had fled—if indeed that had been her intent—she had not chosen to take her horrid soldiers with her.

Maeve's head lolled, and she thought of Calder, and then of Aidan and Valerian. This was the ironic end of it all, then, she reflected, with a strangled sound that might have been either a laugh or a sob. She was wounded, the dawn was inching slowly, inexorably, toward her, and her only hope of rescue was a band of warlocks—*warlocks*, who six months ago, even six days ago, had been her implacable enemies.

She had almost lost consciousness by the time the din ceased, and she could feel the first light of dawn creeping into the cave, finding her with its acid fingers, tearing at her injured flesh.

Then—surely it was only a dream—strong arms lifted her, and she felt a rushing sensation, and the burning stopped.

Maeve opened her eyes slowly, fearing to find that Lisette had come back for her, and brought her as a captive to some place of temporary safety. She found, instead, that she was inside an old crypt—there was no telling what country she was in—and Dathan was with her.

He smiled, though his blue eyes were as cold as ever, and held a golden goblet to her lips. "Drink," he said.

Maeve knew the chalice contained blood, the substance she most needed and that, at the same time, most repulsed her. She hesitated, quite sensibly, for this supposed gesture of mercy might well be a ruse. Dathan might be offering her the poison that flowed through his own veins, or those of one of his multitude of followers.

"Take it," he ordered gently, reading her mind. "It's low-grade stuff—we stole it from a refrigerator in a nearby hospital—but there's no warlock taint to fret about."

Maeve's choices were limited, since she could not regain her strength, or indeed even survive, without ingesting blood. She decided to take the risk and let the stuff flow in through her fangs, completely bypassing her tongue.

When the chalice was empty, she sank back onto silken pillows and regarded Dathan with questioning eyes. Her wounds had already begun to mend, closed by the cool, healing darkness and her own mystical powers, but she was frightfully weak.

"You saved me," she said with emotion. "Why?"

Dathan narrowed his eyes at her and sighed again. He would have made an excellent martyr, it seemed to Maeve.

"Not out of anything so misguided as mercy," he finally replied with a shrug. "We cannot achieve our objectives without you."

Maeve tried to rise, but Dathan pushed her back down again.

"Wait," he said. "You must have more rest and more blood. You will be no use to us without your strength and your powers."

"None of that will matter," Maeve argued, "if our time runs out and Nemesis is unleashed with his sword of vengeance."

Dathan did not look quite so desperate or despairing as he had in times past. He shoved a hand through his thick, maple-brown hair. "We can conclude by the events of last night, I think, that Lisette's new lair is somewhere in the region of that excavation."

Maeve nodded in full, if reluctant, agreement. "How did your warlocks fare against those monsters of hers?"

"Like your encounter with the queen," Dathan answered, "it ended in something of a draw. We fought until dawn was imminent, and then the opposing forces fled, of course, to escape the light. That was when I found you on the floor of that cave—until that moment I thought you'd deserted us."

Had Maeve been mortal, she would have flushed with annoyance and outrage. "Do you believe me to be such a coward? Think again, Warlock—I have as much courage as *ten* witches!"

Dathan laughed and handed her the chalice again; it had been refilled and brought back by a cloaked creature Maeve had glimpsed out of the corner of her eye. "And as much pride, I vow," he said. "Drink up, Mistress Tremayne. I fear we have many frightful adventures still ahead of us."

Chapter

13

Somehow Calder passed the night without awakening William and throttling him, and with the morning came a drizzling rain and a steady stream of visitors. Like crows in their black garb, the mourners passed by the casket single file, peering inside to see how death suited Bernard Holbrook.

All morning and all afternoon they came, the grieving, the curious, the indifferent, the relieved, and the secretly pleased. They ate hungrily of the food Prudence and her small staff had prepared, and speculated among themselves about Calder and William and the bruised state of their faces.

Calder hated every moment of that interminable day and dreaded the one to follow, for that would bring the funeral, the eulogies, the grim and final business of burial. To him, the world looked dark, and it was difficult to believe that the sun would ever shine again.

After the last of the sorrowful callers had left, Calder and William accidentally found themselves alone in the large dining room. William took a piece of smoked turkey from a platter and bit into it, regarding Calder through swollen eyes.

"We'll have the reading of the will tomorrow, after the ceremonies," the elder brother announced, reaching for another piece of meat.

Calder shrugged. "I don't give a damn about that," he said.

"Good," William replied. "Papa was closeted away for hours one day, just last month, with his lawyers. I recall that he was especially exasperated with you at that time, so don't be surprised if you find yourself in the street, with nothing to live on but that pitiful stipend the army pays you."

Although Calder's stomach rebelled at the very sight of food, he knew only too well that he would not be able to think clearly or function well in an emergency if he did not eat. He went to the long table, against his will, and filled a plate, taking slices of turkey and ham, some potato salad, and a serving of Prudence's famous fruit compote. Then, by a deft motion of one foot, learned in boyhood, he drew back a chair.

He paused for a few moments, regarding the food he'd taken and envying Maeve because she didn't have to trouble herself with the stuff at all. As he took up his fork, Calder raised his eyes to William's face.

"Take it all," he said, only a little surprised to realize that he meant it. "Take the money, take this goddamned mausoleum of a house, take the illustrious Holbrook name and the power that goes with it."

William blanched, his fingers tightening over the back of a chair. Plainly he hadn't been expecting Calder's acquiescence, but another fight instead. "You can't be serious," he said.

Calder ate a few bites of ham, chewing each one thoroughly, before answering. "You murdered my mother," he said at last. "And that old man lying in there with his eyelids stitched together covered up for you. As far as I'm concerned, if I never see you or this place again, it will be too soon."

Sweat beaded on William's upper lip. "I killed Marie? Where did you get such an idea?" he demanded hoarsely, pulling back a chair of his own and collapsing into it. "And why is it that you can't speak of our father with some semblance of respect, even now?"

"I loved him," Calder conceded. "But respect is another

thing. As for my mother's death, well, you might say I have a way of looking into the past."

William's hand trembled visibly as he reached for a carafe of Madeira and then a wineglass. "I didn't lay a hand on her," he said.

"You're a liar," Calder replied, still eating. He knew his calm manner was unnerving his brother, and he was pleased by the fact. "She was going to leave this house, and our esteemed father, and you intercepted her. There was an argument, and you gripped her by the shoulders. She struggled, and you wouldn't release her—until you thrust her away from you in a moment of fury. That was when she tumbled backward over the railing and fell twenty feet to the floor of the foyer."

William had managed to pour wine, but his subsequent attempts to raise the glass to his white lips failed because he was shaking. "Pure fantasy," he said.

Calder stared at him for a long, purposely disconcerting interval. "It happened just that way," he insisted quietly, "and we both know it. Kindly don't insult me with your denials."

After casting a yearning look at his wine, William wiped one forearm across his mouth. "If you really believe this— this delusion, then why haven't you tried to avenge Marie's death?"

Calder smiled grimly. "There has hardly been time for that," he said indulgently. "Still, we're young, you and I," he added with a shrug. "There's no rush."

At last William made a successful grab for his glass and raised it tremulously to his lips. After a few audible gulps, his color began to return, and he was steadier. "Is that a threat?"

Again, Calder shrugged, reaching for a platter and helping himself to some of Prudence's cold rice salad. "It might be. Then again, it might not. To be quite frank, I haven't decided how I'll deal with you." He chewed thoughtfully for a few moments, swallowed, and then gestured at William with an offhanded motion of his fork. "Rest assured, though, that I *will* deal with you."

William swallowed the rest of his wine and reached for the carafe while he could. "You don't scare me," he said, though his manner and the pallor of his complexion gave the lie to his words.

Calder smiled again and continued to eat.

That night he waited for Maeve to come to him, prayed that she would, and finally she appeared. She was as ethereal as a spirit, and throughout the magical encounter that awaited him, he feared he was only dreaming.

Without a word she slipped into bed beside him, encircling him in her soft, strong arms. She kissed the underside of his jaw and sent shivers of forlorn desire rushing through his system.

"Maeve," he whispered.

She touched his lips with an index finger to silence him, then trailed kisses down over his chest and his belly. His manhood surged upright in response, and he drew in a harsh breath when she touched the tip with her tongue.

Calder groaned and arched his back, completely in her power. He whispered a plea, and she granted his wish, consuming him, and he writhed in a fever of passion and need. At the last possible moment, she moved astride him, and took him deep inside her, and rode him while his body buckled beneath hers in the throes of triumph. She muffled his ragged shout of release by laying one cool hand over his mouth.

"I love you," he told her when their encounter was over, and she lay beside him, close and slender and solid. "Please, Maeve—don't leave me. Don't work your sorcery and make us forget each other—I can't bear the prospect of that."

She leaned over him and kissed his mouth, but lightly, brushing his lips with her own. Still she did not speak, but in truth there was no need of it. Everything she was thinking and feeling was plain in her dark blue eyes.

Calder's vision blurred as he looked up at her, and he touched her smooth cheek with an index finger. "So incredibly beautiful," he marveled in a whisper, certain he would perish with the loss of her. He wasn't sure, in fact, that he himself would exist at all, without the knowledge and memory of Maeve Tremayne.

Maeve smiled at him, the expression full of sweetness and sorrow, and then removed herself from his arms, from the warm tangle of the bedsheets. Once again she was wearing the soft, gauzy gown she had shed earlier to enter Calder's embrace.

He gave a low, despairing cry and stretched out a hand to her, but between one heartbeat and the next, she vanished.

Calder wept, though he did not make a sound, well aware that Maeve had made up her mind to destroy their love, to tear it front the universe by its very roots.

For the first time in his life he wanted to die.

Perhaps, he thought later, when he'd composed himself a little, she had already begun the mysterious process that would erase her from his memory, and him from her own. Perhaps he would awaken the next morning, or the one after that, with no recollection of the beautiful vampire who haunted his soul, as well as his mind and body.

Even though he knew the transition itself would probably be painless, the prospect of it was the purest torture.

Calder tried to reason with himself. Undoubtedly he would simply go on with his life, treating his patients, perhaps meeting another woman, marrying, fathering a houseful of children. The war, God willing, was bound to end soon, and the sundered land would begin to mend itself into some new and better nation.

No, it wouldn't be a bad existence, and he wouldn't know the difference anyway, wouldn't know what he was missing any more than the corpse of his father, still lying in a wash of candlelight in the parlor, could comprehend that life was going on without him.

Still, for all the dangers and all the terrible things he would see and probably do, Calder wanted to be with Maeve. And yes, he wanted to share her fantastic powers, too, but only because they would enable him to help his patients in ways that were impossible then. He could travel into the future, for instance, into the late twentieth century, the era to which the mystery of time had progressed, according to Maeve, and learn even more about the art of medicine than the miraculous textbooks had taught him. He would be able to bring that knowledge back to people who suffered, along with chemicals, pills, and serums that could kill pain without making the heart race the way morphine did. Vaccinations that would protect small children who in his own time were cruelly felled by maladies such as measles, diphtheria, and whooping cough . . .

He drifted off to sleep, and morning took him by surprise. Confused, uncertain if Maeve had come to him during the night or simply worked some trick of the mind on him and created the illusion of herself.

By rote, Calder washed and dressed and went downstairs to the dining room, but even as he filled his plate at the sideboard and went to the table, his thoughts were muddled. He was not aware of William's presence until his brother spoke.

"Calder."

William had taken a seat at the head of the table, but he wasn't taking breakfast. A hot cup of coffee steamed before him, and he poured rum into the brew as Calder looked at him in cold silence.

William was flushed now, his eyes feverishly bright, like those of an animal approaching the last stages of rabies. "I think you should go away," he said. "To Europe, perhaps, or maybe out West. I'm sure Papa left your enough money to make a new start."

Calder pushed back his chair, dropped his fork to his china plate with a deliberate clatter, and stood. "You've waxed generous, all of the sudden, even reasonable. Why is that, William?"

His brother started to answer, choked on his own words, and began again. "I want to be fair, that's all."

"You want to be fair," Calder repeated softly in a marveling tone. "Of course you do. And General Lee wants to hand all of Dixie over to Mr. Lincoln, tied with Union-blue ribbons." His voice hardened. "Damn it, do you take me for a fool? You'd murder me in my sleep if you thought you could get away with it!"

William closed his eyes tightly for a moment and swayed in his chair. He didn't speak again as Calder turned and strode out of the room.

Valerian sat in the cool, dark dungeon, knees drawn up, back pressed to the dank stone wall behind him. Had his captor been anyone other than Lisette, he'd have escaped easily, but her power was as strong as it had ever been—perhaps stronger, in that peculiar way of diseased minds. It was her magic that held him; the chains and bars and heavy iron doors were just for show.

He sighed, ran one hand through his mane of chestnut-colored hair, and wondered what Maeve and the others were doing, two hundred years into the future in the nineteenth century. It was just possible, he thought with a scowl, that Maeve was glad he was out of the way or, worse, that she hadn't even noticed that he was gone.

Valerian thrust himself to his feet, which were half buried in the fetid straw covering the floor. Rats and mice and a variety of other vermin populated the stuff, rustling and scurrying in the darkness.

"Lisette!" he shouted, his voice echoing in that enormous, lonely tomb of a place. "Damn you, show yourself!"

There was no answer, of course. Lisette had simply dropped him here, sometime in the middle of the seventeenth century, and it was entirely possible that she planned to let him rot. That would probably be a more effective, and more twisted, form of torture than anything else she could have devised.

In the distance he heard a creaking sound and the terrified blathering of a mortal.

Valerian closed his eyes and at the same time tried to shut the sound out of his ears, repulsed and shaken by it, but his efforts were futile. Until that night, he'd been sustained by animal blood, inferior stuff that barely kept him conscious. Now, plainly, Lisette or one of her several lieutenants had apparently decided to serve up a feast.

No doubt he, Valerian, was being fattened up for the kill.

A vampire called Shaleen, a dark-haired minx of a creature Valerian had never encountered before his imprisonment, appeared in the arched doorway of his cell, gripping a half-starved, flea-ridden mortal by one arm.

The boy was dressed in rags, all bones and filthy in the bargain, and he blinked in the darkness, all the more terrified because he could not see the fate that awaited him.

Shaleen, who was beautiful and eminently sane, unlike most of the ludicrous creatures Lisette surrounded herself with, curled her lip contemptuously and flung the unfortunate, blubbering human down at Valerian's feet.

"Here," said the other vampire, quite uncharitably. "Your dinner."

Valerian ignored the pitiful creature groveling in the rancid straw, at least for the moment, and fixed his attention on Shaleen. "Did Lisette make you into a blood-drinker?"

She studied him with insolent brown eyes. Her hair, a lovely caramel color, tumbled to her waist, unbrushed, with a thistle entangled here and there. "No," she answered. "Did she make you?"

Valerian's making was a memory he cherished, and he had never shared the experience with another being, not even Aidan or Maeve. "No," he replied shortly as the mortal clutched at his clothes, begging in incoherent phrases for mercies that were not forthcoming. "Why do you stay here? Why do you help her?"

Shaleen smiled. "I'm a new vampire. Lisette is teaching me her magic—I'm going to help her rule, after she destroys Maeve Tremayne once and for all."

Valerian laid a hand on the mortal's head, stroking him in consolation, the way he might have done with a whining dog. Using the oldest magic he knew, he numbed the poor wretch's mind, thus calming him. "Surely you're not foolish enough to believe it will be easy to stop Maeve? Her powers are as great as Lisette's—perhaps greater, because she isn't mad. Furthermore, Maeve has fate on her side—she is the blood-drinker of legend, the one who will overthrow Lisette."

Shaleen's lovely face hardened, only for a moment and almost imperceptibly, and yet in that time Valerian discerned that she had fancied *herself* to be that vampire. In her heart of hearts, she was plotting against Lisette planning to supplant her.

Valerian smiled. "You are very ambitious indeed," he said. He let the smile fade, for he had not lived so many centuries without learning a few things about dramatic effect. "You are also foolhardy. Lisette will recognize your duplicity, and when that happens, the worst sinner in hell will be better off than you."

She raised her chin in defiance, did the beautiful and treacherous Shaleen, but there was no hiding her fear, not from Valerian.

"Help me get out of here," he said softly in his most persuasive voice, one that had lured many a mortal and not a few vampires into his web. "Your plan cannot succeed, little one. Lisette is too suspicious, and much too powerful, to fall for such bumbling deceptions as yours."

He saw her waver, sensed her indecision, but then she withdrew into the doorway.

"Lisette warned me about you," she said accusingly. "She said you were a better liar than the devil himself, and twice as charming, and she was right. Enjoy your supper, Valerian."

With that, Shaleen went out, shutting the great door behind her, and Valerian looked down at the whimpering, half-conscious, pathetic excuse for a human clinging to his leg. Gently he bent, grasped the lad by his painfully thin shoulders, and drew him to his feet.

"Don't be afraid," he said in the tenderest of tones as he gazed deeply into the terrified blue eyes of his next victim. "I promise you will feel only the keenest pleasure, and no pain at all."

Valerian bared the fragile throat, found the warm, sweet place where a full vein pulsed just beneath the skin, and sank his fangs in deep. Bliss flooded him as he drank, and he felt the specimen tremble in his hands and beneath his lips, not with pain but, just as Valerian had promised him, with an almost unbearable ecstasy.

Maeve was a little distracted; her thoughts kept straying to Calder. She was torn between guilt—she had tricked him, after all—and the hope that, by making him believe she'd been with him earlier in the night, by projecting an image of herself into his mind, she had afforded him a measure of comfort. . . .

She strained to catch hold of what Dathan was saying and pulled herself back into the conversation.

". . . as far as we have been able to discern, the time of his captivity is the middle of the seventeenth century. . . ."

"The seventeenth century?" Maeve echoed, round-eyed, seeing that one of Dathan's warlock spies had brought in a scroll. Closer examination proved that Lisette herself had penned a description of Valerian's exact whereabouts on the crumbling parchment. The message itself, of course, was intended to taunt Maeve, to challenge her. "That's before my birth as a human—and I can go back no farther than my death."

Dathan arched an eyebrow. "Are you so certain? After all, you thought you couldn't escape the vampire sleep, either, but you did exactly that when we traveled to China."

Maeve nodded thoughtfully. More than ever, she wished Valerian was here—he knew about these things. Once, in fact, in an effort to help Aidan find the secret of transforming himself from vampire to mortal, Valerian had actually ventured back beyond his own mortal lifetime. The trouble was, the effort had nearly destroyed him, and he'd been incapacitated by the resultant weakness. Time was running out, and Maeve couldn't afford the long recuperation her friend and mentor had needed.

On the other hand, the war with Lisette was going to be

much more difficult, if not impossible, without Valerian's counsel and moral support. Furthermore, if he perished in the skirmish ahead, then any victory, however sweet, would be tarnished by the loss of him.

Dathan paced. "Surely," he snapped, "you are not thinking of gallivanting off into some other century simply to rescue that worthless Valerian!"

"Your opinion of my friend does not concern me," Maeve said coldly.

"Perhaps it will," Dathan retorted, "if I tell you that we are watching your beloved Calder Holbrook, far away as he is. We can and will take him hostage, Maeve, if you do not listen to reason!"

Maeve trembled with both shock and fury. Stupidly perhaps, she had not expected a threat to Calder to come from this quarter but instead from Lisette. "Here and now," she said, and the even meter of her own voice surprised her, "I make this vow. If you lay a hand on Calder, I will flay you alive and serve you to the devil on a dozen different platters."

Dathan drew back slightly and raised both hands, palms out, in a jaunty gesture of conciliation. "That's a very colorful threat," he said. "And I assure you, I'll keep it in mind."

Maeve narrowed her eyes and leaned toward him. "See that you do, Warlock," she replied. "And keep this in mind as well: I make *promises*, not threats."

Although his eyes snapped with rage, Dathan did not press the matter further. Maeve, for her part, was not in the least reassured, for if she should be felled, as had nearly happened in China, Calder would be left completely unprotected.

Rising from the couch where she'd reclined and then sat, Maeve straightened her gown and ran splayed fingers through her long, loose tresses. "I will send Dimity to check on Valerian," she said quietly, and no nuance of the preceding argument showed in her countenance. "She is medieval, like him, and may be able to reach that time in history without danger to herself."

"Fine," Dathan said, his eyes still glittering with controlled fury. "That will free the two of us to seek out Lisette and make yet another attempt to finish her."

Maeve nodded distractedly. She was not thinking of Lisette, or even of Valerian, but of Calder, far away in Philadelphia. She should make another trip back in time, she knew that, to the night when he'd first seen her, in that grisly churchyard at Gettysburg, where the dead and maimed had been laid out in endless rows. Once there, she would blind Calder to her presence, as she should have done in the first place, and in that moment his attachment to her would be undone.

Knowing what needed doing and actually tackling the task were two different things, however, and Maeve was not anxious to destroy Calder's memory of her. Selfish as it was, she needed the certainty that he loved her, that he wanted her, that he would recognize her if she came to him.

None of those things would be true from the instant she changed history and, for all practical intents and purposes, she'd be alone in eternity once again.

She left Dathan, in his underground hiding place somewhere in the French countryside, and sought out the vampire Dimity.

Maeve found the other blood-drinker haunting London's seedy dockside area, as usual, and they fed together on a pair of deserving louts before retiring to Dimity's graciously furnished cellar to confer.

There, seated in comfortable chairs and cheered by the light of a lively fire in the grate, Maeve told Dimity that Dathan's warlocks had learned where Lisette was keeping Valerian. Dimity nodded when the explanation was through and said she'd attempt a visit to his cell. If possible, she promised, she would find a way to release him.

"I could not ask for more," Maeve said, rising. After offering a quiet thanks, she took herself away and met Dathan in another part of London, one where sleek carriages rolled past through the fog, carrying passengers who would never have believed that such creatures as vampires even existed.

"I'm certain Lisette is in China," Dathan said without preamble, falling into step with Maeve as she passed a street lamp glowing with sickly blue-gold light.

Maeve took her time answering. "I've been thinking about that," she said. "It's possible, you know, that she's found herself another, safer lair. She has to be aware that we'll look for her in that same area."

"She is reckless," Dathan argued, and it was a statement Maeve could not refute. Lisette *was* reckless, making dramatic appearances, taking captives, spawning those dreadful creatures in defiance of the entire supernatural world.

"We'll try again," she agreed with dignity.

Dathan nodded, satisfied that he'd swayed Maeve to his way of thinking. "Shall we meet just before dawn, then, at the circle of stones?"

"I will be there," Maeve said, and in the next instant she realized that the warlock was no longer beside her. In fact, he was nowhere in sight.

She shrugged and set out to feed a second time. In the hours to come, she would need all the strength she could muster.

Dathan idled the rest of the night away in a backstreet tavern, nursing a mug of bitter ale, and watched in detachment as a variety of monsters came and went.

Oh, yes, there were vampires among the revelers, mostly new ones, heedless of the dangers of prowling places they did not know, and one or two warlocks came in as well. Still, it was among the human beings that Dathan found the greatest number of fiends.

He marveled to himself that mortals frightened their children, and each other, with tales of witches and warlocks, vampires and werewolves, while some of the vilest things in all of Creation lived next door to them, or up the street, or just down the road in the next village. And those beasts were not supernatural at all, but other humans, with beating hearts, brains throbbing with mysterious electrical impulses, and, supposedly, souls.

He sighed, lifted the copper mug to his mouth, and drained its contents in one final swallow. Then, suddenly sensing something different in his surroundings, he rose from his bench at one of the trestle tables, tossed a coin down to pay for his refreshment, and went outside into the summer night.

In the street, which was muddy and fouled with spittle and manure, Dathan stopped, sensing rather than hearing the strange, rhythmic chatter of several beings. He smiled, raising the hood of his cape so that his face was hidden in shadow, as well as his hair.

He was being stalked.

Dathan meandered into the nearest alley, drawn there by the vibration in his senses. They awaited him in that dark place, six drooling fiends, newly dead and starved for blood. Any blood.

Lisette's friends were too stupid and too greedy to know of the ancient enmity between their own kind and the warlock.

He pushed back his hood and bared his sleek, white neck to them, and they stumbled toward him, making that odd and frantic murmuring sound he had heard before. He waited, and pretended to flinch when the first one fastened on him.

Infusing a vampire with the venom that flowed through his veins was a ferocious pleasure to Dathan, to all warlocks, and he felt a sweet tightening in his groin as a second monster pushed aside the first to drink.

Dathan allowed that, but ecstasy left him weak and distracted, and those were indulgences he couldn't afford. The poison took effect, and the first two vampires dropped, writhing, to the filth-strewn ground. He killed the other four by a more flamboyant method, one he had not yet exhibited to his reluctant comrade, Maeve Tremayne.

Narrowing his eyes, murmuring an incantation far older than the pillars of Stonehenge, Dathan produced a spontaneous burst of fire. It consumed the vampires, and he watched them twist and flail within the flames, in their gruesome dance of death.

Before the grudging truce, Dathan had consigned many blood-drinkers to the same fate, and he would have destroyed them all if he'd been able; immortals of equal power could, of course, resist his curses. How strange it was to be in league with Mistress Tremayne, when at any other time in history the two of them would have been sworn enemies!

Reaching the street, Dathan raised his hood again, then paused to look back into the alleyway. There was no light, for the fire he'd ignited was a spiritual one, and no screaming, for the vampires' cries could be heard not by the ear, but only by the most sensitive souls.

Most humans had not reached that level of consciousness, and so it was that the passers-by on that London street did not even pause, let alone rush into the alley to watch in their customary helpless fascination while the vampires burned.

Calder stirred uncomfortably in his sleep, dreaming of a night nearly thirty years before. In that dream, he was six years old again, and his mother was still alive, sitting on the edge of his bed, stroking his hair with a gentle hand, saying her tearful farewells.

The boy he had once been opened his eyes, something Calder had not done in reality, and reached up to wrap his arms around Marie's neck. "Good-bye, Mama," he said into the fragrant softness of her neck.

She embraced him, this other Marie, and he felt her tears on his face. Then she stood and walked toward the open doorway, never looking back, yet not seeming to see the young, dangerously passionate William hovering ahead of her. Waiting.

Calder, still trapped in the dream, thrust himself out of bed and ran into the hallway. He'd screamed a warning, putting all his strength into the effort, but not a sound had come from his throat.

He watched, in horror, as William and Marie argued, saw his half brother grab his mother by the shoulders and shake her, heard his father's stern order to let her go. Then, cold as a corpse, paralyzed with fear, Calder had watched as Marie tumbled over the stair rail.

It was torment enough, seeing that horrid spectacle once, but the scene kept repeating itself, over and over again, with a slow, macabre grace.

Calder thrust himself back to the surface of consciousness, unable to bear it any longer, only to feel his heart lurch at the sight awaiting him.

William was standing at the foot of the bed, hardly more than a shadow in the thick darkness, so still that he might have been part of the furniture. As Calder stared at him, still half-asleep, still half-entangled in his nightmare, the clouds that must have covered the moon moved on, flooding the room with an eerie silver light.

A fragment of that light caught on the nickel-blue barrel of the dueling pistol clasped in William's hands.

"I'll say you were killed by robbers," he said in an odd, strained voice, "rebel deserters who broke in looking for gold and whiskey. Everyone will believe me, just like before."

Calder dared not move, either slowly or suddenly. "Put down the gun," he said in a low, even voice. "They *won't* believe you, William. This is murder, and you'll surely hang for it."

He might not have spoken for all the response he received.

"I hope you burn in hell," William said, and then light blazed from the pistol's barrel. There was an explosion, though Calder couldn't tell whether it had come from within himself or outside, and then there was only darkness.

Chapter
14

William watched dispassionately as Calder sank back against his pillows, a strangled, gurgling sound coming from somewhere deep inside him. In the moonlight William made out the torn place just below Calder's right nipple, and saw the matting of dark chest hair turn slick and crimson with blood.

The elder brother moved to turn up the lights, the dueling pistol dangling from his left hand now, resting hot against his thigh, burning right through his trouser leg.

There were murmurings in the hallway, and sounds of rushing this way and that, but William felt no urgency, no fear. Smiling grimly, he drew up a chair next to Calder's bed and sat down to watch him die.

The world, he told himself, would be better off without the likes of Calder Holbrook—if indeed he was entitled to the surname at all—just as it was better off without tramps like Marie.

Calder was unconscious, but even then he struggled, and a muscle in William's jaw tightened. Perhaps, he reflected coolly, it would be necessary to reload the pistol and fire a second bullet. This time the barrel would be pressed to Calder's throbbing temple.

"Maeve," Calder choked, though he had not roused. *"Maeve—"*

The bedclothes were sodden with blood now, William

noted with satisfaction. Surely no one could lose so much and still live.

He settled back in his chair, undisturbed by the continued noise beyond Calder's bedroom door. It might as well have been another country, that hallway. Another world.

William relaxed, stretching out his legs and crossing his booted feet. "I don't suppose anyone will believe that story I made up about robbers," he mused aloud, half to himself and half to Calder.

Just then Prudence burst in, massive in her nightdress and wrapper. "What's happened in here—" she began, but then her eyes found Calder, and she gave a weeping scream and trundled to his bedside. "Sweet Jesus in heaven, you done shot him!" she cried. "You done murdered your own brother—"

William sighed as Prudence tried to staunch Calder's blood-flow with the corner of her wrapper. She was wailing in despair all the while, and when a cluster of other servants jammed into the doorway to gawk, she shouted for someone to get a doctor, and after that a constable.

Meanwhile, a storm was rising outside, and the wind rattled the sturdy leaded windows in their frames.

"I did the right thing by killing him, Prudence," William said calmly. "He's a bad seed—evil, just like his mama was. You'll come to see that, all in good time."

Prudence left her patient long enough to round the bed and snatch the dueling pistol from William's limp grasp. "You gone crazy, that's what," the housekeeper said wetly. "You gone plum out of your mind!"

She stormed back to Calder and laid the dueling pistol on the other nightstand.

"What made you do such a thing, Mr. William? Ain't there been enough grief and sufferin' in this house over the years?"

William didn't mind answering the question. In fact, he was certain that, once he had, no further explanations would be required of him. He looked at Calder, whose flesh was pallorous and gray—except, of course, where the blood soaked him—and could not disguise the hatred he felt.

"I stayed here, all those years, and learned the banking business. I did what Papa wanted, always. I put aside my own wishes, my own dreams, to honor his." William felt his very soul contort within him; it was an ugly pain. "Calder here was the prodigal, fancy free, and his briefest appearance in this house was cause for killing the fatted calf. Still, fool that I was, I believed Papa appreciated my sacrifices, that someday I would be rewarded for my loyalty. And what happened? Papa left everything to Calder—the house, the bank, the fortunes we made together. All of it was Calder's, except, of course, for a pittance of an income earmarked for me."

"Dear Jesus, save us," Prudence muttered. She'd taken off the wrapper now and made a bandage of sorts, but William knew her efforts were hopeless. The white flannel she pressed to the wound was already turning scarlet. "You had no call to do this—Mr. Calder would have done right by you. I don't think he even wanted this old house, nor much money, neither."

William recalled the things Calder had said earlier, in the family dining room. He *had* claimed that he didn't want any of their father's bequests, but William hadn't believed it then and he didn't believe it now. How could anyone fail to want all that surrounded him, and with the full measure of his soul at that?

Monumental as it was, his father's final betrayal wasn't the whole reason for what William had done. Somehow Calder had found out the truth about the night Marie died, and he'd sworn revenge. However mild his tone, Calder had meant what he said. He would have dogged William to his very grave, making him wonder, making him sweat.

William offered none of that to Prudence, though, for she had always favored Calder over him, just the way Bernard Holbrook had done.

"You hold on, precious," Prudence was murmuring close to Calder's ear. "You just hold on—don't you go off nowheres. I won't have you dead and hauntin' this place, and always gettin' underfoot when I'm tryin' to get my work done!"

William closed his eyes as the muscles at his nape clenched.

The constable and an army doctor arrived at the same time.

"It was him," William heard Prudence say, and of course he knew without looking that she was pointing a finger in his direction. "He done shot his own brother. And over money, too."

William was hauled, none too ceremoniously, to his feet, by the redheaded, blue-eyed policeman. "Afraid you'll have to come away with me, Mr. Holbrook," the big Irishman said.

The doctor had already torn off his suit coat and begun working over Calder.

"It's hopeless," William told him pleasantly as his hands were wrenched behind him by the Irishman and bound with heavy iron cuffs.

The physician spared him one scathing glance and returned to his futile efforts.

Lisette's lair, a beautifully appointed tomb intended for some ancient and very important Chinese personage, was empty.

Maeve examined everything—the pyre, made entirely of ivory and inlaid with twenty-four-karat gold, the chests brimming with treasure, the many jade carvings. The mummified being for which the crypt had been created was gone, but in an anteroom she found horrible evidence that Lisette had spent time here.

One of the mortal lovers for which she was so noted, a handsome young man, sat upright in a chair, dead. He looked more like a wax statue than a corpse, and on a small table before him rested a cup and an exquisite porcelain teapot.

"It would seem the poor lad died under sociable circumstances, at least," Dathan observed. "I'll wager there isn't a drop of blood left in him."

Maeve shivered as a spider crawled out the spout of the teapot and scurried across the tabletop to perch on one of the corpse's gray fingers. "There's no need to give an accounting," she said. "I have eyes of my own and I can see what's happened here."

Dathan sighed. "At least he didn't get himself turned into one of those vile creatures Lisette has been plaguing us with these past weeks."

It was a small consolation to Maeve. This young man, whoever he was, reminded her of Aidan. He'd had friends and a family, no doubt, and he'd been allotted a share of too-brief, precious years to live and laugh beneath the sun. Lisette had robbed him, carefully and indiscriminately, of a gift stemming from the very heart of the universe.

"He must have displeased her somehow," Maeve said sadly. She laid one hand on the lad's shoulders and was sickened to feel it crumble like dry clay under the fabric of his well-tailored waistcoat.

"Do you think she'll return?" Dathan asked. "Perhaps we have only to wait for her here."

Maeve shook her head. "No—I'm afraid it won't be so easy as that. Lisette is through with this place—she wanted us to find it, find her dead lover, and be frustrated."

"Well." Dathan heaved out a heavy sigh and thrust one hand through his hair. "Her plan certainly worked."

Maeve was looking at the corpse, now leaning ludicrously to one side because of the damage to his shoulder. "She seems to favor these dark-haired, blue-eyed lads, the younger and more good-natured and gullible the better. My brother, Aidan, was her lover for a while, before she turned him into a vampire, and there have been many others. A striking number of whom were of similar appearance, now that I think about it." She stopped and fixed her gaze on Dathan's grim face. "Have you any warlocks in your army who resemble this poor wretch?"

A light went on in Dathan's eyes, one of irritation. "A

number of them," he confirmed quietly. "You want to trap Lisette, lure her by placing one of my more winsome followers under her nose. Brilliant, except that she'll undoubtedly recognize him for a warlock at first glance."

Maeve raised an eyebrow and then explained patiently, "Vampires recognize warlocks by reading their minds, so to speak. If the warlock in question can be made to believe he is a man, then blood-drinkers will accept him at his own estimate."

Now Dathan looked intrigued and thoughtful. "You're aware, of course, that you've just given me a powerful tool with which to deceive vampires, once this current calamity has been thwarted and things go back to normal?"

"Which means that you owe me something in return."

"What?" Dathan asked, moving out of the mortal's eternal resting place and into the main part of the tomb. He busied himself pocketing gold bracelets and strings of pearls taken from one of the chests while Maeve framed her reply.

"I want you to teach me the incantation that enables you to start fires," she said finally.

Dathan looked at her over one shoulder. "I would be a fool to do that. You could teach it to your vampires, and they'd use it against us."

"I would share it with a select few," Maeve countered. "And you have my word that it would be used against your kind only in self-defense."

"Your word," Dathan mocked, slamming the lid of the chest he'd been looting. "The word of a vampire is hardly something I hold in esteem."

Maeve could feel her strength fading. She sat down on the edge of the ivory pyre where Lisette had probably passed many days. "I have told you one of our secrets. I have trusted you with my very life—you've had numerous opportunities to drive a stake through my heart while I slept. If I can trust you that much, then you can surely give me the same consideration in return and teach me one small incantation!"

Dathan crossed the room and lifted Maeve into his arms.

"No sleeping here, princess," he said with grudging affection. "Our intent is to surprise Lisette, not be surprised by her. Think of someplace in England, someplace dark, and I'll be with you at sunset."

Maeve was exhausted, her head lolling against Dathan's shoulder, but it wasn't England she fixed in her mind, but America. In fact, she focused on Pennsylvania and the dark cellar beneath Calder's house.

Reaching that place, she crouched behind stacks of dusty boxes and crates and closed her eyes.

Only then, when she was helpless, did images of Calder dying come to her mind. She saw him bandaged, lying unconscious in his bed upstairs, his skin bluish from the loss of blood, but there was nothing she could do. She was trapped, mired, in the deepest, darkest part of her own mind.

All during the coming day, immersed in the vampire sleep, vivid pictures came to her, like scenes from a dream, and she heard him calling her name. Calling it over and over again, the voice growing fainter with every passing moment, and more hopeless.

The rain went on throughout the night and the morning, casting an added pall over the circuslike ceremony at Bernard Holbrook's graveside. Word of the shooting in the Holbrook mansion had gotten out fast, and folks had come from every corner of the city, whether they'd known the dear departed or not, to stare and speculate.

God knew, the undertaker thought disgustedly, it would be years before folks stopped chattering about how one brother had shot the other one in his bed, while their dead father lay downstairs in his coffin, and how William Holbrook had been brought to the funeral in handcuffs.

It was a damn pity, all of it, though there was *one* redeeming element in that ugly situation. Poor Bernard was at peace, and he'd never have to know that he'd spawned a murderer.

Not that Calder Holbrook was the kind of son a man

relished having, either. He'd been stubborn his whole life through, that boy, tormented by things inside him that no one else could see, and he'd broken his father's heart on more than one occasion with his cussedness.

The undertaker sighed. Well, Calder was barely clinging to life; that was a fact, for he'd been to the house and seen the young man lying in his bed, unconscious, with half the blood in his body drained away.

Like as not, there'd be another funeral in a few days, and when they hanged William Holbrook, still another.

It made a man wonder, that it did. Bernard Holbrook had worked hard all his life, and if he hadn't always been completely ethical, well, a fellow did what he had to do to make his way. And now it was all gone, blown apart like a house built of matchsticks struck by a high wind.

When sunset came, Maeve bolted upright.

All thoughts of Lisette and the impending disaster of war with the angels were barred from her mind. She cared for nothing and no one but Calder, and she transported herself to his room immediately.

He was indeed dying, just as she had seen in the awful visions while she slept, and his soul had already left his body, bobbing at the far end of the long silver cord that attaches the two, ready to break free. When that happened, Calder would be truly dead, for once the cord is severed, there is no returning.

A heavy woman in simple calico sat next to the bed, weeping quietly, but she did not look up when Maeve approached on the opposite side because she could not see or hear her.

Maeve looked with despair upon her lover and found in the murky shallows of his brain the events that had brought him to such an end. William Holbrook had crept into the room with a dueling pistol, stood at the foot of the bed, and shot his only brother, intending to kill him.

She would go back, she decided, to the night before,

when this travesty had taken place, and undo it. She would kill William if she had to, to prevent this from happening.

When Maeve tried to transport herself, however, her efforts were blocked. In a fury of urgency and despair, she tried twice more, and twice more she failed.

She needed no explanation for what had happened, for Valerian had explained such matters to her long since. Sometimes, for unknown reasons, time travel simply wasn't possible.

Maeve gave up on the attempt to change recent history and instead concentrated on turning herself into a mist, pervading Calder's being, lending him strength. For a while she was truly a part of him, as close as the breath in his lungs and the thready beat of his heart. Then, suddenly, the shimmering silver cord contracted, wrenching his spirit back into its prison of flesh and blood. The sheer force of the event drove Maeve outside of him again.

The housekeeper, probably sensing that something was going on in that room that she couldn't see or hear, grew restless, folded her hands, and began to pray under her breath. Her words were like liquid fire, pouring over Maeve in waves, but Maeve did not flee.

No matter what she had to suffer, she wasn't going to leave Calder.

She huddled in a corner of the room, in the shadows, and presently the housekeeper yawned and went away.

Maeve made herself solid again and hurried to Calder's side, taking one unresponsive hand into both her own. His spirit had retreated again, straining at the invisible tether, trying to escape the pain.

The best and most unselfish thing to do was let Calder go, let him return to his Maker and be received in that place where she could never venture, and she loved him enough to do just that.

She raised her hand to her lips and brushed the knuckles with a kiss as light as the pass of a feather. "Good-bye, my darling," she whispered. Then she rose and turned away, and would have departed forever, except that he spoke to her.

Not with his lips, but with his mind.

Maeve. The name was an entreaty.

She whirled to stare at him, waiting, her whole being suspended. Her soul cried out silently to his, begging him to stay.

Help me.

Maeve was in agony. *I am helping you, darling. Look for the Light, and follow it.*

You are the light.

No! Don't you see? I am the darkness.

Don't leave me, Maeve. Don't let me die.

She took a step closer to Calder, standing at his beside. Without another word, she lay down beside him, covered him in her cloak, and thought of London.

If there was a way under heaven to save Calder, besides turning him into a fiend, like herself, into a being who would one day hate her for her trouble, Maeve vowed she would find it.

Dimity was out of practice when it came to time travel, and she made several abortive efforts before she landed herself in the middle of Valerian's cell.

The place was rank, and a half dozen frail-boned, ragged humans slept in a pile in the corner, like puppies huddling on a cold night. All of them were alive, but they would need to consume a great deal of calves' liver before their blood could truly serve them again.

"Valerian?" Dimity said, annoyed, placing her hands on her hips. "Show yourself!"

He appeared suddenly, directly in front of her, and made her jump backward with a little cry of fright.

"What the—?"

Valerian's grin was a bit wan, but just as audacious as ever. "Sorry," he said, though he plainly wasn't. "It gets boring, being stuck away in a rat's nest like this one, so I've taken to practicing my magic."

Dimity looked around the gloomy cell. "Well, it's no palace, of course, but it could be worse." She nodded toward the pile of rags and flesh in the corner. "At least Lisette's kept you well fed, and you don't look as if you've been abused—only neglected."

Valerian drew himself up to his full and haughty height at that point and glared down his patrician nose. "She's been fattening me up like a Christmas goose," he said, "and I'll thank you not to minimize my sufferings until you've been through a similar ordeal yourself."

She affected a sigh. "All right," she conceded. "If you want my sympathy, you have it. Now, are you through with your travail, or would you like to enjoy it a little while longer? If you're quite satisfied that you've undergone sufficient agony, then let's discuss getting you out of here."

Valerian flushed, a sign of recent feeding more than anger, and narrowed his eyes at her. "You are a most caustic individual, for one who avails herself to the favors of angels."

Dimity glared. "And you are a hardheaded, arrogant idiot," she retorted, standing her ground. She was not acquainted with Valerian, although she'd often heard of his exploits, but she had encountered plenty of creatures just like him, both human and immortal. She knew only too well that if she allowed it, he'd run roughshod over her. "Do you wish me to rescue you, or leave you here to rot?"

The legendary vampire was plainly furious, and no doubt his pride was injured as well. After all, he'd been captured by a vampire of the feminine gender, and now his only hope of salvation was in the hands of yet another female.

Dimity smiled. A little humility was good for the soul. "Well?" she prompted.

"All right," the great Valerian snarled. "*Yes*, of course I want to get out of here—I feel like a mouse shut up in a shoe box! But how do you propose to achieve this magnificent feat? Have you grown more powerful than Lisette and failed to mention the fact heretofore?"

Dimity rolled her eyes. "Lisette grows careless. There are

weaknesses in the mental barrier she's put up around you, or I wouldn't have been able to get in." She crossed the room to the heavy iron door and fixed her gaze on the ancient, cumbersome lock.

"There's no point in attempting *that* old trick," Valerian said. "I've tried to move that lock a hundred times, and it won't give."

A smile came to Dimity's lips as the works splintered inside the lock under the force of her thoughts. "I guess you just didn't try hard enough," she said sweetly. "Who's guarding you?"

Valerian's exasperation was plain, but so was his relief. "A conniving, back-stabbing little chit named Shaleen," he said. "I like her."

Dimity swung open the door and stepped into the stone passageway beyond. "You would," she replied. "Come along. I've found this whole experience a little enervating, frankly, and I'd like to get back to London and my beloved nineteenth century in time for an extra feeding."

" 'I've found this whole experience a little enervating,' " Valerian mimicked sourly, following her along the hall. Dimity imagined it would be quite some time before he got over his pique at being saved by a lesser vampire. "You haven't saved me yet," he said aloud, reminding her that he was an old blood-drinker, like herself, and a skilled one.

"You're right," she replied diplomatically. "Let's try to be civil to each other, shall we? After all, we're both up to our necks—if you'll forgive the expression—in trouble."

As if on cue, a shape rose up ahead of them in the corridor, with a soul-splintering shriek.

"Please," Valerian said contemptuously.

For one terrible moment Dimity thought the creature confronting them was Lisette itself, and that Valerian had further sealed their doom by mocking her, but a closer inspection revealed the little spitfire Valerian had mentioned before, the fledgling called Shaleen.

"Step aside," Dimity ordered quietly. "You must know,

naive as you are, that you haven't the strength to prevail over two mature vampires."

Shaleen seemed to wilt, until she looked like what she'd been before her making, a scrap of a girl who'd never had enough love or food, enough of anything, in the whole brief span of her mortal life. "I want to go with you," she said. "The queen will stake me out in the courtyard to burn in the daylight if she comes back and finds that her prize captive has escaped."

Valerian nudged Dimity from behind. "She'll make a handy soldier in our present trouble, with that fiery spirit of hers."

"I suppose you want to be her tutor," Dimity said dryly. "I don't think you're going to have the time, though. Maeve seems to think she needs your help to prevail against Lisette."

There was a scrabbling sound behind them, and Dimity whirled, as did Valerian, to see the pale boys creeping out of the cell and groping their way along the wall in the other direction.

Shaleen pushed between Valerian and Dimity to stop them, but Valerian caught her arm as she passed. It was then that Dimity got her first glimpse of the peculiar nobility that was as much a part of the fabled vampire beside her as his blatant hedonism and his deft sarcasm.

"Let them go," he said.

Shaleen's face was a study in angry confusion. "But why? Why did you suffer them to live? It's not as though they matter at all—"

"Everything matters," Valerian said, his voice firm but kind as well. "Now, come with us. We blood-drinkers have far weightier things to contend with than a pack of anemic beggars and thieves."

Shaleen cast another greedy glance after the victims she'd no doubt gathered herself for the prisoner she both feared and admired, but then she slipped off in the other direction, leading the way.

"There's a weak place, here," she said finally when they

came to a little chamber at the end of a virtual rabbit's warren of twists and turns. "It's how I get in and out with the lads for this one's supper." She nodded her tousled head in Valerian's direction. "Herself didn't want him to have no supper, you know, but I couldn't stand to think of it."

Valerian grinned and reached out with one graceful hand to muss the girl's hair, and she beamed at this attention.

Dimity was impatient. "Come," she snapped, raising her arms. "Lisette might return at any moment, and I for one do not want to be invited into her parlor for tea."

Valerian found Maeve in the echoing chamber on the uppermost floor of her London house, working feverishly at her loom. The tapestry had lengthened considerably since he'd last viewed it, but the vampire took no time to examine it again. Instead he stared, confounded, at the bloodless, near-dead mortal lying on a pallet beside the towering windows, awash in moonlight.

"Calder Holbrook," he muttered, both irritated and confused.

Maeve whirled, for she hadn't sensed his presence, and in looking at her Valerian knew why. She was almost gaunt, and there were enormous shadows under her eyes. "Valerian," she half sobbed, half whispered, and ran to him.

He enfolded her in his arms, this vampire he had made more than two hundred years ago, and for the first time wished that he'd left her alone that fateful night. At least then she'd have been spared whatever cancerous grief was devouring her now.

"Look at you," she said, her sunken eyes too bright as she took in his splendid tunic of dark gold velvet and the sleek leggings that matched. "You look like a duke or an earl."

"I've been in a sixteenth-century mood of late." The explanation was inane, in light of the suffering he saw in Maeve. "What has happened?" he demanded in an urgent whisper, glancing once again at the mortal still lying senseless on his pallet. "I beg of you—tell me how to help you!"

Chapter

15

"The last thing this world needs is another vampire," Valerian said, the frown he'd worn throughout Maeve's explanation still in place. He glanced thoughtfully at Calder, who stirred on his deathbed, just beneath the surface of consciousness. "On the other hand, the soul in question is his own. If he wants to be a blood-drinker, then it seems to me that he has the right to make that choice."

Maeve had been over the same arguments in her own mind, with tedious attention to detail. In fact, the dilemma had tortured her, sapped her strength and dulled her wits—all this at a time when she most needed all her powers.

She looked at Calder, one hand over her heart, and whispered, "He'll hate me for it someday, just the way Aidan hated Lisette."

Out of the corner of her eye, Maeve saw the great vampire wince—though not, she was sure, at the mention of Lisette, but that of Aidan. He had loved her brother, she knew, with a poetic poignancy that transcended simple sex, vampire or mortal, and it was likely that he still cherished those feelings.

"That's a selfish argument," Valerian observed gruffly. He crouched beside Calder's pallet and touched his waxen face with gentle fingers. "How have you kept him alive this long?"

Maeve hesitated before revealing her terrible secret. "I've been giving him blood—just small infusions of it—in the

541

hope of sustaining him until he rallies from his own strength."

Valerian's magnificent features tightened, and his eyes flashed. "The process is already begun, then," he said in a brusque whisper. "Great Zeus, Maeve, it's a miracle he hasn't become one of those wretched *things* Lisette has been plaguing us with!"

She swayed under the shock of the older vampire's words and gripped the framework of one of the tall windows to steady herself. *"What?"*

Kneeling now, Valerian bared Calder's throat with one hand, all the while gazing up at Maeve with fiery frustration in his violet eyes. "You've never wanted to make a vampire, to my knowledge, so I saw no reason to explain the process." His thumb stroked the fragile skin over Calder's jugular vein gently, almost caressingly, as he spoke. "There is no halfway measure, Maeve. Vampires can give blood to each other, but it is very dangerous with humans. How do you think Lisette made those dreadful creatures of hers? By subjecting them to only part of the process! It's the very reason they have no logic, no individuality, but only unrelenting, terrible hunger."

Maeve covered her mouth with one hand to stifle a cry of pain at what she might have done to Calder. "Why didn't I just let him die?" she pleaded. "Why?"

"There is no time for self-recrimination now, my darling," Valerian scolded, but with the utmost gentleness. "Steps must be taken to rectify what you've done—if not, he'll become an enemy, one we'll have to destroy."

She sank to her knees at the foot of Calder's pallet, watching with both hope and horror as Valerian bent over the love of her immortal life and began the transformation. She wanted to look away a hundred times, nay, a thousand, as the vampire emptied Calder of his blood, but that would have been a form of disloyalty, of cowardice. So she kept her terrible vigil.

Calder was, for all practical intents and purposes, dead

during those moments before Valerian sunk his fangs into that fragile flesh again and restored the blood, changed.

At last Valerian thrust himself away from Calder, a gleam of some unholy satisfaction in his eyes, and rose gracefully to his feet. "Now," he said, "if this fledgling wishes to hate anyone for his transfiguration, let him hate me."

Maeve stood and moved around to the side of the pallet to look down into Calder's face. He was still asleep, but the lines of suffering were smoothed away by some inner magic even as she watched. He seemed larger somehow, his body harder and more powerful.

"We'd best move him to a safer place," Valerian suggested with a sigh. "He cannot bear the sunlight any more than we can."

Maeve nodded, closed her arms around Calder, and willed the both of them to the dank gloom of the secret part of the cellar were she herself reposed. Valerian, a showman at heart, was there before them and in the process of lighting the candles.

"What will happen now?" Maeve asked when Calder had been settled comfortably on the slab. She had had no experience with the making of vampires, as Valerian had pointed out earlier, and did not remember anything helpful about her own metamorphosis.

"The transformation has already begun, of course," Valerian said. "He's lying there, wide awake and cognizant of everything we say and do, but unable to communicate in any way." He moved to Calder's side, touched his shoulder with that same tenderness he had exhibited before. "Do not worry, fledgling," he said gently. "Do not struggle. In a day, or perhaps two, you will be completely functional."

After a moment of thoughtful silence, Valerian turned his attention to Maeve. "I would suggest, my love, that you leave your darling in the care of another vampire, one less vital to our cause, and join the rest of us in the effort to save ourselves."

Maeve nodded, though the reluctance she felt at the idea

of abandoning Calder, especially now, was a keen sorrow in itself. "Yes, you're right, of course—but who can we trust?"

"Trust?" Valerian smiled grimly and arched one eyebrow. "Why, no one, Your Majesty—perhaps not even each other. Still, I know of a fledgling who is most anxious to endear herself to me—a thought should be sufficient summons." With that, he closed his eyes, and an instant later a young, brown-haired snippet appeared in the room with an unceremonious crash, toppling several crates and boxes.

"What the bloody hell?" she screeched in a voice that made Maeve want to put her hands over her ears. The new arrival focused her spritely brown gaze on Valerian, then a glorious smile spread across her smudged face. "Oh, it's you, then!"

Valerian shook his head. "Yes, it's me. Where are those pretty clothes I gave you, chit? And how do you manage to stay sooty as a chimney pot even after a washing?"

The young vampire looked chagrined and, at the same time, very pleased that Valerian had taken notice of her in any way. She would have blushed splendidly, had she been a mortal creature; instead, she simply turned to Maeve and executed an awkward curtsy.

"Pleased to make your acquaintance, mum," she said.

"This is Shaleen," Valerian explained with a smile in his eyes.

Maeve smiled herself, for the first time since before Calder's shooting. Valerian was the most ferocious of vampires and, some said, the most ruthless, and yet he loved playing the mentor. Now that she thought of it, Maeve could not remember a time when he hadn't had some fledgling under tutelage—herself, for instance, and Aidan, and others too numerous to name.

"How do you do?" Maeve said grandly, extending her hand to the feisty little spitfire and hoping she wasn't making a mistake in abandoning Calder to her care.

"Enough of the social refinements," Valerian snapped, suddenly impatient with the whole proceeding. "There is a war on, in case you've both forgotten." He gestured toward

Calder. "This one has just been changed. We'll be wanting you to look after him, stand guard, so to speak. You've had experience with that, now haven't you?"

Shaleen quailed a little under Valerian's fierce glare, but then she made a visible effort to muster her pride and succeeded to a degree. "I'll look after him, all right. Won't no mortals come and stake him. I'll see to it personal—"

Valerian closed his eyes for a moment, a study in impatient grandeur. "We are quite convinced," he said sternly.

His apprentice subsided, chagrined. "Well, then," she murmured, dragging a crate over for use as a chair and taking up her post beside Calder, "I'll just button me lip, then, won't I?"

Maeve's amusement ebbed as she thought of leaving Calder, especially in so fragile a state, but she knew she must not tarry. She went to the other side of the slab where her lover lay, opposite the bristly, determined Shaleen, and bent to kiss his mouth.

"I'll be back soon, darling," she whispered. "Please don't be afraid."

"Great Zeus," Valerian snapped, gesturing wildly with one arm toward the greater world beyond that cellar, "we're about to be overrun by legions of avenging angels! Must we dally in this dusty pit all night?"

Maeve laid her ear to Calder's chest, hearing no heartbeat, feeling no rise and fall of breathing, and knew an infinite sorry, as well as joy. They would be together for eternity, if they were fortunate, rich with power and full of strength, and yet Calder's soul had been stolen this night, and she'd been a party to the theft.

She felt Valerian's hands come to rest on her shoulders, gentle, elegant, and firm. He spoke quietly.

"There can be no looking back now, Maeve. It'll turn you into a pillar of salt, like Lot's wife, and rob you of all your power."

She turned, looked up into his dark purple eyes, and nodded. "You're right," she said.

Valerian took her hands in his own, and they raised their

arms high, in a graceful, simultaneous motion, and then they vanished, Shaleen's parting words echoing in their ears.

"Coo, mate!" she cried, no doubt elbowing Calder in the ribs at the same time. "Did you see that?"

Lisette gave a snarling shriek of outrage when she found Valerian's cell empty, and the new vampire, Shaleen, gone as well.

Fools! Did they truly believe they could escape her so easily? Why, when she found those two she'd bind them to trees and burn them, like Joan of Arc at her stake, as a lesson to all vampires!

She dropped to her knees in the fetid straw, clutching her middle, as the troublesome weakness struck her. It was that rebel Maeve Tremayne's fault that she suffered now—Lisette had not been the same since their battle in that cave, far away in China.

She'd been sorely tried in that confrontation, and injured, and she had had to console herself by lying in her crypt beneath the cellar of her villa on the coast of Spain for several days and nights, with two captive mortal lovers to sustain her.

Even now, curled up in the straw of that miserable castle in the north of Scotland, a bleak spot abandoned even in Bonnie Prince Charlie's day and naught but a ruin in modern times, Lisette smiled at the memory of the pleasures she'd taken.

First, she'd prowled the city in her carriage, finding one luscious boy and then another. She'd taken them to her villa, gotten them drunk on wine bottled before their great-grandfathers were born, and then taught them passion, one by one.

Finally she'd taken them, sated and senseless, to her hiding place deep beneath the floor of the cellar, and slept, waking only long enough to feed off one or the other.

They'd been dead when she left them, both of them, for she hadn't wanted to go to the effort of making the poor lads into vampires.

She frowned, recollecting another experience.

She'd selected Aidan Tremayne for her favors, one night beside a seventeenth-century road, and taught him ecstasy so keen that each of their trysts had left him dazed and drunk with pleasure. Eventually she'd given her cherished Aidan the ultimate gift, immortality, and he'd thanked her by calling her cursed, by hating and reviling her.

Lisette raised herself, both hands braced against the filthy carpet of straw. That, she thought bitterly, was why she'd turned no more of her lovely boys into nightwalkers. They were just too thick to comprehend, those ungrateful creatures, that they'd been translated from mere clay to virtual gods.

A strange exhaustion felled her, and she dropped to the floor again, overcome by the need to sleep. She would find Valerian and the miscreant, Shaleen, later, along with a fine-looking mortal lad to nourish her. In the meantime, though, she'd just rest a little while.

Calder was awake, inside his hardened husk of a body, just as he'd heard Valerian assert earlier, but he could not so much as twitch a muscle or force the weakest murmur past his lips.

He tried to piece together his shattered memories, in an effort to make sense of what was happening, but he remembered only two things at first—William firing the bullet that had in effect killed him, and the terrible, fiery elation he'd known when Valerian had drawn the very blood from his veins and then given it back again, forever changed.

He groped forward mentally, and more came to him. Things were definitely falling into place.

He, the late Calder Holbrook, was now a vampire, an immortal creature with the power to travel through time and space at will. Granted, he wouldn't be able to go backward very far—Maeve had told him once that a blood-drinker could venture only so far as the instant following his own death. Since this had occurred so recently, there was no point in going back.

Still, the future was his. As soon as he was able to move, he would go forward to the final years of the twentieth century and begin soaking up the knowledge he craved. He would soon understand all the newest surgical techniques, know how to mix chemicals into miraculous drugs. Then, *then* he would return to his own century, and save as many of the soldiers, as many of the suffering children, as he could.

Calder's thoughts returned, as he suspected they always would, to Maeve. He knew, even in his distracted state, that he was somehow tethered to her, and he blessed the fact. She would be the center of his life, the sunshine he must now foreswear, the light he warmed himself by, now and forever, world without end, amen and amen.

He tried again to move, and again found the effort to be futile.

Valerian pervaded his mind, that imperious and arrogant vampire whom he had mistrusted and disliked from their first encounter. Like it or not, Calder reflected, with a sigh of the spirit, a bond existed between them now. In a very real sense, Valerian had sired him into the new and exciting life that lay waiting, just ahead.

He struggled, eager to regain consciousness and begin that life, and felt a cool hand come to rest on his forehead, one so small that it might have belonged to a child.

"There now," a youthful, feminine voice chided, "just lie still and don't be so impatient. You'll be prowlin' the night soon enough, I'll wager, and a pretty fellow you is, too."

Calder felt the forces of his changing body trying to overcome him, push him under the dark, glimmering surface into oblivion. They wanted to get on with the business of transformation, those forces, and Calder hadn't the strength or the will to counter them.

He relaxed his roiling emotions, soothed his tempestuous mind, and went under.

The old manse was tucked away in the English countryside, long-deserted, overgrown with vines and ivy, almost certainly purported by the locals to be haunted, and Maeve could see that Valerian loved the place on sight. It would, she supposed, appeal to his macabre sense of humor to make mysterious lights appear in the windows on occasion and send out the odd bone-chilling shriek just for the sake of drama.

Dathan stepped out of a shadowy, cobwebbed corner, seeming to form himself from the particles of dust and darkness that made up the night. He raised his arms, causing his cloak to spread like wings, and grinned.

"Perfect, isn't it?" he asked cordially, though Maeve immediately sensed the chilly wariness that had sprung up between the warlock and Valerian.

Valerian nodded, his jawline unusually taut. "All it needs is a bubbling cauldron and some cackling crones," he said evenly.

Dathan laughed, but the sound had a jagged edge. "Stereotypes," he scolded. "You don't sleep in a casket, do you, Vampire? Nor, I trust, would a necklace of garlic put you to flight."

Maeve interceded, worried by the growing tension. Dathan and Valerian would be no good against Lisette and her forces if they were battling each other. "Stop it," she said, stepping between the pair and laying a calming hand to each of their chests. She gave Valerian a warning glance, then turned to look into Dathan's unreadable eyes. "Why did you summon us here?"

The warlock smiled indulgently, every inch the suave country host, but Maeve was not misled. Dathan was about as warm and welcoming as one of those twentieth-century knives—switchblades, she believed they were called.

"I have something to show you—" he said, shifting his gaze to Valerian's glowering countenance only after stretching the moment to very uncomfortable lengths. "—both."

Beyond the crumbling stone walls of the manse, in the luxurious, black-velvet darkness of that isolated place, something howled.

Maeve and Valerian exchanged a quick glance as they followed Dathan deeper into the old cottage.

No owl, that, Valerian observed in a mental undertone that somehow crept beneath Dathan's level of awareness.

I know you'll protect me, Maeve teased in response.

They had entered what had probably been a parlor at one time, and even though they could all see as clearly as cats, Dathan went through the formality of lighting the nubs of tallow spilling messily from an old candelabra.

Maeve took in the chandelier, draped with dust, the worn organ that only the mice played now, the stained and peeling wallpaper, and imagined the ghostly forms of a dozen long-dead vicars moving about, colliding with each other.

"A very colorful thought," Valerian commented with quiet amusement, making no effort to keep the conversation private this time. "Rather like that attraction in Disneyland."

Dathan cast a scathing glance at the clearly unwelcome vampire towering beside Maeve, and then clapped his hands together with brisk authority.

Immediately two warlocks entered the room from deeper inside the house, the dining room probably, escorting a young man between them.

Both Valerian and Maeve cried out, in despairing shock, for this enchanted wretch was their Aidan, the one they had both loved and lost.

Valerian found his voice first. "What have you done to him?" he rasped, springing forward as if to free the poor captive from the warlocks' hold. He whirled on Dathan, grasped his flowing shirt in both hands, and wrenched him onto the balls of his feet. "God damn your black soul, *what have you done?*"

"It's all right, Valerian," Maeve said gently, for after the first shock she'd realized that, however perfect the resemblance, this was not her brother. She ventured close and touched the seemingly frozen, breathtakingly handsome face tentatively. "Aidan is far away and quite safe. This is only someone who looks like him."

Dathan shook himself free of Valerian's grip, his eyes glittering with a suppressed thirst for vengeance, and nodded. "Very astute, Your Majesty. This is Llewellyn, one of our own. We've tampered with his mind a bit, as you suggested, and when he comes out of this stupor we've so mercifully induced, he'll believe with all his treacherous little heart that he's mortal."

Valerian looked confused, and started to speak, but Maeve stopped him by reaching out to grasp his forearm.

"Ingenious," she said.

"What is the purpose of this?" Valerian demanded, exasperated.

Maeve walked around Llewellyn, studying him in amazement. If it hadn't been for the connection between herself and her twin brother, she would have believed this creature, this warlock, to be Aidan—sweet, stubborn, *human* Aidan.

"Smooth your feathers and think for a moment, Vampire," Dathan said. "How do you believe Lisette would react, were she to encounter our brilliant creation?"

Maeve sensed the quickening in Valerian as, at last, he made the connection.

He muttered an amazed exclamation and peered into the exquisitely molded face of the warlock who would, when fully conscious again, wholeheartedly believe himself to be an ordinary man.

"Did he look this much like Aidan Tremayne in the beginning," Valerian wondered aloud, "or did you alter him somehow?"

Dathan sighed, as if weary of silly questions. "There was a resemblance—rather faint really. We accentuated it, knowing of the lovely Lisette's special fancy for Tremayne. Now the question is, how do we draw her notice to our lad here?"

Valerian flung a testy glance at the warlock. "And I was so certain that you'd thought of everything."

Dathan seethed but, with visible effort, managed to control his temper. "If that were so," he replied in a strange, purring growl, "then we'd have no need of you, would we, Vampire?"

Valerian took a step toward Dathan, and again Maeve moved between them.

"Once Lisette has taken the bait and poisoned herself with the blood of this lovely warlock," she said, "the two of you may feel free to ravage each other. In the meantime, everything we hold precious is at stake, and our only hope is to work together!"

"Take the lad to Spain," Valerian said moments later in a hoarse, grudging whisper. He named an obscure village. "Lisette has a villa there, on the coast. Wherever she is, she's attuned to that place, and she'll sense his presence and come to him."

Maeve stared at him. "You knew of this villa, and yet you said nothing?"

Valerian shook his head. "I had forgotten. Seeing Llewellyn here brought back memories."

It was plain enough that the memories in question involved Aidan, but Maeve didn't pursue the subject because it was so obviously personal.

"To Spain, then," Dathan said, clapping his hands again.

After Llewellyn had been led to the entrance of an especially lively cantina, Dathan broke the spell that had rendered him catatonic, using a brief incantation.

"Hello, George," the warlock said, offering his hand to the lad.

The young man blinked, and then his eyes cleared and he smiled. "Hello," he said, shaking Dathan's hand. "Do I know you?"

The sight of that smile, an eerily exact duplicate of Aidan's, wrenched Maeve on the deepest level of her being, and she suspected Valerian's reaction was quite similar.

"We were acquainted once," Dathan said, stepping back. "Well, I won't keep you—you're obviously bent on meeting friends."

George nodded happily. In their clever, mysterious way

the warlocks had evidently provided him not only with a new identity, but a past as well. Furthermore, they had altered the memories of several mortals to include him. "I don't believe I got your name," he said cheerfully.

"Not important," Dathan said, turning away.

George stared after him in bafflement for a moment, and Maeve feared that the trick had not worked after all, that the youth remembered being a warlock. If that were so, Lisette would not be deceived.

Then Maeve shifted her consciousness, the way she generally did instinctively when warlocks were around, and the signal from George's mind came through loud and clear. He believed he was a man, and, therefore, he transmitted that belief to everyone and everything around him.

Valerian gripped her arm and hustled her away into the darkness. "Much as we might like to hang around and watch," he explained rather tersely, "Lisette will pick up on our presence and smell a trap if we do."

He was right, of course.

Maeve turned to him when they were well away from the cantina. Dathan and his companions had already vanished, probably for the same reason Valerian had mentioned. "What do we do now?"

"We wait," Valerian said, plainly as irritated by the prospect as she was. "We wait and hope that Lisette bites into our lovely warlock's jugular and subsequently chokes to death on his blood."

Maeve was frowning, worried. "It might not be fatal, you know," she said. "When Aidan fed on a warlock, he was very ill, but he survived."

"I remember," Valerian said somewhat gruffly. Talk of Aidan always made him either restive or testy, or both. "Even if she does not glut herself with the poison, in her greed Lisette will be seriously weakened. We will close in then, destroy her, and send her ashes to Nemesis along with our most eloquent pleas for mercy."

He glanced up at the starry sky and smiled wanly. "Do

you suppose Dathan would mind if I explored that delightful old manse?"

"As if you cared whether he minded or not," Maeve retorted, amused, eager to feed and then return to Calder. She would send Shaleen away, lie beside her beloved on the slab, and join her dreams to his. "Good-bye for now, my friend."

Valerian bent and kissed her forehead lightly. "Fare-thee-well," he responded, and then he was gone.

Damn, but he's good, Maeve thought, still awed by the other vampire's theatrical flair.

She raised her arms, then, smiling, and took herself to her favorite hunting grounds—the seediest part of London, where the lowest of the low prowled the night, scheming, indulging in their deliberate evils.

She was drawn to a dark, stinking attic of a dockside pub, a place even rats and fleas would hesitate to frequent. There a drunken man had cornered his wife, demanding the few pence she'd been able to scrape together while he'd been at sea.

Maeve knew in a moment that the woman had been beaten half senseless for her trouble, and her wail was pitiful to hear. "Please, Jack—don't 'urt me no more—I needs the money for the babe that's comin'—"

The lout drew back one booted foot to kick his fallen wife, and outrage surged through Maeve, as hot and sour as bile. She gave a snarling shriek, one fit to wake the dead, and flung herself at the brute, who raised meaty hands to shelter himself.

The woman, whimpering with terror, having no way of knowing that she would not be next, scrambled for the ladder at the edge of the loft.

Jack's blubbery, unshaven face was white beneath a layer of filth. "Saints in 'eaven," he rasped, *"what sort of devil are ye?"*

Only an instant later he found out exactly what sort.

* * *

When his mates from the pub below came scrambling up the ladder to see what poor Mary had been blathering about, they discovered old Jack in a heap, near dead, and him with two bloody holes in his neck in the bargain.

Chapter
—❧16❧—

The cellar where Maeve had left Calder was empty.

Wild panic seized her. Had Lisette, or some other fiend, found him and stolen him away?

Frantic, Maeve searched the room and found Shaleen dozing behind a crate of antique china.

The little hoyden was barely conscious—dawn was so near—but she looked up at Maeve and blinked.

"What happened?" Maeve demanded, crouching and grasping the child's bony shoulders. "Where is Calder? *Where is he?*"

Shaleen scrambled to her feet, visibly struggling against the inertia that overcame most vampires with the approach of sunrise. "He's gone, mum, that he is—and it's been a long time now, too! I tried to stop him, but he wouldn't be stopped—he's a strong one, he is. Why, he came off that slab like a cannon shot!"

Maeve felt herself succumbing to the catatonic sleep and knew there was no point in resisting it. Her terror and despair increased even as she began to lose consciousness— there were so many things Calder didn't know, so many dangers.

Calder had escaped his keeper easily, for he'd been full of strength when he awakened, half wild with curiosity and excitement.

Five minutes after bolting from Maeve's cellar, he stood

on a busy street corner in twentieth-century London, watching in amazement as magnificent horseless carriages rushed past, displacing the night air, making an extraordinary din. There were plenty of people about, too, streaming out of clubs and theaters, strangely dressed and chattering about unfamiliar things.

He was delighted, confounded, awed by his own powers and by the wonderful new world that surrounded him.

A place, he admitted to himself, grimly amused, that he knew absolutely nothing about.

He began to walk, following a high, wrought-iron fence. Beyond it lay a graveyard, the marble stones pristine in the moonlight, the grass well kept. He remembered the sensation of William's bullet entering his chest, and a silent celebration stirred inside him because he was still alive.

Calder smiled as he strode along, reflecting now on the fact that Maeve had evidently come to the house in Philadelphia and collected him, prior to his transfiguration. He wondered what poor Prudence and the others had made of his mysterious disappearance.

Presently Calder began to feel a tightening inside himself, a need for sustenance, but he had no idea how to stalk prey. He knew very little, as it happened, except that he could not survive even the briefest encounter with sunlight.

Calder walked for hours, just looking in wonderment at the strange mix of new and old that was London. He was in the vicinity of Maeve's grand house, which he presumed was still in her possession, when a glance at the sky warned him that it was time to find shelter.

He let himself onto Maeve's property by a side gate, begrudging every moment of awareness he would miss by lapsing into the comalike slumber he could not hope to escape.

He found a narrow cellar window, dislodged the grillwork that covered it with a single wrench of his arm, and crawled through the space, whistling softly under his breath. Perhaps once he got the knack of being a vampire, he would discover a way for blood-drinkers to remain awake in the daytime, or even a means by which they could endure the full glare of the sun.

After all, he speculated, reaching out and pulling the iron grillwork back into place, he was a scientist. He might dissect one of those bumbling creatures Maeve and Valerian were so concerned about, after it was dead, of course, and learn a great deal about the inner workings of all vampires. The prospect filled him with excitement.

Humming softly to himself, Calder found the very chamber he'd left earlier, and he could see immediately that it had not been in use for some time. Odd, he thought, loosening the collar of the shirt he'd awakened in, well over a hundred years in the past, that Maeve didn't seem to favor this bustling, energetic century. It was like a carnival, rife with noise and color; he wanted to see and do everything, to take it all inside him somehow and possess it.

He stretched out on his slab, the same one he'd abandoned only hours before, and yet *decades* before, to go exploring, and considered the paradox of time. How deliciously ironic to be lying there in the cellar, in the very place he was missing from in the nineteenth century.

Sleep overtook him before he could make sense of the enigma.

The day must have passed quickly, for when Calder opened his eyes, it was as if he had just closed them. He felt a violent thirst, a growing weakness, and an unrelenting desire to continue his explorations.

He let himself out of Maeve's house by the same method he'd used to enter it—he crawled through the cellar window—and was nonplussed to find Valerian waiting for him, arms folded, his expression dour.

"Do you know," that august vampire began in a deceptively smooth, even voice, "how foolhardy it was to go rushing off into the world on your own like that?"

Calder felt only mild chagrin, and that was because of the worry his abrupt departure might have caused Maeve. He hadn't wanted to hurt her, and yet the drive to try out his new being had been irresistible.

He began to walk away and would have opened the gate and passed through if Valerian hadn't caught him by the back of his coat and brought him up short.

Calder's temper flared; he bristled and opened his mouth to tell Valerian to go to hell, but thought better of it when he looked into those fathomless violet eyes.

"You have much to learn," Valerian said quietly. "We'll start with passing through solid objects, and then you'd better take your first feeding."

Calder swallowed his formidable pride and nodded. He had trained a number of younger doctors during his career, but there were a great many vital things he didn't understand about this new existence. For the first time in years he would have to play the part of the apprentice rather than the master.

Valerian affected a sigh, then began his instruction.

Calder was so taken with the mechanics of dissolving himself and passing through gates and walls and trees that his mentor finally had to remind him that there were other tasks that must be accomplished in the space of that night.

The finer points of stalking and feeding came next, and a lesson on the proper method of time travel as well. Valerian took Calder to a place he couldn't help recognizing—a field hospital—but this was clearly a later conflict than the one he remembered so vividly.

"World War II," Valerian explained as Calder tried to adjust himself to the sights and sounds of suffering so intense, so terrible that he could barely take it in, even after all the practice he'd had in his own century. "These are German soldiers, technically the enemy, since you were an American, but the pain is the same."

They moved, unseen except by those nearest to death, among the rows of canvas cots.

Calder whispered a horrified exclamation as he looked upon some of the wounds. "What happened to these men?"

"I'm afraid warfare has advanced significantly since your time, Doctor—in this particular period, they used a lot of poisonous gasses and, of course, they were capable of dropping bombs from airplanes."

"Airplanes?" Calder hadn't come across the word in his brief exploration of modern London.

"Flying machines," Valerian answered in a distracted tone. "I'll show you later. In the meantime, you must choose one of these poor, suffering louts and draw from him the blood you need to survive."

Calder had been awash in blood since his first day of medical college and he had gotten past the stage of revulsion long ago. It was medical stuff, blood, full of mystery and power—he believed that with his whole heart. Still, the prospect of drawing on a patient in such an intimate way was abhorrent.

Valerian spoke quietly, standing close behind him. "Trust me," he said. "Your—victim, if that is indeed the correct word, will feel no pain. On the contrary, his agonies will cease, if you choose for it to be so, replaced by that same sense of ecstasy you felt when you underwent your own metamorphosis."

Calder glanced back at the other vampire uncomfortably. He didn't like being reminded of the joy his conversion had brought him, because he had yet to sort out its meaning. He certainly felt no physical attraction to this enigmatic creature who had given him everlasting life, but neither could he deny that he had known indescribable bliss during their unholy communion.

The elder vampire smiled—he'd probably discerned Calder's thoughts—and moved past him to stroke the pale forehead of one of the fallen soldiers. The boy opened his eyes, stared up at Valerian in baffled adoration, and murmured something in German.

Calder recognized the word for *angel*, since he'd had some training in the language while studying to become a physician. He recalled, of course, how Maeve had moved among the wounded at Gettysburg, bestowing her strange mercies, and how the dying soldiers had seen her as a creature of heaven.

"Like this," Valerian said gently, his gaze locked with the rapt, too-bright stare of the lad lying on the rickety cot. Then, to demonstrate, he bent over his welcoming prey, punctured the artery with his fangs, and fed.

When he straightened, Calder was stricken by the singular beauty of his tutor's expression; his countenance seemed to glow, his skin appeared translucent. Tenderness shimmered in his eyes, along with the most brazen glint of satisfaction.

The "victim" lay still, plainly dead, his slender young body slightly arched, as if frozen in the first throes of some sweet passion. He stared, peering straight into the very heart of heaven, it seemed, and his flesh was like ivory, backlit by the flame of an inner candle. His smile was beatific and so tranquil that Calder averted his gaze, feeling that he was intruding on some very private moment.

Calder felt a variety of emotions, as well—anger, frustration, pity, awe, and strangely joy. Still, he had never gotten used to death, its peculiar loveliness be damned, and his most basic instincts urged him to fight against it until the last.

Valerian gestured silently toward another cot, where yet another man-child lay, his once splendid body ruined, his mind fogged with the horror of seeing behind the glorious facade to the true nature of war.

By this time Calder was ravenous, and he knew he could put off the sacrilege no longer. He spoke softly to the soldier, smoothing his hair as he had seen Valerian do, as he himself had done with other dying children, in another war, another time, another life.

He wept inwardly as he bent over the bruised throat, found the pulse point, and plunged his fangs through the thin but stubbornly resistant flesh.

Calder tensed, bracing himself for utter revulsion, but to his surprise the nourishing blood did not flow over his tongue, but through the short, needle-sharp teeth that had once been ordinary incisors. As the stuff raced into him, he was electrified with a pleasure so brutally intense that for several moments he feared it would destroy him. He started to withdraw, in fact, then felt Valerian's hand come to rest lightly on his back, urging him to continue.

When it was over, when he'd felt the life force as well as the pain and terror leave the boy, Calder rose and turned away, ashamed. Paradoxically, for he was well aware that he could hide little or nothing from Valerian, he did not want the other vampire to witness his disgust.

Or his rapture.

Graciously Valerian said nothing, but only went on to another cot and fed again.

Calder could not bring himself to follow suit, even though he yearned to experience once more the inexpressible jubilation that was only then receding, a tide of sweet fire raking his soul as it ebbed away. He left the hospital tent by ordinary means and stood gazing up at the stars for a long interval.

Presently Valerian joined him, and by tacit agreement they returned to twentieth-century London and Maeve's grand house.

Much to Calder's delight, she was waiting there in the formal parlor, pacing back and forth along the edge of the marble hearth. Her hair fell free in wild curls, and she wore tight-fitting denim trousers and a black blouse of some stretchy fabric that clung to her curves.

"Where have you been?" she cried furiously when she realized that Calder and Valerian were there.

Wisely Valerian faded into mist and took himself off to some safer and no doubt more cordial place.

Calder made no attempt to hide his admiration or his curiosity. "I'm sorry you were worried," he said in all sincerity, for he truly loved this glorious being, and even the bliss of feeding for the first time could not compare to the splendors he'd known in her arms. "I was impatient to see what it was like to move about as a vampire."

Maeve's temper seemed to subside a little, though her eyes still flashed with sapphire fury. "There are so many dangers," she sputtered, running the fingers of one hand through her lovely tangle of hair. "Warlocks, angels—the sunlight. And sometimes time travel can go wrong, and it's impossible to return—"

He gripped her shoulders. "I'm safe," he said pointedly, touched by her concern. If anything, the transformation had deepened his love for Maeve, and the emotions she stirred in him were almost too splendid to be endured.

She flung herself at him then, wrapping her arms around his neck and murmuring, "I was so afraid—"

Calder stroked her back, warmed by her love, nourished by it. He laughed hoarsely and held her a little away from him. "What about these scandalous clothes of yours, Maeve Tremayne? What manner of devilment is this?"

Her smile was tentative but genuine. "This is how twentieth-century women dress," she said. "If they choose to, that is. They have a lot more to say about a great many things than their ancestors had."

He took her hand, lifted it over her head, and twirled her about as he had seen dancers do. "Trousers," he marveled. Then he held her close again and kissed her. "I must say, I like the way they look on you."

Calder felt Maeve tremble in his arms, and he kissed her again before saying, "I love you."

Her blue eyes glistened with a sentiment equal to his own. "You taught me to mate as humans do," she said softly. "Now let me show you how vampires give each other pleasure."

Calder pretended to be shocked. "What? Do twentieth-century women seduce their men so boldly as that?"

Maeve touched his mouth with one finger, and with that single gesture effectively set him ablaze with the need of her. "Who cares what they do?" Her eyes, tender before, were smoldering with forbidden knowledge now. "I am a vampire, not a mere woman, twentieth century or otherwise. Come with me, and I will show you passion you have not even imagined."

He did not resist her; indeed, Calder doubted that he could have done that, even if he'd wished to do so. He gave her his hand and then felt himself dissolve, felt his very soul plunging through space. Then, just as abruptly, he was whole again, and they were alone in an upstairs chamber, a vast room that he remembered as Maeve's studio.

She'd brought him there after the shooting, and sometimes when she was working at her loom, unaware that he was conscious, he had watched her for a moment or two before slipping under again.

He moved to draw her close and kiss her once more, but she drew back, smiling and shaking her lovely head, like a mischievous nymph bent on luring him into some enchanted place.

"You're thinking of the human way of lovemaking," she scolded softly. "I want to show you how vampires mate."

Had he still had need of his lungs, or of air, Calder would have drawn a deep breath at that moment. As it was, he simply watched Maeve, struck dumb by her terrifying beauty, and by the depth of his love for her.

She kept her distance, watching him with those magical eyes, too far away to touch him, and yet he began to feel the lightest of caresses. It seemed to him that fingertips brushed the sensitive place beneath one of his ears, made circles around his nipples, whisked ever so slightly across his mouth.

He moaned and moved to reach for Maeve, but she kept herself just out of reach. In the next instant he began to feel her touch in more intimate places, across his belly, the small of his back, along the insides of his thighs.

Calder gasped with pleasure, but Maeve silenced him with a soft "Shhh" and proceeded to tease the length of his staff. He was completely in her power then, as effectively restrained by his own desire as he might have been by iron manacles.

His clothes were not physically removed—they seemed to melt away like thin ice under a spring sun—and not only was Calder's body bared to Maeve's attentions, but his soul as well.

He whispered an exclamation, a plea, and then felt her

touching him everywhere, inside and out, even though physically she was still well beyond his reach. Her mouth drew at his nipples, not one, but both, warm and wet and greedy. At the same time, impossible though it was, her tongue traveled the length of his shaft and teased the tip until he cried out in a ragged, glorious, despairing voice.

Maeve showed Calder no quarter that magical night, as she initiated him into yet another vampire mystery. She was a gentle but relentless conqueror, having him thoroughly, again and again, until it all culminated in one cataclysmic, soul-rendering release.

He lay trembling on the cool, hard floor when she'd finished with him, depleted and yet more fantastically alive than ever before. When his emotions would allow him to speak, he whispered, "It's a good thing you didn't do that when I was mortal, love. I might have died of the pleasure."

She laughed softly and came to lie with him, her own body naked and sleek and glowing in the moonlight pouring in through the tall windows. She took him into her arms and kissed the hollow at the base of his throat. "There are more terrible ways to die," she observed, nestling close.

He stroked her breast, in the human way, and draped one of his legs across hers in a possessive gesture. "Why are you tarrying here with me, Maeve?" he asked, his tone gruff with his love for her, and the sudden knowledge that even eternity can be a fleeting thing. "Has the war been won already?"

Maeve raised herself onto one elbow, her hair a silken mantle in the moonlight, and gazed sadly into his face, as if to memorize every feature. "No, my darling," she said, tracing his mouth with the tip of one index finger. "The war hasn't been won."

Calder asked no more questions, sensing that, for Maeve, this was a time out of time, a place of refuge and restoration. "I think I like the human way better," he said.

She looked puzzled. "Of making war?"

He gave a raspy chuckle and held her close against him,

his chin resting on the top of her head. "No, sweet—of making love."

Maeve drew back to study his face. "Why?" she asked, sounding stricken. "Don't tell me you didn't feel pleasure, Calder Holbrook, because I know—"

Calder smoothed her tousled hair. "I felt more than pleasure," he assured her gruffly, "more than ecstasy. But when mortals make love, they touch, they become one being, if only for a little while. I want that for us."

Her bewildered expression gave way to one of mischievous delight. "Before I decide that one is better than the other," she purred, "I would want you to take me the way you would take a human woman."

He turned her gently onto her back, this beautiful, complex fiend, and gripped her wrists, pressing her hands gently to the floor, just above her head. Then he mounted her, and she parted her silken thighs slightly, her dark blue eyes glittering in the darkness.

"Observe," he teased in a scholarly tone, and glided inside her with one long stroke. Within moments they were both wild with passion, rolling over the smooth wooden floor, first one taking command, and then the other.

The finish of their lovemaking was simultaneous, apocalyptic, a collision and a fusion.

Lisette sensed trouble, but she was intrigued rather than fearful and allowed herself to be drawn back to nineteenth-century Spain, back to her villa beside the sea.

She slept through the day, conserving her strength for battles she knew were coming, and had her carriage and horses brought around only moments after the sun had set. She would feed, of course, but for the time being she would make no more vampires, special or otherwise—to do so would be foolhardy, for her powers seemed to be waning. While she was sure the effects were temporary, she certainly didn't want another confrontation with Maeve Tremayne at this juncture.

Just the thought of that treasonous creature filled Lisette

with fury—she would destroy the rebellious vampires, all of them, and in ways so horrific that tales of them would be told for millennia—but for now she had more immediate concerns. She must coddle herself, feed well, and engage in her favorite diversion—seducing young, firm-muscled mortals, drawing badly needed strength from their unbridled passion.

The carriage rattled its way through sleepy streets and into the small seaside district, where a cluster of cantinas provided lively entertainment for visiting sailors and young noblemen alike.

One particular place drew Lisette, and while she was wary, it was not a new sensation. Over the centuries she had become expert in locating likely prospects—the scent and heat of their rich, sweet blood invariably drew her, even from great distances.

She signaled the driver to stop by tapping at the roof. Manuel was a slow-witted dolt who had—unknowingly, of course—provided Lisette with sustenance on several occasions, when it was inconvenient to hunt far afield. His saving grace was that he never asked questions, even though a great many strange things took place in the villa.

Lisette alighted without waiting for assistance and, clad in a flowing gown of blue silk and a white mantilla made of the finest lace, swept boldly into the cantina that had drawn her attention from the carriage.

Her entrance caused a gratifying hush among the celebrants—even the flamenco dancers stopped to stare—but Lisette did not offer so much as a nod of acknowledgment. Her gaze swept the crowded tavern, seeking the one who had summoned her back from her travels, however inadvertently.

Lisette uttered a small cry when she found him—Great Scot, he was the very *picture* of Aidan Tremayne—studying her speculatively through narrowed blue eyes. He displaced the dancing girl from his lap, and the colorful ruffles of her petticoats swished as she flounced angrily away.

"Aidan," Lisette whispered brokenly, even though she

knew quite well that this mortal was not her lost love, but only someone who looked like him. Still, it was a very attractive quality, an unexpected and welcome bonus.

Silently she summoned him, and he rose from his chair, frowning with bewilderment, to obey. No one else in the place moved nor, it seemed to Lisette, whose senses were suddenly hyperalert, even breathed.

She laid one white hand to his face, felt the lovely rush of vibrant blood beneath his flesh, the warm firmness of the muscles. "Come with me," she said. Then she took his hand, as though he were a child, and led him out of the cantina into the balmy, starlit splendor of a Spanish night.

"What is your name?" she asked when they were settled in the carriage, and she'd smoothed the lines of bafflement from his wonderful face with a gentle hand. Even as she spoke she cupped his masculine parts through his trousers, to make the terms of the game clear, and to give him a foretaste of the ecstasies ahead.

His breathing was raspy, and a fine sheen of perspiration glimmered on his forehead and upper lip. Lisette was gratified to see and feel that he was aroused, eager for her.

"Jorge," he said in soft Spanish.

Lisette preferred English. "George," she said, dragging her fingers along the soft, thin fabric of his breeches, from the top of his muscular thigh to his knee, then back again.

George moaned as Lisette opened the buttons of his breeches and reached inside to stroke his straining shaft with expert fingers, and she was both pleased and touched by his reaction. It had been much the same that other night, long before, when she'd found Aidan Tremayne walking alongside an English road. He, too, had been a lusty young man, welcoming Lisette's skilled caresses, groaning softly as she attended him in various ways and showed him things he'd yet to experience with a mortal woman.

She maneuvered George so that he lay on his back, draped over her lap in delicious abandon, and then just sat admiring him for several moments, thinking what a splendid creation he was.

He writhed with pleasure, the lovely mortal, while Lisette taught him a few basics. Somewhat to her own surprise, she felt a deep tenderness toward the fragile creature, rather than the greedy lust that was usually at the root of such escapades.

Almost gently, Lisette brought the beautifully sculpted human to a satisfactory release. Then she simply stroked and admired him, from head to toe, for the work of art he was, as the carriage bounced and jostled over cobbled streets.

"She took the bait," Dathan said, rubbing his hands together in triumph and delight, when Maeve and Valerian joined him in that splendidly spooky old manse under its blanket of ivy and various vines. "Even as we speak, Lisette is playing her vampire games with our own beguiling 'George.' "

Maeve's attention was wandering; she was preoccupied with Calder, who had chosen to remain in the twentieth century, where they had made such tempestuous love. He was a new vampire, she reminded herself fitfully; he needed time to explore his powers.

Valerian nudged her. "He's fine, your fledgling lover," he said as directly as he would have if Dathan hadn't been there, listening intently. "Stop worrying."

Maeve glared at him for a moment to let him know she didn't appreciate his lack of sensitivity, then turned to Dathan. The warlock stood with arms folded, smirking a little.

"I want you to teach me that fire-starting trick now," she said.

Dathan only pretended to be taken aback by the request, but his glance at Valerian a moment later was genuinely uncertain. The towering vampire glowered at him in quelling silence.

Finally Dathan relented. "All right," he conceded grudgingly. "I will share the incantation. There is no guarantee whatsoever that the magic will work for vampires, however."

"We'll take our chances," Maeve said firmly. She'd betrayed an important bit of blood-drinker lore in letting Dathan and the others know how vampires recognized other supernatural creatures, knowledge that could be used against her kind, and she wanted something in return.

Dathan repeated the chant—the words were from some ancient language, eerie, and more like music than speech.

Maeve attempted the incantation and the simultaneous shift of consciousness a number of times before she mastered it and set a pile of old newspapers burning on the grate.

Valerian, that inveterate show-off, succeeded on the first try.

Chapter

—❦17❦—

The soul-cries of sick children all over nineteenth-century London seemed to ride on the night breeze and rise from the pavement itself. Overcome, Calder sagged against the brick wall of an ink factory and pressed his hands to his ears to shut out the terrible din. Since he was not hearing the sound, but feeling it instead, the gesture was fruitless.

"Maeve," Calder murmured like a man in delirium. "Valerian. Help me—show me what to do."

There was no reply.

Calder pushed himself away from the wall, wavered, and then gathered all his inner forces. No doubt this was a private ordeal, a rite of passage.

The suffering of the children pressed upon him from all sides, and the helpless feeling that assailed him was not unfamiliar. He had known this same frantic need to be more than he was, to be in a hundred places at once, as a mortal, moving among the wounded Rebels and Union soldiers he had attended in America.

Focus. The word came soft and insistent, like a whisper at his shoulder, and Calder had heard it often while Valerian was introducing him to his vampire powers.

Calder started to take a deep breath, realized that his lungs were fossilized within him, having no need of air. He smiled grimly and, as passers-by began to look at him with wary curiosity, straightened his coat. The sorrow of the children was as loud as ever, but he was beginning to cope with it, just as he had coped with the screams and moans of his patients in field hospitals and government wards back home.

Focus.

Calder found a single thread in all that tangle of noisy misery and grasped it with his mind. Then he allowed it to lead him down an alleyway, past a graveyard and a park, into a tenement.

There the horrid music of death and pain was so pervasive that Calder could barely withstand it, but he pressed on, whispering Valerian's word to himself like a litany. *Focus, focus, focus* . . .

The ribbon of consciousness led Calder to an impossibly small room in the back of an enormous, dark, and filthy building. One pitiful wad of tallow lit the stinking chamber, though of course Calder did not need its light to see the pale, spindly boy lying on a dirty pallet beneath the window. A crust of molded bread lay within the child's reach, and he watched with large, haunted eyes as a rat nibbled delicately at the last of his food.

The boy looked straight at Calder, then without a word turned his attention back to the rat. The lad's history flooded Calder's mind, unbidden; he knew his name was Tommy, that he'd been on the streets alone since he was five years old, surviving by picking pockets and stealing food from trash bins and occasionally from street stalls and shops. His mother, who had loved her baby very much, illegitimate though he was, had been a simple country maid, drawn to London by dreams of going on the stage. Instead she'd had to sell her favors to buy bread and milk, and one night she'd been strangled to death by a client who hadn't wanted to pay.

Calder closed his eyes for a moment, grappling with the horrid images. When he had, he kicked at the rodent; the belligerent creature hesitated, then scampered away.

"What do you want?" the lad asked listlessly in a thick Cockney accent, his eyes narrowed. "You're not from 'round here, now are you—not with those fine clothes of yours."

"I'm a doctor," Calder said thoughtfully. "What's your

name?" He asked the unnecessary question in an effort to put the lad at his ease.

"It's Tommy," the child said, trying to raise himself, and failing. "I ain't got no money to pay a doctor, so you'd better just take yourself out of here."

"I have no need of money," Calder answered distractedly, touching the pulse point beneath Tommy's ear. In that instant an image of the child's anatomy exploded into Calder's mind in rich and vibrant color, shining with clarity. Tommy was suffering from a respiratory infection; treating it would be fairly simple, by twentieth-century standards— the prescription was good food, rest, and antibiotics.

Unfortunately Calder's bag, which contained the modern medical supplies Maeve had purloined for him, as well as a few Valerian had collected for sport, was back at the Philadelphia house.

Tommy raised himself onto his painfully thin elbows and with effort demanded, "Why are you lookin' at me that way? You ain't plannin' to saw something off me, are you?"

Calder chuckled and then lifted the child gently into his arms. He could not carry Tommy through time, but space was another matter. He would take him back to Philadelphia and treat his illness. Calder knew a woman there, a widow robbed of three sons by that monstrous war, who would gladly look after the lad.

"No," the doctor answered belatedly, though Tommy had already guessed that he was safe, for he rested lightly in Calder's arms without struggling. "I'm going to take you on a little journey. Hold on tightly now and don't be frightened."

Tommy's eyes widened even farther. "My gawd, governor," he whispered, "you ain't an angel, are you? Tell me I ain't dyin'!"

Calder smiled sadly. "I'm no angel," he said. Then he closed his eyes and thought of that gloomy house in Philadelphia, where there had been so much pain and trouble and treachery.

The place was dark when Calder and Tommy arrived,

moments later. The stair railing was draped in black bunting, and there were mourning wreaths everywhere.

Tommy was in a state of shock; nothing in his brief and difficult life had prepared him for traveling halfway around the world in the embrace of a vampire.

"Shhh!" Calder said when the child would have cried out in amazement. He didn't want to encounter Prudence or any of the other servants; they would be terrified.

Obediently Tommy nestled close against Calder's coat. He was weak, after all, and very sick, and he soon lost consciousness.

Calder treated him with an injection of penicillin, wrapped the wraithlike body in woolen blankets, and fixed his mind on the presence of Ellen Cartwright, the middle-aged widow he'd met in the hallway of the army hospital.

Mrs. Cartwright was downstairs in the parlor of her small but sturdy house when Calder arrived. He settled the sleeping Tommy in a warm bed, summoned the good-hearted widow upstairs with a thought, and stepped back into the shadows.

The lady appeared within moments. Her face filled with mingled joy and concern when she saw the fragile child resting in the bed of her youngest, Albie, who'd fallen at Vicksburg.

"My gracious!" Mrs. Cartwright cried, taking Tommy's hand, blissfully unaware of the vampire looking on. "Where did you come from? Who are your people? My heavens, look at you—you're nothing but skin and bones!"

Smiling, Calder allowed himself to fade. He would return, of course, to give Tommy doses of the medicine he'd need to recover. Mrs. Cartwright could be counted upon to do the rest.

This one was not nearly as smart as Aidan Tremayne had been, Lisette observed to herself as she studied the beautiful, exhausted mortal sleeping in the tangled sheets of her bed. They'd had little opportunity for conversation, of course, but a quick scan of George's brain had revealed a distressing degree of mediocrity.

He had none of Aidan's talent for art, for one thing, nor did he possess his predecessor's poetic spirit and capacity for all ranges of emotion.

Lisette smiled. As far as she was concerned, all these factors were to George's credit—she had no need of another rebellious, troublesome lover, but an obedient companion, one fair of face and countenance, would be another matter entirely. And this one was certainly able to give her the pleasure she craved; he had a seemingly limitless ability to satisfy her.

It might be a comfort to have someone like George at her side, loyal and pretty and stupid, all of a piece. She could pretend he was Aidan if she wanted—she'd done exactly that while they were engaged in passion—and train him to be the perfect consort.

George stirred in the silken sheets, and Lisette smiled fondly and then glanced toward the window. Dawn was still hours away; there was time to enjoy her new toy thoroughly before submitting to the vampire sleep. The slumber would claim her this day, she knew, for although she was often able to evade it, the effort sapped her powers.

She slipped back into bed beside him, began to stroke his belly, muscled even in slumber, and tease his lovely staff back to life.

Yes, Lisette thought as George awakened, gripping her bare, slender hips and moving her so that she was astraddle of him, this one would do quite nicely. She would make him a vampire, of course, because watching him age was a prospect too dismal to consider, and after she'd destroyed the rebels, they would create other, more tractable blood-drinkers to serve as their court, and reign over the new dominion.

Together.

George plunged into Lisette, and she threw her head back and uttered a sound like the cry of a panther, deliberately forgetting, in her need and her ardor, that part of what had attracted her to this insatiable mortal was a sense of danger.

"It isn't wise," Valerian protested as he and Maeve moved along the dark river, deep beneath the ground, that led to the secret chamber of the Brotherhood of the Vampyre, "arriving uninvited and unannounced like this."

Maeve made a soft sound of exasperation. "Since when have you troubled yourself with such trivia? These are the oldest, most powerful vampires on earth. They were present when Lisette was transformed from a woman to an immortal. We've got to convince them to help us, or at least tell us if she has any weak spots."

Valerian's irritation clearly hadn't waned. He was uncomfortable in that dank, hidden place, Maeve knew, but not because he was afraid of ghosts and goblins, or even the Brotherhood itself. No, the cave unnerved him because it hadn't been his idea to venture there, and because he had kept a helpless vigil in that very place, in the earliest and probably most horrifying stages of Aidan's transformation from vampire to mortal man. "Do you really believe they're going to point out Lisette's Achilles' heel, if indeed she has one? After all, she is *one of them.* In telling you how to destroy the mad queen, they'll also be giving you the prescription for their own destruction!"

They were deep inside the cave now, but no sentinel barred their way, as Tobias had the last time they visited. No illusion of sunlight formed a barrier to protect the inner sanctum.

Maeve's spine prickled with an eerie premonition; some shock awaited them, and she tried to prepare herself.

They proceeded into the great chamber where the Brotherhood had held court since Atlantis itself had crumbled into the sea, both silent, both tense.

"Great Zeus," Valerian whispered when they spotted the remains of those ancient vampires, macabre shapes, part charred flesh and bone, part collapsed into naught but pale gray cinders. Obviously the members of the Brotherhood had submitted willingly to their fate, for they lay in a precise row, most with their horrible ashen parodies of arms crossed over their chests.

Maeve recalled Tobias and the others speaking of the old ones' desire to be at rest, once and for all. She had not really believed him; the idea of wanting death, of seeking it out, was so foreign to her that she'd had no frame of reference.

Now, faced with the reality, she felt overwhelming grief.

"Tobias?" she whispered, looking for him among the ruined bodies, unable to recognize his familiar, lithe shape.

"He's not here," Valerian said calmly. He crouched beside one of the vampire corpses and frowned. "Who could have performed this execution?" he mused aloud. "And how could they have lain so still, and yet tolerated the agonies of burning?"

Maeve stayed back, trembling slightly. She had not known these creatures well, nor even held them in particular esteem, but they were the first of her kind ever to exist— ancestors, in a way. "Perhaps they were dead *before* the fire was set," she suggested.

Valerian looked up at her, his violet eyes distant as he pondered Maeve's suggestion. "Perhaps," he finally agreed, rising to his full height.

"Could Lisette have done this?" Maeve asked.

The other vampire shook his head. "Even she would not have dared such a travesty. No, this is the Brotherhood's own work. They wanted oblivion and rest."

Maeve looked again at the horrible figures so neatly arranged on the chamber floor. "Enough to risk the Judgment of Heaven itself? Enough to face the possibility of hellfire?"

"Evidently," Valerian confirmed. "What I wouldn't give to know what they're experiencing right now. Is it nothingness or damnation?" He indulged in one of his pseudo-sighs. "Let's look around a little. There may be scrolls, or treasure."

It was then, as they began the search, that Maeve gave voice to what they were both thinking. "The task of destroying these old ones must have fallen to Tobias," she said.

"Isn't it likely that he would have taken any written record of their secrets when he left?"

"We'll find out, won't we?" Valerian asked, sounding a bit impatient.

"Where do you suppose he is? Tobias, I mean?"

Valerian lifted the lid of a tarnished brass and copper chest and peered inside. "He has probably gone underground to rest. I seem to remember that Tobias wasn't quite so enamored with the idea of giving up the proverbial ghost as the others were." He paused. "Come here. I've found something."

Maeve left off opening other chests and casks, all of which had proved to be empty, and joined Valerian on the other side of the chamber.

Inside the chest were a number of parchment scrolls, carefully tied with shriveled, dirty ribbon. When Valerian touched one of the papers, the corner crumbled into dust.

Feeling a strong sense of excitement, along with a niggling, quiet terror, Maeve drew closer and focused her mind on the contents of those rolls of ancient paper. Opening and reading them in the ordinary way would obviously have destroyed them.

At first she couldn't understand the words that flashed into her mind, for they were not only foreign, but archaic in the bargain. When she concentrated, however, the meaning began to come to her.

Recorded there, by some vampire scribe, were the deepest secrets, sufferings, and philosophies of the Brotherhood.

" 'The truth is ironic,' " Valerian read aloud, his graceful hands clutching the edge of the chest as he, too, scanned the writings with his mind. " 'It is mortals who will live forever, while all blood-drinkers and other unnatural creatures must one day pass over into death.' " He raised himself to his feet and turned to look deep into Maeve's widened eyes. "I guess the joke is on us."

Maeve's attention was drawn back to the treatises inside the chest. "There are other things here," she said in a thoughtful tone. "They lied when they claimed there was no longer a means to change a vampire back into a mortal—the necessary combination of chemicals is recorded here. And they knew, these vampires, how to start fires with their minds, in much the same way Dathan did—"

Valerian stepped back to allow Maeve to move closer to the scrolls, gesturing her forward, his voice gruff with emotion. "Absorb the magic," he said. "You are the true queen."

Maeve hesitated for a few moments, then knelt, as Valerian had done earlier, and spread both her hands out above the parchments, as inscriptions she had already divined instructed her to do. A breath of fire seemed to consume her, and then the knowledge flowed into her like a continuous charge of electricity. She took in secrets and formulas older than the pyramids, and the experience, far from being a sublime one, was shattering. When she had secreted it all away within herself, she used her thoughts to set the dusty scrolls ablaze.

"What the hell—?" Valerian burst out, exasperated, looking wildly about for some way to douse the flames. Of course, there was none. "Why did you do that?!"

Maeve rose slowly, still half entranced. "It was part of the pact," she said, knowing Valerian would not understand—not yet, at least—and unable to fully explain. She had consumed the knowledge of the vampyre, but she had yet to assimilate the majority of it.

Valerian gripped her shoulders, turned her to face him. "We're doomed, aren't we?" he rasped. "Tell me!"

She was still under enchantment, but she sensed the other vampire's desperation and struggled to answer. "Not necessarily," she said in the tone of a mother lulling a frightened child to sleep. "We have choices—more choices than you and I have ever dreamed."

"Go on!" he pressed, giving her a gentle shake.

Maeve shook her head. "Don't plague me about this now, Valerian—I cannot yet speak of it in any sensible fashion, and there are some things I must never say." She turned and looked sorrowfully at the burned remains of the old ones, laid out so neatly, like fallen soldiers gathered from a battlefield. "They perished willingly," she said. "They possessed the power to make themselves burn from the inside, at temperatures so high that the process was over in an instant."

Valerian took her hands in his, gentler now that some of his panic had passed. "What now?" he whispered.

"I must rest," Maeve replied. "It's all like—like a maelstrom inside me—"

A moment later, she collapsed in Valerian's arms.

After he'd left Tommy with Mrs. Cartwright, Calder returned to the grand house where he had died by his brother's hand. There was nothing he wanted from that place or from those people who normally populated it, and yet he needed to put a figurative period to the brief, troubled sentence that had been his mortal life.

He had fed early in the evening, and thus was at the height of his strength when he assembled himself in a shadowy corner of the main parlor of the Holbrook mansion. Before, he had been careful to stay upstairs, out of the flow of normal activity.

Only a few feet from where he stood, a newspaper reporter and the chief of police were conferring over strong coffee laced with brandy. Prudence lingered at a little distance from the two men, taking theatrical swipes at a lamp with her feather duster.

"God knows," the chief of police, and old friend of Calder's father, was saying, "there was no love lost between William and his younger brother, but William couldn't have stolen Calder's body because he was in jail."

Prudence shook her head almost imperceptibly, and in a blinding flash, Calder knew what she was thinking as well as if the thoughts had taken shape in his own mind: These fools were doing a lot of talking, but they were really just covering the same old well-trodden ground. Furthermore, they were no closer to figuring out what had really happened the night Calder disappeared.

I'm all right, Pru, Calder told his old friend silently. *Don't worry about me.*

Prudence started as if somebody had poked her lightly with the prongs of a pitchfork and cast a wild look around the dimly lit parlor, but Calder made sure she didn't see him. She was superstitious, he reminded himself, and even a glimpse of him, lurking in the corner where the gaslight didn't quite reach, might keep her awake nights for years afterward.

She looked at the chief and the reporter, who were still making inane attempts at figuring out what was going on in that house, noted that they hadn't sensed or heard anything, and bolted from the room.

Calder watched fondly until she'd vanished, then transported himself to the jail cell where his brother William sat on the edge of a rusted iron cot, despondency evident in every line of his elegantly slender body, his head in his hands.

Veiling himself from his brother's conscious awareness, if not that deeper, more mysterious part of the mind, Calder stood leaning against the bars of the cell, his arms folded.

Each place he visited, he'd recently discovered, had its own nuances and messages and meanings woven right into the ether itself. In London he had felt the pain and despair of the children; here in America it was the suffering of the soldiers and their families. . . .

Calder shifted his thoughts to the matter at hand. William would not actually hang, he discerned, since no body would ever be found, and he would not be tried and sent to prison.

The immediate future unfolded before Calder's eyes, like a neatly written letter.

William was to be released on bail, put up by Bernard's faithful attorneys, in just a few days. Before he could ever be taken before a judge, Calder saw as plainly as if the actual events were being played out in front of his eyes, William would consume a scandalous amount of bourbon and fling himself over the very railing Marie had tumbled from years before. He would break his neck in the fall.

Looking upon William while he still lived stirred strange emotions in Calder, not the least of which was pity. His half brother was not evil; he was merely weak. His fatal flaw had been nothing more than an unceasing longing for the very distinction he lacked. He'd craved the notice of others, especially Bernard, but tragically his own mediocre personality had rendered him all but invisible.

Calder laid a hand on William's shoulder, knowing all the while that the poor wretch would not feel his touch, or even sense his presence. As always, William's attention was turned inward, and he was unable to perceive Calder as Prudence had done.

Good-bye, he said, *and may God look upon you with compassion.*

With that, Calder left his murderer, the last living member of his family, to his fate and willed himself back to the beautiful house where so much tragedy and heartbreak had taken place. Not wanting to see the place as he knew it, but as it would be, he moved forward in time to the twentieth century.

He was mildly surprised, standing on the cracked sidewalk in the night and staring at the wreck of that once-grand house, to see its degeneration. Certainly no one in the Holbrook family had survived to live in it and pass it down, but Bernard, having been a far-sighted soul, had made provisions for even that. The mansion would be held in trust indefinitely.

Calder stared, feeling an expected pang of regret as he noted that the roof had caved in in places, and the windows had been broken out as well—including the fine stained-glass one that had once graced a medieval cathedral. The pillars supporting the roof over the veranda had long since fallen and disintegrated. The grounds, once manicured, were a tangle of weeds, the roses had gone wild decades ago, and the marble fountain that had once given a certain Grecian glory to the loop of the grand driveway was a ruin, marred by the lewd lettering of vandals.

He rested his forehead against a rusted iron rail of the fence, forgetting to veil himself as Valerian had taught him to do, too engrossed in his own despair to realize he was not alone.

"Personally, I think they should tear it down," a blustery male voice said. "It's an eyesore—brings down the value of the other estates in this area."

Calder looked over his shoulder and saw an older gentleman with bright blue eyes and an abundance of white hair. He was dressed in the garish fashion of the late twentieth century, his trousers plaid, his shirt open at the throat. With him on a leash was a golden retriever that made a whimpering sound and backed away from Calder until the strip of leather would allow it to go no farther.

"What happened to this place?" Calder asked. "It used to be one of the finest houses in Philadelphia."

"Hush, Goldie!" the mortal scolded, but the dog would not be soothed. It knew Calder was no ordinary human, even if its master didn't, and began to leap and plunge desperately at the end of her tether, until the old man could barely restrain her. "They say it used to be downright grand," he finally replied. "But there was some kind of trouble here, a long way back. What it all comes down to is, people started saying the place was haunted, and the rumors stuck. Why, when I was a boy, we wouldn't even *look* toward this house, for fear of being sucked right in and gobbled up by the ghoulies!" By this time the dog was going wild; Calder silenced the animal with an elementary mental trick. The beast's owner stared down at it for a moment, confounded, then finished up his discourse with, "You from around here? I don't recall seeing you before."

Calder smiled sadly. "I've been away for a while." He released Goldie from her spell, and she immediately started barking and pulling at the leash.

"Don't know what's gotten into this mutt," the old man fretted. He nodded in friendly farewell and allowed the dog to pull him on down the sidewalk, calling back with a laugh, "Have a care you don't get yourself bewitched or something!"

"Bewitched," Calder echoed with a somber chuckle. What an understatement.

He looked at the old house for a while longer, remembering—for not all his recollections were unhappy ones, of course—and then turned to walk away.

Valerian was leaning against the nearest lamppost, arms folded, a disapproving expression on his face. "There you are," he said, as if he'd conducted a long and weary search. In truth, Calder knew, the elder vampire had simply fastened his thoughts on his troublesome apprentice and willed himself to his side.

Calder felt a sudden stir of alarm coil itself in his chest, like a snake. "Maeve," he said, stepping closer to Valerian, who still lounged against the modernized lamppost. "Is she all right?"

Valerian arched an eyebrow. "What do you care?" he intoned. "You are hardly an attentive lover, the way you keep rushing off all over time and creation."

The alarm Calder felt intensified and was joined by a dull, pulsing throb of guilt. "Damn you, Valerian, what's happened to her?"

Valerian smiled, but there was a glint of bitterness in the expression, plainly directed at Calder himself and not Maeve. "You are right to be frightened, fledgling," he said coldly. "Maeve truly became the queen of vampires on this very night, when all the knowledge of the old ones was imparted to her, but the weight of it may crush her. She lies dormant, even now."

Calder forgot himself, forgot the other vampire's vastly superior powers, and grasped the lapels of Valerian's beautifully tailored velvet waistcoat in both hands. "*Where?*"

With pointed grace, Valerian freed himself. "For her sake," he said in a low, smooth voice, "and for her sake alone, I will not burn you like a stalk of dry grass for your insolence."

"Where is she?" Calder repeated, subsiding only slightly. Perhaps foolishly, he cared nothing for his own safety, but only Maeve's.

Valerian took his time answering, first straightening his coat and smoothing the lapels Calder had crumpled. "Have you forgotten everything I taught you?" he asked. "Simply think of Maeve and will yourself to be at her side."

Calder *had* forgotten in his anxiety. He scowled defiantly at Valerian, then closed his eyes and permeated himself with Maeve's image.

Moments later Calder found himself, and Maeve, in a vast, echoing chamber that looked like a medieval dungeon. The place was lit by hundreds of flickering candles, and Maeve lay in the center on a long table draped with velvet, like Sleeping Beauty awaiting her prince's kiss.

Her flesh seemed translucent in the candlelight, and the faintest of smiles touched her lips. Calder had seen that serene expression many times—on the faces of mortals who had died with clear consciences, after rising above their pain.

He took up her hand, kissed the knuckles. "Maeve?"

She did not respond, of course, or even stir.

It was only then that he noticed Benecia and Canaan, those horrible vampire children, sitting nearby in ruffled dresses, hair all in curls, swinging their feet. They smiled at him, in unison, but the glitter in their flat eyes was patently savage.

"If Maeve doesn't wake up," they said simultaneously, chilling Calder on some level far beneath his conscious reach, "then Mama will be queen, and we shall be princesses."

Calder glared at them. "Get out of here, you little demons!"

They leaped off their chairs then, fangs bared, making a hair-raising sound that was at once a snarl and a shriek. Calder braced himself for attack, but before they lunged, Valerian materialized, blocking their way.

"Go dig up a grave or something," that vampire said, waving a hand.

Benecia and Canaan looked sullen, to say the least, but they drew in their fangs and vanished.

Calder glowered at Valerian, even though—or perhaps *because*—his creator had just saved him an ugly experience. "What took you so long?" he asked, only then realizing that he was still grasping Maeve's hand, and that his grip was not only possessive, but desperate.

Valerian sighed, as long-suffering as a martyr about to be burned at the stake. "I had forgotten how trying a fledgling's insolence can be," he said. His gaze fell on Maeve then and turned tender in the face of an instant. "I had hoped she would respond to you. Misguided though she may be, she loves you very much."

Calder felt very human tears burning in his eyes as he looked down at Maeve. He had neglected her in the excitement of discovering and exploring his new powers, and he had never felt more remorse than he did then.

"Forgive me," he whispered, not caring that Valerian could hear.

Valerian stood on the other side of the slab. "Come back to us if you can, Maeve," he said with a strange mixture of gentle urging and sternness. "We need you if we are to survive. Nemesis's angels are nearly upon us."

There was not so much as a flicker of an eyelash from Maeve.

"How did this happen?" Calder demanded, as if knowing could make a difference, or somehow undo whatever it was that had brought Maeve to lie there on that slab, unmoving, unresponsive.

Valerian gave a complicated explanation, speaking of vampire corpses and a natural chamber far beneath the earth and a chest full of crumbling scrolls. Maeve had somehow absorbed the contents of those ancient parchments, all the knowledge the old ones had brought with them from Atlantis and gathered since. He finished with another brisk injunction for Maeve to wake up and resume her duties as leader of the vampires.

"Leave her alone," Calder said distractedly. "Just leave her alone."

He bent and rested his forehead lightly against Maeve's, and that was when he felt the spiritual storm raging in and around her. She was struggling, fighting some internal battle on which everything outward hinged.

Calder raised himself and, clasping both her hands tightly in his, willed his own strength into her, without stint or reservation. He grew weak and swayed on his feet, ignoring Valerian's orders to stop.

Maeve heard Calder's voice above the howling tempest within her own being. She struggled toward him, reaching and straining, and finally letting him lead her.

Then she felt the inrush of vitality, as if she were feeding on the mysterious ambrosia that sustained all vampires. She felt him grasp her somehow, and pull her upward with all his fledgling power.

She opened her eyes just in time to see what price Calder had paid to help her. His face was waxen and strangely gaunt, and as she watched, her joy and relief turning now to horror and regret, his eyes rolled back, and he toppled across her, completely spent. Perhaps even dead.

Maeve screamed a protest as Valerian clasped Calder's shoulders and gently pulled him away. She was still weak, and her efforts to sit up were futile.

"Valerian," she pleaded. "Tell me—I beg of you—is he—gone?"

The other vampire's voice was hollow. "I don't know," he answered. "I can't make a connection—"

Fear shot through Maeve and propelled her off the slab. She stood beside it, trembling, and saw Valerian kneeling on the floor where Calder lay, unmoving. She had never seen that terrible stillness in any other vampire, not even the dormant ones she'd occasionally stumbled across when she was abroad and looking for a temporary lair.

She closed her eyes, trying to link her mind with Calder's, but like Valerian, she failed. She could not sense her lover's spirit or his formidable intelligence.

"He did this for me," she said in despair, dropping to her knees. She took his hand and called to him silently with all the force and substance of her soul. And then she felt it— a spark, then a flicker of life, somewhere inside him.

Maeve bent closer and brushed his still, waxen lips with her own. "Come back to me," she told him. "I love you, and I need you—"

Valerian must have felt Calder's spirit rallying as well, for he gave a soft, joyous exclamation.

Calder grew stronger, and then stronger still. Finally, after what seemed like an eternity, he opened his eyes, stared blankly for a few moments, and then gave Maeve an insouciant wink.

With a strangled sob, intertwined with a burst of laughter, Maeve leaned down again and kissed him full on the mouth. "Don't you ever do anything like that again!" she said as his lips formed a smile against her own.

She knew when Valerian left them alone, and was grateful.

Still kneeling, Maeve laid one hand to either side of Calder's face, full of exaltation and love and fury that he'd nearly left her forever. "What happened?"

With considerable effort Calder raised himself onto his elbows. "Nothing," he answered thoughtfully. "All I saw was darkness. My awareness kept shrinking until it was only a pinpoint." He reached up, entangled his fingers in her hair, and tugged gently. "Then I heard your voice, and I followed it back."

Maeve's eyes burned with tears. "You were foolish to expend all your strength that way. Why did you do it?"

He strained upward to give her a nibbling kiss. "You know why," he answered hoarsely.

She did know, and it made everything worthwhile—all the suffering that lay behind her, and all the perils waiting ahead.

Calder Holbrook loved her.

Chapter

—❧18❧—

The knowledge that the old ones were gone came to Lisette as she dreamed in her secure chamber beneath the Spanish villa, and although she had long ago parted company with the Brotherhood, she felt their loss. One, Zarek, had been her childhood sweetheart and later her husband, when they were both still mortal, of course. She had left him behind soon after they became vampires, for Zarek had been something of a philosopher, and he had not approved of the way Lisette used her powers.

She stirred on her cool marble slab, vaguely aware of the luscious mortal moving about abovestairs, helping himself to her chocolates, her brandy, and probably her money as well. She felt mild amusement; when George became a vampire, he would no longer have use for such human comforts. Let him enjoy them while he could, for soon she would be introducing him to much keener pleasures.

One of the first things she meant to do, she reflected, floating just beneath the surface of wakefulness, where mortals and vampires alike are awash in dreams, was change George's name. She must choose something less pedestrian and more suitable—Raoul, perhaps, or Julian, or Nikos . . .

It wasn't unusual for blood-drinkers to eschew their former identities completely, of course. She herself had done just that, shedding her mortal name, Cassandra, and abandoning her profession. Like the other old ones, she had been a doctor and a scientist.

Those ancient memories tugged at her now, pulled her back toward that time lost in mist, like the currents of some vast, unseen river. She reasoned that she was prone to reverie because Zarek and the others were gone, and she was virtually alone in the firmament. In any case, she made no effort to resist but instead allowed herself to drift slowly back, and back, and back . . .

Atlantis.

The doomed continent was real to Lisette, not the nebulous legend it had become in modern times, a green place with gently rolling hills and a curving mountain range edging its northernmost coasts. There were many lakes and rivers on the great island, and animals peculiar to it, curious and beautiful creatures that were lost in the great cataclysm.

Standing mentally on the stony shore of her homeland, Lisette put aside the certain knowledge that everything she looked upon was mere illusion, every stone and stick of wood, every grave and temple. All of it had fallen into the sea so long ago that there was no one to remember, save herself and possibly one other now-dormant vampire, the untrustworthy Tobias.

Lisette gave herself up to the joy of homecoming and climbed a grassy slope to look out over the impossibly blue seas. A fine, cool mist touched her skin and awakened that winsome mortal girl, the forgotten one who'd lain hidden within her all these thousands of years.

Lisette was no longer Lisette, but Cassandra, or Cassie, as she was called by those who loved her. She was young and beautiful, mortal and free, blessed with one of the finest minds in all Atlantis.

Cassie sat in the fragrant grass, drawing up her slim, strong legs and wrapping her arms around them. She did not fit the classical image of the Atlantean, she knew—she wore no toga or sandals, no wreath of leaves upon her head.

No, Cassie wore cutoff blue jeans and a skimpy summer top. She listened to rock music and lived in a split-level house, and her government was experimenting with weapons of terrifying power—bombs and missiles detonated by a process of turning atoms in upon themselves.

Cassie lay back on the grass, gazing up at the azure sky, her long auburn hair spread out around her. She tried not to worry about the tests her father and his colleagues, all top scientists, were conducting, but she knew too much for comfort.

Looking upon her younger self and at the same time gazing outward through that child's eyes, Lisette felt a terrible grief. Cassie was as lost as if she'd gone under the sea with the rest of Atlantis's population, including her father and mother and sisters and brothers.

Despite the pain of bereavement, Lisette was wont to leave this vision of her doomed homeland. She lingered, watching as Cassie grew into Cassandra and married Zarek, her handsome lover. They had joined the secret society, a group of renegade scientists, young and old, who had stumbled on a formula they believed would slow the aging process.

The potion not only met that objective, but also lent the experimenters incredible powers. They could travel vast distances, even to other continents, on the strength of a thought. They could read the minds of others and veil themselves from the notice of ordinary people and, sometimes, even from each other.

The magic had a dark side, but it wasn't discovered until weeks after the members had imbibed the wonderful medicine that made them as strong and intelligent as gods. They developed a penchant for human blood—and soon learned, to their unending horror, that they required the mysterious vitality of the stuff to function. What began as a mere aversion to the light of the sun became a violent and extremely painful reaction. Finally the blood-drinkers found themselves succumbing to a deep, comalike sleep during the day.

They had become fiends, and they named themselves *vampyres* for a terrifying winged creature that existed only in the heart of the continent's southern jungles.

All the other members were alarmed, having foreseen

none of these complications despite years of calculation and experimentation—except for Cassandra. She gloried in her newfound powers, honed them, and enjoyed the unspeakable bliss that always swept over her when she consumed the wine of the gods, the ambrosia that was blood.

She and Zarek, happy newlyweds only a few months before, began to argue violently. An antidote to the original potion was concocted, and Essian, the founder of the society, volunteered to sample it.

In return for his bravery, Essian received a horrible death. He aged while his colleagues looked on in fear and revulsion, wrinkling, caving in upon himself, his flesh drying out until it crumbled like dust. Still, he lived, a rotted corpse, as vile as something dug up from a grave, his eyes peering out of a skull, his screams of terror shrill and echoing.

After witnessing such an atrocity, volunteers for other experiments were not forthcoming. The Brotherhood of the Vampyre was formed, and Cassandra, who had taken to ranging over the whole of that hemisphere in search of victims and playmates, was tolerated but not, as the name of the fellowship indicated, really included.

She was not on Atlantis the night the accident happened, but in a village that would become Athens, battling with Zarek, who wanted to live quietly as a scholar, instead of wandering the earth with her, while the two of them explored their magnificent powers.

While these vampires argued their cases, the land of their birth trembled on the brink of disaster.

A power station had been built over a fault line, the vampire Tobias reported later. When the first explosion occurred, it set off a chain reaction of other blasts, violent enough to shift vast geological plates far beneath the surface of the land. There were quakes, and great fissures formed, snaking out in every direction. Tidal waves lashed the continent from every side, and volcanoes, long believed extinct, erupted all over the once beautiful land. In a matter of days Atlantis had cracked like an eggshell and literally fallen to pieces.

The people and the visible continent were gone, swallowed. The earthquakes continued for weeks, however, and great walls of sea water struck lands thousands of miles away, wiping out other civilizations as well.

Zarek and the others had been grief-stricken, holing up in a cave with primitive paintings of animals and birds on the walls, lying dormant for centuries. Cassandra, unwilling to waste a moment mourning a time and place that no longer existed and would never exist again, except in fairy tales, changed her name to Lisette and set about forgetting all that had gone before.

Now, lying prone and dreaming in her villa on the coast of Spain, the ancient vampire wept—for Zarek and the others, for Atlantis, and, most of all, for herself. Only now, when it was too late to stop the Brotherhood from choosing death, did Lisette realize that they'd all been interconnected in some mystical, inexplicable way. With the passing of her colleagues, Lisette had been diminished and perhaps had even died a little herself.

Far away, in a different land and century, in a vault beneath a forgotten grave, another ancient one lay slumbering. His was a deeper trance than Lisette's, dark and rich and vital, meant to last for months or even years.

Tobias also dreamed and remembered and grieved for his lost brothers. There were times when he regretted his decision to choose the healing sleep instead of death, but there were still too many mysteries on this plane of existence, troubled as it was, too many puzzles and possibilities he could not bring himself to abandon.

One night, in five years, or fifty, or three hundred—he was so old that he no longer needed blood to survive—he would stir, leave his burrow beneath the moldering bones of some English dowager, and venture abroad. When that time came, he hoped to encounter the magnificent Maeve Tremayne again, and Dimity, the enigmatic blood-drinker who consorted with angels, and even that most exasperating of vampires, Valerian.

Ah, Valerian. Fascinating creature, even if he *was* irritating. Tobias knew much more about him than anyone else did, including, perhaps, Valerian himself. Yes, indeed, that vampire's story was rich and complex, crying to be told.

Tobias settled himself deeper into his private enchantment and turned his thoughts to his own happy mortal youth, spent long ago and far away, in a verdant land overlooking a sapphire sea.

Maeve found Calder in the late twentieth century, a time she despised for its busyness and crass, materialistic orientation, just an hour before dawn. She was weary from warfare, for Lisette's creatures were spawning others like themselves, helter-skelter, and for every ten she and Dathan and Valerian and the others managed to destroy, it seemed a hundred others cropped up. Although there had been no further communication with Nemesis's forces, the deadline was mere days away, and the Warrior Angel, seeing the mindless vampires multiply, absorbing innocent mortals into their ranks, was surely straining to fight.

For a few minutes Maeve just stood there in the shadows of the famous medical college's library, watching as Calder took volume after volume from the shelves, absorbing the material as quickly as he could flip through the pages. He was greedy for knowledge, the way most vampires were greedy for blood, and that troubled Maeve.

Despite Calder's declarations of love, and his heroic sharing of strength when she'd needed it so badly, Maeve still had her doubts about his motives. She wasn't sure, in fact, that Calder himself truly understood them.

At last he sensed her presence and turned to smile at her in the comforting darkness, at its richest now that dawn approached. He slid the volume he'd just scanned back into its place and came toward her.

"I'm sorry," he said, taking her hands, bending slightly to kiss her cheek. "I was supposed to meet you in the circle of stones—"

Maeve smiled and touched his face tenderly, wanting to

memorize it with the tips of her fingers as well as her eyes. "But you became so engrossed in your studies that you forgot," she finished for him in tender exasperation. "Did you even remember to feed?"

Calder kissed her lightly on the mouth, and Maeve felt the same pleasant shock she always did. "Oh, yes," he answered finally. "I am at the height of my powers, fledgling though I am. Would you like me to show you?"

She nodded, almost shyly, and, by tacit agreement, they took themselves to their new secret lair, the wine cellar of the now rundown Holbrook mansion in Philadelphia. There they made love in the vampire way, with Calder putting Maeve through the same demanding paces she had so often required of him, and again in the mortal fashion. This time Maeve was the aggressor, kneeling astride Calder's hips, riding him hard, taking him deep inside her and holding him there until he cried out and arched beneath her.

At last they slept, limbs entangled, on the old, scratched trestle table that was their vampire bed.

"I want to give you a new name, my darling," Lisette purred to her mortal lover only minutes after sunset. They were on the terrace of her villa, overlooking the warm, star-splashed Spanish sea.

George enjoyed a hearty dinner of roast pheasant and new potatoes, among other delicacies, while Lisette perched on the stone rail, letting the soft breeze dance in her hair and in the delicate folds of her gown.

"I like my own name," George said, licking his fingers.

Lisette felt a surge of temper, but brought it quickly under control. There was no need to worry about this one; he wasn't clever enough to give more than the occasional amusing ripple of trouble.

"It doesn't suit you," she told him moderately, reaching out to touch his lovely ebony hair. Like silk it was, fine and glossy, sliding smoothly between her fingers.

He looked up at her with impudent blue eyes, Aidan's eyes, and Lisette's heart tumbled a few times before catching itself. "What would suit me?" he asked in Spanish, chewing as he spoke.

His manners were atrocious, Lisette reflected, but she didn't care about that, either. He would suit her purposes just fine, poor manners and vacuous brain notwithstanding.

She gazed upon him thoughtfully for a few moments, a finger to her chin, even though she'd long since decided that he would be called Nikos. "Have you noticed anything—well—*different* about me, darling?"

Nikos, formerly George, settled back, draining a glass of the finest Madeira in Europe before answering, "You are always gone when I awaken in the morning."

Lisette smiled to herself. "Is there nothing else?"

Nikos frowned beguilingly. "You are unusually strong for a woman, and your skin is like iridescent stone when the moonlight strikes you."

She leaned to trace the underside of his jawline with one fingertip, then slid it slowly down the length of his throat and into the dense, dark hair matting his chest. It was pleasant and diverting to watch him squirm in his chair, already wanting her.

"Would you like to live forever?" she asked, unbuttoning his silk shirt to the waist.

Nikos made a throaty sound of surrender as she worked his belt buckle easily and opened his trousers. "Yes," he rasped.

Using her mind and not her hands, she began to stroke and tease Nikos, until he was bucking in his chair and, at the same time, groping for her.

She withheld herself, although she wanted to be ravished by the eager young brigand as much as he wanted to ravish her, at the same time intensifying his arousal with ruthless skill. "Would you like to be just as you are tonight—young and hard and full of fire—for the rest of eternity?" she whispered close to his ear.

He groaned, and Lisette knew what he was feeling because she was inducing those sensations that made him so feverish and fretful. "Yes—*damn* you, Lisette—what are you doing to me? I feel your hands cupping me—I feel your lips, your teeth, and it's as if I'm about to be swallowed—" His words fell away as he gave an involuntary cry of savage need. "By the saints, I beg of you, give me mercy—"

But Lisette was not inclined toward mercy. She compounded the battery of sensations, toying with his nipples, laying a wreath of kisses on his hard belly, squeezing his powerful buttocks and lifting him, driving him deeper and deeper into his own senses.

The one thing she denied him was satisfaction.

Finally she pushed him to the point of madness; he rose from his chair and overpowered her—or at least, she let him think that was what he'd done. He tore her clothes away, cleared the table with a sweep of one arm, and hurled her down onto the surface, taking her with deep, angry thrusts.

Lisette's release was instantaneous and violent. She pitched beneath Nikos's plunging hips, arching her back and crying out in animal ecstasy as he punished her for her teasing.

He was not satisfied with once, however—that was one of the things Lisette loved about Aidan—no, she must remember, this was *Nikos*—he was insatiable, just as she was. Thus, he turned her on the table, so that her buttocks touched his groin, and put himself only a little way inside her, just far enough to drive her wild with wanting him.

He fondled her breasts as she begged, denying her in a low, murmuring voice, telling her that she was his and his alone, that he would have her when he was ready, and no sooner than that. He told her that she was a beautiful whore, pinching her nipples lightly and giving her another inch of his staff when she pleaded, and said what she needed was a proper hiding, and he had a good mind to give it to her.

Lisette moaned, desperate, despairing, delighted. It was this explosive pleasure that gave her such tremendous power.

"What do you want, little whore?" Nikos whispered, caressing her breasts, weighing them in his palms, chafing the nipples with his thumbs. "Tell me what you want."

She gripped the edge of the table. "You," she wept. "I want all of you—oh, please—I want it all . . ."

Nikos teased her some more, venturing a little farther inside her—but only a little—then withdrawing until he had almost left her completely. While he subjected her to this sweet torment, he pretended to ponder her request.

Lisette was certain she would perish, she wanted him so badly, and when he suddenly thrust deep inside her, she shouted with avaricious lust.

Nikos told her what a brazen wench she was, behaving in such a way, actually begging to be taken, making her whimper and whine, grasping her hips and holding her when she would have increased the tempo by thrusting herself against him. Finally, however, he lost control of his own need and pounded against her with greater and greater urgency, greater and greater violence, until they were fused by the heat of their fury, completely joined, each jerking against the other in instinctive surrender.

"You are a very naughty boy," Lisette said minutes later, when she had gotten down from the table and collected her shredded gown.

Nikos pulled her close and bent to kiss her lightly on the side of the neck. "I think I'll take you that way from now on," he said in a husky whisper. "Like a stallion, mounting his mare."

Lisette was weak with satisfaction, and yet she felt her intimate places heating again as he talked on and on about all the sweet, sinful things he wanted to do to her, weaving his lover's spell.

Only when Nikos had draped her roughly over the wide stone railing of the terrace and put her through all the same exquisite little torments again, only when she was buckling against him in the throes of brutal pleasure, did she wonder—just fleetingly—how a mere man could so bewitch a great vampire like herself.

Dimity was waiting when Maeve and Calder came up from the cellar at the setting of the sun and into the kitchen where Calder had eaten as a boy, well over a hundred years in the past.

Maeve was slightly troubled that the other vampire had found them so easily; she had made every effort to veil herself and Calder in the hope that they would sleep in safe anonymity.

"What is it?" Maeve asked.

"The angels have come," Dimity said. "They are encamped everywhere, waiting to attack us. Gideon says that Nemesis himself has come from the higher world to participate in the greatest purge since the war in heaven!"

Maeve felt chilled and cast a quick glance toward Calder. He was strong and brave and most willing to fight, but he was a fledgling, his powers were new to him, and he was unskilled at wielding weapons of the mind. If he tried to aid in the cause, the results were likely to be disastrous, for himself and for other vampires.

"There is more," she said, looking Dimity straight in the eye once again.

The angelic nightwalker nodded. "Yes. Nemesis wants to see you, Maeve. He's issued an order that you are to come to him this very night."

Even as a mortal child Maeve had been intrepid, walking the high crumbling walls of the convent where she grew up, running away with a caravan of gypsies on one occasion. She'd battled Lisette herself and lived through the terrible pain of losing her brother, but this was by far the greatest challenge she had ever faced.

"What is my assurance that I won't be taken prisoner?" she asked quietly, raising her chin.

Calder erupted in sudden protest, leaving the falling mantel he'd been attempting to right and rushing to her side. "You can't seriously be *considering* such a thing—"

Maeve used her superior powers to render Calder mute, though only temporarily, knowing that reason would not reach him.

Dimity answered Maeve's question as if Calder hadn't

spoken at all. "You have Nemesis's word. The promise of the high angels cannot be false, you know that."

"Yes," Maeve said as Calder struggled to speak, glowering at her, knowing she had somehow frozen his vocal cords. "Where is Nemesis to be found?"

"Gideon said you are to go to All Souls' Cathedral in London and wait. You will be contacted."

Maeve nodded as Calder made furious strangling sounds and grasped her arm as if to restrain her. She turned her gaze to Dimity. "Look after him," she said, meaning Calder, and the other vampire nodded, her lovely eyes wide with sympathy.

Forming an image of the cathedral where she and Valerian had been attacked by warlocks, Maeve raised her hands slowly over her head and vanished. Calder could not cry out to her, it was true, nor could he follow with Dimity using her considerable might to restrain him, but Maeve felt his protest in the center of her soul all the same.

He would not soon forgive her for restricting his freedom again.

Maeve kept to the twentieth century, knowing that angels preferred the current moment to all the past combined.

The graveyard of All Souls' was not empty—here and there a derelict slept, curled up behind some headstone or monument, and all the benches were occupied as well.

Maeve scanned the place with a quick sweep of her thoughts, finding naught but mortals who would sleep until morning, and more mortals who would sleep until Gabriel sounded his trumpet. A Dante-like picture came to her mind of wavering, vaporous souls rising from all the graves to be judged by their Maker, and she shivered.

"Quite a dramatic image," a male voice said.

Maeve spun, taken by surprise, and looked upon the countenance of a tall, powerfully built angel. He was dressed in modern clothes, a tailored suit, an overcoat of the finest wool, a white cashmere scarf.

"Nemesis," she said, half in greeting, half in awe.

He actually smiled, and Maeve noted that he wasn't handsome in the standard sense, though if she managed to survive this night, she knew she would never forget a single detail of his features. He had brown hair, attractively shaggy, and green eyes; like Gideon, he shimmered with the light of a kingdom that could only be reached by traveling inward.

"At your service," he said with a slight bow of his head.

Maeve's awe began to give way to suspicion, annoyance, and plain ordinary fear. "I didn't expect you to be quite so courtly," she said.

"And I didn't expect you to be beautiful," Nemesis replied smoothly. He sighed. "Unfortunately, neither my manners nor your loveliness has anything whatsoever to do with the business at hand."

He began to stroll along a stone pathway, and Maeve kept pace. The mortals around them slept on, unaware that their fate, as well as that of vampires and warlocks and all other immortals, was being decided.

"What do you want?" Maeve finally dared to ask.

Nemesis seemed amused by her bravado, even a little taken with it. "Surrender," he answered in a cordial tone. "Nothing less than the complete surrender of every evil creature walking the night."

The idea was foreign to Maeve, but she had others to consider besides herself. "What would happen then? If we gave ourselves up, I mean?"

"You would be cast into the pit, where you could do no more harm," Nemesis answered, as calmly as if they were two humans deciding whether to have biscuits with their tea or scones with jelly.

Maeve shuddered.

"You'll end up there either way, you see," Nemesis went on with quiet, terrible reason. "Surely you realize that you cannot resist legion upon legion of angels."

She nodded but was careful to hold her head high. "Of course we know that," she replied. "Our hope is to stop Lisette and bring her to you. She is the guilty one, after all."

"Every last one of you is guilty," Nemesis argued pleasantly. "Even if you do destroy this devil's spawn, this Lisette, why should I let you go on?"

Maeve thought fast. "Because if there is to be a kingdom of light," she said, "there must be a kingdom of darkness to balance it. You protect your Master's beloved mortals, you guide and teach them, but it is the so-called evil creatures who make them strong by giving them adversity to resist."

Nemesis was quiet for a moment, thoughtful. Then he gave a low, bone-shaking burst of laughter. "You are smart, Vampire—like your father, Lucifer."

She stopped, furious. "I'll thank you not to credit Lucifer with siring me—I've never met him, let alone sat at his feet to learn evil magic as you seem to be implying. Before I became a vampire, I was *created*—by the same God who made you."

The great angel glared at her for a moment, but then it seemed to Maeve that something in his bearing softened ever so slightly. "There is no time to argue semantics, child. I urge you again—surrender, and bring your dark followers with you."

Maeve shook her head, wondering if she was being brave or just foolhardy. "No, Nemesis," she said. "I will bring you Lisette, and then I will storm heaven itself with pleas for mercy. If you do not grant us clemency, perhaps your Master will."

"Such a waste," the warrior said, his eyes sad as he looked down into Maeve's upturned face. "You would have been a fine angel." With that, he shook his head once in apparent sorrow, turned, and walked away into the night.

Chapter
19

Cobwebs swayed in gray scallops from the great chandelier in the entryway, but for the time being, Calder was not concerned with the condition of his erstwhile home. Although his voice had been restored, he was still as much a prisoner as if he'd worn chains and manacles, and the fact outraged him.

"Maeve is only trying to protect you," Dimity, his jailer, remarked distractedly when he'd joined her in the parlor. She was standing beside the time-ruined harpsichord, running one finger over the keys.

Damn, but he hated the way they could look straight into his mind, Maeve and Valerian and Dimity. Was he to have no private thoughts at all?

"Not until you learn to veil them," Dimity replied as if he'd spoken, smiling that angelic smile.

Calder made yet another futile attempt to crash through the unseen barrier Maeve had erected around him, around this memory-haunted house, and it left him feeling as though he'd been struck by a train.

He collapsed into a dusty chair, rubbing his temples with a thumb and forefinger.

"Stubborn," Dimity said, turning back to the harpsichord, drawing eerie music from it. If the sound was heard by mortals, there would soon be a new spate of rumors about the spooky old mansion.

"I am Maeve's mate," he muttered. "I belong at her side—*especially* when she's in danger."

Dimity drew back the spindly-legged bench and sat down to experiment further with the harpsichord. "You would only be a liability to her at this point," she said, her attention mostly focused on that mouse-eaten old instrument. "Perhaps later, when you've learned to use your powers more proficiently—"

"Damn!" Calder bellowed, bolting from his chair and startling Dimity, who jumped and then turned to look at him over one beautifully shaped shoulder. "No one, not even Maeve, will rob me of my personal liberties—I will not endure it!"

"It seems to me," Dimity observed diplomatically, smoothing her brown silk skirts, "that you haven't much choice in the matter, at least for the moment."

Calder went to the warped, filthy mantel, which had once shimmered and smelled pleasantly of the oil Prudence used to polish it, and gripped it with both hands. His head was lowered, and his pride, like the exquisitely expensive mirror that had once hung over that fireplace, was in shards at his feet.

"You're right," he said hoarsely after a long pause. "I have no choice—now. But tomorrow night, or the next one, or the one after that, I will be free. And love Maeve though I do, with every grain and fiber, with everything that makes me who I am, I will not sacrifice my freedom of choice to her whims." Calder turned, knowing his bleak decision lay naked in his eyes, unable to hide the torment he felt. "I'm going to leave her, Dimity, if we survive this present trouble. I'm going to venture out on my own and learn the things I need to know, and work out just what sort of a vampire I mean to be."

Dimity's lovely face reflected both misery and understanding. "It will kill Maeve to lose you," she said softly. "She does love you, you know. Her passion is a part of her, as much so as her, powers, even her soul."

"I feel exactly the same way about her," Calder replied

grimly, "but that isn't enough. I need my right of choice, and Maeve's trust, as well, and she needs those same things from me." He paused, shoving a hand through his rumpled hair. "I don't think either of us is capable of giving them—not willing."

Slowly, gracefully, Dimity rose from the harpsichord bench and came toward him. "Maeve would give you anything," she whispered. "Anything."

"Except the holy right of deciding my own fate for myself," Calder replied. He escorted Dimity to a round table where his father and William had once played games of chess, the winning of which had been inordinately important to both of them, and drew back a chair for her.

When she was seated, Calder sat across from her and folded his hands on the rain-warped, dirt-covered table-top.

"Since we apparently have considerable time at our disposal," he said, "tell me about yourself. How were you made, and when? Were you changed against your will, or did you give your consent?"

Dimity laughed good-naturedly. "I see you haven't studied vampire etiquette yet," she said. "It is very rude to ask a blood-drinker about her making—the topic is a sore spot with so many of us."

Calder was undaunted. He had never worried much about protocol in his human life, and he didn't plan on doing so as an immortal. "Is it a sore spot with you?"

Dimity shook her head, as if amazed and a little scandalized by the bluntness of the question, but there was a mischievous light in her blue eyes. "No, actually—it isn't. I became a vampire by my own choosing, in the late fourteenth century . . ."

It was silly, Lisette decided, as she watched Nikos parading back and forth in front of her, showing off his expensive new velvet coat and doeskin breeches, to deny herself the pleasure of creating a prince consort for even one more night.

She thought of the process of changing a mortal into a

blood-drinker and felt a rush of dark desire, almost as compelling as the passion Nikos could so easily stir in her. With him, she would bring the full extent of her powers to bear, and the experience would be exquisite for both of them—no more of those clammy corpses, quickly made and left to their own devices.

Lisette shuddered and then put the vile creatures out of her mind.

Oh, yes, she would take her time with Nikos. She would give him the powers and the prowess of a pagan god and teach the little scoundrel all—make that *some*—of the glorious skills and tricks she'd acquired throughout century upon century of adventuring.

She rose a little unsteadily, for she'd been feeling a strange sensation since the Brotherhood had perished, as if she were being pulled down and down into some black morass of the spirit.

"Come, darling," she said, holding out one alabaster-white hand. "It is time to give you the gift."

Nikos arched an eyebrow, but he understood the word *gift* only too well and was plainly intrigued by it. He came to her, in his lovely tight breeches and his fitted coat, and it was all Lisette could do not to gobble the delicious creature up the way some mortal women did chocolate.

She told herself there would be time for that later—all of eternity, in fact—and raised her hands to his sturdy shoulders.

"Do you trust me?" she asked softly.

He laughed, a delightful scamp of a lad, so hard and warm and beautiful, and for the briefest moment Lisette doubted her own plans.

"Of course I do not trust you," Nikos replied, grinning, so engaging and sweet that Lisette's heart threatened to crumble within her. "You are like me—you think only of your own wishes, your own pleasures. When you find another lover that you like better, you will abandon me."

Lisette smoothed his hair and spoke softly, hypnotically.

"Oh, but that is not true, Nikos," she said. "I will never leave you, and you will never leave me. Not ever."

He looked puzzled; his grin faltered a little, and a shadow of bewilderment moved in his Aidan-blue eyes. "How is this possible?" he asked. "We are flesh and blood. We must grow old, we must die."

She took enormous delight in contradicting him, in heightening that delectable confusion in his eyes. She shook her head and murmured, "We can live forever."

He seemed troubled now and moved to step back from her, but she took his shoulders in a grip calculated to be inescapable but also without pain, and would not let him go.

"What madness is this?" he whispered, and the flush of emotion under his warm, pliant skin made Lisette half wild with hunger and blood-lust. "No one lives forever!"

She calmed herself, made soothing, murmuring sounds, as a mortal mother might do for a child, pushed Nikos into a chair, and perched lightly on his lap. "Vampires do," she said, inwardly tensed for his reaction.

Instead of flying into a temper, Nikos laughed. He was scoffing at her, and that was worse, in some ways, than a storm of petulance would have been. "Vampires!" he mocked.

Lisette showed her fangs, both delighted in his recoil and despaired because of it.

He tried to throw her off then and escape her, but Lisette, by her own reckoning at least, had indulged him long enough. She took his head in her hands, as she had done so often before, but this time she was not gentle. No, this time a slight, quick motion of her wrists would have broken his neck.

"Do not resist me," she said in a crooning voice. "I will destroy you if you do."

The sound of Nikos's heartbeat seemed to fill the whole room with a pounding, steady *thumpety-thump, thumpety-thump*, and his beautiful eyes were wide with horror and, even then, disbelief.

The rushing of his blood, audible now, drove Lisette into

madness. Her control was gone, and she bared Nikos's delicate throat and sunk her fangs into the vein, drawing on him greedily, nearly swooning with the ecstasy of their intimate communion.

Nikos cried out when she took him, stiffened slightly, then went utterly limp beneath her.

Lisette was moaning inwardly as his blood flooded her own empty veins, and she began to rock against Nikos, the pleasure so savage she almost couldn't bear it. She nearly forgot that if Nikos died in her arms, she would not be able to complete the transformation. Should that happen, he would be lost to her forever.

It was actually painful to draw back from that continuous, buckling euphoria. She expected Nikos to be waxen—she'd so nearly drained him—and certainly unconscious. Instead he was gazing at her with eyes too old and too wise for the face of a lad of some twenty years. . . .

At that moment the suffering began. It was as though there were small, vicious fish inside her, tearing at her vampire flesh, at the atrophied organs that should not have been sensitive to pain.

Lisette shrieked in rage at Nikos's betrayal as well as in the agony of being poisoned; this was no mortal lad, no innocent lover and playmate, but a warlock!

Even as she screamed and clutched at her middle, she saw the knowledge of his own identity returning to him, the awareness. That was how he had fooled her, her pretty Nikos—he himself had not known who or what he was!

Now his foul blood was burning Lisette's insides like acid; she fell to her knees, still shrieking like a wild jungle cat caught in a trap, and, clutching the rungs of a ladderback chair, pulled herself upright again. Through a red fog of misery and the most primitive fury, she saw Manuel, her mortal carriage driver, loom uncertainly in the doorway for a moment.

She reached out to him, desperate; he crossed himself and fled.

Nikos, for his part, had risen to his feet, and he was

backing away from her, not fearful, but repulsed. There was even a hint of mockery in his eyes, the blackguard. If it was the last thing she ever did, she would see him suffer for that effrontery, as well as for his efforts to murder her.

Lisette struggled to remain conscious; the sun would rise soon, and in her weakened state she knew she could not survive its rays. Then, like a distant bell pealing somewhere far off in the Spanish countryside, she heard Maeve Tremayne's voice.

Come to me. Let us finish this.

Maeve, the enemy. The usurper. This was her doing, this betrayal, this physical and spiritual torment. A surge of hatred raced through Lisette's system, strengthening her.

She saw Nikos, laughing at her now, taunting her, but she could not hear his voice. No, all she heard was Maeve calling to her, calling and calling.

She could not tolerate the humiliation of looking upon her betrayer another moment, and she wanted Maeve Tremayne to suffer. Oh, how she wanted that traitor, that Judas, to suffer!

Gathering all her strength, which was greater than it might have been because of her rage, Lisette closed her eyes and willed herself to Maeve's presence.

Lisette took shape on the low rise behind the circle of stones, framed by the light of the moon, and Maeve readied herself for the battle of a lifetime. Unlike Valerian and Dathan and the others, she did not believe that the ancient one was already defeated.

"She is magnificent," Valerian whispered, clearly awed, as they all watched Lisette raise her arms gracefully against the dark sky, a shimmering angel of hell, to summon her multitude of followers.

They began appearing, those dreadful walking corpses, a score here, a hundred there, bumbling and stupid and deadly in their unheeding obedience.

Dathan, who had been prepared for this confrontation, called to his own warriors, and they came out of the thin shadows, silent and ominous, anonymous in their hooded cloaks.

The vampires, Maeve noted with nervous irritation, were seriously underrepresented. It would serve them all right, she reflected, Benecia and Canaan and the other cowardly ones, if she left them to Nemesis without even *trying* to defend them.

Maeve looked up into Valerian's eyes, seeing sorrow there, and fear, and then into Dathan's. He smiled at her and nodded his encouragement.

"Maeve Tremayne!" Lisette called in her hollow, unholy voice. She loomed on the hillside like a living flame, her pain palpable in the cool night air.

Taking up her skirts, Maeve answered the summons, and the two of them stood facing each other on the line of the hill.

"Why have you done this to me?" Lisette rasped, more dangerous in her suffering, rather than less. Her eyes were enormous in her gaunt face, and sunken. "Why? To save a lot of ungrateful blood-drinkers from the just vengeance of heaven?"

Maeve felt a strange urge to reach out to the other vampire, even though it would be like trying to touch a she-wolf caught in a trap, and wisely resisted it. "I have not done this to you, Lisette," she said reasonably. "It is by your own recklessness, your own treachery, that you've come to this end."

Lisette swayed, but at the same time Maeve could feel power emanating from the creature, pulsing and throbbing like another entity, an ominous reflex that might function even after the wounded vampire had died.

She gave a snarling shriek and stumbled toward Maeve, who stood her ground even though she was mortally afraid.

Then she heard Valerian, just a few feet behind her, his voice as smooth and even as velvet. "You are the rightful queen, Maeve," he reminded her.

Calder's voice joined Valerian's and, although Maeve dared not turn to look, she knew that he, too, had come to her somehow, and she blessed him for it, and drew strength from his presence.

"I love you," he said gruffly, and it seemed to Maeve that there was a certain sorrow in the tone and texture of those precious words. "Be strong, beautiful Maeve."

Dimity spoke next. "We are depending on you," she said softly but firmly. "The weak and the strong, the good and the evil, all of us."

Lisette screamed again and started past Maeve, delirious now, like a wild animal in the last stages of hydrophobia. Her thoughts were clear; before she collapsed, she would kill as many of the rebels as possible.

Maeve stepped in front of her then, and the mental struggle that had been brewing for centuries finally began.

There was a great, ferocious sweep of invisible fire, encompassing Maeve, smothering her with its heat, singeing her marble-like flesh. She endured, and called upon all the things she'd learned from the scrolls of the Brotherhood, and the sky itself thundered with the power of her command.

Lisette dropped to her knees, then struggled back to her feet again. At her back Maeve heard the chilling sounds of combat as the warlocks and the handful of courageous vampires engaged the sharklike beasts formed and shaped from madness itself.

Maeve did not wait for Lisette to attack again, but struck ruthlessly herself, crushing the other blood-drinker to the soft, fragrant ground, bringing the weight of all the stones in the circle to bear upon that one ill-fated creature.

Lisette wept—it was a frantic, mindless sound—and, rolling onto her back, raised herself up onto her elbows.

Again Maeve was moved toward foolish mercy, but again she resisted. Never taking her eyes from Lisette, holding the wounded one to the ground with the power of her mind, Maeve raised a hand in the agreed signal, and Valerian came forward.

He gave Maeve the stake and mallet they'd brought for this very purpose.

"You mustn't lose your courage now," he said, reading

her mind again, seeing the pity she felt for Lisette. "And you must not turn from this task."

Maeve hesitated for a moment, then nodded and accepted the instruments of death. She took a step toward Lisette, who made a whimpering sound and tried to crawl away.

"Do not be deceived," Valerian warned, staying close. "She is a beast, fit only for the bowels of hell. If your positions were reversed, she would not hesitate to finish you!"

It was all true, Maeve knew that, but knowing did not make the duty before her any less distasteful. She trembled a little as she advanced on Lisette, thinking of Calder, of Valerian, of Aidan and his lovely mortal, Neely—all their fates were in her hands, and she must not falter.

Maeve dropped to one knee in the dew-laced grass, placed the point of the spike directly over Lisette's heart, and raised the mallet. After only a moment's hesitation she struck the first blow.

The stake pierced Lisette's papery flesh, and she shrieked in pain and in fury, and Maeve trembled, but she raised the mallet again. And again.

Lisette screeched and struggled, and Maeve watched in horror as the dying queen's beautiful face went gaunt, then turned to dust and crumbled. Finally only a skull remained, but with Lisette's blue eyes peering out of the charred bone, glowing with unholy fire.

The screams echoed through the night long after the staring eyes had turned to cinders and dissolved.

Maeve knew triumph, but she was shaken and sick as well. She knelt in the grass, still clasping the mallet, chilled to the center of her soul.

After some time had passed, Calder gripped her shoulders from behind—she would have known his touch anywhere, for it always reverberated through her like the toll of a great bell—and drew her to her feet and away.

Maeve watched, spellbound and horrified, until Lisette, half corpse and half skeleton, had disintegrated into a pile of ashes, a ludicrous parody of the human shape. The stake protruded from between those discolored ribs, and the mallet fell, forgotten, from Maeve's fingers.

A shout of victory made her turn at last and look first into Calder's solemn eyes, then at the battlefield beyond. When Lisette had ignited herself, in the same way the members of the Brotherhood had done in their death chamber far beneath the ground, she had also destroyed her followers.

The grassy clearing was covered with grayish-white forms, and as she watched, the wind came and spread them over the grass, and only the warlocks were left—the warlocks, and the few vampires who had been willing to stand behind Maeve in her time of greatest need.

"The dawn comes!" one vampire cried.

Calder and Valerian collected Maeve between them, sheltering her with their larger bodies, and she felt herself dissolve into particles. Moments later she was in a dark place, as cool and welcoming as a grave. When her dazed eyes adjusted, she realized they had brought her to a chamber beneath the circle of stones itself.

At one end of the small cellar was an altar, probably druid, so old that it was crumbling. Valerian stood before it and executed a truly regal bow.

"My queen," he said.

Maeve was lying in Calder's arms, and she was definitely grateful for that. "Get up," she snapped. "I am nothing of the sort!"

Valerian laughed and spread the fingers of one graceful hand over his chest. "Anything you say, Your Majesty," he replied.

Maeve closed her eyes, inexpressibly weary, and let her head rest against Calder's shoulder. "Leave us," she commanded, "and find a lair of your own."

He obeyed, that troublesome, beloved vampire, dissipating into smoke with a finesse only he could have managed.

Maeve lifted her mouth to Calder's, and he kissed her hungrily, furiously, and with unutterable despair. There was no time for lovemaking, however much they might want each other, for the sun was about to spill its light over the countryside above.

They lay entwined, Maeve and Calder, in the rubble of the old religion, and let the vampire sleep take them.

There were no dreams, at least not for Maeve.

When she awakened at sunset, Calder was already sitting up beside her, looking upon her with despair naked in his eyes.

"You're leaving me," Maeve said, certain that this was not reality, but merely what mortals called a nightmare.

Calder nodded once and reached out to caress her cheek lightly, with just the tip of one finger. "It will be better for us both," he said hoarsely. "I love you, Maeve—more than I ever dreamed I was capable of loving—and I understand that you've held me prisoner only to protect me. Still, I cannot be subject to your will, no matter how benevolent."

Maeve swayed, horror-stricken. It was real.

For an instant Maeve wished that she'd died in battle the previous night instead of Lisette, but her instinct to live was perhaps her strongest trait, and it prevailed.

She raised her chin. "I see."

Calder looked away. He was already withdrawing from her, even though they shared that small chamber. He started to speak and then stopped himself.

"We could change," she suggested tentatively.

His gaze returned to her face; his eyes smoldered with dark conviction. "Never," he said. "You are too strong, and I am too stubborn." He paused to sigh, and the sound was filled with heartbreak. "I wanted to be your true mate, your equal, but now more than ever I know that isn't possible."

Maeve closed her eyes. "But you are my equal."

"No, darling," Calder said gently, shaking his head. "You are the vampire queen, and I am a fledgling."

She was really losing him. It was unbearable, incredible, after all they'd been through. And they loved each other so much!

"How did you convince Dimity to bring you to the circle of stones last night?" she asked, needing to back away from the heart of the situation for a few moments, to gather the scattered pieces of herself and try to fit them back together somehow.

"I didn't," he said. "I sensed the danger you were in, and I guess my desire to be at your side was greater than your power to keep me away. I thought about you, and I was there."

"How do you intend to live without me?" Maeve asked in all seriousness. "How shall I live without you?"

Calder left her side, rose to his feet, and dusted off the legs of his trousers as a mortal man might do. "I suppose we'll see each other, now and then," he said, taking care not to look at Maeve. "In time we'll forget."

She shook her head. "When the last star collapses into dust, my darling," she said softly, sorrowfully, "I will still love you."

"Don't," he said, turning away. "Please. Just let me go."

"That's not so easy," Maeve replied, standing, laying her hands on his broad back where his shoulder blades jutted beneath his flesh. "I love you, Calder. I need you. Don't you care enough to forgive me, to try to understand?"

He turned then and looked down into her eyes. "It would only happen again and again—your trapping me somewhere every time you thought I was in danger—until I came to despise you as my jailer! The only thing we can do is end it now, before we're both destroyed!"

With that, Calder disappeared, but his words echoed in Maeve's mind.

Before we're both destroyed.

"Too late," Maeve said softly. Then, with no one to see, no one to lend comfort, she buried her face in her hands and wept. She had won so much in that final battle, and lost everything.

Nemesis was waiting in the graveyard of All Souls' Cathedral three nights later when Maeve arrived. He might have looked quite ordinary, in his conservative overcoat, with that simple but frightfully expensive black umbrella unfurled against the chilly rain, except for the luminous quality that came from inside him.

Looking upon this magnificent creature from a little distance, Maeve could see why the great masters had graced their painted angels with halos and bright auras. They must have been aware, some consciously, some unconsciously, of their own heavenly guardians and comforters.

She wondered if she'd had a guardian angel as a child, and what he or she was doing now, when his or her services were no longer required.

Or were they?

Nemesis smiled his cordial, benevolent smile when at last she stood facing him, feeling the fiery heat of his aura. "You did have a guardian, you know," he said. "Every mortal does."

Maeve covered her trepidation with bravado, for something about this powerful, mysterious, implacable being made her feel as defenseless as a child. "Fat lot of good it did me," she retorted somewhat testily. Losing Calder had made her even more reckless than usual; she had so little to lose.

The warrior angel chuckled, and the sound was throaty and rich. "We are not infallible creatures," he explained, and Maeve thought it was rather generous of him, considering the circumstances. "Sometimes we make mistakes."

The rain pattered on the roof of All Souls', the gravestones, and the ancient walkway that had been worn smooth by the passage of generations of saints and sinners. Maeve looked directly into the angel's eyes and felt a strange, entrancing peace.

She shook it off. "Then perhaps you will be more understanding of the errors of others," she said. "We have destroyed Lisette as you probably know, and all but a very few of her vampires—which are being gathered by my friends at this moment."

Nemesis regarded her steadily, revealing none of his thoughts or emotions—if indeed angels had such things. She honestly didn't know.

"A great deal of damage has been done," he said.

"And there will be more still," Maeve reasoned boldly, flying blind, "if you unleash your forces on the dark kingdom. Granted, you'll eventually prevail, but we will fight you, you may be sure of that, as long as we have the strength to raise our swords."

"Insanity," Nemesis replied. "You cannot win!"

"No," Maeve agreed calmly. "We cannot. But remember this, Warrior Angel: We, the warlocks and vampires, have met your demands, and we plead without shame for peace. If you refuse us, and thousands of mortals die in the resulting fray, whose fault is that? Yours or ours?"

Chapter

—❦20❦—

Maeve did not have to seek out the Warrior Angel to hear his final decision; she was in her studio, working feverishly on the tapestry she had yet to properly study, when he appeared in the center of the floor.

There was less fanfare than she would have expected of one of the most powerful angels in heaven, but she was startled all the same. Somehow all Valerian's abrupt entrances had not quite prepared her for this particular surprise.

She let go of the shuttle and stepped down off the high stool, her eyes wide. Everything depended on this meeting—everything. Either heaven was satisfied that Lisette had been stopped and her minions destroyed, or the end was upon them all.

Nemesis, who wore a good nineteenth-century-style suit, including the tight celluloid collar, did not immediately speak or even look at Maeve. He went, instead, to the tapestry, now spilling, almost complete, from the back of the loom, and examined it thoughtfully.

"What does this image mean?" he asked after a long and, for Maeve, difficult silence.

Maeve had not looked at the tapestry in weeks, although she had worked the shuttle often in moments of intolerable stress. She felt stupid for not being able to answer the question—her pictures were never planned, they simply came out through her fingers—and they were often prophetic. She rounded the loom to stand beside Nemesis, and what she saw brought a small, strangled sound to her throat.

The tapestry showed herself, in a flowing dress, holding a lush bouquet of ivory roses. Some of the petals had drifted to the ground, which was covered in leaves of brown and gold and crimson, and behind her was a low stone wall, perhaps waist high. Sitting on the wall, with the casual grace so typical of the vampire, was Calder. He was smiling back at Maeve, who wore an expression of radiant joy, but it wasn't those things that moved Maeve. It was the beautiful, dark-haired child, perhaps a year old, who sat laughing on Calder's shoulder, small, plump arms reaching out to Maeve.

A child.

She laid her hands almost reverently on her stomach. A child? But that was impossible—no vampire in all of history had ever given birth.

Nemesis, probably weary of waiting for Maeve's long-delayed answer to his original question, had by then divined the meaning of the tapestry for himself. He reached out and touched the likeness of the little one with the gentlest brush of his fingers.

Maeve gazed up at him, in wonder and fear, because everything in that tapestry, every dream it represented, was in his hands. "Please," she said hoarsely. "Tell me what has been decided."

He heaved a great sigh and turned to look down on Maeve with a peculiar combination of sympathy and love and reluctance. "Were it up to me," he said, "I would still purge the earth of all night creatures—vampires, warlocks, werewolves, all of those things. But, alas, it seems there is some truth to that theory you expressed before—the Master feels that you have your place in the scheme of things." He was studying the child again, an expression of troubled amazement on his face. When he turned to meet Maeve's eyes once more, he said, "You will live and fulfill your destiny, and if you are to be destroyed, then it will have to be by one of your own kind."

Maeve felt a great surge of joy, closely followed by an equally powerful rush of fear. "This infant—" Her words fell away, and she laid a hand to Calder's woven image and then the baby's.

Nemesis heaved another sigh. "One of their poets said it—'There are more things in heaven and earth . . .' "

"But vampires do not have children," Maeve mused, as much to herself as to Nemesis, "and certainly I would never transform a mortal child. . . ."

"This infant *will* be mortal," Nemesis said, frowning at the tapestry again. "Perhaps conception occurred before Dr. Holbrook was transformed."

Maeve was in a daze. There would be no war with the angels, and a miracle of the sort she had never dared to dream of was happening. She, a vampire, carried a living, *human* child within her.

And the father of that little one, she reminded herself brokenly, had gone away.

Having delivered his message, Nemesis vanished in the blink of an eye, and Maeve was alone with her thoughts and the mysterious tapestry.

Dathan and Valerian must be told that the danger was past, that Nemesis and his Master had relented. Maeve would leave the spreading of this good news to them, however, for she had other things to do.

She stared into the tapestry for a long moment, her heart swelling with happiness and anticipation, then focused her thoughts on Valerian.

He was in a smoky saloon in the nineteenth-century American West, wearing rough-spun trousers, an old woolen shirt, six-guns, and one of the biggest hats Maeve had ever seen. A long, thin cigar protruded from one side of his mouth, and he was frowning at the hand of cards he held, as if the fate of the world depended on that very game of poker. A dance-hall girl hovered behind him, simpering and at the same time massaging Valerian's broad, powerful shoulders.

None of the mortals saw Maeve; she made sure of that.

Valerian, however, looked up at her over his hand of cards. The merest shadow of a smile touched his mouth, and his eyes twinkled.

You and your games, Maeve told him.

He settled back in his chair, a gesture meant for the assortment of mortals sitting at the table and standing around it. *Eternity would be very dull without games,* he replied.

Maeve laughed. *I suppose you're right,* she said. *Nemesis came to me a little while ago—he and his Master have decided not to make war on us.*

Valerian laid his cards out on the table in a flamboyant fan shape, and the mortals groaned in sporting despair and threw down their hands. *I am your creator, remember?* the great vampire finally said. *The instant you knew what had been decided, so did I.*

Maeve put her hands on her hips and tilted her head to one side. *Then you know about the child, too.*

Valerian gathered his winnings and tossed a chip to the dance-hall girl who was attending him so faithfully. *My dear,* he answered, *if you'd only troubled to look at the tapestry you were weaving, you would have seen the truth long ago. I've been aware of your delicate condition for days.*

Mild irritation moved in Maeve's spirit; sometimes Valerian's seeming omniscience really got on her nerves. *Well,* she retorted, *just tune out for a while, won't you please? There are things I want to settle with Calder, and I'd rather you weren't a witness to the whole encounter.*

He raised one shoulder in a shrug too elegant for the surroundings. *I have interests of my own,* he replied. *In fact, if you don't mind, I'd like to concentrate on my poker game.*

You'll tell Dathan and the others about the truce with Nemesis? Maeve pressed, eager to go but at the same time determined to accomplish her original purpose in coming to that rough, smoky place.

Certainly, Valerian answered, but he'd become absorbed in the new hand of cards he'd been dealt, and the dancing girl was perched on his knee. *The first time I see the warlock, I'll tell him. Then I'll tear his throat out.*

Maeve shook her head. *Have a care,* she warned. *Dathan is more powerful than you like to think.*

Valerian shifted his thin cigar to the other side of his mouth, clamping it between his white teeth. *I've been taking care of myself for centuries, Maeve,* he reminded her distractedly. *Believe me, I'm very good at survival. Now, get out of here and let me finish my game.*

She hesitated, then went to Valerian's side, bent, and kissed his cheek in gratitude, affection, and farewell.

Maeve found Calder in that same century, in a field hospital in northern Tennessee. He wore the uniform of a Confederate officer and carried a black leather bag packed with modern instruments and medicines.

When Maeve revealed herself to him, he was injecting a powerful painkiller into the arm of a boy who should have been at home, playing ball, doing chores, and going to school.

Calder raised his eyes to Maeve's face, and she saw his love for her in them, and his pain.

"Can they see you?" she asked.

Calder smiled sadly and withdrew the needle from the man-child's arm. "Yes," he answered softly. "They believe I'm a mortal, like them."

She looked down at the soldier. "Will he live?"

Calder nodded, then rounded the cot, took Maeve's elbow in one hand, and led her outside into the balmy southern night.

"That's quite a uniform," she said, noting his gray tunic and well-made trousers. "When did you switch sides and become a Confederate?"

"I haven't," he answered, studying her through narrowed, worried eyes. "I've always been on the side of life—I go back and forth between the two armies, helping where I can. Why are you here, Maeve?"

She hesitated, then said bravely, "Because I love you."

"And I love you," Calder answered, setting his bag down and laying his hands on Maeve's upper arms. "But I can't

625

let you hold me prisoner, no matter what dangers you might be trying to protect me from. I need the freedom to be myself, Maeve—without that, I might as well not exist."

"I understand," she replied. "And I'm sorry for those times I held you captive. My intentions were good, but I realize now that I was wrong."

Calder raised one hand to touch her face. "Perhaps we could try again, you and I," he said gruffly. "You let me take my chances with the world, and I'll let you take yours."

Maeve felt unvampire-like tears burning in her eyes and clogging her throat. "We could always find each other," she said, "with just a thought."

He bent and kissed her lightly on the mouth, and she felt the old, savage passion stirring. "Always," he agreed.

She took his hand. "Would you come away with me, just for a little while?" she asked almost shyly. "There's something I want very much to show you."

"Of course," he replied, looking puzzled.

"I'll meet you in my studio," she said, feeling as though she could fly home on the wings of her joy, needing no other magic than that.

"To London," Calder said with a grand gesture of one arm, as though inviting Maeve to precede him.

She was standing in front of the tapestry when her mate appeared, and she watched his eyes widen as he took in the images and their meaning. Finally he turned to her in wonderment.

"A child?" His voice was low and gruff, and he sounded as though he were trying to restrain his rising hopes, to avoid disappointment.

Maeve caught both Calder's hands in her own and arranged them flat against her stomach. "Nemesis says the baby is mortal," she said.

Calder looked at once joyous and baffled. "But how can that be?" he whispered.

She put her arms around his neck. "I don't know," she said with a smile. "You're the doctor."

He ran his hands up and down her back, his eyes full of

wonder. "It's a miracle," he marveled, and then he kissed her again.

Maeve was intoxicated when he finally drew back, and so weak that she clung to the front of Calder's tunic to keep herself upright. "How will we manage, Calder?" she asked. "How can vampires raise a mortal child?"

"The same way mortals do," Calder replied, smoothing her soft dress away from her shoulders to reveal her white, full breasts. "With a great deal of love and patience."

"But—"

Calder bent and took one of Maeve's nipples boldly into his mouth, effectively cutting off her words and swamping her doubts in a storm of physical and spiritual sensation.

Maeve threw back her head, abandoning herself to Calder's attentions, glorying in the wild appetites he had aroused in her. He smoothed the rest of her clothes away without leaving her breast, and then Maeve was clothed only in moonlight.

"Here's something else mortals do," he said gruffly when both Maeve's breasts were throbbing and wet from his tongue. He dropped to one knee before her, like a cavalier acknowledging his queen, parted the veil of silk that hid her most sensitive place from view, and kissed her there.

Maeve cried out, half in protest, half in glorious surrender. Calder's hands cupped her bare buttocks, and he pressed her hard against his mouth and suckled until she was trembling against him, whimpering softly in her need.

Calder lowered her to the bare wooden floor finally, and his own clothes were gone, quite literally, in a twinkling. He poised himself over her, and she parted her thighs for him willingly, even eagerly.

He entered her in one hard, desperate thrust and, as quickly as that, Calder's own control snapped. He and Maeve moved together in a graceful dance of passion, their sleek bodies rising and falling, twisting and turning, as each worshiped the other.

It ended with a simultaneous, white-hot melding, not only of their physical selves, but of their souls as well, and afterward they both lay stricken and exhausted on the hard floor.

Maeve was the first to move. She put her clothes back on, reached into the pocket of her gown, and took out the pendant the gypsy had given her, long, long ago. Crouching beside Calder, who was still splendidly naked and had managed to raise himself onto one elbow, she put the chain around his neck and then kissed him softly on each side of his face.

"This is my pledge to you," she said. "I will be your wife, now and throughout eternity, in heaven or in hell, in life or in death."

Calder sat up, took Maeve's face in his strong hands, and kissed her earnestly. "And this is my pledge to you," he replied then in a hoarse voice, drawing back only far enough to look deep into her eyes. "I will be your husband, faithful and brave and patient. I will love you beyond forever, and my soul will be a part of yours."

Maeve moved back into his arms. It was the closest they would ever have to a wedding, this exchange of vows they had just shared, but she and Calder had agreed to love each other for all eternity.

Forever sounded just right.